# In Sunlight
and in Shadow

SELECTED TITLES BY MARK HELPRIN

*Freddy and Fredericka*
*The Pacific and Other Stories*
*Memoir from Antproof Case*
*A Soldier of the Great War*
*Winter's Tale*
*Ellis Island and Other Stories*
*Refiner's Fire*
*A Dove of the East and Other Stories*

# In Sunlight
# and in Shadow

## MARK HELPRIN

HOUGHTON MIFFLIN HARCOURT
*Boston • New York*
2012

Copyright © 2012 by Mark Helprin

All rights reserved

For information about permission to reproduce selections from this book, write to Permissions, Houghton Mifflin Harcourt Publishing Company, 215 Park Avenue South, New York, New York 10003.

www.hmhbooks.com

*Library of Congress Cataloging-in-Publication Data*
Helprin, Mark.
In sunlight and in shadow / Mark Helprin.
p. cm.
ISBN 978-0-547-81923-5
1. Triangles (Interpersonal relations)—Fiction.
2. New York (N.Y.)—20th century—Fiction. I. Title.
PS3558.E477515 2012
813'.54—dc23
2012016242

*Book design by Melissa Lotfy*
Printed in the United States of America
DOC 10 9 8 7 6 5 4 3 2 1

The quotation and its translation from Lucretius on page vii are from Henry Adams, *The Education of Henry Adams,* edited, with notes and an introduction, by Jean Gooder, Penguin Classics Edition, London, 1995, page 434 (Latin) and page 541, note 15 (translation).

*Amor mi mosse, che mi fa parlare*

— *Inferno,* II

*Alma Venus, coeli subter labentia signa*
*Quae mare navigerum, quae terras frugiferentes*
*Concelebras...*
*Quae... rerum naturam sola gubernas*
*Nec sine te quidquam dias in luminis oras*
*Exoritur, neque fit laetum neque amabile quidquam....*

Life-giving Venus, who beneath the gliding stars of heaven
Fills with your presence the sea that bears our ships
And the land that bears our crops...
You alone govern the nature of things,
And nothing comes forth into the shores of light
Or is glad or lovely without you....
— Lucretius, *De Rerum Natura,* I

# CONTENTS

| | | |
|---|---|---|
| | *Prologue* | xiii |
| 1. | Boat to St. George: May, 1946 | 1 |
| 2. | Overlooking the Sea | 11 |
| 3. | Her Hands and the Way She Held Them | 22 |
| 4. | The Moon Rising over the East River | 28 |
| 5. | Catherine's Song | 43 |
| 6. | In Production | 53 |
| 7. | And There She Was | 66 |
| 8. | What You're Trained to Do | 89 |
| 9. | Georgica | 99 |
| 10. | Distant Lights and Summer Wind | 116 |
| 11. | Overcoats | 132 |
| 12. | Changing Light | 142 |
| 13. | Billy and Evelyn | 149 |
| 14. | Conversation by the Sea | 170 |
| 15. | Gray and Green | 184 |
| 16. | The Abacus | 192 |
| 17. | The Glare of July | 197 |
| 18. | The Whole World | 209 |
| 19. | Spectacles | 215 |
| 20. | The Gift of a Clear Day | 226 |
| 21. | The Beach Road | 234 |

| | | |
|---|---|---|
| 22. | Young Townsend Coombs | 241 |
| 23. | The Settee | 254 |
| 24. | The Economics of Hot Water | 265 |
| 25. | The Wake of the *Crispin* | 276 |
| 26. | Speechless and Adrift | 301 |
| 27. | The *Evening Transcript* | 307 |
| 28. | Lost Souls | 324 |
| 29. | James George Vanderlyn | 344 |
| 30. | Baucis and Philemon | 350 |
| 31. | Crossing the River | 364 |
| 32. | The Highlands | 393 |
| 33. | Pathfinder | 400 |
| 34. | Glorious Summer | 424 |
| 35. | Vierville | 455 |
| 36. | Snow | 467 |
| 37. | Catherine | 506 |
| 38. | Counsel and Arms | 521 |
| 39. | Office in Madison Square | 558 |
| 40. | The Train from Milwaukee | 569 |
| 41. | Red Steel | 580 |
| 42. | A Passion of Kindness | 586 |
| 43. | The Letter | 606 |
| 44. | In the Arcade | 634 |
| 45. | Catherine Rising | 652 |
| 46. | The Horse and His Rider He Hath Thrown into the Sea | 675 |
| 47. | In the Arms of an Angel | 693 |
| | *Epilogue* | 703 |

# In Sunlight and in Shadow

## PROLOGUE

IF YOU WERE a spirit, and could fly and alight as you wished, and time did not bind you, and patience and love were all you knew, then you might rise to enter an open window high above the park, in the New York of almost a lifetime ago, early in November of 1947.

After days of rain and unusual warmth, the skies are now the soft deep blue that is the gift of an oblique sun. The air is cool but not yet dense enough to carry sound sharply. From the playing fields, the cries and shouts of children are carried upward, sometimes clearly, sometimes muted, like murmurs, and always eventually to disappear. These sounds inexplicably convey the colors of the children's jerseys, which seen from the eleventh storey are only bright flecks on grass made so green by recent rains and cool nights that it looks like wet enamel.

Coming in the window, you might wonder who had left it open, for the apartment is empty, its silence, to a spirit, thundering like a heartbeat. Perhaps you would turn back to glance at the gulls bobbing in the reservoir, as white as confetti, or to see how the façades of Fifth Avenue across the park and over the trees are lit by the sun in white, ochre, and briefly flaring yellow.

The wind coming through the window, as you do, unseen, moves a shade to and fro as if gently breathing, its circular pull occasionally leaping up enough in contrary motion to tap against a pane as if it wants to speak. No one is in. In a breeze that enters and dies before it reaches the back rooms, you ride above particles of dust propelled across polished floors like snowflakes tumbling in a blizzard. In the air is a remnant of perfume, strongest by the door, as is often the case. The lights are off, the heat not yet been turned on, and the brass front-door lock silent and immobile, waiting to be turned and released.

In the room overlooking the park the bookshelves are full. Hanging above the fireplace is a Manet seascape with flags and pennants snapping in the wind; in a desk drawer beneath the telephone, a loaded pistol. And on an oval marble table in the entrance hall near the immobile lock and its expectant tumblers is a piece of card stock folded in half and standing like an *A*. Musical staffs are printed on the outside. Inside, sheltered as if deliberately from spirits, is a note waiting to be read by someone living. On the same smooth marble, splayed open but kept in a circle by its delicate gold chain, is a bracelet, waiting for a wrist.

And if you were a spirit, and time did not bind you, and patience and love were all you knew, then there you would wait for someone to return, and the story to unfold.

# 1

## BOAT TO ST. GEORGE: MAY, 1946

IF A NEW YORK DOORMAN is not contemplative by nature, he becomes so as he stands all day dressed like an Albanian general and doing mostly nothing. What little contact he has with the residents and visitors who pass by is so fleeting it emphasizes the silence and inactivity that is his portion and that he must learn to love. There is an echo to people's passing, a wake in the air that says more about them than can be said in speech, a fragile signal that doormen learn to read as if everyone who disappears into the turbulence of the city is on a journey to the land of the dead.

The busy comings and goings of mornings and late afternoons are for doormen a superstimulation. And on a Friday morning one Harry Copeland, in a tan suit, white shirt, and blue tie, left the Turin, at 333 Central Park West. His formal name was Harris, and though it was his grandfather's he didn't like it, and didn't like Harry much either. Harry was a name, as in Henry V, or Childe Harold, that, sounding unlike Yiddish, Hebrew, or any Eastern European language, was appropriated on a mass scale by Jewish immigrants and thus became the name of tailors, wholesalers, rabbis, and doctors. Harry was one's uncle. Harry could get it at a reduced price. Harry had made it into the Ivy League, sometimes. Harry could be found at Pimlico and Hialeah, or cutting diamonds, or making movies in Hollywood, or most anywhere in America where there were either palm trees or pastrami — not so much leading armies at Agincourt, although that was not out of the question, and there was redemption too in that the president was named Harry and had been in the clothing business.

The doorman at 333 had been charged with looking after the young son of one of the laundresses. As a result of this stress he became talkative for a doorman, and as Harry Copeland, who had maintained his military fitness, began to increase his velocity in the lobby before bursting out of the door, the doorman said to Ramon, his diminutive charge, "Here comes a guy. . . . Now watch this guy. Watch what he does. He can fly." The boy fixed his eyes on Harry like a tracking dog.

As Harry ran across the street his speed didn't seem unusual for a New Yorker dodging traffic. But there was no traffic. And instead of relaxing his pace and executing a ninety-degree turn left or right, north or south, on the eastern sidewalk of Central Park West, he unleashed himself, crossed the tiled gray walkway in one stride, leapt onto the seat of a bench, and, striking it with his right foot and then his left, pushed off from the top of the seat back and sailed like a deer over the soot-darkened park wall.

Knowing extremely well the ground ahead, he put everything into his leap and stayed in the air so long that the doorman and little boy felt the pleasure of flying. The effect was marvelously intensified by the fact that, because of their perspective, they never saw him touch down. "He does that almost every day," the doorman said. "Even in the dark. Even when the bench is covered with ice. Even in a snowstorm. I saw him do it once in a heavy snow, and it was as if he disappeared into the air. Every goddamned morning." He looked at the boy. "Excuse me. And in a suit, too."

The little boy asked the doorman, "Does he come back that way?"

"No, he just walks up the street."

"Why?"

"Because there's no bench on the other side of the wall."

The doorman didn't know that as a child Harry Copeland had lived at 333 with his parents—and then with his father after his mother died—before he went to college, before the war, before inheriting the apartment, and before the doorman's tenure, though this doorman had been watching the weather from under the same steeply angled gray canopy for a long time. In the spring of 1915, the infant Harry had dreamt his first dream, which he had not the ability to separate from reality. He, who could barely walk, was standing on one of the glacial, whale-backed rocks that arch from the soil in Central Park. Suddenly, by neither his own agency nor his will, as is so often the lot of infants, he was lifted, though not by a visible hand, and conveyed a fair distance through the air from one rock to another. In other words, he flew. And throughout his life he had come close to replicating this first of his dreams—in leaping from bridges into rivers, or flying off stone buttresses into the turquoise lakes that fill abandoned quarries, or exiting airplanes at altitude, laden with weapons and ammunition. His first dream had set the course of his life.

Because he was excellently farsighted, no avenue in New York was so long that the masses of detail at its farthest end would escape him. Over a lifetime of seeing at long distances he had learned to see things that he could not physically see: by reading the clues in fleeting colors or flashes, by close attention to context, by making comparisons to what he had seen before, and by joining together images that in changing light would bloom and fade, or rise and fall, out of and into synchrony. For this fusion, which was the most powerful technique of vision, it was necessary to have a prodigious memory.

He could replay with such precision and intensity what he had seen, heard, or felt that these things simply did not lapse from existence and pass on. Though his exactitude in summoning texture, feel, and details could have been bent to parlor games or academics, and in the war had been made to serve reconnaissance, he had realized from very early on that it was a gift for an overriding purpose and this alone. For by recalling the past and freezing the present he could open the gates of time and through them see all allegedly sequential things as a single masterwork with neither boundaries nor divisions. And though he did not know the why or wherefore of this, he did know, beginning long before he could express it, that when the gates of time were thrown open, the world was saturated with love. This was not the speculation of an aesthete, or a theory of the seminar room, for this he had seen with his own eyes even amid war, darkness, and death.

To see and remember life overflowing and compounding upon itself in such vivid detail was always a burden, but, that May, he was able to carry it easily. Though a bleak, charcoal-colored winter had been followed by an indeterminate spring, by June the beaches would be gleaming and hot, the water cold and blue. The streets would flood with sunlight and the evenings would be cool. Women had emerged from their winter clothes and one could see the curve of a neck flowing into the shoulders, actual legs exposed to the air, and a summer glow through a white blouse. In the weeks before the solstice it was as if, moving at great speed toward maximum light, the world had a mind of its own. It clung to a reluctance that would slow it as the brightest days began to grow darker. It is perhaps this hesitation at the apogee that lightens the gravity of sorrows, such as they are, in luminous June evenings and on clear June days.

As the half-dozen or more people who had swum that morning rushed back to work, the shivering clatter of slammed locker doors momentarily overwhelmed the hiss of steam escaping from pipes in locations that would remain forever hidden even from the most elite plumbers. Why steam still charged the pipes was a mystery to Harry, because the heat had been off for more than a month, and a string of cold days had chilled the unheated pool to the taste of polar bears. As he removed his clothing and floated it across the gap between him and the hook in his locker, the tan poplin undulating slightly as it met the air, the last of the other lockers was closed, and after a long echo the hiss of the steam pipes restored the room to timelessness. He was alone. No one would see that he did not shower before entering the pool. That morning as always he had bathed upon arising. He walked through the shower room and onto the pool deck, which like the sides and floor of the pool itself was a mosaic of tiny porcelain octagons, every edge rough and slightly raised.

The last swimmer had left the water ten or fifteen minutes earlier, but it was still moving in barely perceptible waves repelled by the walls and silently rocking, lifting, and depressing the surface, though only a keen eye could tell. Unlike in winter, when the air was saturated with moisture and chlorine, it was cool and dry. Standing in front of a huge sign that said *Absolutely No Diving!* he sprang off the edge and hit the water, gliding through it like an arrow. As the body's sensual registration is not infinite, the shock of falling, the feel of impact, the sound of the splash, the sight of the world rushing past, and even the smell of the water he aerated in his fall crowded out the cold, and by the time he began to feel the chill he had already begun to warm in exertion.

He would swim a mile, first at a sprint, then slowly, then, increasing his speed until he would move as if powered by an engine, all vessels open, every muscle primed and warmed, his heart ready to supply whatever was asked of it. He swam twice a week. Twice a week on the bridle trails and around the reservoir he ran a six-mile circuit of the park. And twice he took a racing shell out on the Harlem River or, were it not too windy, on the Hudson, or upstate on the Croton Reservoir, for ten exhausting miles in the kiln of summer or in the snow, fighting wind, water, wakes, and the whirlpools of Spuyten Duyvil, where the Harlem and Hudson join. And on Saturday, he rested, if he could.

Although he had played every sport in high school except football, and in college had rowed, boxed, and fenced, it was the war that had led him to maintain the strength, endurance, and physical toughness of the paratrooper he had become. Whereas many others long before demobilization had abandoned the work of keeping themselves fit for fighting cross-country and living without shelter, Harry had learned, and believed at a level deeper than the reach of any form of eradication, that this was a duty commensurate with the base condition of man; that civilization, luxury, safety, and justice could be swept away in the blink of an eye; and that no matter how apparently certain and sweet were the ways of peace, they were not permanent. Contrary to what someone who had not been through four years of battle might have thought, his conviction and action in this regard did not lead him to brutality but away from it. He would not abandon until the day he died the self-discipline, alacrity, and resolution that would enable him to stretch to the limit in defending that which was delicate, transient, and vulnerable, that which and those whom he loved the most.

Though as he swam he was not thinking of such things, they conditioned his frame of mind upon reaching the state of heat and drive that sport and combat share in common. Upon leaving the water, however, he was a study in equanimity. As he showered, a fragrant gel made from pine and chestnuts, and bitter to the taste — he had brought it from Germany just after V-J Day not even a year before — made a paradise of the air. The pool had been his alone, and no old men had come to paddle across his path like imperial walruses. In the glow of health, he dressed, and the bitter taste became more and more tolerable as it receded into recollection.

To be in New York on a beautiful day is to feel razor-close to being in love. Trees flower into brilliant clouds that drape across the parks, plumes of smoke and steam rise into the blue or curl away on the wind, and disparate actions each the object of intense concentration run together in a fume of color, motion, and sound, with the charm of a first dance or a first kiss. In the war, when he dreamed, he sometimes heard the sound of horns, streetcar bells, whistles, claxons, and the distant whoop of steam ferries. All rose into a picture attractive not so much for the fire of its richness and color but for the spark that had ignited it. He had known in times of the greatest misery or danger that his dreams of home, in which all things seemed beautiful, were in essence his longing for the woman for whom he had been made. That was how, as a soldier, he had seen it, and it was how he had come through.

In the five or six miles down to South Ferry the life of the city crowded around him and no one could have been more grateful for it. From the arsenals of history came batteries of images bearing the energy of all who had come before. They arose in columns of light filled with dust like the departed souls of hundreds of millions agitating to be unbound; in sunbeams tracking between high buildings as if to hunt and destroy dark shadow; in men and women of no account, the memory of whom would vanish in a generation or two, and who would leave no record, but whose faces, preoccupied and grave, when apprehended for a split second on the street were the faces of angels unawares.

For a moment in Madison Square, he had locked eyes with a very old man. In 1946 a man born in the last year of the Civil War was eighty-one. Perhaps this one was in his nineties, and in his youth had fought at Antietam or Cold Harbor. Fragile and dignified, excellently tailored, walking so slowly he seemed not to move, just before entering the fortress of one of the insurance companies through an ancient ironwork gate he had turned to look at the trees in the park. No one can report upon the world of the very old as the old comment upon that of the young, for no one has ever been able to look back upon it in reflection. Who could know therefore the real weight of all the things in this man's heart, or the revelations that had begun to surge from memory, to make the current that soon would bear him up?

In Little Italy, Harry saw half a dozen men loading heavy barrels onto a wagon. The sides of the wagon were upright two-by-fours joined by chains in symmetrical catenaries. Two dappled grays stood in their braces ready to pull. The barrels were lifted in coordinated rhythm, rolled along the wagon's bed, and righted. For these men, the world was the lifting of barrels, and nothing could have choreographed their moves more perfectly than had the task to which they submitted. And when finally Harry broke out from the tall buildings of Wall Street at South Ferry, the harbor was gray and almost green, the sky a soft blue.

At a newsstand in the ferry terminal he bought a paper, folded it, tucked it under his elbow, and so armed walked through a patch of sunlight in the center of a room blackened at its edges by shadow, to stand at a folding steel gate beneath a sign that read, *Boat to St. George*. From there he could see out to the slip, where iron railings and ramps and walkways of riveted steel plate were hung from chains and ready to clamp an incoming boat to land and release its passengers, by the thousands, who would then descend into subway tunnels hundreds of miles long.

Though it was already hot, every grown man wore a hat, and the calendar had yet to reach the magic, variable date when the gods gave license to the men of New York to switch to straw boaters. Perhaps this permission had something to do with the proximity of the equinox, or the sum of temperatures above a certain level, or the sexual maturity of cicadas had there been any in the masonry canyons. But when it happened, it happened all at once, and it hadn't happened yet. Men were still imprisoned in felt hats and in coats and ties, and women wore fairly long dresses and skirts, jackets, and summer shawls to cover partially the luxuriance of arms and shoulders that soon would be bare.

In the hundreds of times that he had watched the docking of the Staten Island Ferry, almost never had he heard speech in the procession upon the ramps. Though once or twice, young girls had spoken excitedly of their plans for the day, those who were habituated to the run took the walkways in funereal silence. But because they were coming to Manhattan from Staten Island—and whatever one might think of Manhattan it had so little about it of the dead, who for centuries had not been accepted for burial there and were forced instead to spend eternity in Brooklyn, Queens, or New Jersey—their silence as they shuffled over steel had to be something else. Even cows, Harry thought, lowed and mooed when they filed through their gates and pens.

And that was just it. They weren't cows. Their silence was their dignity, their protest of being herded through channels of industrial iron, ramps, and chains along which they—living, breathing men and women—were moved like wood or ores. It was their reticence and dismay at being compressed into a crowd and swallowed by a dark, tight tunnel, something especially trying after half an hour over open water. Many times, the younger Harry Copeland had hurried through the terminal and rushed out to the street rather than into the subway, whether he would take the subway later or walk the eight or more miles home.

Now, his direction was opposite that of the incoming crowds the boat would disgorge. He was going out into the harbor and the problem of confinement did not exist forward of where he stood. When the gate opened he would be released to walk onto the ferry, seek the upper decks in the sun, and glide in the wind across to Staten Island, within sight of the ocean sparkling through the Narrows.

Before he saw the ferry, it cut its engines. Then it cleared the plank walls and piles, bow first, stern sliding into alignment, a crown of spray tossed toward Brooklyn by the breeze. In the interest of efficiency and speed the ferries came in too fast, and as a result the wood walls that guided them to their berths always suffered. For, most times, despite the hysterical reversal of the screws, the boats coasted too uncontrollably to do anything but smack and push the wood. Again and again, they mimicked a drunk trying to park a big car in a little garage. Half the people at the bows were there not because they were in a hurry to disembark but because they wanted to be present if, as each landing seemed to promise, the boat in all its magnificent tonnage would finally snap the wood and hurtle into the pages of the *Daily News*.

As the arriving passengers filed past, he closed his eyes and saw again the spray lifting from the water in the moment when the stern swept gracefully to starboard. Were there a choice—between the steel walkways lowered with deafening racket, and the toss of spray in the air; between the silent, graceful coming to rights of the stern, and the crash of the boat into wooden palisades; a choice between the great heaviness of the city looming behind him, and the gravityless air above the water—he wanted to make it. And if there were a way to come from darkness into light and to stay there as long as life would allow, he wanted to know it. He was thirty-two, the war was over, and he wanted to leave even the shadows that he himself had made and to which he feared he was becoming a lifelong apprentice. But he could not imagine how.

The gate was rolled back and he and a large group of passengers went through it and streamed down the ramp. He chose the port side and would head for the bow. As he stepped into the sunlight between the terminal and the deck, he saw a woman off to his right, just beyond the ramp on the starboard side. Although distance did not allow much detail, he could see certain intricacies across it.

She walked with her back so straight and her head held so high that it was as if she had studied for years to be a dancer. But though she had studied, the effortless way she carried herself had been born with her. She was a flow of color. Her hair trapped the sun and seemed to radiate light. It moved in the wind at the nape of her neck and where it had come loose, but was otherwise gloriously up in a way that suggested self-possession and formality and yet also exposed most informally the beauty of her shoulders. She wore a blouse with a low collar that even across the gap he could see was embroidered in pearl on white, and the glow of the blouse came not only from its nearly transparent linen but from the woman herself. The narrowing at her waist, a long drop from her shoulders, was perfect and trim.

She carried nothing, not a newspaper or a purse, and the way she walked was so beautiful that an angry man berated Harry for stopping on the ramp, where he was oblivious of everything on account of a woman who then vanished, and left him as if struck by a blow. She was more than image, more than the random beauties by which he lived through his days and of which he had never been able to make more sense than a shower of sparks. He had long known that to see a woman like this across the floor in receptions or gatherings is as arresting as if a full moon were rising within the walls of the room, but this was more arresting yet. And what was a beautiful woman? For him, beauty was something far more powerful than what fashion dictates and consensus decrees. It was both what creates love and what love creates. For Harry, because his sight was clear, the world was filled with beautiful women, whether the world called them that or not.

As the sound of a claxon that had whooped in Brooklyn seconds before now echoed off the buildings of lower Manhattan, he remembered at last to breathe and to walk, and the breath came in two beats, one of astonishment and the other of love, although what right had he to love the brief sight of a woman in white who had crossed a crowded deck and disappeared in shadow?

# 2

## OVERLOOKING THE SEA

As even the moon has its virtues, so too does Staten Island. But except in declarations erupting from the crooked faces of politicians, the borough of Richmond was no more a part of the city than Mars is a part of Earth. If New Jersey, linked to Manhattan by tunnels and a bridge, could not make a claim of attachment, how could Staten Island, the humpbacked child of the Atlantic? It couldn't. But it did.

As they sat in her garden overlooking the sea from a high hill, Elaine, Harry's aunt, the widow of his father's only brother, put down her glass and asked, "Now that you've returned to the light of day, what will you do?" He thought this was a widow's question and perhaps a touch envious, for although he had come out of the war she could not come out of old age. He meant to comfort her by lessening the contrast.

"In some respects," he said, speaking carefully — for she had been a Latin teacher and she listened clause by clause — "there was more light and air in the war than now."

Via a slight tilt of her head, she asked why.

"When you did see something of beauty, when you did love, it was more intense than I can describe. Perhaps wrongly so, I don't know, but it was. And in the fighting or when you came out were islands of emotion such as I had never experienced: in short takes, in fragments that pierced like shrapnel."

Not wanting to go deep, she just smiled, and the setting carried them through. A shingled house on two acres of garden shielded from other houses by thick hedges, on the eastern slope of a hill overlooking the sea, with three parterres of lawn, fruit trees, flower beds, and white shell paths, this was a paradise with a view to the horizon forty miles out and 140 degrees in expanse. The ocean breeze that came up the hill was artfully broken by ranks of boxwood until all it could do was gently sway the profusion of red and yellow roses on their long and threatening stems.

Elaine, and Henry, the brother of Meyer Copeland, Harry's father, had fled to Staten Island because each had married outside the faith. Neither the Irish on her side nor the Jews on his were hostile or unforgiving, but the couple felt discomfort, disapproval, and tension. Not wanting to spend their lives this way, they exiled themselves to Richmond, where, in the City of New York, they lived as they might have on the coast of California or Maine, and prayed every day that no bridge would ever be thrown across the Narrows.

After Harry's mother died when he was a boy, he had spent a fair amount of time in this house. When his father went abroad to buy leather or hire craftsmen, this was where Harry would stay, arising at six to make his way to school on the Upper West Side, studying with such concentration on the ferry twice a day that he seemed to make the crossing instantly. It was on Staten Island that Harry had first encountered a lobster and eaten it. Now he sat in the sunshine at a linen-covered table, encountering another one, in a salad by the side of which was a glass of iced tea and, although he did not ask for more, not quite enough bread and butter for someone who had swum a mile and walked eight.

Not long before, he wouldn't have noticed any effect after several times the exertion and no food whatsoever. He had learned in the war to unlink the output of energy from its intake, resulting in the conversion of hunger into a feeling of warmth. Which is not to say that, after a lobster, four rolls with butter, two glasses of iced tea, and a large salad, he was in danger of starvation, but that he was still drawing on his reserves.

"I went out to the cemetery," he said, leaning back in his chair so that the full sun was in his face. He knew that because his aunt didn't drive she seldom could visit her husband's grave, which was not far from but invisible to Manhattan, on land that rose gently westward from the Saddle River.

"I haven't been there for a while. Are they taking care of it?"

"No. There were perpetual-care medallions on every stone, but they weren't taking care of it. I went to the office. They apologized. They said that half the workers are still in the service. What with the demobilization, I thought at first this was just an excuse. But the mortuary detachments are still busy. Graves Registration has got to find gravesites that weren't always well marked, dig everyone up, and move them to war cemeteries over there or bring them back home. And it's not like digging potatoes. When they were buried, with artillery deafening the gravediggers and the bulldozer operators, there wasn't much ceremony. Now they're making up for it. They take them out carefully, as they must."

"So what will they do? At the cemetery."

"It'll straighten itself out in a year or two. Meanwhile, since I complained, they offered to attend to us at once. But I wouldn't let them. It would make it worse for the graves that no one comes to visit, so I did it myself. They had tools to spare, and they let me use them. I think they were embarrassed, that they feel they owe us. They don't owe us."

"They don't. I know."

"I cut the grass. I repaired the rails that go around the plot, cleaned the markers, weeded, I even planted ivy. It's all done. And I said Kaddish for my mother, my father, Henry, my grandfather, grandmother, and my mother's father and mother, wherever they are. By myself of course, no *minyan*."

"A lot of people would not approve," she offered.

Elegant, almost formal, and prepossessing in his suit and angel-blue tie, he contemplated for a moment and said, "Well, then fuck them."

After lunch, as Elaine carried several trays into the house, and he, at her order, remained in the sun, he thought about the woman he had seen walking onto the ferry. Even as he had been in conversation, her image would brighten and fade, rise and fall. Although he did not know her, he longed for her. The memory might last a week or two, or perhaps forever, but he was sure he would never see her again. He hadn't been able to find her on the ferry, when instead of standing in the bows as he usually did he walked around the decks as if taking exercise. There were enough levels that had she moved casually from one to another only once or twice, he could have missed her, and he did. And when he tried to find her as she disembarked, the crowd was moving too fast through the four exits all at once. Though she may have been visible for a moment, concealed among the rapidly trotting people whose heads bobbed up and down like a flock of birds floating at the edge of the surf, the sight of her had eluded him.

"The business," his aunt said, as she returned to her chair. "How is the business going? Is that colored man still there? What was his name?"

"Cornell."

"That's right."

"That really is right. His name is Cornell Wright."

"After Meyer's death, was he able to bring everyone through?"

"He was. It was weeks before they told me that my father had died. I can't blame them. They usually didn't know where I was, because we were often seconded to other divisions. So I don't hold it against them, even if they forgot. When I found out, it was a comfort to know that he had long been at rest. I hadn't known, but still it was as if I had grieved in that time and was beginning to recover. I'll never be able to explain that. It's as if the world is running according to some master clock. I felt like a character in a play, and for some reason I was offstage when I should have been playing my part, but when I returned things had moved on without me, and I had, too.

"We were fighting in deep winter. It took awhile before it occurred to me that the business was on its own. But then I didn't worry in the least.

"I own the voting stock, but only thirty percent of the dividend-paying shares. Cornell owns twenty percent, and fifty percent is in a profit-sharing trust. Everyone there has a stake."

"How was he able to run the company?"

"You're saying that because he's colored?"

"It would be difficult."

"Elaine," Harry said, pausing as if to drop what he was going to say and then catch it, bringing it up high, "Cornell could run any business. He's very much underemployed. If he worked anywhere else he wouldn't have ownership, and they might make him push a broom. That was my father's genius and luck, that he saw Cornell as a man rather than as someone who, when he comes into a room, makes people breathe differently and talk carefully in his presence. It happens to me when they find out they're sitting next to a Jew. They stiffen and distance themselves even if they don't want to."

"I used to see that with Henry," she said. "Sometimes people reacted to him as if he was polluted or dirty. He didn't even know it."

Harry looked at her and smiled just a little. "Yes he did."

"It's convenient that Cornell can run the business. Entirely without you?"

"He could. He did."

"Your father would have wanted you to finish." She was referring to what was going to have been his graduate education.

Harry shook his head and looked down, addressing the ground. "I can't go back. Not after the war. I wouldn't have the patience. Not now, anyway. Things have been moving too fast, there's been too much change, and my heart wasn't really in it even then. We have problems, all of a sudden. I don't know what to do. Cornell doesn't either. Maybe my father wouldn't have known, although that's hard for me to believe. I've been trying to make the right decisions, but it's difficult.

"We were lucky during the war that whoever made the contracts didn't throw us the kind of business they gave to others. It may have been because my father didn't wine and dine anyone, much less kick back. I don't know, I was a world away. But because we're known for our quality they didn't give us the staple contracts, the millions of holsters, rifle slings, binocular cases, and that kind of thing.

"We were given luxury orders — general officers' belts, Sam Brownes, attachés, wallets, map cases, presentation portfolios, the top end. So we weren't raking in the money, we didn't overextend, we stayed perfectly stable. Our civilian carriage trade declined to almost nothing, but all of the slack was taken up by the top-end production for the military. We neither expanded nor contracted. As a result, we haven't had to lay anyone off, we haven't relaxed our standards, we still produce the finest leather goods in the country, and we're still connected to the right sources of supply. Everyone else is in chaos."

"Then what's the problem? It sounds ideal."

"Europe. The first industries to revive are not the steel mills and automobile plants—it takes time to rebuild something like that—but the ateliers, the small workshops and family businesses like ours. They're back up already. In Europe now people will work for nothing. The exchange rates are such that even with import duties and excise taxes an Italian briefcase of a quality similar to what we produce, or better, will soon go for half of what we can price ours if we pull in our belts. And the United States is not going just to sit still while Europe teeters and the Soviets keep their armies mobilized. We'll have to help them. How will we do that? We'll liberalize imports, for one. And when we do, the big industries here will bribe Congress to go easy on them, but small companies like ours, in small sectors like ours, won't be able to."

"Then what can you do?"

"I don't know. If we cut prices, which we can't anyway, it would destroy our image. I don't want to lay people off, and if we scale back production it wouldn't solve the fundamental problem. In fact, it would hasten our demise by reducing volume at the same time that margins are shrinking. A lot of companies are farming out work to the Italians. That just puts off the day of extinction, and it means layoffs, or shutting down. Any temporarily advantageous deal you make with your competition will run only as long as the date on the contract, if that.

"A Cypriot who said he knew my father—although Cornell had no memory of it—came onto the floor a couple of weeks ago. He has workshops all over Italy, and wanted to take our production and mix it with the lines he's importing here. He's done it with other companies. It would be the end for us. He was arrogant in the way that people who suddenly make a lot of money can be arrogant, all puffed up — mania. He looked at me and said, 'Oh, I thought you were Clark Gable, until my eyes came into focus.' Can you imagine? That's how he greets me, in my own factory, in my own country, where he's a guest."

"You do look a bit like Clark Gable, when he was younger," she said.

"I do not. For Chrissakes, Elaine, when he was young, without the mustache, Clark Gable looked like a mouse. He still looks like a mouse."

"Some mouse."

"Elaine, nothing I've ever done or thought has had anything whatsoever to do with what I look like."

"I know. You have no prettiness. I'm not saying that."

"Be that as it may," he continued, "I don't know what to do. But it'll come clear one way or another. It always does."

"And marriage?"

"What does marriage have to do with it?"

"When will you get married? You're thirty-one years old."

"Thirty-two."

"All right."

"I'll marry a beautiful girl I saw on the ferry."

"Oh?"

"She disappeared." At this, Harry stood and offered his arm to his aunt. "Let's take a walk," he said, helping her up.

"Take a walk?"

"Just around the paths. You don't have to leave the roses. The shells are so white. How do you keep them that way?"

"We don't use oyster shells," she said. "They have a lot of black and gray. What we use is more expensive, but worth it. And we put down about twenty percent fresh every year. I mean, I put down."

"I know."

"Harry," she said, as they rested at the top of a short flight of bluestone stairs from which they could see waves breaking white on the beach far below, "never forget that the time is always short."

He walked down to the ocean, reaching it at about one-thirty, with his jacket slung over his shoulder and held by one finger, arm cocked, sleeves rolled up, and tie loosened so much that the normally long ends were short enough to have been the flourish beyond the knot of a scarf. Were it not for the wind, his shirt would have been wet even though he had been going mainly downhill. Enforcing its own protocol, the beach slowed his pace before he reached the water. Fast walking, the universal pace of Manhattan, had the edge planed off it after he had left the pavement and crossed a weathered and neglected boardwalk onto glassy sand that forced him to half speed. He felt his weight as he pushed on toward the ocean, but as if taking strength from the roar of the waves he grew lighter as the sea filled his eyes. Although he stood on dry land, he could see only the ocean. The strong wind neither ceased nor changed direction, and no sail driven before it would luff. As steady and invariable as the air from an electric fan, it seemed to cover the world uniformly.

He had intended merely to touch by the sea and then walk north to St. George and get the ferry, although no one expected him back at the loft that day. But just as upon his return from the war he had found the world still and becalmed before the century (and perhaps his life with it) would accelerate toward the gleam of fire at its end, his intentions were directed entirely apart from his will.

When he had returned home, the troopship had pushed through the Narrows with everyone on deck, as impossible and unstable as that may have been, Brooklyn to starboard and Staten Island to port. He had had no idea what he might find, but it felt more like a beginning than an end. Perhaps after tests and deprivations, fighting on land, over the sea, and in the air, it would be settlement, the founding of a new family, and love. Yet nothing seemed to happen and everything seemed ordinary: subways, restaurants, telephone calls, business, the paying of bills. Now, however, on a beach where he had not planned to linger, some mercurial spirit held him as if by the leaden anchor of one of the ships that passed through the pillars of Fort Hamilton and St. George.

He had never liked reading a folded newspaper as one did on the subway, and here he was on the beach with not a soul in sight, not even the ghost of a coast guardsman in one of the abandoned watchtowers or concrete fortifications, and certainly no passengers pressing on all sides, but the wind forced him to the subway rider's origami, and until sometime after three he read the news in his usual disciplined fashion, pausing to burn into memory important facts and figures. When he had no more to read, he collapsed the paper into a pillow, and as he stretched out and relaxed on the sand everything became quieter, the apparently immutable wind having been thrown off its game by the imperfections of the ground. Listening to his own heartbeat, he fell asleep in the sun. And in the airy, unburdened moments before sleep, he saw her in full.

Throbbing from hours in the open, he sat in the dark ferry hall, impatient to pass through the gates and out to bright water. In the harbor and under a shield of inconstant smoke, ships by the hundreds moved in and out, each bent upon its purpose, crossing a surface brocaded by the sun into flashes like a forest of leaves turned up by a sudden blast of wind. The only time he had ever been in the presence of more ships had been during the invasions of Sicily and Normandy, and these he had rapidly flown over. Unlike the invasion fleets that had been silent and immobile as they rested on surprised seas, the ships and boats in New York harbor were as loose with their horns and whistles as if they were desperately trying to speak.

Pigeons that had been trapped inside rose against the dark green walls all the way to the highest windows, glanced off them, and fell back to the rafters to rest. The floor glinted with ground glass that had been mixed into the concrete to give it traction. A hundred electric lights burned steadily to relieve the darkness even as the sun beat against the roof and walls. Footsteps, and the sound of a clock ticking. Claxons, engines, wind, water, wings flapping, the sound of breathing, the beat of the pulse, the rush of one's blood.

Harry closed his eyes lest he lose his way in the confusion. As the gate swung wide at the call for the next boat and he opened them, he saw a flash of white in the air, like a hawk cartwheeling in a turn, and then it vanished. As he stood, he apprehended in a split second that it had been a newspaper that, with the speed and certainty of a throwing knife, had been propelled into a trash can. And he apprehended just as suddenly that this perfect, powerful, nonchalant shot had been made at a fast clip by a woman walking toward the boat, it seemed, angrily.

All sense, propriety, and inhibition left him as he bolted forward, pushing through the crowd to close, determined not to lose her again.

She went to the top deck, to port, where the sun would be. He followed, embarrassed and troubled that he was following, not knowing what he could say or if he would be able to utter a word. He had yet to see her face, and yet he knew that she was beautiful. Walking past her, not two feet to her right as she took a place near the rail, he looked toward the bow and waited for the gates to close, the boat to shudder, and the harbor to splay into view. He stopped ten or fifteen paces away from her, put on his jacket, restored his tie, and placed his forearms on the rail, clasping his hands in front of him as if in relaxation. He would casually turn to his left, glancing to see that the last passengers had cleared the ramps, and he knew that when he did this, and if she were still in the same position, he would see her profile. What he would do then, he did not know.

Far more slowly than someone who might be checking to see if the ramps were up, he turned, expecting to see her, if at all, in profile, fifteen feet away. But when he came around he saw that, having moved forward, she was close enough to touch, and was looking right at him, her penetrating eyes magnified in her clear lenses, a neutral, almost disapproving expression on her face, which seemed to indicate a fine judgment hard at work on subjects far from sight.

He had fallen in love with her at a distance and in an instant, and now, as he saw her for the first time in the shade of the wooden pilings and palisades, with a diffuse sun making her hair golden and casting muted shadows within shadows, what had been playing upon the surface began to plunge deep. He found himself staring at her without the ability to feign looking elsewhere. As seconds passed, he thought she was returning his gaze, perhaps waiting for him to introduce himself as someone whom she had already met, for no one but someone she had already met would be so forward and rude as to lock his eyes upon her like this.

And then he realized that she understood from his expression and his stance that in fact they hadn't met. And yet she didn't turn away. She was simultaneously curious, irritated, expectant, and reserved. To save his life, Harry would not have been able to say something clever or even appropriate. At that moment, as betrayed by his expression, he hadn't the ability to say anything at all. He remembered being told, If you want to meet somebody, drop a sheaf of papers, but he had no papers to drop.

Not one woman in a thousand would have failed to retreat, perhaps resentfully. But she had read him as finely as he had read her. The ferry whistle blasted, catching even daily ferry-goers unaware and making them jump as if they had been jolted by an electric current. It shook the two of them and made their lungs tremble as it seemed to hammer them down into fixed positions on the deck and separate them from the world. As the ferry started to move and the wind came up, the sun broke out. And when the harbor appeared she stepped toward him, moving in the direction of their travel. Not taking her eyes from his, she held her right hand within reach for him to grasp, which he did, as if in a formal introduction. To touch her hand was overwhelming. And then, in the most beautiful voice he had ever heard, she said the most beautiful word he had ever heard: "Catherine."

# 3

## HER HANDS AND THE WAY SHE HELD THEM

AS THE FERRY strained forward to reach top speed, it left behind long garlands of white water at the edge of a turquoise wake. A rope hanging loose from a davit swung back and forth in the crosscurrents of wind and with the slight roll of the boat as it reached open water. He had been waiting for her for the longest time, although he had not known he had been waiting. And there she was, standing before him, too beautiful for words.

She spoke first, accusingly, but enjoyably. "Have we met?"

"No, we've collided."

Lost in infatuation, he had moved incautiously ahead to the point where he was in love with even the smallest detail of her. Had she known of each or perhaps any one of the specifics, she would have had the evidence that she had begun to sense, and that had begun to sweep over her in the rare feeling of being adored. Although she had neither designed nor sewn her blouse, nor accomplished the sinuous, restrained embroidery, nor given to the embroidery the gray and rose color of mother-of-pearl, she had put it on, and it embraced her hour by hour, absorbing the heat of her body and the scent of her perfume. The collar, the buttonhole, the button, the threads that made a basket knot within the button's ivory recess, became for him more than just a symbol, for he had never loved just a symbol, but a part of her — touched, regarded, accepted, and chosen by her.

And of other things about her that overwhelmed him there were many. Her hands and the way she held them, unconsciously. And yet her fingers never existed in relation to each other except beautifully, no matter how they moved or where they came to rest. My God, he thought, she has beautiful hands. Every syllable she uttered, the way she pronounced every word, the bell-like quality of her voice. Her grace when she moved, or when she was still. Even the few wrinkles in her skirt. The line of her neck as it rose from the top of her chest. Her bosom, though he hardly dared look, but did. And beyond all that, far beyond it, he took the greatest pleasure in anticipating the surprise, delight, fascination, anger, and love with which she would greet all that she would encounter for the rest of her life. He wanted to listen to her history, to know her microscopically and also from afar, to see her and also to see through the eyes that now held him in thrall.

This unreasonable heat was chilled only by the occasional currents of his fear that he would assume too much and move too fast, or that she was spoken for and would not transfer her allegiance, or that if she did abandon someone else she would someday abandon him. But each anxiety was outweighed by the moment itself, which gave rise to an uncalculated grace in which even their silences were perfect and needed no saving.

"I have no idea," he said, "how old you are, what you do, or where you live. The effect is that, somehow, you do everything and you live on the Staten Island Ferry. So I don't know where to begin."

"Begin what?" she asked, her severity in reserve but detectable in response to his having stepped over the line.

"A conversation," he responded, barely saving himself.

As they sped over the water toward Manhattan, she said, "I could say that I didn't expect to go back to the city today, or to see you again."

He was astounded. "You saw me earlier?"

"I did. You were moving swiftly around the decks. I thought you were chasing someone. Are you a policeman? Whom were you chasing?"

He made no comment except a slight, self-incriminating smile.

"Oh," she said. "Uh-huh. In that case I can confess that I threw my paper in the trash can near you to wake you up. I hadn't finished it."

"If you want to do confessions, I can do better than that," he said.

"I was thinking of taking the ferry every day, all day long, though it would have been really inconvenient."

"Do you live on Staten Island?"

"No. You?"

"Not even slightly."

"You were going to stay there a while?"

"No."

"You were going to stay there forever, immigrate?" he asked.

"There is another possibility," she said. This game meant nothing for either of them other than that it was an opportunity to remain in one another's presence, and a way for him not to ask, intrusively, what she was doing on Staten Island, a question that may have choked the bud of many an incipient romance.

"You were going to go on to someplace else. Elizabeth?"

"Catherine," she said, teasingly, as if he were an idiot.

"Elizabeth, New Jersey?"

"Catherine Sedley."

"Catherine Sedley." Just saying what he thought was her name (it wasn't) gave him pleasure. "Where were you going to go when you got off the island?" He drew back a little and surveyed her — a lovely task — as if trying to solve a riddle. "You're flushed with sun. You were on the beach." She seemed pleased by his desire to work through this. "You weren't waiting for a boat, were you?" She brightened, impressed by his sharpness. "The boat would have to be either very small or large enough to launch another boat to pick you up."

"A hundred and five feet," was her response.

"That's the length of a corvette. Was it? Canada has been decommissioning them, and people are making them into yachts."

"No, it was built in nineteen twenty-eight for the America's Cup."

"But it didn't show."

"It didn't win the Cup, either. It travels with the wind, and the wind is unreliable. I waited my appointed hours, and then I left."

"Today," he said, "the wind moved as steadily as a conveyor belt."

"Perhaps yesterday the wind was not so steady, or the boat lost a mast. Things like that happen on the sea all the time. Meanwhile, I'm unexpectedly on my way home."

"You have no luggage. The boat is yours?"

"Hardly."

"But you have things on board."

"A whole set. In my own cabin."

"I did notice," he said, "that you carry nothing. Not a purse, a bag, an umbrella, or a ring on your finger. No jewelry at all."

"No jewelry," she repeated.

"The effect is beautiful," he told her, touching the line but not crossing it — for it had been moved.

"Are you one of those people," she asked, "who think everything is beautiful?"

"No. That would mean that nothing is beautiful, or that I would have an eye like God's. And then, more simply, everything is not beautiful."

"What about that?" she asked, indicating the cliffs of lower Manhattan three-quarters ahead, shining in the western sun. "It's commonly perceived as beautiful. People say that it is, and take pictures with their Brownies. What do you think?"

"I think," he said, anticipating the point and going beyond it before he would answer her question, "that one of the finest things in the world, a saintly and holy thing, is when someone sees the beauty in something, but especially in some*one*, who is commonly taken as having no beauty at all. I once knew a woman who in the instant she understood that she was loved and that her beauty was perceived, hardly survived the intensity of her emotions. She was shaking in disbelief — one side of her face had been forever disfigured — because it was as if in that moment God were there. This was in Germany, in the Black Forest, just like a fairy tale, but it was true. My friend, who was with me and who fell in love with her, loves her to this day. He married her. They live in New Jersey."

Catherine was disturbed because she knew her life was going off course, and she didn't like things to go off course. He went on to finish what he was saying and move to a lighter note, not wanting to diminish in any way the feeling almost of weightlessness that he had had since he had first seen her.

"I do believe, then, in that sense, that there's beauty in everything other than in evil, but that it would take a perfect and perfectly compassionate being to see it."

"And what about Manhattan?" she asked, not as the test she had originally intended, for he had already passed that, but to bring him back. She, too, did not want to compromise what she was feeling.

"Don't like it."

"How come? Everyone else does."

"It's square, rectilinear, blocky. These buildings with their hard, unbroken planes are like lives in which nothing happens. Modern architects apparently haven't heard of either nature or human nature."

"You don't like modern architecture?"

"No, but don't worry about the architects. They'll always be prosperous because they'll never run out of bad taste."

"I don't like it much either," she said, "but I don't feel passionately about it. You must be an intellectual."

"I'm not. The war saved me from that."

"And what would be so terrible if you were?"

"They don't go outside enough."

"They don't, do they."

"Not nearly enough."

"And you do?"

"I try," he said. "And so do you, I think. I can see it in the way you carry yourself, and in your face—unless you got too close to your toaster."

"I have one of those toasters that doesn't get hot unless you're out of the room so it can burn the toast," she said parenthetically and as if addressing someone outside their conversation, and then she returned to him. "You mean then that what we see ahead is never beautiful, that breathtaking mass, those heights?"

"Oh, no, it is," he said, "when the sun shines against its windows and they echo it. It is, when seen as a whole from certain angles and at certain times of day or night. When it snows, or when you consider the souls that inhabit it. Beautiful not on account of itself, of its design, but in the way nature showers it with unexpected gifts. And the bridges, with the double catenaries, running parallel, high above the rivers...."

He wanted to move more cautiously and slowly, which meant paying decent respect to the mundane, so he tried. "What I do like, much more than art, is, for example, water running over rocks in a wilderness stream. Just the sound of it is more beautiful than all of Manhattan." As he said this he swept his arm backward, briefly and tightly, to indicate the city. "There's something about rushing water that I can watch for hours and feel as if I need do nothing more. It's alive in a way that's greater than any description of it, like what you see in someone's eyes or expression, or hear in her voice."

"Do you actually speak this way?" she asked him, rattled by the nature of his reply. Before he could answer, the ferry blasted its whistle three times, and as the first blast echoed off the cliffs of lower Manhattan the boat began to skate into alignment with the slip, its stern skidding toward Brooklyn Heights.

"When I'm nervous, or in an exam," he said. "But I also do short answers and multiple choice."

"You do? You can answer simple questions, simply?"

"Yes."

"Good, because I think I have a lot of them."

# 4

## THE MOON RISING OVER THE EAST RIVER

NEITHER COULD DISENGAGE. To part now would be like lifting the tone arm in the middle of a song, the sudden silence inexplicable. And yet, as they had passed through the terminal they hadn't exchanged a word. The darkness above, deep and cool, was broken by the repeated flash of wings as jagged and quick as lightning. Catherine felt as if she were in a cathedral. She would remember for the rest of her life the friction of her shoes against the rough floor that sparkled like the Milky Way, which the lights of the city had banished long before, and how despite the arbor of sound—boat whistles, ferry engines, water lapping, waves breaking, the jingle of gates opening and closing, taxi horns, the flutter of birds—they had been encased in their own magnificent silence, aware of almost nothing except one another, electrified with a sense of beginning.

The air was charged with sunlight, and the streets were crowded with office workers released from financial houses and shipping companies. So that they could stay together, and because the custom had yet to die, Harry offered Catherine his arm, and she took it, lightly, their second touch, a high, intense pleasure out of all proportion to what anyone casually passing may have guessed. He feared that were he not to introduce some sort of conversation as a guide and to slow the rush she would vanish as if in a dream. So he asked her where she would like to have dinner.

"At four o'clock?"

"They're having dinner in Spain."

"Where would you suggest, other than Spain?"

"We could gamble. The first place we see."

"I don't eat at lumberyards or hardware stores. I'm not a termite."

"Look," he said, "the automat." A block and a half away, it was announced by its marquee of electric lights glowing weakly in the daylight. No man had ever taken Catherine out to dinner at anything other than an expensive restaurant that was thought to match her station, and never at four o'clock. "There," he said, gesturing at Horn & Hardart, "for a first date."

She disengaged from his arm, as if regretting all that occurred, and said, severely, "It's not a date. It can't be."

He thought she might turn and walk away. It would have been exquisitely painful had she done so. Instead, she said, "The automat has the best iced tea in the world, somehow," and led him inside. He felt as if he had just liberated Paris, and then Catherine told him her second untruth.

It wasn't exactly a lie, and though it made her uncomfortable, it was something she had to do. She was troubled not because she would be misleading him but because it was necessary to mislead him. Despite her belief that they could not progress much further, she began to weave the deception. "At least it's familiar," she said. She had no knowledge of the automat other than what she had been told by people who had been there. "I eat here a lot. It's wonderfully cheap, which is why I like it. And it's pretty good."

"And no one bothers you," he told her, "although sometimes I bother them."

This made her more than slightly nervous. "How do you mean?"

"I'll show you." They walked over to a bank of little glass doors in the hot-food section. He guided her to the counter in front of a rank of empty windows, put his hand in his right jacket pocket, took out a nickel, and rolled it into the slot of a "Frankfurter and Baked Beans" chamber.

"Why did you do that?" she asked. "There's nothing in there."

"There will be," he answered.

After standing with his left hand holding the metal-framed glass door slightly ajar for a minute or so, it shuddered, and a pleased smile came to his face. All the other doors locked shut, but not his. Soon, oval green ramekins holding little chariot-loads of baked beans with a hot dog reclining in the middle, like a very thin Prussian in an old-fashioned bathtub, were flipped like pie plates into each heated chamber. They came from the mysterious food-producing precincts behind the wall of little glass doors and the porcelain knobs one had to operate to unlock them.

When it was the turn of the chamber that Harry oversaw like a Brazilian Indian watching a rapids for the appearance of a fish, the back door opened and a hand appeared behind a loaded green dish. Harry grabbed the hand.

A scream came from behind the wall. "Lemme go!" It was a woman with the voice of Ethel Merman. Her fingernails were polished.

"Not until you put an extra hot dog on the plate," Harry told her. "That's the ransom."

"Are you crazy? I can't do that."

"Why not?"

"Because we're not supposed to."

"Did anyone actually ever tell you that?"

There was a pause. "No."

"Don't you have discretion?"

"Let go of my hand! What's discretion?"

"It means you're not an animal or a dummy. You can think for yourself, you can act for yourself, you can protect your own interests, you're not a creature of the boss."

"What are you, Willie Sutton? Batman?"

"Batman." He glanced at Catherine, whose eyes were wide. "Say something, Robin."

"Hello!" Catherine said in a high, lovely voice, after clearing her throat.

"I'll getcha one, but you gotta let go. I can't reach it."

"I've heard that before," Harry said. "Can't do that."

"Then no extra dog. I've got discretion."

"How can I trust you?"

"You can keep my ring as hostage."

He looked at the ring. "Where'd you get it, Woolworth's?"

"Tiffany's," said the voice, lying (and it knew it was lying).

"How do I know you won't go to the police or the FBI?"

Suddenly, a second hot dog entered the chamber and dived onto the plate. "I took it from another tray."

"Thanks," said Harry. "You're a sweetheart."

Catherine looked at him in a way she had never looked at anyone before, truly, and then she asked, "Do you always do this?"

"Not when I'm in a hurry."

She was speechless, but then she began to laugh, and the laugh came back as she bought herself iced tea and a buttered roll, and even when she rejoined him and sat down at a little table that wobbled every time either of them touched it or put something down. "Really," she said.

"It doesn't seem too outrageous to me," he replied, "given that a very short time ago the law required me to jump out of airplanes and shoot people whom I didn't know, and who were the sons, fathers, husbands, and brothers... of women just like you."

It was a lament. The war was so close, and so many had served. She closed her eyes briefly in acknowledgment.

Other than the effortlessly surfacing memory of her, all he had was her name, which was not real, her telephone number, which was, and an invitation to call her on Sunday night: at eight, she had said, with alluring precision. That weekend he wandered in and out of the complex shadows of the Els, in the Saturday-quiet districts of deserted factories and lofts, in a chevron across and down Central Park beneath a canopy of new leaves coloring the air light green. He walked forty miles in those two days, and though he spoke to no one, words came silently in torrents.

In every residential neighborhood, he imagined that she might suddenly step onto the sidewalk, and at every market or store, that he might see her buying whatever she might buy — a scarf, a book, an emerald, it hardly mattered. He would round a corner, wanting to see her amid the shelves of roses and peonies banked in front of a florist's. He would peer far ahead on the avenues and wide cross streets, hoping to catch sight of her at a distance. And dreaming that she would appear, he would scan crowds exiting theaters or moving through the parks in the armies of leisure and their stray battalions relaxedly ambling in all directions.

Manhattan and its vassal boroughs tirelessly generated images. Even smoke and steam rose beautifully, slowly unfurling in the play of wind and light like a silent song to redeem the memory of forgotten souls. As pictures endlessly flashing were the telegraphy of a superior force, so his infatuation, light and all-possessing, was the prelude to something finer. By what magic in the expression of a woman one could pass through the door to her heart into the heart of the world, to and fro in time, he did not know, but it was true.

On Sunday before he called Catherine he walked to the Battery, crossed over to Brooklyn on the Brooklyn Bridge, and recrossed on the Williamsburg. Behind and to his left, the Navy Yard was frozen into silence, the ships unfinished and the cranes stopped in their tracks as much reminders of the war dead as would have been white crosses. In the park, across from his apartment, he rested on a bench overlooking the playground in which he had played when a child. At four that afternoon the air turned rather cool for late in May, and mothers and nannies farseeing enough to have brought coats and hats put them on their children and their charges.

Watching the children, he noticed two things especially. A girl of about five, and her sister, who was no more than three, wanted to drink from the pebbled concrete fountain at the playground's edge, but it was too high for either of them, so the five-year-old, who was fairly heavily coated and had a cloche hat, jumped up and, resting her stomach on the edge and grasping the sides, began to drink. But she was neither strong enough nor oblivious enough of the pain to hang on, and she began to slip off backward. At this, the three-year-old, in knit cap and pink coat, advanced to her sister and, also grasping the edge of the fountain, placed her forehead against her sister's behind, straining to hold her in place, eyes closed, body trembling, curls spilling from her cap. Her sister drank for a long time, held in position by an act as fine as Harry had ever seen on the battlefields of Europe.

There were swings for older children, the kind with open seats suspended from chains, but the swings for infants were almost like cages: little wooden crates with safety bars, hanging from four ropes. On one of them a mother had placed her baby girl. In a camel's hair coat, mittens, and a dark knit cap, the child was no older than eighteen months, quite chubby, and seemingly half asleep. But she awoke when her mother pushed her on the swing and it gained speed, gently rising higher with each push. Away from her mother, and back, but always rising, always returning, her eyes on the trees and sky. As she flew, with little wisps of her hair pressed back by the wind, she squinted, and as she rose it seemed that she easily apprehended something for which he had to strain and sacrifice to remember even as a trace.

That weekend, Catherine was not as sanguine as Harry, for although she might easily have had him at her door, by her side, or in her bed, merely by invitation or command, such power is not only the power of attraction but the cause of hesitation. In the automat they sat across from one another oblivious of everything else, except that, because it was too early on, they would break their easy silence with conversation. And then they would fall into it again. That as love commences all couples must make bowers is written in the blood. And in New York they make them invisibly in restaurants, where, surrounded by a shell of something like glass that mutes the sounds of the world and blurs and intercepts its light, they would hardly notice if Vikings or Visigoths sacked the adjoining tables and set the place on fire. This obliviousness she had tried to resist, and by nature, in an act written in the blood just as deeply, she put him off until Sunday.

Though he wanted to call her and was able to wait only because he knew that he could and would, she could not have called him had he not called her. Thus, she tacked contrary to her character, which was otherwise and notably hot and decisive, and waited as if disinterestedly until Sunday night at eight, the expectation of which, despite her purposeful discipline, lifted her incessantly. For her, it had not been a minor encounter. There was something about him, something in his eyes that led far beyond his shy and careful manner upon meeting her, something momentous and grave enough to lead to a great deal of trouble, heartbreak, and anger. For she was already betrothed.

To pass the time, she did what she ordinarily would do. On Saturday, she went swimming, and though the water that washed over her as she dolphined through it sometimes became his embrace, with almost every stroke she also swam away from him, and at the end of her mile as she lifted herself up from the pool onto the mosaic deck, removing the horrid bathing cap, dripping, lightheaded, and strong, as the water ran off her it was as if they had parted and she was alone. And then came sorrow, longing, and a contentment bought by the borrowings of optimism, which she knew would be paid back with interest and then some were he not to call. As she walked home, every sight and sound was intense. At the corner of 57th and Park, on Saturday afternoon in the sunshine, her right hand unconsciously over her heart, she stood through two lights, oblivious of the cars and people coming and going, surging forward, stopping, starting. She stared down the south-shadowed side of 57th Street toward the East River, watching flags and clouds in the wind, the former as rebellious as a wild horse on a rope, and the latter sailing like weightless galleons.

The servants who had not accompanied her parents to East Hampton, where she was supposed to have been as well, had been dismissed, and she was alone in the house. On Saturday night she descended the five flights from her rooms on the top floor to the kitchen in the basement, and on the wide marble stairs between the first and second floors she danced — because she could dance beautifully, because the stairs were challenging to the choreography, because she liked the sound of her shoes clicking against the glossy stone, and because she imagined that he was watching her, and, better yet, that someday, though it seemed impossible given the situation, he really would watch her as she descended these stairs. She wondered if, in what she hoped had been his infatuation, he had noticed her body, through which she could express a great deal both effable and ineffable. Then, still on the stairs, she paused, recalling that he had.

In the kitchen, dangerously happy as she listened to the radio, she made herself a light dinner, which she ate standing up at a limestone island beneath a huge pot rack. On a bed of lettuce, greens, and cherry tomatoes, she put two enormous prawns, two sea scallops, and some crabmeat. This she dressed with olive oil — no vinegar, she did not like vinegar — a pinch of salt, pepper, and a sprinkling of paprika. To the left of her plate she placed a linen napkin and silverware — she did not like to put silverware on the right, without a napkin upon which it could rest — and to the right a wine glass three-quarters filled with Champagne. Champagne seemed to follow Catherine wherever she went. She opened the metal bread drawer in front of and below her, took out a roll, put it on a small bread plate, and stepped back. The bubbles in her glass seemed to rise and dance in synchrony with the songs on the radio. She was so happy she was silly, and she sang her version of a song that, even after she sang it, she could not get out of her head:

> Picka you up in a takasee honey,
> See-ah you abouta halfa past eight!
> Picka you up in a takasee baby,
> Donah be late!

She would not have eaten while standing up and moving to music had she not been overbrimming with expectation. "Goddammit," she said out loud, encouraged by just a little Champagne, "if I have to throw him over, I'll throw him over." Then she stopped, two feet from the plate, staring at it as if it were a calculus problem. "No one," she said, "has ever thrown Victor over. He doesn't throw over." And then she said, "But I will!" and she was happy again, lightened, confident.

The next day, Sunday, she walked from Sutton Place to the tennis courts in Central Park to meet a friend and college classmate, a beautiful, unpredictable, Cuban blonde who was scandalously married to a Jewish neurologist, the scandal being not that he was Jewish, for so was she, but that he was a neurologist, which by her family's standards was insufficiently dynastic. Her mother had once said, "To live without chauffeurs is to live like an animal."

Catherine and Marisol in tennis whites turned so many heads that they were embarrassed. The male tennis players, sometimes missing their shots, could not refrain from glancing at them, first at one and then at the other, like spectators, rather than players, at a tennis match. Had Harry been home and looked out his windows fronting the park, he could have seen them, distant but dazzling. Instead, he was half searching for her on every street in the city. As he was walking home, they were finishing their game, and as he passed the playground and came out onto Central Park West, Catherine was a few hundred feet to the east.

On her way home, she continued to hear in memory the tennis balls that, struck by earnestly wielded rackets, sounded like a continual and uneven popping of corks. When she crossed the bridle path literally in the shadow of the San Remo, two horses trotted by, high and handsome. On one was a man perfectly attired in riding boots, jodhpurs, a tweed jacket, a tie, and a very fine hat. With a carnation at his lapel, and an expert seat, he was turned in the saddle, speaking to his daughter, a girl of seven or eight, just as elegantly attired but in miniature. Though her horse was somewhat smaller than his, she was confronted with the universal terror of rich young children, a terror that Catherine herself had faced and mastered, that of sitting on a spirited horse proportionately two and a half times higher, faster, and less amenable than her father's horse, with her legs having no chance of gripping its sides to keep her steady. The father had seemed as fixed in the saddle as a fact of gravity, but his daughter just rested there, balanced only by her grace and that of God. She was, however, unafraid, for she trusted him, and as they rode he gave good and learned advice, and by his love and by the grace of God, she stayed on.

A majestic staircase, with shiny white balusters and a red-brown chestnut rail, was set against the Sutton Place wall of her house, rising in switchbacks from the second floor to the sixth, past large windows that looked out onto the street. Thus she had been told, ever since she had been moved from the nursery to the sixth floor, never to take the stairs while dressed immodestly, lest the "poor people" who lived in the cooperative apartments across Sutton Place catch a glimpse of her *déshabillé*.

Once they reached their destination, these stairs opened onto a generous landing that ran the width of the building south to north. A left turn would take one along a gallery lined with lighted paintings to an architraved door at almost the north end, the entrance to her rooms. A long hall led into the depth of the building, and off this were a bathroom and dressing room, a study, and a bedroom together taking up less than half the floor. The major part and major room, into which the hall spilled as naturally as a brook, was an immense living area that led two steps down to a terrace. From this room, with a fireplace, grand piano, and American and French impressionist paintings glowing like jewels, one could look easily out over the river to Queens. The view was industrial and grim, but the water was wide and the sunrises almost blood red. The ships and barges that raced by, their speed doubled by the fast current, were close enough so that it was possible to see the color of the helmsmen's eyes.

Very few captains wanted to take their boats upriver when the current was running against them or downriver when it had shifted, but often they had to, and often they did. And when they did, vessels that at other times might appear and disappear in seconds would labor for five or ten minutes to move through the waters directly in her view. Where ordinarily when they rode on the current the pilots seemed breathlessly to guide them as they fell, pilots who guided them against the current were breathless as if from the exertion of climbing.

Immense volumes of foam in an oxygen-white avalanche were disgorged from straining propellers as they churned the river, which did not cease its resistance for a split second. The strain was so great and the force streaming against the prows so steady that the main task of the pilots was to keep the current dead ahead lest they be swung around and hurled sideways downriver or onto the rocks. Catherine had many times seen a barge and tug forced to come about. Mostly they had saved themselves, surrendering their hard-fought battle to run apostate with the current they had opposed, but more than once she had seen a panicked boat beach itself against the unforgiving banks.

And all this from the tranquility of her living room. Or from the terrace, which now that it was warm had a line of potted orange and lemon trees joining the evergreens that had remained outside through the winter. Cushions had been restored to chaises and chairs, and glass tops to wrought-iron tables. When she returned from playing tennis with Marisol, she closed the French doors to the terrace because a cool wind from the sea had pushed the warm air out of Manhattan like a croupier's rake moving chips across a felt-covered table.

Although the sun had yet to set, it was low and all her views were by now in shadow. She left the lights off until shortly after eight, when she switched them on because she wanted to make sure that without knocking anything over she could get to the phone if and when it rang, and because she had to be able to see her watch so that she would not sit for hours bereft, unknowing, and like an idiot, if he failed to call. If he didn't call, she would be very angry but heartbroken all the same. The lamp she switched on had been mounted on a Chinese vase. Though the shade was off-white and pearly, the white of the porcelain was absolute, and the blue like that of the ocean on a cold day.

Not having brought a key with him into the army, when he had returned from Europe Harry had to ask the super to make a new key for the apartment. During the time it took to find the super, go down to the workshop, and have the key made, he was stricken with grief, for he knew that his father's death would come home to him with finality only when he stepped over the threshold. But as he turned the key in the lock, he was unprepared for what he would see.

Virtually nothing remained. Other than walls of books now stacked on the floor and covered with dropcloths, there were several boxes of files, letters, and photographs. Another box held a few cameras, some watches, his father's folding knife, and a pair of binoculars, all familiar to him. Gold, silver, bank notes, stock certificates, and a small amount of precious jewelry were in a safe-deposit box to which the lawyer would give him the key when making out the papers that lawyers prepare in such circumstances.

But in the apartment itself, other than the boxes and books and a few pieces of good furniture, nothing was left. Even the curtains had been removed, and the walls were freshly painted white. He had to open windows to vent the paint fumes and, early in September, cool the air. His father had had warning and enough time to dispose of his clothes, the contents of drawers, and things that would be difficult for his son either to throw away or to keep. The message was clear: start over and anew. Harry might not have understood this as well as he did had he not just been through four years of war. Now he knew, and he was grateful to his father and loved him all the more.

One of the first things he did was something he had vowed to do if he came back alive. Having fought through France, he loved it immeasurably, and had always loved its painters. So, with a not inconsequential part of his inheritance, he went to an auction at Parke-Bernet and bought — for $6,000, the price of a house — a Manet: sea, sky, and flags whipping in the wind. It would have been frightening to spend that much money had he not just returned from North Africa, Sicily, Normandy, Nijmegen, and the Bulge, where money didn't mean much. He put the painting above the fireplace in his L-shaped living room overlooking the park. Well lit and deep blue, the Manet drew the room into a placid infinity. Every other thing — an English partners' desk, sofas that he re-covered in damask, new drapes and carpets — seemed naturally to fall in place around it and become more beautiful because of it.

He reshelved the thousands of books on the newly painted bookcases that lined the south and west walls of the living room, and had shelves built in what had been his father's bedroom, which he made into a study. He refinished the dining room table, replaced the icebox with an electric refrigerator, and made his old room at the back austere, with, however, a double bed.

He lived quietly, with almost no visitors, waiting on events. Deciding not to take any important steps until he had passed at least a year in civilian life, he had spent nine months without the need for action or decision. At work he did little, leaving almost everything to Cornell Wright. He attended to his health, read, and spent a lot of time sitting in the park or in his apartment, thinking and remembering. He knew that his capacity for action could be unleashed in a flood, that the world could instantly become demanding and dangerous once again. But this was his holiday and his rest, for which he was grateful even as he knew it could not last.

Contrary to her every impulse but with complete certainty that it was the right thing to do, at eight Catherine rose, walked to the table that held the instrument of which she had been thinking for two days and at which she had been staring for half an hour, removed the handset from its cradle, and rested it on a notepad beside the phone. Then she opened wide the French doors, crossed the terrace, and stood at the railing, the glossy leaves of a potted orange tree touching her on one side and those of a lemon tree brushing against her on the other.

A ship moved fast in the current, riding from Hell Gate at speed and under lights. It came into sight like charging cavalry, passed as fast as cars on a highway, and rushed downriver into the gathering darkness. She followed it with her eyes. When it had passed, she went in, picked up the telephone, and took it out to the railing, handling the long cord carefully because she didn't like unnecessary tangles. Before replacing the handset, she crushed a lemon leaf in her fingers, closed her eyes, and inhaled the scent. Now ready, she mated handset and cradle. Checking her tiny watch, which was never accurate despite the several times each year it was repaired, she saw that almost fifteen minutes had passed since the appointed time.

Uptown and west, Harry sat in his living room. The park was visible through four large windows, its lights twinkling as new leaves put them in and out of view according to the wishes of the breeze. Over the reservoir the canyon-front of Fifth Avenue and the higher buildings behind it began to come alight, a red sun having left the stone in shadow and the lights dim but rising. In the corner of his eye was the blue Manet framed in gold and shining like the sea. He had determined not to call until 8:20, but it was difficult to hold fire.

Overcome with the sudden conviction that he had already waited too long, he dialed at 8:15 exactly. The switching and relay took long enough so that Catherine's phone rang a little after, a great relief to her, as even the short time she had waited after freeing her line had filled her with apprehension that he had tried to call and would not call back, or that he hadn't called and never would. She let it ring six times, picked it up, and, as if she had been surprised and had no idea who might be calling, casually said hello.

"Is this Catherine?"

"Harry?"

"Where are you?" he asked. "I always ask, when I don't know, where the people are to whom I'm speaking on the telephone. It makes them less disembodied and abstract, and brings them closer."

"East Side," she said. "Fifties."

"Near a window?"

"Looking out."

"What do you see?"

She said, "I see a park: flower beds, trees. There are white, pea-gravel walks." She had deliberately tilted her head down so as not to see the river and Long Island on the opposite bank, and she had omitted to mention that this was a description not of a public park but of the largest private garden in Manhattan.

"I have no idea where that is. I thought I knew every inch of Manhattan. Is it a corner of a park, or a park that I missed? It's not Bryant Park, which is west of Fifth Avenue, and isn't in the Fifties. Where is it?"

"You'll see, someday. What about you?"

"I see Central Park as if from the bridge of a ship, a hundred and ten feet up — which is high enough to remove you from the noise of the street but low enough to keep the expanse of the park immense and the leaves visible one by one. Because it's dusk I can see the lights glowing in the mass of buildings on Fifth Avenue."

Her heart beat fast as she waited for what would come. As he looked out at the cliffs, now shining, and she at swift ships backlighted by the newly risen moon, Harry Copeland said to Catherine Thomas Hale, through the copper lines that tied together with electric current every cell in the body of Manhattan, the words—which though simple were excitingly charged with many meanings—"May I see you?"

# 5

## CATHERINE'S SONG

HER INSTRUCTION WAS that as the music came up she was supposed to take a breath, the kind of breath, as if in shock, that signals great emotion. It had to come just before the percussionist sounded the automobile horn, which elided into a trolley bell, which then became a torrent of music that transformed the dark theater into the streets of Manhattan in a blaze of light.

"Can you do this?" the director asked. "Think of yourself as, remember, the girl from Red Lion, Pennsylvania, or somewhere, somewhere where they have chickens. You step out of the station, and there all at once is the city. You've never seen anything like it. It's overwhelming. It takes your breath away. That's what we want."

"They have chickens in New York, Sidney," she said.

"Live ones?"

"Yes."

"Not in the restaurants where I eat. I'm asking, can you do it?"

"I can do it," she said, "but I'll have to practice."

"Practice taking in a breath?"

"If you want me to express what you want me to express...." She paused, and looked up at the darkness beyond the blinding spotlights that pinned her onstage. She waved her hand in a questioning spiral. "The whole city. If you want me to convey the life of the city, on this stage, in a single breath—I mean, really—you'll have to have a little patience."

"The music has something to do with it too, dear," the director told her condescendingly. She was the youngest member of the cast, and it was her first part.

But, with one great exception, which she had not overcome, it was both easy for her and in her blood to hold firm. "The music, Sidney, has more than just a quarter of a second with which to work."

He relented. "All right, everyone take a break so she can practice breathing. At Bryn Mawr, didn't they teach you to breathe?"

"That's not what they do at Bryn Mawr. It's a college. You learn to breathe way before that. *Capisce?* I need fifteen minutes." This was just the beginning of her song, as hard as it was, and the song itself, arrestingly beautiful, would have to follow with just the right tone, the right pacing, and the right gloss.

She hurried backstage to stairs that rose to the grid, and as she ascended she realized that, never having been there, she didn't know if she could reach the roof this way. Even if she could, the view might be blocked, and even were it not, would she find enough in what she would see, because in Manhattan after the war the great and the heroic had given way to tranquility and rest. She drifted up through the darkness, unsure. The higher she climbed, the more the activity below, seen through a black matrix of ropes, bars, wires, and flats, seemed like a miniature of the city itself. Lighting technicians brought up crazily timed sunsets and sunrises in orange and gold, and replicated the terra-cotta-colored rays that in late afternoon make the high façades of city blocks into cathedrals of light. The people moving in the wash of the kliegs seemed to flutter like masses of wings, and in the flare of tungsten fair hair looked like the gold that sparkles in sunlit rock.

At the top of the stairs was a door. After pushing it open and stepping out she found herself high above the street, with neither rail nor parapet to guard her from falling. Because of what she saw from the roof of the theater she did not need to practice as she had thought she would. For as she beheld what lay before her, the sharp infilling of her lungs, divided into a short beat and a slightly longer one that followed and concluded, was as lovely a sound as any living being has ever made. She had had no idea that a single breath could be so magnificent, that it could outdo the clearest notes of the greatest soprano, or the perfection, down below, of a brass section manned by balding and ever-hopeful rejects of the New York Philharmonic.

She had mastered her part in an instant, but, still, she stayed, held by the time and place, for although she was only twenty-three, she had a history of looking into the heart of great scenes and busy prospects as if she were at the end of life and these were something that she had yet to decode.

Down long streets in a hundred shades of gray, in clouds of fast white smoke and in flights of pigeons that with the twitch of a thousand wings were like the turning of a skyscraper's worth of venetian blinds; at the foot of piers where ferries skated-in over silver water, their top-hat stacks billowing smoke that trailed across a whitening page of sky; in the tangle of the streets; in the traffic autonomous, fighting for complete independence, yet ever moving as a herd; amidst sound too broken and complex to interpret except as a twin of surf perpetually effervescent on the beaches of Long Island; and in the miracle of faces, to which even the greatest painters cannot do full justice; there was the city almost at midcentury, as one age had begun to elide into another, and the innocent forms of the past, though numb from the deep cut of war, were still alive.

She felt so strongly what she saw that she tried to hold its impress in memory until she was able to puzzle it out, even if that would be never. To see things and long for them, shadows in gray, people who will never return, days of sun and clouds that vanish like smoke... this was what she wanted.

What she saw was not random, and not chaos beyond the deepest power to make clear, for the threads of beauty and meaning that ran through it shone brightly in the dark, the whole a work greater than art, its consistency assured. This she knew because she had seen it and felt it since infancy, and would not be turned from her faith and trust even by all the war and suffering in the world, even were the suffering her own, which, although in her view it had never been, she knew eventually it would, in that it comes to all. All souls, she believed, blinded and blown into the air like dust and tumbling without gravity, can nonetheless find their bearings and rise as intended into the light. But despite this glimpse of the years to come in a vision of the ceaseless shuffling, transfer, and transaction in the streets below — like spangles of light on a sunlit river — she had to go back down into the theater to play her part, and she did.

She had taken the breath as instructed, and night after night would reproduce it onstage. Though she did not have the lead, in a quarter second she would have to supply the transcendent moment upon which the production would rise or fall. From her lungs and breast would come a gasp, a cry, the beginning of a song that would bring into view in a dark theater the machinery and friction of one era breathing its life into another, of light mixing with light, and sorrow with sorrow. And all conveyed in one sweet breath of Catherine Thomas Hale.

Which was not, however, the name by which they knew her. Her stage name was Catherine Sedley. They were unaware that she had chosen to call herself, professionally, after a mistress of James II. This was not because the original Catherine Sedley was virtuous but because this Catherine Sedley loved the sound of the name, because it took her family out of the picture, and because from a scandalously young age she had understood the travails of being a mistress.

She was, in her way, although not everyone thought so, very beautiful. It was not a soft beauty but, rather, sharp and delicate, with a backing of unseen strength that was not quite fully developed as she came into womanhood. In isolation, the pure, heartbreaking beauty of her face, though hardly perfect, could almost be an object of worship. Her body was strong and vibrant, and when she moved, or laughed, or settled back into a chair, she became sexually radiant. It is possible to have eyes that are carelessly unobservant, that in failing their task betray a listless soul. In contrast, the hazel eyes of Catherine Thomas Hale (or, if you wish, Catherine Sedley), though neither large nor opalescent, which would have made them commonly beautiful, were clear, alert, and ever active. They seized at a great rate upon the details of images that most eyes overlook even in things that appear in plain sight.

Though glasses were off limits onstage and there she was slightly myopic, other than when she was in the sea or in the shower she often wore a pair of round lenses held in delicate black metal frames that her father had brought from Paris before the war, and that seemed as thin as the locks floating at her temples, where these had escaped from a mass of reddish-blond hair, the color depending upon the light and sometimes as dark as auburn or as bright as gold, kept exquisitely up and partly braided at the back in a magical combination that was both classically arranged and randomly loose, almost windblown, as if she had come in from a deck or a beach.

The lenses, plumb-set and perpendicular to the plane of the floor, were a foil to the sharp assertiveness of her nose, which was small, perfectly formed, gracefully projecting. Her upper lip was larger than the lower, which suggested imminent speech protected nonetheless by careful reticence. Her teeth, unnaturally white in the glare of the spotlights, were even, straight, and large, in alluring palisades that cried out to be kissed.

As a rule, her bearing was uncompromising, and she held her head as if her name had just been called. Her breasts, not large, had as a result of her long, firm back and superb posture a perpetually attractive thrust. When she sat at table she had the habit of lightly grasping the edge with both hands, thumbs beneath the tabletop. This aligned her in a way that was ravishing. Even had her hands not been so beautiful, had her hair not been so glorious, had her face not been of breathtaking construction, had her youth not enveloped her like a rose, had her eyes not been so lovely, even had all this been different, the way she held herself, and her readiness to see, her fairness of judgment, and her goodness of heart would have made her beautiful beyond description. She was, like many, though not everyone by any means could see it, beautiful, just beautiful, beyond description.

Passing through the mitered beams of spotlights that convened upon the stage, she was now ready to take up her task. "So fast?" the director asked as the musicians walked sideways to their places amid a forest of metal chairs. The happiness of her expression betrayed her answer and her certainty.

"Okay," he said, "from the top, and when you're ready. Remember, what you see is the streets, the traffic, the mass of buildings — not a nineteenth-century drawing room." He had described the set that would be there months later, after they had opened in Boston and if they were fortunate enough to get back to New York. They had the theater in the daytime on days without matinees, and the play that was running in the space they hoped eventually to occupy at night was a drama about what one critic had called "the discovery of physics." The set in which Catherine was to represent the miracle of a city was at the moment displaced by a London drawing room in which, by nine that night, fake German accents would contend with fake English accents in arguments about the atom: "I have izolated zeh atom in zeh zspecial zserum!" "Bloody not!"

His front bathed in lectern light, the conductor took up a white wand and, without a tap, quickly lifted and depressed it to make his musicians ready. Then began a coordinated rush: a blast of brass, a piano tremolo, a horn, bells, and Catherine's marvelous breath, the finest note of all, and so full of life it was like God breathing into Adam, a woman in the midst of love, a cry of astonishment, or the sound made by a swimmer who bursts into light and air. For in her quarter of a second she outdid the instruments, the plan, the setting, the lighting, the book, the music itself. That she could do this so readily and so well, stunned her listeners, but then came the song, so different from the brassy start, so terribly moving and entrancingly slow. It was, at least in that very moment, the most beautiful song in the world.

"That was . . . ," the director said, unable to find words when the music ended. "That was. . . . Can you do it again, just like that?"

"Yes."

"From the top," he commanded.

The conductor lifted his baton a second time, the music started with the same professional consistency, and at the right instant Catherine came in, playing a note that, though it was common to everyone who had ever lived, here was played astonishingly well. When she finished her song, the director, thinking of Boston and Broadway and his apotheosis, spoke as if from the thrones of Hollywood.

"It couldn't be better," he told her. "Keep it just like that. And the beginning. . . . God, I was looking at this *fahkahkteh* set, but I saw Madison Square."

"I have a suggestion," Catherine said, though not because she was taking advantage of the quick rise in her stock, for she would have spoken up anyway. "I arrive at Penn Station from God knows where. . . ."

"Chickens," the director filled in. This was his opinion of anything west of the Hudson and east of Santa Monica Boulevard.

"Yes, you said that, but where?"

"Pennsylvania."

"Why Pennsylvania?"

"Are you arguing with the book, Miss Sedley?"

"The book doesn't specify."

"So we can supply anything we want. You can't be from the South, you don't speak that way. Most of Pennsylvania is rural, and you really are from Pennsylvania."

"I'm from New York," Catherine said. "I went to college in Pennsylvania."

"Where'd you learn to speak that way? Don't ask me for a raise, but it's gorgeous."

"Thank you. I don't know."

"Bryn Mawr," the director said, pointing at her with the index finger of his left hand as if he had solved a mystery.

"No, Sidney," she replied. "New York, with possibly a little Bryn Mawr, although I doubt it."

"New York City?" he asked, pointing the same finger now at the floor. Her voice and manner of speaking were so aristocratic that he looked at her for a long moment as he realized that he didn't really know who she was. He might have resented her refined mien and speech, but he didn't, because he knew that though the country had long before given the forbears of people like her their chance, and that obviously they had taken it, it was now giving him his. "Whatever your speech," he said, "keep it."

"I arrive from Pennsylvania," she stated, moving on. "I set the scene. The audience sees the city through my eyes and in the breath. Then I meet Wilson in the automat."

"Who the hell is Wilson?"

"I mean Charles. I fall in love with him, I go to work at Lord and Taylor, he falls in love with Amanda, the society girl, and I'm out, finished, smunk"—they wondered what she meant by *smunk*—"and I can be home by nine-thirty, despite my song, which is really great, and makes people cry even way at the beginning of the play. It should be at the end of the play."

"You can't rewrite the book, Catherine, and a lot of actors would die so they could be home at nine-thirty."

"Wouldn't it be better," she asked, as if he hadn't said anything and as if he hardly existed, "if I, and not Amanda, married Charles? Because, the way it's written, Amanda is kind of a bitch, and I'm the underdog. She's got the money, a mansion, a chauffeur, and she's really a God-awful bitch, really. I'm a farm girl, from a chicken-keeping place in Pennsylvania, who becomes a shop girl. This is a play, Sidney. I should marry Charles." She seemed dumbfounded at the injustice.

"You are going to argue with the book."

"Well, yes."

"Look," said the director, "Charles is a returning soldier. The play is called *Homecoming*, right? He's a poor Irish boy from Hell's Kitchen. You're right, this is a play. *He* gets the society girl. That's the way it's supposed to be, because that's what people like."

Knowing that she would not prevail, Catherine looked to the side as she spoke, which was what she often did when she knew that her words would be spoken in vain. "But what do I get?" she asked, as if she and her part were the same. "What about me? It would be a better play if Charles married me."

"And you would have a bigger part. And we would have to rewrite the play, change the lyrics, and add new songs. It doesn't work that way, Catherine. We've got investors."

"All right," she said, "though if you did, I would be happy to switch parts with Amanda."

"No," the director decreed. "Especially not after today. We need you for your song. We need you for that breath. We need you for that one note, Catherine. Catherine, on that one note, this play depends."

She hadn't been unhappy with his assessment. How could she have been? Still, she found it galling that he had his eye on her, and every time he spoke to her or looked her way she wanted to say, "Sidney, there are many buttons that never should be unbuttoned, and never will be, at least not by you." In her dressing room, in front of an electrified mirror that bathed her in incandescent light, she tried to mark her position and think ahead through the confusion of Harry, Victor, and God knows what else. And she found herself struggling, hardly for the first time, against a competing image, a picture that was moving and yet somehow still, of a boy swinging on a rope tied to the girders of an elevated train platform on the East Side. It was somewhere near 100th Street. Moving from sunlight into shadow and shadow into sunlight, he made a perfect inverted arc. She had seen him sometime in the twenties, as she passed in a car that seemed as big as a room, on her way south to her house overlooking the garden and the river. He was older than she was, but it didn't matter. Though she was only a little girl and had no hope of ever seeing him again, something had happened. She had looked through the glass and seen him just as he had come into the sunlight at the top of his arc, and for an instant, in a flash that to the conscious mind is incomprehensible — behind him, to his left, merely from the corner of his eye and through the window of a moving car — he had seen her.

As he reached the top of the arc his feet pointed gracefully but unconsciously to the path he would then follow. He had had no idea that she had seen him, and no idea that, as he flew from light to shadow and back, she had taken his image into her eyes as if with the decisive click of a camera shutter.

The boy on the rope, by her long, insistent memory, by what he was and how he had lasted, was fighting hard not to be forgotten. Somehow, he had seen her through shame and grief, and she had never betrayed him. She saw herself behind the polished glass reflecting the lace-like girders. She saw his face, and her own, and though she knew that he was long gone and she would never see him again, when he had flown silently from light to dark, and back again, rising and falling beneath the steelwork, he had come into her life forever.

# 6

## IN PRODUCTION

OTHER THAN HAVING to be there less, one of Harry's chief pleasures in arriving late to work was to traverse the narrow blocks west of Fifth Avenue at midmorning. Here, industrial lofts were stacked twenty storeys or more in massive buildings that kept the street in shadow except when, rising or setting, the sun was low and its light golden red in rifle-shot alignment east to west or west to east. To a practiced ear, the noise of this district was divided and comprehensible. By listening as closely as if to birds in the forest it was possible to disentangle the weavings of sound and give each thread its due.

The wind, above all, when it whistled past, moving in great volume through the high canyons and meticulously touching everything, provided a background of ascending or descending notes determined by the speed of the air, its temperature and density, what windows had been left open or closed, what chains were hanging, what ventilators revolved at what speed and with what squeak and shriek due to oil or its lack, or friction, malfunction, or rust. Adding to the roar were trucks by the hundreds, never in the same permutation, with different types of engines at various rates of idle, diesel or gasoline, shaking, jangling, or smooth, and parked in different patterns, and automobiles from limousines to motorcycles, not to mention carts, bicycles, and garment racks with little wheels that made more noise than locomotives.

Like the bleats of Tibetan sheep, the car horns of Manhattan echoed across the cliffs. Conversation and argument in a dozen languages mixed with cries, shouts, and commands to back or stop, load or drop. Freight elevators were in constant motion, surprisingly rising and falling, sometimes emerging magically and unfolding from the sidewalk, their steel frames sprouting like beanstalks. Their castled gates opened and closed, slammed and shut, in iron and wood, solid and grid. Presiding over this were hundreds of men and scores of women who passed in and out of building entrances and stood by their trucks or pushed racks and dollies loaded with boxes, clothing, tailings, and bolts. This was a society that only they could fully understand. On every block, hundreds of companies, each more or less unknown to the other, went about their complex work, the thousands of employees divided into sections and subsections, cliques, groups, and friendships. Cross-banded by ethnicity, language, and past acquaintance, they mixed together on the street. When they came out for lunch, left for the day, or arrived in the morning, it was like Coney Island in July as thousands jostled against thousands. But at other times it was less crowded, and most often when Harry arrived at the Copeland Leather loft on 26th Street he would pass the chiefs and capos, those workers who absent formal powers managed to stand in charge and run the action of the street.

Their networks were invisible, and they seemed to know one another whether they did or not. They inspected everyone who passed, and controlled their building entrances like guards at the White House. They worked sporadically, the casts they supervised changed every few minutes, and they could speak in concussive bursts that enabled them to carry on a conversation with someone across the street and a hundred feet down the block as if they were standing shoulder to shoulder. They greeted one another explosively. "Hey! Vinnie!" they might shout, as if Vinnie, whom they had seen half an hour before, had just come back from the dead. "Hey hey hey!"

He — Harry, not Vinnie, not yet — could have joined the Harvard Club, sat in its vast main room and, surrounded by crimson and gold and bathed in the cocktail light of late afternoon, listened to the ticking of the clock and the play of the fire. He could have gone there pretending to have arrived, the rough edges of the city smoothed and its sharp sounds muted. But each time he received an invitation from the Harvard Club to join he was seduced instead by the industrial lofts stacked one upon another, their society, their industry, and their vitality, and he postponed his application for the time when he could do little but rest in the kind of comfortable chair that is to the end of life what a cradle is to the beginning.

Although the unwritten code was that if you were in a suit you took the lobby elevators and pressed buttons, he preferred to ride with the freight. And now, because the freight elevator was waiting disengaged at street level, he seized the webbing strap with which to part the gates, pulled it down, and watched one rise and the other fall until he could step through. Then he cleared them and guided to the fourteenth floor the immense box in which, though it could have held the weight of three or four elephants, he was the only passenger. The whole fourteenth floor was his, not leased but owned by Copeland Leather, and other than Cornell he was the only one who had been present since its beginnings. Having played there as a child, he knew the place in microscopic detail as only a child can. Though it changed day by day according to the needs of the moment, though walls were put up and taken down, lights and machines moved, reorganizations accomplished, and though he had been largely absent for six years before the war and entirely so for four years during the war itself, it was imprinted on him as on no one else. He was aware of things there that adults skated over, having learned them in other places and filed them away. Despite the changes, he could have found his way in the dark, as one can in one's childhood home, and he was as comfortable here in his early thirties as he had been at six.

The loft was a rectangle of approximately twenty thousand square feet, and its north and south sides had rows of windows that went all the way up to a twelve-foot ceiling. The core, around which the workspaces were arranged, comprised the ventilating ducts and electrical panels, storage, bathrooms, the passenger elevators, and offices. The freight elevator was at the eastern, windowless base of the rectangle.

The gate that faced south into the street opened on the ground floor only: inside, access to the lofts was via a west-facing gate on the elevator's longer side.

No signs or receptionist greeted a visitor arriving on the fourteenth floor, who found himself in a workshop as busy as a Central American market. Depending upon health, the vacation schedule, and whether the leather buyer was in or out, up to forty-eight people would be at work on a given day: a leather buyer, supply clerk, wood joiner, boxer/packer, stock manager, mechanic, two sweepers/cleaners, three leather cutters, three hardware fabricators, two truck drivers/deliverymen, six stainers/waxers/polishers, two bookkeepers, Cornell, Harry, and twenty-two leathersmiths.

No one had ever taken a census, but had one been taken it would have identified the largest ethnic grouping as Italian, then, in the terms of the day, Porto Rican, Jewish, Colored, Irish, and Protestant, meaning anything from Dutch and English to Czech, German, and Scandinavian. The Jews were all Russian, and one of the cutters was Chinese. Meyer Copeland had offered his workers a choice between ownership without voting rights of half the company, or unionization. Even apart from their dividends, their wages were higher than union scale. This created a source of ongoing conflict with the unions themselves, which didn't know what to make of Copeland Leather and tabled the question, carving out an exception that existed year by year not by right but by sufferance. Some in the union leadership viewed what Meyer had done as a noble socialist experiment, others as a clever capitalist trick, and they could never come to agreement, because it was neither.

Production was arranged in a circle. At the left of the freight elevator, purchased leather was received, inspected, sorted, and held for the short term if it were soon to be used. Each flat or roll was viewed under incandescent, fluorescent, ultraviolet, and natural south light because north light was too even. The buyer, who had seen it before, used his hands and eyes and could tell certain things by smell. The next step was the cutting room, where long-experienced cutters placed their patterns on the leather so that the finer surfaces would be exposed most conspicuously in the final product.

The cut and patterned leather then went to the twenty-two leathersmiths according to their specialties, and they did the bending, fitting, and stitching, mating the occasional wood frames provided by the joiner, and the brass and nickel hardware provided by the metal fabricators, to the briefcase, handbag, belt, or valise. Wallets, portfolios, and blotters required neither wood nor brass. The leathersmithing stage was by far the most time-consuming and took up the most physical space, with each leatherworker stitching, cutting, planing at his own capacious bench, his bank of machines, and his cabinet of tools.

In the next step, the leather was stained, dried, waxed, and polished. Then it sat and breathed for a while in an area between the wood and metal shops until it was wheeled past the business offices in the middle of the north side and brought to the boxer and packer, who put each item in a felt bag, wrapped it in crisp tissue paper, and placed it in a deep brown, navy blue, and gold Copeland Leather box. These were then stored in a set of large rooms with high shelves, and were eventually packed into cartons for shipment to accounts all over the country and the world, not least the Copeland Leather store on Madison Avenue just north of St. Patrick's Cathedral and the Villard Houses. There, two ancient Yankees, though one was pretty much Dutch, gentlemen's gentlemen whom Meyer Copeland had pirated from Brooks Brothers, somehow did a land-office business at a slow and dignified pace. Working on commission, they did very well, as they deserved, for they were the face of Copeland Leather to its loyal and habitual clientele.

Henry Livingston, the one who despite his name was pretty much Dutch, spoke in the ancient and elevated New York dialect in which Catherine spoke. And he knew how to use his speech as a kind of lullaby by which to mesmerize into buying briefcases the stockbrokers, lawyers, and rentiers who had come in for just a wallet. Both salesmen, if one could call them that, were silver-templed and tall, their heads held erect and thrown back like a pigeon's. Henry Livingston's colleague, Thaxton Thrale, was as intimidating as the headmaster of Groton or St. Paul's, as tall as a Masai, and as dour as a hogshead of lemon juice. His almost total silence, in combination with his doubting, provisionally contemptuous glance, made the carriage trade so desperate for his approval that they spent money like demons. That was the trick. Henry was the soft cop and Thaxton the hard. Henry lived on Park Avenue, and Thaxton in Ardsley, in a greystone house, with a pale and terrified wife who jumped like a cat when he twitched, and three children who called him *sir*.

Though Harry often stopped by the store to see how things were going, and though ultimately he was in control, they were to the company what chiefs are to the navy, of low rank but admirals in their own right.

Cornell had known Harry since the infant Harry had learned to walk, and had always been as affectionately tough with him as an uncle. "Well," he said without looking up, as Harry swept into the office on Monday morning, ruddy and smelling of chlorine, "it's sleeping beauty."

"I wasn't sleeping, I was swimming."

"I know. I can smell the chlorine."

"What am I supposed to do, cut the leather a second time?"

Cornell turned and looked at him directly. "You're supposed to do *something*," he said, and turned back to the work at his desk.

"When I said I'd need a year, you didn't object."

"Why a year?" Cornell asked, pivoting in his almost-yellow swivel chair, which squealed like a mouse. "I was in the First War. I went to work the day after I got back. Right here." He paused and, to be clear, added, "Not here, when we were in Paterson."

"It's different."

"Why is that?"

"How long were you in the army? How long were you overseas? And how old were you?" Harry asked, knowing that Cornell, who was Jesuitically precise, would know exactly.

"When we entered the war I was your age now. I was in the army a little over a year, and in France for seven months."

"There's the difference. When we entered the war this time I was twenty-six. I was in the army for four years. And I was overseas for more than three. I need the time, because I don't know what to make of what happened. It isn't that I don't understand it: I'll probably never understand it. It's that I haven't yet absorbed it. I need a rest not because I'm tired but because of what I've seen, and there's no direction in which, at present, I have ambition."

"Necessity will show you that direction or you'll live a wasted life."

"It hasn't 'til now. The business is running efficiently: I couldn't manage it the way you do. I have no desire to duplicate what you do. I don't even know if I want to stay. I know how it works, but to cut or stretch as well as they can" — he meant the workers beyond the glass partitions — "would take twenty years, and what would be the point?"

"We're running efficiently," Cornell said, "but selling less."

"We're not a mechanized business, we're a craft. The only way to compete with people whose labor costs are a fifth of ours or less," Harry said, "is for all of us to take less. The workers are closer to the margin, so you and I would really have to tighten, but the two of us can hardly do it all. If we reduce their wages, the unions will rescind the exception and strike us. We'll go out of business or pay up, after which we'll go out of business anyway, just as we may now if the trend continues. I don't know what to do. It'll take Europe decades before it catches up to us and prices align. Maybe never."

"There could be another war in Europe," Cornell said. "We've just had two."

"Stalin would attend," Harry added, "as Russia has yet to demobilize. But if there were another war, when it ended and we stopped making belts for generals we'd be right where we are now."

"If we were a different kind of business, if we were an industry, we could pay off Congress and they would raise tariffs to protect us," Cornell said. "But we're too little. We don't matter like General Electric."

"I wouldn't want to be General Electric."

"That's not the point." Cornell stared out the window, into the north light. "The store's okay."

"Because we've got the only two clerks in New York who don't raid the till. It's a miracle."

"We could open in other cities."

"No cash, Cornell. With our sales the banks won't loan us any money, and we couldn't afford the interest anyway. At this point they probably wouldn't lend to us if we were doing well. I have a hundred thousand dollars to my name. With that we could open stores in Chicago and Boston. People know Copeland Leather. We'd probably do all right. But it's all the money I have, and if we open stores, we lose accounts."

"We're losing them anyway."

"So maybe we'll do that. But it makes me nervous, because if it didn't work I'd have no reserves, either for the business or myself. And where can we get a Henry or a Thaxton? There aren't people like them anymore, who have the manner and appearance of a chairman of the board but will work in a store and behave like a butler."

"They make them in Boston," Cornell said, "but we'd have to import them to Chicago. And we know New York, Harry, we don't know any other city. We could really sink fast. Maybe we should sell to that schmuck from Cyprus."

"That sounds like a musical," Harry said. "*That Schmuck from Cyprus.*"

"It would pass our problems on to him, and keep everyone employed."

"You think so?"

"No. He'd take the name, the store, the accounts, and move all the production to Europe."

"I wish my father were here."

"Maybe for his sake it's better that he's not."

"You don't think he'd know what to do?"

"He might, but that's not the point. What are *you* going to do?"

"I don't know."

"I mean today."

"Oh. Today. Today, I'm going to meet a girl."

The very second he turned north on Seventh Avenue, though he was still in the garment district and had to take care not to be battered by high-velocity clothing racks, everything changed to the world of the theater — a world that, though not part of it, he and so many others knew almost as much as their own. It was theater's task as it portrayed its audiences to make them its intimates, and it succeeded so well that just the turning of a corner and moving in anticipation toward Times Square made him see differently. In the many ugly buildings, behind garish marquees, on narrow, undistinguished streets, worlds were in production, plays that when they opened were like new life and when they closed were like death.

When Catherine had told him, on the phone, that she was an actress rehearsing in a musical destined for Broadway, he was surprised. Although he knew little about her, it seemed that she was the kind of person who would not have been an actress. He suspected that though she was now poor, as she had intimated more than once, she had at one time been of a class that could look down upon a lot of things, and that, therefore, for her to have entered the theater would mean that she must have a transcendent understanding of dignity and was directed by a strong sense of what was real. For the poetry of the theater was that by indirection it found directions out, that with the conflagration of artifice and insincerity it generated a coherent light in which were held truths that can elude even the light of day. People who were comfortable and long established, or wanted to be, often did not understand this. But now, despite her well-spokenness and aristocratic bearing, she may have been forced to it. Perhaps her family had lost everything in the Crash and the Depression. If he could help her, he would. If he could give her security and provide for her, he would. If he could give her everything, he would. He already loved her.

He arrived at the stage door an hour early, because the time he spent at the loft had not passed quickly and because of that he had left before he might have. "Is this the rehearsal for *Homecoming*?" he asked the doorkeeper, a man who looked at anyone who asked any question to which he himself knew the answer as if that person were an idiot for asking a question the answer to which was already known.

"Yeah."

"Miss Sedley?" Harry could hear the music coming from within. As it was being coaxed into shape it stopped and started in a way that audiences never know.

"Yeah."

"I'm supposed to meet her," he said.

"So?"

"I just wanted to know."

"Why?"

"So you would know that I'm supposed to be here. I'm supposed to meet her at six."

"You're early."

"I know." He was getting uncomfortable.

"You're going to stand here for an hour? Why not go get a hot dog?"

"I don't want a hot dog. We're going to have dinner."

"So why don't you go in and sit down?"

"I can go in?"

"What is it, Fort Knox?"

As Harry passed him, he heard the doorkeeper say "Stupid!" under his breath. It was okay, for the doorkeeper now had the satisfaction that would enable him to get through the rest of the day and go back to his grave in the Bronx, and it hadn't cost Harry a thing.

The drawing room had been raised to clear the stage for the maneuvers of a chorus, and in semi-darkness, illuminated in the absence of scenery only by the stage lights reflecting from the boards and the players, he found a seat in the back and sat down unnoticed. Five minutes after he had settled in, the director commanded that Catherine do the song that just a day before she had accomplished with such stunning perfection. She appeared, rouged and lit as if the production had really made it to Broadway, which, in fact, this was. They rehearsed in makeup so as not to be disturbed by it later. Harry figured this out, having often been told to "train like you fight."

The music began. First it was a short, deep bow from the string section, and then it rhythmically took to the waves. But it would recede, leaving Catherine's voice alone to fill the theater and arrest every onlooker. Twelve beats after her introduction, she began to sing. Onstage, the light, the color, and her song exaggerated her presence almost beyond belief. And though he knew that her speaking voice was beautiful, when she had spoken to him she had not been singing. Her voice was so trained that it was able to carry throughout the theater the deepest emotion and truth, powerfully and yet gently, her enunciation clear, silken, and strong. On occasion she lessened the clarity and misted her expression, only to go back into the clear, which gave her a range for which musicology had yet to come up with a name, for there was no term for the glory within reach only of a woman's voice.

It said so much about her that could not be said in words, that he was battered. Until now he had been in love because he had been infatuated, entranced by her manner and appearance, excited by her presence, drawn to her by invisible attractions. Until now it had made perfect sense, for she was interesting and alluring. But now she took him far beyond sense. Her voice — its quality, its clarity despite the frequent mistiness of slightly offset double notes riding together, like the complex sounds of distant breaking waves — led far beyond her, enlarging her worth and depth by its embrace of seemingly all things. Her voice summoned and fused images in their thousands: memories, colors, views, other songs, fading light, blooming trees swaying in sunshine and wind. It united past, present, and future, limning and lighting faces and souls, their expressions carried forth over time, holding them as long as it could until they would vanish except for a remnant in the exhausted air, almost invisible, like smoke that hangs over a valley until the winds passing above pull it after them and it disappears. And when this knitting together of all things was gone, what was left was Catherine, the source and spring of life itself — daughter, wife, mother — to be loved and treasured above all else.

In the perfection of her song, by the voice that sprang from her, speaking words as he had never heard them spoken, he now loved her as he had never known he could love. He might never see her again, and decades might pass, yet he would love her indelibly, catastrophically, and forever. If half a century later he were alive, he would remember this song as the moment in which all such things were settled and beyond which he could not go. As she sang, and he understood that he loved her as he had never loved anyone in his life, he was almost frightened, because he knew that actresses and singers have such an effect quite commonly, and that most often it simply comes to nothing.

Then hers was subsumed in the voices of others. She sang in a higher range when she sang with them, and when their feet hit the boards in unison, precisely striking and precisely lifting in the glare of the spotlights, it was electric. With the help of the chorus, the deep emotion of her song had become celebration.

"Stop!" the director shouted. As if in midair, they stopped, mortal again, silent. "I want to break up this line so it doesn't look like the goddamned Rockettes." He turned to the choreographer. "Can't that be done?"

"We can do it in three," the choreographer answered immediately. "That way it's not symmetrical, and the eye won't be frozen. Someone looking on will always feel that it's out of balance, so it'll seem to be that much more in motion."

"Two parts stage right, one left?"

"It would have to be, because the pillars of Penn Station will be stage left."

"It's better that way, isn't it?"

"Yes," said the choreographer, "I think so."

"Where should Catherine be, in the center of the middle line?"

The choreographer ascended to the stage. He was as thin as a thread. "Divide up," he said, directing with his hands, and when he had marched them into position he looked at Catherine, who had remained standing, as straight as a column, stunning in the light.

"Catherine, why don't you take the left position in the middle line." She walked over and linked arms with a young man who seemed not to notice. "That's great. You become the center point, no matter how much you move." He turned to the director, though because of the lights he could hardly see him. "How about that?"

"Let's try it," the director said.

"From Catherine's song?" the conductor asked, twisting his body so he could get his question across clearly.

"No," said the director, "from the end of Catherine's song. We don't need to do her song again. Her song is just right."

The conductor raised his wand, and off they went in the sharp white light. As actors have always known, though a show may be perfect and triumphant, rehearsals, less than perfect but closer to the heart, are better.

# 7

## AND THERE SHE WAS

SHE WAS STANDING in front of the theater, near but apart from a small line at the box office, where people who had been unable to get tickets for musicals were unenthusiastically buying them for the physics play. Now dressed more for dinner than the beach, she was in an elegant gray silk top lightly gathered at the neckline, with two ribboned panels hanging down from the collar at her left, and a pleated skirt of matching gray, which was shorter than the fashion of the moment and made him think of the twenties, in the latter years of which he had been an adolescent newly intoxicated with women. No more an adolescent, he had a great deal of self-control and was used to disappointment, so he knew or at least believed that no matter how much he might be knocked akilter by her he would not reveal it, which is not to say that he would not feel it.

Even for an actress, she showed a great deal of leg in the soft, light wool skirt that, because it was classically tailored, was enjoying a long run and had survived the fashions of the times. After she had left the stage and gone to change and to remove her makeup, he had walked around the block. He was a minute or two late, knowing that one could always safely be that late when meeting a well dressed woman, because she wouldn't have a watch or it would be too small to fit the blazes for minutes. Coming from the west, he saw her in profile, her posture undiminished, as straight and strong as he had remembered it, her face, though lit harshly by the lesser lights of the marquee, both gorgeous and thoughtful, and her legs as smooth as Jean Harlow's pajamas. How lovely that the woman with whom he was so deeply in love was also so sexually exciting.

She seemed agitated and displeased, but when he stopped at her left and she turned to him, her dark mood simply faded. He sensed that this was involuntary, and had broken her determination to be grave. Her eyes showed that though she may have decided to reject him, as long as he was in her presence she could not. Why she was torn so early on he could and did not imagine, but, like her, he brightened at the instant they met. "Hello," he said. Even in heels, she was somewhat shorter than he, and she looked up at him, thus softening her posture and her stance, so that she seemed very young. He had thought that she was in her late twenties and still youthful in many respects, but she was very womanly and had not struck him as girlish until this moment.

She was about to speak, but then, late like Harry, the church bells in Clinton rang out from the west and the full lighting of the marquee went on, with the sound of the relays — metal thrown against metal — in counterpoint to the bells, the electric currents fusing with a knock. It seemed strange, because the sun was fairly high in the sky. Her greeting displaced by sound and light, she stared at him and asked, "What happened to your eye?"

A long cut traversed almost the entire length of his left eyelid. It had begun to heal, but, unlike most wounds of that size, it was still red. "From a machine," he said.

"What kind of machine?"

"A leather punch, a kind of stamping machine."

"Did you put your head in it?"

"I was changing the belt. It snapped and whipped across my eye. Another eighth of an inch and we could go to a pirate restaurant."

"When did this happen?"

"Friday after we met. I wasn't paying attention."

"I see."

He wanted to kiss her right there as she stood in the middle of the sidewalk. He wanted to draw her to him, to feel her body through the silk, and he thought that she would have let him, and that she would have kissed him back with the same urgency and heat, but he dared not, and instead just let it wash over him. An inimitable pressure would build up until the slightest touch, or even its imagination, would echo throughout his body and hers, blinding them to the practical.

Though they hardly knew it, they were already walking east. "I'm used to it," he said, coming back to the cut over his eye.

"How so?" She had no idea where they were going, and neither did he.

"In the war."

"Did you work in a factory?"

"A factory in its way, the Eighty-second Airborne, though I was often detached and sent to other formations. The cuts, abrasions, minor contusions . . . were continuous."

"From what?"

"Branches snapping back, not only when you parachute into trees or brush, but in moving across country. Under fire, you move when and where you have to. You don't notice things like brambles. And if there's gunfire directed at you, you throw yourself into all kinds of places without knowing where you're going to land. But that's not the half of it. Breaking windows, making cover, loading and unjamming weapons, attaching winches and trailers, fixing recalcitrant jeeps, pulling them out of the mud." He stopped and turned to her. "Shaving with a safety-razor blade held between the fingers. When bullets hit walls, rock, or stony ground, lots of little particles zing around. Mainly they sting, but sometimes they draw blood. Oh, and then there are animal bites, sheet metal cuts, trying to move around in the dark in places you've never been."

"What about bullets?" she asked.

"Well," he said, bashfully, it seemed to her, "those, too."

"Where are we going?" she asked, as if disenchanted with his catalog of minor wounds. He felt that his list had put her off, that he had sounded boorish and boastful, and, worse, that he was talking at her, which hurt him more than the little wounds.

"I know a lot of restaurants that were good, anyway, before the war, but they're closed on Monday. The French ones, that is."

"It doesn't have to be French," she told him. "It doesn't have to be fancy. I really can't afford that."

"I'll pay," he said. Of course he would pay. The man always paid.

"Not for me" was her reply.

"Why?"

"There's a reason," she said.

"I know," he answered. "I have to tell you about it."

"*You* have to tell *me*?"

"When we sit down."

She was puzzled. "Okay," she agreed, "but where?"

"There's a place in the Twenties between Fifth and Sixth that's open Mondays. Their specialty is fish (which they pronounce *fis*) grilled on charcoal." She wanted to go there. "Shall we walk or take the bus?"

They were at the corner of Fifth Avenue and 44th Street, and at that instant a double-decker pulled up to them and opened its doors with the sound that seals make at the zoo when their keeper arrives with a bucket of squid. Catherine leapt onto the steps and was up the spiral staircase and out of sight before the doors closed. He paid and followed.

Appropriately for a couple that had come on together and would leave together, they sat next to one another. Their thighs were close enough so that when the bus occasionally lurched from side to side they touched, and for both of them this was enough to erase the previous awkward moments. Each touch, she felt, was as powerful as two shots of gin.

"What did you do in the war?" he asked, his gaze fixed on the side of her face as she deliberately looked ahead. He had misjudged her age: the construction of her face was such that, even when she was fifty, she would look thirty-five.

"I went to college. Other than rolling bandages and giving blood, I didn't do much for the war effort."

"That's okay," he said. "The war effort was for you. We were fighting for you."

"For me and not democracy?" she asked archly.

"I never met anyone who fought for anything but the flesh and blood of the living and the honor of the dead."

"What about the Atlantic Charter?"

"Who the hell knew or cared about that?"

"I just wish I could have done more," she told him.

"By your existence, you did more than enough."

"You're a flatterer," she said, half accusingly.

"No, I'm not" was his answer.

"You don't know me."

"Yes I do," he said. "I know you very well. And you know me."

Early on a Monday, the restaurant was nearly empty. As they waited to be escorted to the terrace, it was the first time they had been together in a small, quiet room. Until then, it had been in the open air, or the automat, which was noisy and busy, with a forty-foot ceiling and whirling fans. Here it was almost silent, the air still. Standing next to Catherine, Harry breathed in. Catherine often smelled like a good department store: new cloth, expensive perfume, fresh air, and, when she carried a purse, fine leather. And when at times, which he would come to know, she would have a gin and tonic, the scent of juniper coming from her lips was far more intoxicating than the alcohol. He wondered if women understood that their apparently insignificant attributes often have a power greater than that of armies. It was what he had meant when he had said that the war had been fought for her. Like the atom, which in its internal bonds contains the essence of matter and energy, in her glance, the sparkle of her eye, the grasp of her hand, the elasticity of her hair in motion, the way she stands, the blush of her cheek, sweep of her shoulder, tone of her voice, and snap of her locket, a woman is the spur and essence of existence.

They sat at a table in the garden, opposite a long brazier from which a fire cast up white smoke. Sometimes the wind blew the smoke around them before it rose. When this happened, and they were enveloped until they could barely see one another, they couldn't stop laughing, because sitting in a restaurant was not supposed to replicate the experience of being trapped in a burning building. Immediately when they had come in, the maitre d' and waiters had sized them up and judged that they were just beginning a love affair. The staff knew to keep out of sight even if the couple would be locked in one another's gaze, pay no attention to anyone else, and stay for hours, and even if the tip, either fantastically large or fantastically small, was anyone's guess, because such couples almost always handled money unmindfully.

Bread, olives, a dish of olive oil, a bottle of mineral water, and a bottle of retsina were brought to the table. In a heavy Greek accent, the waiter who put them down said, "In how many minutes — hours? — tsall I come back to take your order?"

Harry looked at Catherine, who merely smiled, and he said, "Twenty."

"Minutes or hours?" the waiter asked, knowingly. Harry didn't answer. "If you want sooner, call me."

After he left, he came charging back, beginning to speak as he was halfway across the flagstones. "Forgot. Spessal dinner tonight. Oktopadi on grill, kotopolou fornu, salat, very good." He turned to go.

"Wait," Harry commanded, and, turning to Catherine, asked, "Would you like that?"

"What is it?"

"Marinated octopus on the grill, chicken from a clay oven. The octopus, like many people, is better than either its name or its appearance."

"Yes," she said, and then, to the waiter, "I'll have that."

"Two, then," Harry told the waiter, holding up two fingers, like Winston Churchill. "*Duo.*"

"When the waiter disappeared, Catherine asked, "You know Greek?"

"A little."

"Demotic Greek?"

"Enough to get by as a tourist. I was in Greece before the war."

"Doing what?"

"Supposedly studying."

"Studying what?"

"I was a graduate student, what they call an 'advanced student.'"

"Where?"

"Magdalen College, Oxford."

"Aha."

"What *aha?*"

"Just *aha*. What were you doing?"

"I wanted to write a doctoral thesis on the Mediterranean as a historical force unto itself. The civilizations that ring it have so much in common other than just the olive, and half of what they are they owe to the sea. It's certainly worth a book, which would be interesting, beautiful, and sensual."

"You wanted to write a sensual doctoral thesis?"

"I did."

"You expected it to be accepted? I majored in music at a girls' college in Philadelphia...."

"Where?"

"Bryn Mawr."

"Aha."

"And I'm not exactly Ph.D. bait. But even I know that you could never get something like that through."

"You think I didn't?"

Her jaw dropped a little, but she kept on with her train of thought. "It would collapse the professoriate."

"You say that because, you see, you're a girl, and girls don't have what boys have, which is a goat-like capacity to bang with the head against heavy objects that will not move."

"Isn't that pointless?"

"Yes, except that, once in a million times, it does move."

"Did it?"

"No."

"What happened?"

"In general?"

"We have time."

"I was the class of 'thirty-seven...."

"Where?"

"Harvard," he answered, like someone anticipating being struck. It was always that way.

"Oh no," she said, very annoyed.

"Why do you say that?" he asked, but he knew why.

"Harvard boys think they're semi-divine, and they aren't. They used to ride down to Bryn Mawr like Apollos in their chariots."

"I wasn't like that," he stated. And he wasn't.

"I know." Then it dawned on her, and she said, "You're eight years older than I am."

He did the arithmetic. "You were graduated last year?"

"Yes."

She seemed much older than twenty-three, and she thought that he seemed much younger than thirty-one or -two. The shock, however, was only momentary. "To write on the Mediterranean that way, how many languages would you have to know?"

"One."

"How many do you know?"

As he spoke, he counted on his fingers.

"That many?"

"All badly, except perhaps English. Unfortunately, I don't know Turkish."

"What a tragedy," she said. "How can you possibly get around in New York?"

"I manage, but what I know is nothing. Your song...." He had to stop and start over again. "Your song... in its few words. Your enunciation. The way you sang those words, the way you expressed them. Nothing I've ever done can compare. I've never experienced anything as perfect. Just the caesura in the second stanza is the most extraordinary...."

"But it's only a half-note," she interrupted.

"It may be only a half-note, but it's infinitely beautiful and it tells all." He meant, *about you,* and although he did not say it, she understood it.

And she, of great self-possession, could hardly breathe, much less speak, because it was true, because she had not realized it, because of what had been sent to her. Rather than go deeper, she made for the surface. "You heard me?"

"I did."

After turning her eyes toward the tablecloth, a silence, and a few deep breaths, she looked back at him and said, "I majored in music and studied voice. I have a rich midrange. Seems to be expanding. I can't do opera, yet. I'm barely good enough to sing one song in a careless Broadway musical. No one has said to me, about my singing, what you said."

"The director thought it was perfect."

"How long were you in the theater?"

"I got there early and the idiot at the stage door invited me in."

"He is an idiot. We've got to get a new one. Did you pay him?"

"No."

"Usually, people do. That's his racket."

"He let me in for free."

After Harry had said what he had said, she could hardly look at him, and could not believe that her emotions were so strong. It frightened her, so she tried to slow the momentum. "Why didn't you write that book? What could be more lovely than writing a book about something you love?"

"I was in England for two years. I spent a lot of time in the Mediterranean and I got an M.Phil., but my father got sick — my mother died a long time ago — and I had to take care of him and the business. I was going to go back, but there were a lot of problems here — he never really got well. And then the war. I enlisted in 'forty-one, before Pearl Harbor."

"That was early. A lot of people were waiting to see, even after."

"I had an English sense of the war. My father died soon after we breached the Siegfried Line. I got out last year. I've been involved with the business since then."

"And what business is it that has a leather punch? Oh!" she said, making the connection, if late. He watched as it unfurled, knowing what was coming. "Copeland Leather. You're Copeland Leather."

"Actually, I'm just Harry," he said, waiting for what he knew she would do.

She held up her purse as if it were the golden fleece, looking at it in astonishment. "This," she declared, "is Copeland Leather."

"I know."

"I was carrying your purse. Why didn't you say something?"

"I was thinking of other things."

"It's beautiful."

"Thank you. So are you."

They dipped some bread in oil, and had some water and some wine. They were already in love and both of them knew it, but for both it was too fast. "What's the greatest mystery of the universe?" he asked.

All she could do was ask what.

"That Popeye's girlfriend is called Olive Oyl. What insanity led to that? Who can ever say? It's a question that, by its nature, probably can never be answered."

"By the way," she said, "we split this."

"I understand."

"You said you did, and you may be the only man in New York who does. Why?"

"It's a long story."

"Do you think I'm rich?"

"That would be a short story. And, no, I think you went to Bryn Mawr, you speak magnificently, and you wear very expensive clothes from another era because you may be living in reduced circumstances. Maybe you were rich, but not now. That means you don't envy the rich or have contempt for the poor, and it means you know a great deal even though you're young. Maybe it explains the depth of your song. I don't know. It has to come from someplace, an understanding, a compassion. You see very clearly. You feel deeply. You're older than your years."

"All right," she said, moving the candle that was dead-set between them to her right, so that nothing was between them, and then leaning forward a bit, "so tell me why I pay."

"As I said, it's a long story."

She shrugged, which said, *I'm here, I have patience, tell it.*

"When I was in France, in the war—and it seems to me now, as it did when I was a child, that Paris was and is the center of the world, and as if I'm dreaming now and if I wake up that's where I'll be—when I was a soldier, I would see women on the street, many of whom were young and attractive. I would make an instant connection with them, through the eyes. When you're in the army, fighting, you get that way. There are many men who are very crude, and they get cruder. They always thought of women as sort of prey, and in the absence of women, apart from civilian life, apart from civilization, that is, it gets worse, much worse. But, for me, suddenly coming into a city in France or Holland... a woman became as beautiful and venerable as.... I mean, why were we fighting if not... if not to protect...."

"I understand."

"That June, the weather was magnificent. I used to look up at the moon at night, at rest, in battle, wherever I was. It was weightless, satiny, the color of pearl, feminine. It saved me. But, anyway, I would see women on the streets of liberated towns, and because everything had broken down, and for a while there were no supplies, and the soldiers coming in had money, food, and chocolate.... Love can't exist in servitude."

"If you bought me dinner it wouldn't be servitude."

"I know. There's more. I don't want to talk too much."

"I want you to talk to me," she told him. "I really do."

"It's a long story to make a point you already understand."

"What I'm saying to you," she said, "is that you can read me the telephone book if you want. And I would be perfectly happy."

"How about the Yellow Pages?"

"I prefer the White."

Smoke from the fire circled them like a veil. For a moment they sat in silence, but then he continued. "It was worse in Germany, much worse, although there were relatively peaceful islands in the war. We were southeast of Munich, pressing up toward the Alps in a country full of lakes and long roads through uninhabited stands of pine. I was with a guy who had been born in Germany and spoke German fluently. We had a jeep, and were supposed to make a reconnaissance all the way to the Swiss border. They wanted to know what was going on in the forests. G2 was obsessed with forests after the Ardennes, the Bulge, the Hürtgen. Who could blame them? And after Market Garden they put less faith in aerial reconnaissance, so they sent us and others through the allées in the pines.

"But there was nothing there, the forests were empty. This was one of those pockets that, except for a scarcity of goods, had been untouched by the war. You live for that, for the time you have when you pass through places like that, and there are lots of them, much more than people imagine. You find them in clearings and copses, and little groves of trees, and sometimes over a whole plain as far as you can see.

"It was the first really warm day in spring, and we were riding down what seemed to be an endless dirt road. Though we could have been shot at from the trees at any moment, we were happy. The air was a pleasure. I remember thinking how insistent it was. Most of the time it lets you forget it's there, but on that day the breeze embraced us. And you could smell the pine needles. They exhaled everything they had held on to during the winter. It was sweet like you can't believe.

"As we were driving between huge ranks of pines, we saw two figures up ahead. Off go the safeties, we slow, we go back to war — but they were girls. Who knows how old? Late teens? Early twenties? They had that peculiar charm. . . ." He looked at her, and smiled. She knew. "That explosive, happy, embarrassed charm that only a young woman can have.

"We offered them a ride. When they understood that we would not hurt them, that we would treat them with great deference and politeness, they were shocked and relieved. They were going to Munich, although they didn't tell us at the time. Munich was still in enemy hands, and we were alone, relatively nearby, but it was almost as if we were in Switzerland: no feeling of war, no tension.

"We came to a restaurant and hotel in the middle of the forest, on a hillside that overlooked a reservoir and the fast stream that filled it. I've always loved rivers...."

"I know," she said. "You told me. And so have I. I don't know why anyone leaves them, but they do. I don't know why I leave them, because they've always made me very happy. Go on."

"We were the first Americans they had seen since the beginning of the war. The place was filled with refugees who were trying to get into Switzerland. Switzerland was close, but they weren't going to get in.

"There was a main dining room, with tablecloths and silver, and ninety-year-old waiters in black jackets like French waiters in a bistro, and then there was a bar in another room overlooking the river. In the disturbance created by the arrival of two armed American officers, the girls disappeared into the bar. We were led ceremoniously into the dining room, where everyone tried not to look at us, and the waiter came to take our order as if nothing were out of the ordinary.

"All they had was chicken, soup, and bread, which, then, was a lot. They had wine, too, but we couldn't have more than half a glass. We didn't know who would be around there. The German army could still shoot, we were in Germany, and the other half glass of wine was not worth dying for.

"After we ordered, my friend said, 'Where are the girls? Why don't we ask them to eat with us? The food will be better here, if it's not poisoned.' I jumped up. '*Bitte, essen mit uns,*' I said to my friend, to see if it was correct and if it would do, and I left before he replied, because I knew it would.

"I passed through the dining room, saying '*Bitte, essen mit uns, Bitte, essen mit uns,*' and then through curtained glass doors into the bar overlooking the river. The girls were sitting at a wooden table, alone because the bar was closed. They didn't have enough money to get anything to eat. When I looked at them, I loved them for what they were, what they had been through, and what they were going to go through. One of them had been badly scarred on one side of her face. I mentioned her when we met."

"Yes."

"It didn't matter. She still had the charm of youth. They were happy to eat with us, to eat at all. I remember how amused they were when I asked them in my rudimentary German to join us. And I remember how the sun sparkled on the river, blinding me and warming the room. The river grew shallow just before plunging into the reservoir, and rushed over a bed of small, rounded rocks with the color and blur of a school of fish. Polyhedrons of light backlit the girls, backlit their hair.

"We could have been killed so easily, because at dinner we forgot everything. The four of us together, with my friend interpreting and me speaking fractured German, and the girls speaking fractured English, and everybody speaking bad French.... They would consult on a word and then sally forth; we would consult on a word and then sally forth. It meant the end of the war, the restoration of everything... the restoration, to their rightful place, of love and kindness.

"Naturally, we had to pay for them, and they were in our debt. We were conquering—and I really mean conquering—their country. We were taking them on the road, feeding them, carrying them under our protection. When the waiter came and we paid him, in dollars that he took so eagerly it was a sure sign they had lost the war, I glanced at the girls, and the expression they had was that now the bill had come due. All the lightness I had felt suddenly drained.

"What can I say?" He hesitated and looked away, and then back at Catherine. "When you love someone, even if it's only infatuation, even if it's only immense respect, the last thing you want is subservience, obligation, dread, payment. I thought to myself that I never wanted to see that expression again. Never."

"So you don't mind if I pick up my half of the check?"

"I'd prefer it, although it's hard to explain to someone who assumes I'll follow the custom."

"I think you've explained it quite well. They didn't pay the bill, did they?"

"No. They expected to, but we weren't like that. My friend ended up marrying the one whose face had been disfigured—in a bombing raid, one of our bombs, or a British bomb. She was sixteen when it happened. He loves her, he really loves her. . . ." He couldn't finish.

Harry was apprehensive that he had spoken too much, that he had fallen too fast, that he had been too suggestive, too forward. Although he sensed that she was attracted to him, she moved on tides that he could not read. As comfortable and warm as she became, she was at times reserved, distressed, almost disdainful. She used the expression "Oh please," which he did not, and which he now realized was a class marker with the power to freeze him cold. It was the language and enunciation of someone who either needed nothing or had come from a society in which the norm was to need nothing. It was dismissive yet charming. It stunned him, almost frightened him, and at the same time made her infinitely desirable. For the way she said it was rich in intonation and expression—like her song. Of course, he was in love, even with the way she brushed her hair back from her face. Like her speech and diction, her emotions, hot and cold, were held in magnificent balance.

He thought he saw what was coming, and was determined to get through it successfully. It was like watching a big wave moving dangerously fast right at him. She looked down, gently clenched her left fist, closed her eyes, and shook her head very rapidly from side to side. "I shouldn't be here," she said. "I can't do this. I can't do this to Victor."

"Victor," he repeated.

"Yes, Victor."

"I hope it's a cat."

She tried hard and in vain not to laugh, and then said, resolutely, "It's a man," which made her laugh again.

"Oh," he said. "I'm not surprised that his name is Victor. Everyone I've ever known by that name has been able to beat me at one thing or another. It's as if there's something they know that I don't. I think it may be more than just coincidence, but rather that their parents gave them that name as part of or a prelude to a mad program of education in winning. Wouldn't you think that someone who cared about winning would name his child Victor? I see the Victors at age five being solemnly — desperately — instructed in how to cheat at tennis, how to play a sharp hand of poker, flatter a teacher, dress perfectly, and, above all, assume that they're going to win, and that they have no other choice, as it is their destiny. Winning is what they do, and all they can do. It stops there. Never have I failed to have been beaten by a Victor, even at chess, where, throughout the whole game, they smile like Cheshire cats.

"And yet, what victories have Victors achieved? Napoleon wasn't named Victor. It wasn't Victor the Great who conquered the known world, or Victor Caesar. For that matter, it wasn't Victor Nelson or Victor Wellington, Washington, Eisenhower, Montgomery, or Grant. Nor do we have Victor Shakespeare, Victor Einstein, Victor the Baptist, or Victor Christ. Victors are in fact in short supply as victors, except that they always make more money than I do, beat me at games, and get the girl.... But maybe not this time."

"You stun me," she said. "You drive me crazy."

"And you, me," he returned. "So Victor isn't a cat?"

"No," she said, "he isn't a cat."

"If he's not a cat, why are you laughing?"

"I shouldn't be. He's my fiancé. Victor Marrow."

"Victor Marrow?"

She nodded, no longer laughing but almost crying.

"That's a name?"

"Yes. He's a Mellon."

"He's a melon," said Harry, deadpan.

Again, she nodded, and even sniffled.

"What kind of melon?"

"A Pittsburgh Mellon."

"Is that like a watermelon, or a cantaloupe?"

"No, you idiot," she said, with more affection than she could bear absent an immediate embrace, which could not and did not materialize.

"I thought his last name was Marrow?"

"His mother's a Mellon."

"Well, if his mother's a Mellon and his father's a Marrow, how can he tell if he's a watermelon or a squash? He must have had a very difficult childhood." He looked at her. "It's not something to laugh about."

This made her laugh more.

"What does he look like?"

She came to and assessed Harry straight on. Then she drew in a breath both pleased and resigned, and said, "You're much handsomer, damn you, and he went to Yale."

"I'm glad you got that right, about Yale."

"He wouldn't agree."

"Deep down he would. They know."

"Yes," she said, "they do. I've noticed it myself. It's as if they know they can never catch up," and then she looked away. "Can I," she asked, "can I . . . take a break? Can we just not talk for a while, and maybe eat. There's too much, too much going on. I'll be all right, but I just need a . . . a minute."

"I myself need a week," he told her.

"You don't have a week," she said. Then she took a long drink of water. As she raised her glass, he could see her heart beating against the silk of her blouse.

"God," she said, partly because of the retsina, "this is wonderful. It doesn't taste like what you would think grilled octopus would be. I never would have ordered it."

"Nor would I."

"Why did you?"

"The first time I had it was in a tiny village in the Peloponnesus. It had taken several days for me to walk there over a high, deserted spine of mountains, but it was on the coast, not that far by sea from Piraeus. When I arrived, however, because of the difficulty and loneliness of the journey, I thought I had come to the end of the earth. Then a yacht full of Germans appeared, flying a big flag with a swastika, and the shutters were suddenly flung open in what turned out to have been a little waterfront restaurant that served whatever it could to the yachting trade.

"I didn't like it when the Germans came ashore. They were all so tall, and there were so many of them, and while I had a walking stick, they had a yacht."

"Victor is even taller than you are," she said, "and he has a yacht."

"The yacht that didn't show?"

She confirmed this with a lifting of an eyebrow in an unmistakably condemnatory, and yet fairly hopeless, expression. And she saw very clearly and could not banish from her mind the yacht coming up from the south on humid and silvery air, bringing with it insistently another age, the rear guard of time, moving across the sea in force and at a different pace and as arrestingly as a ghost. Haunting, seductive, easy, it called for many kinds of surrender, each comfortable and tragic. Were she to have been rowed out, she would have been lost to this. She would have regretted and grieved for the rest of her life. She had come that close, and would have disappeared had it not been for the winds and tides.

Not knowing what she was thinking, Harry snapped her back to the restaurant, and then off to Greece before the war. "You know what happened to the Germans?"

"They lost."

"That, too, but before that, maybe as an omen, they couldn't start the outboard on their dory. They tried, each of the men taking turns, for a whole hour. Nothing. It was a delight to watch, because I knew they would have to turn to me."

"Did they?"

"Of course. It was an Evinrude, which they pronounced *Ayfinwootah*. No wonder they couldn't start it. And they were really obsequious when they asked me to see if I could. I got into the dory and looked it over. Practically the first thing I saw was that the bleeder valve on the bulb in the gas line was open."

"What's that?"

"To prime the engine you have to pump some gas into it by squeezing the bulb. It has a bleeder valve, as on a blood-pressure cuff, that's circular, and you can't always tell if it's open, but I saw that the threads of the screw were half shiny and half dull. The shiny ones had normally been inside the valve, protected from the salt air."

"And they didn't see?"

"They were not people who are used to doing things for themselves."

"Oh," she said, thinking of herself, her family, and Victor.

"So I knew I could do it, but I wanted to make it seem more complicated. I removed the engine cover and used my fingers to move and palpitate the most mysterious-looking parts. I didn't know what the hell they were, but I was jiggling them around at blinding speed like playing the piano. The Germans were looking at me, their mouths hanging open. Then I put back the cover really fast, and sort of set things up, including closing the bleeder valve and squeezing the bulb. It was empty at first, and then it filled, and I knew I had it. I set the choke and the throttle, turned to the audience, said *Alles klar!*, and gave the starter rope a single pull. The engine started with a roar before the rope was halfway out. If they were alive at the end of the war, when they saw the American flag on our vehicles, over our camps, and above their ministries, they might have thought once or twice of that moment."

"Why are you telling me this?" she asked, not because she hadn't wanted to hear, but as an encouragement for him to close the circle.

"Because, when they left, they thanked me in stilted English — I acknowledged in worse German — and they gave the restaurant owner a wad of bills. I hadn't been able to afford the restaurant. I was on a tight budget, and while they were being served grilled fish and lamb, I ate a can of sardines that I had carried with me.

"So the 'restaurateur' ran over to me and, picking up my pack, herded me onto the concrete dock where his restaurant was. The village was called Nea Epidavros. There were some very flimsy tables and chairs on the pier. He told me in Greek that the Germans had paid for my dinner. And the next thing he did was take off his shoes and shirt and dive into the water. I thought he was nuts. When he surfaced he was holding an octopus, which he then spent half an hour tenderizing by smashing it (dead after the first blow) against the concrete. He looked like a madman, or maybe a Guatemalan woman doing her laundry on the rocks by a river. The rest of the afternoon he marinated it, and by dark I had one of the best meals of my life, done on charcoal just like this, with retsina and all the rest. I could see the stars there so brightly I felt I was sailing among them. I was alone, and the Germans had disappeared over the sea." He paused. "I really wish you had been there."

"I never would have ordered it," she said.

"Neither would I. Like quite a few things in my life, it was the result of unforeseen action by Germany."

Riding the troughs and peaks of the waves, they were happy in one another's presence, with little awareness of anything else, frightened that it would not last, frightened that it would, staring at one another with great draughts of what felt like love, and then withdrawing coldly in the face of practicalities. For her, loyalty, prudence, staying the course, the expectations of her society. For him, the fear that she was so much unlike him, although she wasn't, and that even were he to win her she would soon stop loving him.

"Did Victor earn the money to buy his yacht, or did he inherit it? I'm not trying to set him up. I inherited my father's business, after all."

"Then you should know."

"Know what?"

"That there's no division in such things. With the Marrows, the Mellons" — she hesitated — "and the Hales," naming three families famous for their wealth, "no one has any right or claim to the money any more than anyone else. It's just there, and each generation is trained to ride it. Victor's father didn't make the money either, but on the other hand he did, as does Victor. No one feels either proud or ashamed, although, in this set, one feels as if one is truly better than people who don't have money — as if they live half blind in the underworld and only the Marrows, the Mellons, and the Hales are free and can see."

"Would you feel that way?" he asked, wondering about the Sedleys.

"No," she answered. "I've been educated away from things like that."

"By what?"

"Love," she said. "If you can love, you can't think that way. Even when I was a very small child, I played with the Bonackers' children. I loved them, and understood that I was no better."

"The Bonackers?" He thought they might be a family.

"The farmers and fishermen of the eastern tip of Long Island."

"You lived there?"

"We did, for a time."

"And this is a strong and durable feeling?"

"This is the root of my life."

"I want, more than anything else," he said, "to know you."

"In the biblical sense?" She was embarrassed, but excited, to have said that.

"Yes, but that isn't what I meant."

"You can't," she said, "because I'm going to marry Victor. Last weekend, when you and I met, he was going to take me on the boat to East Hampton—his house is in Southampton—where he was supposed to announce our engagement at the Georgica. It's a club, on the beach. There was a gale off Norfolk and he had to run into the Chesapeake. The reception was canceled, but it's on for Sunday, a second time: two hundred people. We can't cancel. He's got the ring, a diamond the size of a ping-pong ball. He didn't give it to me, because he thinks I might lose it."

"You can end it with the flick of a finger," Harry said. "There's no law. You can at least postpone it. He's young, you're young, it's allowed, even expected."

"He's thirty-eight, closer to thirty-nine. His birthday's in September."

"He's got as many years on me as I have on you."

"And more if you count his character and his health. He seems much older. I'm supposed to like that."

"Do you?"

"No."

"Catherine, do I have a chance with you?"

"Of course you have a chance. But I have to marry him. Everyone expects it. I'm more or less married to him already."

"No, you're only twenty-three."

"Since I was thirteen . . . ," she said, sorry that she would have to change the course of things this way.

"Since you were thirteen, what?"

She didn't answer.

"When you were only thirteen?"

"Almost fourteen."

"And he was thirty."

"Twenty-nine."

"You were a child."

"Not for long."

"Do your parents know?"

"When I started in the theater, my father took me aside. He walked me out into the garden, where he explained to me that theater people have different mores than we do, and that actresses are expected to be loose, but that I should not be ashamed of, and should guard, my virginity."

"You don't owe Victor anything. He should be imprisoned. He should be shot. You certainly don't have to marry him."

"There are other reasons."

"Like what?"

"I'm an ingénue. Do you know what happens to ingénues?"

He didn't.

"Most of them," she said, "not being strategic thinkers, don't either. By the time you're twenty-five, they drop you. One in a thousand make the transition to leading lady, and the rest live the remainder of their lives in thrall to the brief period when they were in full and fragile bloom. But no one else in the world remembers, and no one cares. I don't have illusions about my career, even if I have hopes."

"I don't see the connection." He understood that she might be enchained by a number of things that he could not simply dismiss, but it seemed that the prospect of her freedom, and her right to it, had never been simply stated. "You don't have to marry so soon. You don't have to worry about finding a husband. And, God knows, you certainly don't have to marry Victor."

"My clock is different than yours," she told him, "and I'm not exactly fresh."

"That's absurd. It doesn't make any difference."

"It does. It does to most people. It does to me."

"It doesn't to me, and I'm right here."

"I know you're right here."

"Postpone it."

Her expression darkened. As she spoke, she trembled from emotion and anger. "You want me not to marry a man who has been . . . *fucking* me . . . for ten years, since I was thirteen years old, who everyone in the world thinks is going to marry me, who has bought the ring, invited two hundred people, hired the caterers, reserved the club, and told the goddamned, the goddamned *New York Times*? And this, this you want, on our first date?"

"I do," he said, as if it were a vow, which it was.

# 8

## WHAT YOU'RE TRAINED TO DO

HE REMEMBERED HER song in every particular, how she carefully pronounced each word, and that each word was like a work in itself. He had never heard English or any language spoken with such lucidity, care, and dignity. The skillful enunciation and timing rode on the river of her voice, a voice that was so arresting because although it was of her body it was almost as if her soul were carried on it for an excursion in the air. It would not fade along with youth. Nor was it corruptible. Nor was she, in contradiction of her own opinion, corrupted.

She had insisted halfheartedly that he not see or call her, but she had allowed him to take her home. On the way, she said, "I've been telling you my stage name. It's not my real name." He then expected a multi-syllabic Eastern European name, or perhaps, given her accent, a name like Phelps or Horsey. "It's not Catherine Sedley," she told him somewhere in the Fifties, as they passed a French restaurant with a Chinese-red awning. "It's Catherine Thomas Hale."

Just the sound of her name was for him as beautiful as a wave slowly curling in the sun. Perhaps because he was so disarmed, he failed to make the connection to the Hales she had mentioned along with the Mellons and the Marrows. And, besides, he wasn't thinking along those lines. She had had him walk her home because she wanted to stay with him as long as possible, and she wanted to shock him, to show him the house so that the battlements of wealth and family might make it easier for him to withdraw. When he saw it, he did see that there was a great deal to overcome and that he was on almost unfamiliar ground. But he wasn't turned back, because although he was quiet, courteous, and contemplative, he had another side as well, to which he had been educated by jumping out of airplanes into battles with a most capable enemy.

After they parted, he hadn't the slightest idea of what to do, but he had the happiness of someone who knows what he loves. And although she was nearly certain that her course was determined, and that for what had happened with Victor she would pay the price she was sure she owed, she too was unaccountably happy, oppressed and joyous in alternation, like the rhythm of a scythe sweeping to and fro in a field of wheat, or the pendulum of a clock as it clucked back and forth.

But they carried forward and did what they had to do — she at rehearsal, singing; he at his loft, the machines spinning — and for each the city was filled with the presence of the other.

On Thursday she was delayed because she had walked to rehearsal in a daze and stopped to look up at the racing clouds as she listened to the sound of buses, and watched horses pulling wagons, and knife sharpeners at work at their whetstones. The traffic, as usual, fought like charioteers at the Circus Maximus. As she blithely walked-in late without noticing him, the director yelled at her. And then she, like the all-powerful star she wasn't, said, "Hi, Sidney," and laughed, defusing his anger merely by showing it could not reach her.

Though at every go-round she sang without fault or imperfection, she was distracted; and though consummately professional and admitting no variation in technique, she seemed fragile nonetheless.

"Are you tired, Catherine?" Sidney asked, in fear that his question would unleash the tirade of an indispensable leading lady, though it unleashed no such thing.

"I'm not tired," she said sweetly, and, of all people, when she said something, she could say it sweetly, firmly, seductively, authoritatively, mysteriously, or any way she pleased.

"How are you? Is everything all right?"

"I'm fine, Sidney," she said, and then, with eyes closed and a slight smile, she turned her face up as if the beams of the spotlights were the warmth of the sun, and took in a long breath. She had the angelic expression of a mother nursing a baby. No one could figure her out, and the orchestra was silent, listening for something.

"Catherine, would you like a long weekend?"

"A long weekend?" she asked, coming partially out of her reverie.

"Would you like to take a rest tomorrow? You've had your song down for weeks. We can put an understudy in your place for the day." He thought she might bristle at that, because understudies are to performers what colonels in dictatorships are to their chiefs of state.

"Okay," said Catherine, and abruptly walked offstage.

"Catherine," Sidney called out, "not now. Catherine? Tomorrow!"

She didn't hear him.

"She didn't have her glasses on, Sidney," volunteered the playwright, who was there too much.

The director lowered his head and opened his hands as if releasing a pigeon. "She can't hear without her glasses?"

"When I can't hear something very well, Sid, I put my glasses on," the playwright said, truthfully, if lamely. "Don't you?"

"No, Barton, I don't."

Catherine was already on the street, having changed but having forgotten to remove her makeup. She walked as if above the sidewalk, in full faith and as if she knew the future, or as if she did not have to know it.

Harry kept thinking about the ferry, that it had delivered her up to him, that everything had happened quickly, that everything seemed set so strongly. As she exited the theater on Thursday he was in the loft, a little more than a mile away. As he circulated from task to task, filling in where he was wanted, the windows were open and he could hear bells and traffic and the rumbling of the Els at a far distance rising and falling with the wind. Somewhere in the sea of sound she was walking or sitting, or perhaps looking in her dressing room mirror, with electric light flooding her face.

As Harry was helping to carry an anvil, Cornell glided up to him.

Perhaps because he was tall and thin, and old enough to be respectful of arthritis, Cornell had a light step. "Could you come into the office?" he asked, as a command.

Having put down the anvil, Harry closed the door to the office, because Cornell's expression seemed to indicate that he should.

"We just lost half of Saks Fifth Avenue," Cornell said, referring to their long-established Saks account.

"We did?"

"They called on the telephone. Not even a letter. Just like that. Our display space is going to be cut by half, and, naturally, the orders, too."

"They never liked that we have a store around the corner," Harry said, beaming.

"What are you so happy about? Are you out of your mind?"

"No."

"Well, what?"

"Nothing."

"Did we get another account?"

"Did we?"

"What? Look at you," Cornell said in exasperation. "We could save on electricity if we plugged a few lamps into you. It must be a woman."

"It is. A woman."

"Jesus. Are you going to go out of commission? This is a big account."

"I think so."

"You think what? That you're going to be out of commission, or that it's a big account?"

"Both."

"Can you put it off for a while?"

"No. On Sunday she's going to be engaged to someone she doesn't love, someone who's been sleeping with her since she was . . . very young, and who's twice her age."

"How'd you get mixed up with someone like that?"

"I don't know. I guess I'm attracted to the lower orders of society."

"It sounds like it."

"I can't stop thinking of her. She's only twenty-three and yet she thinks and feels with neither feeling nor thought degraded but rather each elevating the other. Most people can't begin to do that. It's as if when they see they can't hear, and when they hear they can't see. We haven't been educated into separating the senses, but we have regarding the heart and the intellect. I told her this. She thought about it. It was while we were eating dinner in a Greek restaurant. I thought she might not even have heard me, but then she looked up and said, 'Without thinking, there's no clarity; and without feeling, there's no purpose. Why would I starve them of each other? Why would anyone?'

"Can you imagine what she'll be like when she's thirty?"

"Can you imagine you when you're sixty?" Cornell asked. "You'll be a moron, if you aren't already."

"And Cornell, she's so much more than what she says. Every gesture, every adjustment of her body, every lifting of a brow or movement of her eyes...."

Cornell interrupted. "God," he said, "you're gone."

"I am," Harry agreed.

"Fine, but you'd better come down if you don't want to lose everything."

"The business?"

"The business, *and* her. You don't want to lose her, do you?"

"Of course not."

"So what are you going to do?"

"What can I do?"

"Who is she? How long have you known her?"

"I've only seen her...." He thought about it. "Three times," he said, counting the time he had seen her before having spoken to her.

"That's not really a lot."

"I met her on the ferry. We went out to dinner twice. The first time was at the automat."

"Elegant."

"It was great."

"How much can you really love someone, Harry, if you know her that little?"

"I know her much more than a little. I fell in love with her a long time ago."

"You fell in love with an image you've carried, an image of your own creation."

"No. With her. When I saw her, it was very strong. I caught just a glimpse of her: she was walking away from me. And then I saw her later, and we met, and it was as if I had known her all my life."

"Infatuation happens all the time. Sometimes it happens to me, and I'm sixty-one."

"She's an actress."

"Oh boy," Cornell said. "Here we go."

"She trained in music, and she has the most beautiful voice I've ever heard. When she speaks, I have no power of resistance. I went to the theater to meet her before dinner. Because it was early I went in and I heard her sing. Cornell, if I were married, I would have to leave my wife. If going to her meant that I would die, I would go to her."

"You can't judge a woman by her singing, Ulysses."

"You *can*. You can, by her singing, know her absolutely."

"No. The song isn't hers. The music isn't hers—unless she wrote it. Anyway, even if she did, the song is alive in a way that the person who's singing it can never be. I know about that. For the first half of my life, we had no electricity. My relatives in South Carolina still don't have electricity. Until I was your age the light I saw by came from a wick—the wick of a candle, an oil lamp, or a kerosene lantern. The flame rides above the wick, it doesn't touch it, it doesn't consume it. No doubt that when she sings, her song has all the qualities you say it has. I believe you. But her song isn't her. If it were, it would consume her. The flame is never inside the candle, which is something else entirely. Stage-door Johnnies fall in love with that flame, but it can never be touched or possessed. It neither lasts nor can it be loved.

"You're just back from the war. For four years you lived on the edge. You still live intensely, and you see everything in heroic terms. But you're home now. It's different. It won't work here."

"Guide me, then," Harry said. "I'll listen. But I give no guarantee."

"That's what I've been trying to do. That's what Meyer would have done."

"I know. But you're not my father. You can stand to see me fall, which is good, and why I can probably take your advice a lot better than his."

Cornell sighed, and then entered the problem. "If she's interested in you, why will she not cancel or postpone her engagement?"

"Expectation, family, security, inertia. But mainly he has the kind of hold on her that you might expect of a pimp. I should kill him."

"You can't kill someone you don't know."

"Oh really?"

"I mean, you don't know enough about him to know if he really deserves to be killed. And anyway, if you did, even if you could get away with it, you'd never have her."

"How do you know?"

"I've seen the very thing."

"Then what should I do?"

"Win her. You have to take her from him right in front of him, and without hurting anything but his pride. Hurt him otherwise, and you break her love for you."

"How can I do that with so little time?"

"How much does she love you? Does she love you at all?"

"I suspect she loves me very much. I hope so."

"But she hasn't told you?"

"Not in words."

"Then you've got to risk everything."

"By Sunday?"

"*On* Sunday. It'll be more dramatic. That's what you need to break a lock."

"How? It's going to be announced at the Georgica Club in East Hampton. I've never heard of it. I don't know where it is. Probably the only Jew to come within a mile of it is their accountant."

"But I'll bet they've got plenty of us working in the kitchen," Cornell said. "She's not Jewish?"

"Catherine Sedley?" Harry asked. He loved both her names, but he had fallen in love first with Catherine Sedley.

"Who's she going to marry?"

"Me, I hope."

"Who's she scheduled to marry at the moment?"

"Victor Marrow."

"Marrow as in Wall Street?"

"Apparently. He's a thirty-eight-year-old Marrow—I have no idea what his position is. Perhaps her father wants to unite the two families' bank accounts in the little Marrow she's been practicing to bear, although she didn't say so directly."

"Oh, so she's an *heiress* from the lower orders of society."

"I guess she is."

"That's convenient."

"No, because I won't take money, if that's what you mean."

"Harry, the money's always there. It can pull you out of trouble."

"I wouldn't let that happen."

"In any circumstance? At any price?"

Harry thought. "The way I feel about her... yes. What I have right now is the best time of my life. I wouldn't trade it for anything, much less certainty or ease, which eventually disappear anyway."

"That's the war speaking, Harry."

"Not just the war, Cornell. It's love speaking."

"Love or not, what do her parents think of you, a Jew hurtling toward insolvency?"

"Now we're hurtling? They've never heard of me."

"As merciful as that may be," Cornell said, "it won't last and it doesn't make it any easier."

"You don't have to tell me. There'll be two hundred guests there, all WASPs, like some sort of Indian tribe with Champagne. I spent a lot of time with them at school and I know how to talk to them. Sometimes they mistake me for one of them, which I always found flattering, because they're admirable in many respects, but they'd never let me *be* one of them even if I wanted to be, which I don't."

"Then how are you going to do this?"

"That's what I'm asking you."

"You think I have an advantage here?"

"You're a Christian."

Cornell drew back. He put his left hand up to his forehead as if shielding his eyes from the sun. "You are truly," he said, "a piece of work."

"You're closer to them than I am."

"You really think so?"

"Yes. You are, and always will be." He was sincere.

"I've got to say," Cornell said, astounded, "that's an eye-opener."

"She made me promise not to call her or go to her house, and I did promise."

"Well then you're all set."

"And yet I think she really loves me, maybe. And, for some reason, I don't think I'm going to lose her."

"You're not."

"I'm not?"

"No. If you hadn't said what you said about me being a Christian, I wouldn't have known what to do. But now that I know you're as crazy as you are, I do know. Meyer wouldn't tell you to do this, but I'm not Meyer, and I can. It's simple. It's obvious. It came to me when you put me in shock."

"What?"

"Do what you're good at, what you know, what you're trained to do."

"And that is?"

"Go on a raid."

"A raid? What kind of a raid?"

"I don't know. You're the pathfinder."

"I can't do that."

"Why not? It's on the beach, isn't it? It must be on the beach. It's probably on a bluff above the beach, to catch the wind."

"There's no bluff there. She said it's in the dunes."

"That's great. It's like Normandy, but there isn't a bluff and there aren't any Germans."

"In Normandy I was dropped deep in, nowhere near the beaches, and I don't have a plane."

"You don't need a plane or a parachute. You have a train. Get out there. What can you lose?"

"Her."

"And if you don't get out there?"

"Her."

"Need I say more?"

"War is different. I have no license."

"You're not going to kill anybody."

"I could still end up in jail."

"So what? The food's good in jail." Cornell stopped and brought himself up short. "No it's not."

"Just to think about it makes me nervous."

"Tell me you weren't frightened in the war."

"Initially, always."

"So was I. And when the things you had to do frightened you, what did you do?"

"I did them anyway."

"That's right. So do it. But be careful, be gentle, because it's all about a woman."

# 9

## GEORGICA

Perhaps it was the rhythm of the wheels clicking past the joints of the rails, or the lurching and swaying of the coaches, or the weaving of steam and smoke as they painted the brush and the sandy banks through which the train sped. Or perhaps it was the fields newly ploughed and newly cut, or still in hay and waving like the sea. Or perhaps just the great mass of the train pressing forward, but he was thrown back to a time not long before, when he had ridden powerlessly with the fortunes of war and nothing was left of what he had been. He was a pathfinder, whose job was to go first and set the flares and smoke that others would follow. With the first major actions in Sicily, and then in France, Holland, and Germany, he discovered that no matter how well he might show the way, he was following a course that had already been set. So many times he would look back toward the echelons that he guided in and know that just as they were tracing his path he was tracing another; that it had all come before, and that he was merely following the first soldier. He remembered — he could never forget — that in the fiercest fighting the casualties were so many that you could feel the souls of the fallen rising all around you, lifting upward as gently as snow falls.

The fields between sea and sound were in their silence like the fields of France where he had been broken, and now he was racing through them, still alive. The window was open full, and sometimes cinders from the steam engine came in and stung his eyes. The larger ones, more than just grit in the wind, were hot enough to burn where they touched. Farmers had made long windrows at angles to the rails, and the land was in the state of perfection it knows only in early June. Clouds and sun made the light that burst through the windows of the train flash as if from a heliograph, and now and then the train would run near the ocean, where the sea air was as fresh as the water was blue.

With one telephone call he had found out the schedule for the event, the requirements of dress, and, although he hadn't asked, the menu. Whether Victor or Catherine had chosen the salmon with sauce verte he did not know. At the station, the detraining passengers were met by fleets of taxis and private cars (some of which had "Georgica Club" painted in gold on their maroon front doors) and ferried to the reception and dinner.

Had he been dressed properly he would have chanced riding with them, but he was in street clothes, with his formal outfit in a musette bag strapped across one shoulder and hanging at his side. With time until a taxi would return, he could change at leisure, which was good, because changing in a train station toilet stall was bad enough, but to do so in a rush was worse. Once he had done this in Philadelphia when it was 105 degrees and he was late for the wedding of two people he hardly knew. Exiting the fetid toilet stall and dripping with sweat, at risk of being less on time than he was already, he had stood in front of a giant fan in the hall that led to the men's room, his dinner jacket open like a bat's wings, as he enjoyed every second of evaporation.

At the East Hampton station he was neither sweating nor late, and when he emerged from the men's room the taxis were gone and he was dressed and dry, with not a hair out of place. His heart, however, was beating fairly fast. The stationmaster agreed to store his bag, and told him that the taxis would be back. "There's a big thing at the Georgica Club. Is that where you're going?"

"I might stop in later."

"I think it's pretty full unless you're invited, even if you're a member. I don't know how it works. Are you a member?"

"Of course, and members can attend," Harry said, making it up out of whole cloth, "if they respect the privacy of the event." He pronounced the word *privacy* with a short *i*, in the English way.

"It's a Marrow getting engaged to a Hale."

"I know."

"You brought your own bottle and a glass?" the stationmaster asked, eyeing the bottle of Pol Roger and a flute hanging from Harry's left hand.

"I'm stopping someplace first," Harry told him, truthfully.

"A housewarming gift."

"It makes my arrival more appreciated."

"One glass. I hope she has another one," the stationmaster said, wanting to tease out something erotic.

"She drinks straight from the bottle," Harry told him, more than fulfilling his expectations. A taxi was pulling up.

"She must be some kinda woman."

"Oh, she is," Harry answered as he got into the taxi, which drove off before the driver even knew where he was going, which seemed appropriate for the evening.

"A Marrow is marrying a Hale," the taxi driver said.

"Like hell," Harry told him.

"No?"

"Not if I have anything to say about it."

"Uh-oh. You want me to take you to the Georgica Club."

"No. I want you to drop five hundred to the east, on the beach."

"What?"

"Can you put me a quarter of a mile to the east of the club, on the beach?"

"I can't get to the beach on the east. It's private all the way to Amagansett. There is a road about half a mile west."

"That'll be fine."

As Harry came out of the dunes and onto the strand the sun was riding just above the horizon and evening light had begun its conversion to banker's gold. The wind was steady at his back from the west, the beach totally empty, and the Georgica Club, where the first act would be cocktails until dusk, the second a late dinner, and a third the announcement and dancing, was visible to the east, perched on the dunes and garlanded by golf links. The building itself, of gray stone like an Edinburgh townhouse, was enormous, each of its many large wings as big as a ministry. Paper lanterns glowing imperceptibly in what was left of the sun were strung across its terraces, and lights could barely be seen in the windows of shadowed areas from which the sun had been blocked.

As it had done night and day without cease for hundreds of millions of years, the surf broke in a war of blue against white. And because the season had not yet begun — early June was too cold for most — the beach was unswept and the detritus of fall hurricanes and winter storms was everywhere. There were the ordinary tangles of driftwood, fishermen's floats, nets, and dried kelp, but with the war less than a year in the past the beach was littered as well with shattered life rings, sections of raft, and items of clothing scattered at different levels of the tide. Tins of food and provisions, unopened but somehow empty or partially filled with salt water, bore witness to torpedoed ships, and planes downed at sea. The print on all these was fresh enough to read — in English, military English, and sometimes German. The sea had rid itself of most of the markers of six years of war by sending them up onto the beaches as if onto shelves in a cupboard. Some may have been still afloat, but it would not be long until every surface of the ocean was clear, for that which could be waterlogged would sink, and more buoyant things would eventually be cast onto dry land where they would be worn down by sun, wind, rain, and blowing sand. The print would fade, colors bleach, nails and metal rust, structures collapse, and wood rot. In twenty years or so when the children of those who had crossed and recrossed safely over the sea were young women and young men, hardly a trace would remain, and of the traces virtually nothing identifiable — sea, air, and sun having swallowed and vaporized everything but memory.

He stopped in front of a black shoe missing its laces. It was preserved well enough so that with some softening and polish it might have been put back in service. The heel was hardly worn. He thought that had things gone differently it might have been his shoe, and that someone else might be standing in front of it as if at a grave, grasping the lapels of his tuxedo in a tight grip and pressing a bottle of Champagne close to his thigh. As if he were the one who was dead, he spoke to himself, the one who was living, urgently charging him with life. He let the breeze force its way into his lungs, and looked ahead at his objective, now strongly shining. Catherine was inside, not a quarter of a mile away. She would almost certainly be in a strapless gown — it was the fashion — and he realized that he had never seen her bare arms and shoulders, the top of her chest, or her back. And with this in mind, he stepped over the black shoe and went forward.

The straight course of the beach, which wanted to run unbroken from Coney Island to Montauk Point but did not, was cut by an inlet just short of the Georgica Club itself, a channel a hundred feet wide through which the tide was receding in a fast stream.

About to cross this, he calculated. First he approximated the distance. A hundred feet was a good guess, which he checked by throwing a smooth stone. It went almost the whole way, but he was wearing a dinner jacket and was unaccustomed to throwing things. A sidestroke while carrying with one hand his bundled clothes, the bottle, and the glass in the air would take him across in about a minute and a half. Then he threw a piece of driftwood upstream and timed its passage. In a minute and thirty seconds it was carried into the surf, moving approximately three hundred feet. Thus, were he to have any hope of crossing and keeping his clothes intact, dry, and in his possession, he would have to start from the marsh at the neck of the pond. And the wider the neck, the slower the water, so the farther inland he went, the better his chances — except that he could not go too far without sinking into the mud.

He stripped, laid out his clothes on the sand — shoes, socks, pants, braces, shirt, cummerbund, tie, jacket — and tied everything into a bundle that, were it to be swept away, would put him in a very embarrassing position. When it was secured and tightened with the braces, he picked it up and stepped into the rust-colored sand at the edge of the channel. His feet felt many sharp shells, but none sharp enough to cut except bloodlessly and shallow.

And then he heard, "Trying to come over?" Across the channel was a man of indeterminate age, tall, sandy-haired, and drunk, with a brigadier's mustache and a dinner jacket.

"Unless you know of a bridge."

"You could walk around the pond, but you'd be trespassing multiply and it would take you forever. No, this is good."

"I don't suppose the club has a boat?"

"All locked up and unreachable," the man said, glancing over his shoulder at a line of sheds.

"Then I'll swim. I didn't know about the channel."

"Coming to the celebration?"

"Yes."

"We don't get too many naked people at this club. It'll shake things up. I'm all for that. Which side are you on?"

"Is it a war?"

"Not yet; they're still unmarried."

"I'm on Catherine's side."

"Wonderful girl, Catherine."

"Yes. I love her."

"Have a good swim. With luck, we'll be at the same table." He turned to go back, staggering elegantly.

"See you," said Harry, remembering the idiom of the final clubs, to which he would not have been admitted, and he continued to walk, anxious about his nudity and wanting to get to the other side of the channel and dress. He went into the marsh and reeds of Georgica Pond's ocean side, and on his right the club came alight in the dusk.

Away from the wind, which anyway had diminished with the sunset, he could hear music coming through the many French doors that opened onto the terraces, and when he lowered himself into the water, which though not warm was a great deal warmer than the ocean, he found himself swimming to the cadences of Cole Porter.

By the time he was halfway across, he was also halfway down and moving more and more rapidly to the sea. The minor weight of the bundle, held unnaturally, was a torture similar to that of holding a rifle at arm's length. His left arm pumped desperately, his legs moved like egg beaters, and just as the water grew frigid and he felt the timing of the waves, he grounded on the sand, safely across, close to the edge of the surf.

Breathing hard, he struggled to his feet. His clothes were dry. He moved inland at a run, to a prominence in the dunes, where the wind was strongest. There, he threw the bundle down in the sand and stood in the breeze to dry. Ahead of him was the Georgica Club, now rising massively and shining like a Christmas-lit house in the snow. Through the clear glass of its doors and windows he saw gilt-framed paintings, fires leaping in the fireplaces, and flashes of color as guests and servants moved about. The sound of the orchestra came and went at the discretion of the wind, but as he listened in the semi-darkness, its swellings and disappearances, alternations, sudden interruptions, and sudden surges, like those of the surf, seemed especially poignant. Expensive cars were gathered like herds of cattle in the parking lots, and the golf links, now deserted, had been conquered by an evening mist coming off the Atlantic.

Inside, they were celebrating. For someone who is happy, celebration is yet another channel or instrument through which happiness may course. For someone who is not, celebration is a tedious parody of existence that seems pointless and false. Concentrated inside were fame, riches, and power, all of which were nothing more than forms of multiplication. But as the lights sparkled and the music ebbed and flowed with the deaths and resurrections of the west wind, Harry understood that Catherine was embraced by these things and lived within them, that she was protected by ancient and tested privilege, and kept from him by forces of great weight, seriousness, and long standing.

What exactly was he doing, naked, almost in the dark except for the faint rose light of a sun that had set, with the wind coursing freely over him. All he had was himself. With water still streaming off him, his body hard and his eye keen, he realized that he had nothing and could not have been more naked, and this allowed him to lose all apprehension and fear. As soon as he was dry, he dressed. He combed his hair with his fingers. After popping the cork of the Champagne, he drank a third of it directly from the bottle so as to bring himself close in spirit and demeanor to the people he was about to join. Walking in from the beach, holding the bottle by the neck and the glass by the stem, seemed as natural as anything he had ever done.

The surf crashed in the dark several hundred feet away, its broken front further disrupted by the current rushing from the inlet. This cruel sea stretched for thousands of miles with more mass and power than was comprehensible. A simple shrug, no more than a turn in its sleep, a barely perceptible movement of its world-spanning flanks, an adjustment of a millionth of its mass, would instantly swallow the third of civilization sitting at its edge and by its leave. When Harry had stood in the wind, stripped of everything, the eternal ocean had been on his right, and the club, delicately perched on sand, to his left, pulsing with light and warmth and in the scheme of things all told just a brief flare. Though the building in front of him was destined to disappear as surely as the tens of thousands of ships, pieces of which now lay bleaching on the shore, women in lovely gowns now glided across its Persian carpets and its polished floors.

As he moved from the dunes to a path compacted in the sand, to a boardwalk, to a stone terrace, and then to shiny heart-pine and antique Isfahans, he forgot the sea. Once again in uniform, just like more than a hundred male guests and waiters also dressed like penguins, he acquired the confidence of anonymity. No one would challenge him. He could move freely, more than freely, because he had no position to protect, no investment, no membership to preserve, and no agreement to keep. He felt as invulnerable as if he had come back from the dead and was walking invisibly. He was a ghost who could without detection flip trays loaded with full glasses, trip pompous dowagers, and launch baked potatoes through the air like artillery shells, and he drifted forward in the oncoming air of scandal he was determined to create.

Though he had told Cornell that there would be no Jews within a mile, with his ability to recognize other Jews even when non-Jews could not (something that he thought would disappear in a generation or two), he became aware of several of the musicians and the woman who was singing. Perhaps it was something in their eyes, the way they moved, or the very shape of them, and in her voice: he was of course unusually sensitive to a woman's voice. She was singing "Someone to Watch over Me," and as one of the Jewish musicians brushed the surface of a snare drum to soften the plaint, another sharpened it with his violin.

All he had now was light and music as he wandered from room to room in search of Catherine. Everything there — the glossy white millwork, the rich colors of the walls, the silver and crystal, and the carefully tended fires — was only a frame for her. And yet, in half a dozen capacious rooms and long halls, he couldn't find her. Perhaps she'd been moving away from him at the same speed he'd been moving toward her, and they had circled never to meet. Perhaps when breaking this pattern and crossing his former paths at random he had simply missed her. That the two of them could be in an enormous, busy place for half an hour and not meet did not seem unreasonable. It had happened on the ferry.

He stopped to consider this. In the center of a large library a fire was burning and twenty or thirty people were talking in small groups. His glass was in his hand, empty. Some time before, he had abandoned the bottle to a table with fifty others. He might have felt self-conscious standing alone in the middle of the room were it not for the fire, what he had drunk, and the thought that had come to him that it was likely that in the years before they met they had passed on the street, or sat in the same subway car, or waited next to one another, as New Yorkers say, on line. Although he had no memory of such a thing, and as far as he knew it had never happened, he believed nonetheless that it had, because he did have a memory that he could not quite remember, and suspected that he had created it only in honor of something he would never reach. And yet it was very strong and stayed with him. It lasted no longer than the snap of two fingers or the clicking of a camera shutter, but it was repeated over and over: a flash of clouds and sky — the sky pale blue, the clouds like a pigeon's lightest gray. He was falling through them, as when he parachuted in the war. It was a winter sky, and the sun was shining.

Then a hand clasped his shoulder. He started, and turned. "It's you," said the man, neither more nor less drunk than he had been at the inlet. "You made it."

"Barely." The pun vanished unrecognized. Harry was, himself, slightly drunk.

"Did you have a good swim?"

Harry stepped close to him and said, softly but with the deliberate clarity of someone speaking to a drunk in a noisy room, "Very cold. And I was almost swept out to sea. Can we keep this quiet? It's somewhat embarrassing, not being aware of the inlet, and having to go around naked."

"Absolutely. Wouldn't dream. . . ."

"Good."

"Were you in the war? You must have been."

"I was."

"So was I. I flew transports in the Pacific and went down twice. What about you?"

"Airborne. I went down, too, but it was part of the plan."

"Where?"

"I was in the Eighty-second, and never got to the Pacific."

"Where'd you go to school?"

"Harvard," Harry said, his attendance, in this circumstance, the equivalent of a perfect knowledge of German after being parachuted into Berlin in 1944.

"I mean where did you prep?"

"I didn't prep. I was found in a shoebox, brought up by welders, and educated by wolves. Then I went to Harvard."

"Welders!" said the transport pilot, delighted. "I never knew anyone who was brought up by welders!"

"Yes," said Harry. "My mother and my father. They taught me, among other things, how to weld. Have you seen Catherine?"

"I did at first, but I haven't for a while. Either she gets invisible to me when I've had too much to drink, or she and Victor snuck off to the beach or upstairs" — he pointed with his left index finger and followed drunkenly with his eyes—"because I haven't seen Victor either."

"There are a lot of people. What's she wearing?"

"A silver and black thing that sparkles. At engagement parties it's always better when the woman is beautiful. It puts everything in focus. If Victor were going to marry a mop, what would be the point? And Catherine is beautiful, in her way."

"I think," Harry said, with the lunacy and conviction of someone deeply in love, "that she's the most beautiful woman in the world."

"I wouldn't say that. She's attractive, but she's also kind of funny-looking."

"I don't think so. I think she's the most beautiful woman in the world."

"You said that. Why do you keep saying it?"

"I told you before. I love her."

"You did? That's very friendly of you. I mean"—he said this conspiratorially, swaying a little—"maybe too friendly. Why do you say you love her? I thought...."

"I love her," Harry answered, as if testifying not to an inebriated, High Episcopalian transport pilot, but before God, "because of, among other things, her amplitude of reflection and the richness of her mind. That's what makes her infinitely beautiful."

"Wo!" said the transport pilot. "Her what?"

"Her amplitude of reflection, her richness of mind. And I just love her."

"Wo," he said again, as much to his drink as to Harry, "you ought to marry her, not Victor." He was now a partisan, fully convinced.

"I'm not going to marry Victor, and I am going to marry Catherine."

"Does Victor know this?"

"Victor," Harry said, "has no rights in the matter."

"Of course he doesn't. He's her fiancé. Why would he?"

"Even if he had rights, they would terminate tonight."

"Don't they begin tonight?"

"Same thing. The last person to leave the ship is also the last person not to leave the ship."

The transport pilot struggled. "That's right," he said. "How did you figure that one out?"

"I figured it out as I was waiting at the door to jump out of a Dakota."

"Do you think, do you, that as the war recedes, that five years from now, or ten, things will be less insane?"

Harry considered this carefully. "No."

A bell called everyone to dinner. In the stream of people heading toward rooms of which he had not been aware until unfolded doors revealed flower-laden tables, she was nowhere to be seen. Had the transport pilot not mentioned that this was the engagement party, Harry would have thought he had come either to the wrong place or to the right place at the wrong time. In a dining room to his right he saw a table with a chair leaning against it, and a place card folded so that the outside was blank. He pocketed the place card, righted the chair, and stood behind it, ready to assist any ladies who might appear. Scanning the place settings, he saw that four people were due, and shortly they arrived.

One was a woman in her thirties, who, depending upon her expression, was either not attractive at all or excruciatingly so. Another was a dowager of profound visual neutrality. And the third was a young woman who was heavily made up, which can be magnificent if it is done well, but it wasn't, and unfortunately for her and everyone else it looked as if she had been dipped in flour, and her lipstick made her lips into red bicycle tires. Some men liked this, Harry did not. He and a bald man with glasses pulled out chairs for the women and exhibited the required deference. All was well as they began to talk and eat. Harry longed for Catherine, and, wondering where she had gone, hoped that he wasn't too late.

"We came all the way out here," said the older woman, "because my husband says that this presages the formation of the largest firm on

Wall Street." She was clearly resentful and willingly indiscreet. Necessity may be the mother of invention, Harry thought, but liquor is the father of indiscretion.

"We have a house here," the woman in her thirties said. "It was no trouble." In wrestling, this was called a *smackdown*.

"I'm out of school," the youngest said. "I don't care where I am. What about you?" she asked Harry. "Do you care where you are?"

"Of course I care where I am."

Discovering him sexually, she said nothing except everything that could be said with an averted glance.

"I came to see Catherine and I have yet to see her," Harry said.

"I saw her," the youngest woman offered. "Then she disappeared. But she's here. How could she not be here? What about you?" she asked the bald man with the glasses.

"I own taxi fleets," he said, not taking his eyes off his salmon. "You've ridden in my taxis."

"I didn't ask what you did."

"I know you didn't," he said, still not looking up. "I know what you meant, but I'm just a friend of Willie Marrow, which isn't very interesting, so I skipped to the good part. What work do *you* do?" he asked Harry. It was impolite to ask the women what they did. If they did anything, which was unlikely, they would probably be brassy enough to volunteer it.

"I've been back for only a few months," he said. "Demobilized. I'm not really doing anything." It was, in this circle, an answer neither unexpected nor unadmired.

"Demobilized? Weren't you an officer?"

"I resigned my commission."

"I resigned my commission at Sweet Briar two years ago," said the young one, and then, like a pack of hunting dogs making a sudden turn upon a scent, the conversation turned to Sweet Briar, horses, and hounds. Harry, who liked horses and dogs, though he rode neither, listened with the detachment of an anthropologist. What his dinner companions knew about animals could have filled an encyclopedia.

They had a real connection to nature and the land. Even the owner of the taxi fleets, who had houses all over and took taxis between them, spent long days in high boots, in reeds, blinds, boats, and brush.

Then another bell rang, melodiously but with the timing of troopship claxons dictating shifts in the dining halls and on deck. Dinner was over — all nine hundred carefully wrought calories of it, including a chocolate mousse in a cup the size of a half dollar — and the dancing was about to begin.

Everyone had had a great deal to drink, and half the women now walked like beagles. Harry had gone far beyond his normal limit. So when the music swelled, it would be easy for anyone to find a willing partner provided he or she could stand up, and the ballrooms would quickly fill. The tedium of tight, confining clothes and small talk, which are to the soul what acid is to metal, would soon disappear, as ordinary mortals, if they could, seized upon the opportunity to move like angels.

As he was getting up, Harry saw that the dowager of profound visual neutrality was sharing something with the taxi-fleet man, and it was about him. "I think he's a Goatly," he heard her say.

"Which Goatlys?" was the response.

"The ones with the dean of St. Michael's."

"You think he's Warren Goatly, Edmund's son?"

They drifted off.

Harry imagined that he might see Catherine dancing. He both dreaded and desired this. He had seen her dance to a bar or two during rehearsal, just a twirl, really, as a transition from her song, and what he saw in those brief moments was what dance, when not too studied, not too disciplined, can accomplish as if by nature and in defiance of it — the movement, by the deepest commemoration, to another plane; the transcendence of the body by its own art; the giving over of oneself to the invisible wave that runs through all things.

He imagined her dancing to the music coming from the ballrooms, her movements both poignant and irresistible, as impossible not to love as when the wind slightly lifted her hair. And what would he do if she was paired with Victor? He feared witnessing them in the greatest and most intense intimacy that is both allowed and takes place mostly in public.

With little scope of what was going on, who was who, or what he himself was going to do if faced with Catherine across a room as time stopped still, he began to move toward the sound of the music, a route that took him through the main dining room. As he was wending his way past tables that waiters had begun to clear, he saw at what appeared to be the head table five people in animated conversation and distressed withdrawal, with speech and silence alternating in a tapestry of disconsolation. The scene was anchored by two older men who had the restfully stiff bodies of those who, even if still athletic, paid the price for it. And yet their wives, handsome women beyond their prime—one still comely—seemed to direct whatever action there was. These he took to be the Marrows and the Hales, the more attractive and younger couple, who were also physically smaller, being the Hales. The third man, who looked to be in his forties, with little hair and a big, square face, he took to be Victor. It seemed that they didn't know where Catherine was, either.

Victor looked like a building on Pennsylvania Avenue. At this moment at least he was so stolid and gray that he could easily have been mistaken for a post office. He seemed neither cruel nor kind, intelligent nor unintelligent. He, too, was distressed, but not so much as the others. Nor did his presence give Harry any clue of attack, and Harry could think of nothing to say should words become necessary. The anger that had sometimes grown to storm subsided, and he feared that he might laugh.

As he observed from a standstill and as if from invisibility (for they would hardly be aware of a stranger amid the waiters), Catherine stepped from the path onto the boardwalk and increased her speed. When she crossed the terrace, its hard surface made her realize that her shoes were filled with sand. She was breathing through her nose, as her lips were tightly closed lest they tremble, and her hands were gently gathered into fists. Although a few stragglers who were not by then dancing greeted her as she passed, she neither heard nor saw them. Her hair was slightly disheveled, and the sea wind had brought to it pearl-sized drops of clear water that sparkled in the many lights. The sequined top, which fit her closely and sent out dozens of communicative flashes, was like some sort of glorious feminine armor. Her arms and shoulders, which seemed capable of wielding a two-handed sword, were bare in a way that was not vulnerable but the sign of martial confidence and courage.

When she entered the dining room, the families rose. She was behind Harry and to his right. He saw her in the periphery as a fast-moving, sparkling orb, and as she went past he smelled her perfume. She glanced at him and continued forward as if he didn't exist. About to follow her, he checked himself and remained in place.

Her father stood and took several steps toward her. Before anything was said, they embraced in the embrace that can exist between fathers and daughters, all-forgiving even as they fight. Her mother, having seen without doubt in the way Catherine moved that whatever was going to occur was inevitable, merely smiled.

Catherine whispered something to her father, who, looking as if he had just been hit by a bullwhip, wearily pulled back. Then to her mother, who as if pleased that whatever she had correctly foreseen was now about to come and go, smiled yet again, in resignation.

Victor was inert, but with the patience of a hunter. His parents stepped forward graciously to greet the young woman who was to be their daughter-in-law. They didn't know what was coming, and had no impulse but that of kindness and respect. Seeing this, and hurt that she would have to rebuff them, she shook her head to warn them off. They understood instantly. And Victor, though inert, knew as well. As if the whole thing were unimportant to him, he said, so that it was audible to Harry and half a dozen waiters, "Oh crap."

"That's what you say?" Catherine asked, infuriated. "That's what you say?"

She seized a half-full wine glass with her right hand and pitched it into his face. Although it shattered, brought up blood, and covered him with red wine, he hardly flinched.

"Oh, God," her father said, not in distress but as he would have in reaction to a particularly garish pair of golf pants.

The Marrows were paralyzed.

A dozen guests were now looking on, having been drawn in by a sixth sense of scandal. As a covey of thrush in the fall woods suddenly rises, its wings mastering the north wind, so the Georgica Club would erupt that evening in the flutter of having found something to talk about other than real estate, horses, and problematic servants.

Catherine pivoted angrily and walked toward the exit. After a short distance she turned back and shouted, "That's what happens when you do what you did, you bastard. It sleeps. But then it wakes."

As she marched past Harry, she said to him, as if to a dog that had followed her down the lane and was going to make her late, "Go home!" As far as anyone knew, she was addressing all the onlookers, who had no idea that Catherine would never speak to a dog in that fashion, or care that it had followed after her, unless she loved it.

# 10

## DISTANT LIGHTS AND SUMMER WIND

"I swam here," he said, over the sound of the motor furling the roof of her convertible. Standing by the passenger side, he watched the top rise and fold.

"You swam from New York?" Even in her present state she could not help but think this was amusing.

"Across the inlet."

"In a tuxedo?"

"I held it above the water. I was naked. I was almost swept out to sea. And now I need a ride."

The top was down and tucked in, the motor silent. Victor watched from the main entrance. He had heard her laugh.

"How is it," Catherine asked, "that when I'm most upset, you can make me laugh?"

"You know," he said, "if your eyebrows were like woolly bears, and your lips were thick, and you spoke like a dunce and couldn't sing a note, I'd still be in love with you. You know that."

"And then you make me cry," she said. "What are you trying to do?"

"Nothing."

"Well you're not succeeding."

Quietly, he said, "I came out here and I was going to do something. I didn't know what. But I didn't have to. You did it. You didn't see me until you were going full steam, did you?"

"Actually, I did," she answered. And then, like a taxi driver, "Where're you going?"

"Home."

"Get in."

After he had become accustomed to the shock of her driving—"That's all right," she had said, "I know this kind of road: I grew up here"—he asked if the car in which they were riding belonged to her parents.

"Not a Chevrolet convertible." It was black and boat-like. "My mother wouldn't have a convertible, because it would muss her hair, and my father has to have a Rolls or, before the war, a Mercedes. It's my car. I keep it out here."

"Where are we going?"

"You tell me. What direction are we headed in? You think I know?"

He looked up at the stars, and, unperturbed by the sea wind except to sparkle, they told him. "West-northwest."

"That's just because the road bends that way."

"So, where are we going?"

"New York."

"We won't get there until three in the morning, if that. Do you know the route?"

"Past Southampton it's anyone's guess. No one knows. It's like never-never land."

"Really?"

"Yup."

"Then let me ask you this. How much gas do you have? Gas stations won't be open."

She looked at the gas gauge, moving only her eyes. "Half a tank."

"That won't get us to Manhattan."

"It'll get us to Hauppauge," which she pronounced *Hop Hog*, "and past there it's a kind of hell where gas stations and diners stay open all night, at least along the big road."

"You drive pretty fast."

"I always have," she said.

"It makes me a little nervous, even though I do, too. I don't knock down mailboxes."

"Was that a mailbox? I thought it was a dead branch."

"It may have been a branch, but it had a metal flag and it said *Lucastrino*."

"I should send them a check. Would you like me to slow down?"

"I would. And you didn't eat, did you?"

"I was having a crisis on the beach. When I have a crisis, I don't eat."

"We'll find a place that's open late, somewhere in Hop Hog. We'll take it easy, we'll go slow, I'll drive some, and we'll pull into Manhattan at dawn and see the sun reflecting from a million windows. I've seen that at the end of the day more times than I can count, but never at sunrise."

"Nor have I," she said. "You see, we look right into it."

They took many wrong turns on roads that bisected huge fields of potatoes or hay, and they would come to unmarked junctions where great oaks were clustered after several centuries safe from the plough, and there in the dark, the new leaves choking the moonlight, they would have to choose. When they chose wrongly, they would still come to a beautiful end, overlooking a bay, inlet, or the sea itself, the waters ruffling in moonlight and summer wind.

Slowly, they made their way west, through a silent and benign landscape just sixty or seventy miles from the largest city in the world. The roads gradually became wider and less rural, and they had the sense that they were nearing a paved highway that was connected to the industrialized maze, as macadam always was. But they were wrong, for they came to yet another barrier of water, a dead end where the road disappeared into a bank of sand.

Braking to a stop, she said, "Less than a quarter of a tank."

"Let's see where we are," he suggested, opening his door.

She turned off the lights and engine and joined him as he climbed the bank. When they reached the top they saw an immense bay, its little waves sparkling dimly in the moonlight. The wind blew through the sharp dune grasses and made them bend, and on the other side of the water two radio towers, black against a slightly bluer sky, blinked in red, their distant lights beating rhythmically. Beyond, somewhere invisibly to the west in an endless volume of darkness that its throbbing lights would make as pink as coral, was New York. "This reminds me," she said, "of the kind of scene they light when they make a sunrise. They always start with dawn, and hold it proportionately longer than would nature. When I was a little girl I wanted to go into the theater because of the music and the light. I didn't have many friends when I was growing up — none, really. But then my mother took me to a play, where the light and music seemed better than the world itself. I'm so stuck on that, that when I see the real thing it makes me think of the imitation. When you watch from the dark, as I did for so long, that's what you get."

The wind blew her hair back as she stared across the water — her posture, without deliberation, unrelenting, her arms crossed against the sequined top to protect her from the chill. At first, concentrating on her face, and watching the distant lights reflected in her eyes, he hadn't noticed that she was cold, but as soon as he did he removed his jacket and laid it over her. She pinched closed the satin lapels and was relieved not to have the wind flowing through her almost insubstantial gown.

He put his arm on her left shoulder and turned her until they were facing one another. She thought — she was sure — that he was going to kiss her, as she wanted him to, and he did, only once. The shock of it was such that, for the moment, once was enough. Many kisses, days of kisses, would come. Now he pulled her close to him, and with his left hand he took her hand as it clasped the lapels of his jacket. And then he looked at her, bowed his head, and closed his eyes as if in prayer. By the time he straightened not long after, she had accepted him as she had never accepted anyone else in her life. "I wanted so much," he said, "this evening at the Georgica Club, to dance with you for as long as we could. I really wanted to dance with you."

"You will," she said. "You will. Ten thousand times."

The night now had a different quality. They were happy to leave the oaks, the silvery fields, and lights that beckoned from the other side of windy bays. You never reach the lights across the water, but their beauty on the summer wind is such that you never have to. The forward progress of the car homing in on Manhattan, where its engine would be like a bee in a hive of innumerable others, was as cheerful as being in love, which, of course, they were.

Somewhere way to the west of Hop Hog they found an open gas station and filled up the car. Twenty minutes farther on, they were on roads blazing with neon and incandescents and crowded with tire shops, furniture stores, and huge cylindrical tanks the sides of which moved up or down as they filled or emptied, but only very slowly, so that many people and nearly all children were mystified by the empty steel frames where once solid tanks had stood, and then by the return of the solid tanks. Farther on, where the ground was shadowed by streetlights and split by railroad tracks recessed into the streets, and the overhead trolley wires were like bolts of lightning that had been stilled and straightened, cleaned and pressed, they saw a diner. It was elevated on a platform, with four wings in a cross, like the Georgica Club itself, glowing from within like a window at Tiffany's, and open to serve policemen, cleaning ladies, and emergency returnees from the Hamptons.

"Stop here," she commanded. He pulled in. As their doors slammed and they stood bathed in white light, she said, "This light reminds me of how we found out the war in Europe was over, just before it was announced. We were in East Hampton last year at the beginning of May. It was very warm one night, so we decided to walk home on the beach after we had dinner at the club. If you walk slowly it takes about half an hour. As we were turning toward the cut in the dunes that leads to our house we noticed a kind of glow, and we could see our shadows against the sand. The three of us turned at once. Not far from shore was a ship that had come up behind us from the west. The ship was ablaze, but not burning, as we had seen on the horizon many times during the war. It was close, with electric lights strung from the bowsprit to the masts and down to the fantail. It was so beautiful, for so many reasons. For years, everything had been blacked out. You could hear freighters, battleships, whole convoys — but at night you never could see them.

"My mother said, 'Someone's going to get a ticket,' but my father told her, 'No, no one's going to get a ticket. That's Henry Stimson's yacht.' I remember. He said, *'That's Henry Stimson's yacht, Evelyn'* — my mother's name is Evelyn — *'and if the secretary of war turns on his lights like a Christmas tree in the middle of the ocean, the war's over.'*

"You've had dinner?" she asked as they took their seats in a booth. They wanted to sit side by side, but also to face one another. They ended up facing. It was three o'clock in the morning and they felt no desire for sleep.

"That was yesterday," he stated as he scanned the menu, "and it was Champagne. I'm going to have a club sandwich and a milkshake, to bring me back to earth."

"I'll have the same."

"Do you always do that? You did that the last time."

"It's a habit left over from Victor, but last time and just now it's what I really wanted. Maybe we have the same tastes. We'll see. Tell me, what were you going to do tonight? Were you going to disrupt the announcement? Punch Victor?"

"I wouldn't have punched Victor, he's as big as the *Hindenburg*. I had no plan. I thought that when I saw you I'd know what to do. Then I didn't see you and I thought I was in the wrong place and had missed my chance."

"I saw you," she said.

"You did?"

"I did. As I was coming out of the ladies' room. I was resigned to everything that was about to happen, and not too unhappy about it, either. I've been with him for so long I'm used to him. It would have been like an arranged marriage. There are worse things.

"And I hadn't thought about you . . . for at least two or three minutes. I was putting you out of my mind. I could have. Maybe I would think of you every now and then for the rest of my life. Maybe, if I lived to be eighty, I would regret that I had not lived with you, and maybe not. If I had nothing to remind me of the past few days, my memory of them and you would eventually have been shorn of detail. . . . That's what happens. People say, Think if we hadn't discovered Emily Dickinson. I say, Think of all the Emily Dickinsons we've never discovered. The greater part of things is secret, lost, undone. I do believe that.

"And then, as they were playing that song—I would like to sing it; I think I could sing it very well—I stepped into the hall and nearly had a heart attack. There you were, awkward and out of place, a bottle in your hand, held by the neck. Even a waiter wouldn't have done that. You looked like someone who had walked into the club from the beach to crash the party. People do it now and then, and it's easy to spot them."

"I was spotted?"

"Like a leopard. They knew. I heard them, but you were too prepossessing, too good-natured, to kick out. You were wandering alone, it was obvious, until that idiot Ross Underhill got to you and you started talking to him. He's a nice idiot who, like most idiots, doesn't know he is one, but even other idiots won't talk to him, because since he got back he's been trying to raise money for an expedition to catch the Abominable Snowman—in Austria. It was very kind of you."

"I thought he was just drunk."

"He was. He always is."

"And, besides, even idiots have souls. Even idiots can be loved."

She hesitated, enjoying the seconds that passed as one enjoys time elongated in music. "Then I had to decide. It didn't help that I had numbed myself with expensive alcohol, and that the ocean was close by. It made me think, This is what is important, this is what we live for. And then I went out to the ocean. Do you know what it was like? The waves broke, and each time they did, as they slapped against the sand, I could feel it all through my body. And each time they broke, and each time they thudded down, they said, You have only one life, you have only one life."

Soon after they began to eat, she got up and crossed the empty diner to a telephone booth from which she called her parents, a sudden rush of love and regret prompting her concern that they might be worried about her. But they hadn't been as concerned as she had thought, and had not only gone to bed but to sleep.

Her father told her that the garage at home in New York was full. She knew this already. "Don't park the car on the street," he said. "It's a convertible; you can get into it with a penknife. Put it in the garage on First." She would. They said nothing about what had happened. They would wait until she brought it up, as she would have to, but in saying nothing they had lifted a weight from her. When she returned from the telephone, Harry's jacket casually draped over her shoulders, her purplish-black sequins an earthquake of elegance in the diner in Commack or wherever they were at four, now, in the morning, it was as if her life had opened up in the clear. She showed it. Her smile was almost as beautiful as her song, which was to say a lot.

"They're all right?" he asked.

"They were sleeping."

"No explosions?"

"No."

"Reprimands?"

"None."

"Got off easy."

"Got off easy," she repeated, "especially considering that this is the end of Willie and Billie."

"Enlighten me."

"My father is William Hale III, and Victor's father is William Marrow III."

"What happened to Victor?"

"His older brother was the Fourth, but he was killed in the war. People call my father Billy and they call Willie Marrow Willie. So the joke was that when Victor and I had a boy he would be William the Fourth, and the firm he would inherit would be Hale, Marrow — like Hail, Caesar — but otherwise known as Willie and Billie. I think that name would have stuck. Wall Street is like that. Don't tell anyone, but my father hates it."

"Hates what?"

"The Street."

"Oh. But it was all planned out?"

"On a track."

"How do you know Victor's not following with a posse?"

"If he is, he probably went the wrong way. Besides, he doesn't do things that aren't carefully engineered. Insult him, and two years later you'll find that your checks bounce. You know how some things are warm to the touch, like wood or wool, and some aren't, like marble or steel? Victor is marble."

"I'll keep an eye on my checks. By the way, why Catherine Sedley?"

"My stage name."

"I know, but why didn't you tell me?"

"I wanted you to think I was poor. It's a reflex we have, to protect ourselves from insincerity."

"I didn't think you were poor, just not rich."

"But you didn't think of me the way so many people do, did you? It's disgusting when they do. In freshman year in college, it would make me cry."

"I didn't, and I don't now. I never will. You blind wealth right out of the picture. Do you understand?"

"No," she said, although she did.

"Catherine, I want to court you, slowly."

"Court," she echoed, thinking of the word and idea. She felt deep emotion, for what she had lacked and what she now might have.

"Victor certainly didn't. Has anyone?"

"Harry?"

"Yes?"

"Victor raped me. Not figuratively."

Taking this in, Harry was silent. Remarkably, she had said it unemotionally. "Then maybe I should kill him."

"No. It was a long time ago. I can never put it behind me, but I don't want to take it forward. And no, no one ever courted me."

"During the war, when you were in college?"

"We danced with servicemen at the USO in Philadelphia, and some fell in love with me, but it was inappropriate. They were boys, and I didn't meet the right one. The sailors got back on the bus and so did we. The Harvard boys had to go back to Cambridge to study and drink. And Victor managed to be there whenever we were free. I would meet him at the Benjamin Franklin Hotel. I didn't go in chains, Harry, and no, no one ever courted me."

"I would like to, if you'll let me."

"Out of charity?"

"Charity!" He was amazed. "My God, not out of charity. I would like to show up at your door, in my best suit—not a tuxedo—and take you out. I would like to meet your parents, and get you back before midnight, or one, or whatever, gently."

"They don't care."

"I do."

"You're not bloodless, are you? Are you?" she asked.

"Oh no, Catherine, hardly, but I know when to hold, to go slow, and I really want to court you as you have not been courted. Every little thing. Every touch. Every word. I felt that the first time I saw you, as you were walking onto the ferry, before I had any reason to."

"How did you know?"

He shrugged.

"We were told," she began, "that courtly love...."

"Told by whom?"

"By our professors... that courtly love is twisted."

"How so?"

"Demeaning. Controlling."

He straightened in his seat, lifting himself until he seemed taller, unconsciously positioning his upper body as if for a fight—not with Catherine, but with an idea. His eyes narrowed a bit as they seemed to flood with energy. "I don't know who told you, but I do know that whoever said this was a fucking idiot who must never have seen anything, or risked anything, who thinks too much about what other people think, so much so that he'll exterminate his real emotions and live in a world so safe it's dead. People like that always want to show you that they're wise and worldly, having been disillusioned, and they mock things that humanity has come to love, things that people like me—who have spent years watching soldiers blown apart and incinerated, cities razed, and women and children wailing—have learned to love like nothing else: tenderness, ceremony, courtesy, sacrifice, love, form, regard.... The deeper I fell, the more I suffered, and the more I saw ... the more I knew that women are the embodiment of love and the hope of all time. And to say that they neither need nor deserve protection, and that it is merely a strategy of domination, would be to misjudge the highest qualities of man while at the same time misreading the savage qualities of the world. This is what I learned and what I managed to bring out with me from hell. How shall I treat it? Love of God, love of a woman, love of a child — what else is there? Everything pales, and I'll stake what I know against what your professors imagine, to the death, as I have. They don't have the courage to embrace or even to recognize the real, the consequential, the beautiful, because in the end those are the things that lacerate and wound, and make you suffer incomparably, because, in the end, you lose them.

"And then, you know, I'm not talking about Sir Lancelot. It's different now. What I mean is deep consideration, devotion. That's hardly demeaning, and not controlling," he said, falling back in his seat. "I'm sorry. All I want is to be with you."

"And you are," she said. "And it's four-thirty in the morning and we're in a diner in — where is this? Commack?"

"I think it's Commack. It looks like Commack."

"You know what Commack looks like?"

"No."

"I didn't think so. Come on," she ordered, "we can time this for sunrise."

"You drive even faster than I do," she told him from the passenger seat.

"I've never had an accident."

"Neither have I, apart from things."

"Oh, things. Who cares about things? Did you ever knock down a house?"

"No, not yet."

"And you're only twenty-three."

"Well, you were gone for four years."

"But I drove."

"You did?"

"Sure. Sometimes I had a jeep. I took them all over Germany. I told you. And half the time it wasn't on roads but through open country. I got to know jeeps so well I could use them to take out a splinter. You would hit fewer mailboxes if you didn't move in bursts — foot on and off the accelerator. It's not a potter's wheel. And you don't have to whip it. Hold it steady and it'll run steady. That would give you more hope of survival. Would you like me to drop a few miles an hour?"

"I feel perfectly safe with a dullard driver like you."

"Catherine, when you were driving I could look at you, and that compensated for any peril." It was true.

"Today," she said, "I'll sleep until noon and then go to rehearsal. But tomorrow there's a matinee of the physics play, so we can't use the theater and I'll be free. Call me."

"I will."

"Next weekend, can you come out to East Hampton? We won't go anywhere, just stay in the house and at the beach. I don't want to humiliate Victor any more than I have. In a few weeks, no one other than Victor will care, but next weekend all the mousetraps will be set."

"I'll pick up the clothes I left at the station."

"Do you play tennis?"

"Not really."

"Good. I'll beat you. Then I'll train you. Chess?"

"Not too badly, but you have to practice. My chess is dormant because in the army everyone played cards."

"Good, my father can beat you."

"Why is that good?"

"Give him something. You've already beaten him in that you've got the future, and he worked for Bernard Baruch in the First War and was too old for the Second."

"But he's your father, one of the leaders of the economy. I don't even have a profession."

"No matter what anyone else may think, he's not very impressed with himself. No one who inherits can be. And when he looks back, he's unhappy. That binds me to him as nothing else."

"Why is he not, if not impressed, at least content with himself? How far do you have to go before you forgive yourself for how you were born?"

"I'll tell you," she said, engaged in a way that showed him that when a beautiful woman speaks beautifully it becomes all the more devastating for one who is in love with her. "I've thought about that a lot. You don't want to be content with yourself. People who are, are insufferable, the walking dead. But you don't want to be entirely driven, either, because then you just skate over the world and never touch it. My father works not to get money but to work. But real work is valued in money, so he does work to get it—as a measure. But there's always someone richer, always someone better at something than you are. We judge narrowly, by measures rather than by the soul. It wouldn't matter if you were at the top of everything. You know why? I figured this out because so many people approach me with the idea that I've got it made. No. You see, everyone, no matter what his accomplishment, is made to feel insignificant by the scale of things. Not by nature, which is miraculously kind in this regard—but all the things that are done by groups of people and nations. The economy. War. Cities."

"The economy? Cities?"

"Yeah," she said charmingly, sweeping her hand to reveal the kingdom around them of small grocery stores and car repair shops. "People do little things, like making change for the sale of a muffin, sweeping up a tenth of an ounce of lint, putting a stamp on an envelope, or brushing a dog. Then they look about and see vast constructions and efforts: huge airplanes crossing the Atlantic at three hundred miles an hour; buildings that rise a quarter of a mile into the air; networks of roads that cover millions of miles, a single square foot of which a human being would be hard-pressed to lift; armies that invade and conquer continents; cities that stretch to the horizon; causeways; bridges; atomic bombs; huge buckets of molten steel, as big as locomotives, gliding noiselessly through the darkness of a mill; and money that sloshes in the billions past back-office clerks who worry about the next dollar.

"Every time you open your eyes, everywhere you turn, we've built immense cities to inhuman scale and thrown bridges across rivers and straits, and yet, individually, well, most people can't even *draw* a house, much less build one, or the Empire State Building. No wonder everyone feels like an ant. So the ants, indomitable of spirit, set out to correct that disproportion, and wind up throwing their lives away in competition with the other ants. I've thought about it, you see, 'cause I had to."

"You think about things a lot, don't you, but not clothes, and parties, and jewelry, and shows...."

"I think about shows. Are you kidding?"

"Movies, then. Like someone your age."

"No."

"You're pretty serious, you know."

"That's what a lonely childhood does. It screws you up and makes you suffer forever, but it makes you think. Not that I ever came up with anything much."

"But you're driven to it. By what?"

"By memory," she answered, turning away from the things on the road and toward him. "Love. I fight to hold some things in place, to keep them from being swept away. You can't really win, but you can fight."

"And this you know, at twenty-three?"

"I knew it," she replied, not triumphantly but sadly, "before I knew numbers, before I could speak."

It was a lovely moment that nonetheless she wanted to cap with sunshine, so she said, "And so did you, or you wouldn't be driving my car, with me in it, at four in the morning, down the boulevards of Hop Hog."

Quite happy, she longed for the radio, and when she turned it on she knew the song that was playing and sang along with it, in the proper key. When it ended and before the next one began, he said, "When I sing to myself it makes me happy but embarrassed. For you, it's different. When you sing to yourself it's a lot better than listening to the radio."

She blushed. She was, after all, only twenty-three.

Ahead, the sky was pink with artificial light, and as they closed upon it, it grew less intense as the dawn had begun to rob it of its powers and would soon burn away the color like mist. Factories were changing shifts, and there was traffic on the roads. For a long time they paralleled a railroad track over which a freight was moving at their speed, its empty boxcars making a thunder like the thunder that echoes through the canyons of Utah. Airplanes, marked by lights that hung silently in the air like burning lanterns, rose and fell from a half-dozen fields and airports, and early commuter trains with sleeping passengers leaning against the windows rumbled west to a city sleeping in gray.

At first they saw the flash of the towers as distant flares or out-of-place pieces of the sun, but as they sped without cease and when they rose on ramps and viaducts and were elevated into the air as effortlessly as aircraft, a gilded city appeared as the sunshine dropped its rays from the cliff tops of Manhattan to the depths of its streets.

In strengthening light, they sped over vast cities of the dead to the left and right of the raised roadways that kept them airborne. The crowded tombstones seemed to propel them upon their rising trajectory and to bless and condone every risk they might take. Amid the constantly working transfer of light, the unceasing shuffle of ships, trains, and traffic gliding and glinting silently along the arteries, amid lives playing out, clouds twisting and floating, tugs whistling, they were carried forward.

The top was down and the morning air was warm and promising of the heat and blue of a June day, and as the black convertible crossed the Queensborough Bridge a million windows flared with sun, and the sounds of the city came up as they descended into it. With the passing of each second, the gold and orange light of sunrise was refined to yellow and white.

Crossing the park was as splendid, because of the trees, as any part of the drive. They went up Central Park West, made a U-turn at 94th Street, and rolled to double-park in front of the Turin. The doorman didn't come out. It was too early, or he was remiss. Harry pulled the brake and turned to Catherine. She had already moved toward him, but as they drew together a siren sounded from directly behind them. A police car they had forced to a halt was telling them, in the fashion of police cars that one forces to a halt, to move on.

So their kiss was a brush of lips that lasted no more than a quarter of a second, and when she drove off, the trees at the edge of the park swaying slightly in a stirring of the wind, he was left standing in the road as the police car slipped by and the traffic lights turned green and marched into the distance. He replayed her kiss as a wave of oncoming cars drove him from the middle of the street.

# 11

## OVERCOATS

When Harry walked in at ten-thirty, Cornell said, "Hurry up. Let's go for an early lunch."

"It's ten-thirty."

"I want to get there before they run out."

"Who runs out?"

"The counter at Woolworth's."

"Of what?"

"American cheese."

"Cornell," Harry said, his voice expressing disbelief, "when Woolworth's runs out of American cheese it'll only be because the universe has exploded. There's no way I can eat lunch this early. I just won't."

When a few minutes later they sat at the counter at Woolworth's, Cornell said nothing until the counterman took their orders: grilled cheese sandwiches, Coca-Colas, and chilled grapefruit salads, all of which Woolworth's did surprisingly well, including the Coca-Cola, which could vary from fountain to fountain and was often either flat or too sweet.

"I wonder what the Negroes are doing today," Cornell said, speculatively and as if he had just opened a newspaper, which he hadn't.

"One, anyway, is obsessed with American cheese."

"I just wonder how today dawned for us. Something's going to happen, even if it's little, somewhere, every day, because the world is not going to stand still. Do you remember when your father took you to Florida?"

"I was in high school. It wasn't that long ago."
"Before the Crash or after?"
"Before. High times."
"And what happened at that hotel."
"Which hotel?"
"Where you drove up. . . ."
"The one in Boca Raton? The sign?"
"Yeah."
"I was driving. My father made me turn around."
"Your father and I used to have debates about that sign. He said that because it said *No Negroes, Dogs, or Jews,* that Jews were at the bottom and therefore the least welcome." Cornell slowly shook his head. "That's not how it goes. I said that we were the least welcome, then dogs, then Jews. He said that that was impossible. They like dogs. Jews wouldn't be more welcome than dogs. Then I told him," Cornell said, rapping the counter, "if that's so, why would we be more welcome than dogs? He said proximity. We were house slaves and servants. The dogs sometimes were allowed in, and sometimes not. Jews weren't servants, so they aren't used to them, and that's why they were at the bottom — because they caused a kind of revulsion. Go to Darien or Scarsdale, he said, and you'll see Colored people all over the place, working in the houses, taking care of the children. A Jew they think of as unclean, and they would be horrified to have one in the house, like a pig. It was hard to argue with your father, but well meaning ladies' maids and cops never said 'Here, boy,' to him. I come from many generations of free men. Sometimes, the way people act, you'd never know it.

"If power corrupts, Harry, I'm going to exit this world totally uncorrupted. It will change. It has to change. But I don't like change. I don't want to be distracted by adjustments. I just want quiet in the time I have left. I'm too old to want to fight, although I will."

"Cornell, it worries me when you talk like the Sphinx."
"You want me to talk like the Sphinx?"
"No. I *don't* want you to talk like the Sphinx."
"I'll talk like the Sphinx." He folded his napkin, and ran his big

hands over the smooth counter, which was waxed like a bar top. Then he looked at his watch. He was upset.

"What?"

"Overcoats."

"Overcoats," Harry repeated.

"Two came this morning just after we started work."

"Two overcoats?"

"Two men in overcoats."

"It's June. Why would anyone wear an overcoat?"

"You tell me."

"I don't know."

The food was put down before them. "Why would anyone wear an overcoat in the summer?"

Being in love, Harry was so happy that he couldn't hold the weight of Cornell's anxiety. "Because they're cold."

"When it's eighty degrees?"

"Perhaps they just got over an illness, or had some sort of serious mental damage, or they live in Hawaii and by comparison it's cold here. If an Eskimo came here in the winter he might wear a Hawaiian shirt."

"That's about the stupidest thing I ever heard you say."

"Then you tell me."

Cornell took a sip of Coca-Cola from a glass that said *Coca-Cola* on it. "To conceal weapons. Guns. Baseball bats. I don't know."

"Oh, them."

"Yeah, them."

"What did they want?"

"Did you ever wonder how we spend five hundred dollars a week in cash?"

"We pay for lots of things in cash."

"Maybe a hundred a week, maximum."

"Payoffs? What? Garbage? Police? Inspectors?"

"Only at Christmas, or when the inspectors shake us down. Mostly they're too busy with new construction."

"Protection? How long has that been?"

"Since about 'twenty-three or 'twenty-four."

"My father paid?"

"He did."

"What a waste."

"Four hundred a week to Mickey Gottlieb."

"I know the name. I thought he was my father's friend."

"Harry, with friends like that there's no need for diphtheria."

"Why didn't he tell me?"

"He didn't want you involved in that kind of thing."

"And what other secrets?"

"How should I know?" Cornell said. "These are new people. I used to pay Gottlieb's collectors and that was that. I knew them. I got used to them. Believe it or not, they were nice. The ones who came today are going to crack the whip."

"What did they say?"

"They wouldn't talk to me."

"Why not?"

"Come on, Harry!"

"Did you tell them you're an owner?"

"I did."

"What'd they say?"

"They laughed. I could have shown them the documents and they still would have laughed. They're going to come back, and they want to see a white man."

"That's no good."

"Who knows what they want? The war's over, there's inflation, everyone expects more. Something's got to change."

"How did my father handle them?"

"Your father was tough."

"He was."

"The best negotiator I've ever seen."

"What did he do?"

"He paid them what they asked."

"They're not a force of nature, you know," Harry said. Cornell craned his neck to glance at the clock at the end of the counter. With his head at that angle, he looked somewhat like a turtle. "The problem is that they can take anything. They don't care. And they've come at just the wrong time. Can you do this? Are you scared?"

"A little. And the strange thing is that just a week ago, ten days ago, I wouldn't have been."

"The girl?"

"Yes."

The charms of a young woman are natural, without diligence, and unending. They arise effortlessly and in great abundance and can leap across an abyss of silence, or inhabit memory until it glows as in a dream. Because of Catherine, for most of the afternoon Harry was unable to think of the visitors he expected. Except as empty overcoats moving like puppets on sticks, their image remained unformed in his mind, and even had it been formed precisely and with perfect menace it could not have outdone his continual recollection of her as if she were there. He was in danger of losing his balance on ladders and his hands in machines. He walked as if lightly drugged or slightly drunk, preoccupied with his imagination of her, in which he could recall and project views, short clips of motion, sound, speech, and scent. He didn't know how many minutes he spent at the top of a rolling ladder, boxes piled on the last step, remembering in a burst of microscopic detail the two kisses, every word she had said and how she had said it, every move she had made, her face, her clothes, her perfume, the bracelet at her wrist. It was a band of woven gold to which three tiny gold signets were attached. The body of one was carved into a vaguely leonine shape, the other into a bird of some sort, and the last a human figure, each holding at the base a flat stone — a ruby, a sapphire, and an emerald — for pressing the inlaid seal into wax. The work was so fine that, thinking that she probably wouldn't know, he asked anyway to whom the signets had once belonged. "The red one to the Duc de La Rochefoucauld," she said, "the green to Queen Anne, and the blue to one of the Medici, I've forgotten which one. Their provenance isn't absolute. I've had them since I was little." It was possible for her to have such things without amazement.

"Do you know," he asked, "how they look on your wrist, near your hand, set off by the rest of you?"

She showed by her expression that she had never thought of it.

"It doesn't matter to whom they belonged," he said.

"I'm a little afraid of losing them," she had told him, "but, with this top, I needed something strong for balance."

As a gleam of adrenaline woke him up, he caught himself as he was about to fall off the ladder, but had he fallen he would surely have felt no pain. Even when Cornell appeared in the stockroom and said, "They're here, in the office. They walked right past you. I sent Rose out to the stationery store," Harry was lost in the memory of Catherine and thinking of nothing else.

But now he had to deal with an opposing force. Their faces were huge, and had a quality that made him think of the exfoliated tops of the stakes that anchor circus tents; and of a butcher shop with heavy cuts of meat hung from hooks, gravity coaxing their dense flesh into a downward bias and red bloom. These men looked as if they were starving for violence that the world in its cruelty refused to provide. They seemed almost as big as elephants, they moved like wolves, and their little eyes really could have fit into the head of a rat.

"Hello," Harry said, offering his hand, which they didn't take. They were offended that he hadn't divined the spirit of their visit, although of course he had, and that his payments to them would not include compensation for the lesson he was about to receive free of charge. He sensed all this, but some unplanned instinct kept him fearlessly on a steady course. Cornell could see that he was hard at work at something, although Cornell didn't know what, and doubted that Harry knew either. And the overcoats didn't understand that Cornell's worried look had less to do with them than with him.

"Would you like a cup of coffee?" Harry asked, pressing his luck, because they had signaled with their expressions that he should relinquish the initiative. "I can send the boy out for something to eat."

Facing away from them and toward Cornell, he signaled, though his voice did not, that this was part of an act. "A Danish, a cruller?" he asked, playing the fool, but also defiant. They could not know which.

"We came for the money."

"The money?"

"You're the owner, right?"

"I just took over from my father."

"Talk to him."

"I can't. He's dead."

"Before he was dead, he was dealing with Gottlieb, but Mr. Gottlieb has transferred this account to us."

"What account?"

"We provide security."

"From what?"

"You never had a problem, right? You could."

"What happened to Gottlieb?"

"Mickey Gottlieb is gone."

"And now we pay you?"

They nodded, bored.

"I'm not being uncooperative, but how do we know that you're not just two guys who walked in off the street?"

"Because if we were just two guys who walked in off the street and did this, we'd be dead before his birthday," said one of them, pointing to the other.

"When's his birthday?" Harry asked.

"Thursday."

"Happy birthday," Harry said. Cornell raised his eyebrows. "Cornell, can you get the money from petty cash?"

Cornell went to the safe and, shielding it with his body, quickly worked the combination.

"You let him know the combination to the safe?" one of the overcoats asked Harry.

"Ya."

The overcoat wagged his finger. "I wouldn't do that if I were you. That's crazy. They steal."

Cornell thought this was painfully funny, but he didn't dare laugh. He counted out four hundred dollars in twenties, put the remainder back, walked over to Harry, and handed him the money. Harry counted it again and offered it to them.

"How much is that?" asked the one whose birthday was coming.

"Four hundred."

"It went up."

"To what?"

"Two thousand."

In the dead silence, Harry could feel his heart beating, even now a pleasant sensation. "Two thousand a month?" he asked, suspecting that a four-hundred-dollar increase might not be what they had in mind.

"A week."

"How can that be? That's five times what it was."

"I don't care how it can be, it is."

"We don't have two thousand."

"You can give it to us Friday, a whole day after my birthday."

"Two thousand a week and we'll be out of business before the end of the year."

"Things change," said the other overcoat. "Everywhere. Prices go up."

"I need to talk to your boss."

"It doesn't work that way."

"Look, could you please tell him that I just took over this business, I've never had any experience with this kind of thing, and I need his advice? Okay? I need his advice."

"We'll tell him, but you better have the two thousand by Friday. Got it?"

"Can I deliver it to him personally so I can have a moment of his time?"

"No."

"Two thousand dollars!" Cornell said, clenching a fist. "Two thousand dollars a week! We'll be finished by October."

"What are we doing these days?" Harry asked.

"About six thousand a week, but it's going down. Expenses have been a little more than six thousand a week, and they're going up."

"Has the four hundred been included in expenses?"

"Yes, but that leaves sixteen hundred to break us, and break us quick."

"With what I have, I can keep us going for a year."

"Then you'd have nothing left, and then what anyway?"

"My father would want me to keep the business going. It's his money. I didn't earn it."

"But there's no point."

"There is a point, a very important point. When you're in what seems like an impossible situation and it looks sure that you're going to be overrun, you have to keep in mind that only half of what the enemy does is actually going to put him in a position to overrun you. The other half is to communicate this so you'll do his work for him."

"What good would it do, if he really can overrun you, to ignore the message?" Cornell asked. His had not been a war of maneuver.

"If you ignore the message, it changes the situation. He now has to consider the cost, change his focus and pace. He has to suspect that maybe you're in a better position than he thought. Therefore, he becomes more cautious. The price goes up for him. The timeline changes. You, for your part, have resolved upon dying, and so because of this he hesitates, and you're still alive. In that moment, which may be short or long, something can happen, and it usually does. If you can hold, and time passes, things change and you have a chance. They can change from without, in the enemy force or by some agency impinging upon it from elsewhere. They can change in the objective situation—the weather, an accident, action on the part of other echelons—or in you, in what you figure out and in what you resolve. Which is not to say that we'll survive, but that the field of maneuver is just opening up. I'm not going to give in and do their work for them, not before I know the conditions."

"Harry, they've been doing this for decades. The whole city pays off. They own the politicians and the police. Nothing's going to change."

"You yourself said that every day something changes. They don't own every crack and cranny. They don't do everything right. They're not invincible."

"You're going to fight them? You can't fight them."

"I want to see what ground we're on. I'll see first if I can get them to lower the amount. They may have been mistaken. When I was talking to those guys, I felt a kind of mortal pressure. I felt defeat very strongly. I've felt that way before, not long ago. And look, I'm still here."

# 12

## CHANGING LIGHT

From the moment he had been apprised of the sickening amount of money he would have to pay regularly and indefinitely to someone whose name he did not even know, he felt a continual pressure that became the background of all events, something only half forgotten even in sleep, that then, when he became fully awake, became fully awake itself.

Each time he did the kind of calculation that people who worry about money do over and over again, the results, varying only slightly according to an only slightly varying range of assumptions, told him that it would be impossible. And as each calculation was followed to its end, its end was some form of death — of the business that was the last remnant of his father's life, of the commercial equilibrium that kept half a hundred families secure, of his savings, and of his chances with Catherine. He could not offer himself to her bankrupt and in decline, and would never seek an excuse for his catastrophic failure at such an early age. As he walked, and he walked a great deal, he went over the numbers. For hours and hours, they took their places like eighteenth-century soldiers in highly structured battles. He hadn't been made to be the kind of person who can think all day in numbers, and their ceaseless ballet in the air weakened him as they crowded out the world. He was going to bleed to death slowly so that the overcoats could fill and expand, their faces riding above their collars, puffy, stuffed, overfed, and red.

Sometimes, despite his anxiety, nothing seemed to have changed.

At other times he would imagine almost joyously half a dozen ways not merely to extricate himself but to triumph. As he returned to these again and again, however, the difficulties became clearer, the risks more forbidding. Having failed to prevent the decline in revenues, he was at a loss to engineer the dramatic increase that was the only thing that would keep him solvent. Cornell understood the checkmate far better. The period of waiting for developments was familiar to someone who had waited his whole life and never seen the unfair lock on his fortunes dissolve. Harry alternated between dejection and euphoria, the euphoria coming with his temporary excitement at schemes he would then have to abandon. It seemed natural to want to kill Gottlieb, except that Gottlieb had apparently already been killed or pushed aside by someone of greater power, someone who, in the midst of civil society and in a country at peace, killed people as part of his business.

How could this person, whose name Harry had never heard, whose face Harry had never seen, have enslaved him in the space of an afternoon? The answer was, if not encouraging, nonetheless uncomplicated. Amidst the peace, his opponent lived in a state of war and dared others to do the same. If they did, he would fight them as he had habitually fought to reach his place. If they did not, he would take from them. It was how the knights and lords had lived off the substance of the peasants. As old as man, the technique had come to the New World and made its home beneath the happy, lighted surface of things.

By his own account, Harry had a year's grace in which to see what he might do. What happened, he asked himself, when the peasants came back from the wars and knew how to remove a knight from his horse with a pike and dispatch him with his own sword? In those times, peasants had seldom fought, but now wars were democratic and the city was filled with former soldiers who knew a thing or two even if, having fought, they loved peace dearly.

And Manhattan seemed to welcome his distress, as if it had somehow been constructed for the story of such a thing, had seen it an infinite number of times, would see it until kingdom come, and with perfect calm use it to build the invisible webs of its history. The beautiful prospects, galaxies of lights, and scenes and feelings that an observer felt overwhelmingly, were composed not of stone, steel, and electric current, but took their charge and made their fire from the mortal struggles within its impassive folds. The city would stay the same were Harry Copeland to be buried in a potter's field and Gottlieb's successor watch the lights come up over the skyline as he sat on his high terrace, or were Harry somehow to triumph in overturning the reigning design. Forever neutral, the city would favor no one, promote no one, mourn no one, remember no one. And as everything within it that had occurred before or was yet to be would be set as in stone and unalterable, it seemed that the only thing that mattered was to do right. The only thing left to anyone would be an echo that would not even be heard, and, therefore, whence pleasure and pride except in doing right? This was a conclusion that Gottlieb, his predecessors, and those who would follow would never understand, and for which, therefore, they could not be as fully prepared as they would have to be to survive it if it came at them by surprise.

"Come at two," Catherine had said, and, partly because of this, in the morning he had run so well on the bridle paths that he had been able to pass cantering horses. As he was running, Catherine was speeding through flat water as if swimming down a fast stream. When she combed out her hair in front of the mirror and lifted her arms to braid it, she turned her head as if posing for a photograph, and then, ignoring her image in the glass, felt that whatever was within her that was beautiful was like a fire sweeping to and fro, its light changing, its life fleeting. As a singer and a dancer trained from an early age, she wanted both to sing and to dance, but had she done either she would have been stopped or asked to leave by the ladies of her mother's club, who could do neither. Nor would she ever sing or dance except where it was appropriate: in the rehearsal hall, at home alone, on the stage itself.

So she made the rhythm, sang the song, and inconspicuously mouthed the words, in silence. But she could hear as if the orchestra were there, and the music, only remembered, was more powerful for want of an outlet, its compression driving it deeper into her than if it had filled the air. As she closed her locker door, she watched it move in the deliberately slow arc in which she had propelled it, her arms tense and engaged as she guided it, her left foot extended forward, her back magisterial and straight, her entire body moving as gracefully and rigidly as a gliding swan.

He was in love with her. And he had come to her so strongly, having seen her in a flash, knowing nothing of her but what she was as she stood before him. Despite its obvious dangers, his sudden, thoughtless, and intense attraction was the one thing she had wanted most in life, more than comfort, achievement, longevity, or triumph — this one thing, this one perfect imperfection. As she walked home, the world came alight. Trees on the sidewalk seemed in their slight swaying to be dancing to music she could not stop, the rhythm of which she could not escape. In the shadows of Grand Central, the beams of light flooded down in mitered columns to illuminate golden dust hovering like gnats. Her heart rose with the changes of color and form with each new view down long, sea-horizoned avenues glittering with sun on glass, or in the narrow blocks choked with green, and with the precise and astounding choreography of the scores of thousands who moved with quick step interweaving and never colliding.

For Harry's part, it was like war, in which every second alive was a triumph, every sight indelible, each inhalation a blessing, all light magnified and overwhelming, motion stilled, and stillness put into motion. Once, somewhere east of the Rhine, his helmet dripping with cold water, he had lain in a cradle of wet leaves, watching his breath come out white in the air as he was soaked by windblown rain. He had hardly slept in days; he was filthy, thin, and under fire. But his body was hot and the rain not unpleasant, because his heart beat like an engine. Every drop sparkled. The past was crowded out, the future projected no more than a second or two ahead. With nothing guaranteed but the present, it expanded and intensified, as if a balance of force were faithfully maintained, until the cold rain became a shower of stars.

As he walked east on 57th Street, its shop windows glowing like miniatures in illuminated manuscripts, air that had ducked beneath the great bridges came to meet him from the East River and lifted his spirits like a sail on the wind. Far ahead, at the end of the street, was a window of pale blue sky.

Anxious to see her and wanting her to know, he pressed the button for the bell five minutes before two, and in the time between the sounding of the bell and her appearance at the door his pulse escalated. When she opened the door and he saw her, though not for the first time, in full light, some of her features, which had led Ross Underhill, the transport pilot, to declare her "funny-looking," and might have disqualified her from thoughtless admiration, made her so beautiful to him that he was unable to break the silence.

Nor was she. Her thoughts of this moment had distracted her from sleep and work. Each time she had imagined it, it had possessed a quality of lightness and effortless musicality. But she had moved beyond infatuation. And when love does move this way it assumes almost a tragic quality as the deep investment signifies to an alert mind the inevitability of a deeper loss.

"May I kiss you?" he asked, still properly unsure of how things stood.

"It would break my heart if you didn't."

Recognizing the seriousness and courage of this reply, he mounted the first step, and the next, until he was standing by her, and there they embraced for the first time, only slightly tighter than if they had been dancing. The first kiss was just a light touch, as it had been in the car, as if they were going back to find the place in the music where they had been forced to stop. Then the next, and the next, rhythmically, until they lost their sense of time and forgot where they were. A passerby would have seen two people on the limestone steps, pressed up against a column and kissing. But the street was empty and they were oblivious of it anyway when they stepped behind the column, hands caressing faces and pushing back hair, lips touching again and again. With his right hand he pressed against the small of her back, and with his left he went between the yoke of her dress and the nape of her neck. On the back of his hand he felt the roughness of a label, but next to his fingers and palm was skin as soft and taut as sateen. Now he knew very well the smallest detail of her upper lip, which, slightly projecting and angular, was the perfect imperfection of her beauty. He knew it wet, and he knew it relaxed, and he knew its sweet taste. She smelled so fresh, and the cotton of her dress sprang back crisply when touched. Her body, firm and trim, overwhelmed the cloth between them.

After half an hour they moved to disengage, but it took ten minutes of last kisses that were not last kisses until they sat down next to one another on the highest step, his right hand and her left tightly entwined. She burned red. Her hair was slightly disheveled. He switched hands and put his right arm around her. As she leaned into him, he asked somewhat wryly, "I forgot to ask, but are your parents in?"

She liked that. "Only the servants," she said.

He looked to his right and then to his left, and in the wonderfully clean but old and wavy window glass he saw faces disappearing like fish darting from the wall of an aquarium. "The maids wear black and white?"

"Yes."

"I saw them."

"Don't worry," she said. "They're responsible and meticulous."

"Meaning?"

"They'll be sure to tell everyone in New York. Even the newspapers."

"Why would the newspapers be interested?"

"They wouldn't, but that doesn't mean that Margaret won't give it a try."

"She's the enterprising one?"

"Well, there's Tim," she said. "He siphons gas. It's part of the deal. The struggle never stops. The trick, my father says, is to make it livable for everyone: laws are like trees in the forest, and the animals in the forest move between and among the trees."

"So he lets Tim siphon gas."

"Yes, and Tim takes more than a couple of gallons. It's like a tip. He's a really good driver, and despite the fact that he's a thief he would defend us to the death." She pulled back, looking at him directly. "What are we going to do now?"

"All I want to do," he answered, "is walk with you. There are ten thousand places where I want to kiss you."

Not wanting to be easy, she smiled slightly and said, her tone only ambiguously echoing the double entendre, "There are ten thousand places where I want you to kiss me."

They walked south on Sutton Place, arms comfortably around one another's waists, shoulders touching, the Hale maids in black and white pressed against the windows until the angle of the couple's travel took them out of sight as they disappeared into the city.

# 13

## BILLY AND EVELYN

For Harry, Penn Station was a gate to the underworld. When he and Catherine had been in the automat and their conversation had returned to architecture rather than drift into anything too revealing of what had been rapidly building between them, or, rather, what had somehow always been there, he had said of Grand Central and its great counterpart, "God help the city if they tear them down. It's been proposed. I don't know why. It would be the first act of national suicide." But instead of setting foot inside Penn Station he had taken the subway to Jamaica to board the train that had taken him to East Hampton and the Georgica. Now, however, he was to meet Catherine amid the great columns and arches. On every square foot of Penn Station's expansive floor, someone had been seen for the last time, someone had been embraced by his family, and then, as surely as if he had been lifted up and passed through the ceiling so high that to see it one had to tilt one's head way back, he had vanished. For too many soldiers and their parents, wives, and children this had been the last place.

Meyer Copeland had overruled his son, who, in uniform, a duffle bag on his shoulder, had come to the loft to say goodbye. They had decided on the loft and then Meyer had gone back on his word. "You want to ride with me on the train?" Harry had asked rhetorically. "All the way to Georgia? Do you want to join my unit?"

"I would, if I could," his father had answered, meaning not with his son but in his place.

They stood numbly near the gate, the son busy with thoughts of the future, the father wanting to hold on to the present. When the train was called, they embraced. Meyer was wearing a tweed jacket with patches at the elbows. He was old, bearded, not in the best of health, and the years had taken from his height. He told his only child that he loved him, and then Harry had to break away lest he miss the train. As he went down the stairs he turned briefly and saw his father, as hundreds of people passed him, standing absolutely still.

The last spot where he had seen his father drew his eye magnetically as he descended the stairs for the first time since 1942, now not to go back to the army but to wait for Catherine. A policeman was watching him, perhaps because the invisible burden he carried had distorted his step. On the very spot, two young mothers had corralled three children and some luggage, and were adjusting hats, tying shoes, and pulling objects out of their suitcases. From the way they were dressed and the toys the children dragged it seemed that they were going to the Jersey Shore, unless they were so free-spirited that they could wear straw hats and sundresses in downtown Philadelphia. They covered the marble where his father had stood, and he knew that his father would have been happy had he seen the children there.

He looked up from the rose-patched cheeks of the infants, and the mothers' bare shoulders and arms, past the ironwork and the rays of sun streaming in through soot-encrusted windows, to the space immediately beneath the vaulted ceiling. And there he heard from amidst the incomprehensible mixing of echoes and voices a sound like the singing of the surf, as if this were the barrel into which the memory of everything that had happened below, all that had been said or felt, had risen to be kept. There trapped like smoke were the faint traces of when he had been held for the last time by the man who had held him when he was born.

For a few minutes he watched quietly as soldiers, sailors, and civilians passed by, each intent on meeting the requirements of his ticket and proceeding according to schedule. They nervously sipped sugar water passed off as orange juice. They ate at wagons and counters, rushing to finish even though they always had more time than they used. And they hurriedly bought newspapers and magazines, all the while checking their watches as if these were gauges for their steadily rising blood pressure.

Then he saw Catherine coming down the stairs, a young woman not much older than a girl, who moved unselfconsciously, in whose eyes you could see the qualities of thought and reflection, of woundedness and optimism, of kindness, and of love. Though she was young, the woman she would become was present in the way she held herself. Dressed elegantly in white with pearls, she walked modestly through the light streaming over the stairs.

Her pace quickened as she crossed the floor, and her observant and tentative expression changed. As she closed, he saw the tiny double crescents that framed her smile, and although he disapproved of publicly demonstrated affection he forgot everything and kissed her not once but three times, the last certainly long enough to elicit attention. But kissing was allowed in a station, even over the limit.

"We've got ten minutes," he said.

"I would have gotten here earlier, but there were a million people on Thirty-fourth Street. Sales."

"Why aren't we driving out?"

"Because the car is and always has been a symbol of my independence, and now I've used it to do something that gravely embarrassed them. I don't want to arrive in it. It would just start things up. If we come on the train it will be less provocative. When I was a little girl, I would come on the train, because they would go out before school ended. Better. And I think I want to keep the car in the city from now on so I can use it to go to Philadelphia or drive around upstate."

"Isn't it faster to go to Philadelphia by train?" he asked.

"I like to drive in the country, especially now. Do you know the Pine Barrens or the Delaware? We'll go to Philadelphia. We'll leave early and walk around the Pine Barrens, swim the Delaware up where it's narrow and clean, and then get some of my college friends and eat at Bookbinder's."

"And where will we stay?"

"Anywhere but the Benjamin Franklin Hotel." She had had a hard gloss when she said this.

"You're quite grown-up about that sort of thing."

"I am. I'm like a divorcée. Does that trouble you?"

"No." He bent to lift his luggage — she had none, as usual, a characteristic of the Hales, who hated to carry things and so left toothbrushes and coats stashed seemingly all over the world. The train had been called and the rush to it began, a river of seersucker, pin cord, sundresses, and straw hats. Jackets over the arm. The beaches were much cooler, and people had begun to flock to them. The smell and humidity of steam from the boilers of the locomotives idling in tunnels beneath rose through every passage. "It doesn't bother me."

"Good," she said. "I don't have to be coy, or worried, I hope. Just love."

For him, the word *love* was the most beautiful in the English language, even if not the most gorgeous or sparkling. It would last beyond all privation, and surface after years of repression as gamely as a glass float shooting up from beneath the waves. As a word, it bloomed before his eyes as red as a rose, and was as round and cupped in hand as a buff-colored dove.

Though the Friday-afternoon Hamptons train, the Cannonball, was packed, they sat facing one another in single seats in the parlor car. She had reserved the tickets with that in mind. And though many people were smoking, and Catherine and Harry never had, the windows were open and the sun-filled air was as fresh as the wind above the dunes. As people who are in love often do, they stared at one another like idiots. She kicked his small suitcase with the toe of her shoe. "That's a hell of a suitcase. Where'd you get that, I wonder?"

"Finished today." It was the richest, darkest leather she had ever seen. "This is the best one we make. FDR used them, but they were all battered. The Roosevelts didn't take very good care of their things. He wouldn't buy new ones, either, so we offered to send a stainer, a polisher, and a leathersmith down to the White House to clean them up. The president himself received our guys, they got a great lunch, and by the end of the afternoon the whole set looked better than new because of the patina. Wherever the president went, people saw our product."

"How about Truman?"

"We're working on it. He doesn't like fancy things, but he does like good things. One of our leathersmiths lives next door to Joe Micelli, Truman's barber and friend at the Carlisle, but it's delicate."

"My parents are allergic to luggage," she said. "We don't like burdens. But they know something beautiful when they see it."

"So do I," Harry said. She turned the color that Russians call "blood and milk," and he loved it. "This morning I started out with a pack, but then I stopped in and traded."

"It must be convenient to own Copeland Leather."

"It was today." He paused as a train flew by in the opposite direction, rattling the windows in their recesses. "Catherine?" He deeply enjoyed just saying her name.

"Harry?" And she his.

"What did you say to your parents?"

"About you? What do you think I said to them?"

"I think you said that I love you and that I want to marry you." Before she responded he was able to count twenty-three sections of rail over which the carriage clattered as they flew by.

"That's what I said."

In the high summer heat of February, 1888, Billy Hale was born in the harbor at Rio de Janeiro, in the sickbay of a United States naval vessel with paddle wheels, masts, and sails. Now fifty-eight, he and his friends of the same age rationally expected to die within five or ten years. The weight of this expectation took from him, as it did with most of the men of his generation, much of the fire that he had managed to bank despite a youth that had not been touched by it.

He loved his daughter and only child, and watched as time and necessity properly carried her away from him to make a life of her own. With no need to struggle, never much ambition, and the clear understanding that even had he an ambitious nature the few years remaining would mock it, he was lost. Except that, as if by nature or just the way of things, he was drawn to his wife anew, and sometimes with more force than in the earliest days of their marriage.

Ten years younger than her husband, Evelyn Hale was blond and, in a kind of miracle, delicate, indestructible, kind, and severe. Her hair was pulled back, but she did not look in the least horsey; she dressed magnificently; seemed always to be made up, perfumed, and bejeweled; and had only recently comprehended that her husband's renewed obsession with her physicality would not die until he did. In public she treated him with an indifference marred only by a hint that she was irritated by everything he did, which was not true; and he treated her, with the same impulse to preserve their privacy, as if she were nothing more than a paperweight. But in private they comforted one another and confided. And of late what their bed, the pool, and the deserted beach witnessed was in appearance as desperate as a death struggle. At one point she had asked, glistening with sweat, "Billy, what's come over you? Are you some sort of salmon or something?" And then, under her breath, though they were alone, "You're a goddamned sea turtle."

"A sea turtle? Is that a compliment?"

"*I* think it is."

By his reckoning, he was indeed a salmon, or a sea turtle, or an electric light that flares before it burns out. As a son of a prominent family, he had always been underestimated, but he was like any other man. He loved his wife and his child, he appreciated the beauty and decorum of the life he had lived, and wanted it to last into time. It would be a gift to those who succeeded him, as it had been a gift to him. He had as much courage as most, but because it had not been put to the test he doubted it. Now he was going to meet his daughter and her surprise fiancé. He thought it too soon after the war to drive the Mercedes except to sneak it out at night to keep it in shape, and he didn't want to overdo it in the Rolls, so he showed up at the East Hampton station in a dark green MG, its top down and its chrome untarnished.

Catherine went to her father as if Harry did not exist, something to which Harry could hardly object, especially when, like a wave that breaks against a sea wall and is instantly thrown back, she retreated to him. Billy put out his hand, and Harry took it. They were both nervous. "Can you fit in the back?" Billy asked, pulling the passenger seat forward and exposing the luggage compartment.

"I may stick out a bit," Harry answered, his phrasing almost British, as if to match the car. First he put in his suitcase and what he had retrieved from the stationmaster, who had been astonished to see him with Catherine, and then compressed himself into the narrow space that was left. When the seats were returned to position they bound him in like a swaddled baby. As Billy picked up speed, Harry freed his right arm and tried to catch his sky-blue summer tie, but soon gave up and let it trail like a flag in a hurricane. Billy drove like a fighter pilot, rounding turns with such speed that the wheels screeched before either the left or the right pair would momentarily leave the road. And on straightaways he would shift like a racing driver and run down the fortunately empty lanes as if he were immortal. They went so fast through the back streets and cool, moist air, its heaviness a gift of evening and the sea, that the few people they saw would disappear in a blur of madras, canary yellow, or pink. The lawns were so green, tight, and cold that Harry wanted to stroke them. And the trees out there, near the ocean, had just come into full leaf.

"Have you been here before?" Billy shouted into the wind, which easily carried his question to the back seat. Still, everyone shouted.

"Yes. I had friends here, in college."

"Anyone I know?"

"Watson Dickerman?"

"East Hampton?"

"South."

"And what college was that?"

"Harvard."

"In what?"

"English. I was a student of Howard Mumford Jones, but I was too dumb to understand him."

"It doesn't matter. Evelyn will appreciate it. I was never quite good enough for her, being Princeton, class of 'ten. Her father taught there, so to her we ranked somewhat below yeast. What year were you?"

The wind forced itself into Harry's lungs. His answer sounded as if it were coming from underwater. "'Thirty-seven."

"A good deal younger than Victor then, who was . . . class of what, Catherine?"

"'Thirty,'" Catherine said, somewhat annoyed. "But Victor was a stayback at Andover, so he's actually older."

"Really," said Billy. "I didn't know that."

"A D in trigonometry, D-plus in French, and nothing higher than a C," Catherine said.

"What are *you* laughing about?" Billy asked, repressing a smile.

"Nothing," said Harry.

"You'll meet Victor if you're out here for more than half an hour. Everyone does. He's always lumbering along the beach. I feel sorry that he's lost someone like Catherine," he pronounced over the wind, "but I'm actually glad she's found someone else on her own. It smacked of an arranged marriage."

"It more than smacked," Catherine called out.

As they turned into Further Lane, Billy slowed the car. "It was your choice," he said. "No one pushed you into it, and no one blames you for pulling out." Harry looked at her as her father continued. "The wine in the face was a tad dramatic, but what's a little drama after four years of war? On the other hand, it was a Lafite. I hope it was worth it."

"Believe me, Daddy, it was."

He slowed to a crawl when he entered the driveway, to make it seem longer, cool down the motor, and restore the decorum he had thrown aside while speeding. Orchards on the left, newly ploughed fields on the right. Dense hedgerows compressing both into a long rectangle leading to the sea. A quarter of a mile later they pulled up to the house, beyond which the dunes were visible. Billy halted the car on an apron of beige gravel and it came to a stop with a concussive rasp. After the engine was switched off, and in the silence before Evelyn appeared, they heard the wind and felt the thud of the breakers. Beyond dunes covered with sparse, sharp grasses, the world was at war in the white of the surf, and the wind curled the tops of the waves.

Always apprehensive in social situations, Harry wanted to escape to this pounding surf, for in fighting he was never awkward. It would have been much easier and less dangerous to be leading an infantry squad or sailing into a gale than to meet Catherine's mother. He looked over at Catherine, who had turned her head toward the house, and the sight of her, her hair pulled up at the back of her neck, changed his thoughts of war, which were easy, into a longing for her, something that was in its way far more risky. As her father walked around the front of the car, facing away, Harry reached over Catherine's right shoulder and pulled himself forward. She briefly squeezed his right hand with hers, and he kissed the side of her head. Her hair was sweet, and when he kissed her he heard her lips make the sound of a kiss, barely audibly. As he fell back and began to extricate himself from the luggage compartment of the little car, he saw that her mother had been watching.

Knowing from previous experience how radically girls can differ from their mothers, he had no idea what to expect. He knew that any natural discord with Billy could be quenched in fishing, launching a boat, or building a stone wall, for he had seen that Billy was not so full of himself that the two of them would be unable to revert in the face of such things to something resembling boyhood, and thus make their peace. But there was no way he could so engage an older woman except by wit, and that would not do, as it was too close to flirtation. Thus, Evelyn, were she in the slightest bit malevolent, could concentrate upon him the female death ray that only a mother-in-law or potential mother-in-law can deploy, that comes from frustration of a hundred types, that is as old as the monkeys, and for which there is no antidote.

And Park Avenue and its environs—granted, the Hales, nonconformists, had decamped for Sutton Place—were full of caked and powdered reptilian women and florid, panting men who lived to shop and eat, with muscles evolved mainly for approaching a maitre d', lifting a poodle, or carrying glistening packages. At home these people did not breathe. There was no air, no room to move, no space to stretch out an arm without shattering Lalique, no sunshine, no water, no waves, only a coffin-like *bella figura* of life as still as a wax dummy.

How surprised he was, then, as Evelyn came into view. For although she was done up as if she had just walked out of the Colony Club, she was girlish as she descended the steps gracefully and fast, and beneath the mature and knowing planes of her face was a softness and kindness that bloomed in the presence of her daughter, whom she adored. Immediately, his apprehensions fled, although he knew just as instantaneously that though he might get along with her and develop a kind of affection, he would never, ever, understand her, no matter how perfectly and naturally he could know Catherine.

After all, he had never been a woman. He had never been a mother. He had never been middle-aged. He had never been a socialite. He had never been a Christian, a debutante, or had cellulite (although she didn't either). He had never been trapped in the delicacy and inadequacy of a woman's clothes and shoes. Because of their clothes and shoes they could hardly take a step in rough terrain, running was out of the question, and God help them if they had to throw a punch. He hated what he called "little pea-brained sandwiches sized for canaries"; he thought a dog was something you should be able to wrestle with rather than use to dust a Fabergé egg; and he had never been an aspirant to, much less a member of, either the Georgica Club or the Four Hundred.

On the other hand, she was the child of a prominent theologian, and had grown up—without radio, without movies—with much of her entertainment the complex disputes of moral and religious philosophers, in contrast to whom and as a gift of nature and her sex she was much wiser. Wise enough to absorb and comprehend—eventually—all of what they said, wise enough seldom to comment, and wise enough to reject it in favor of a knowledge that, exactly according to her father's ideals, came directly from God and without intermediaries—though at times intermediaries might be advantageously consulted.

Catherine remembered an evening long ago, and her mother sitting by a fireplace in their house on Sutton Place. A silk gown, of a color hard to describe except that it glistened slightly Roxburghe in the firelight, surrounded her like a soft throne. All the dinner guests were men. They were talking about bridges and steam pressure and electricity. The first to leave was Evelyn. Then Catherine could not take it any longer, and found her mother. "Don't worry," Evelyn told her. "It's all very interesting, what they're talking about...."

"I don't think so," said the child.

"You will. But, Catherine, everything that's true despite us — the things they're talking about, natural laws — will always remain true despite us. What matters is what's true because of us. That's what's up for grabs. That's where the battle is. One remembers and values one's life not for its objective truths, but for the emotional truths."

"What do you mean?" the child asked.

"I mean the only thing that's really true, that lasts, and makes life worthwhile is the truth that's fixed in the heart. That's what we live and die for. It comes in epiphanies, and it comes in love, and don't ever let frightened people turn you away from it." Though Catherine had not understood the words precisely — she was still too young — the meaning had been conveyed, and it stayed with her for the rest of her life.

So if Catherine did not entirely understand Evelyn's lesser pronouncements, she did the greater ones. Nature does not require children to understand their parents, and may require that they don't. Still, just like Billy — who although he was fifty-eight was older than that when he was born, and yet seemed in many ways to be much younger, perhaps because of his fondness for practical jokes (most of which were incomprehensible to anyone not an enthusiast of croquet) — Evelyn was as mutable as the ocean weather but as solid as Manhattan bedrock.

When she greeted Harry, she said, "The only other person who's ever done to the Marrows what you did was Al Smith, who went after Victor's grandfather like a rabid dog, bit his buttocks, and threw him from his golden den."

"What?" Harry asked, his hand still in hers.

"A stock scandal when you were too young to remember or care. Long over." She turned to her daughter. "Catherine, take Mr. Copeland to the guest house. I don't mean to hurry you, but we've been roasting a tuna that your father caught this morning and I don't want it to dry out."

"I'll take him," said Catherine.

"Don't stay too long. Dinner at six-thirty. Come as you are."

The guest house lay beyond the pool and was encased like a jewel in a crucifix of shell paths dividing up a garden about to come into bloom. Before he was established there he put down his suitcase and they passed through a gate in a waist-high stone wall and onto a cedar boardwalk that led to the beach. No guest except those who arrived in a squall could resist the ocean. To settle in at East Hampton without looking at the ocean, even at night, was the sign of a crippled soul.

The boardwalk crossed the hump of the dunes to a small deck with benches and an outdoor shower. Overlooking the water from this spot, they saw fast flights of gulls and terns sweeping parallel to the strand and colored by the setting sun into half a dozen shades of deepening red. The breeze was steady and the sea roared with unimpeachable authority. Every board was heart of cedar, and its scent mixed with the salt air. "This is magnificent," he said.

"Not as much," she replied, "as when you come from the sea and lie on the cedar as it bakes in the sun. Two of my favorite places in the world are this long run of boards and the Esplanade in the park. The way their straightness aims you down their lengths I find pleasurable and comforting."

"What's the Esplanade?" Harry asked.

"You know, in the park, with the trees on either side meeting high above in the middle?" She illustrated with her arms upraised.

"You mean the Mall?"

"I've always called it the Esplanade. So has everyone in my family. *Mall* sounds like *maul*, the horrible verb, or something you split wood with. *Esplanade* is beautiful."

Thenceforth, Harry was content to call it that. What he did not yet know was that the Hales substituted, changed, or eschewed many words at Evelyn's behest. Often she was proved right by logic and history. An esplanade, for example, was originally the flat plain between a castle's battlements and the city that had grown up around it. In Europe, esplanades were the parks and greenswards, the epitome of peace, where people paraded in their finery and even the poor could pretend luxury. And yet they had been the battlefields and siege grounds of previous ages. The Mall in Central Park pointed like an arrow at the Belvedere, a replica Scottish castle on a hill to the north, separated by a lake as if by a moat. The fletching of the arrow was midtown Manhattan, the city. The Mall, according to Evelyn, was therefore the Esplanade.

Sometimes, however, her word preferences — dictated to or unknowingly inherited by Catherine from early childhood — were less substantiated and perhaps a touch idiosyncratic. "I will not say the new and disgusting word that purports to represent a combination of breakfast and lunch. Nor will I say the disgusting, coy, and contemptible word that rhymes with the aforesaid disgusting word and pertains to the chewing and eating of crisp foods, often, unfortunately, slowly. Nor will I say the P-word."

The P-word was *popcorn*, which Evelyn hated. She went to the movies only at private screenings or premieres, where popcorn was *verboten*. She didn't like the smell. She didn't like the sound. And she didn't like exiting a theater in a crowd of people whose hands and lips were covered with rancid butter. If young Catherine said *popcorn*, Evelyn would look at her with the expression of a hawk mulling its options in respect to a mouse dancing in an open field. This resulted in Catherine, at age six, briefcase strapped to her back, walking to school through the Upper East Side while chanting "Popcorn, popcorn, popcorn."

Alone for ten minutes in the guest quarters, Harry looked over the length of the pool, now almost black, at a shingle-sided house every window of which glowed with a different color — red, dark green, gray, peach, chalk, blue, yellow — set off by luminescent white millwork. He had seen no servants, but (to take the chill from the night air by the ocean, even in June) fires were burning in several fireplaces, including his own; huge arrangements of flowers had not a single dead petal or any leaves lying by them; and to someone who, although he knew little about keeping up an estate, was good at estimating required labor for any task, the gardens appeared to have received the attentions of many more than one full-time gardener.

Rather than come exactly as he was, he changed his shirt and put on a deep violet tie that he thought more appropriate to evening and darkness than what he had been wearing. He anticipated with growing pleasure the sight and presence of Catherine, though she had been absent for only a few minutes. And the Hales seemed quite approachable. Probably the dinner would be painfully conventional and quiet — fish and roasted potatoes ladled out by servants speaking occasional pleasantries. Correctness above all. At the Dickermans' and like households, he had always had to rein himself in and adapt to the quiescence, like a dinosaur bumped ahead a few eons, lest he terrify them with the comparatively loud rough-and-tumble of his own background, lest he eat more than nine peas, or stare with disbelief at the one-ounce cutlet of beef centered on his plate like Hawaii in the middle of the Pacific. He had been only partially polished and contained during his years at Harvard, and had often broken from his confines while there. But tonight he wanted to be at his most diplomatic and dull.

As he walked past the pool, the black water enticingly alive, he straightened his tie. At first he couldn't find the right way in, and walked into the kitchen, where four servants — two men and two women — were working smoothly and fast. After backing out, he found the correct entrance and, like someone reinserting the pin of a grenade, gingerly closed the door behind him.

The Hales were in the living room, in front of the fireplace, arranged like a family portrait. Evelyn sat expectantly at the edge of a white, satin-covered chair, her hands placed royally together and resting on one of the thick arms. Billy was standing by the fire. None of them had changed clothing: Billy was in the navy polo shirt he had been wearing. Catherine, leaning against a brocade wing chair, had the self-effacement of a stage actress who must stay relatively silent in a scene that belongs to someone else, but whose presence is the essence of the play. The part she played in her play required this of her, and she vibrated with life even when she had no lines.

At first it was rather awkward. No one knew how things might or should proceed in the new constellation in which they found themselves. To break a silence that grew more brittle with each second, Evelyn said, "Does your family own Copeland China as well as Copeland Leather?" In every Hale household were plenty of both.

"No," said Harry. "No connection. Only leather."

"Each is the best of its type," Evelyn offered.

"Thank you. That's kind of you."

"It really is, really."

Breaking this rhythm, Billy said, "You changed your tie."

"The other one doesn't behave at meals."

"I have ties like that."

"Harry," Evelyn asked, "can Billy get you a drink?"

"Not if you're not...."

"Oh, but we will."

"Then straight Scotch, please."

"Single or blend?" Billy asked, gesturing toward a huge silver tray resplendent with single malts, crystal glasses, sterling ice buckets, and bar things, and backed by an ebullient, almost blinding floral arrangement that Harry could smell from all the way across the room.

"Single."

"You have a preference?"

"Surprise me."

The surprise was that Billy handed him a tumbler with at least four shots of Glenlivet. It was practically overflowing. "Here, take it in to dinner. You know, Scotch is the second cousin of the potato."

"I didn't know that."

No further explanation was forthcoming. Billy poured himself a Scotch of equal size, and Catherine and her mother were provided with gin and tonics that Billy dressed with some sort of sweet, pinkish-yellow syrup that foamed slightly pinker.

"What is that?" Harry asked, somewhat crestfallen because he seemed to have nothing to say.

"I have no idea. It was brought to us from Africa in the thirties, and I'm trying to use it up."

"What does it say on the label?"

"It's in Arabic," Billy said, enjoying the stop this statement would put to subsequent investigation, as it always had.

"I can read it."

"You can?"

"Yes, although I may not understand it."

Billy brought him the bottle. After a minute or so, Harry looked up. "It's for malaria," he said. "It's a pharmaceutical made in the Sudan in nineteen seventeen."

"I didn't think it had a date. I looked for one."

"Arabic numerals," Harry told him, "are not what we think of as Arabic numerals. For example, the zero is just a dot."

"The poor things," said Evelyn, taking a sip from her tumbler, "they must be so confused by freckles."

"Are you sure you want to drink that?" Harry asked.

"We've been drinking it for a year now," Billy said. "We broke it out on V-E Day, when supplies were scarce. I thought it was for a Tom Collins. It's delicious."

Catherine took a long draught. "It hasn't hurt me," she said, "up to this point. And I haven't gotten malaria, either."

At this, Evelyn rose and suggested that they go into the dining room. They followed her and took their seats, although Billy cracked open a pair of French doors that appeared to lead to a sun porch, and made a pronouncement into the darkness: "At the second bell."

"What does that mean?" Harry whispered to Catherine.

"You think I know?"

Billy glanced at Evelyn, who then rang the bell. A man and a woman entered with silver serving platters. "A beach dinner night," Billy announced. "No soup."

"Do you say grace?" Evelyn asked Harry.

"I live alone," he answered, "and so have forgotten."

"Would you like to remember?"

"I would, but it's Friday and I don't have the proper equipment. Besides, I'm not a woman."

"No," said Billy. "You're not a woman. Okay." They hadn't the slightest idea what Harry was talking about.

"It's a long and complicated ceremony."

"To become a woman?" Billy asked.

While Harry was amused by this, Evelyn, only slightly put off in feeling left out, said, "Billy, why don't you say grace, then?"

"Because we don't really do that," Billy protested. "It's mainly for him, and I don't know what the hell *he* does, but it sounds like he doesn't do it either, so why don't we just skip it?"

"No, Billy. Grace is hanging over us, and now it has to be said. It's like pulling back the hammer of a gun. Don't keep yourself all cocked up."

"Oh, I wouldn't," Billy answered. "Why don't you do it?"

"It's your serendipity to do it," his wife told him.

"It is?"

"Yes."

"Catherine?" her father asked.

"Don't look at me," Catherine said.

"All right. I'll say it. But . . . let's see. It should have music."

"That's just an excuse so you won't have to . . . ," Evelyn began. "And what do you mean, 'music'?"

Billy held up his hand like a traffic cop. "No, it isn't an excuse. We have music. Ring the bell."

"I don't know any tunes," Evelyn said, "and it's only one note."

"Just ring it."

She seized the bell and moved it back and forth like a dog shedding water. At first, nothing happened, and Harry took some Scotch, hoping to relieve at least a little of the tension and that he might after a dazed moment or two begin to understand what was going on. But then everyone but Billy nearly jumped out of his seat as an immense volume of music swelled from the sun porch. The lights went on, and the French doors were thrown fully open from the outside, after which the marimbist rushed back to his seat amid an eighteen-piece orchestra packed against the screens and the furniture that had been stacked out of the way.

The music enveloped the room like a tidal wave that had breached the dunes. The servants, who somehow had been kept in the dark, almost dropped their platters. The clearly professional orchestra was playing a kind of ersatz Brazilian music of the "Flying Down to Rio" variety, but had put it in a minor key, so that despite its happiness and urgency it had a sad, ghostly quality that nonetheless was so spirited that it filled the room and made everyone want to dance. Thus, everyone was moving, at least slightly, and the tension was carried away on the music like fallen leaves upon a rain-swollen kill.

"We thank you," Billy said, eyes closed, swaying rhythmically, "for the fish I caught in the sea, and the dolphins that flew above the waves as I pulled him in. For the rice that is a cousin of the dune grass that grows here. For the vegetables, especially the salad and Louise's marvelous dressing. And for the dessert, and for making it possible for me to have rented this orchestra. Really. Amen."

Harry took another drink of Scotch, a big one. "Do you do this often?" he asked.

"Oh, certainly not," Evelyn said. "He didn't even tell me."

"I wanted to give Catherine her party," Billy said. "I asked Clayton—you know, the one who was surprised when he saw me surf-casting, because he thought it was below my station—where I could get in touch with these people, because he's the one on the board who approves the hiring of musicians. He was true to form, and said, 'People like us don't do things like that. Why don't you just put a Victrola in the sun room and have a servant turn it on?'

"Well, people like us do all kinds of things. And people like us don't have to run in narrow tracks that people like us, and people not like us, may think we have to run in. I wanted the music to be full, to surround us, to lift us like the swell, so I rented a bloody orchestra. You only live once.

"They're going to play at the club tomorrow night, and came out today to get settled. It was easy to hire them. That's what they do.

They play every night for money. Not a bad life, if you like music and you don't have too many days when you're unengaged."

"It's the life I've chosen, Daddy," Catherine said. "It's not for money or fame. It's for the music."

"But in the end, where does it leave you?" her mother asked.

"In the end, it leaves you where everyone is left, but with a full heart, I hope."

"I hope so, too," Evelyn told her, touching her hand. "And do you agree, Harry?" For decades it had been her job as hostess to direct the conversation felicitously, touching upon what was serious but always ready to lift and carry it, like music, beyond the reach of gravity.

"Those questions," Harry said, "were like the questions I asked myself before the war."

"And what was your answer?"

"I thought I had come up with an answer, and then I was swept away."

"Yes, of course."

"And ever since, before I can ponder such things, I've been swept away. I met Catherine on the Staten Island Ferry, and since that unplanned second, everything has changed."

"You can't surrender completely to chance," Billy said.

"I know," Harry agreed, "that God is on the side of those with the biggest battalions, and I don't believe in chance anyway. Chance is ugly and ragged. What I believe in holds things together beautifully as they run."

All this was said almost lightly as they rode on the music as if on a boat in the waves. "And I try not to surrender entirely to anything," Harry continued. "I find that it's like jumping from a plane. You can plan on your landing zone, you can partially collapse the chute to influence your course, but overall the jump is blind and you go where the wind takes you."

That led to much talk about many things, and as they ate and drank, everyone, including Catherine, ventured beyond safety. "I caught this fish this morning," Billy told them. "It was a great cast. I was relaxed and the throw was easy, but more than that, the wind took the spoon. I followed it. It just carried forward like a bird in flight, and when it landed it was taken by the rip. I watched my reel unwind as if the hook had snagged a boat, until it jerked to a stop because I had run out of line. That spoon was two thousand feet from the beach, which is how I was able to bring in a bonito: they don't run close to shore. He took the line about ten seconds after it had played out. I was half expecting the reel to wind itself. It didn't. I had to work. And in the hour it took to land the fish, it was surrounded by leaping dolphins. I thought they wanted to save it, and if I hadn't worked so hard I would have let him go to oblige them. I almost did."

Luckily for their consciences, they had finished the main course and were speeding through a lemon cake. "It's for dancing," Billy said. "The orchestra. Catherine, you didn't get a single dance last week. Even though the whole thing blew up, the orchestra continued to play after you left, and people danced until well beyond midnight. It was like a wake, I guess. And they had come all the way out here. Why shouldn't you get a dance, too?"

Catherine drew back in her chair and pushed her empty plate away. As Harry helped her up she rose directly into his arms. The orchestra had started a euphoric, fast-paced Mexican song with a lot of whoops, brass, and flutes. "I don't know what dance to do to this," she said, looking up at him.

"That's all right," he said, "because we're already dancing, and this dance is called 'Just Don't Knock Over the Table.'"

With Billy and Evelyn now up on the floor and almost oblivious of Catherine and Harry, Harry and Catherine, oblivious of Billy and Evelyn, danced their first dance. They were as smooth and free as if they could fly. They moved together naturally and without plan.

"Do you like it?" he asked.

"Do I like it? I think I'm going to faint."

"I don't think so, Catherine. People like you don't faint. But go ahead, I'll faint, too."

"No, don't," she said. "I hope the song never ends."

It did, however, and when it did he really didn't want to let her go, but they switched partners and he found himself dancing, far more carefully, with Evelyn. "Will Catherine be as elegant as you?" he asked, for in her youth Catherine was not as stringent as her mother, if only because she did not need to be.

Self-possessed even as she was spun around the small space between the dining room table and the sideboard, Evelyn answered, "Catherine will be more so, because Catherine is better than I am." They glanced over at Catherine, who was dancing with Billy as only fathers and daughters can dance. No matter how old the daughter may be, the father is dancing, in joy unparalleled, with his child when she was little.

Then they switched back, and when Catherine was again in his arms, in the white dress in which she had come on the train and which now nonetheless seemed as if it had been made for the dance, and when they were lost again, moving together in a rhythm that cut out everything else, they knew why dolphins breach the air above the sea.

## 14

### CONVERSATION BY THE SEA

HE HAD EATEN lightly and had had only a little more than half the Scotch Billy had poured him and less than a full glass of wine, so when he awoke at sunrise to the pounding of the surf his body was untroubled and his eye was sharp. Dressed in khaki uniform trousers and a polo shirt, he walked slowly along the length of the pool, now blue and slightly rippled by the morning wind. In banks of flowers bordering the slate that surrounded the pool, bees suspended in the air like hummingbirds alighted to load nectar, and patrolled in paths as precisely curved as if they had been laid out by a nautilus. Freighted with the remnant mist of breaking waves, the air beyond the dunes glowed like the sky above a distant city. And, as always, the heartbeat of the surf continued. It vibrated the ground beneath his feet, reverberated through his lungs like the sound of cannon fire, and was carried away on a reviving wind.

Inside the house, Billy stood in his robe, teacup in hand, as still as an Elgin Marble. Instead of greeting Harry, he remained motionless, gazing into the strong light from outside. Had Harry looked closely enough, he could have seen two perfect pictures of the terrace, the pool, the gardens, and the line of dunes, miniaturized and bent to follow in faithful color the orbs of their owner's eyes. Fearing that Billy's impassive demeanor meant that he had decided against him, Harry carefully said good morning, but Billy just stared in his direction, until he quoted, "'The air was literally filled . . . the light at noon-day was obscured . . . and the continual buzz of wings had a tendency to lull my senses to repose.'"

"I beg your pardon?"

"Audubon. The passenger pigeon. There."

Harry turned around. Behind him was what captivated Billy, the Audubon engraving of the passenger pigeon.

"Audubon reported that there were so many of them that they darkened the sky. But now they're gone. The very last one — they had her in a zoo, in Cincinnati, and they knew that she was the last of her kind — died at one in the afternoon on the first of September, nineteen fourteen. I was probably . . . I don't know what I was doing then. If it were a weekday, I may have been trading stocks. What were you doing?"

"Probably sleeping or drinking milk."

"Were you born in Cincinnati?" Billy asked hopefully.

"No, but had I been born there, I don't think I would have been her."

Billy seemed disappointed. "Look at this," he said, walking over to a flat tin box, as gray as lead and scarred by time, resting on a cherry-wood desk. "It's one of the boxes they used for sending prints to subscribers. I have all the prints, the complete set." He opened the lid and propped it up with the dowel that came originally for the purpose. "Wow," he said, meaning the life still to be felt in a wild goose, its plumage as dark as velvet and as white as raw cotton, its neck bent in readiness for combat, the red tongue vibrating between the halves of its beak like flame, its cry almost audible, and the background of marsh plants as lonely as in a Japanese print. Harry bent to the caption, which read, *Drawn from nature and published by John J. Audubon. F.R.S. F.L.S. & etc. Engraved, Printed, & Colored by R. Havel.*

"Sometimes I regret that we so readily eat birds and fish, which are beautiful, and perfectly suited to the water and air. But, then again, when they can, they eat us, and with no regret."

"And we're ahead in the game," Harry said.

"Not for long," Billy answered. "Humankind, or at least American-kind, will lose its edge as we produce more and more pipsqueaks and everyone gets nicer. Whole generations of pipsqueaks will be so fucking nice you won't be able to tell a man from a woman."

"You won't?"

"Nope. And it will get worse and worse as people mistake nice for good. Hitler was nice, supposedly, most of the time. A lot of good that did. Luxury and prosperity breed pipsqueaks. A century from now the country won't even be able to defend itself."

"Do you think that my generation," Harry asked, "that just conquered the world, are pipsqueaks?"

"That's why the pipsqueaks are on their way. The universe isn't homogenized. Everything changes, and there's only one direction in which we can go in the near future. Brace yourself for a different world, where you'll be totally out of place, and hope that your children are strong enough to carry through to the hard generations that will protect your line from extinction."

"I'll do my best," Harry said, unconcerned about the virility of his sons, and, given Catherine, the femininity of his daughters.

"Mark my words," said Billy. "Within a decade the British Empire will have vanished."

And then Catherine appeared. She had been standing close by and listening to their discussion. She, too, was in a robe. "Okay," said Billy. "To hell with the British Empire. Let's have breakfast and get to the beach before the sand fleas." He left quickly, like Santa Claus.

"Are sand fleas a problem, like pipsqueaks?" Harry asked, aching for Catherine even as she stood before him.

"That's what he calls the talky people who bunch together in groups to lie in the sun. It's a semi-nude cocktail party, with seaweed. Listening to the two of you, one would think that you were both slightly out of your minds."

"You're his daughter, and I came out of nowhere. In the natural order of things, that's difficult. What you witnessed was civilization overcoming the impulses of nature. Even birds have patterns of behavior and ceremonies that save them."

"It's just that he feels wanting because he missed both wars," she said. "You should get into your bathing suit."

"So soon?"

"In our house, breakfast is a grapefruit, and that takes a minute and a half because it's pre-cut. Daddy frowns upon reading the paper at the breakfast table. He thinks it's slovenly. So in the morning the Hales are always out like a shot. And now the idea is to do the five miles before getting trapped in the seaweed party. If we go soon, we'll escape them."

She was iron-straight in her pink silk robe. A strap, silvery pink with a metallic sheen, rose from beneath the robe's shawl collar and looped around her neck. "Are you in yours?" he asked, meaning her bathing suit.

A second or two passed as her expression changed from something light to a deep, slow stare. Rather than speak, she undid the loosely tied belt, took in a long breath that she did not immediately expel, lifted her hands to open the collar, and let the robe drop to the floor.

She was in a two-piece bathing suit, in the French style. The pleated top took the shape of her breasts with enough force to iron out the pleats, and her nipples, pressed back, showed sharply nonetheless through the sheen of metallicized fabric. The lower part was deliberately a scandal—two triangles meeting on the side of the hip in just a narrow band, the front bulging gently and softly, arrestingly beautiful.

Her body was lithe, sharply defined for a woman, and of ideal proportions. She had wanted him to see her, and the way she had shown herself was stunning. Pleased by his reaction, she said, "Harry, you can breathe now."

From a distance, the knot of people arrayed in a rough circle on the high, level part of the beach, where tire tracks showed that fishermen's jeeps had passed by at dawn, might easily have been mistaken for a hump of colored rock. Almost a dozen of them had coalesced from east and west, from the Georgica Club, the houses inland, and the houses to the east along Dune Road. Artists and theater people came from the east, loping in from Amagansett like camels and stopping magically near the Hales' as if repelled by the Episcopalian energy belt that emanated from the Georgica Club. Being artists and theater people, they often had psychiatrists in tow — not always their psychiatrists, but psychiatrists just the same. From the west came the investment bankers, lawyers, and rentiers, pouring into what Billy had christened the Demilitarized Zone, where they gathered with the others to sit in clumps and talk in the sound of the wind. From the east, fame and art; from the west, power and wealth. Each probed the world of the other in search of advantages less likely to find them than would a direct meteorite strike.

By definition, the artists, writers, and actors were so desperate for money that, had a decent amount been offered for doing so, they might have taken the few steps to the Atlantic Ocean and swum it, and yet they never talked about money in the presence of those who had it, lest those who had it think that they might need it. And those who had the money came because, having crested the top of the hill and seen that on the other side was nothing, they wanted to feel the touch of life they had left on the slope behind them. This was why they spoke so little. The artists thought it was because the monied were deracinated WASPs who somehow had less soul than others, and that, at least in comparison to the newly arrived and deeply engaged, they had nothing to say. But it was not so. It was only that success had introduced the bankers and lawyers to futility, and they could do nothing but look back, as if from the land of the dead, and with gentle envy and equal affection, at those still animated in struggle.

The Hales were there, having failed to get out quickly enough; various Marrows; a lawyer named Cromwell, without the wife who had left him because he won every argument and was never home; a Hollywood leading man and his Eastern European acting coach, who looked astoundingly like a monkey, both from a distance and from very close; a truly great representational painter, his wife, and their daughter of five or six; the psychiatrist *du jour,* who was bald and to compensate had grown a beard of the kind, common to nineteenth-century whalers, that could have served as a brush for reaming out barrels; two very strange Mediterranean dogs that looked like bulked-up greyhounds, one chocolate brown, one light khaki, both stretched out miserably in the sun with the resigned elongated necks of dogs who sleep stoically while suffering through human conversation; and Victor.

Victor Marrow's dreams were set and glazed in the spring of 1929 when, as a junior at Yale, he sat in his room, at the edge of his bed, staring at his closet, the doors of which he had (and not for the first time) opened fully to reveal his carefully attended wardrobe. Carpenters had constructed this closet along an entire blank wall. He felt a surge like that of an opium/caffeine cocktail that a chorus girl once had shared with him at Chumley's: tiny, microscopic, warm, almost infrared rays coursing through his body, like the species of sexual pleasure that is primarily the province of women, who, unlike men, are more apt to take long rather than wild rides. But he didn't know this. All he knew was a marvelous, ecstatic, pre-orgasmic contentment, white foaming oceans of it frothing in his mind as the birds outside sang of Eli. As he hummed in low tones like a Tibetan chant, "Boola-boola, boola-boola, boola-boola, boola-boola, boola-boola, boola-boola, boola-boola, boola-boo!" over and over again, he surveyed the eighty Savile Row suits, the Peal shoes, the walking sticks, spats, umbrellas, and hats, the pumps, braces, cummerbunds, and coats, the gloves, shirts, and sweaters of the wool of angora goats. And when he combed his hair, not a single one of the brass-colored straight strands rode up or was even vaguely crossed with another. Perfect parallels to the end of the earth, he thought, just like Euclid. Better than Euclid. Of course, Victor knew that his hair would soon start its emigration to other worlds, leaving strand by strand to race down the drain of a shower or sink, like a cross between Alice in Wonderland and a very skinny snake. He was well educated, clever, and marvelously inane. But beneath these qualities was a callousness, a disregard for all living things (as a boy he had used frogs for shuttlecocks), a malice as sharp as Angostura bitters, and a hold over women that, surviving the process of his body going to seed, paralyzed them as if they were staring at a swaying cobra. Although no man could see or understand this quality, it worked upon the feminine in a way that must have begun at the beginning of time. Although men like Harry were born to protect women from men like Victor, in perceiving no threat, they often failed.

"The sand fleas," Catherine announced to Harry as they approached on the hard-packed part of the beach that the water strokes twice a day and then abandons. They had become so comfortable walking tightly together that it seemed to be less difficult than walking independently, and that morning they had gone all the way to the Coast Guard station at Amagansett and back. As soon as they came in range of the group, however, they separated.

"Do we have to show?" he asked.

"They saw us come out of the dunes at our house. We can't avoid them or it'll look like we're afraid. We just have to do it," Catherine said. "Victor is on the right. I can't fear him or seem ashamed. I won't turn around. If we remain standing, we can leave after not too long. Just don't sit down or we'll have to stay there an hour."

"I thought that was a rock," Harry said, referring to Victor. "Does he go anywhere without his parents?"

"That's not fair. You've only seen him twice now."

"But many times in my dreams."

As they ascended to the flat ground, conversation stopped. "Who are they?" the acting coach asked with a mixture of excitement and envy that could have come only from someone who looked so much like a monkey that when very small children saw him they thought they had been taken to the zoo. "They're too strong to be dancers. Are they gymnasts? God, look at them."

The leading man tensed his abdomen lest he be upstaged. Only the artist and his wife, a couple of superior temperament, were undisturbed in any way. Even the lawyer was made unhappy, as he had no wife but the law, and no one actually has the law. The daughter of the artist, platinum-haired, lay asleep in his arms, and the dogs didn't look up. Victor did not, like the leading man, prepare for meeting Harry by tightening all his muscles, but by letting himself go slack as a sign of contempt. He so let his jaw slacken that his jowls expanded.

Evelyn made the many introductions over almost five minutes, at the end of which, as a rainbow dimly formed in a cloud of mist over the waves, and then floundered on the wind, she introduced Harry to Victor. Like a dying crab, Victor lifted his forearm without taking his elbow from the sand. Harry extended himself into a cantilever and reached for Victor's hand, which was as limp as a lamprey. But when Harry grasped it firmly and quickly, Victor just as quickly and unknown to anyone but the two of them bent his index finger and scratched Harry's palm.

Harry was not pleased, and then posed this question to the group. "What does it mean," he asked, "when someone, while shaking hands, scratches your palm with his index finger?"

"It means he's interested in you," immediately said the acting coach, whose name was Arthur Tawney, although he had been born Szygmunt Przyemskl. When everyone looked wonderingly at him, he added, "In some circles . . . I believe."

"Victor, what do you think it means?" Harry pressed.

"It means," said Victor dismissively, "that the person who scratched thinks the other one is a shithead."

"This is among four-year-olds?"

"This is among forty-year-olds."

"Is that where it stops?"

"No," said Victor. "It stops when the shithead is dead."

"From what? Rabies?"

"From whatever you'd like," Victor continued. He glanced at Catherine, who was obviously annoyed, and who, in the blush of morning sun, looked spectacular. "Maybe from choking on a breast." Suddenly aware that even his parents were horrified, Victor added, "Of chicken," and lapsed into determined silence.

"Of chicken!" exclaimed Arthur Tawney.

"Harley," Billy said, ignoring Victor, this is my daughter, Catherine. She's in the theater." He did not have to introduce Harley to Catherine. Everyone in the United States knew Harley. His eyes went as briefly past her as a basting brush, and his mouth tightened in contempt. Catherine was obviously hurt, though she tried not to show it.

"What was your last movie, Harley?" Harry asked, with a delicate edge and having lost no time.

"*Delilah.*"

"Was that the one with the talking dog, or was he in *Fire over Bulimia*?"

"Rumania. *Fire over Rumania*. I played the bomber pilot who...."

"I liked the one with the talking dog. He stole the show."

"And what do you do?" Arthur Tawney asked, like acid on metal.

Harry turned to him, put his finger to his lips, and said, "Shhh! Let the organ grinder speak, or he won't feed you."

At this, the psychiatrist interrupted authoritatively, addressing Harry both as if no one else was there and as if he were in front of an audience. "I can tell," he said, "that until recently you were a soldier. Is that not correct?"

"It is."

"And that you were in for years?"

"I was."

"The war is over," he said, kindly rather than with rancor.

"Then tell that to the fat palm-scratcher over there who called me a shithead and 'threatened' my life. And to George the Fourth and his chimp, who treated Catherine like the dirt they are." For Harry, who had seen a great deal of war, this was not really fighting.

"What *do* you do, anyway?" Harley asked, sensing that this was how he might trump Harry, in that he was famous and Harry was not.

Harry said, "I wanted to be a movie critic, but during my training I saw a lot of films that made me so ill — you might know them — that I changed my profession and now I'm a monkey hunter and a hippopotamus slayer."

"Are you talking about my son?" Willie Marrow asked indignantly.

"I beg your pardon?"

"Obviously I'm not the monkey," Victor said, as if from sleep.

"Who's the monkey, then?" Arthur Tawney asked, without a clue.

"I can't believe it," the lawyer announced. "This man has been here five minutes and we're all about to kill each other."

"It's not his fault," Catherine asserted.

"Don't be defensive," the psychiatrist said.

"Why not?" Catherine asked. "When you fence, Doctor, do you stab yourself?"

"I don't fence, Catherine, I listen."

"Oh please. Spare me," she said.

"No, it's not his fault," Victor's mother declared, addressing Catherine. "It's yours."

"I can solve this, I can solve this," the psychiatrist said, putting his professional pride on the line.

"You can?" Billy asked, skeptically and somewhat amused, for he had been in too many negotiations to believe there was a solution, to whatever this was, other than time and separation.

"Yes. I guarantee that if Victor, there, and Harry were to walk together to the club and back, by the time they return we'll have peace between them, between Catherine and Harley, and between the Hales and the Marrows."

"Are you insane?" the lawyer asked. As a named partner in a leading firm in New York, and a rhino-hided litigator in his day, he spoke as he pleased.

"I'm the psychiatrist and you're the lawyer. Does that answer your question?"

"Yes it does," the lawyer said confidently.

"Look," Evelyn observed, "now they're fighting, too."

"No no no," the psychiatrist insisted. "It'll work. He turned to Victor, who got up by placing his hands in front of him on the sand, one at a time, like an elephant coming to its feet. "No one's going to kill anyone. Take a walk. Go ahead."

As they left, not exactly arm in arm, Catherine sat down and sighed. The artist turned to her. He was tall and slim and his hair shone silver in the sun, just as Catherine's shone in gold and deep red. "Catherine," he said, able to elevate her above Harley and everyone else, because he was the only one there who would be remembered in history, and they all knew it, "I'd like to paint you. Billy, what do you think? She's in full bloom."

• • •

"This is ridiculous," Victor said.

"So are you," Harry shot back, tranquilly.

"You realize," Victor threatened, "that I could beat you silly. I boxed at Yale."

"What'd you box, lunches?"

"You've got a nerve, coming out of completely God-assed nowhere and stealing Catherine from me. How long have you known her, ten minutes? I've known her since she was born."

They moved down to the compacted sand. The sun was high enough so that the wind had largely died and the surf quieted. "It's true, Victor," Harry said, deliberately containing himself, "that I haven't known her very long, and you have. But I didn't rape her. That gives me a kind of advantage."

"Is that what she told you? That I raped her? I didn't rape her. She seduced me."

"Of course she did. In fact, she probably raped you, right? After all, she was thirteen and weighed all of a hundred pounds and you were thirty-one and weighed—what?—a thousand? And you know, I know what she was like when she was that age, because I know her now. I know what she likes, I know her favorite poet, I know her heart. She was quite delicate, remember? Deep in her Emily Dickinson phase, which always puts young girls in the raping and seduction frame of mind, especially since she was so coarse and worldly. Who would believe her instead of you, who claim to have been 'seduced' at thirty-one by a thirteen-year-old? You just couldn't help it.

"She was not even out of puberty, you son of a bitch. Be grateful for law, Victor, because were it not for law, I would kill you."

"You wouldn't kill anybody. And you'll find that you can't take her from me," Victor said confidently and smoothly. The authority of the pronouncement was for Harry a window into what Catherine had seen for so long when she beheld Victor, and it made Harry both more careful and more determined.

"I'm not taking anyone from anyone. If she comes with me it'll be because she's decided on her own. I've made no effort in that regard."

"The hell you didn't."

"Not in the sense you mean. She's not a yachting trophy or a bank you're trying to buy."

"What would you know about banks?" Victor asked condescendingly, and because he had little to fall back upon.

"I know a lot about banks, I owe them a lot of money. I know about banks as much as a rabbit knows about foxes."

"What banks?" Victor asked.

Harry immediately regretted what he understood to have been a dangerous indiscretion. Victor's eyes had lighted, it appeared to Harry, like the flicker from a peephole in a woodstove in Vermont.

"I think I will get Catherine back, because I think you're afraid to fight," Victor stated as they increased their speed yet again. They were now walking so fast that Victor was almost out of breath. Harry had decided that if Victor actually would attack him, because of Victor's size and weight it would be best to face him when he was winded.

"Victor," Harry began, pressing ahead even more rapidly, but not so much that Victor would catch on: the trick was to keep his mind occupied as he was made to walk faster and faster. "I spent the last four years fighting. I hate fighting. I'm scared of it. You can have all the skill in the world, but something can happen in an instant, and then everything you are, all the training and the experience, all you know, all the love and all the memory, gets turned into rotting meat. And you don't come back again. It's not like tennis, where you can start another game. I don't know what you did in the war, but I know what I did. It's going to be very difficult for anyone these days to get me to fight. I truly hate it. But . . . if anyone does force me, push me, and I do have to fight, you know what I'm going to do?"

"What are you going to do?"

"I'm going to kill him. I've put that part of me to sleep, but if you wake it up, which I don't think you yourself can do . . . but if you do, I will kill you. I won't want to, but I will."

They had reached the club, where they quickly turned on their heels. "I'll get her back," said Victor, "because I don't think you're fit to live in the world. What kind of name is Copeland, anyway? It's suspect, somehow. What kind of a name is Harry? Are you like that pussy in the White House?"

"You mean the pussy," Harry asked, "the officer of horse artillery in the Great War, the tough and taciturn farmer who dropped the atom bomb and is facing off with Stalin?"

"He's still a pussy," Victor said, "and so are you."

"You don't know me well enough to judge."

"I think I just may. And whenever you kiss her, Copeland, you can think of how many times she's held my cock in her mouth."

Harry recoiled briefly, as if struck. After a few waves had broken and receded, he said, "Love has burned all that away, and it's as if you never touched her. The first moment Catherine and I beheld one another, we shot ahead of all the years you had her in your bed. And lately, you know what she said? She said 'Victor?' as if I had mentioned a farm animal. She said that now she felt as if she had been in a sanitarium in Switzerland or New Mexico, and that her system was cleansed and you were completely out of it, as if you never touched her, as if she never knew you, as if you never existed. She said, 'And, besides, when I was with him, it was horrible. It was like digging ditches and washing dishes. I was unhappy all the time.'

"Would you say that was a good review, Vic? And, you know, everything we do in life is subject, one way or another, to review. It's not just Brooks Atkinson who gets to pass judgment or close a show. Yours is closed, curtain down, lights out."

"What do you do, anyway?" Victor asked.

"Do you know how many times I've been asked that in the last hour? What kind of people are you?"

"Perhaps we're people who can sense a weak point."

They were back at the group, which was expectantly quiet. The psychiatrist glanced at them, sighed, and said nothing. Harry felt good being near Catherine.

As he stood apart, he surveyed this group not for what it was but for what it would be in memory. How beautiful were the women, ranged in the sun, hats and hair luffing sometimes in the breeze, their colorful robes and scarves glowing in the beating light that in time would carry them away on the wind. They spoke, but he could not hear them. He saw them from afar, in colors as if enameled in a kiln and still glossy and hot. The blue behind them was so dark with heat that it was almost like the night sky.

He hoped that from amidst these people, all of whom were worthy in one way or another, even if not all to the same degree, Catherine would rise in the present daylight as if from the unretrievable past and come to the place where he was standing. He had no desire to separate her from her mother and father or from the world she knew, but the separation was already under way, and he could see it in the picture before his eyes both breaking and still.

They spoke to him, but he didn't hear. The painter had watched him, and understood that in taking in the true composition of the scene he had stopped time, which is what the painter did day by day. He, the painter, smiled and held his daughter tight as he watched Catherine rise from the group and, as if loosed from the moorings of gravity and time, glide across the sand until, hardly knowing what she had done, she had clasped Harry in her arms as though no one had been watching, because they had all drifted away long before.

"Catherine?" her father called out. "Catherine? When will you come for lunch?"

Though she turned, she couldn't hear him, for as once he had been, now she too had been taken on the flow.

# 15

## GRAY AND GREEN

THE THIRD MAN to come from the storefront was the first to hesitate at the threshold and survey the street. Sharp-featured, he wore a Panama hat, white bucks, a white suit, black shirt, and a tie that looked like wallpaper in the bathroom of a lounge where people drank in the daytime. As nervous as a tree frog, he seemed relieved when after a few steps no one had shot him. For three-quarters of an hour, Harry had perched on a low brick wall half a block up Prince Street, reading the *Trib* and drinking from a bottle of club soda. He never once turned his head completely in the direction of the doorway he was watching, but as his eyes looked left he had counted five men in and out.

They seemed like gangsters, because they were gangsters, but on a sunny morning in June they looked as much like everyone else as they ever do. With the exception of the nervous one, they apparently forgot what kind of world they lived in and who they were. So, papers tucked under their arms, they walked in the newly awakened streets almost like normal people, and when they saw what everyone else saw — children in green plaid with briefcases half as big as they were, moving like a tide into school doors surmounted by Christ on the cross; heavy trucks loading, unloading, purring, and rumbling; shopkeepers in the sun, washing their sidewalks clean; old people perpetually staring, their elbows welded to their windowsills — when they saw these things they forgot for a time what it was they did, and what would come during the rest of the day and at night. For at night, like cats, they found their essence.

He hadn't planned to observe, but reconnaissance had been burned into him in the war. As a pathfinder, his job was first to see and then to mark the route that others would take. He dropped in darkness, fully outfitted for combat and loaded as well with flares, smoke, and tape for marking arrows and codes on the ground. He was unknown to those who followed, almost always alone, and usually so far ahead that the people who had sent him tended to forget he was there. He was one of the few who fought the war by himself much of the time, until he would halt and rejoin his stick of paratroopers, who could work together nonetheless with coordination that seemed telepathic.

He had come early. While counting and categorizing, he noticed that no one moved cautiously or was alert to being followed, except for the third man, who, as anxious as he may have been, was unaware that he was being watched. On a battlefield, because they didn't take the trouble, by now they would all be dead.

At eleven he folded his paper, took a last drink from the soda bottle, and rose from his position. As he walked, his clothes uncreased and fell into a comfortable drape. He tossed the paper and the bottle into a trash can and moved faster and with more concentration, until he slowed just before the door. He wanted to go in neither submissively nor aggressively, and at an even, unagitated pace. He was there not to react but to collect information, and would not give whoever it was he was to see the satisfaction of creating in him either fear or defiance. He was concerned, however, that his very lack of common reactions might mark him as someone not to write off, so he began to think of what to feign so they would forget about him after he left.

When no one answered his knock, he turned the knob and slowly opened the door. As his eyes adjusted to lesser light, he entered a sea of luminous gray and green — the gray of a rock dove or a felt hat, with shades darker or lighter depending upon light that came through various windows. And green the dark green of tenement paint half a century old or more, in many shades on a single wall: enamel green, bottle green, seaweed green, verdigris. He had seen it many times, but never had he seen it softened by gray as if in a painting, though he had never seen in a painting such a fusion of otherworldly colors. The men standing within it, as if they were submerged in a lit aquarium, were completely unaware, but Harry was so taken by the color that he almost forgot why he was there.

Two men were settled at the bar, and the bartender, his hands working a towel over a glass, deferred to them. One turned to Harry and said, "This is a private club." But a man at a table in the back and to the left of the bar signaled with a flick of his head, and the second bar sitter jumped off his stool and turned his very wide front to the interloper. "You got an appointment?"

"Yeh," Harry answered. He thought they might not understand *yes*.

"With who?"

"I don't know. They just said be here at eleven."

"That's him," the man at the table said.

"Okay," the second bar sitter explained, and moved a step forward for frisking.

"Don't bother," the man at the table told him. "Come over here," he commanded.

Late off the mark, the one who had moved to frisk Harry said, "Mr. Verderamé will see you now."

Harry approached the table. "Si'down," Verderamé said. "You want something to drink?"

"No thank you," Harry said. "I just had a whole bottle of club soda."

"Whad'ja do that for?" He pointed. "The bathroom's over there. You shouldn't pee on the street. You don't want cops to see." He was amused.

"It's okay, I don't pee on the street."

"Yeah, but why'd you drink a whole bottle? It's not that hot."

"I was early, so I bought a paper and sat on the wall up the block. Then I got thirsty. The only size bottle they had was a big one and I didn't want to waste it." He was watching Verderamé's eyes. When he had given away his reconnaissance the irises hadn't moved a millimeter.

"You shoulda come in here. We'd give it to you by the glass, for free, no waste."

"Thank you." Harry hated to be thanking the person who was robbing him. Verderamé enjoyed it.

"No problem. Any time." In his middle forties, Verderamé was tall, his black hair pushed back on his forehead in a slick as smooth as the smoothest wave in a Hiroshige print. He appeared to be highly alert, intelligent, and trim, with elevated cheekbones, hollow-seeming eyes, a tenor voice, and delicate hands. He spoke in almost a singsong, as if he enjoyed revealing to people miraculous things that they didn't know. He was dressed conservatively in a dark blue suit of European cut, an oxford shirt, and a blue tie. "I told you. You shoulda come in here. Next time, you come in here."

The exquisite tension in Verderamé's manner and presence that turned solicitous comments into orders and threats told Harry that he was one of those people whose reservoirs of anger, though covered with humor, good nature, or curiosity, are so deep that when they erupt nothing can contain them. When people like this work in an office or a factory everyone is afraid of crossing them. If they yoke their anger to ambition, well, then they are Verderamé, someone who when he was younger had had to relieve the pressure on his soul by every now and then beating some other one to death. For him, innocence was insolent provocation, and lack of aggression an indictment that had to be violently suppressed. Verderamé's eyes sparked. Like so many of the short-fused and explosive, he was often charming, graceful, and captivating. The pit viper betrays how it will strike not in its movements, which are feints, but in its eyes.

Harry saw that Verderamé was looking in his eyes with the same care with which he himself had earlier looked in Verderamé's. Nor did Harry's irises move a millimeter, as he had retreated into complete neutrality and suspended his emotions to the point where he felt he could have been in someone else's body.

In a heavy Sicilian dialect, Verderamé called out to the men at the bar. "Who did we send to this boy?" In the same dialect, they answered that they weren't sure, that it could have been Marco or Sammy, or John, the new guy.

Harry understood, and kept them from knowing that he did. He had thought that perhaps by speaking in Italian he could make some headway, but now he would not give up the advantage of being privy to conversations they thought secret. And, beyond that, to them his academic Roman dialect would no doubt sound pretentious. "Copeland Leather," he said.

Verderamé drew his head back and opened his eyes a little wider, quickly restoring his expression, to show that he was familiar with the subject.

"I asked the guys you sent if I could see you. Until last week, we were paying Mickey Gottlieb a fifth of what they told us. It's not as if business is suddenly good. We're competing with cheap European labor. What we make is on a par with the best leather goods in the world, but though we're as good as England or Italy, we can't do better, and as their product begins to come in cheaply, they're killing us."

"What does that have to do with me? What are you telling me this for?" He was already angry, not with reason, but because he could be.

"If . . . we pay that amount every month. . . ."

"Every week, it's always by the week."

"Every week. God, every week. We'll be out of business in six months, and then we won't be able to pay anything."

"Do you know how many times a day I hear this?" Verderamé asked, his irritation deliberately exaggerated to shift the ground. "All these guys, these people, who come to me and complain about the price of my services. Nobody I protect has ever been forced out of business because I protect them, but they all whine about how they're going to go bankrupt. What has that got to do with me except that they wanna Jew me outa what they owe me? Even if they do go bankrupt, what do I care? Someone else is going to take over the space."

"This will break the back of my business and put fifty good men out on the street." Harry's neutrality was ebbing. He stared at the table.

"Well," said Verderamé, "you're young. Did you just get back from the service?"

"Yes, sir."

"What did you do?"

"I was a clerk, in Washington. Supply," Harry said. "It wasn't exactly...."

"But you served, right?"

"Yes."

"So I'm gonna cut you some slack."

Harry stiffened against expecting too much.

"I'm gonna drop it to two thousand."

"It already is two thousand."

"Twenty-five hundred."

This hurt. "They said two thousand."

"They made a mistake. Whata they know?"

"Two thousand is what I was talking about. Two thousand is what will kill us."

"I did you a favor. I cut what you owe by twenty percent. Where else can you just walk in and get twenty percent off? You wanna be greedy?"

"I still don't understand. Gottlieb charged so much less."

"Okay," Verderamé said. "Someone did us a favor, and now we're doing them a favor. That's all."

"You mean you're making me do the favor for you."

"Don't tell me what I mean."

It was too dangerous for Harry to follow this line, so he became silent, not knowing what to say next. In the pause, Verderamé's right hand, which in perhaps a conscious effort had been kept either beneath the table, under his lapel, or clenched in a cloth napkin, emerged for a second or two. Verderamé saw Harry's eyes settle upon it and follow for the brief time it was in the open. His right thumbnail, and just his thumbnail, was dark yellow, and extended at least an inch beyond his thumb. That Harry had seen it was mysteriously embarrassing to Verderamé, and Harry knew immediately that nothing further would be accomplished.

"Two thousand?"

"Two thousand."

"My father paid four hundred."

"I collected for Gottlieb then. Your father and the nigger paid six hundred. Maybe it went down in the war. Your father begged like a fuckin' dog."

"My father did what?" Harry didn't seem so weak when he said this.

"Your father, kid, begged like a dog. But he still paid the maximum."

"I don't think he did that," Harry said.

"I think he did. Where'd you bury him, in a pet cemetery?"

Then came the sound of the creaking and scraping of chair legs as the heavy men at the bar dismounted. Expressionless, Harry whitened, which seemed to them to be the most dangerous of all signs.

"You just got back from the war," Verderamé said, "where you fought at a desk. Lemme tell you something. I'm still in a war that I've been fighting since I was ten years old. It's all I know. I can't do anything else. I don't want to do anything else. And I won't pretend to you that I don't love it in the same way that, no matter what he says, a cop loves what he does. I don't know you. I don't care about you. You don't mean anything to me. But you just entered a game that I've been playing since before you were born. How you play is up to you, but you have no fuckin' idea—I guarantee it—of what it took for me to get to this table. You just keep in mind that I've got the wall at my back and you've got the door."

His anger rose again, inexhaustibly. "So I wanna know, who the hell are you? Some fuckin' guy, some fuckin' guy walks in off the street, you walk in here looking for a break from me, based on what? I'll tell you, because I know. Because you think I might feel bad about what I do. You think so? You wanna ride a white horse? Look around you. You think the mayor doesn't get a piece of both of us? The commissioner? Everybody is fucking everybody else. It's what they call a circle jerk. If you stop, *you* die, but *it* keeps on going. The war's not over, kid. It was never over, even before it started. And it's right here, every day. You see?"

"There's a difference," Harry said, crossing the line, "between starting something . . . and finishing it."

"I don't like what I hear," Verderamé told him tensely.

With no more than a second to react, Harry said, "We made the first payment. We'll make the rest."

"You were five hundred short."

Harry was stunned. "I'll have five hundred on Friday."

"Then you can go back to two thousand," Verderamé said. "Merry Christmas."

# 16

## THE ABACUS

After the interview on Prince Street, Harry and Cornell went to the accountant. The one joke that the accountant had told even before the turn of the century, and would tell until he no longer breathed, came always upon the saying of his name, Ludwig Bernstein. "I'm not a law firm," he would croak, "I'm an accountant!" The more he repeated this, the more droll he thought it was and the less other people did, a small part of the comprehensive unhappiness that had been killing him longer than most people had been alive.

On the seventeenth floor of a building on Third Avenue in the Forties, his offices had the June sound, contented and comforting, of half a dozen fans of different sizes that pushed the air until the hum as it was concerted from room to room was like that of a steady wind far out at sea. Harry and Cornell sat in a waiting area from which they could look up from reading the only magazines supplied—*Boys' Life* and *Good Housekeeping*—to see buildings across the way baking in the sunlight until they were almost silver. The ceaseless sounds of traffic came from outside, and in a corner of the waiting area a fan the size of Achilles' shield stood on one black-and-chrome leg and swept back and forth as if it were saying not merely *no* but *tsk-tsk*.

"It says here, Cornell, that you should never wear a poncho when riding a horse, because the horse may get spooked if the wind flaps the poncho. That makes sense."

"It's good to know," said Cornell, "for Manhattanites."

"What are you reading?" Harry asked.

"Tips for baking pies."

"You think he puts these magazines out here to irritate his clients or to make himself seem more interesting by comparison?"

"I think these are the magazines he subscribes to."

A tall woman whose hair was done up in a kind of lacquered mantilla suitable only for a giant flamenco dancer came in to announce that Mr. Bernstein was now available. They stood up quickly, and as they walked from the waiting area they heard the fan beginning to shuffle through the abandoned pages of *Boys' Life* as if it were trying to find an article.

Ludwig Bernstein was a full five feet tall, with only enough bramble-like hairs on his head to make it look like a switchboard. He wore tweed as if there were no such thing as heat, and though on his lapel he sported a little card that said he had epilepsy, he had never had a fit. Although as immobile as if he had been filled with vertical rebar, he was both friendly and smart.

"Ludwig, this is Harry," Cornell said, "Meyer's son."

"I'm Ludwig Bernstein — not a law firm, but an accountant!" A laugh gurgled up in him and then he got down to business. "The numbers you gave me, assuming they're approximately correct, are hardly encouraging. But before we discuss them I should tell you that due to circumstances we can't control, our fee is going up from twelve to fifteen thousand dollars."

"That's just ... it's ...," Cornell said.

"You know it's not us, Cornell. We don't see a penny of the increase. It's them."

Cornell nodded in resignation.

"Who's *them?*" Harry asked, feeling more and more beleaguered by the minute.

Bernstein turned to Cornell as if to ask, He doesn't know?

"He doesn't know," Cornell answered.

"So tell him."

"The IRS."

"Why would our taxes go up if our earnings are reduced?" Harry asked. "And how would you know in advance by how much? And you said your fee."

"It's not taxes," Bernstein stated.

"Then what is it?"

Bernstein depressed his voice so that no one beyond his door would hear. "Copeland Leather enjoys an advantageous tax situation because of its utilization of various depletion allowances."

"You mean for materials?" Harry asked.

"Minerals and timber."

"Minerals and timber? What minerals and timber?"

"Subsidiaries that invest in the Southwest, Wyoming, and Montana."

"We don't have any subsidiaries."

"You do. On paper."

"Since when?"

"For a long time. It was the only way you got through the Crash. It started with real investments your father made. I wouldn't worry about it."

"But now it's not real."

"Nothing is real," Bernstein said, immensely pleased that he could reveal this to Harry. "God made the world, and we have to operate as if it is real. Maybe it's not, but we have no choice. The Congress tried to ape God when it made the tax code, and if you don't like it, the IRS will put you in prison. If you fight not to go to prison, eventually someone will shoot you. But, unlike God, because they're almost human, they have weak spots."

"You pay off the IRS?" Harry asked, astounded.

Bernstein was totally immobile, but Cornell leaned forward and said in a low whisper, "Revenue agents in Manhattan."

"Christ," Harry said, "what if someone finds out?" He felt both naive and unclean.

"First of all," Bernstein said, "you don't know. You're relying upon my advice. Second, to whose advantage would it be to tell? Anyone who tells goes to jail. Anyone who doesn't tell makes money. And, by the way, it didn't come from us. They started it. They shook us down. If we don't cooperate we spend the rest of our lives being audited. It would bankrupt you, but you wouldn't know, because by the time you were bankrupt you'd have totally lost your mind. It's kind of like your problem with whoever it is, but the government is a lot more reasonable. Whoever is taking a bite out of you, no matter how well he's doing, is struggling to survive. He's got a lot of enemies and he knows he can't last long. The government, on the other hand, has no predators and will last forever — maybe not until the hour the sun goes out (I read in a magazine that the sun is doomed), but until a quarter of."

"I have to pay off Verderamé, I have to pay off the IRS, I have to pay off the cops, the garbage men. . . . They're all corrupt. But what's worse is that I'm corrupt."

"You forgot the building department," Cornell reminded him, "and the Teamsters, the fire inspectors."

"We're not in compliance with the fire regulations?"

"Of course we are."

Harry turned to the accountant. "You're not a law firm, you're an accountant, right? If we didn't have to make all these payoffs, we'd be solvent, isn't that so?"

"For the moment, nicely."

"And as it is?"

"In reality? The only way you can last more than three months is to increase your revenues by fifty percent and keep your costs stable. Can you do that?"

"The buyer from Macy's came by the other day," Cornell announced. "He told me that they're making more things, even wallets, from artificial fibers. The big chemical companies are going to build on their work during the war. He said in twenty years cotton and leather will be like whale oil."

"That's not so," Harry insisted.

"Maybe not, but Macy's cut back on their order. We're going down a little bit at a time, no blow unbearable, just down, down, down, nothing fatal until the end."

"I don't understand," Harry said to both older men, hoping for assurance that he knew would not come. "We make a wonderful product. It's finely crafted of the best materials. We work hard. We don't let imperfections pass. We should be prosperous."

"People don't want it as much as they used to, and then there's Europe," Cornell said.

"All right, that's one thing, but why do all these people impinge upon us? They don't make anything themselves. Their whole energies are devoted to tricking and forcing money from other people."

"That's human nature," said Bernstein. "It was never different. Look, I have a house in the Catskills. My wife and I killed ourselves and spent a lot of money to make it nice — great view of the mountains, quiet. Last spring a neighboring farmer put sewage all over his fields. He didn't ask, he didn't care. The smell is impossible, you can't drink the water, you can't eat. Forget guests. I asked him about it, and he said he'd switched to this kind of fertilizer, and would use it every year. We're going to have to sell the house, almost give it away. Guess who's gonna buy it. And guess who'll mysteriously stop using the new kind of fertilizer."

"So what do we do when these people despoil us, just sit here and die?"

"That's what you do," said Ludwig Bernstein, whose work had overlooked the busy streets of Manhattan since the nineteenth century. "You play their game or you die, or sometimes you play their game and you die anyway."

"What about," Harry asked, "not playing their game, and not dying?"

"Don't get me wrong," said Bernstein. "I'd love to see that. I'd give anything to see it. But it doesn't happen. What you said are the words that young men speak before they go down. Some die literally. Most just die a little inside." And then he added, with a quivering smile, "Like me."

# 17

## THE GLARE OF JULY

In the heat of July, the ocean was cool, and after a day in the moist glare of Amagansett beaches it was possible to believe that this was all of life and ever would be. For the talent of the sea in monopolizing perception is not limited to its empty reaches, but spills over and inundates the shore. The waters of lakes, streams, or the ocean bring contentment enough to tranquilize even someone who has always moved at the speed of New York — that is, walking as if chased, talking like a tobacco auctioneer, eyes darting, heart racing, skeptical and alert even as he sleeps. But take him out to East Hampton in July and he becomes a peasant with neither clock nor calendar, whose temperament is calibrated at the speed New Yorkers know only when they're dead. There, on the beaches, away from what he thinks he treasures, he is truly happy for a week or a month, until he makes the mistake of going back, although it is true that the city itself can make someone happy if, like the ocean, it is seen with awe.

At three o'clock, Catherine and Harry came in from the beach. For seven hours they had walked, they had swum in the bracing, boxing surf, and now they were burnished with sun and throbbing with health. Whatever reservations the Hales may have had because they still did not know Harry, his background, or his prospects — this was only the second time they had met him — these were held in abeyance as the young couple stood before them, a gift of nature in its prime, their youth, strength, and love enlivening the house like the summer colors that drifted through the rooms in yellows and blues.

"Will you stay for dinner?" Evelyn asked. Billy was content to remain mute. "We haven't really had a chance to see you. Unfortunately, the Holmeses are coming, but because you went out last night and are leaving tomorrow we have no other time. They've been on the calendar since April, and since Rufus may die at any moment we really can't cancel."

"That's fine," said Catherine. "They're horrible, but maybe he'll fall asleep like last time, and we'll all eat in absolute silence, hoping that he hasn't slipped away. I suppose some people think that's fun."

"Rufus has some sort of mucous condition," Evelyn said to Harry. "His heart goes to sleep and so does he. He can't drive."

"He's a real live wire," Catherine said, "like Pancho Villa."

"And he has emphysema," Evelyn added, "which makes him hard to hear, and when he talks he does so very slowly, especially when he's smoking."

"He's a veritable amusement park," said Catherine, "and when he's awake his chief enjoyment is to stimulate a bitter argument among everyone around him."

"Your father has known him since they were boys. You don't turn your back on someone because they're in ill health. There are many things about him — one thing in particular — that we find difficult, but we just let them pass. Souls are complicated things. No one is perfect, Catherine. Your father sees him as he knew him when they were children."

"What thing in particular?" Catherine inquired.

Evelyn glanced at Billy, who said, "It has to do with your mother, but it's ancient history."

"Were you involved with him?" Catherine asked, alarmed.

Evelyn found this amusing. "No. Not Rufus. Really, Catherine, what do you think I am, a wildebeest?" Then, changing the subject, she said, "The lobsters were just delivered, but will you and Harry pick up the clams and the corn? Our corn isn't ready yet, but the corn from further inland is. Because it's hotter away from the ocean, the corn is sweeter."

"Doesn't Frank usually pick up the dinner things?"

"Yes, but his license was suspended last week — going too fast on the Montauk road again because he didn't want the lobsters to die. We tell him that they're hardier than that, but he grew up in an era before refrigeration."

"Strange to see a Mercedes without bullet holes," Harry said as he guided Billy's open car through the lanes that led into town in paths of beige macadam, "and stranger yet to be driving one. I've actually shot at these a few times. This one's in really good shape."

"It's an American citizen," Catherine said as they pulled up to the market, "and it sat out the war. With the Bund and everything so close it had to keep a low profile, so it stayed in the garage and out of the salt air."

"Are you selling it to me?"

As they kissed before they got out, a little boy saw them and it made his heart beat fast and his face turn the color of lipstick.

Extremely busy on a Saturday in July, the market was tense with class. Those who came in a particular kind of car and were dressed in a certain way were addicted as if to heroin to the need to assert their position. They did not so much want to be envied as they wanted their rank to be known. For many it was the reason for living, and for some there was nothing else. Harry knew the facts of his position here, which in some respects was unassailable. He had come from a house of great wealth, with a woman of extraordinary elegance, vitality, and beauty. Physically, they outranked everyone in the crowded store. People looked at them, but they themselves did not look back. His academic credentials and military record, although unknown to others, were known to him. And they had arrived in a car that some might criticize but that he could justly claim as the spoils of war.

And yet he felt kinship only with the grocer and the Puerto Rican assistants who stood behind the counters or were stocking shelves that investment bankers and their wives, or delegated servants, were stripping like locusts. He had neither money nor a profession. The business he had inherited was on the verge of bankruptcy. And in the eyes of the people who surrounded the Hales, Harry's father, his uncle, and his grandfather would be viewed, if they were lucky, as servants, assuming that one might have Jewish servants, which was unlikely.

It was an old and intractable problem with which he was never comfortable and which he suspected would not and could not be solved. But it was one of those problems that came and went in one's life, and could be forgotten as one lived.

"It makes my flesh crawl," Catherine said as they spoke about this on the drive home, "when I think of the lengths people go to, to keep themselves puffed up so they don't feel bad when in the presence of someone with more diamonds on her bracelets."

"It's the nature of man," Harry said, "and baboons."

"Snobbery is human nature?"

"Insecurity and competition. I guess snobbery is different—the profit and joy of invidious comparisons. It's cowardly. Like contempt, it's always directed downward. It comes from lack of experience and lack of generosity. You can think you're superior to others only if you're blind to their inner lives, and, by extension, to your own—assuming you have one. Though they're educated differently, the men with whom I served and the workers on my factory floor are just as intelligent and capable as my classmates at Harvard. And yet my classmates at Harvard, for all their fashionable egalitarianism, think they're truly better than everyone else, as some of your father's friends undoubtedly think that, because they're wealthy, they're better than everyone else."

"And my father?"

"You tell me. I'd imagine not."

"He's not like that, which might be viewed by some as quite remarkable."

"Not in view of you. You're above all this. But take, for example, a Wall Street magnate—call him Chase—who needs to have a painting authenticated. He calls in a professor—call him Salmon. Chase thinks of Salmon as an impoverished, blinkered, powerless, naive, super-specialized tool without the dynamism to meet moving challenges or weather a fight. To Chase, Salmon is a glorified clerk or butler. He needs him, but he may also need a truss.

"Salmon, on the other hand, thinks of Chase as a lucky, vulgar idiot who runs after money and can do nothing himself, who must rely totally on others who can actually do things while he merely directs. People like Salmon are necessary to explain the world to people like Chase, and making money is for corrupt simpletons. Salmon thinks it's so easy he won't even try. It's too far below him.

"They deny the virtues, necessities, and realities of the other, and thus they deny the world and blind themselves to it," Harry said. "Sorry. I tend to speak in aphorisms when I'm driving a fancy car."

"Would you prefer to drive a less fancy car?"

"In a way. It wouldn't make me think, I'm driving a fancy car, I'm driving a fancy car. It's like that with hotels. I don't like cheap ones, but in the super-luxurious ones your attention is commanded far too much by the details.

"I'd rather be working in the kitchen of an expensive restaurant, or as a waiter, than to sit there and be served porcupine gelées. Really. Luxury not only makes me uncomfortable, it frightens me."

"It frightens you?" Catherine asked. She had taken such things for granted since birth, had never wanted them in either sense of the word, and preferred—when she was able to tell the difference between the rough and the smooth, which her background made sometimes a difficult task—to do without them. But they had never frightened her. "How can you be frightened by a watercress sandwich at the Brook Club?"

"I'm frightened, for example, to be entombed in stiff, expensive clothes that make it impossible to run, jump, climb, fight, or swim, or engage with half of the things in the universe. I don't want to be a fancy person, because fancy means you can't lie on the ground to look beneath something, or to rest: there is no ground anywhere near anyway; you've forgotten the ground. You have to sit relatively still because the presumption is that it's better to let other people do things for you. Your muscles get croquet-weak, your nerves and reflexes, all bottled up, get lazy and unpracticed. You don't strain or sweat, or ever work with your hands, so you don't get to stretch beyond yourself. And then you have no reserve capacity. You're in a semi-exquisite paralysis, far too aware of how other people regard you, separated from nature, from human nature, challenge, storm, sun, rain, life. I'd really rather be in the kitchen, or a mounted policeman in the park, or coiling rope on a tugboat speeding through Hell Gate."

"The upper class pays a price," she said, "of vertiginous paralysis. But there's a kind of thrill to it. It's dangerous."

Harry's expression showed that he found this strange. "That thrill is totally alien to me. Were we immortal, I might try it. But time is limited and I don't want to let go of the texture and feel of things. I don't want to watch as other people serve me. The war pounded into me that you have to be as alert and independent as you can be, or you die one kind of death or another."

"Why don't you come along with me sometime?" she asked. "Are you sure that the habits of a thousand years make certain things impossible for you? That it's not just a question of blind loyalty?"

"Even if I marry up," he said, turning to her rather dangerously given that he was driving, "I don't want to live in that kind of breathless, delicate world."

"Hold on, Harry," she insisted. "Tell me what's dead about running across a gleaming sea on a sailing yacht that you'll race to Bermuda at risk of your life, conscious every second of a change in the wind, a jibing boom, or a rising storm? We do that kind of thing, too."

"That," Harry admitted, "I could get used to."

"You see, we can make deals. It doesn't have to go just one way. I'll give up the watercress sandwiches — I won't give up watercress entirely — if you'll take the yacht. We'll split our own wood and tend the fire if you'll accept complete financial security. I'll shoot with you, if you don't mind a Holland and Holland. I understand. Real life must be classless. Friction, motion, risk. I know. I want that, I always have. The Hales, actually, are as tough as cypress or ebony."

"What about hickory?"

"What about it?"

"Are you as tough as it?"

He loved how this animated her. "Tougher," she said, like a five-year-old, but it was true.

Billy spent an hour or two preparing for the arrival of his oldest friend by enlisting the aid of gin and tonic. In the midst of the greatest comfort and security — on a hundred safe acres by the sea, in a house that glowed like a jewel, in a room filled with paintings, and on a chair that with a football field's worth of satin damask banished every touch of arthritis — he sipped from a crystal glass for the purpose of freeing his mind from his body, something he had done from an early age and that he no longer could do without.

"Why do you drink so little?" he asked Harry in a tone both benevolent and accusatory. "You haven't even had half that. Are you planning something?"

"Even a little alcohol can make me ill, Billy."

"A hillbilly? What?"

"*Ill*, Billy." He thought Billy might take him for a Cockney. "Anything more than half a glass, sometimes just a sip."

"That's worse than being allergic to water."

"My father was the same way. I live dangerously if I have a glass of wine. In a social situation, just the obligatory little bit can make me look as if I've drunk myself under the table. Unfortunately, I like Scotch. I like the smoky taste. Sometimes I have some, but then I pay for it."

"It must be unbearable. How do you unwind?"

Harry looked down at the floor.

Billy didn't comprehend, and said, "Well?"

Then Harry said, "Exercise."

"Don't tell that to Rufus, who thinks exercise is the leading cause of death. He'll have another heart attack. I remember him when he was so skinny the doctor told him to drink cabinets — that's what they call milkshakes in Rhode Island, where he's from. We were at Groton together. He added rum and drank a lot of them."

"What else does he do?"

"Bank notes."

"Bank notes?"

"He prints money for chickenshit countries all over the world that can't even stand up a press. Do you realize the potential of that? He does. Put it this way: sometimes it's necessary, for technical reasons, to keep samples. He inherited the business from his father in the days when things were loosey-goosey. When we were kids, we found an unusual room in his barn. It was behind heavy wooden doors that were padlocked, but we were small enough to squeeze through the hay chute. Instead of hay, that room was filled with money. Wonderful, colorful, wrapped in packets. We rolled and swam in them and couldn't get to the bottom. The pile was at least eight feet high and it lapped up against the walls. There must have been a hundred million dollars in that barn. I mean, wouldn't you?"

"I might."

"Depending on how much he put aside, the effect would be to elevate prices a bit in Bolivia or Mongolia. If their governments had an inflationary monetary policy, which they usually did, he was just helping them along. It was sweet, but I wouldn't mention it. And no one can prove it."

"He prints money."

"He does. Everyone's dream, and it's legal."

"How long can that last?"

"Forever, Harry, in one form or another."

A car moved slowly up the driveway, through sea air that was salty and flashing with fireflies. When it stopped, nothing happened. It was as if it had driven there by itself, turned off its lights, and gone to sleep. Head cocked, Billy said, "I can guarantee you that they're not necking. Rufus has yet to wake up. Give it a couple of minutes." He listened. The waves sounded close in the silence. And then a car door opened and closed. "That's Bridget, getting out." There was a faint crunch. "She's walking around the car. The other door." A minute later, they heard people coming up the steps. Evelyn met them. Bridget and Rufus fell through the front hall into the living room. She guided Rufus to a chair, and he collapsed into it with a single wheeze.

He wasn't that big, but he was shaped like a buoy, and his threadbare gray hair was arranged in lines across the splotched but glossy top of his head. With eyes that were jaundiced and red, he looked at Harry, and then turned to Billy. "Who the hell is that? Is that Victor's replacement?"

Rudely ignoring Harry, Rufus started to talk to Billy in short, incomprehensible exchanges that, almost a code, were ungrammatical and heavily laden with names, terms, and grunts. But just as this was heating up, Catherine appeared on the porch and beckoned to Harry. A second later the screen door banged shut, and they were walking through the garden.

In a gray silk skirt and a white, pleated blouse with closed collar, she glowed in the incidental light from the house, and as they moved he heard the skirt rustling about her legs. Perhaps because so many theater people came out to East Hampton — the stars and producers to almost stately houses, the rank and file to little cottages in Springs and shared lodgings in the village — and because, at parties and other gatherings where there was a piano, impromptu performances easily erupted, with the beat of the waves in counterpoint, and singing more poignant than anyone might expect, Broadway was so near that if you listened you could hear the creaking of the boards, and if you looked you could see as if by stage light.

Like the trained dancer she was, Catherine walked with a controlled grace that emanated from her whole body. When she turned and spoke, only to say when dinner would be ready, he fed on every vibration of her voice. Putting his left hand against her back, he placed his right hand flat against the top of her chest. "Speak," he said.

"Speak?"

He unbuttoned two pearl buttons hidden among the pleats, and gently rested his palm against her bare skin. "What are you doing?" she asked, not displeased.

"I fell in love with your voice the first time you spoke to me, with the very vibrations in your chest as you speak. When you say a one-syllable word I hear five or six variations in it that are so beautiful each makes me fall in love with you more. There's nothing you can do that drives me deeper than that."

The wind made the fruit trees sway and strain. In the dark the house was lit like a marvelous set. "In every word I speak?"

"Or sing."

"I don't know what to say," she said. "I've never been adored."

He felt the words as they arose within her, and then he withdrew his hand and stepped back to look at her in the dark, to be away from her for a moment so he could return. When they came together they kissed, revolving on the lawn, one step at a time. He was in love with every part of her body, every stray hair, every plane or curve as much as he loved each individual part of every word she spoke or sang, and he was sorry for the years he had spent in the grip of lesser enthusiasms. Dropping to his knees, he lifted her skirt and pulled her to him. She tilted her head back as far as it could go and closed her eyes, for never had she been so adored and never had anything been more loving or pure.

After Evelyn called them for dinner, Catherine came in, scarlet and red and wholly unconcerned. Everyone else had already been seated, with Rufus breathing like a cross between a Komodo dragon and a steam engine on the Holyhead–London run; Evelyn fussing with this and that and especially the little bell that signaled for the first course; and Billy trying to diagnose the soft, out-of-focus gaze in his daughter's eyes, and noticing that she and Harry, as if they were fifteen, were holding hands beneath the table. He had never seen her touch Victor, much less insist that the touch not end.

Bridget had learned long before that she did not have to double her conversation to make up for Rufus's lost consciousness, but commenced nonetheless, and despite his unusual animation (he was still awake), with a question to Catherine. What was she doing now? Hadn't she been graduated from Bryn Mawr a year ago, or was Bridget mistaken?

"I'm in a play," Catherine said.

"Summer stock?"

"No, Broadway. At least that's where we rehearse and where we're booked to open. We're trying out in Boston in September."

"How wonderful," said Bridget, "for one so young."

Catherine smiled her gracious smile, and Rufus, like a geyser, as if he were a machine into which someone had put a nickel, as if he were speaking to the gods of the air but not to the people in the room, said, "Lots of Jews in the theater."

Harry saw Billy and Evelyn wince. Then he focused again on Catherine, who took a spoonful of consommé, returned the spoon flaccidly to the bowl, and said, "Lots of Jews."

"And in the movies, too."

"Lots of Jews in the movies," she said.

"You're not going to make it a career, are you?" Rufus asked.

"The theater?"

"Yes."

"I already have."

"You don't want to spend your life in that kind of society. Even Gilbert and Sullivan were Jews." To the pained laughter that this provoked, Rufus answered, "They were! You see, the theater is saturated with them. You don't want to pick up their habits. You don't want to accustom yourself to that kind of degeneracy."

"Why don't you just leave off, Rufus," Billy said.

"Well, it's not your table, Billy, it's Evelyn's table. What says the hostess?"

With no hostility but rather a complex gravity that Catherine had never seen in her and that Harry could not interpret, Evelyn said, "Rufus, you may say whatever you wish."

"I told you," said Rufus, as triumphantly as a child who has won five hundred baseball cards.

"What habits?" Catherine asked. "What degeneracy?"

"Oh," Rufus said. "I can see that you're a real liberal." (The Hales had been Republicans since before the Civil War.) "I don't want to generalize, but as a class the Jews are associated with particular behaviors."

"Such as?"

"Such as . . . reading and writing all the time, excessive cleanliness, hoarding, grasping, pushing, stealing, bullying. Stealing not openly, mind you, but with trickery, always with trickery. Highly distasteful."

"You mean," Catherine said, for she had heard the story of the barn filled with bank notes since she was four, "trickery like extending the press runs for pesetas and cruzeiros?"

Rufus was unaffected by this, or at least he did not respond to it except to pop like a firecracker, and when he popped he said, "Moneylenders, they keep to themselves, and they're dirty. Don't you know? You can tell by looking at them. Their faces aren't clean. Haven't you ever been on the Lower East Side? They flooded into this country and ruined it. It will never be the same again, and because you don't know what it was like before, you can't know exactly what I mean."

Perhaps from a desire to defuse the situation, or simply to put an end to this kind of talk, Catherine said, "Well, don't worry, Rufus. I won't marry one."

# 18

## THE WHOLE WORLD

VERY OFTEN AT the end of summer and sometimes briefly in July, the air in New York, which for weeks has been dulled by haze and mist, suddenly clarifies and cools into a shock of well defined lines and vivid color. Wind from Canada streams down through the blue-green corridors of the Hudson Highlands to snap flags, jingle halyards and hardware against their staffs, and push the harbor waves into whitecaps. While spring can at times last only a day, the heat and haze of summer come as gradually as cataracts, until one morning when the wind turns clear you realize you've been blind. Then the view is sharp all the way out to Staten Island, its battlements suspended above water as if on clouds, and from high buildings it is possible to see as far as the north country.

On a day when the July haze was briefly clarified, Harry and Catherine, in her car with the top down and the sun flashing warmly against the chrome, crossed the Hudson on the George Washington Bridge. As the wind gusted, she held down her ribboned straw hat, slightly turned her head, looked to the north over the great expanse of river, and waited for the breeze to subside.

"They were the whole world to me," Harry continued as they drove so high above the pale blue Hudson that it was as if he were piloting a plane. "The whole world." He was speaking of his mother and father.

"It was that way for me, too," she said, regarding her own parents. "I love them so much, even though something keeps me from expressing it, and even though I'm not much like them anymore . . . yet."

"You know the photograph to the left above the fireplace?" he asked. She did. She had once studied it when he was not in the room, and had wanted to take the child in it into her arms. "That was the three of us when I was about four. I had no idea, no conscious idea anyway, that it would be only temporary. Time seemed not to pass. But, of course, they knew. You can see it in their eyes."

"They seemed happy," Catherine said, "in the way a couple with a small child should be happy."

"It was before my mother got sick. I'm not sure we were happy, but we were where we were supposed to be, and not one of us wanted anything else."

"That's what I would call happy."

He elevated his left arm straight in the air to signal a right turn. "Yes, even if you suffer through the days. Difficulties don't preclude happiness. You really come to understand this only when those you love have died. Catherine, if we marry, you should know some things about me beforehand."

"I know enough already, unless you rob banks."

"I don't, but you should know more."

"Like what?"

"Three things in my life I'll never get over, that won't heal, that I don't forget. I keep on going back, even if it makes no sense and brings me nothing. I would rather be destroyed for the sake of these things than abandon them and prosper: you, the war, and my parents. I love you. The war will always haunt and puzzle me despite our having won it. And I lost my parents. It all mixes together, and each of these things has a deep hold on the other."

"But you have to live," she said.

"I know. I try not to shrink from much."

"That's for sure. You're the first person in the history of my family, that I know of, not to think it inappropriate for two people to lie on the same chaise."

"No one saw," Harry assured her. "They were still on the beach."

"Did you see that?" Billy had asked Evelyn as they went in to change for dinner. "They think they're invisible."

"So did we."

"Not like that."

She looked at him as if to differ.

"No, I wouldn't have done anything like that in front of your parents."

"But you did, exactly that."

"I did?"

"The bathing costumes weren't as brief...."

"Brief? She's practically naked."

"It was the same thing. We didn't know what we were doing either. They're really in love. What could be better than two people equally in love and without limit? She didn't love Victor, and Victor didn't love her. Now she's been saved from that."

"I suppose so, but at least Victor's prospects are assured. We don't know about Harry's."

"Don't count him out. You wear his belts, carry his wallet, and put your papers in his briefcases. And you're not the only one."

"That's small stuff, Evelyn."

"Our families, Billy, started with nets and fish hooks, with little sacks of seed, and reused nails: small stuff. It's good enough, and he has his whole life ahead of him. He's a brave man. He's devoted to her. They're the most handsome couple. And she's happy, Billy."

"How long will it last?"

Evelyn thought for a moment. She was not in public, and not playing a role. She did not have to entertain with malapropisms or verbal mysteries. Most people weigh carefully what they say in the open and speak with less consideration in private. She did more or less the opposite. "I hope it lasts for the rest of their lives," she said, "but, as we know, even when the silver wears away and you're left with copper, if you attend to it every day it has a gleam all its own."

Harry and Catherine rolled through the streets of Englewood as if in the excitement of fall. Though it was still weeks from the heat-kill of August and not a leaf was down, it seemed like the end of summer. Descending the ridge from the Palisades, they drove toward the first of several valleys and rivers to cross, the final one being the Saddle River, on the banks of which, near Lodi, Harry's family was buried in the cemetery to which his aunt in Staten Island found it difficult to travel.

Because the start of the day had seen most of their inhabitants drain east toward the cliffs of Manhattan backlit by the rising sun, the towns were strangely empty, the landscape in its way more deserted and tranquil than that of New Hampshire or Oklahoma. Leached out of their hills and dales and from Victorian houses with screen doors banging shut to signal silence until evening, legions of office workers magnetized to heat and light, crossed on ferries, and emerged from dark and choking tunnels into a city that made them as jumpy as crickets.

But in New Jersey it was quiet now. The little rivers moved languidly. At the top of a second ridge, Harry saw in the silver of his rearview mirror the upper halves of skyscrapers ranged like a row of tombstones. Closer, but in perspective equidistant, were the palisades of gravestones ahead, though the road did not lead straight to them but rather through a shaded valley where the river wound unpredictably. Once across, they would be there. They started down, and soon were on a level stretch.

Like the roof of a cathedral, trees arched over a long, deserted road so little traveled that grass grew in the cracks between the pebbled slabs. The river was somewhere beyond a line of evergreens to their left. They could hear the water and smell it and feel currents of cool humidity in the air. Not far away, pine branches were burning, and the fragrance of the smoke covered the road, sometimes turning the air white before the sky burst into blue.

"Why did you stop?" she asked.

"When I don't have a car, I walk this road, so I'm used to taking it slowly. Not once have I ever met anyone on it."

"It reminds me of the Via Appia," she told him, "where you can go for miles, and there's no one, and all you hear are cicadas in the dry heat."

They fell naturally into an embrace, their heads touching the way horses nuzzle, all contact on the side. He looked down the back of her dress. Her taut shoulders were smooth and smelled fresh. The arch of her back was firm and tan, with the tiniest and most delicate of white hairs, invisible but for an irresistible silvery-white glaze. Although neither he nor she had intended to kiss in this place and at this moment, they kissed for a long time, stopping for less than a second to turn off the car. They might have made love had they not understood that someone could happen upon them, though all they could see were ribbons of white smoke drifting among the trees.

He had never entered the cemetery in an open car. There were willows by the river, and as the car passed through the gates, Catherine, looking down a long prospect running south, missed the sign with the cemetery's name. "This is where your parents are buried," she said. He hadn't told her that he was taking her there.

"I hope you don't mind."

"I don't mind. As we grow older I'll become more like my mother and you'll become more like your father. I would have liked to have met him, and your mother."

He threaded the car around tight circles and turned sharply down narrow alleys between the tombs until he stopped in front of a plot near the cemetery's western edge. Through a line of arborvitae that muffled the sound, they could hear the road that formed the closest boundary. Before she opened her door, she saw everywhere the Hebrew lettering that she had not seen on the way in. Her lips parted slightly and her eyes narrowed as she discovered this. "Oh," she said quietly, almost in a whisper, "oh."

He watched her as she moved toward the Copeland plot, which was marked by a huge cut stone bigger than the headboard of a bed, and he concentrated painfully upon her in case this would be the last time he would see her. It had happened twice before, with others, in the same way that he now feared, although they had been nothing like Catherine. How beautiful she was as she walked closer to the graves. What elemental mechanism was at play to give him such pleasure, even here and at this moment, merely at the sight of Catherine in a straw hat. The effect on her coloring, the enclosure of her face in a halo of shadowed, sun-glowing gold, and the scarlet ribbon with unpredictable twitches in the wind breaking the perfection of the circle, were attractions that arose in ancient reflexes of the body and spirit, part of the continuous play of small and vivid things that are the true action of the world.

The individual headstones were in English and Hebrew. She knelt at his mother's grave, and said, "When you were ten...."

Standing behind her and to her left, he nodded, knowing that she knew he had done so, though she couldn't see him. She turned to read his father's stone and then lifted her hand and traced the Hebrew that paralleled the English on his mother's gravestone. "What does it say?" she asked.

"Esther, a daughter of Israel."

After a long moment, Catherine, still kneeling, twisted her body and turned to Harry. She put her right hand on the ground to steady herself, her expression expectant but disciplined, giving nothing away. It was as if she were waiting for something from him even though now everything that mattered had to come from her. Never had he seen so neutral an expression. She looked tranquil, yet he thought that much was going on within her, that she was weighing past and future. And indeed she put everything in the balance, not just her life but the lives of those who had come before her and those who would come after, the weight of principle, belief, and love. And how marvelous it was, and an indication of her quality, that she came to judgment in utter stillness and without the slightest hint of difficulty. She said nothing for a long time, and then she smiled so softly, so subtly, that it was barely perceptible. And in this barely perceptible smile was a courageous declaration as wide as the whole world.

# 19

## SPECTACLES

OTHER THAN CATHERINE, the only person in the room who, everyone knew, was not Jewish, was a lyricist from Nebraska, a young man with a red face and military haircut, who tried desperately to fit in to the society of blindingly demonstrative Jewish theater people, all of whom either wore spectacles or, when they didn't, bumped into furniture, and some of whom habitually called one another *dahling*. Not a single one of them failed to keep a detailed journal of his own thoughts and speculations, in the unexamined yet invincible belief that future historians of the theater would painstakingly disentangle their loaf-like stacks of pages by the thousands, in beer, gin, or vodka handwriting, the fashions in liquor lasting each less than a decade and thus giving to their lives an almost geological stratification.

The cast had recently discovered, though no one seemed to know how, that Catherine Sedley was in fact Catherine Hale. Not only was she a Hale, but *the* Hale, in that she was the only child of William Hale. It was no crime, and stage names were more common than locusts in the Bible, but now that they knew she didn't need her part as they needed theirs, and that she came from such great wealth as to be able to finance hundreds of plays like the one they were struggling to keep alive, they did not know quite what to think of her. She became at once both desirable and detestable. She threw everything off balance, and suddenly they tried to be careful when speaking to her, although, thanks to her natural kindness and wit, they would soon forget what they had intended.

Sidney, the director, had invited Catherine to dinner at his Bank

Street apartment before the revelation of who she really was. When he found out, assuming that a society girl would have a thinner version of a Victor, some sort of aging St. Paul's boy, to escort her, he had called her up and said as offhandedly as he could, given that he was himself in love with her, "and bring your beau." This was poker. He wanted her to show up beau-less and thus, confessing the emptiness of an heiress, cleave to him, drink his wine, and perhaps stay the night. He thought that even were she to have brought a beau of her class — he pictured a tweed-covered bow of the kind that shoots arrows — Sidney would make quick work of him, because the person he imagined as Catherine's escort would be so privileged as to be infinitely dull. Yes, he would be tall, strong, and blond, with a chiseled face flat of plane, because people like that, of a certain heredity and culture, played a lot of violent and invigorating sports, ate like canaries, and drank like goldfish. But he wouldn't have a chance in a garret where he couldn't fully stand, surrounded by lightning-fast, mercurial Jews who for two thousand years had been banned from sun and sport and exiled within the book, where in its confines and shadows they could swing and swoop with the speed and agility of orangutans. Not a chance had this tweedy bow of St. Paul's against Sidney Goldfarb, orangutan of the theater, a man who could talk an octopus into a straitjacket.

But when he had buzzed Catherine in and she came up to the landing he was so overcome by her presence that he completely lost his wit. And when he saw the beau she had brought, he despaired, for she had betrayed her obligation to bring someone watery and weak. The man standing behind her shyly, and appropriately for a guest who knew no one, was immediately if not intentionally dominant. Though he wanted only to be inconspicuous, power issued from him unstoppably. The instant he was perceived by the others, their conversation dropped by decibels and its velocity slowed to a creep.

He was six feet tall and as solid as rock, with the build of an army Ranger lost in training for many months with no comforts and an increasingly difficult daily regimen. His physical power alone would have been impressive, but it was only a part of his presence. He was dark and angular, and he could look severe, although his kindness passed readily through the strength of his features. More to the point, he was one of those people from whose eyes it was possible to see that he might be thinking ten things as you were thinking one, and that his intellectual labor consisted not in generating an answer, something to say, a *bon mot,* but in choosing the best and most appropriate from an ever-proliferating stock of striking observations and ideas that came effortlessly to the fore.

And yet he was shy, and wanted to listen rather than speak, which among theater people is a trait so rare as to astound. Catherine had had to maneuver him to the gathering by claiming that Sidney's apartment was so small no more than a few people could be accommodated for dinner. In fact, there were eight. It made him very nervous, but she stayed close, which made anything possible — she, who governed the nature of things, but was too modest to know it.

Upon sensing that Harry was not only a soldier returned from the real war — it was undeniably apparent — but also a Jew, Sidney moved to ally himself with the lyricist. In Sidney's calculation, were the Nebraskan to become his ally, which the Nebraskan would be glad to do, as he was otherwise bamboozled by Jews, Catherine might gravitate to Sidney and her coreligionist. And, undoubtedly, Catherine's beau, a sort of Achilles, would have a soft spot that Sidney, who spent his days observing from the dark before darting to intervene, could readily recognize.

Sidney's hopes were dashed once again, even if not absolutely, after Catherine introduced Harry, and Sidney was forced to announce, to murmurs that though unintelligible sounded vaguely Japanese, that Harry Copeland, whose name Sidney said as if it were Attila the Hun, was Catherine's fiancé. The Hales themselves had not yet been formally apprised of this, though clearly they knew, if only through the agency of hardly perceptible smiles.

There is not much air on Bank Street because of its narrow gauge and the way it winds. The houses with their black roofs and brick fronts absorb the heat of blast-furnace days and echo it onto every living thing in radiative agony until midnight or beyond. All the windows in Sidney's apartment were open and a tiny fan in the tiny bedroom moved the air only a little from the garden side to the street. Because they were on the top floor and under the roof, it was as hot as hell, but from the tiny living room with walls covered by abstracts and Buddhist line drawings a pair of French doors opened onto a deck, slightly bigger than a lifeboat, that looked over the ill-tended gardens in the back courtyard. "Walk gently," Sidney said to every guest, "a violinist lives below."

At the dinner table on the terrace, sitting with drinks and cigarettes, talking now with less animation but nonetheless in party voices that while saying one thing really said another, were Andrea, a Barnard senior and the script girl for the play, who was pretty, precocious, and well read, if hesitant to contradict the older people even though she could run rings around them; Rolvag, the lyricist, who made fun of Nebraska, where he was born and where his mother and father still lived, and who would regret that he did and, each time that he did, feel sorrow and shame, and yet persist, sadly; a woman whose name sounded something like *Surrealya,* but who looked like her name should have been *Cat Woman from the Moon,* and who had a perpetually injured, calculating, semi-malicious expression — no one knew what she did except that she had once been married to a lawyer who collected stamps and she was an intellectual: her face said, *I am a lesser being, I avert my eyes, I am aware of your superiority, and I am now moving into a deadly ambush that you cannot possibly escape.* And then there was Tommy, a playwright deeply influenced by the Weimar avant-garde, although he did not know a word of German; and AT, his mate, a fashion designer of great talent and instability, who depended upon Tommy's gentleness and patience to keep him sane. They were often introduced as *AT&T.*

Wary of embarrassment, wanting to shine, lonely, fiercely competitive, savagely ambitious, and as tense as pulled crossbows, they were the typical guests at a New York dinner party, suffering like soldiers in the trenches of the First World War, and, like them, forced by close combat to be fully alive to what was around them — the greatest gift that New York gives.

And yet the air was languid and lyrical; the street noises, starting out sharp, muffled; the sounds of bus herds on the avenues, their diesel engines rasping like ten thousand sore throats, distant. Blue was becoming black, the fat candles in glass globes were brightening, and an occasional breeze would materialize for a moment or two, from where no one knew, as if someone had opened and closed an icebox.

Fragrant smoke arose from ranks of skewered lamb cooking slowly over fading coals. Although Harry had had none of the abundant chilled white wine, and Catherine only a little, it occurred to them both, though neither knew that the other had had the same thought, that the hours of conversation to follow would be unnecessary. The settling darkness, the lifting heat, the scent of the few flowers that had lasted into the height of summer in the ragged garden below, the sounds of the city dampened by distance, the dirty pink sky through which only a planet could shine, the waving white smoke, and the wine that momentarily removed the weight of the world but deepened emotion and regret, begged for silence. But this was New York. Talk was inevitable, insuppressible, and not without its pleasures.

Everyone knew more or less who everyone else was, which was the cause of numerous upwellings, some obvious and some not. AT was alert and full of hope that Catherine would commission him to design at least a dress or a suit for her, if not a whole wardrobe. And then there were her mother and her mother's friends, so AT purred for Catherine like a cat that thinks it's an electric motor. This inexplicably necessitated his savage clawing of Andrea the script girl, who was so stunned that she let Cat Woman from the Moon defend her in facing off with AT by means of a structured and panic-inducing flirtation with Tommy, who had once been straight.

Rolvag had focused on Andrea, but then could not take his eyes off Catherine, though this disconcerted Sidney, who had hoped Rolvag would act more or less like a eunuch. Except for defending Andrea,

Cat Woman from the Moon was at sea, with no one but AT to slay ... and so on. The net of things said and unsaid was woven as if in a square dance, but a lot tighter, with all the dancers inevitably colliding.

Harry was a surprise to everyone, unknown except by what they could immediately sense and see. Though at first he was silent, they were going far too slowly for him. He wanted to be running, walking in the sun, propelling himself through the pool, or even fighting — anything but to be confined to a chair and talking obliquely. He had too much energy, too many cares, and was too fit and too fast just to sit, unless it were pure rest. But he was soon relieved when a match began that pitted him against Cat Woman from the Moon, who took the first cloaked step.

Harry's initial utterance after "Hello" was to respond to young Andrea's self-congratulatory pronouncement, stimulated by wine, that she would only live in "an arts neighborhood," surrounded by "people in the arts: artists."

Harry could not resist. "I would rather live," he said, "in a tarantula box, surrounded by arachnids in a box: tarantulas."

At first, almost joining in, they thought he was mocking people who were not they, but then they realized that he was mocking the people who they were. Cat Woman from the Moon asked poisonously, "And why is that?"

"Because tarantulas are less vicious, more intelligent, less conformist, more interesting, and not as hairy."

"You're being ironic, aren't you?" Rolvag asked. He was from Nebraska.

"No," said Harry, "I'm not, and I wouldn't be. Anyway, irony is only a term for a cowardly mocking of someone else's true conviction. If I'm going to mock, I'll be direct."

Of course, Harry was now the center of attention. "You were in the service, weren't you?" Sidney asked, rhetorically and almost compassionately. People seemed to know. It was disconcerting, and made Harry think that perhaps something really was wrong with him. "For a long time, yes? It's hard to adjust, isn't it?"

"Not that hard. In fact, it's rather easy to adjust to the idea of not getting killed, of sleeping in a bed, having an ice cream soda, walking in the park without a rifle and a forty-pound pack. Not so hard. Soldiers when they come back are not really crazy, they just seem so."

In having returned from the war and combat, he was hardly unique. But he was by now interesting in the pure sense and as a target. They ached to probe further.

"Are you in the theater?" Cat Woman from the Moon asked, despite their lack of recognition, and other signs that he was not.

He answered her with a short, negative shake of the head, and almost a smile.

"What, then?"

"What price glory?" he answered. He didn't like it when people asked him what he did. He didn't like his dinner companions, and even before the war he often met concealed hostility bluntly rather than, as Evelyn had once put it, "dueling around the bush."

Cat Woman from the Moon also could be direct. "Terrific. You know the name of a play. But I asked if you were in the theater."

"And I said no."

"And then I asked what you do."

"In what circumstance?"

"Probably to make a living," Sidney said. "That's what the expression means in America, generally." He thought he had Harry here, and he almost did.

"You mean other than marrying heiresses?" Harry asked, tacking right into the gale.

"Is there anything, these days," Cat Woman from the Moon asked, "other than marrying heiresses? Which explains why I'm no longer married and probably never will be?"

"There is," said Harry. "Leather goods."

"Ah, leather goods!" Cat Woman from the Moon said with equal and immense volumes of surprise, disbelief, faux puzzlement, and contempt.

"Copeland Leather," said Andrea, the script girl. "I can't afford it."

But now they had him. "Did you inherit it?" AT asked.

"I did."

"And that's all?"

"What do you mean?"

"You run Copeland Leather, and that's it?"

"I've just started running it. I had no intention of doing so, but my father was inconsiderate enough to die. So, for the moment, I have no choice."

"What did you do before?"

"I was involved in something called the Second World War. Before that, I was mostly a student."

"So you have no profession," Tommy said, astonished that a man Harry's age could be so unformed.

"I have no profession other than manufacturing and selling leather goods, which is far more difficult than I imagined."

"But, still," Cat Woman from the Moon said, "what is it?"

"What is what?"

"What do you leave behind?"

"Leather goods," Harry answered.

"Are you people out of your minds?" Catherine asked. "We just walked in the door, and now he's on trial for his life."

"Why not?" the lyricist asked. "We all are, all the time. We may hope not to be. We may pretend not to be. But we are. When I write the lyrics of a song, and people don't like them, that hastens my death...."

"No it doesn't," AT interrupted, "but it should." AT didn't like either Rolvag or his lyrics, both being, to him, inaccessibly Norwegian, though in fact AT himself was Norwegian, or at least of Norwegian extraction.

"The same with me," Tommy added. "I don't escape the critics. Why should he? And you, Sidney, if your play's a flop... and Catherine, if they don't like your singing...."

"You don't like my briefcases?" Harry asked, with evident enjoyment.

"It's not that," Sidney told him patronizingly. "What they're saying is that whether one likes it or not, what one does with one's life can be judged, and there are hierarchies of value."

"Oh," said Harry, "I hadn't thought of that."

Catherine began to regret that she had convinced him to come, and to believe that when he said he didn't like social gatherings he really meant it. Still, what they were doing was unfair, especially because it had a great deal of truth to it. So she abruptly chimed in.

"Do you know the line," she asked, "'What had Rome after its many centuries better than cicadas singing on a golden afternoon'? Or something like that. The glories that people seek are dross. Real glory, in unlimited quantity, is simple and free. You can't show it off, because it isn't yours. When you come into a room and people say, because you want them to say and you work all day to have them say, 'Oh, it's so-and-so. She does . . . whatever,' you've done nothing but indict yourself. And I mean you," she said to everybody.

"Wow," said AT. "It's like the Battle of the Bulge."

With Catherine having covered his flank, Harry pressed on against the main body. "I don't think a life can be judged by what one leaves behind," he said.

"What about Mozart?" Andrea asked.

"Who here is Mozart?" Harry asked back. "I'd yield to him, but not to you. For the rest of us, what's important is conduct, how we carry ourselves given the circumstances we face. There are people, for example, who spend their lives working until death to try to get a small fraction of what is guaranteed to someone like Catherine entirely without effort. Does that make them better than her? Worse? Tell me that I'm wrong to look first to what one makes of one's life in the absence of choice: if you're crippled so that you can't walk or speak, or you're impoverished, caught up in war, or, like Catherine, born rich. All these, including the last, are burdens."

"About that last," Sidney interrupted, "can you tell me where the burden is in being born to great wealth, and where I might pick it up?"

Catherine jumped in before Harry could begin to speak. Unlike most heiresses, who are bred to be apologetic, Catherine in defense of herself was concise, stern, and combative. Her brows tightened and she leaned toward Sidney as if ready to strike him. "Being the object of envy is a burden, Sidney. Being separated from other people and treated more roughly or more tenderly than one deserves is a burden, Sidney. And the biggest burden, Sidney, is that everything you earn you have to earn twice or three times over, because no one thinks you have to earn anything." Then she came slightly unhinged, speaking passionately and fast, and it was delightful to watch. "Because people look at you like you're a goddamned ostrich in the goddamned zoo, that's why. How'd you like that, Sidney, starting in infancy and following you for the rest of your life? People assume too much about you, always. They don't see you, they don't hear you. They put someone in your place, someone who doesn't exist, and they take that person in your stead. So in the end what you face is a continual pressure that tells you more or less that you don't exist. To hell with that, Sidney. And to hell with you if you think it's easy to be me."

Silence. She reverted almost to her polite self. "Harry, did I interrupt?"

"Sort of," Harry said. "But, as I think I was saying, I look to conduct also when there *is* a choice: what it is that you do when you have the power to decide. And then I look to the balance. You must help others in distress. If you're not compelled to that, you're more a casualty than those whom you pass over, although to make a self-announcing career of it is sin. To begin with, if it's all you do and you live no life beyond it, you're guilty of murdering your self.

"As long as I retain the capacity to act independently of my own interest I need not be ashamed, either of the things I make or the limitations I face. But leather goods are hardly my whole life. If you take as your whole lives the plays you write or direct, the lyrics you provide, the dresses you design, or the articles you publish, then you're the vulgarians you like to think businessmen are. You, then, are the acquisitive, the blind, unconscious, lesser men and women, and not the better, ethereal selves you take yourselves to be."

"How can you say that," young Andrea asked, the purist among them, "in a city that's red hot with movement and competition, where getting and spending is — are? — everything?"

"It isn't what you say," Harry answered, with Andrea awaiting his further explanation, "if you draw back in distance or in time. Then the moment stills, the struggle ceases, and the qualities of which I speak rise: beauty, courage, compassion, love. Like a song, such as Catherine sings," he said, looking across the table at Catherine, "which stops the show. There's nothing better than that, and you're not the ones who've made it, even if it sometimes flows through you."

They were mystified.

He turned to address Catherine as if they weren't there. They were amazed at his ability to ignore them. "Once, I sat just inside the doors of Schermerhorn Hall at Columbia — it seems like a very long time ago, a war ago at least. It was a summer afternoon and hardly anyone was there. For hours I listened to faint sounds from outside and within: pipes shuddering when someone, somewhere, drew water, and then going silent; the squeak of a door opening and closing; someone on a higher floor, coughing twice; a plane so far away it sounded like a mosquito. Only a few people went in and out, but when they did the changing air seemed as momentous as a tidal wave. I used to think about that, in the war. I'd put myself back there. It was nothing of account, but it was peace."

No one said anything. What was he talking about? It didn't matter. He was talking only to Catherine, unembarrassed to do so, and so much in love with her that it had actually shut them up. But he would wait to tell her later, on Bank Street, with not a soul in sight, that in the cemetery, when she had turned to him as she knelt, and with the briefest, slightest smile, changed everything, she had had the greatest courage and the greatest beauty he had ever seen.

"I wish I had someone who would talk to me that way, as if no one else were in the room," Andrea said, not caring how vulnerable she might appear in the eyes of her friends and acquaintances, for she had no one who would, and at that moment she would have traded everything in the world that was clever for one simple thing that was true.

# 20

## THE GIFT OF A CLEAR DAY

That summer had more than its share of the unusual days when almost cold winds rush in like cavalry and waters that have become nearly emerald turn back to blue. The wind was like a long letter from Canada, and in the cool air that helps athletes Harry ran more than his accustomed miles, went home to shower and dress, and then walked down to the loft. Despite the worsening situation, he was optimistic and happy, for in the evening, as almost always now, he would see Catherine, and as almost always, the first glimpse of her was enough to disconnect him from his troubles. She might come to the door and stand in shadow, or on a corner in full sun. She could be wearing a suit or a dress, or her arms could be left bare and framed by a snow-white blouse or sleeveless gown. The first sight and first touch would be both anaesthetizing and electric.

When he arrived at work he went from station to station, reassuring everyone, much like the generals who, before a battle they are destined to win even if they do not know it, pulse with inexplicable confidence. He put his hands on everything, moving them across piles of leather sheets or over glossy boxes, touching the soft flannel bags for finished cases and belts, resting his palms on the anvils, running the tips of his fingers over stitching to see that it was tight, lifting polished objects close to smell the wax and examine in detail surfaces he tilted to refract the light.

He greeted each of his employees by name and spoke with some at length, eventually joining Cornell in the office not long before lunch.

The clock said eleven-thirty, and to its left, even so high above the ground, a sunny, iron-framed window was alive with ivy moving in the unaccustomed breeze. Light green shoots and young leaves rocked back and forth and gently slapped the glass, recoiling like drunks who bump into lampposts only to come at them again and again. The newly emerging leaves had never been in the wind or known the cool, the clear, or the unfiltered sunlight that showed their infant green to perfection.

"How are we doing, Cornell?"

Cornell, too, was inappropriately cheerful. "Blazing along and headed down. Today things are slightly worse. What else?"

"Just since yesterday?"

"A six percent increase for the sheets from Cronin in St. Louis. Found that out this morning. Six percent."

"Is there anything we can use in their place?"

"Not on the attachés, unless you want to change the color and texture. You know what that does to repeat buyers."

"We've got to stick to it. That's what we're known for."

"We are," Cornell said, licking a stamp and pressing it onto an envelope. "By the way, Tony Agnello said he would come for lunch."

This was the owner of a shirt manufacture on the floor above, a young man in his middle twenties, whose company made the highest-quality men's dress shirts for a wide variety of stores that sold them as their own and under their own labels at vastly differing prices calibrated according to perceived prestige, despite the fact that all the shirts were exactly the same.

"What else is new?" Harry asked.

"Nothing."

"What are we going to do?"

Cornell shrugged his shoulders. "We can't survive if we pay two thousand dollars a week. It would take a miracle."

"What about half a miracle, and we do the rest?"

"I'd be happy with a quarter, Harry, but we've got to have something, a little handhold, some sort of break. I think about it day and night. I'm approaching the point that bankrupt merchants reach when they consider shedding their inventory for anything they can get."

"We're not there yet."

"Harry, it's not good to be headed down when you're old, when you're on the way down anyway."

Harry had known Tony Agnello since childhood. Their fathers' long friendship began when they discovered that they came from similar backgrounds (one an Italian, the other a Jew), were the same age, and were engaged in much the same profession, but, as Meyer Copeland had said, crosswise. Contrary to what might be expected, the Italian sewed shirts and the Jew worked in leather. When visiting one another's lofts, one directly below the other and as high off the street as tree houses, each had had a sense of the other's business as if in the blood, and they believed that though they had crossed over they were absorbed in the same task. One made shirts of silk or Egyptian cotton, the other briefcases, portfolios, women's handbags, and belts. Their products often went to the same stores, where they were bought by the same people. Their underlying desire was not to satisfy the demands of the market, something with which they struggled and that neither of them could ever get quite right, but to satisfy the demands of their crafts.

Because Tony was almost ten years younger than Harry, Harry had often been assigned to take care of him. Whenever the boys found themselves at their fathers' places of business, usually in summer, Harry would be relieved of polishing leather or making boxes in the almost dead air, and his father would say, handing him a dollar bill, "Take 'Ant-knee' someplace. Buy yourselves lunch. Go to the zoo. And bring back the change. He's going crazy up there because he's too young to sew."

So Harry would go upstairs, get Tony, and take him out into the world. Sometimes they would ride the subway all day, standing at the front window as tunnels rushed at them. At Coney Island they looked for dimes that had slipped through cracks in the boardwalk. Once, they got off a train at Van Cortlandt Park and tried to walk to what they imagined was Canada but turned out to be Yonkers. Even now, after both their fathers had died and both boys had been through the war, Harry was still the older boy, and Tony's face seemed hardly to have changed. As in childhood, he had dark, sunken eyes, a gentle smile, and jet-black hair that had the look of sable. He was getting heavy, but then again, he had never been thin.

"What?" he said as he came into the office. "The girls gone out again?"

Harry and Cornell had been deserted, as usual, at noon.

"What's today's beauty secret, Tony?" Cornell asked.

"Never get involved with a woman who keeps a snake," Tony responded, not missing a beat.

"You had to learn this by experience?" Cornell marveled.

"And tattoos. You couldn't see them when she was dressed." He was carrying a shopping bag, from which he withdrew two bottles of beer, a bottle of Coca-Cola, and three deep, thin-walled, tinfoil pie dishes crimp-sealing white cardboard covers.

"What'd you get?" Harry asked.

"Porta Rican," Tony answered, not looking up as his tailor's fingers rapidly uncrimped the foil around the cardboard. Steam rose and disappeared as the cooling dishes became approachable. "*Arroz con pollo.*"

"No salad?"

"You don't like it?"

"I like it, but next time bring a salad. If I don't have a salad I feel like I've betrayed my country."

"How many miles did you run?" Tony asked.

"Twelve."

"Twelve!" Cornell exclaimed, beginning to eat.

"What are you gonna kill yourself? What's it gonna get you?" Tony asked.

"It keeps me fit, so I don't get *ant knees.*"

"Harry, the war, I heard, is over."

"And if we have another one?"

Tony had a built-in delay, but could always come up with an answer. "You'll be too old."

"But you won't."

"So that's why you run twelve miles?"

"Six for you and six for me. When they get off their asses, the Germans and Japanese...."

They ate their *arroz con pollo* contentedly, as if that portion of the conversation had ended, but then, after a long drink of beer, Tony said, "I don't think so."

"You don't think what?" Cornell asked with the touch of severity he had to have in the presence of the younger men.

"It'll be the Russians."

"Whoever it is," Harry said, "if I'm pulled into that again...."

"And you would be," Cornell told him, "because you were an officer."

"I don't want to have to relearn everything. It took too much out of me."

Agnello said, "I hope so."

"What do you mean," Cornell pressed, "you 'hope' so? You hope what?"

"That it's not the Japanese."

They thought Tony had said this because he had served in the Pacific, and they also thought that he might be claiming too much for someone who had been a clerk. But he surprised them. "The Japanese are going to save us."

"Save what, America?" Cornell asked.

"Lexington Shirtwaist," he told them, referring to his archaically named company.

"How is that?" Harry asked, pushing away his tinfoil dish.

"We bombed their cities and their bases. The cities burned and the bases were destroyed. Half the men of a certain age are dead. But there was no mission against the mulberry trees, and the silkworms weren't in the army. Even when Tokyo was in flames, they were working away as if there was no war. And the women who take care of them, who spin the silk and weave the cloth, they didn't fight. The whole damned industry's intact except for some of the mills, but there are plenty in Korea, and what could happen there? In a few months we'll be getting silk so cheap it'll offset the rise in labor costs. God bless Japan."

"You wouldn't happen to know if the Japanese were left with herds of cheap, leather-producing cows?" Cornell asked.

"Yeah," Tony said. "You won't get off that easy, will you? But you'll make it. Our fathers made it through the two crashes. So will we. It's not even a crash."

"If we can make the payoffs. Do you get a discount for being Italian?"

"Why would Mickey Gottlieb give me a discount for being Italian? He'd give the discount to you."

"That was then. I'm talking about Verderamé."

"Who's that?"

"The guy we pay off to."

"Since when do the needle trades pay the Italians? It would be like the produce wholesalers paying the Jews. I pay Mickey Gottlieb. I always did."

"Gottlieb's dead."

"I don't think so. I paid him last week. Who do you pay?"

"Verderamé. You don't pay Verderamé?"

"No. Never heard of him."

"How much do you pay?"

"The same as always, four hundred. You don't?"

"No."

"What are you talking about?" Tony asked. "I was in the elevator as his guys, the same guys, Mickey Gottlieb's, went from floor to floor. One got off on two, the other on three. Ten minutes later, they came to me. They work all the floors. Who's Verderamé?"

After Tony left, Cornell said, "Hold on." He stood up—tall, thin, and crooked, but still strong—and left the office in a way that said he'd soon be back. Harry tried to order the situation as best he could. How often in tight straits new information promised a way out but then failed to deliver. He didn't want to be seduced by relief, because he knew that whatever his conclusions he would have to ride upon a guess.

When Cornell returned he sat down as if to punish the chair. "We're the only ones. Everyone else pays Gottlieb. And it didn't go up. I don't know the stationers on six, and it's just a warehouse anyway, but for everyone else nothing's changed."

"Why us? Maybe we're the first. Maybe the whole building's going to go one at a time and we're just the first."

"Couple it with the fact that it's so unreasonably high," Cornell said, as it was beginning to come clear, and then it did. "To drive us out of business."

"No," said Harry, "not why, *who*. The Cypriot. He was so cocksure and excited, and I thought, Who the hell is he? We just conquered Europe and he's strutting around as if he owns New York. I don't even remember his name."

"The little fat guy in the expensive suit?"

"Why would he have to?" Harry asked. "They've got so many advantages as is."

"Maybe because it's easy," Cornell speculated. "We don't know. Maybe a friend of his is Verderamé's cousin, and he suggested it. Verderamé's got everything in place. This is what he does every day, only he doesn't kill his cows, he milks them. But so what if he kills just one? Farmers do that. Everyone else will keep quiet as long as it's not them. It makes perfect sense."

"But what about Gottlieb?"

"He does it as a favor for Verderamé and gets something in return," Cornell said. "Maybe he's getting all the money, or half of it. Look at it the way Bernstein would. Verderamé gets a hundred thousand from us before we go under. Fifty thousand, let's say, goes to Gottlieb, who, after we vacate, gets his normal take from whoever buys our floor. It's not something they can do on a regular basis, only now and then. Why not? Maybe Verderamé's getting paid by the Cypriot, they're not connected in any other fashion, and another thirty or forty thousand is going to Verderamé. The Cypriot buys our name, or at least takes over our accounts after we're gone. You can run through it in half a dozen ways, but these bastards have all the options and they always come out ahead. I almost wish I were in that business myself."

"This is only speculation. How can we know? We can never know."

"What else have we got? Who's going to tell us, who's going to bail us out?"

"The government?"

"Tell me you didn't say that, Harry. Every business in New York, including the police, either pays off or is paid."

"La Guardia was on the take?"

Cornell shook his head from side to side. "All right, La Guardia wasn't on the take. Neither was Theodore Roosevelt. I mean, I don't know. But even people like that can't do a thing. They make some noise, it shrinks a little, and then it comes back. In a hundred and fifty years it'll still be the same."

"I don't understand," Harry protested.

"What don't you understand?"

"If they can do this, why can't the far greater numbers of people they steal from rise up against them?"

"Because they're willing to kill and be killed. Are you?"

"I was."

"But that was then, in the war. You had license. You were forced to it."

"I don't want to, but if I had to I could go back in a minute and it would be as if I'd never left."

"Maybe you could. But would you? That beautiful girl, she's such a beauty."

# 21

## THE BEACH ROAD

In blazing sun at eleven o'clock on a weekday in August, when few people had come out from the city and the beaches were empty, Catherine and Harry had walked a few miles up the road to Amagansett and turned toward the sea. Following a deep sand track churned by the jeeps of fishermen and the Coast Guard, they passed through juniper and shoulder-level laurel across the sand until they reached an opening that led to the beach. Windless and concave, with the dunes reflecting the high summer sun upon a reflective floor, the route was unbearably hot until the breach gave out to the sea, where the temperature dropped by forty degrees or more.

Halfway there, she in her satin-tight, two-piece suit that had knocked the breath out of him when she had dropped her robe, and still did, and he in khaki naval swim trunks, they began to feel the heat to the point of distress. In a totally windless bowl, pinned by rays of sun, the temperature was close to 130 degrees and the radiative heat could be endured for only a few minutes. Covered with sunscreen that made them as glossy as the sand, they began to sweat until the water ran off them in droplets and the scent of Catherine's perfume mixed with the salt and juniper that pervaded the air.

Tramping about the sand in canvas boat shoes was strenuous, and she walked in front so as to set a slower pace. He watched her through the glare. Deeply tanned for someone of light coloring, her skin was smooth and flawless, as much rose as brown, pulsing with life and color. The gloss of the sunscreen made her shine with light, and golden flecks of sand had gathered in random places like glitter. Clear droplets sparkled and grew until they plunged in rivulets that soaked the small of her back.

On the previous trip, they had walked from the house to Accabonac, swum to Cartwright Island, and thence across a chain of sandbars and shoals to Gardiners Island, five miles of swimming all told and twelve miles of walking: more than a full day of sun, wind, and water. When they returned they played tennis before dinner, and Catherine won. She was very good. He couldn't drive from his mind how the wind that evening had carried braided within it dance music from the Georgica Club, sometimes faint, sometimes swelling. He couldn't drive from his mind her burnished hair, made full by the salt air, sunlit and shining. As they made their way to the ocean, his knowledge of her, his sense of what she was and what she would be, was overlaid upon the woman who walked before him, the sea wind carrying back steady seductive traces of scent.

Following the path she made through the waving air, he increased his pace. After a step or two, he caught her elbow. She turned, with the expression and stance appropriate to someone who was about to be drawn to something practical or of interest, such as an alternate route or a bird gliding above. But as soon as he closed upon her she relaxed every muscle and felt in every cell an upwelling of expectation and a lightness that separated her from the world. Clear perspiration, sparkling in the sun, rolled over her upper lip. She tasted the salt, and knew that in a moment he would too.

"Not here," she said, "we'll die of the heat," but as soon as he began to kiss her they fell into a gravityless, hallucinatory state they did not want to leave. Dropping to their knees in the hot sand so as to be pressed together without effort, they entered into competition with the sun for domination of the flats and dunes that surrounded them. And if the power of love and adoration can outshine light, for a few moments it did.

When he had said that he would court her, he meant it. He recoiled at the thought of what Victor had done, and though now she was not thirteen but twenty-three, and had been through ten years of an apprenticeship that had fully acquainted her with any and every part of sexual mechanics, they held back.

Once, on a quiet evening when time was unusually slow even for New York in summer, they had lain together, alone, eleven floors above Central Park West. A warm breeze came through the open windows and brought the sounds of evening. They were tangled in their disheveled clothes, wet, and engorged everywhere appropriate. Her breasts were turgid, her nipples taut, and she throbbed. And yet, as difficult as it was, they went no further.

"Why?" she asked, as if drugged, although she knew exactly why.

"To go back to where you started with Victor, and do what people are supposed to do, but to be brought along slowly," he said.

"I would have thought it would be impossible to erase what happened," she said, "that it was indelible."

"Is it working?" he asked.

"It's working."

"You see?"

"But we will?" she asked.

"Of course we will. Have you noticed" — he propped himself up on his elbows — "that we can make love for hours, and we just want more? Every time we touch, it's more intense. Have you ever felt this strongly?"

"No, but my friends in the theater would think we were prudes."

"Your friends in the theater fuck like a bunch of rabbits playing musical chairs. They go from one person to another because no one is sufficient. You should throw Victor into the pot. He'd probably be very happy there."

"He had me pretend to be other women."

"I'd feel cheated if you were another woman."

"So would I," she said.

"Did you used to go into three-hour-long trances with Victor?"

She laughed cruelly.

"How long did it take before he finished and turned to the business pages, ten minutes?"

"That would have been a world's record."

"So when he had sex with you it wasn't as if you were dancing, was it?"

"No."

"And it wasn't a conversation, right?"

"Right."

"It was a lecture."

"A short lecture," she added. "*Thirty Seconds over Tokyo.*"

"Did you tell him that?"

"No."

"You should have."

"I couldn't. He was the lecturer. I was the audience. But," she asked, sweetly, "Harry, when we finally, completely, totally . . . fuck . . . will all this quite wonderful preface have gone to waste?"

"What do you think?"

"I think maybe not," she said, her eyes slightly glazed, and then they fell back into one another and lost track of time.

They were astounded whenever they came into one another's presence, and amazed when they touched. When they did—a kiss slightly slower than custom would countenance, or with fingers entwined as they went down the stairs of the subway, or when he brushed her hair from her eyes, or touched her lightly through her suit or her dress, even once when he touched the aquamarine brooch pinned to her linen jacket—the touch was as exciting as if they were falling through the air, a sensation Harry knew well.

Now, on the shadowed slope of a dune that was the last wall of land to face the sea, on silken cold sand, they sat together, thinking that the way they felt would last forever. Far out on the water, a distant sail glided silently, true to the speed of the wind and heading into the horizon. Tranquil, remote, and, above all, silent, it moved toward a great open space. "If that's death," Harry said, "then I look forward to it. I confess that when I see a sail shining in white, moving in the distance toward the shadows as if to go from this world to the next, I want to follow."

"Harry," she said, intent upon bringing him back, "it's a sailboat. It's not death. Don't follow. Just stay with me as long as you can."

"You don't always have a choice in the matter," he said, remembering.

"I know. But . . . just drop it. We have a sailboat, you know."

"I didn't."

"We do, and you can go on it far beyond the horizon and you don't die, you come back. It's at our house in Maine. It's fifty-four feet — what the man who built it called 'a bonny yacht,' and more than seaworthy. You can sail all over the world in it."

"I didn't know you had a house in Maine."

"We have a cabin, sort of, on Mount Desert Island. We keep the boat there in summer. In October after hurricane season it goes to Florida."

"You have a house in Florida?"

She nodded.

"Where don't you have a house?"

"That's not fair. We have houses," she counted on her fingers, "only in New York, Florida, Maine, and London. Like an isosceles triangle."

"A triangle with four angles."

"*Like* an isosceles triangle."

"What's the name of the boat?"

"The *Crispin*."

"It is a lot of money," he said, "isn't it."

"It's a very lot of money."

"I don't want any of it."

"I'm the only child."

"I know."

"If you marry me, you're going to have to learn to live with it. That's a job in itself — although most people don't know it — because it can easily ruin you. Are you going to let it ride?"

"Let what ride?"

"That my parents don't know you're Jewish."

"No, but I'm overwhelmed now. . . . It's more of a problem that my business is almost insolvent."

"It is?"

"It is."

A minute passed, until Catherine said, "My father could take care of that with the stroke of a pen. Eventually, I'll be able to take care of it with the stroke of a pen. Actually, I think I can now. I'm not really sure. But you won't allow that."

"If I did, you'd be marrying nothing."

"When that horrid Rufus said what he said, and I foolishly went along with the tenor of it, why didn't you protest? Why didn't you defend yourself? Are you ashamed?"

"Not ashamed, fatigued."

"At not even thirty-two?"

"At not even thirty-two. And I won't let people like him dictate my focus, take me from the ability to live my life as I please. Some people think it's their responsibility to fight every fight, and it becomes their lives. I want to live otherwise. At the moment I don't feel that I have to take up every challenge. Anyway, it would be impossible. And then there was the matter of mercy. Rufus has an appointment to keep in the very near term. I have no desire to disturb the little peace he may have left."

"So you let it go."

"I let it go."

"And with my parents?"

"Will they object? You tell me."

"I don't know what they'll do."

"What would you like me to do, Catherine, announce it over the lobster course? 'Oh, by the way, I'm a Jew, how do you do?'"

"You might think of a more graceful and considerate way."

"I don't feel apologetic."

"I didn't mean that. I mean that they come from a different era, and they don't love you. They're my parents, and I love them. What if you had told your father and your mother that you were going to marry a Christian?"

"My father would have been at sea: the line of five thousand years coming to an end—I don't know what he would have done. But it wouldn't have mattered."

"We have a line, too."

"I know that. But before I do this difficult thing I would like at least not to be bankrupt. I may never be rich, especially as it has never been my ambition, but it's one thing for a Jew to ask the hand of Catherine Thomas Hale, and another for a bankrupt Jew."

"How long until that might be settled?"

"At this point it seems like eternity, but if there's no way out it won't last for much more than a year, possibly a lot less."

"That's too long. I want to marry you sooner: today would be fine with me. And anyway, in a year they'd find out somehow and think we were keeping it from them. You're going to have to find a way to fight two fights at the same time."

## 22

### YOUNG TOWNSEND COOMBS

BILLY AND EVELYN usually came out early on Fridays, but an engagement in New York had delayed their arrival until Saturday evening, when a cold supper would await them in a quiet house. That afternoon the remnant of a southern gale had raised the waves to ten feet or more, and in bright sun they struck the shore like hammers. Since childhood Catherine had called these the hurtful waves, for they hit as if with a lifelong grudge. They turned the ocean into an enemy, and made swimming in it a combat in which life could be taken. Though Europeans did not swim in waves like this, Americans did.

She had gone into the breakers with Harry, holding out her hands to him when she sighted what looked like a particularly vicious wave coming at great speed, which is what she had done in milder conditions when her father had first taught her how to maneuver in the surf. She was not embarrassed in violent waters to hold out her hands for protection, because she was no more reluctant to rely upon him than she was to give herself to him entirely.

After half an hour of tense fighting, she sat on the beach, a towel draped around her, and there she regained her balance and sense of gravity as she watched him duel with the swells. At a disadvantage when he was looking out for her and lost in calculations of when a front of water would strike, or whether to advise diving into it or riding over it, now he merely fought. Huge masses would loom over him, and he would either dive into their momentarily gelatinous walls or stand his ground and disappear for a full minute in a hell of foam as he was tumbled head over heels and banged against the hard sand floor.

Sometimes he was smacked from behind by a wave curving unexpectedly and snapping like a whip. Sometimes he punched back, as if the ocean could feel. And sometimes he swam hard to catch a wave at its crest before it broke, launching himself into the empty air behind it and dropping six feet or more, as if he had leapt from a rock. She knew from watching him in the water that he was not only the kind of man she wanted but the very one; that though, because she loved him, she would marry him even were he weak and unable to endure, he had great resources. He had what her heart cried out for, and strength that was bred in the bone.

When they came in from the beach she went to wash her hair and to dress. He dived into the pool to rinse off the salt, combed his hair, and put on shirt and shoes. Sitting in his customary khaki shorts as they dried, on a teak bench in the garden by the pool, he heard the patter of her shower. After an hour—first of cascading foam; then dressing in clean, pressed clothes; the application of light makeup; and choosing of jewelry (she was now free to wear her beautifully worked diamonds, sapphires, and gold)—she would have come as far from the sea as possible while it was yet close. Eventually she would appear in the garden, so graceful, civilized, and powerful that he imagined that the Atlantic, still striking beyond the wall of dunes, might be held at bay.

He stared out over the fields, his balance not completely restored and the roar of the ocean that he heard within almost as loud as its actual static carried by luffing winds into the garden. As if he had not left the waves, if he closed his eyes he didn't know where he was. For a moment, a cloud of humid, perfumed air from the second floor of the house traveled past him. He heard the water slapping the base of the shower after she had gathered it in her hair and it had overflowed and fallen. Then that receded as the wind moved along the compass rose. As he sat in the garden set like an emerald in fields of row crops planted daringly close to the ocean, he was slowly coming back to land.

In a distant field between a line of oaks and the first rising of the dunes he saw a deer grazing in shadow. He knew that with a rifle he would be able to bring it down with a single shot at three hundred yards. He could calibrate range and elevation and compensate for the easterly wind. He had almost a sixth sense that would tell him when the animal would take a step or if it would stay still. But even had he had a rifle he would not have taken this beckoning shot, for what he knew of shooting he had learned as a prelude to and in the practice of killing men, and he wanted never to hold a rifle again.

The night before, fireflies had woven through the trees in great profusion, blinking in the darkness, crossing overhead as if to find refuge in the camouflage of the stars, and at a distance passing for the traces of meteors. Now, in full sun and heat, the fields seemed solid and immutable, gravity was aligning itself properly in his inner ear, the surf fading, and dreams burnt away by the afternoon sun. This was a tranquil place where beauty, tradition, and wealth were like the walls of Holland that kept back the sea. Surrounded by the great stillness of the fields, he was about to fall asleep.

But then, from the east, with the suddenness of a pistol shot, a brightly colored monoplane came roaring at him, six feet above the ground, as straight as if it were on a track aligned with the cultivated rows. Just beyond the garden, not fifty feet away, the mass of this plane, with blood-red trim but otherwise as yellow as the yolk of an egg, streaked over the hedge in a blur, the engine noise vibrating in Harry's chest and rattling every pane of glass in the Hale house. Catherine pushed her bathroom window fully open and peered out at nothing.

Then it came back from the other direction, still flying astonishingly low. After attacking the fields with spray, the plane closed its nozzles, flew for an instant in the clear, and, just before it would have ploughed into a dune, pulled up, rolled, and doubled back, dropping low and releasing spray as it thundered by. Catherine returned her window to its former position ajar, and Harry stood up, following the plane to the end of the field and longing for its return.

• • •

As mist rose from the ponds and began to cover the lawns of Further Lane, and the ocean thudded nearby like a metronome, it was for Harry the eleventh of July, 1943, at the height of summer and after the triumph in North Africa. The sun rose over the Mediterranean east of Tunisia, changing the color of the sea, first from a furious gray inappropriate to summer heat, to a kind of melon green, and then to cold blue. Far away and in silence, fleets of fighters rose and fell like swallows, dipping over the swells, rising in great arcs, and suddenly turning. Inland at Kirwan, the traffic was immense and unceasing. Dappling the sky like dense flak, British and American planes of every type moved intently upon their separate missions, going to or returning from the invasion of Sicily.

As the sun climbed, the sea became a canvas wet with color, dotted with ships still disappearing over the horizon to mate the rear echelons of the armies to their advance guard fighting in a battle that threw its electricity back upon the troops waiting to take part. To a paratrooper at his assembly point, it was miraculous. Never did the planes not fill the sky; never did they cease forming up, only to move north and away; never did they collide as they swarmed; and never did they not inspire as they lifted from the runways, their engines at full power, each plane rising until it was a silent black speck, then silvery white, then an afterimage, and then nothing. When they returned it was as if they were born out of the same nothingness, though unlike that which is reborn, when they finally touched down they seemed heavy and tired.

That day, the paratroopers rested and checked their equipment over and over. The 504th and 505th Regiments of the 82nd Airborne were already fighting the Hermann Göring Division north of Gela on the coast of Sicily. Though the battle was fought far from sight, it was possible to feel the tension rising and falling, and though the remnants of the 82nd, held in reserve at Tunis, were supposed to be at rest, their exhaustion began as the first of the other regiments departed for Sicily. They could not help it.

As the day wore on, a messenger delivered orders. Between 2230 and 2400, they would be dropped onto the beach at Gela to reinforce troops already landed and fighting. Harry and the seven pathfinders with whom he shared a tent would fly on and jump at Ponte Olivo, perhaps, depending upon the course of the next hours' fighting, beyond a line that the 504th and 505th had not been able to breach. The object was to get behind advance elements of the Hermann Göring Division that had descended to defend the coast, mark drop zones for subsequent landings, scout the terrain, cut telephone wires, change road signs, and blow bridges.

The waiting was difficult in itself and made more difficult in trying to decide, for example, what to eat, a problem no one had ever solved completely. Rough air, natural anxiety, and day-long intermittent nausea dictated that they should not eat much, and the temptation was not to eat at all. No one wanted to drop or land, much less move and fight, on a full stomach. On the other hand, their strength was already draining from them, and in just hours on the ground it would be much more rapidly depleted. A proper balance was hard to achieve, true rest improbable.

As the commander of his small detachment, the oldest, and an officer, Harry had to take charge, an improvisation that he himself had to believe so as to give others confidence. Everyone had tried to sleep, but even had it not been too hot in the tent they wouldn't have been able to, and they worried that when having to draw upon all their resources to stay alive they might instead surrender to fatigue and death. This, in turn, made sleep, which had been merely unlikely, only something to dream about.

He told them that they should neither try to sleep nor be anxious for lack of sleep. "Your anxiety will disappear in the roar of the engines," he said. "From the moment of takeoff you'll want to make the jump more than anything in the world, and when you exit the plane you won't be afraid. You'll work your skills, move as you've never moved before, and wonder, How did I get from there to here if I can't remember it? And you won't be weak or tired for at least a day or two."

As always and often, they checked and rechecked their equipment: their many times cleaned and well oiled carbines, their pouches of ammunition, the radio, grenades, explosives, and harnesses. They counted their rations and calculated days. They opened pouches to make sure that the bandages and morphine they had seen there twenty times that day were still in place. And every time they looked up they saw the planes beginning or ending their missions, circling slowly in the far distance almost over the sea, rising quickly, descending sharply, and, nearer the field, turning in vertiginous arcs.

In a vast, prayerful order of silence, thousands of men went about their separate tasks. Even before battle they had entered into a deep connection with those, past and future, who had found or would find themselves part of a great host, moving as if without will, coordinated and sanctified by death. This pointless and tragical fugue had rolled through history since the beginning. The pace may have varied, but the harvest was steady over time, its momentum increasing and undiminished. It moved evenly, treated all passions equally, and was as cold and splendid as the waves in winter.

What force, he wondered, could paint such a canvas and command such dedication while never failing, again and again, to take sons from mothers, husbands from wives, and fathers from children? Unable to hesitate or protest, he looked toward the weapons and equipment he had made ready many times over, and felt love that would forever abide for all those he had followed, and all who would follow after, in thrall of this tide.

Townsend Coombs was too young for his name, which properly belonged to a portly, middle-aged insurance salesman in a small town, though not the one in New Hampshire from which Townsend Coombs had come, but perhaps in Indiana or Ohio, or some other place that sophisticates, having visited for perhaps an hour, would then mock for eternity.

His town had a name like that of one of Fenimore Cooper's Indians, and neither Harry nor anyone else could ever get it straight. In writing reports that called for this reference Harry had to look it up each time and carry the spelling verbally from where he saw it written to where he himself would write it—Ashtikntatippisinkinkta (truly) —as if it were water that would run through his cupped hands. He never managed to spell it the same way twice, and neither did anyone else, and the only one who could actually say it was Townsend Coombs himself. This and other things suggested very strongly that Townsend Coombs should have been in that town rather than in North Africa somewhere south of Tunis. He was more than ten years younger than Harry, who, not yet thirty, seemed to him to be heavy, slow with age, someone who knew what was over the wall. Townsend Coombs hardly had a beard, and his face was almost as round as a child's. He did — often unconvincingly — what the older men did, and adopted their expressions, their language, and to some extent the way they moved, although his age allowed him to move with a smoothness he could not banish even when he tried to imitate what he thought was the weariness of experience. As the youngest, he had no choice but to follow. This was to be his education, and he took to it not from a tendency to imitate but as a means of staying alive. They were much older, they were still living, and theirs was the only story available to heed. And as he discovered in training and their time in North Africa, the other seven were watching out for him.

The great assemblage and activity on and above the land and the sea were more exciting for him than for the others, whose view was colored by their knowledge of things he had yet to experience. For Townsend Coombs, all this seemed not the potential end of things but their beginning. He was proud of the strength of his country, comforted and assured by the vast numbers and their balletic efficiencies. He was fascinated by the British, from whom he had sprung, and delighted by colors and climates so different from the white and slate-blue New Hampshire winters and its short, cool, entrancingly deep green summers.

Harry often listened patiently and respectfully when Townsend Coombs told him what Harry already knew, or, wanting to impress, about the triumphs of his sports teams, or mischief he had done with his friends. Putting a skunk in a teacher's mailbox, things like that. Harry had tried to steer him to the soldier's craft and draw his attention to what he would need in battle. It was sad to heavy the heart of a youth, but it had to be done.

Sometimes Harry was not patient with him, and would revert fully to rank, ordering him to do something unpleasant or criticizing him in ways that he suspected he himself would regret for the rest of his life. Once, when the boy was acting foolishly, Harry had snapped, "Not that way, you idiot!" which, although it had hardly been a mortal wound, had shamed and hurt Townsend Coombs in front of the others. And because Harry was his commanding officer, he could not, and did not, apologize.

In evening light forty miles east, the sea turned a color blue that hid details shown by day. From beaches and bluffs it was no longer possible to see wave lines sweeping in on winds from the Levant, or whitecaps spilling over, though one could see night hanging over Palestine and Egypt as the sky above them tended to violet as it cooled. On the airfield, as far as the eye could make out, long lines of men blended into the desert and dusk as they moved with military patience into fleets of transports and gliders. Though assembled en masse, they would fight in much smaller groups, and at times individually. But gathered in thousands for a flight that would end with thousands of parachutes silently blooming in the dark, they felt the great pride and elation of battle that battle itself almost always destroys.

If you looked ahead or back, right or left, you saw on the rust and ochre desert sinking into the dark thousands of armed men quietly boarding the planes to sit in facing rows. Insane and guaranteed to break hearts into eternity, there it was nonetheless, war inescapable, elevating the sense of being alive like nothing else but love. The engines started with such great noise that cheers were made silent and doors closed and bolted without sound. They felt the brakes strain as the throttles were opened, and then the transports moved slowly into lines to await their turn to rise. It seemed to take forever, but in a steady rhythm the aircraft ahead of them in the queue began their runs and screamed past. Then they themselves turned. The first ninety degrees put them on edge. The next promised everything at the end, and, almost to the degree, they knew when the turn would flatten out. For most the timing was perfect, and the engines came up to full exactly when they expected. The airframe shuddered as if all its rivets would pop at once, but the more it vibrated the more it moved, and soon it was racing down the runway, following the path of the other planes rising in the half darkness like fat, olive-drab dogs.

Its propellers spinning in occasional flames of exhaust, the plane lifted. The last thing Townsend Coombs saw in the light was the illusory basketwork of the spinning propeller blades, as gold as a woven bracelet. Soon they were over the sea, which despite the fact that evening had long sunk into violet and black, somehow held a trace of powder blue where it ran beyond the shadow of the cape.

Dim red lights in the cabin illuminated two rows of men as overwhelmed by their equipment as babies in snowsuits. Part of the allure of the drop would be that when down they could shed parachutes and harnesses and move unburdened except for the weapons and packs to which they had long been accustomed. They knew they might die, but at least they were moving, and in movement was the chance that they would live. Because each time they jumped it was as if they were given a new life, they yearned to exit the planes. The moment they stepped into darkness was the moment they began to fight. At first it seemed from their expressions, when you could make them out in the red light, that they were almost euphoric. Far from their families and prepared to die, they were nonetheless without care. Only in the last part of the flight did joy harden into determination.

As the 144 transports approached Gela from the sea, each man stood and hooked his static line over the cable that ran through the center of the cabin. Everything was checked and rechecked so many times that doing so in itself began to make them nervous. Some now began to be afraid, and though they were in the minority, this reminded the others of fear and laid them open to it. All anyone wanted to do was get into clear air. The jumpmaster issued a string of orders for moving them out of the plane expeditiously, and also to distract them. It worked well, and the imminence of the jump had lifted their spirits.

And then they heard the first muted booms. A few to begin with, up ahead, soon there were many, and in less than a minute they were everywhere in front, behind, underneath, and above.

"We weren't told," someone began to say, but was cut off by a burst that knocked half the men down and left the others swaying and confused. Pieces of flak hit the plane, piercing its skin in several places, but leaving it intact and still flying.

"Sit down!" the jumpmaster shouted as the plane began evasive maneuvers that had little chance of protecting it but were certain to nauseate everyone on board.

"How much can they have?" a paratrooper asked, shouting from close to the open door.

Townsend Coombs, who had never been in flak, looked to Harry, who hadn't either, and by silently moving his lips, Harry said, "Don't worry."

After peering out the door, the jumpmaster announced in an angry, emotional voice strong enough to carry through the sounds of exploding anti-aircraft rounds: "We're still over the sea. Those are *our* ships firing at us."

The words *Christ* and *Jesus* were said so many times and in combination that the narrow cabin was more like the nave of a church than an aluminum airplane now taking enough hits that it yawed and pitched as air forced its way through holes in its skin.

"It's Americans, and they're firing at us from the beach as well." No one knew who said this, but it was true, and just as he finished, a huge explosion bounced the plane thirty feet straight up and fifty feet to the right, taking a piece of wing and a piece of the fuselage. Suddenly, where part of the side and underside of the plane had been, there was nothing, only a gap five or six feet in length and three or four feet high. Nothing, that is, except the upper half of Townsend Coombs, briefly suspended in air, as if in a dream, before it fell into the void and down to the sea. His face had upon it the expression he had had before the blast. He looked calmly ahead, eyes open, with neither grimace nor shock. Harry didn't know whether, in that instant, still in his helmet and harness, young Townsend Coombs had been dead or alive. And then the air took him, and he was gone. He would become a telegram that would be pressed to the hearts of those who loved him, and saved until their deaths, or perhaps beyond, until sometime, somewhere, someone would read it and feel little or nothing.

He was simply gone, and wouldn't have a grave. For an instant the air came up cool and clean through the hole. Flashes of white light illuminated vacant space and flapping pieces of metal. But before he could think, Harry was being rushed to the door. The jumpmaster pushed him and a dozen others out almost all at once, just before the plane broke in half and cartwheeled slowly through the air, its flames extinguished only by the sea.

That night, American guns downed twenty-three American planes carrying paratroopers of the 82nd Airborne. Someone's boot kicked Harry in the head, but his parachute opened, and the wind swept him over the beach, over the American lines, and onto ground held by the Hermann Göring Division. No one saw him land. He was safe. Almost as a reflex, he gathered and hid his chute, made ready his weaponry, sought initial cover, and swept the view 360 degrees. At first he didn't know quite where he was, or who he was, or what had happened. Only when his pulse began to slow did he begin to understand.

He had no time to think of young Townsend Coombs. Later he would think of him now and then, still as shocked and puzzled as when he had landed hard in the rocks and scrub. He had no answers, and could imagine none. He had hardly known the boy, and neither had anyone else except perhaps his father and mother, who were left to grieve for him with the hopeless grief of parent for child, and to look forward to joining him as soon as a decent interval might allow.

In the dusk, Catherine knew not to touch him and not to speak, but just to sit down to his left on the teak bench without saying a word. That she knew at all, without an obvious sign and without having been with him in the four years that now possessed his thoughts, was a confirmation of the quality and grace that in Catherine was far greater than education, breeding, and luck. He stayed still, turned to her only briefly, and then looked out as he had before.

And when the time was right, she asked, "What are you thinking about?" She could see in profile his expression changing subtly as he answered.

"A soldier named Townsend Coombs," he said, focusing on the distance the way one does when speaking of those who are lost forever. "There was nothing I could do, but, still, I failed him."

"Townsend Coombs?" she asked, driven somehow to be precise about the name. "Dead?"

"Yes." He told the story, in full.

A gust rippled the surface of the pool enough to make it sound for a moment like the bell-like lappings of a lake.

"Look," she said, gesturing to their left. "You see that dark mass? The bank of hydrangea?" Flanking the pool was a thick rectangle of hydrangea, now in bloom. "Hydrangea is a Linnaean name, I guess, very unattractive, as are so many words with a *g*, either soft or hard."

Harry had never thought about it, but he agreed.

"As a child, I didn't like hydrangea because of the name and because the flowers, purplish blue, seemed so cold. I let that prejudice continue in force until just recently. That kind of blue, almost violet, is like the color of death. Not merely because of the color of the dead, but because, if you look really closely at it, it takes you past the known colors of the world. It bleeds right off the spectrum into light we can't see. But before you lose it, it takes you someplace where you yourself begin to lose your bearings."

He waited for what she might say.

"But not long ago I found that I couldn't avert my gaze as I had in childhood. It had become my time to look, and to be disconcerted. It was my responsibility to see ahead, to see what, eventually, was coming. And I was no longer afraid. So I stopped, and I looked hard.

"Tomorrow, if you come out here in the morning when the sun is beginning to get hot and no one is around, when the pool water is always clearer than at any other time, and the sound of the surf the most energetic . . . if you come out at that time, and walk along that thick barrier, look closely. The light is disconcerting, and leads to another world, but you'll see hundreds of thousands — literally hundreds of thousands — of bees of all types: fat bumblebees, drones, carpenter bees, and little ones of various sizes, some almost as small as a grain of sand.

"You stand close, safely, enveloped in their hum, which becomes louder even than the surf. They work intently and as if they have a plan. I've never seen people working as smoothly or well. They're so rich in color — yellow, gold, black, and red — that they break the spell of the ultraviolet and move among its waves as if working above water at the edge of a fall, fearlessly and without accident, collecting their nectar, while the sun is high.

"Stay in the light while you can. It's not that far from Townsend Coombs. You can hover in the sunlight at the edge and still be very close, which should be a cause not of regret, but of happiness."

"How can you know this?" he asked. "How could you possibly, at your age?"

In her clear speaking, the very sound of which he realized yet again was miraculous and thick with import, she said, "I stopped to look." And then, inexplicably and perhaps inappropriately overcome by emotion, she closed her eyes, from which tears were streaming, and she said, "God bless Townsend Coombs," as if she had known him, and as if she had loved him, all her life.

# 23

## THE SETTEE

ON A SUMMER morning in New York, between the rush to work and just before crowds of people made their way to lunch, even the shadows that had held remnants of cool night air were windless and hot. And on a side street echoing with the muted traffic of the avenues, the honeycomb of windows was filled with hundreds of steadily turning fans, some moving slowly and others racing invisibly. Midtown was almost never empty except very late at night and early on Christmas Day or the Fourth of July, but every day at this time it was made to feel empty by the immense unseen activity in its high buildings. Descending like rain, the whitened heat brought peace, contentment, and the hope that a downpour would light the lights, cool the air, and break the chain of days each hotter than the last.

According to the New York idiom, Catherine and Harry were *in* Saks. In London, one might have been *at* Harrods, but in New York one was *in* Saks or Macy's, though, inexplicably, *at* Gimbels. No one was ever *in* Gimbels. It was ninety-eight degrees and they were sitting on a tufted leather bench in a room off one of the selling floors, watching people with dazed expressions go in and out of the bathrooms.

"I'm going to splash some water on my face," she said to Harry. And then, after thinking about it for a moment, she added, "Not a single one of the women who has gone in and out as we've been sitting here has been able to do that."

"Why not?"

"Makeup. My mother wears makeup on days like this when she goes out, and sometimes at home, too."

"Your mother is as consistent as the meter stick in Paris."

"All for dignity," said her daughter, wondering about what she herself might be like in twenty or thirty years.

"At least women don't have to wear a jacket."

"Why don't you take it off?" she asked.

"For the same reason that every morning I make my bed without a single wrinkle, though from morning to night the only one who'll see it will be Morris the pigeon, who sits on the windowsill all day while I'm gone. That I make my bed to please a pigeon shows both the power and difficulty of civilization. I do, however, have a fairly uncivilized trick for keeping cool." He waited for her to ask what it was. In the Copeland family, rhetorical questions and leading statements had always called forth a response freely given with the next beat in the music of conversation. The Hales, however, were more economical, and that beat was skipped in favor of a Christian caesura as clean as Occam's razor.

"Don't you want to know?" he asked.

Her answer came silently, in her eyes. She had changed her hair at Elizabeth Arden so that it was cut to float near her face like the crown that sun and wind had made of it at the beach. Were it not for the balance of its form as it framed her features, it might have looked anarchic. But the masses of hair casually arranged — some purely shining; some in shadow and almost red; some in wave-like curves; some straight; some in white gold riding in the light that filtered in through the high windows — were overwhelmingly beautiful.

For a long time, nothing was said as people came and went on the periphery like ghosts. Distant jackhammers, faintly sounding, ceaselessly pausing, sighing, and exploding, forced upon them by recall alone the presence of white dust rising in the sun, the concussive blasts, the loud, low jingling of the metal as a jackhammer snaps back like a whip when it has shattered concrete. "What trick?" she asked, eventually.

"I take off my shirt, soak it in cold water, wring it out, and put it back on. It darkens evenly, doesn't bleed through to the jacket, and the cooling effect lasts for half an hour, with no one the wiser."

"You should tell that to my father," she said.

"He probably won't do it, for the same reason that on a day like this your mother wears makeup."

"You'd be surprised. This is a man who, well, I'm not supposed to say."

"What?"

"I can't tell you."

"You can't tell me what?"

"I really can't."

"You started. That means you have to," he said authoritatively.

She fell for it. "I suppose it's all right if you promise not to tell anyone — because he's dead."

"Who's dead?"

"Roosevelt."

"The president?"

"Promise not to tell anyone, ever."

"I promise."

"Okay." She paused, as if aligning the story. "Our families were fairly close, beginning in the nineteenth century, but when Franklin became president things changed. The New Deal was what did it, but we go so far back that it wasn't sufficient to cause a complete break. And both Daddy and Franklin were raised by Groton, which is like having a common set of parents, although Franklin was much older. The point is, when Daddy was little, Franklin used to trap him and tickle him until Daddy's throat was raw from shrieking. Everyone thought this was very funny, and it ended with Franklin throwing Daddy, way high, into the pool, river, lake, or whatever body of water was convenient. This was a summer thing."

"Where?"

"I don't know, a lot of places. Daddy loved to swim, but when Franklin was around he would get extremely nervous when he came out in his bathing suit, looking about as if he were walking through a field of cobras. And then, usually just before he got to the point where he might have thrown himself into the water, Franklin, who had been hiding, would appear. And my father would say, in his seven-year-old's voice, 'Oh no! Oh no!'

"Then the chase would begin, with Daddy, often in flippers and water wings, desperately trying to escape — which, if you've ever seen a little boy in flippers furiously trying to get away from being tickled, is alone worth the price of the ticket. My father never forgot this, of course.

"Sometime in the thirties he was called to the White House as part of a move to put pressure on what was left of the banks. The meeting was in the Cabinet Room, where the weight of the president's power was set against that of the assembled bankers and financiers. My father, as usual, came in late. It was already very tense, so, to the horror of the other bankers, what does he do? He immediately runs around the table and digs his fingers into Roosevelt's ribs, and doesn't cease tickling him even after the guards burst in, practically in cardiac arrest, because the president... of the United States, is shrieking like a hyena. 'That's all right! It's okay! Stop it, Billy!' the president is shouting. No one knew what the hell was going on. The financiers were white — of course they were white, but I mean with shock — and at the president's command the guards just stood there like ice sculptures, while he took his punishment.

"'It's quite all right,' the president said, dismissing them. When he had finished shrieking and laughing so hard he had tears in his eyes, he asked, 'How many times are you entitled to do that, Billy?' 'I think about a hundred, Franklin,' was the answer. The president made everyone promise not to tell, but I'm sure they all will, eventually, if they live long enough. But you can't."

"I won't."

"I hardly knew FDR. When I was little he hadn't become governor and he was in a wheelchair. He was very nice to children. There were always a lot of us around, and we would sort of form into gangs and go away to play while the adults talked, and to us he was the most adult in that the wheelchair scared us, or me anyway. After he became president, he became very remote. Obviously he was busy, and he was always castigating people like Daddy, so I didn't like him, but Daddy said, no, despite that, the personal is more important. Anyway, Daddy says that he was much more like TR than people realize, and you know that TR was perpetually six years old. The meeting that followed may have been the most relaxed and delightful ever held in the White House. Who knows? It may have been good for the country: everyone stretched, everyone gave. It was quite something. That's what my father says. Now do you think my father wouldn't wet his shirt?"

"I think he might take a bath in the sink."

"So should we," she said. "Let's cool off." And they left to do so, even if not by bathing in the sinks. When he reappeared, his shirt was wet through and wonderfully cool. She had splashed so much water on her face that it had run down the curves of her neck, splotching the shoulders of her dress, and fallen in cool rivulets past her open collar, across the top of her chest, and between her breasts.

As she emerged, she and Harry looked at one another, the sound of jackhammers hypnotic in the distance, the faint ringing of their metal like bells in a meadow. He could not separate his gaze from the splotches of water on her dress, and from her eyes in their extraordinary setting.

"If I were to die right now," he told her, "on a settee outside the bathrooms on the fourth floor of Saks, and if this moment never ended, the sun didn't move, and people worked their morning's work for eternity, I would be happy. But, eventually, this morning will be lost."

"So much the better," was her response. "It's one of a kind."

They had been going from department store to department store to look at the leather goods and their pricing. Catherine was impressed to see Copeland Leather well represented everywhere, and everywhere the most costly, but Harry had been disturbed. What she could not see, not knowing how things once were, was that Copeland's display space had plummeted and sales had followed. Once, their pricing had held up and they had had half the floor space in the appropriate departments. Now they occupied twenty percent at best, and were outsold by cheaper imports comparable in appearance and quality.

Before Saks they had made a stop at the Copeland store on Madison Avenue, where Thaxton and Henry were impotently upset and yet proud to divine that the owner was affianced to Catherine Hale. They knew Billy. They had known Catherine's grandfather. They were possessive of such people and would mention their names and exaggerate their connections so as to feel important, as feeling important is the one treasure for which everyone in Manhattan has always been willing to lie, cheat, and kill. It is the chief thing for which New Yorkers work, money and goods being only subsidiary. They will do without food and water, and if necessary thrive anaerobically as long as they can touch, see, or hear someone of greater social status, someone whose fame will rub off on them microscopically atom by atom, a lingering odour imperceptible to a bloodhound but for them sufficient unto the grave: *Myron and I once took a taxi in which Francis X. Bushman had ridden only a week before.*

Thus, Henry and Thaxton were pleased to have sensed the engagement. But they were also thrown into deep anxiety that the daughter of an exemplar of their kind would stoop to marry a Jew (which was almost as distressing as if she would marry a Negro), even if he were their employer, even if they had loved his father, even if they respected him immensely and he was fairer to and more generous with them than anyone ever had been. Blood is the thickest. She was so beautiful, in her way, stunning in mien and character, almost not of this world. She was light where he was dark. Her eyes were like jewels and his were like coals. She was bred to perfection, and he, by definition, could not have been bred at all.

Thaxton spoke reflexively, asking, "If you and the young lady were to marry, would it be in a church?" This was not only highly impertinent, it was almost insane, but he couldn't help it.

Though he was shocked, Harry answered, "As things stand, we'd have a civil ceremony."

"Oh."

The *oh* was like the slamming of a thousand doors, but Harry, unlike Catherine, whose eyes flashed with anger, was immobile. Soon, however, they became absorbed in talk of commerce, and she separated from them to wander about the store.

It was as polished and impressive as a gold piece. Every item was of the highest quality, every surface shiny and rich. From across the room she noticed that Henry and Thaxton were actually dressed in morning coats, which gave the place the air of a vicarage, and although she pitied these two she could see that Harry needed them. Were he to man the counters, he could never be elegant and comfortably self-demeaning in their way. And she wondered if this unseen advantage, an inbred confidence that could not be eroded by defeat, would be denied to her children even though they would be of her blood as much as of his.

Later, on the settee, as water ran down the front of her dress and the cooling evaporation stimulated her subtly and deeply, she brought up the subject indirectly. It spoiled the moment, for she had hoped that they would get in a cab; that upon arriving at his house she would exit, semi-delirious from kissing all the way up Central Park West; and that on this day the courtship would come to a close. The most natural thing, soon enough, would be for them to lie pressed together, pinioned at the groin, bathed in sweat, exchanging breaths from one set of lungs to another, for hour upon hour. Soon enough, it would come, for it had been held back with hallucinatory discipline and pleasure that would color and elevate their lovemaking for the rest of their lives. And now it was time. But she could not help asking, again, "Why didn't you fight?"

"Who this time?"

"Rufus, Henry, Thaxton, me, my parents, Victor, the whole world that says and feels that you and I are not appropriate for one another, that for you to mix your blood with mine would be a pollution."

"Your parents haven't said that."

"Don't you understand? It runs under everything. Why haven't we let them know? It's been months now."

"Not that long. I told you. I'd find it hard to announce such a thing.

You make it sound as if I would say something like, 'Oh, by the way, I have a wooden leg.'"

"But it's you who must tell them. It's not for me to do."

"They're always surrounded by guests or just rushing off someplace. If you want, the next time I see them I'll make a declaration and ask for your hand."

"That's not good enough."

"Arm?"

"You know what I mean."

"Shall I send a telegram?"

"I mean it doesn't explain why you don't fight. It doesn't."

"I'm tired, Catherine, I'm tired. I've killed men. I spent four years of my life preparing for it and doing it. And now I find myself in the safest place on earth, a place that I nearly died to preserve and protect. I'll fight when I have to, but I've been at peace for a year and I like it. If I can avoid several actions at once, I will. I have enough to do without trying to cure anti-Semitism. I think I've cured my share of German anti-Semitism."

"What other actions?"

"I can't live on your money. If I can't pull my weight, we can't last."

"I don't care about the money," she said. "I hate the money. I'll give it all up."

"No you won't, and you shouldn't. You're the only child. You can't cut the line like that."

"And I can cut the line by marrying a Jew?"

"That's different," he said.

"Why?"

"You'll know when you see our sons and daughters. Nothing that's admirable in the line will cease, and they'll be the proof. Those who would say no will have to look them in the eye and back down.

"Out of decency, you have to accept the wealth your parents bequeath, and pass it forward to our children. But not to me. I have to make my own way, or it's finished."

She was distressed, so he tried to explain. "I had a friend in college with whom I used to study languages. He would come to my room, and because it was so small we'd go up on the roof and sit in the open air, drilling in declensions and vocabulary — and syntax: you can never know enough syntax in a language that's not your own.

"When I would go to *his* house, a Bulfinch greystone on Brattle Street, we would sit in his garden or in the library and servants would bring us iced tea and hors d'oeuvres. His father was, or still is, the forest ranger in charge of Mount Moosilauke in New Hampshire."

"I used to climb that mountain," Catherine said, "in camp. But I didn't realize forest rangers made that kind of money."

"They don't."

"I do know that, Harry."

"They were as poor as you might think a forest ranger's family in the thirties would be."

"What happened?"

"There was no school nearby, so they had to send him away at an early age, and St. Paul's took him on scholarship. He became indistinguishable from his classmates and stuck with them at Harvard, where he met and fell in love with a Radcliffe girl early in freshman year: Alison Ranley."

"Chemicals."

"And everything else. Out of California."

"I know."

"She was a lovely girl, and by sophomore year he had decamped to Brattle Street and was pushing around a very expensive English pram with a beautiful baby in it. They didn't have to rent the baby."

"Not a bad ending," Catherine said hopefully.

"No, but that's not the end."

"I hope they're all right."

"They're not. Once, we were up on my roof — we were really young then. We were in the middle of vocabulary. It was a beautiful day. He looked at his watch and jumped up. 'I have to go,' he said, and gathered his books. 'We have a dinner tonight.'

"'Who's coming?' I asked. I think I was trying for an invitation.

"'The dean of the law school.'
"'Harvard Law School?'
"'Yes,' he said. 'Alison is endowing a chair.'
"'Oh.'
"As he was about to go down the stairs, he turned to me and said, 'Harry, I love Alison more than anything in the world, and I wouldn't have it any other way, but if you can help it, don't marry money. Maybe for people who're older it's different, but for me it's a little like the lid sliding over a sarcophagus. The money takes from you far more than it gives. Trust me.'"

Because she was both hurt and frightened, Catherine became cold and reserved. Harry went on. "In November of 'thirty-nine they were living in London, where he was working in one of the family's subsidiaries or banks — I don't know. He joined the Royal Air Force, was trained as a pilot, and flew in the Battle of Britain."

"That's impressive."

"Yes, and he died in the Battle of Britain. He left behind a young child and a young wife. That's not unusual, but her family and his had begged him to come home. It wasn't his war at the time. It didn't have to be."

"I see." Catherine could be quite severe. She now simultaneously instructed, challenged, reprimanded, and risked him. Even in her incomparable voice, she was clearly calling him out. "Harry," she said, "you're not marrying money. You're marrying me. If you don't know the difference, there will be no marriage."

Proud of her strength and infatuated with her courage, he said, "I do know the difference. How could I not? And thank God for it. At the same time, I have to make my own way."

"But you are, so what's the problem?" She was gripping the edge of the settee very hard.

"We find ourselves," he said, without fear, but without hope, "in a very unusual situation. I have yet to make it completely clear to you." Then, with the sound of the jackhammers coming faintly from uptown and out toward the East River, and as the sun wheeled through the summer sky illuminating the dust of the streets, he told her in detail for the first time how and why he was rapidly going under. One did not have to be an accountant to understand. It seemed so unnecessary, but there it was. For him, and now for her, the world, which since the war had ended, since he had returned from the army, had become beautiful and calm, had now taken a somewhat different turn.

# 24

## THE ECONOMICS OF HOT WATER

WHATEVER THE OPIATES he was given, they confounded gravity and time and relaxed him with glimpses of eternity that slipped through his fingers before he was fully conscious. When the evening dose wore off in the morning, the hot, irritable feeling beneath his skin was as welcome as a cool rain, for it meant that, even if not for long, he was about to come into the clear. Though in August the city was half emptied, at eight o'clock the buses crowded Amsterdam Avenue, the bells of St. John the Divine banged out the hour, the sun was still low enough in the east to be not entirely white, and the eastern face of every block was propped up by a wedge of black shadow.

Slipping in and out of relaxed memories and dreams, he couldn't tell one from another. Though the sun had begun to bake the western façades of every avenue in the city, Harry was with Catherine at Amagansett, where it was a July night, the sand and the wind were cold, and the waves were thudding at the shoreline. To the left the ocean was surging and black. To the right, running on its straight track through the dunes, the New York train sounded its whistle in a mournful note before it shot through the crossings, its light blinding whatever lay ahead. They reclined on the slope of a dune. Sometimes a summer night speaks longingly of the clarity of winter and the hardness of things, from which respite is only temporary. As they warmed in one another's embrace, they knew this.

He was alone. The walls of the room were beige. A Protestant cross — wood without Jesus — was hanging on an interior wall facing two large windows filled with the sun, which would soon climb above the clouds and spend the day diffused as if by cotton, but now was like a dam-burst of white gold. Most hospital rooms do not have airy spaces, flowers in Chinese vases, or fine English furniture. He had had no idea that such accommodations existed, until he had awakened in one at St. Luke's, to which Catherine, after a telephone call to her father, had had him transferred.

When he was able to speak, he told her that most of the hospitals he had seen were in humid tents where forty men, many of whom would die, lay in undistinguished rows. Rain leaked through frays in the canvas and was caught in buckets that nurses and orderlies tripped over and kicked. The dead had no mourners, and were taken out in sacks. Wind shook the walls, and the thunder of artillery echoed back and forth in duels that helped to keep the tents always full.

"When you endow a hospital wing, you get to have a room like this," she said, "with the payment of an extra charge so modest it's basically fraudulent. When the people who endowed it aren't in it, South American dictators are."

"I didn't endow anything."

"Neither did I. Neither of us deserves it, but we've got it. You can worry about the inequity when you recover."

Every day she came at ten A.M., and with the exception of three half-hour breaks in which she walked briskly around the Columbia campus, she stayed until five unless she had rehearsal. He felt strength and energy whenever he would awake. Then it would quickly drain from him and, unless diverted, he would drift back to sleep. Even with Catherine there, he slept while she read on the sofa beneath the cross. It was back far enough in the room, and the room was big enough, so that in storms when the light disappeared as if in an eclipse she would have to switch on a lamp to read by it as sheets of rain lashed the windows.

Such steady, heavy rains, which in August were plentiful, would put him to sleep like nothing else, and because her practice was to leave without waking him, she seemed to appear and disappear supernaturally. He wanted to get more of a grip on things, but his body's insatiable need for rest, the opiates, and the tranquility of his room won out.

The door opened and a day nurse entered, a matronly Irish woman with green eyes, gray-blond hair, and the distinctive speech of a woman one generation away from an unadulterated brogue. It cascaded upon itself like water spilling down rocks, full, echoing, and clear. "The young lady comes at ten. Who is she, then, that sits with you like an angel? You're a lucky one. And you should have a bath, if only for her. Can you walk by yourself today?"

"I think so."

"There was a gas leak on the street side, so the kitchen will be an hour and a half late with breakfast, but that has nothing to do with the hot water, which is made by the boilers, oil-fired I'm told. I'll have the sheets changed and the room done while you're at it. You don't run Argentina, do you?" she asked, used to dictators with heart ailments.

"I'm working on it," Harry said. He began, exhaustingly, to get himself out of bed. As she opened an armoire to his right, he felt the breeze made by the door. Swaying slightly as he stood, he let her help him into a robe of navy-blue cashmere, a gift from Catherine after he had told her that he had never owned a bathrobe.

"Are you capable?" the nurse asked.

"I'll go slowly."

After she left, he sat in a chair and laboriously put on his hospital slippers. Then, getting up, he shuffled across the floor until he reached the door, breathing heavily, his heart pounding. He knew from previous experience that it would be all or nothing, that when recovery took hold it would seem unbelievable that he had been so weak. Using the wall for support, he made his way to the bathroom, turned on the light, closed the door, and breathed as if he had just run up every flight of stairs in the Empire State Building. Then he went to the tub and twirled the faucet handles. Water gushed as if from a fire hose. While the tub was filling, to save his strength he closed his eyes as he undressed. A bulb behind a frosted glass fixture made the light in the bathroom pearly, and when the tub was half full he grasped scored handles on the wall and lowered himself into the hot water. Then, in a half sleep, he heard a stream coursing through the overflow.

Thought and dream came together as he lay in the bath. He saw a stream of black water, choked with flowers and green stems. It was busy, slow, and quiet, with a life of its own. He thought of things, like seawater or a clear lake, obviously featureless, inert, and pellucid, that in strong light show upon the bottom a motion-filled gray marbling like a silent after-action report of desperate goings-on above—the battles of currents, eddies, fronts, and waves in three dimensions even a small patch of which all the physicists in the world could not analyze precisely, but that the light makes easily apprehensible.

Taken all together, the oceans, seas, rivers, lakes, and rivulets, even water dripping off eaves or rain upon a tin roof, but especially the surf and the wind out on the open sea that whips the tops of whitecaps and spreads them back in spray with a sound like that of gently shattering icicles, but softer. . . . Taken all together, the insistent lapping of little waves on inland lakes as if protesting imprisonment by the land, the roar of hurricanes across the Atlantic, typhoons in the Pacific, and the breaking of waves all over the world. . . . All this, in volume and variation too great to imagine, is the earth singing unceasingly, giving off not just light reflected from a star to mark its existence in the void, but also a lovely, comforting, continuing song.

In strong incandescent light that made the water sparkle, he took stock. His left knee was swollen and purple, with a dozen black stitches projecting in ugly knots as if from a rotted fishing net. His right thigh, unevenly mottled and red, was the color of a split pomegranate. Above four broken ribs distributed with a bias for the right side were fields of bruises and a stitched laceration ragged with more black thread. The marks on his arms and shoulders were inconsequential except over contusions of the bone, which ached deeply. His right eye was blackened, three tiny stitches held the left lower lip together where it had been split, and the dental lab was fabricating crowns for two back molars on the left, which had been painfully shattered. And he had a fever.

As he moved his arms in slow motion to carry water for splashing on his face, breathing hard from exertion, he wondered whether anyone who made movies had ever been beaten. No artistic license could justify the immediate leaps back into action of heroes who had sustained the equivalent of half a dozen fatal beatings. Beyond the will of its speakers, the English language had conflated two meanings in a single word, and whatever the final outcome, to be beaten, if not actually then to be beaten, is to feel beaten, and for a long time afterward.

Now that he could hardly move, he sought refuge in unprotected sleep, and was aware every moment that by their not coming for him and not having killed him, his enemies were merciful and had powers far beyond his own. As long as a slow, careful shuffle across the room would leave him breathless, or he might die from an embolism or an infection, the idea that he might take retribution would seem impossible.

Hospital water ran from huge boilers in the enormous quantities needed every day for washing, cleaning, and bathing. No one anywhere would know the difference if he turned off the tap or he did not. The sound of the inrush, the outflow, and the stirring of the water was pleasant. Their action aerated his bath and made it bearable despite its high temperature.

He knew that the water came from holding reservoirs in the city and the vast lakes upstate that in times of drought he had seen with their banks advancing and the ruins of farmhouses suddenly emerging after many years. Those reservoirs now were full, so he fixed his attention on the oil that fueled the boilers. To sustain the river of hot water, a fire had to burn hard, and for that, oil had to be drawn from the ground, refined, shipped to New York, distributed, stored, and paid for. If all the taps at St. Luke's were left open, would it be only a matter of time until, without intervention, the hospital would go bankrupt? It was privileged with the immortality of institutions; with the loyalty, participation, and resources of thousands; and with a tax exemption. How many years might it go on if the taps were opened full? He tried to calculate an answer, but for lack of pertinent facts he could not.

In his own case, however, the facts were available. He had no contributors, no endowment of any magnitude, no institutional immortality, no multiplicity, no freedom from taxation. Eventually and soon at his rate of flow there would be no more money, water, or blood. With their vast reservoirs, the Hales had at any moment much more coming in than going out. The excess grew every day of every year, and there was so much left that to be decent they could only give it away, which they did. Here, for example, they had paid for a great deal more than all the water the hospital could use even had the taps been left open all year. What a feeling—more coming in, always, than draining out. The rich are different, he understood, not because they have more things or more freedom, but because they are not confronted with the perpetual metaphor of death by exsanguination. Our time runneth out always, but theirs doesn't, until it does. Of course, most people, by discipline, hard work, or, at the very least, self-denial, could adjust the balance and create equanimity. In this sense, the chief treasure of the wealthy would always be available via simple modesty of desire.

The admirable basis and sound practices of Copeland Leather would ordinarily have been able to see it through at least a decade of difficulties, but not now. They had a year at most, after which the business would fail and he himself would have nothing. What was the difference, he wondered, between him and the Hales and the Marrows? Success begat success, optimism begat optimism, cheerfulness begat cheerfulness, and all begat confidence, which incestuously begat them over and over again. Were they brought to this state solely by luck? He would not allow himself the luxury of believing that, if only because he was horrified by the prospect of relying on luck alone. Work, discipline, suffering, fortitude, brilliance, courage, risk—all these were to luck as tugs are to the docking of an ocean liner.

Thus, when purely by accident one evening while making his way through Madison Square he saw Verderamé, he found it impossible not to try to talk to him once more. It wasn't a matter of thinking. The instant he beheld him dressed to go out on the town he was struck by a rush of optimism, and immediately ran toward him, leaping over an iron fence, crossing a flower bed, and closing—from behind—before the bodyguards were aware of his presence. Harry could run very fast, and he took obstacles like a hurdler.

"Jesus Christ!" Verderamé exclaimed, startled, then embarrassed to have been startled. Shamed and irritated, the bodyguards surrounded Harry and immobilized him. Two had drawn pistols, and held them, cocked, against either side of his gut.

"Mr. Verderamé," he said, not having had the time to be frightened, but breathing hard from his sprint. "I saw you from over there. I just want to talk to you. I didn't mean to scare you."

"You didn't mean to scare me," Verderamé said, weighing the words. "You didn't mean to scare me."

"No."

"You didn't scare me."

"I just got excited because" — Harry tried to find the right words — "we may not mean anything to you, but you're very important to us. You have the fate of a lot of people in your hands."

"Who are you?" Verderamé asked.

Harry looked at him not in disbelief but with the feeling that comes just before despair, and he told him.

The guards stepped back a foot. Verderamé no longer looked like someone just missed by a bullet. Turning his left hand in the accompanying gesture of an exasperated question, he asked, "What do you want? You're making your payments, what do you want?"

"I wanted to ask you," Harry said, "why we're the only ones in the building who pay you rather than Gottlieb, and why we pay ten times what everyone else pays, and if maybe you think we're a different business, or another kind of business, or bigger — much bigger — than we really are, and if it's all a mistake."

"A mistake? It's not a mistake."

"But, then, *why?*" Harry pressed, tempering his argumentative recklessness with a deferential way of speaking that was so unnatural to him that not only was he ashamed of it, but it didn't communicate deference as much as it did defiance.

Verderamé looked up and turned his head quickly, snapping it in anger and disgust. Harry knew exactly what it meant. The bodyguards knew exactly what it meant, and at the south end of the square two cops who knew exactly what it meant turned away as the four of them began to beat Harry, who, had he attempted to fight back, could not have prevailed without a weapon, and, knowing this, sought only to escape. When he couldn't, he tried to protect himself with his hands, arms, and pulled-in legs. They took long, considered, well aimed strokes, choosing a target on his body and thrusting for it as if they were splitting wood or hitting a golf ball.

Circling like a tiger, Verderamé held up his hand to signal a pause. They stopped. Harry struggled on as if they were still landing blows, a cry emerging from lungs filling with fluid. Verderamé said, "When I get out of that restaurant, I don't want to see you on this sidewalk. So no matter how you feel, no matter how unconscious you wanna be, walk off. That's my answer to your fuckin' question."

Then they resumed. Even had they the hands of pianists it would have been a terrible beating, but their fists were thick and hard, and at the end each one got in one last kick and a laugh, like children playing soccer with a ball they had not yet learned to control.

Harry tried hard to remain conscious, but he couldn't, and the last thing he remembered as he lay bleeding on the sidewalk was his fear that he would still be there when Verderamé came out. He could neither move nor stay awake, and he just let go.

The two cops walked over, tapped Harry with their feet, and, when there was no response, one went to a call box to summon an ambulance. The ambulance drivers were told, and the police report said, that an unruly drunk had attacked passersby, fallen, and injured himself. Eventually, Cornell found him in Bellevue, unconscious and filthy with blood, and when Catherine came she took him up to St. Luke's. After a while, by the time he could walk, he could converse, although he couldn't do both simultaneously.

Now, as someone else's hot water ran richly, it was also clear. It was possible to lose everything in an instant or over time. It was possible to be confronted by forces, natural or otherwise, that one could not overcome by virtue. Courage, greatness, honesty, all could be defeated. He had understood this on the field of battle as it was illustrated by the way death chose among the soldiers. But after such a war, in which scores of millions had died, how could anyone tolerate corruption? How could Verderamé's tiny army rule a city of eight million? How could such a thing, after so much sacrifice, in a country where millions of men were now hardened soldiers, be allowed? There was no good reason, and yet it was so, and as the hot water cascaded over the lip of the overflow and into oblivion, so would his money and so eventually would the water of his life.

When Catherine arrived at ten he had had his long bath and was very tired. She had never been seriously ill or wounded, and did not understand the weakness and alteration of time with which such things are accompanied. Impatient for him to recover, she had no idea that once he did he would need space in which to catch up, and that in some ways he never would. As lonely and kind as she had been, always, she had known mainly victory, even (eventually) over Victor, and she assumed that for Harry it would have to be the same. He found her conversation rapid.

"We're going to open at the Schubert in Boston on the twenty-third."

"Of August?" he asked, as if it could be possible.

"September, Harry. Sidney says it's perfect, because everyone is back from vacation, including the college students, who are just starting their courses and have very little anxiety."

"Where does anxiety come into it?"

"Because they're not worried about grades or falling behind, they go out a lot."

"I suppose they do."

"Didn't you?" It was clear that he hadn't. In the condition he was in, he looked like he never could have. Still, she pressed. "Why not?"

"At the beginning of each term I worked as if my life depended upon it. I used to work for the first five or six weeks the way people work before exams." Tired, he stopped.

"Why?" she asked gently.

"For the foundation."

Thinking reflexively of her family's foundation, she was momentarily confused. "Of the course work," she said, clarifying for herself.

"You master a subject at the beginning or not at all. I would read all the required readings and take volumes of notes—not précis, but questions, arguments, answers—all above and beyond the call. I would read the suggested readings, too. I would memorize passages, tables, equations...."

"Was there a particular reason?"

"Had to get all A's."

This upset her. It was against the ethos of the Ivy League, almost anti-social. She came to her reaction naturally, without knowing why, but her questions, though unspoken, were unambiguous: Why were you so driven? Why did you have to stand out? Wasn't this somehow dark and aggressive, a kind of warfare that was uncalled for?

He read the questions in her eyes. "It was expected of us in the thirties. We weren't really welcome. If a Jew didn't shine academically, the implicit question was, Why do you think you deserve to be here? Where's your ticket? I had to have a ticket, and I had to punch it myself."

"Didn't people hate you for working so hard?"

"Yes," he said, remembering, "and then what could I do but work harder? I rowed and fenced with the same intensity, gained as much as I lost, lost as much as I gained."

"But didn't you ever do anything or go anyplace just for fun, without the fight in you?"

He thought for a moment. "Girls could make me forget—their goodness, and gentleness. They were sometimes so kind that I wondered what the hell I was doing. But it never was quite enough, as the world was rougher than they were, and I knew this, so I stayed in the fight. I worked the hardest in September and October. It's a good time, however, to open a play. Sidney's right."

The talking had exhausted him, and his eyes closed. While he slept, she read the paper until he stirred, and then she virtually leapt out at him with the announcement that she would be staying at the Ritz: "The whole cast. You have to do it to impress the newspapers and put yourself on the highest level. We're almost broke and we should be staying in South End boarding houses, but if the *Globe* comes to do an interview in your boarding house, they assume you're not at the top of the game on Broadway, and write it into the article. The Barrymores don't stay in rooms to let. *Bella figura.*" She came closer as he lay in bed. "We rehearse in Boston beginning after Labor Day. My parents have invited us to Bar Harbor for the weekend. If the weather's good, which is always iffy in Maine, it'll be perfect. You'll be well enough by then to get around and to sail. No one else will be there. It's more modest than East Hampton, no servants, and very quiet. My parents know that you've been ill."

"Did you tell them why?"

"No, that's for you."

"I'm going to deliver a hell of a package."

"They already know about the other thing."

"They do?"

"Someone told them. Then they asked me, and I said yes."

"What did they say then?"

"They didn't say anything."

"Nothing?"

"What should they have said?"

"I don't know."

"They're civilized people."

"They are, I know, and I won't approach them as I did Harvard."

"Have you ever been to Maine?"

"I knew a girl in Maine once, on an island near Portland. It was in summer. We were both twenty, but she was nothing like you."

"That's good," Catherine said only teasingly, "because, had it been the other way around, you'd be in hot water."

# 25

## THE WAKE OF THE *CRISPIN*

SOMETIMES IN THE WAR, will exhausted, faith depleted, and death seemingly imminent, Harry had bowed his head, closed his eyes, and prayed. Not for victory, not for survival. He asked nothing. He just prayed. And having thus surrendered he was lifted and empowered, with a foresight of ensuing battles that then ran before him as if in slow motion, the enemy's moves almost as still as a painting.

Now, as then, although on a lesser scale and in a lesser register, he waited to be shown the way ahead. Though his broken ribs would take months to heal completely, within a few days of coming home he had begun to run and swim, carefully. And though it was still hot, the declining sun announced that autumn was gathering somewhere beyond September.

Just before the Labor Day weekend, Catherine called to say that if he could be ready she would pick him up in a taxi (she had added "honey"), not at about half past eight but in an hour. Someone who had lived out of a knapsack for years and felt little privation even though half its weight had been ammunition, could of course be ready in an hour. "I'll be out front," he said, assuming that she had changed their reservations and booked an earlier train. As it had stood, they would not have arrived in Bar Harbor until the holiday was half over. Now they would have an extra day.

The taxi stood at rest across the street on the park side, facing north. He thought that the driver, instead of making a U-turn and cutting across at 86th, might want to gain an extra six blocks on the meter by using 96th. It could actually be faster, in that getting over to

Park higher uptown would be easier, and shooting down Park rather than Central Park West would be better in that Park was wider and they wouldn't have to cross at midtown.

They did take 96th, and when they sped across the southbound lanes of Park he then assumed that they would turn north and go to the 125th Street station to get on the New Haven and Hartford, but they crossed the northbound lanes as well and continued east. "Where are we going?" he asked, with the anxiety of someone, misrouted in a taxi, who knows he will have to pay both for the driver's mistake and for correcting it. He looked at his watch as if he knew what time the train was leaving.

"Lunch," she said, "at a great restaurant I know. It's not crowded, but it's a little noisy. I hope you won't mind."

"We're not booked on an earlier train?"

"No."

"But we do have reservations," he said, suspiciously, as the taxi turned north onto the East River Drive. "In the Bronx?"

"No, Harry. They're mostly in South Dakota and places like that," she said, "where there are Indians."

He knew something was up when she got like that. "Are we going to eat in Queens? Has it ever been done?"

"Wrong."

"Westchester? Not Connecticut."

"No."

"Where? A nice German restaurant? They're always popular after a war, because people love a light German lunch on a hot summer day — ten or twelve pounds of potatoes, a pound or two of wurst, sauerkraut, and a gallon of dark beer. Then we can play tennis."

She had her family's characteristic smile when amused. It was generous, restrained, and mischievous. "It's not German."

"Then what is it?"

"It's American."

"What's it called?"

"N-something, I don't really remember. I've been there only a few times."

"N-something? N-what?"

"Seven six two eight?" She looked at the roof of the taxi. "Seven six two four? Does it matter?"

"That's a peculiar name for a restaurant."

"I admit that."

"Perhaps it's Maison N — seven six two eight? Or Chez — seven six two eight?"

"No," she said, "because it's American."

By this time they were speeding along the deck of the Triboro Bridge. To their right, over the East River, Manhattan formed a spectacular palisade of brown and gray, still glinting in the eastern sun. It was so immense and of such great mass and depth that they leaned slightly toward it as if by the command of gravity, and they felt as if they were flying above the river, now a cool gray tinted with the blue of the sky and flecked with gulls. The next thing they knew, after a shock of cool air on the bridge, and then a long, lovely embrace, was coming to a stop at the Marine Aviation Terminal. "I see," he said, "but I'm really not used to getting into a plane if I don't have a parachute."

"Steel yourself," was her answer. "It's a new world."

At the end of a wooden pier sloping toward and then projecting into a back bay of Long Island Sound, a huge gray clipper, its wings projecting into fine points far from the fuselage, faced outward toward a run of open water. Several men were working atop it, some now more than a hundred feet apart, inspecting the four enormous engines, the ailerons, and the flaps. In comparison to the plane they looked like the figures on a wedding cake, and, dressed in what looked like naval uniforms, they glowed in white.

"That's quite a restaurant," Harry declared, reading the black letters on the right wing, or perhaps, because it was a seaplane, the starboard wing: *NC 18604.*

"I knew it began with N," she said.

"Whatever it begins with, it's a great way to get to Boston."

They walked faster than they normally would have, and their heels knocking on the wood planks of the pier made the sound of departure.

"It doesn't go to Boston until it drops me off on the trip back. It's a charter. We'll pick up my parents in East Hampton."

The whole plane was for them. "I've never lived like this, Catherine. It's unsettling."

"Would you rather spend twelve hours on a train?"

"No."

"Does flying bother you?"

"Only through flak."

"Come on, then," she told him. At the door they were greeted by two stewardesses in pale blue uniforms of French-tailored, superfine wool. Each of them had straight blond hair that seemed almost lacquered and was pulled back on the left side, and each was heavily made up.

Stepping into the cabin, Harry and Catherine saw a small room with leather banquettes and, at one end, a table covered with white linen. Vases of flowers were held on gimbals, and the interior was lit like an expensive restaurant on the Upper East Side. As soon as they sat together on a banquette and strapped on their seat belts, two men jumped down from a forward hatch, closed it after them, and went to the flight deck. The main door had already been shut and bolted. Engines were started one by one and brought up to equal tach. The stewardesses took to their folding seats, snapped closed their buckles, and the engines came alive, moving the plane out onto smoothly rippling water.

The dominant shades of blue and silver on the bay were compressed by the heat into an opalescent mist, and by contrast any touch or smattering of gold was breathtaking and hypnotic: the stewardesses' gold earrings, rich in the sunbeams and shadows of the salon; the distant skyscrapers, some yellow-gold; and the ordinary, highly polished brass cabin fittings. Their effulgence in the blur of silver light made a glowing fume around them not in halos but in orbs. And although Catherine's earrings were diamonds the size of buttons, her hair was gold and it glowed.

The plane pivoted and then strained forward, throttles open, engines deafening. A ray of sunlight tracked steadily through the cabin, seizing upon a rose in a gimbaled flute that slowly turned as if to meet the light that warmed the rose to the color of a fire engine. As the enormous plane lifted from water into air, everything was aglow.

With military timing, the stewardesses unbuckled at the same instant, one moving briskly toward the galley and the other offering her two passengers Champagne. Catherine declined, sure that Harry would follow suit, but he surprised her.

She signaled to the stewardess that she would join him. "But you don't really drink."

"There's no way I could forgo it now."

"Why?"

"Because I'm sitting on a web bench, weighed down with parachute, carbine, pack, ammunition, flares, food, and all kinds of other things. My harness is so tight it compresses my body painfully and makes me even more claustrophobic. I have to wear my lousy helmet because there's no room for it on my lap. My carbine keeps slipping into a tilt because of the vibrations. The sound is deafening. I'm surrounded by scores of men, the cabin smells, we're about to jump into battle, the flak has started, the evasive maneuvers, the nausea. I'm doing my best not to throw up, and some people are not as successful as I am, and I see only a devilish red light, the black gleam of oiled weapons, and blinking eyes.

"So, if now, two miles above the ground, a beautiful woman with hair that shines in the sunlight offers me a glass of Champagne, there's no way that I'm not going to take it, because you don't look an angel in the gift eye — whatever that means. I don't really know what it means."

"But I do," she said, and then the clipper banked.

It followed the Sound for a few minutes before making a chevron across Long Island at Islip, gaining altitude for a short time only to begin its descent over Westhampton. It flew parallel to the beach, as if after many years of spanning the Atlantic, Pacific, and Indian oceans it was impelled to strike out for Europe. As they descended, the surf came more clearly into view. From a high altitude it had looked steady, deliberate, and slow: it crawled. But from near its own level it was like herds of horses galloping toward the beach. It had from this perspective a persistent, wide-fronted, and purposeful urgency. To see it frustrated on the shore and pushed back in cataracts of foam was like witnessing the frustration of an invading army.

A relatively calm sea state allowed them to land on the ocean rather than the bay. Their first bounce came at the Georgica inlet, the second far past the Georgica Club, and then a series of closer and closer touches, the distance between them diminishing as it does when a stone is skipped across the surface of a pond, until the plane ploughed a steady white furrow deeper and deeper as it slowed. They came almost to a stop opposite the Hales' beach. Then they turned left ninety degrees and taxied toward the path that led through the dunes to the house, halting about a thousand feet offshore and idling the engines as the waves slowly pushed them toward land.

From the air as they approached, and then at each upward skip, they had seen the house. Beyond the dunes, sheltered from wind and surf, the gardens, fields, and pool—a clear sapphire—looked even better from afar than from close up. For her it was home, but for him, because he knew he would have to earn it and that he might never do so, it was especially beautiful in the foil of its inaccessibility.

What they saw next was Billy and Evelyn and one of the gardeners dragging a light rowboat across the beach and into the water. In a sundress and carrying her pumps, Evelyn waded to the stern, climbed in, and made her way to the bow as the boat rocked and yawed at the edge of the surf. The gardener, in Montauk fisherman's khakis and visored cap, stepped into the boat from amidships and took the oars. Then Billy, in a blue pin-cord suit with the pant legs rolled up above his knees, threw his shoes and socks onto the floorboards, loosened his tie, and pushed the boat over the shallows, keeping its prow pointed at the waves.

When a breaker would hit, he would push down with his hands on the top of the transom, lift himself high enough not to be soaked, and kick like a hysterical frog, his swimming motions acting as a rudder to stop the prow from being swung around by the waves. Then he would drop down and run forward, pushing the skiff ahead of him until the next wave. When finally the water was too deep, he threw himself into the boat and took a seat and an oar amidships, and he and the gardener rowed hard through the surf to reach open water. Then the gardener took over. He had been born a fisherman and was a gardener only because of fate and change. It would be easy for him to keep the lightened boat straight when speeding back to the beach and cresting the waves.

When they came alongside they were helped into the plane by the copilot, who stood by the door, carefully watching the rise and fall of the sea. Evelyn's dress was half wet from the waves and foam that had been battered into the air above the prow, her hair slightly disheveled. Billy was dry only from the waist up, and the triangle at the bottom of his tie was as dark with brine as if it were a strawberry dipped in chocolate. They were pleased that they had rowed out in such a way and with such skill that it seemed like something they did every day.

One could not fail to note not only that they took things in stride, but that they possessed immense resources of all types, and that Evelyn, though her dress was half wet and her hair disheveled, like her daughter and like any woman, looked more beautiful in the wind than she did in perfect presentation. The door was closed before they knew it, and the plane took off southward, climbed, and banked north. They would fly over the inner Cape, with Boston to the west shielded by its many islands and peninsulas, and then dash above the sea to Mount Desert Island.

While the sun was still high, the huge plane landed on Blue Hill Bay and taxied to within a hundred yards of Seal Cove. Engines idling, it sat gently rocking as its passengers were rowed to shore in two trips of a rubber dinghy. Then it turned around, brought itself to full power, and skimmed the top of the sea until it lifted and disappeared southward. A few hours before, Harry and Catherine had been in a taxi on the East River Drive in heat that seemed eternal, and now they were in Maine, with only the sound of a cold breeze in the pines. They started walking against the wind, with Evelyn clasping her arms together, as if in the pose of refusal, to warm herself.

Along the empty road it was fresh in a way that only the northland can be. Billy bent down and pressed his palms into the earth, inviting the others to do so. They did. It was cold. "The soil in East Hampton," he said, "and certainly in Central Park, is still hot. By the middle of September it'll be just warm, and not like this until the end of October." It was fine dirt, reddish black, and it muted their steps as they moved between thick walls of trees.

At the northern tip of Seal Cove Pond was a large cabin that for sixty or seventy years had sat on eighty acres at the end of a long, winding road. It had four bedrooms, four baths, and a lodge-like center room in which could be found the kitchen, a woodstove, a huge fireplace, a dining area, and wooden cabinets, some sturdily locked, keeping everything from bedding to rifles, provisions, jackets, fishing gear, books, lanterns, and games. Other than the food, half these items had descended from the nineteenth century, but as they were all of the highest quality, their age was only an asset.

The floors and walls were unfinished wood, there was no electricity, and the water came from a cistern in summer and, in winter, a hand-pumped well. Light came from lanterns, and the heat, hot water, and cooking depended upon fired wood, which meant a great deal of work and constant tending. From a southward-looking porch, the pond below was visible down its length of about a mile, a narrow and even stretch of water far warmer than the sea and now, though quickly fading, at its warmest. On both sides, walls of granite were fragrant with pines rooted like mountain climbers clinging to crags.

A jeep stood by the house, fueled and maintained by a caretaker who was seldom seen and who had stocked the pantry with groceries and fresh food. They threw open the doors to let in the air, which seemed to carry oxygen better than air in the city, perhaps because it came off the ocean and was free of the many millions of rooms, tunnels, and cul-de-sacs that in the city captured, tortured, and enslaved it. Billy built a fire in the woodstove while Harry was tasked with starting a medium-sized blaze in the fireplace as a primer for the larger one that would come in the evening. Billy watched him discreetly, wanting to see how he would make a fire, and thinking that he might not be very good at it after having been brought up on Central Park West. To the contrary, Harry quickly hatcheted some split logs into kindling and tinder, built a structure expertly, and brought it to an almost explosive conflagration with just one match and not a single breath.

With Catherine looking on, Billy asked, "Where'd you learn to do that? You make a fire like an arsonist. Bring me a brand so I can get this going."

Harry put a burning brand in the cast-iron shovel used for ashes and carried it across the floor to the woodstove. As Billy positioned it and blew until he was dizzy, he asked, "In the army?"

"No, when I was ten my mother died, and after that my father and I fled into the wilderness as often as we could, usually in a canoe. We started on the Hudson and went all the way up to the Adirondack chain of lakes. We did the Connecticut River, then Lake Champlain, and as time went by we went into Canada. I think we were probably Abercrombie's best customers who didn't go to Africa. Sometimes we'd be out for two months at a stretch. My father spent his youth on a farm and worked with his hands all his life. You couldn't have anyone better or smarter to take you through the wilderness."

"How could he have left his business unattended for so long?"

"He had a partner to help him run it, who still does, and manufacturing leather goods doesn't require split-second timing like trading on Wall Street. It wouldn't have mattered anyway: we had to get away, and we did. I'm not skilled at the social graces — as you may now know — but all we had and all I wanted day after day were paddle, rod, rifle, ax, and book. If you're out for months, when you make a fire you make your home."

"It must have served you well in the army," Evelyn said from the couch.

"On occasion."

"What's for dinner?" Catherine asked. And then, opening the icebox, she answered herself: "Half a dozen lobsters. Not again!"

"We're in Maine, Catherine. What would you expect, enchiladas? Oh, and I forgot to bring the bread from the plane," Evelyn announced. "They never have decent bread here."

"Oyster crackers will do," Catherine said.

"Only," Billy added, "if you like them. I don't, really." He was disappointed. "I'll bet that tonight it drops into the thirties. If the weather holds, we can sail tomorrow, or the next day. No rush."

"Where?" Harry asked.

"Just out into the Atlantic, beyond the sight of land. Ever since Catherine was a child she's loved to be on the sea. And if the weather's bad we can sail on the pond. A Winabout in a gale can give you a hell of a ride."

"And what does one do here at night other than read?" Harry asked.

"Games," said Billy, "and dinner — which takes a long time to cook and eat, and you have to boil water to wash the dishes. If our minds have slowed enough, as they tend to do up here — which is the whole point — we'll turn up the lanterns and play Monopoly. When Catherine would bring one of her friends or if her cousins were here we always used to play board games and do charades on the first night. Once, Honoria — quite a name — a very Mediterranean-looking girl for a Hale, lost a diamond as big as a golf ball as she was swimming in the pond. Well, not a golf ball, but children shouldn't have such things. It's still there.

"We didn't finish those games, because the children would fall asleep and we would carry them to their beds. We would try to preserve the board for the next night, but with three or four kids, a dog, and the wind, good luck. Once, the money blew into the pond, I guess to be with the diamond, and for years thereafter the game was much harder, but that seemed appropriate as the Depression dragged on. We probably won't finish tonight, either, because we'll have too elaborate a dinner and start too late. But the main thing is that we'll sleep a sleep such as no one in New York has ever slept. The air will be cold and it will be bitterly quiet. No appointments to keep tomorrow, no taxis, no garbage cans making a symphony at four A.M. All in all, the effect is like that of anaesthesia."

"I think I've outgrown Monopoly, Daddy," Catherine averred.

"Nonsense," said Billy, slyly. "No one ever outgrows Monopoly. What do you think I do all day?"

"Yes," Evelyn added, in the same self-deprecating tone, "for people like us, it's like looking at a family album."

While Billy and Evelyn sat on the porch in the sun, Catherine and Harry went through an unmowed field to a dock from which they swam (gently, for his sake) a mile down and another mile back up the pond. The water was comfortable, sweet, and slightly rippled by the wind. Had the distance been shorter or the surroundings less entrancing they might have increased their speed, but swimming slowly past the granite walls, determined to get to the end and back, their pace was as leisurely as if they were drifting on a slow current. They were in the water for almost three hours.

Halfway back, feeling as if she had been born and raised in the lake, Catherine asked, "Do you know what we could do? My father could deed the house to us. Just with the money I have now, we could stay here in perpetuity, with neither doubt nor wants. We could fill it with books and music, sail on the *Crispin*, swim, run, catch lobsters and fish, and live with silence, the wood fires, the pure air. We could buy a tractor and have the best garden the soil would permit. We could import soil. We would have no schedule. We could throw away clocks and watches and lie together for as long as we wished. Our children would go to the local school, and we would supplement their education carefully and well. We can do this if we want."

"You would have to give up your career," he said. "You wouldn't be able to sing."

"Yes I would."

"Not in the theater, not with a live orchestra, not lifting a thousand hearts."

"I'd give that up to lift just one."

"You're scared of the opening?"

"Everybody's scared of the opening. It has nothing to do with that. And you'd have to give up your career, too."

"That would be easy, since I don't have one."

"Not yet, but you will. You could give your share of the business to Cornell."

"And where would we find the friction, the sparring with the world, that you need to feel alive?"

"Where is it now, in this swim?" she asked. "There's no strain. We're moving slowly and yet we're covering a large distance, enjoying every moment of it, and we'll be hungry tonight."

"Can't do it," Harry said.

"Why not?"

"I'm too young for that, and so are you. We can come here for vacations, long ones, a month or two. And then we'll go back to New York in the fall. How could we do without New York in the autumn? How could anyone?"

Harry was nervous at dinner because he thought the conversation might turn to him. It did, but not in the way he expected. The temperature had dropped ten degrees and everyone was grateful for the fire. The lobsters, slightly charred, sizzling upon pewter chargers, had shrunk in their shells and smelled deliciously of brine. The three Hales, like the three bears, had wine in proportion to their size, sex, and age. Billy had carried up a bottle of white Haut-Brion wrapped in the *New York Times,* which got so wet in the surf boat that it became like papier-mâché, and news about troubles in the Mediterranean was fused with a report of a tennis match and an ad for garden gnomes: it would have been an odd story had anyone been able to decode it. Wine, Billy explained, could not be left in an unheated house in the winter, not in Maine, although Scotch presented no problem. "Too bad you can't take advantage of that," he went on. "Sitting on the porch with a tumbler of Scotch is more salutary than three years in a Swiss asylum.

"By the way," he went on, "why were you hospitalized? I asked Catherine but she said to ask you. Did you have an accident? You've got the remnants of. . . ." And here Billy made a gesture with his hands to indicate the bruises and areas of stitching.

Harry replied with a question. "Please don't take this the wrong way, but did you ever have any problems with organized crime?"

Evelyn stiffened in her chair. "Uh-oh," Billy said. "No, I didn't."

"Why not? I would think that, as you're in the business of money, vast sums of which can be carried on a slip of paper, they would find Wall Street and the banks irresistible."

"The Mafia?"

Harry nodded.

"They do. They hunger after us. The more abstract an activity, the easier it is to appropriate it, if, like a forger or an accountant, you know the procedures, you have the skills, and you're patient. We get around that with controls and exclusion. Our people come from Harvard, Yale, and Princeton. It's a different world, with different thieves, and to the Mafia it's unknown and as yet impenetrable. They would stick out, you see, much as I would in their society."

"What about the back office, where Harvard, Yale, and Princeton don't ever set foot?"

"They do when they're young, but, it's true, not as a career. The back office is all Irish, the kind of people who have been honest cops for a hundred years. Most of our employees are related, and everyone knows everyone else. It's like a tribe. It is a tribe, and these people, the salt of the earth, have the integrity of saints."

"Do you keep out Italians, Daddy?" Catherine asked.

"We haven't reached the stage of keeping anyone out, and when the ice does start to break up on the American rivers, which it will, we won't do that. But for now it's us and the Irish, and we're in a different universe than the Mafia. I don't know how the Jewish firms handle the Jewish gangsters, because the Jewish firms employ Jews almost exclusively, so there's opportunity for penetration at all levels."

"I didn't mean fixing or embezzlement," Harry said, skirting the subject of ethnicity, a subject that had made Catherine nervously roll her knife back and forth over the tablecloth, "but of pure extortion, protection. The Jewish gangsters run the garment business, Irish gangsters in Boston run the government, and the Mafia extorts protection money from practically every establishment in New York. But not yours?"

"No. You take from people you know. You've got to know who they are, how their business operates, where they live, how they think, and what they'll do when pressed. There's a Turkish neighborhood in the Twenties. I guarantee you that the Mafia doesn't touch them. They're closely knit, who the hell knows what they're saying to each other, and they'll fight and die rather than surrender to extortion."

"How do you know this, Billy?" Evelyn asked.

"From living in New York all my life."

"But so have I."

"I've lived more on the outside, Evelyn. My job has been to protect you and Catherine. I sometimes deal with harsher things and rougher people." Turning back to the subject, he continued. "We're the last stop on the line. Like the Turks, we have our own culture, our own neighborhoods, our own organizations, and we are, to the new arrivals, the most mysterious of all, because we've been here longest, we have power, and we — not I — wear mauve-colored pants and canary-yellow blazers, which I'm sure scares them the way you might be scared by the regalia of a New Guinea headhunter. How the hell are they going to read somebody who dresses in madras and a boater? They can't. It's like the Rosetta stone without the Greek. The tribe is very strong, its powers unmatched and supreme. Pastels and madras are its plumage. Still," he went on, "Mafiosi know how to fight both aristocracy and its government. That's why they came into being in the first place. And even if we are to them the most impenetrable and most mysterious, we're also the richest prize. From time to time, they lunge for us."

"And what happens?"

"The first time was in the teens. They set up an extortion scheme on a narrow front, with the idea of breaking off one branch at a time. They threatened individuals and their families, but only people in the two weakest and smallest firms. In those times, however, there was both more structure and less. The big firms — Morgan, Stillman, and all the others — realized that they would be next. So they had a meeting, and what a meeting it was.

"They said — my father was at that meeting, and told me this. They said, more or less, 'These people get what they get because they have a secret and loyal army and they're willing to kill and, if necessary, die. So what we'll do is match and exceed them.' And they had the money, so they fielded *two* armies. Their reserve, army number two, was the United States Army itself and the whole government, which they had already partially purchased for various other reasons. I mean, everybody knows that. But now they gave even more to the politicians, from the president on down to the police commissioners and the precinct commanders, and the message was, keep these people off our backs. That would hardly have been enough at the time, given the powers of the government, which, domestically, were pretty feeble. So what did they do?

"They fielded their own army, literally. More than a thousand, mainly Irish, but plenty of Yankees, Southerners, Rough Riders, former marines who had served in the Philippines, cowboys. They armed and trained them at ten camps upstate, and, to keep them under control, organized them into ten separate command structures. Then they brought them to New York in the guise of bank guards and detectives. You should have seen Wall Street. It was an armed camp.

"The extortionists already felt pressure from the police. It was relatively straightforward: 'Do what you will, but don't touch the financial sector.' To really drive it in, they were called to a meeting at which they were told that the private army, the power of which they could not begin to match, knew their neighborhoods, knew who they were, where they lived, and that if they laid a hand on the financial sector, they and their families (you know, in their code, they don't touch families) would be massacred. Not hurt, not just killed . . . massacred. It was more horrible than they were, and they were told of it by very serious men who had done very terrible things in parts of the world they had hardly heard of, men who, if you saw them in the street, would give you a fright.

"For more than a decade, they didn't touch us. In the late twenties, however, after they had built themselves up during Prohibition, a new generation of their leaders came at Wall Street again. The army had melted away, and Morgan—that is, Junior—being old, tried a different tack. Not only had the power of organized crime increased, so had that of the government, which now had the means to go after them. With the government as its sole agency, the financial sector, at a cost of only a few millions, sent the same message, almost the same anyway, and it worked. Had it not worked, there were plenty of war veterans to be assembled once again into another private army. After all, the money and investments of the United States pass through us. If we're broken by the mob, they'll run the country. Not that we do, but they would, because in regard to such things they have no ethics whatsoever."

Catherine was amazed. That she hadn't known much of her father's world had been his intent.

"I expect that they'll make another run at us. Why not? But the response will be the same. It has to be." He cut a seared lobster tail in half and looked up, muscles tight from the determination he fell into by placing himself in the battle as he narrated it. "Why do you ask?"

The *Crispin*'s wake rolling out on the sea was as soft as the glint of polished silver. "Money," Billy said to Harry, while Catherine and Evelyn were forward, stretched out and asleep on cushioned benches in the mild sunshine, "is a net in which sometimes you can catch something as splendid as this."

"It also feeds you, keeps you sheltered, and cares for you when you're sick," Harry added, "keeps enemies at bay, protects the ones you love, and allows you to live without constant anxiety." He said this with some resentment.

"I know that," Billy said. "I was speaking of money in excess. It's the only thing for which excess money is good, and it's a risk to character, because you can do the same thing with hardly any money at all. The more civilized a civilization, the more that moments of beauty and contentment have no price and are accessible to everyone."

"That's right," Harry said. "In a park, in the lines of a building, in speech, in a dish that's cooked, in the way the days are laid out. In France even during the war everything stopped in the early afternoon and people would return home for lunch and a nap. Families reconstituted each day at the same time. It was a source of strength and continuity that no one and nothing, not the Germans, not the war, could break. I wanted us to do that here, working to live rather than living to work."

"Theater people say they live like that, don't they?" Billy asked.

"They do, but they're always 'on.' What kind of life can you have if you yourself are calculated for effect? And at lunchtime they're not yet out of bed."

"You don't like theater people, Harry?"

"I take them as they come. I'm just being accurate."

"I'm concerned about Catherine," her father admitted, "because I think it's a bad crowd."

"Not as bad," Harry said, "as the sons of some investment bankers."

"Obviously you don't like Victor."

"I'm not fond of him, no."

"I understand. He always struck Evelyn and me as being overly polite, hiding something, or perhaps a lot of things. Since the age of two. Is that possible? At that age? Politeness is wonderful if it's deep and quiet like a lake, but not if it gushes like a waterfall. He never called me Billy. He's known me all his life and he never called me Billy. Everyone calls me that—it's my name, for God's sake. I don't stand on ceremony. You call me Billy. . . ."

"I try not to."

"When we first met, you didn't, which is proper, but you should now."

"Billy," Harry said.

"What?"

"Just trying it out."

"Right. Look, they're sleeping. You never got to what happened. Maybe I can help."

"I appreciate that, but it's something for which I can't accept your help, just as I could never work in your firm or live off Catherine's money, either her own or her inheritance, in that it would make me unworthy of her."

"And what makes you think that you're worthy of her otherwise?"

"She does. And I trust her, I want to fulfill her expectations."

"Did she tell you that you're not to live on her money or work for me?"

"To the contrary, she wants to help in any way she can. She's generous. She has a good heart. She'd give everything."

"But you won't accept?"

"I won't."

"And what happens — if the Mafia beats you up it's a rather strong signal — what happens if you go down? I mean, if they kill you?"

"If they kill me, for a time Catherine will be like a war widow, of which there are plenty. Then she'll start anew. This is all around us right now."

"What do they want?"

"They want me out of business."

"Are you sure they don't just want money?"

"They're taking much more money than we can afford. They want to milk us and then kill us off."

"Why kill a cow rather than milk it like a long bond?"

"As a favor to a constituent, maybe a cousin, I don't know."

Billy moved the tiller and altered course by a few degrees. The sail stiffened, the wake doglegged, and, like a spotlight that had been turned with a crank, the sun began to shine more fully into the cockpit. "So what're you going to do?"

"Everyone asks me that, because no one knows the answer, and neither do I."

"What if I gave you the money? Set you up in another business? Or took you into the firm?"

"That's precisely what I can't accept."

"I understand, but this is an extraordinary situation. It could save your life. Catherine loves you. I'll do whatever's necessary, and it wouldn't be a strain."

"You wouldn't be saving my life, because I would hardly be alive.

And more is at stake than you allow. My father built this business. It took him his whole life and then he bequeathed it to me. That means they're attacking my father, his will, and his hopes. Thus, they attack my mother as well. And Catherine. 'You take my house when you do take the prop that doth sustain my house. You take my life when you do take the means whereby I live.' They would rob me of my past, present, and future. I won't let them do that."

"You're not an industry. You can't hire a private army, you can't bribe the whole government."

"I know."

"So how are you going to manage? You won't run. You won't accept my help. You're in a very difficult position."

"Very."

"And do you expect that I would approve your marriage to Catherine?"

"I would hope so."

"How will you raise the children?"

"Meaning?"

"As Christians or Jews?"

"I see."

"No you don't. There's a great deal you aren't aware of, and my question is perfectly appropriate. How would you raise the children?"

"We haven't discussed that."

"You'd better discuss it, because you've got to make a choice. They'll be either Christians, Jews, neither, or some messy hybrid, which is also neither. They will be one thing or the other, which, initially at least, you and Catherine will determine. I'm not the one who poses this question, it's posed by circumstance."

As calmly as a diplomat, Harry said, "What are your objections?"

"In theory, I would object if they were raised as Christians, and so were distant from their father. I would object if their father converted, and thus betrayed his family all the way back to Abraham. I would object if they were raised as Jews, and thus were distant from their mother. And I would object if their mother converted and thus became distant from me. And, certainly, if they were nothing, and had no belief, and were part of no tradition, I would be heartbroken that lines so loyal, stubborn, and courageous for so long would come to a vacuous end."

"We haven't dealt with this," Harry said, "because we love one another so much that in comparison it seems minor. I may be blind and proud, but I see it as a matter of faith."

"How so?"

"I believe in God. Not as a manifestation of man but as an omnipotent power. If He made the world in such a way that it results in the love I have for Catherine, I trust that He will take care, and that all will come right in the end. His commandments are fundamental and of the heart and soul even if man has drawn them out into orthodoxies of his own making in a forest of dry reeds. Sometimes a storm rises and flattens the reeds to open the world to the sky."

"With what theology, exactly, does that comport?"

"God's theology."

"How justified and confirmed?"

"By all nature, rich in life. I haven't arrived at this belief via reason. I was brought to it, carried like a child in benevolent arms."

"That's heresy, of course."

"Oh, you mean that though you yourself can speak to me, and professors can teach me, and the town council of West Hempstead can dictate laws that govern me as I drive through it, though Western Union can send me a message, the Mafia can force, a poet can entrance, a logician can convince, and an orator can enthrall me, God lacks these powers and is compelled to be forever mute and indirect. Who compels Him?"

"Perhaps it's His choice," said Billy, who, although Harry didn't know it, was used to theological discussion much more than most people would have thought.

"How justified and confirmed?" Harry returned. "And if it was, or is, or will be His choice, can He not change His mind, make exceptions, operate on more than one plane, sustain contradictions, or set up blinds, puzzles, and traps? My tradition, Billy, if I may, considers intermediation secondary. And so, I believe, does yours."

"But the more you depart from intermediation," Billy said, "the more you risk madness, pride, and error."

"Very risky, I agree, and one of the most dangerous things in the world"—and here he drew out his words and spoke them firmly—"from which the chief protection is God's grace."

"Okay, I'm impressed," said Billy, "but what about practical things? The world is so constructed that, as you well know, in many respects you can't move in it as freely as I can. Your children will not have the same freedom as I have. It's wrong, but it's true. You can't live in certain places, go to certain restaurants, work in certain fields, go to certain schools...."

"I know."

"And the long courses of both our families would be altered forever. It's only natural for someone to want his children and grandchildren to be like him and those who came before him, not slavishly, but at least a faint echo after he's gone. And not just he, but she. Evelyn, too. Continuity is not an unreasonable thing to want, is it? Is it anti-Semitism? Wouldn't your father have felt the same discomfort in a like situation?"

"Yes, and I won't say that it should be addressed only by trying to make the world perfect, because that evades the question by substituting for it an obvious impossibility. Of course we want continuity of belief, appearance, tastes, predilections, way of life, morals. My father would agree. I have no answer, nor would he, but he would admit as well that marriages are made in heaven, which is why they cause so much trouble on earth. My only answer to these questions, my only answer, which to me proves sufficient, is my love for Catherine."

They were forty miles out, but Billy held his course and didn't come about. It was relatively early and the radio had predicted magnificent weather. The sea moved in a gently rolling swell no higher than a foot, and all was pellucid and blue. After five or ten minutes during which he seemed to be weighing things gravely, Billy asked, "Am I to take it from this conversation that you and Catherine *do* plan to marry?"

"We do."

"Why haven't you asked me for her hand?"

"I had hoped to straighten out my affairs."

"No one ever straightens out his affairs. There's always something, and if marriages are made in heaven, why would you let it stop you?"

"Shall I ask you now?"

With a gesture of the hand that was not on the tiller, Billy said to proceed.

"But we're on a boat. Catherine's sleeping. I thought I would be formally dressed, that we would be in your library and she would be waiting in the next room, in a gown or a suit."

"To hell with that."

"All right, Mr. Hale...."

"You might as well keep it *Billy*."

"Not for this. I love Catherine more than anyone in my life, more than my father, more than my mother. In a way, that breaks my heart, but it's true, and I have to admit the truth. I promise that I'll always care for her, that I'll always put her before myself, that I'll never betray her, that I'll protect, honor, love, and defend her. The world can be unimaginably violent, and, therefore, this is required. I say it not only in the heat of love but because of what I've seen. I say it as an oath before God and on my honor. I ask for Catherine's hand in marriage. She fully concurs. And I pray that you'll give us your blessing."

Billy kept him waiting in the sound of the wake and the wind as they skated primevally across the border of sea and sky. And then he said, "You have it. Evelyn and I have discussed it deeply and at great length."

Harry was visibly moved, and quiet.

"There's something," Billy replied, slightly lowering his voice, "that you should know, that even Catherine doesn't know, but that she will, God help us, when she wakes up, because it's time." He leaned forward, keeping the tiller, which was highly varnished and as yellow as butter, in his right hand. For the first time, Harry looked closely at him, to take in his features so as to guess their influence upon children yet to be born.

"Here," Billy said, for no apparent reason other than just to start. "Evelyn was born in eighteen ninety-nine. Her mother was born sometime in the late seventies: we don't know exactly when." This seemed strange to Harry, as people such as the Hales knew the particulars of their ancestry. "I met Evelyn in the summer of nineteen twenty, when she was twenty-one. I was your age. It was at a dinner on the North Shore. I can still hear the clinking of the glassware and the little waves of the Sound striking the gravel beach, and I can still see the roses on the table. God, she was much more than beautiful, and I fell in love with her instantly.

"She fell in love with me, too, but I had to chase her. At first I thought she was just shy, or that she wanted to set the barb tight, but no, she really did pull away. I was determined enough, and followed her to Princeton. I didn't actually follow her: I knew where her family lived, and it was believable that I would be in Princeton, having been an undergraduate there. I called the house and asked if she would see me. On the evening when I met her family, the lawns were deep green and soaked with newly fallen rain. I was terrified. Her father was a Protestant theologian. I had never encountered him, as I had majored in economics, which despite what a lot of people I know might think, isn't quite the same thing. I had heard of him, though, as at the time he was very well known.

"So there was Evelyn Thomas, and there were her father and her mother, and there was I. I was fairly presentable, they knew of my family of course, everyone does, and it was clear that Evelyn and I were in love, even if she was doing her best not to be. But they, as well as she, were very disturbed, as if an equilibrium precarious for many years was about to be shattered.

"The problem was that Evelyn's marriage would bring out something they had let coast for want of ability to do otherwise. Evelyn's grandparents on her mother's side were, in fact, distantly related to my family in Boston. You needn't be concerned with the complexities of that. Nor should anyone else be. They, the grandparents, were childless until, in the early eighties, they adopted a blond, blue-eyed girl who had been orphaned in northern Europe. On the Baltic someplace, perhaps Estonia, or maybe St. Petersburg—I don't know. They knew. She probably would have remained in Europe were it not for the fact that after the Kishinev pogrom there was a massive exodus of Jews from all of Russia, and not just the Moldova. She was swept up in it, and landed in an orphanage in Springfield, Massachusetts, where they found and adopted her.

"This child, Evelyn's mother, was born a Jew. Nonetheless, as she was only five or so, they planned to raise her as a Christian and save her soul as a daughter of theirs would deserve. But she would have nothing of it. She remembered her parents indelibly. She knew enough so that, even at the age of five, she would have died rather than abandon the remnants and memories she had of her — God — her infancy.

"They could not and would not force her, and so allowed the question to be subsumed in their love, and it was never addressed. Sound familiar? When she grew up she married the liberal theologian Thomas, whose love for her surpassed any other consideration. They then raised *their* daughter, my wife, 'neutrally.' It's what happens when things mix and people take their cues from God instead of man. Thomas was a Protestant theologian who, just like you, believed in God's omnipotence and direct address. Just like you, he thought God would take care. And because he was a theologian, no one questioned the religion of his daughter, assuming that she would of course be a good and elevated Christian, and that she went to church and Sunday school.

"Well, she didn't go to church and she didn't go to Sunday school, and then I came along and married her. We were not married in a church, and we got away with it because of the war, the influenza, and then everything just coming loose in the aftermath. Evelyn was always loyal to her mother, but she hadn't practiced any religion, and when Catherine was born I asked and was allowed to bring her up — lightly, because that's how I was brought up — as a Christian, or an Episcopalian. Take your pick. On the rather rare occasions that I've appeared at a church service, I've taken her with me — when she was young. She thinks she's a Christian, she feels she's a Christian.

"But the fact is, her grandmother was a Jew, and her mother, *pace* the Colony Club, the Georgica, and the Social Register, all of which would throw us out if it were public — I don't care — is a Jew. So, if her grandmother was a Jew and her mother is also, tell me, what does that make Catherine?"

Harry had drawn back as if in shock. "Are you just saying this?" he asked.

"No," Billy said, as casually as though refusing an hors d'oeuvre. "It happens all the time, racial mixing, intermarriage, adoptions of children from other religions. People don't talk about or advertise it, so it may seem rarer than it really is. I know a cabinet member whose maternal grandmother is named Hadassah Levy. He thinks he's Episcopalian. Actually, he's so drunk all the time he may think he's Egyptian."

"Still," said Harry. He didn't know why he said that. He was quite stunned. The wake of the *Crispin* seemed to be saying a million things at once, as if it were a choir so immense he could not see the end of it. All he could manage was a simple question. "She doesn't know?"

"Not yet. I thought that, with her marriage, almost certainly to at least a deracinated Protestant, which is the way they come out of Yale, she would put us back on our ancient track. That after their two generations of perturbation, the planets would stop vibrating and settle into smoother orbits. Had she married Victor, all this might never have been known. Even had it later somehow been revealed, it probably would not have been believed. Let me correct myself. She doesn't know on one level. But she chose you. Maybe you just came along by chance. Hell, if marriages are made in heaven, who's to say?" he asked. "Why wouldn't I bless your marriage? Among other things, it's more religiously consistent than my own."

Graciously resigned to the force of the wind, Billy pushed the tiller over hard and the *Crispin* came about with a huge shudder, waking Catherine and Evelyn. Having come about, they all headed home over the open sea.

# 26

## SPEECHLESS AND ADRIFT

When Catherine, for a brief oment upon awakening, returned to the world of mother, father, and child, Harry looked on at the fleeting equilibrium of a family as once it was, sorry that he, no less than time, had broken and would yet break it. As surely as the *Crispin* drove north, a trail of sea singing quietly behind it before softening into the depths, the forward momentum of things would break apart all families, as it had broken his own, and as in the future it would break it yet again. Watching Catherine make her way astern, he knew what would be revealed to her, and that it would change her life.

Moving along the deck and followed by her mother, she was as happy as if while she slept all her cares had been washed away. Kneeling on one of the benches, she seized a pair of binoculars and began to track birds gliding above the water near the entrance of the bay. "Two gannets," she announced.

"Take the tiller, Harry," Billy commanded, rushing to join his daughter and his wife. The Hales knew a lot about birds, and could identify them when others saw just specks in the sky.

Harry took the tiller.

"We don't have to tack yet." Billy lifted his own pair of binoculars and lapsed into silence.

After a while, Catherine said, "See the yellow? A remnant of breeding."

One of the gannets' head-and-neck plumage was yellow. The other's was so intricately checked as to be an optical illusion. They were fishing near a beach littered with driftwood silvered by Maine winters. Their nearly divine economy of movement, their speed above the waves, their darting, their effortless suspension and decisive plunges were evidence that they had received their instruction from the angels.

Billy was the first to break off, because finally he did have to tack. He gave his binoculars to Harry, who then saw his first pair of gannets, and as the *Crispin* surged forward he watched them weave above the water in their primal state, a mated pair at their peak.

"I can't think of a more perfect setting, Catherine," Billy began, with surprising formality, "in which to tell you that, although it was not intended for the sea, and we just fell into it — not the sea — Harry has asked us to bless your intended marriage, and, having discussed it beforehand with your mother, I did."

The passage of the *Crispin* between islands of rock cliffs and pine took place in the sun and in full air. Catherine closed her eyes. She cried easily, and didn't want to. But every breath was an elevation she hoped would last forever. "Something else came up," Billy said, "which Harry now knows and you don't, although I should — we should — probably have told you long ago, and certainly in advance of Harry, because it concerns you foremost. I hope you'll forgive me, although if you don't I'll understand. We kept it from you for many reasons, not least because it's a difficult and complex subject that's best dealt with by an adult. And we kept it from you, to be truthful, because we didn't want it to come between us as you were growing up."

"What?" she asked, apprehensive but unafraid.

"We didn't want to introduce...."

"Am I adopted?" she interrupted, almost stridently, slightly losing her composure, and, for some reason, amused.

"No, nothing like that. Well, a little like that."

"I'm a little adopted?"

"Of course not. You're our child entirely — biologically, legally, historically, completely. A hundred percent. Not a problem."

"But you're Jewish, dear," Evelyn said in a preternaturally Episcopalian way.

Catherine laughed. She didn't think it was a joke: she knew it was serious, but, still, she laughed, because it, whatever it was, was so much a shock as to be incomprehensible. "But I'm not adopted."

"No."

"So," she said to Billy, "you're Jewish, too." This struck everyone as funny.

"No," said Billy, "I'm Episcopalian."

"I always thought so, Dada. I always thought you were." She hesitated. Seconds passed. "That means, Mama . . . that means, that. . . ."

"Yes," Evelyn told her.

"Oh God. You were adopted by Grandfather Thomas?"

"My mother was adopted. She was born a Russian Jewess, and never converted. That means that I, which means that you. . . . You see? Had you married Victor we might never have told you. But when you chose Harry, how could we not have?"

"It's the strangest thing in the world," said Billy. "My grandson, for Christ's sake, as I understand it, will be a hundred percent Jewish. The Hales, in one fell swoop. . . . I mean, had my classmates known what was to happen, they would have ostracized me. Had my grandfather known, I hesitate to tell you. One wants one's children to be at least a little like oneself. To carry on. You want your grandchildren to be like you, too." He looked at his daughter and her fiancé, and said, "And I think they will be, no matter what the world may say."

"Is this true?" Catherine asked, not waiting for an answer. "Why didn't you tell me? It's such a shock, such a shock, to find out that so important a part of you was unknown to you. I don't know what to think." She stood up and made her way to the bow.

There she sat at the root of the bowsprit as the boat flew forward and sometimes, obliging a surge of air, pitched gently into the swell. Harry was content to wait amidships, watching the wind blow through her hair as she stared outward, until she would call or come to him.

They had long passed the island where they had first seen the gannets, but now, on the port side, many more appeared — dozens, perhaps scores — the lords of small green isles, whitened driftwood, and pine, going about what they did with simplicity and the perfection of a hundred million years in which they had come to know the elements so well that it was as if they had never been cleaved from them, although they had, and that was the beauty of it, their separation from the wind and the sea, but their never having left them.

Instead of returning home, they found a cove and anchored there out of the wind. Evelyn cooked dinner while Catherine remained at the bow, as if in grief, but with an expression of concentration. At risk to his extremities in the numbing water, Billy took the dinghy to shore and walked about in the shallows, digging up quahogs. The meat of these enormous clams looked like boned chicken breast, and, cut up with potatoes and celery, made a buttery New England chowder more than a match for the Riesling that went with it.

Every once in a while, as the quahog chowder cooked in its pot, Catherine would turn her head. And when dinner was ready they didn't have to call her. She was neither angry nor hurt, but had fallen into a deep rest in which speech had no place. Thus, as the *Crispin* kept its anchor line taut in a current that entered the east-facing cove on its south side and exited north, the dinner was silent. They felt the tranquility that comes of being close to the sea, a steady heartbeat that substitutes for activity and noise. It was what Catherine needed, and as they watched her, if only with glances, she seemed simultaneously subdued, wounded, content, and amazed. No one dared speak, until she said, "After dinner, I'd like to row to the beach, and cut some wood, and build a fire there next to a rock."

"Who speaks?" asked Harry, "a cave woman or William Butler Yeats?"

"Be careful, Harry," Billy said. "This reminds me of when I had had a bit too much to drink — which is always — and I called Evelyn *Elephant*. It took several years to get over that one." He paused. "And a diamond necklace. The lesson I learned is that you can't call even a svelte woman an elephant, even by accident."

"That's all right," Catherine said. "I don't mind if he calls me an elephant, or a cave woman. Flattery will get him nowhere."

Billy and Evelyn stayed aboard to clean up and go to bed early, as one can do easily on a gently rocking boat, and Harry and Catherine rowed to shore. He was relieved that she had spoken. She didn't have to speak in torrents. Out of sight of the *Crispin* they found a huge rock and built a bonfire against it. Sun-dried driftwood lit easily, and though it did not burn hot the fire was big enough and the backing reflective enough so that as night fell and the temperature dropped they remained warm. Shadows danced against the rock but the firelight was too weak to dim the Milky Way. By starlight undiminished, and yet able to see one another's faces softened as if in candlelight, they listened to the waves, the wind in the pines, and the crack of the fire.

"What have you come up with?" he asked.

"How long has your family been Jews?" she inquired.

"Five thousand years or so, I guess."

"And what have you come up with?"

"You got me."

"In the last five hours I've been doing my best," she said.

"Tell me."

"You really want to know?"

"Or we could go bowling."

She looked at the base of the fire, where the coals were already in agony. "It changed me instantly," she reported, "neither completely nor because I wanted it. I didn't want it. It was very sad to leave what I was — not in terms of belief, which, compared to what I'm talking about, is superficial, but in terms of what I am.

"I looked at my reflection in the water and didn't get much back from the swell, but there I was, the light moving past me like a river, and everything obscure. I looked at my hands. I turned them slowly and opened my fingers. And at my legs. You may have seen me: I crossed my arms and held my shoulders as if steadying myself, holding myself, discovering myself. And I could see my hair in the periphery as the wind lifted it in and out of view. And I thought to myself, Who is this girl, whom I haven't known, who's come from someplace that I never thought about, 'til now?

"I can't ignore them, all the people who came before me, who lived in hovels in Eastern Europe — in Poland, the Ukraine, Moldova, Russia.... I thought we came from Scotland. Well, my father did. But I'm more deeply like my mother, and I can't forget the people from whom she came, even though I'll never know them, because they're me — rabbis in caftans and fur hats, their wives, the children dressed in black, with sparkling, tragic eyes, it's unbelievable. And, Harry, I'm them. Whatever I had thought about them before, now they're with me forever. I don't have to do anything. I don't have to believe anything, as far as I can tell, though deep inside it's all working as if on schedule. Today I became as rooted as a tree, with no voice of its own except the wind that moves through it. It's an extraordinary thing, what I've just learned, which is the patience of five thousand years. For the past few hours I've been motionless but time has been moving through me. Am I talking nonsense?"

"No."

"Those skeletons in the newsreels, the children stacked dead at the sides of ditches, their legs like firewood.... They're me."

"They are."

"It changes everything. It really does." She held her head high, refusing to collapse beneath the weight of emotion while tears rolled down her cheeks. Catherine, she cried easily.

## 27

## THE *EVENING TRANSCRIPT*

"This is not a goddamned college production of Gilbert and Sullivan," Sidney said with simultaneous anger and joy as he led Catherine and the other stars of the play across the Public Garden and through Boston Common toward Washington Street. "We are the American musical theater. We are Broadway. Others look to us, aspire to be us. We're professionals." They were walking four abreast with stragglers of the cast grouped behind them, the rhythm of their step in keeping with people who habitually worked at singing and dancing, and at this moment Sidney was their general. It was cold and dry for late September, and as the lights came on in buildings that flanked the Common they sparkled in place as if in winter.

"Catherine, are you anxious? I hope not. You've got it down. All of you have it down, and it was that way before we left New York. In the weeks here, it's been almost flawless."

"I am anxious," Catherine answered, "but I can't wait to go on. The only daunting thing is the time between now and then."

Though everyone but Sidney would change into costume, they were dressed beautifully, and they could hear music so faithfully that it was as if they were already in the theater and the orchestra lay in wait in the black space between the audience and the stage, bridging with music the gap between them. If the production were half as good as the Boston rehearsals had been, the audience would be sure to be delighted most of the time and now and then know bliss. Sidney was in a double-breasted greatcoat and Liberty of London scarf. Charles — handsome, strong, and as dumb in real life as onstage — was in Harris Tweed, ready for his heiress. Amanda, the heiress who was not an heiress, was coatless and dressed as a leading lady should be, in a gown too flimsy for the cold, too high at the knee, too low at the bosom, and just right for the party. And Catherine, the simple girl from Red Lion, Pennsylvania, who really was an heiress, and who, every night, would lose Charles, was in a French dress so wonderfully tailored and arresting to the eye that as she walked across the Common everyone turned to her as if slightly startled. Her colleagues — people of ceaseless and merciless charisma, directors and Broadway performers — were made to seem like postilions.

But as they marched forward in natural light giving way to galaxies of electricity shining through the trees, Catherine didn't know. At the stage door they encountered a group of people who had assembled an hour before curtain to see Amanda but who either missed Amanda or thought Catherine was the lead. Amanda smiled royally at glances directed past her. Then, the power of opening night having propelled them, they were pulled into the theater as if through an airlock, the cold of New England pouring onto the busy and expectant stage like some kind of magical fuel.

Just being in the theater began to change their voices into the powerful and perfectly calibrated instruments that project strongly and, as in the mechanics of seabirds riding on the wind, are elevated as they push against resistance. For the singers, this was the echo of their own voices. Catherine had said to Harry that one of the most wonderful things in the world was to meet her own voice and adjust to it as if in a duet, so that something there was, that was not she, that would sail above the audience and astound both the actress and her listeners. Yes, she wanted stardom, from the vanity that she was too honest to deny; and, like every child of wealth, she wanted to earn money on her own; but most of all she wanted this — to be able to project her soul outside herself for those moments, enchanted and free, when it would play among the beams of light flooding down through the proscenium. If she could do this seven or eight times a week now and then in productions yet to be born, it would be well worth all the tortures of the theater.

· · ·

As he walked up Newbury Street, beneath trees shuddering in the wind, their dry leaves as stiff as cymbals and shuttering the city lights like stars, Harry understood what she faced. With nothing to do but wait for the curtain and then sit and watch powerlessly, he was more agitated than Catherine herself, and began to know a little of what women felt when they had waited through the war for their men to come home: an anxiety that found no relief in action. He was thinking mainly of Catherine. But, with no loss of force, both love and prayer tend to embrace all those who are deserving. So, in the Boston autumn, on streets that seemed charged with life, Harry was moved as well by George Yellin, one of Catherine's fellow cast members, whom Catherine had taken under her wing. George was a slight, short, older-than-middle-aged man with a minor role that required him to don a pencil-thin mustache. He performed this small part faithfully, never faltering, always going nowhere as he aged and others rose. He had almost been a star, though not quite. Now, everyone was careful to be kind to him. His face was a symbol of certain and inevitable decline. Harry had watched Catherine protect him, at times at her own expense.

Once, when the actors were gathered in a Romanian restaurant, consuming large amounts of wine as they waited for marinated steaks from a ten-foot grill, George Yellin, who had forgotten to remove his pencil-thin mustache, had said, "You know, now most Victrolas run off electricity, with a cord." The shock of this statement, decades out of phase, reduced the gathering to stunned silence. It was as if he had announced that someone had invented an apparatus to replace the gaslight. One could feel a burst of mocking laughter on its way, with nothing to stop it but Catherine, who reflexively leapt in to cover him. "That's true, George," she said, a young woman protecting a man old enough to be her father, "and what I'll bet no one at this table knows is something my father, who works with people who fund these kinds of things, told me: that they've begun looking into a way to make radios and Victrolas without tubes. Daddy said that they will, and that when they do, the radios will be so small you'll be able to carry them in a purse, and so rugged you'll be able to throw them out the window without breaking them. And you won't need a cord, because they'll use much less power and will be able to run on batteries." She looked around the table, surveying all whose laughter she had dammed in their throats, and she said, "I'll bet you didn't know that, did you?"

Even though Sidney would explain why what Catherine had described was, given his knowledge of physics, impossible, George was saved, and this was but one reason of many why Harry loved Catherine as he had never loved and would love no other. Perhaps had his own circumstances been not as bleak he wouldn't have been concerned, but, confronted with imminent failure, he was frightened by the possibility that Catherine might fail as well. The theater was full of terrors — of fashion, opinion, retribution, politics, and perversity. It was one of those things, like so much of life, that cut down many more people than it raised up. Catherine might protect George Yellin, but who would, or could, protect her?

Though Harry could not, he was comforted by the fact that God had given her a shield not only in beauty and talent inborn, but in qualities that far exceeded them and would last beyond them. So it was back through the darkened, star-ravaged streets to the theater where he could confidently witness at her turn the woman for whom his love was the closest thing he had ever known to a prayer directly answered. It was commonly agreed that such things did not happen. But, of course, they did.

The usual wearers of furs and topcoats had assembled beneath the marquee, stirring with excitement like a wave rocking between two yachts. Napoleonic ranks of incandescent bulbs rained down on them a certain gleam that made them seem larger in number and louder in speech. Amidst the automobiles dropping them off came a carriage or two laden with unchangeable dowagers and delicate male companions who carried canes and dressed in white shirtfronts with pearl buttons. The horses sensed the excitement, and, though silent and enslaved, they were the most expressive of all. Meyer Copeland had once said to his son, "I have often prayed that you will grow up to be as dignified as a horse. You could do a lot worse."

"A horse!"

"Yes, Harry, your kingdom for a horse. Their temperaments are governed by God. They skip a lot of nonsense. They're strong, gentle, and just. You'd be lucky. I think you will be lucky."

"But they're stupid."

"Maybe they're merely quiet."

When the brass doors were opened, the sounds of an orchestra warming up came through them so entrancingly that the crowds were drawn in as if by a vacuum cleaner. Professional musicians do not limber up with scales, but with quick remembered passages and cadenzas as impossible to resist and sometimes more beautiful than the compositions from which they are drawn or upon which they are based.

Almost before he knew what was happening, Harry found himself in his seat, surrounded as if in a jewel box by cushiony furs and satin, by matrons from Marshfield, accountants from Newton, dyspeptics from Natick, and Harvard undergraduates and the girls at their sides from Wellesley and Wheaton. In the real boxes sat the dowagers and their men who looked and dressed like ringmasters, Irish gangsters and their molls, and young Brahmins looking handsome, impatient, and drunk. The Porcellian had a box. This Harry knew by their youthful pink faces, their dinner jackets, the way they threw back their heads when tippling, and the little flashing pig of gold tied to the chain of a pocket watch that one of them kept pulling from his vest because he thought it was a flask. Harry had lived next to their club, and although he had never shot any of them, he knew them the way a gamekeeper knows his pheasants.

Time was kept by orchestral riffs growing fuller and fuller as they skated by like puffs of smoke; by the thump of ropes and wood muffled by the heavy curtain as scenery was adjusted at inhuman speed; by lights that blinked ascendingly; the filling of seats; the sounding of chimes; and, finally, by the falling of darkness.

This darkness mixed with silence for a breathtaking moment until music cascaded inversely with the quick rise of the curtain — part of Sidney's brilliance was his disdain for darkened overtures — and the appearance of a set radiating daylight that, no matter if it is supposed to be as white as June sun, in the theater cannot avoid a touch of incandescent yellow. The beginning was auspicious and strong.

Though they were in Boston, New York appeared in chaos and perpetual motion. The skyscrapers and bridges the set designer had launched almost to the peak of the proscenium arch were only backlighted canvas, but as envoys of the real thing they claimed the theater for New York. Brass, bells, horns, and a sudden flooding of the stage with dozens of people, yellow and checkered "taxis," "horse"-drawn carts and wagons (some horse: the man inside was named Irv), policemen blowing whistles, criers hawking their wares, and a canvas subway train inching across a box-girdered bridge in the background, all came at once. It would have been nothing had it been nothing but chaos, but it was as choreographed as the ballet of real life it represented.

Into the light and brass, parting the action onstage like the Red Sea, emerged Catherine, stepping out from the portals of Penn Station. With perfect timing she accomplished the inhalations that had made Sidney fall in love with her, and they went straight to the hearts of the audience. Harry was proud that these sweet and powerful breaths had come from a mouth that he had kissed, that he had inhaled them deeply into his lungs, and that she had taken his.

The stage cleared as she surveyed the city. Harry realized that as she peered stage right, took a step forward, peered stage left, looked up, and raised her left hand as if to shield herself, that, though it was short and tight, this was a carefully accomplished dance. In just a few moments, her wonder at the city was transformed into an incipient mastery over it. As she was pleased by what she beheld, she relaxed. And as the music beat through the air, she moved to it almost imperceptibly, and smiled. She had arrived. She had beheld something magnificent, as if it were her first glimpse of the world, and she had learned to love and master it all in an instant. The focus could not help but shift from the vastness and power of the city to the eyes of the girl who had come to it, and the lights now left the others in darkness and shone upon her until the stage was enveloped in silence.

In this silence, she had them, and she knew it. So she stretched out her cue, withholding it from the conductor himself, wanting to stay longer, driving the hook deeper. And when the time was right she began to sing her heartbreakingly beautiful song. The musicians, rallied by the long caesura, played more than the music. It became one of those great moments, a triumph. Catherine's singing was so magnificent, far more than in any rehearsal, her presence so arresting, that time was vanquished. Well versed in just about everything, the audience knew — even if, to protect themselves in a complicated and atrophied social system, hardly any one of them would have admitted it — that Catherine Sedley's simple song was on a par with the "Ma di'" of *Norma,* the "Deh! Non turbare," of *La Gioconda,* and the "Soave sia il vento" (perfectly mirroring her introduction) of *Così Fan Tutte.* They could not contain their honest emotion or their enthusiasm, and when Catherine finished, there was a brief breathless silence followed by a thunder of applause and the rising to a standing ovation that would last two full minutes and more.

As the rafters shook, she remained absolutely still, finally acknowledging the great tribute to her with an almost sad smile that bound to her forever anyone there in that moment. For as high as she herself had been lifted, she had carried along with her more than a thousand people.

By the time she sang her two other songs, one a duet that had been added only in Boston, the momentum of the play had made standing ovations inappropriate, but at the end she had so many curtain calls, and applause like a deafening waterfall close up, that there was no question of either the play's success or hers. Harry was so proud he could hardly rise from his seat, but when he did he found himself borne along on a current of satin and topcoats until at the exit he almost rammed into Billy and Evelyn, who were both furtive and aglow. "Harry!" said Billy. "Wasn't that spectacular! My God, my own daughter. I didn't realize who she was. She's got everything ahead of her. *She's* the one who will make our name, not anyone but her."

"She will," Harry replied, certain that it would be so.

"Don't tell her you saw us," Evelyn said excitedly, kissing Harry as she spoke. "We promised not to be here, but we had to see her, so we sat way in the back beneath the balcony. It didn't matter. She came through as clearly as starlight." As they were separated by the crowd and the distance increased, Harry heard, "Don't tell her. We're going back to New York. We've got to get the train. God bless."

"I won't, I won't," Harry heard himself say, and then they were gone. Eventually, he would tell her, but only much later. How could he not? And then, as the tides thinned and he found himself outside, relatively alone on a stretch of black pavement, he took in a deep, satisfied breath of cold air and began to walk to Locke-Ober, where with Catherine and the others he would wait all night for the morning papers. Sidney had reserved Locke-Ober with the last of the production funds. Now, that money would seem like nothing at all.

Winter Place was cold and black, the lights of Locke-Ober so dim that the vast amount of silver within hardly seemed to shine, but the calm would shelter and stabilize the cast as they waited. Had things gone badly, the brown darkness of the interior would have been insufferable, but now they needed to be tranquil, as far as they could be. They would enjoy their success no less if their euphoria were countered than were it accelerated, quiet triumph being infinitely stronger, as Harry had learned time and again in the years just passed.

The first to greet him was George Yellin, who was happy for perhaps the only time in the last twenty years. "How did it go?" George asked, knowing full well how it went, which was betrayed by his expression as sharply as the pencil mustache he had once again forgotten to remove.

Catherine was trapped in the voluble crowd, and when she and Harry caught sight of one another they felt the peculiar rush of feeling that two people in love feel when they are politely separated and cannot wait to be close. Nonetheless, the time until they came together stretched out pleasurably, and when finally they embraced and were swept into the restaurant, they said what they needed to say in their eyes and in their touch.

Seated at a table that ran the entire length of the wood-paneled downstairs room, which women ordinarily were not allowed to enter, Harry noticed in the corner of his eye several figures passing outside, clothed in tweed and caps. Their speech was faintly audible as it vibrated the glass. He knew them instantly, as he always had, and felt that he almost belonged with them more than with his own. Locke-Ober, he thought, was dimly lit so that those privileged to be inside would be able to see others not so fortunate passing in the cold, and so that those in the cold would not have so pretty a picture engraved upon their eyes by too strong a light. So many bottles of Champagne were uncorked that, though no one would ever know, one of the youngest girls in the chorus actually looked around for a popcorn popper. Catherine quaffed two glasses like a tonic. She was thirsty, used to it, and she knew she had earned it.

"Don't you want something to drink?" Sidney asked Harry.

"I want it, but I shouldn't have it, so, luckily, tonight I don't need it."

"You should be jealous of your girl," George Yellin said. "She's on a rocket to the moon."

"I'm not jealous, George," Harry said tranquilly.

"Why not?"

"George, if you were lucky enough to be betrothed to Athena, would you be jealous of her?"

"Athena who?"

"Goldberg," Harry said.

George was panic-stricken. "I thought, I thought...."

"The goddess."

"Oh!" he said.

Catherine blushed, and surveyed her fiancé with "such war of white and red within her cheeks" that her deeper commitment was betrayed.

"Well," George Yellin said. "Now I see, now I see. Catherine, you're an angel. I don't know how you did it, but you saw me through this, and I feel good about tonight. I've always been afraid of Boston. They slaughtered me here once, you know, and you never forget."

In New York, many theatrical people have cardiac crises when, coming out of the theater, they see and rush for the next day's paper and discover no review of their year or two of work, in that the review will run in a later edition. This is because in New York newspapers are launched upon an immense mass of readers and they spread their weight over the waters in confusing multiple runs, assaulting the public in waves that, like the oceans', never cease. Not so in Boston, a city where the rich strive to make do with less, and those who have enough proudly disdain the luxury of sufficiency. In Bostonian eyes, to have only one edition was to flirt with excess. So all the reviews would come that morning, and the wait stretched until five, but most of the cast was young and bohemian enough not to feel it.

As they descended from the charged heights of opening night they began to entertain their doubts. "Don't get your hopes up," Sidney announced at four. "As you know, theater critics are capable of anything. Criticus may leave his house one evening with the unquenchable desire to see a play about a talking lobster. When the production he is to judge is instead about Pope Innocent the Tenth, he may be disappointed, insulted, and outraged."

"That's right," said someone who, slumped in his seat with a bottle, fluently supplied an excerpt from the review: "'The author has failed to impart to the Pope a redness of color, the touch of vitality, and the briny wit we expect. Nor is his Innocent capable of the immensely powerful grasp, pinching the life out of his enemies, that he is reputed to have had. And where is the depiction of the New World fishermen, risking their lives to gather their pots and traps, which so sustained Europe and the papacy at the time? All in all, a grave disappointment from a writer whose previous play, *Gloucester and the Cape St. Ann*, I found first rate.'"

"Is that what he wrote?" George Yellin asked. "How dare he!"

"But the audience," Harry protested.

Sidney was glad to be able to bring his experience into play. "Not disoften" — he knew this was not a word, but thought it should have been — "critics will take the opposite tack of an audience just to show who's master. Word of mouth may reach ten or twenty thousand people over a period of weeks. The critic speaks to half a million the next morning. I've seen critics delight in their power to bring the audience itself to a different view, simply to see if it can be done. It can."

And then everyone, having responsibly considered the worst, went back to expectations of glory. In the still black shades of morning, Locke-Ober became as quiet as an opium den. Catherine leaned into Harry and slept. There were only murmurs now, and few of those. Intermittent snores dueled as nasally in the air as Sopwith Camels.

The spell was broken by the explosive thud of a bundle of papers thrown at the doorstep of a building across Winter Place. One of the boys in the cast rushed out, lobster shears in hand, to steal as many as his pounding heart would allow. They watched him cut the twine and run back in with three papers under his arm as if they were a football in the crucial moments of the Harvard-Yale game. He almost forgot to open the door as he was about to sail through it. The *Boston Herald* was slapped down in front of Sidney. He opened to the right page as if it had been bookmarked, and, trembling slightly, he read.

First, the headline: "'A Triumph of the Postwar.' Wow!" he said, as everyone sat straight and awakened. "'Only a few times in the life of the theater comes a play, or, even less frequently, a musical, that is so powerful and moving that when it ends you are heartbroken to leave it and step back into your own life. Very seldom does one come to love the characters so much as to long for sleep and the opportunity to dream oneself back into their midst.'"

The review continued in this vein, unreservedly praising every aspect of the production — the music, the book, the staging — and the actors, who bathed in one or two glorious sentences as if they were Cleopatra bathing in milk. But after progressing euphorically, Sidney stopped short.

"Wait a minute," he said. "This can't be. I don't understand it." He read something over, silently. As his expression changed, Catherine, who had not been praised, felt the floor beneath her fall away.

"Read it," she said.

"You don't want to hear it," Sidney told her.

"No," she sighed, "but read it."

He looked down slowly, and read: "'The only wrong note in all this perfection is one Catherine Sedley, whose performance, fortunately not essential, is so overburdened with lack of talent as to serve as a kind of obstinate anchor. Blame nepotism, for this Catherine Sedley is none other than Catherine Thomas Hale, who likely got the part because her father, namesake of the famous investment house, is rumored to have backed the production.'"

Catherine was stoic. She neither dropped her head nor, as she easily might have, and as many would have, cried. She said only, "It's not true."

"Not a penny," said Sidney. "Her father had nothing to do with it."

"It's a freak," said George Yellin. "Wait for the *Globe* and the *American*."

"The *American*'s a Hearst paper," someone said, negatively.

"So what?" Sidney replied. "Their critic won't be the critic of the *Herald*."

Two thuds, one closely following the other, and the boy with the lobster shears ran out and came back almost instantly with the *Globe*, the *American*, and the *Boston Daily Record*. These three, with the *Herald*, would be decisive. With the *Herald*'s stunning praise, all they needed was one merely good review from amongst the three others. They got more than that. All were ecstatic. Sidney read them, assuming that the *Globe*, which was the first, and the other two would treat Catherine fairly.

They did not. Each and every one slighted her performance. The *Globe* said, "I couldn't wait for her to stop spoiling the production and leave the stage. Her voice is so peculiar, her movements so strange, and her appearance that of a not very pretty society girl, which is what she is and reportedly why she got the part, when she is supposed to be a country girl. Her presence throws an otherwise glorious production off track every second she appears. Perhaps New York will not have to suffer through this if the producers are wise, although they probably dare not trample upon the paternal affections of their investors."

After making Sidney read them all, Catherine stood, the silver light of Locke-Ober gleaming onto her hair. She said, "I want everyone to know that, first, I truly am happy for you: congratulations. Congratulations, George." She smiled at him. (The papers had noted his performance. One had said, "Even George Yellin, who has not appeared in Boston — with good reason — since 1924's *The Empress Eugénie,* is wonderful, if small.") "And, second, I'll go. I don't want to ruin it for anyone else."

"No you won't," Sidney said, followed by strong murmurs of agreement. "No you won't. You were superb. There's no explanation for these reviews, except that sterile imaginations and closed hearts never forgive those unlike themselves. You're going to open in New York. We'll all be together. Fuck them and fuck the money. You come with us."

"But Sidney," Catherine said, "I don't need the money, and everyone here does. It's not...."

"Do you know why?" Sidney interrupted. "Do you know why all these crazy Jews in the theater, and me, and the Nebraskans and Alaskans, and Irish Catholics, and George Yellin, whatever he is, don't have any money?"

"I'm Jewish," said George. "Why am I a special category?"

"Because when it comes to this kind of thing we always say fuck the money, and the money goes away. It goes away, but, listen to me, Catherine," he said, and paused, "it's worth it."

And Catherine, who until that moment had been composed....

The next day, bright and warm, brought back a touch of summer, flooding its light upon the Public Garden as the sun filtered through the trees and then rose above them, burning away shadow. Catherine's room looked east over the Common. On the desk and tables were a dozen vases of flowers, some from people she didn't know, with unread notes praising her performance, wishing her good fortune, asking her to dinner. She sat on the edge of the bed, still in her elegant clothes, still in makeup, with hardly a sign that she had been up all night. She drew for this upon nothing but her youth.

The sun illuminated the flowers from behind, infusing them with the kind of glow that cinematographers induce with fine gauze. The colors intensified with the light, pulsed as the sun strengthened, and seemed almost as if they were moving. "Did you see the look on George Yellin's face," Catherine asked, "after he said it wasn't over until the reviewer from the *Evening Transcript* had his say, and Sidney told him that the *Transcript* had folded at the beginning of the war?"

"I did. How can a living human being be so continually surprised by the present?"

"It's because he's so sad," Catherine averred. "Because he's been moving down for so long, he doesn't want to move at all, so he lives in stilled time. It reminds me of my cousins, little girls — Hales — who hesitate at doorways. They don't cross thresholds until they check with their parents. They love what they have and are suspicious of change. I don't know why George touches me so, but he does."

"Because he's old, he failed, and he can't afford to quit the field. He has to eat, so he struggles through one beating after another until, not so long from now, he won't ever get a part again. He'll become theatrically extinct, and no one will ever think of him or his descent from a profession in which one is always courting adoring eyes."

"Then what?"

"He'll live in an apartment the size of a steamer trunk, surviving on a tiny bit of food. He'll spend the day on a bench in the Broadway median, watching pigeons, and go home to the little apartment, where on summer nights he'll sit by the open window listening to a baseball game on the radio, drinking one Rheingold, looking out at windows across the courtyard. He'll do this for five or ten years, maybe twenty. Then he'll become ill, struggle with that for a while like a fish trapped on deck, and then he'll die. The *Times* will give him one and a half inches, no picture. 'George Yellin, a bit-part actor.'"

"And his mother and father?"

"His mother and father, long dead, loved him perhaps as he should have been loved — I hope so — and as the world has not. That is, without regard to his success. In the end, that's what you come back to, the only thing that matters, those who love you though you have failed."

"Is that how you love me?" she asked.

"It's exactly how I love you, although you've hardly failed."

"I feel as if I have."

"You haven't. But even if you had, it wouldn't matter to me, because what I love was with you the day you were born."

She wasn't really listening. Adjusting her hair exactly as her mother did — Harry noted this — and mesmerized by the glow of the roses, she said, "I'm going to quit."

"Just because of nine bad reviews?"

She couldn't help but laugh. "Nine out of nine, and what reviews! I was the only one."

"Who said it would be easy? You work it through, as you told me yourself, for the few moments of almost divine grace. The rest is either monotony or agony."

"Still," she said.

"Still what?"

"You can't argue with that kind of fierce unanimity. Every single one, and they were all so hateful."

"But that's your sword and shield."

"How so?"

"Nine reviews."

"Yes?"

"Each hateful."

"Yes?"

"Each coming to the same conclusion."

"And?"

"Each one, without exception, an angry reaction to the belief that you were bought into the part. Nine reviewers. Where do you think they live?"

She began to awake as if with anger. "Who, the reviewers?"

"The reviewers. Do you think they all live together in the same room? In the same building? I'll bet they live all over the place. I'll bet they live in Mattapan and Somerville and Swampscott. That's only three. This is Massachusetts. They probably live in places called *Mooshacumquit* and *West Fishcake*. They're theater critics. Maybe some live on Beacon Hill, maybe one lives in Back Bay. They don't all read the same things, or talk together: they're in competition; they probably hate each other."

"If it's like New York, they drink together while they think of nasty things to say."

"No, it's Boston. They're too stupid to do that. Maybe the rumor appeared somewhere in the press, or maybe it didn't. If it did, who put it there? And who made sure all the theater critics in Boston knew about it?"

"I can't believe it," she said. And then, upon only a little reflection, "No. No. I can."

"He's capable of it, isn't he?"

"He is," she said. "And what you don't know is that at Marrow he's responsible for financing newspapers, of which they do a lot. But we can't be sure. We can't know. We'll never be able to prove anything. And even if we could, what could we do?"

Harry shook his head and pursed his lips, as if to say, This is something I know about.

"What?" she asked.

"They would hide," he said, "in churches, hospitals, convents, schools...."

"Who would hide?"

"Germans. They would shoot from these places. They wanted us not to be sure. They wanted us to die because we were not sure, and because we were good."

"And what did you do?"

"We discovered that we were not good."

Now the streets were filling up with workers in gray, secretaries getting off streetcars, people walking to take their places in offices, factories, and shops. Ships were heading out to sea, and steamers coming in. Trains from the western suburbs and the North Shore clattered east and south to the stations, and shadows continually wheeled with the passage of the sun. As they advanced like a tide, light followed in exact and equal measure. All was at risk and nothing would stay the same. The flowers in Catherine's room at the Ritz would glow and stop glowing as the sun changed position and its rays shot through one window and then another.

They spent much of the morning tight in one another's arms. It comforted her. And when he left to make the one o'clock train to New York she was ready to go onstage again with neither fear nor apprehension, though she knew that everyone who came to the theater would be eager to see a great production and primed to wince when she appeared. As difficult as it might be, she would hold steady. She would make them forget. That was her task now, to hold through, with no guarantee, like all those in gray who filled the streets on the way to their jobs, anonymous from birth to death and thereafter, the little people, so called, who so often were as brave as soldiers and as great as kings.

# 28

## LOST SOULS

When the new haven and Hartford train from Boston pulled into Grand Central, Harry stepped onto a platform in air humid with the remnants of summer heat. On the great Sargasso Sea of the main concourse, where rush hour had already begun beneath the twinkling constellations in the ceiling, late-afternoon light cut shafts through animated dust beneath the vault. Harry felt at home among the ten thousand racing creatures in gabardine, with newspapers and portfolios under their arms, and the grim, penetrating expressions of New Yorkers in the battle of market, office, and street. The portraiture of the thousands and millions who might someday overleap mortality was never-ending. For perhaps with the ignition of eternity every single vanishing moment and the blessedness of each man, woman, and child lost to memory would awake to be engraved on the black walls of time by joyful Niagaras of light.

He stood on the marble floor of Grand Central, turning as slowly as a tourist, while on the eastern side of every block the lights of Manhattan came up as day slid into evening. Through cascading armies of commuters, he fought his way up the Vanderbilt Avenue stairs. Outside, the streets were golden with sunset, crowded with taxis, and flashing with doors opening and closing as office buildings emptied faster than if they were on fire.

Rather than move only up avenues and across side streets, he took a complicated route through lobbies, atria, arcades, and alleys. It was almost possible to go from Grand Central to the park along these back ways that mercifully scaled down the city, especially if one were not shy about opening a door or two or leaping a fence.

As he walked through a long hall beneath a gilded ceiling, the arcade of an office building in the Forties not far from where he had started, he passed a reweaving shop. Though he had been aware of its existence, he had never given it a thought. Because he didn't smoke, there were no holes burned in his suits. And moths were rare on the upper floors of Central Park West, perhaps because of the rent. As he sped by, he merely glanced to his right.

But before he was able to slow his pace he was whipped around as if he had run out of rope. He slid on the polished floor after he turned, and came to a stop in the dim glow of alabaster chandeliers dirty with soot and dust. Drawn to movement in the window of the reweaving shop as if he were a cat in front of a goldfish bowl, he looked in and saw a woman he hadn't seen in going on fourteen years. He had loved her when they were both young, and perhaps because he had never told her, never touched her, never kissed her, the love had inconveniently survived. Her name was Eugenia Eba. It was not the most beautiful name, unless you knew her.

Two fields of black were painted on either side of the window, each with three clear ovals exposing a lighted shelf with before-and-after samples of cloth that had once been holey and then were redeemed. In the window itself, next to an ebony-and-gold sewing machine, Eugenia Eba was bent over the sleeve of a man's jacket. It was rust-colored tweed with a touch of blue, and she was intently holding it at a remove and then sliding it beneath a goosenecked magnifying glass before choosing from a little tray of fibers to match those to which she would join them. Except for what he took as a weariness and patience she had not had as a girl, she seemed the same as she was at eighteen, and because he could not see himself, which might have been a check on transportation to another time, her appearance threw him back as if nothing had changed.

Other than at commencement, the last time he had been near her had been at the class picture, in June of 1933, when ninety-two seniors were arrayed in front of a wall roughly the color of the jacket Eugenia Eba was now repairing. For years, whenever Harry had looked at this picture in black and white at the center of the yearbook, his eyes had bounced between his own image and hers, and with each transit came realization and regret that she was impossibly beyond him.

Knees drawn up and hands casually clasped, in suit and tie, with a handkerchief in his breast pocket, he sat on the ground, in the center of the first row, and she was seated on a chair in the row behind him, over his left shoulder. How could he have been so small, so tense, so pale? How could his chin have appeared so weak, his skin so smooth, his frame so diminutive and childish? To the fully developed man, now virile, powerful, and magnetic, his seventeen-year-old self seemed eleven or twelve, despite the hints in his brooding expression of gravitas to come, unrelieved by the lightness that also came with it. He remembered that this expression was a result only of the fact that she was near and he was aware that he meant absolutely nothing to her.

For her part, it was as if she were of a different species, or a goddess among lesser beings. No one who did not know her had ever thought, upon seeing the picture, as his eyes moved instantly to her and stayed, that she was anything but a teacher among her students. She seemed at least ten years older than anyone around her, and so much larger, even if, although of handsome proportions and noble height, she was not nearly as large as some of the girls whom somehow she appeared to dwarf. And whereas almost every other girl wore a broad lace collar, with or without a kind of sailor's tie, she wore what looked like a Gibson Girl's formal jacket, with long, crossed lapels, their velvet a deep and seductive black. Resting against the top of her chest, halfway to the plunging neckline, a necklace cascaded over bare flesh. Her hair shone in the sun like hammered brass in blinding light. Her expression, unlike that of very beautiful women who because of their beauty are receptive and kind, had an edge. It said that she knew she was different, and that she would, though graciously, hold herself apart. It was the inimitable expression, Harry realized many years later, of royalty.

And now she was working in the window of a reweaving shop in a midtown arcade that never saw the light of day, repairing a man's suit at six in the evening, when everyone else was on the way home but she had to stay so people could drop off or claim their garments. It was a shock to see her at her bench, her hair still golden as if she were yet in the class picture and trying not to squint against the sun.

This was deep, unfinished business, and simply to speak with her would hardly betray Catherine, whom he was not able to betray. He had to know where Eugenia Eba had been, although it seemed not far; what she had done, although it seemed clear; and what she felt. He wanted to hear the sound of her voice, to see if now she wore perfume (for her to have done so then would have further stopped his education in its tracks), and if she would remember him. He wanted to see if over the years their powers had come into balance, if she would react to him — not differently but at all. It was dangerous, but he opened the door anyway.

A sleigh bell that was sprung on a metal strip snapped in announcement, and Eugenia Eba raised her head in a way that she would not have had a woman walked into the shop. Her hands settled as if in slow motion, she breathed in, her eyebrows lifted ever so slightly, and she smiled. It seemed that the seconds beat longer and harder.

"Eugenia?" he asked.

Her eyes narrowed. She tried to place him. "Yes?"

"Are you Eugenia Eba?"

"I was." She had a wedding ring that, though he had seen her hands before, he now saw for the first time. "I am."

"Harry Copeland."

She looked at him uncomprehendingly, struggling to remember the name. He said it again, and when she showed no affect, he said the name of the school. "Oh," she replied, as if to cover herself. But it was clear she didn't know him.

For a moment, he looked down in defeat, but then, in a deliberately light and reportorial tone, he said, "Every sport that I played, every catch I made, was with the patient hope that you would be watching. I would walk home, way out of my way, so that I could pass your house—with the idea," and here he paused, "that you might choose to look out the window."

"I'm sorry," she said. "I didn't know." She was not overjoyed to be held to account for something, decades before, of which she had been totally unaware.

"No, no," he said. "Boys do that. I did, at least."

"You were in love with me?"

"Everyone was in love with you. You must know that."

"I do. It wasn't fair." She shrugged her shoulders, as if to say that it didn't matter now, which it didn't.

"Then you went to the Brenau College Conservatory?"

"Now I remember," she said. "You went to Harvard. How could I forget? It was very difficult . . . for Jews. As far as I know, it may still be. You seem so different."

"You seem much the same," he told her.

"I'm not." She turned her head to direct his glance to the area above the sewing machine. Because it was dark in contrast to the work-lighted reweaving table, he hadn't noticed it. Hanging from a tack fastened to the edge of a shelf was a miniature flag with a gold star.

"Your husband."

"Missing, presumed killed, on Saipan."

"I'm sorry."

"You needn't be, because although they presume, I wait. And although I don't have him, and may never, the waiting is sacred. It's been a while. I'm not unhappy. Do you know what it feels like?"

"No," he said, so quietly she almost didn't hear.

"Like being in love."

He nodded. "Children?"

"Unfortunately not," she said. Only silence could follow.

Then she looked at him, in an unexpected reversal, with compassion. She was more out of his reach than she had ever been. "I'm still a married woman, but perhaps, sometime, you could stop by, and we could cross the street to the tearoom, and have tea."

"I'm going to be married myself," he said, to put things right, "and I would like that very much."

In the golden arcade, in a wash of indistinct sound saturated with murmurs, the whir of motors, and heel clicks coming from nowhere and sadly fading to nothing, she glanced at the star behind her, and then turned to Harry. Moved by her own words, but resolute, steady, and defiant, she said, "I believe . . . that when all is said and done . . . love that won't quit is more important than triumph, than time, than life itself."

Billy and Evelyn had been out when he had called, so the housekeeper in charge had smoothly connected him with Billy's executive secretary, a woman with an extraordinary presence over the telephone and everywhere else, one of those elegant, self-possessed, and inexplicably unmarried women who was so obviously efficient and intelligent that had she not been a woman, Billy would have been working for her. Sensing the importance of the matter before Harry had a chance to state it, she said that though Billy had meetings all morning, both Billy and Evelyn would be in the office for lunch, and would he care to join them?

Perhaps it was just a style left over from the thirties, but the Hale offices from the lobby all the way up to the forty-sixth floor exuded a certain shine that Harry, who had never been to either place, could associate only with South America. On the forty-sixth floor every piece of furniture was English or eighteenth-century American, the paintings American or French, the porcelains Mings. The decor being entirely Episcopalian, there were no colors or shapes that said, for example, *Brazil,* and yet the wood-paneled rooms with masses of flowers lit from above by recessed reflectors faintly tipped everything south. Almost blinded by the silver-blue harbor mist through which ferries were sweeping at remarkable speed, Harry supposed that the South American part was the result of the luxury, the color, and the airy view, with the coup de grâce supplied by Art Deco elevator fixtures that, quite mysteriously, looked like Carmen Miranda. All in all, although it may not have struck everyone the same way, entering the Hale offices was as relaxing and exotic as flying down to Rio. And then Harry remembered, drawing in a quiet whistle, that Billy had been born in the harbor there. As he waited in the reception room, he did not have to close his eyes so as to see nothing but blue sky and a monocoque plane heading south, its slipstream sparkling white in the sun.

Soon the capable woman to whom he had spoken that morning appeared and welcomed him. She would have been just as gracious even had she not known that he and Catherine would someday own the Hale Company. She took him into Billy's office, which was fifty feet long and almost as wide. A wall of windows glowed sapphire. One could see ships beyond the Narrows, moving as silently as clouds. Billy sat at his desk, his back to the windows, talking on the telephone. He gestured to Harry as if to say, I'm on this call, but you're more important: I'll be off in a minute.

Evelyn was ensconced in a wing chair covered in Williamsburg-blue jacquard. She was dressed, as he had never seen her, for Manhattan, but seemed harried and tired. She smiled, having accepted not only Harry but the new era he would bring. She looked over at her husband, then at Harry, and patted the air as if to say that he would finish soon, as he did. A waiter in a white jacket was setting up lunch in another part of the room. They rose and went to the windows, where they looked down at traffic and pedestrians moving noiselessly on the street far below. "What a beautiful place," Harry said.

"Yours if you want it," Billy told him. He and Evelyn, it seemed, had been discussing the future, and it is remarkable how quickly parents can move from being prepared to close ranks against a suitor to sudden warmth and trust in regard to a potential son-in-law. Still, Billy's statement was astonishing.

When Harry was silent, Billy said, "You'll have plenty of time to decide."

In Billy's office, as high above the harbor as a Pan Am Clipper and as quiet as and more spacious than a blimp, they sat down to eat. After the waiter served, he left through a door that clicked shut in assurance of absolute privacy. "We know," Billy said, "if what you want to talk about is the review."

"Reviews," Evelyn added.

"The only one that matters is the *Globe*," Billy insisted.

"No," Harry contradicted. "What really matters is that they were uniform and they all said that you bought her into the play."

"Of course I didn't."

"Where did it come from?"

"Don't you have a feeling about that?" Billy asked.

"I thought," Harry said, "that it might have come from Victor."

"Maybe." Evelyn stared at a golden roll sitting forever safely on her bread plate. "But it was in Winchell's column more than once. That's how all the Boston reviewers knew, probably."

"Winchell, that evil idiot," Billy added, "called Catherine 'an investment angel.' Investment has nothing to do with it. She is what she is, and she can sing."

"I had thought," Harry said, "that because Marrow lends to the press—"

"You don't need to make loans to the press to start a rumor," Billy interrupted, "but perhaps if you do, and you have a lot of contacts, it would be that much easier. The damage...." He shook his head.

"What can we do about it?"

"If I did anything at all it would appear to verify the original charge."

"You could write a letter stating the facts."

"I did. I wrote to each paper. Not that it would have helped—the reviews are in—but to set the record straight."

"What happened?"

"They don't like to admit they're wrong. Look, they slay people every day. For them it wasn't worth a moment's thought. They know we won't sue, because in court they fight like dogs, and by the time a verdict came down, even if in our favor, Catherine would be thirty and the play long forgotten."

"Can't you talk to someone—you must know people—so that it won't happen in New York?"

"I would, except that if I so much as approach them they'll back off as if from a leper. The one thing they claim never to do is to bow to outside pressure. It's their rightful pride. If they took account of what people do to influence their coverage one way or another, nothing would ever get printed."

"Even when they're wrong?"

"Especially when they're wrong. The point is, Harry, that on these questions opinion is divided. When they make an egregious mistake, which might cost thousands of people their livelihoods, or a number of people their lives, they won't respond, because of what it would look like. They'll say to you, and I've been through this, 'These are the people I hired. I trust them. They have integrity. Their job is to seek the truth. Write a letter.' They never publish a letter when they're wrong enough to be embarrassed."

"Winchell seeks the truth?"

"Winchell is his own special case. He libels a dozen people a day and you can't touch him. This kind of complaint wouldn't even register. To show his irritation he would probably write that to protect my untalented daughter from the justified criticism of the production I unethically bought for her, I tried to suborn the press. With something like this, the harder you pull, the tighter it gets."

"But . . . Catherine."

"Catherine is my daughter. We won't be able to sleep at night because of this. I'd kill for her, but we're powerless to help."

"If it's Victor, can't you talk to his father?"

"You're going through all the options, aren't you? Willie Marrow will never speak to me again, which is all right with me. But even if he would, he doesn't control Victor and never has. When you think of Victor, you have to reckon with the fact that he has so much money he knows that his children, his grandchildren, and their grandchildren will never want. If there's a depression, he has cash. If there's inflation, he has real property. If there's a revolution, he has gold. If there's war, he has minerals, rubber, armaments, and food. If there's peace, he has consumer goods. If there's prosperity, he has luxuries. In hard times he has staples. It's like an armored vehicle, and the brain that drives it is very clever, even if not that big."

"Though he's much more dreadful," Harry stated, "he still sounds like a cross between Sears, Roebuck and Santa's workshop. What does he want, anyway, other than Catherine?"

"Money."

"But he has it."

"Yes, but getting more of it is the only exciting thing left for him to do."

"For me," Harry said, "money has always been difficult, but simple. I need relatively small amounts, and struggle to get them, but I've never thought about getting a lot. I think that Victor never will be rich enough to know what I know, which is that money is highly irrelevant. Do you see what I mean?"

"Certainly I do," said Billy. "I have from the beginning. That's one reason why you're sitting here. We don't just take raccoons off the street, especially greedy ones."

"If you look at him," Evelyn said, getting back to Victor, "you can see that no one controls him, least of all himself. He refused to be disciplined as a little boy. Once, long before Catherine was born, the children were playing a game of throwing cards down on the floor, and if yours landed on top of another you got to keep everything. Practically the whole deck was waiting to be won. Catherine's cousin, a boy Victor's age, threw his last card, which appeared to land on the pile. Victor jumped down and put his head close to the floor. In his version, a loop of shag rug had kept the last card from touching, but before he could make his case Catherine's cousin snatched up the winnings, destroying the evidence. Victor was probably telling the truth, but from the grownups' perspective it did look as if the cards had been touching.

"Willie told him to be sportsmanlike and accept defeat, but he wouldn't have it. He insisted that he'd won, grabbed at his winnings, and flew into a rage. Willie had to throttle him down and, because Victor was kicking and biting so savagely, actually hit him. Victor was nine. He ran away, got on a train, and spent a week alone in Manhattan. The Marrows barely survived this."

"And so did Manhattan," Billy said. "He was returned to them only after he was apprehended by the police."

"For what?" Harry asked.

"Robbing Chinese merchants," Billy said. "They were more or less his size, and he knew they were afraid to go to the authorities. When one finally did, the police found Victor living in a shipping crate in an alley, with a bag that had more than a thousand dollars in it. Willie never had any influence over him after that. He couldn't disinherit him: like Catherine, he's now the only child. His brother was killed in the war. Really, the only way to deal with Victor would be to do away with him, and that would be out of proportion and rather dangerous."

Evelyn leaned forward. "And we really don't know that it was Victor, although I think it was. We can't think of what to do. Can you?"

"I've never had to deal with anything like this," Harry said, "but the same sort of thing now seems to be popping up all over the place."

"Don't you know," Billy asked, "that this is how life is? The world is made up of insoluble problems, of things that are beyond the influence of heroic action — of bitter loss, and no recoupment."

"I did know that," Harry said. "I thought you were the ones who didn't."

"Even Catherine has a sense of it. The world screwed up," Billy said, half to Harry and half to the ice in his glass. (Evelyn already knew.) "And what's going to happen is, it's going to have to make amends in suffering and further confusion. You can't just have wars like these and not feel the recoil. It'll be a hundred years before the crying stops. You have to be prepared to ride the storm."

"I've been doing that for a while now, Billy. I had hoped it was over."

"Harry, it's never over."

Walking up from Wall Street to the loft and occasionally catching sight of distant bridges spanning the rivers, Harry felt both his own powerlessness and the inexhaustible energy of the streets in which the work, emotion, and concentration of millions gathered in a magnetic wave that enlivened everything it touched.

The Cypriot, Victor, Gottlieb, Verderamé, and the other things that seemed to hold him and even the Hales in check were like a part of nature. Were they simply to vanish, others would take their place. These were the forces that assaulted all that he was obliged to protect. There would be no profit in remarking upon their injustice, but rather he should enjoy them as much as he could, no matter how painful, if only because, lacking opponents, fencers cannot fence. The more he accepted them as ordained in and organic to the life of the city, the freer he would be to deal with them however he could. Nor, he thought, walking fast and feeding off the vitality of Manhattan, must he win. Rather than merely win, he would engage, move, and fight. He would dodge, strike, rest, hide, and strike again until the end, the sole object being to continue the story in which he had a part.

When he arrived at the loft he guided the elevator slowly past active workshops appearing and disappearing beyond its gates until he stopped at his floor, where no one was working. Instead, people were scattered about in small groups, standing by the windows, and talking. He took a few steps into the workspace and, saying nothing, lifted his hands to inquire what was going on. It was neither the lunch hour nor a holiday nor the end of the workday. Those of whom he had inquired waited until one of the polishers/stainers/waxers was summoned from around the corner to offer an answer. Born in a country in South America that during the war had, like most, stayed neutral (Harry had forgotten which one), he had a mustache and a full face, and his hands were dark with stain. His expression was that of a man whose life easily eclipsed his job.

"You know Velez, the polisher, Clementino Velez?"

"I didn't know his name was Clementino."

"That's because no one calls him that. They call him Guada."

"Oh, yes. We make out the pay packets to Guada. From Porto Rico."

"He was hired just before you got back."

"What about him?"

"He was coming from lunch. Two guys stopped him downstairs in the hall and asked how to find us. He told them. Do you work there?

they asked. He said yes. Good, they said, and then they punched and beat him. For a long time. They put him in the passenger elevator, pushed the button, and it stopped on this floor. Guada was lying in a pool of blood that was moving, because the floor of the elevator is a little" — he made a gesture with his hands.

"Tilted."

"Yes. For when you wash it. The blood ran over the metal edge and dripped into the shaft."

"Where is he?"

"St. Vincent's."

"Who saw this?"

"No one. He told us before he went out."

"Lost consciousness?"

"Yes, and he couldn't hardly talk. Blood in the throat."

"Is Cornell with him?"

"Cornell and some others. Someone went to get his wife."

"Did you call the police?"

"Detectives from Manhattan South looked at the blood, but no one here saw anything they could say. They said they were going to the hospital. We told them what happened. Then I think they went to the hospital. You know what he said?"

"Velez? What?"

"Not to call the police. But we had called them already."

More people had gathered. "Okay," Harry said. "Clean up, and everybody go home. Tomorrow, come in early. Be right at the door downstairs exactly half an hour before the usual time. No one goes out alone. Key the elevator. I'm going to the hospital." Before he went, he stopped in the glass-paneled office, opened the safe, and took out a thousand dollars.

He knew that though she would have no cause to be, Velez's wife would be frightened of him, so he went in to see Velez first. The woman in the waiting room, a peasant such as still existed all over Europe but not among even the poorest of the poor in the United States, didn't know who he was. Harry was reluctant to face her, because he knew she wouldn't understand him and because an oppression of man that had begun at the beginning of time would make her unnecessarily grateful and obsequious. He anticipated that were Velez's condition to worsen, his wife would wail hysterically. The poorer and less powerful a person, he had observed, the more expressive. Had the wife of an English duke been apprised of her husband's death, she might have clouded over, perhaps stiffened a little, or trembled momentarily, and in the stillness the bearer of the bad news might hear a leaf drop somewhere on the soft and capacious lawns. But not here. Were Guada to die, the screams and flailings would be like those of torture, and then, not long after, would come the exhausted silence of utter defeat, a silence where, courtesy of death, all classes meet.

Velez was different from his wife. He worked, spoke English fluently, circulated in the streets, ate at the automat. Though he may have grown up cutting cane, he would know that the rules here were not the same, and that for anyone who played by these rules, as did Harry, there were neither masters nor slaves. It is true that a discrepancy existed, and, as he had arrived only recently, not in his favor, but all Copeland workers knew that Harry was well aware that he was himself almost a new arrival.

Velez was hardly awake. He breathed with difficulty in extremely slow flutters. His face was swollen like a puffer fish, slit, stitched, and so heavily mottled with red, black, and cyanotic blue that it looked like someone had spread different kinds of jam over it. His left hand, right leg, and right arm were in plaster casts. Blood and saline dripped into him from bottles suspended above the bed.

"This is what we get," Cornell said from a low chair near the window, "for paying what they asked, when they asked."

"It was the right amount?"

"It was. They came to get it Friday. No complaints."

"Did you speak to the police?"

"I did. A nigger speaks on behalf of a spic who was beaten up by people he can't name, for a reason he can't say. No one saw, no robbery, he's not dead, no weapons. We won't see the cops again. They have nothing to go on. And if they did, and they found them, they would stop out of fear or because they've been bought off. Now what?"

"We have to take care of him," Harry said. He approached the bed. Turning back to Cornell, he asked, "He'll be all right? Does my experience fail me?"

"You've seen a lot of beaten-up waxers and polishers?"

"I've seen a lot of chewed-up soldiers. He looks bad, but he doesn't have that faraway stare that comes when your outside is calm but your inside is bleeding out like a stream and no one can see it. He doesn't have that look, yet."

"The doctor said he was at the edge."

"Verderamé is precise. He could have been a jeweler or a bomb fuser." Harry went to the bed and leaned in. "Velez? Guada?"

Velez opened his eyes. Harry looked in them and saw morphine. "Wake up, wake up." He did. "Do you recognize me?" Velez nodded as best he could. "I'm going to give your wife a thousand dollars," Harry said, taking the money out of his pocket. "When you get better, come to collect your back pay. You may not remember this, but we'll tell you, and tell you again. We'll keep you on the payroll for six months until you find another job. And if you want to come back, you can at any time, for a job and a raise — if we're still in business. Is that clear to you?"

Velez tried to say something, but it came out as a hiss from between dry lips.

"Later, then. I'm sorry this happened. You know that it happened to me, too? Not as bad, but probably the same guys. We'll take care of you if we can." He patted Velez's uninjured hand, and left, followed by Cornell, who assured the patient, whose eyes were now closed, that he would be back the next day.

As Harry and Cornell stood outside the hospital room, Harry kept his hand tight against the packet of bills. "Does she know you?"

"Not from Adam," Cornell replied.

"Doesn't she wonder what you're doing in there?"

"I think she thinks I'm a cop."

"I'll do it."

When he gave her the money and, in a most peculiar Spanish constructed from Latin, Italian, and French, explained what he would do, she knelt and tried to kiss his hand. He wouldn't let her get below him, and knelt with her, and as they were having a sort of contest in which he wanted to win so that she wouldn't lose, he thought to himself that Verderamé's actions and existence were pushing history backward and running time in reverse.

To drop off Mrs. Velez, they took a taxi, because Cornell had miraculously come into possession of a fifty-pound hamper of food for her and they didn't want to struggle with it in the subway. The three of them sat awkwardly in the turtle-backed cab, the hamper at their feet, the smell of leather brought up from the seats by a sudden drop in pressure that had come with rain and wind from the direction of New Jersey. They knew it had come from there because it smelled like burnt coffee. In summer, weather usually arrived from the south, billowing up over the sea in clouds that were as enormous in proportion to the rest of the world as a painter's tube of white is to his smaller tubes of more intense colors, like a whale surrounded by porpoises. In winter, memorable weather came from the north with sterilizing clarity and immersed the whole world in a sea of shining glass. But in spring and fall it tended to roll in from New Jersey as surreptitiously as if it were ashamed. The clear wet air that had crossed the fields near Princeton, dipped down into abandoned canals, and strained through willows dripping with rain, often arrived with the foul smells of marshes, bogs, factories, refineries, tanneries, and landfills. Most people could not begin to guess what it was they smelled on those winds, but the rain would eventually clear it away.

Now, early in the afternoon, the streets were slick and the lights in the commercial districts had blinked on. Farther north, it was different. Most apartments and houses were dark. Sometimes a light appeared where people were at home — a woman ironing, small children too young for school, an invalid, a widower, a widow, or perhaps a musician who worked at night — but overall the premature dusk was undisturbed—except all the way up Broadway, where old ladies were shopping, and pulling old-lady wheeled wire baskets behind them through the rain. In midtown, Harry and Cornell, unable to comfort Mrs. Velez, who was as tense as a piano string, leaned toward their respective windows and scanned the blocks as they passed. The streets glistened, the windshield wipers were hypnotic, the lights, yellow in cast or burning red neon, were doubled or tripled by watery refection. The taxi passed a gun store on the second floor of a building on the east side of Sixth Avenue. It had a neon rifle in the window. Harry bent his head to look up at it, and followed with his eyes as it receded.

"*Rifles*," he said in Spanish, to make conversation of a sort with Mrs. Velez, who was sitting in the middle, drawn up against herself for fear of touching either of the two *patrons*. She had not seen the sign, and had no idea why Harry had said *rifles*, but she smiled to be polite. Thinking that this had made her more comfortable, Harry said, as they passed a hairdresser on the second floor on the other side of the street, "*Parrucchiere*," as if, because it was Italian, she would understand.

Although she didn't, she said, "*Sí*."

"*Bueno*," Harry replied.

"What the hell are you talking about?" Cornell asked.

"I don't know," Harry answered, and then the taxi rounded Columbus Circle and slingshotted up Broadway. In a minute or two it turned on a side street and disgorged them in front of a tenement. They carried the hamper up four flights of stairs, past brown walls that had aged into black. There was hardly any light, and the floorboards creaked like the timbers of a ship. "What's in this, anyway?" Harry asked.

"Ham, biscuits, cheese, bread . . . ," Cornell told him.

"Where'd you get it?"

"My church. They keep them for when someone gets sick or dies. My nephew brought it down."

"In a truck? Why didn't he wait?"

"He carried it in the subway."

"He must be a giant."

"He's as skinny as a chicken leg, but he's fourteen years old. He could probably carry the *Titanic*."

Mrs. Velez did not want them to go into her apartment, and they were about to put down the hamper and leave, when one of her children opened the door. A girl of about five or six, she stood on the threshold, her eyes seeming very large for her size, her dress simple and stained, her face smudged. She looked hungry, numb. As they carried the hamper in and put it down, they could hardly make out the apartment's two small rooms. One was filled with mattresses, some covered and others with the ticking exposed, on which sat or lay half a dozen children, doing nothing. The other room was a kitchen, with a bed in it and a small table covered with dirty dishes.

"Okay," Harry said, about to repeat what he had told Velez, but he realized that his ersatz Spanish would be insufficient to communicate it, so he just said, "Okay, okay," as she thanked him in Spanish. They left quickly because they were afraid that she might try to kneel to them again. The children had a great task ahead, and this would be something they would be better off without witnessing.

When Harry and Cornell came out on the street, the light rain and now cooler air were welcome. "That was my family, sixty years ago," Harry said, "only my grandmother would have kept the place spotless, piecework shirtwaists would have been in neat piles, and the children, far fewer, would have been reading or sewing."

"And it was mine," Cornell added, "working or studying. My father told me that my first commandment was never to be a slave. And that there's only one just way not to be a slave, which is to be a master — neither of another nor of the world, but of oneself."

"I feel the tenement pulling at my heels," Harry said. "All I'd have to do would be to close my eyes, and I'd be there."

"That's where we'd all be," Cornell answered, "rich or poor, white or colored. Some people don't know it, but they find out."

"In a matter of months, at this rate," Harry told him as they were striding up Broadway in the rain as darkness fell, "I will have lost all that my mother and father and their mothers and fathers worked to build in the New World."

"Except you, Harry. The business is just a business. You should close it down and keep what you have."

"I can't."

"Why not?"

"Defiance."

"You're not being very defiant as far as I can tell."

"It's more than that. I could never live on Catherine's money, but that hurts her and she says that everything she has is mine. The problem is the imbalance. All I need is to be a Rockefeller, and we'd be even. I can't throw our people out of work. I don't want to close down or give up this business that means such a great deal to so many and has helped so many rise, including me; that makes useful and beautiful things; that's something into which my father put so much of his life and his heart. If he were alive it would be different. I could. I could pull out and do something else. But he's not alive, so I have to see it through."

The rain was heavy enough now that it ran down their necks, backs, and inside their clothes. "My mistake, Cornell, was to think that I was home safe. It just takes different forms. You're never home, never safe."

"If you know that," Cornell said, "then you are home."

This encouraged them, and they parted. As each walked in the storelight of evening, in the excitement of the end of day, in the freshness of the rain-washed air, neither could know that when they set the hamper down for Guada's wife, she was a widow.

To the extent that Harry had known him—a conversation or two—he understood that Guada was quiet in the way of someone who, believing that he himself cannot rise, is determined that his children will. Though his English was not perfect and would always be accented, though women on the street or the bus would not look at him or simply did not see him, and though the winters in New York drew him away from his childhood on the south coast of Puerto Rico, he did whatever he could in the hope of the future.

He was a good and dependable worker. He never missed a day and he worked hard. He would fade from the world's memory faster than those whose lives are spent trying to trick this memory into keeping theirs fresh an instant longer, but his triumph, every day, was his children, whom he loved.

There might not be much to note about him, yet one could not help but notice that this well broken horse was kind and good, and always identifiable by his one indulgence: he smoked cigars, perhaps the only thing he did not do for others. They were small, but not the cheap kind that smell like badly cooked cabbage. Even people who didn't like the scent of cigars liked these Cubans, his indulgence, his signature, almost like a cologne. A rich scent it was, of the tobacco-drying shed, a combination of earth, wood, smoke, and honey.

The white smoke around him sometimes seemed like gossamer robes, and was the constant frame for his black hair, his khaki clothing, and his patient, ever-enduring expression — except when in winter the merciless winds shot through the canyons, and cold dry air without the slightest compassion for either sight or the preservation of scent made away with the soft white cloud as if it had never existed.

# 29

## JAMES GEORGE VANDERLYN

Though his life was calm and gracious, and everything around him was beautiful, he lived in sorrow. Having come out of the First World War with high rank and great distinction, and the Second with greater distinction still in running a major portion of the clandestine services of the United States against enemy fronts in Europe, he was now in his late fifties and content with investment banking, serving his sentence there for the sake not only of his compensation, but of family, propriety, and the part of his soul that had yearned for peace. He had not had to serve, but when with the father's exploits in mind his son had gone into uniform, it became impossible for the father to sit out the war.

Although his wife lived with him in the same house and slept with him in the same bed, she had begun to leave him before the war had permanently sealed their lack of a bargain. She was a charming hostess, still physically attractive, and always amusing, but love is indifferent to talent, and the something deeper from which love springs had in the case of the Vanderlyns become dust billowing in the air. Like an ancient and abandoned nest beneath an eave or at the inside peak of a barn roof, their marriage, held by inertia alone, was a powder ready to be taken on the wind, a very sad thing.

He believed that the best things he had done, he had done. In the years remaining, having missed his further chances, he would find satisfaction where he could — in modest beauties that passed unnoticed and without acclaim, in small symmetries, private action, remembrances of early sensations and loves. These now seemed so much more important than they had when he had left them in the wake of his striving. In the powerlessness of childhood, life had been most vivid, and as he began to fade into the powerlessness of old age it was becoming vivid again, if less surprising and less sharp. Despite certain things moving into place, he thought that for him action and accomplishment were over. He would be proven wrong.

On a Friday morning late in September, when hurricane season was not entirely finished and a storm against which all mariners had been warned was tracking up from the Outer Banks, having missed Florida but neither the Bahamas nor the Carolinas, Vanderlyn walked across the wide porch of his house in Oyster Bay and went down a path to the water. Past lawns as closely clipped as carpets, rhododendron long out of bloom, and a thick stand of fragrant pines planted to weaken gales as they came off the Sound, he descended to a cove made by the left hook of a pristine beach. There are some days at the end of summer, after the heat has broken and everything is dry and gleaming, when the crickets sound as metallic as bells. But those had passed, and even at midday it was wet and dark.

After tossing a rucksack into his sixteen-foot Winabout, he loosed the painter, dropped the centerboard, and when the wind in bare rigging had pushed him halfway across the inlet, raised mainsail and jib, tacking out to open wind-lined waters already running with a two-foot swell. Despite the weather and size of the boat, his plan was to sail to New London and up the Thames, leave the boat for the winter with a friend, and pick it up on the way home from a trip to Boston in late spring. The winds ahead of the storm went northeast. It would be a quick but dangerous run, and he would take the train back on Sunday, having been through enough difficulty and privation, he guessed, to keep him for a few months, and having touched upon the state of life in which nothing was assumed, all was at risk, and even things thought dead can come alive.

The track of the storm, however, had moved unfavorably and confused the winds, which now clashed in the Sound in unexpected violence, deepening the swell almost unbearably for the little boat and subjecting it to life-threatening concussions. This was before the rain and the dark, and just the work of the wind, when land was close by and easy to reach, though far enough away for drowning. Vanderlyn could have come about and made for home. To go east he had to tack now anyway. He could have sought shelter on any of the beaches to the south, the mansions behind them unperturbed by the winds through which, like his own, they had long held.

But he didn't, guiding his boat instead between the two pillars of Greenwich and Oyster Bay and out to the middle where small boats were in great danger. The wind screamed through the few short stays. The boat ceased to be propelled solely by the air, and was made by gravity to slide down the slopes of swells, sometimes fast enough to luff the sails, sometimes fast enough to give rise within Vanderlyn to a giddy feeling of disconnection, as if physics were abridged and this boat were soon to be lifted into the thin of the atmosphere.

Perhaps it was adrenaline or something greater, but in the storm the world seemed full, and he slowly cut his way east, tacking now broadly, now tight, according to what was happening far out at sea and its repercussions in the Sound. Somehow the eastern-driving winds were a narrative of his life, and opened the truth of it to him in their pattern and their beat, and thus the truth of the lives of others, which in essence were the same.

For eight hours until dark he struggled every second, always alert, ignoring everything but what was instantly required. The first thing to go was the jib, nipped at the base until it broke half free and flew hysterically from the top of the mast like linens on a clothesline. He let it go — daring to leave the tiller and dash to the mast for the seconds it took to uncleat the halyard — and watched as it climbed on the wind. Rather than flopping upon the waves and sinking like a handkerchief, it rose violently, lines snapping, compressing upon itself in folds, falling back and unfolding as if in regret, and then, when open, rocketing up again. It would take two steps down but twelve up, and in this way it ascended until he could no longer distinguish it from the streaks of gray and white that scored the charcoal-colored clouds.

He had never seen anything like that. Sails were heavy. No matter what the force of the wind, when detached from the rigging they hit the water within a boat's length or two at most. The departure was welcome. Like watching for the largest wave or listening for the loudest crack of thunder, it served more than curiosity or entertainment but something related to a greater expectation. Things lifting on the wind, seas violent such as no one had ever seen, the world shaken by majestic events: this was the way out. In this seemed to be answers, although they were not clear and perhaps never would be. But on the edge — rain now lashing, the rucksack overboard with his possessions, the shore no longer visible, the ribs and stays threatening to explode with strain — nature seemed just, its elemental assertions against which he now struggled the theme and answer he had sought all his life. It was good to get such a strong answer from such a strong hand. He imagined that unexpectedly and contrary to all the fixed laws by which the world lived, he might possibly follow the ascending sail, and that this would be his death. Though in general he could barely see, he did see when the friction and collision of two great waves sent up columns of oxygenated white water, bursting the darkness like fireworks that bloom, upwell, and disappear with a sigh.

At almost three, when, had he been sensible, he should have been camped in a harvested field close to the water, with the boat pulled up safely on the sand, he checked his watch. It glowed back at him, and he tapped it, thinking it had stopped in the afternoon, though he didn't bother trying to listen for ticking that could not possibly be heard. Had he guessed, he might have said it was not the middle of the night but no later than eight in the evening. Perhaps he had been taken so fast that he had sped past Montauk and Block Island and was now in the open sea. The water seemed very wide, the waves were of a class that lifted great liners, and there were no lights, horns, ships, or ports. And then, in a blast of wind like a hammer blow, the mast cracked and knifed into the water, pulling the tiny bit of mainsail with it and the boom as well. Like a sea anchor, drawing after it wire stays far too strong to unfasten at a stroke, it swamped the boat and sent Vanderlyn into water that, though cold, seemed to him to be a pleasing temperature and, rather than a shock, a relief.

· · ·

Though by now beyond the realm of deliberation, he still had to decide whether to stay with the boat or let himself be carried by the sea. Like his life, were it not to sink completely, the wreckage would keep his head above water if he could but hold on to it, for in daylight the swamped sailboat would be far more visible than a man alone. From the rails of many an ocean liner on the North Atlantic he had seen clumps of flotsam stuck in place as he steamed by. In comparison to the empty expanses they were an irresistible target for the eye. Even on a destroyer pressing thirty knots one scanned these things for clues of life. The crews of fishing boats, freighters, or warships would look closely, the watch-standers lifting their binoculars. So he clung to the gunwales, now at water level, and stayed with the broken vessel.

This was not easy. The water had retained enough of the summer heat not to be that cold in early fall, but it eventually numbed his hands and fingers. Waves struck with great force, threatening to break his hold. The mast twisted, clubbed at him, and sometimes wrapped its guy wires around him like the tentacles of a squid. Salt water was shot into his mouth by high-pressure winds and attacking waves. And at four or five, after what seemed like a week, the lightning began, bringing intermittent floods of illumination that froze the swells as if in a slide show.

But the lightning enabled Vanderlyn to make out a coastline so low it might have been an illusion were not the land of eastern Long Island shallow after epochs of grading by the sea. It was unlike a hallucination in that it was homely and indistinct. And then, still offshore, the remains of his boat caught on a shoal. The waves broke over him, but the varnished timbers dug into the sand and held fast, and he knew they would stay.

At dawn he found that his grip had closed like rigor mortis around the half-broken gunwale that had saved his life. The sky was the color of long-tarnished silver, and the waves now were only a foot high and running as evenly as if they were apologizing. He looked about. The shore was a mile or two away, a concave necklace of beach and low dunes, in the center of which was an inlet. He recognized this. Sitting on the sand, the little waves crossing over him never more than chest high, he turned his head as if he were rowing, hands still on the gunwales, and saw behind him, at the same distance as the shore, the southern tip of Gardiners Island. As a child, passing by on sailboats, he had seen workers there harvesting grain by hand, like medieval peasants. No one was allowed to land, but his father had beached their boat and gone in to speak to them. "Either they're all Shakespearean actors hired to amaze trespassers, or we've stumbled upon a remnant of the Elizabethan age," he had said. In college, Vanderlyn had sailed there at night with a girl from Vassar, and, in for a penny, in for a pound, they had swum naked in a warm freshwater pond, as disconnected from the world as if they had been shot back a million years.

Breathing hard, worrying about his heart and whether it might stop, not confident that in his state and in the wind and current of even the denatured storm he could reach shore, he thought back to 1910, before the great wars, when he had swum at the height of summer under a full moon in the Gardiners' bath-warm pond. In the moonlight the Vassar girl was flawless. He had thought at the time that he would marry her, and eventually he did.

At eight o'clock by his still-running watch despite the paradox of the description, he abandoned what was left of the Winabout and, at first half walking, half swimming over the bar that had saved him, found deep water and began a slow, two-hour crawl toward Napeague Inlet.

Were he to make it, he would burrow into the side of a dune and sleep, and when he awoke go to the highway and then East Hampton, where among the many people he knew, someone would be at home despite the season and the storm. He had nothing but his clothes, neither shoes nor socks, which had been stripped off by the sea as easily as a two-year-old's shoes and socks are shucked from his feet by a mother's well practiced and affectionate hands. In the cold, dry sides of a dune, he dreamt of the island pond, moonlit, warm, and ruffled by the wind.

# 30

## BAUCIS AND PHILEMON

CATHERINE NOW DISPLAYED a delicacy that made her parents unusually tentative in her presence. They refrained from speaking when ordinarily they would have spoken, they shot glances at one another, and were as careful about what they said as if they were disarming unexploded ordnance. The more fastidious they were in her regard, the more fragile she seemed to become, until, faced with this realization, they pretended unsuccessfully that nothing had changed. But it had. Silences in conversation were now much longer, the resumption of speech more abrupt, the endings unnatural, the atmosphere brittle. Her insoluble problem, that of injustice working upon a single human heart, threatened to transform her. Forced to change, she longed not to, and in sorrow and in anger could only observe what was happening. An unknowing onlooker might have thought that she was angry at the people she loved, but it was just that when she struck out at enemies she could not reach, her frustration found its target among those who were closest to her.

At first that Saturday, she hadn't wanted to ride out to the docks at Montauk to buy dinner from the incoming boats. "Why don't you send *him?*" meaning Harry, she had asked her father, who, instead of upbraiding her for her startling rudeness, stated patiently that he and Evelyn would be going, and it would be good to get out of the house on a rainy day. In East Hampton, storm days wore out playing cards and electric lights, and by late afternoon the roads were filled with restless people who, as if it would be their salvation, wanted to look at storefronts.

Harry loved Catherine too much to be hurt that she had referred to him as if he were a disliked servant or an untrusted stranger. "Why don't you come?" he asked. "We can look at the storm waves from the Montauk Road."

"We can just walk out here and look at the waves," she answered, her tone half combative and half a cry for him to take her in his arms.

He remained practical. "It's far more interesting and dramatic from a height." He should not have said *dramatic*. Billy and Evelyn winced.

"The storm is over," Catherine stated.

"But on the ocean side," Harry responded, trying not to be argumentative (which was somewhat like walking over a bridge of eggshells), "the highest waves are born at sea and they come after the storm. They'll be at their maximum, and you can face them knowing that they can only back down."

"Yes," said Billy, "and from inside the Rolls, where you'll be quite comfortable."

She had seen too many wonderful things while looking out through the windows of that car not to go, and, announcing that she would, she seemed closer to her old self. "I don't want lobster," she said. "I want something that's comforting."

"Lobster's not comforting?" Billy asked. "I guess not if you use it to clock someone in the face."

"Lobster is for triumph, for people who don't care. I'd like something like chowder, and rolls."

"Oh," Billy said. "I see." He didn't.

"Of course," Evelyn added, knowing how simple it would be to make what her daughter wanted.

At Hither Hills the waves were once again cavalry charging against the dry world as line after line of galloping white attacked beaches that somehow remained intact. The water on the bay side was comparatively still, and there fishermen driven by habit and necessity had gone out before the storm was over, baiting smaller hooks, dragging lesser nets.

At the docks, Catherine seemed connected to the fishermen in a way that Harry, having come from the war, well understood. He was neither jealous of her love for them nor disturbed by their love for her, for it was the kind of thing, glancing and pure, that he had seen make hardened soldiers worshipful of feminine beauty they had mistreated and misapprehended all their lives, and would again, perhaps, when their privations came to an end. Catherine had always understood the difficulties of the fishermen, and she had always been kind, but now it was deeper, as if she had been riding with them in their boats or waiting at home with their children.

Billy bought fish, and they started back. She was placid and silent. It was raining lightly. Either dusk had fallen or dense clouds had replicated evening light. Billy flipped the switch for the headlamps, and as he did so Evelyn leaned forward and turned on the radio. At the tip of Long Island they were more or less halfway out to sea, with neither hills nor mountains to obstruct radio signals as the storm-driven atmosphere did to these what wind did to escaped birthday balloons. A station in Chicago faded in and out, its ghostly dance behind the warm yellow light of the dial finally disappearing. French then filled the car as if a miracle. "Montreal," Billy said after listening a moment to the transmission, disappointed that the broadcast had not leapt the ocean. And then Evelyn turned the dial and stopped its lighted bar on a strong New York station from which Beethoven's Violin Concerto in D issued amid lonely cracks of static from lightning over distant seas.

As if by instinct, and like a pilot checking his gauges, Billy directed his eyes to the bar to see the number of the station. He was a good driver, and had looked ahead. The long, straight road was empty as far as he could see, and he would have noticed lights a mile off. He was comfortable and relaxed, as one is in driving on a straight and empty road even at dusk. Billy was the only one who had not been able to identify the music almost instantly—it took Catherine two bars—and as he narrowed his eyes and listened, trying to pick out patterns and the characteristic use of various instruments, the car drifted toward the side of the road. It was a very big car, and although the right wheels had yet to touch the sandy shoulder, the body of the automobile was planing a six-inch strip through air where it should not have been.

Evelyn was the one who grabbed the wheel and sent the Rolls veering over the center line so as not to hit the dark form of a man they would have killed as he walked right next to the pavement. It would have been hard for him to have heard them. The wind was high and the Rolls's large engine, which did not have to strain, was exceedingly quiet.

"Son of a bitch!" Billy screamed, bringing the car back to its lane as the adrenaline coursed through him so that he could hear every note coming over the airwaves. "I knew it was Beethoven. That son of a bitch, what was he doing walking in the road like that?"

"We were almost off the road, Daddy," Catherine said severely.

"But we weren't," Billy replied. "We weren't. You don't walk right on the road, where you can get hit by a car." Billy was expecting a male-female division in this debate, and waited for Harry's support, but Harry had turned around in his seat and was staring out the back window.

"Stop," Harry commanded.

"For Christ's sake, Billy, you hit him," Evelyn declared, out of panic.

"I did not. I didn't hit anybody." Still, he braked as if he had, and the car came to a stop. "Why stop?"

"His tunic is from the Hundred and First," Harry announced. "He doesn't have any shoes." The figure was just visible in the darkness, coming toward them in what the ocean wind and rain made to seem a threatening, discomfited gait. Billy pressed the accelerator, and the car moved silently back onto the road.

"Wait," Harry called out, as if to the man outside.

"What do you propose?" Billy asked.

"Let's give him a ride."

"To where? The last train's already left."

"The village."

"An immediate arrest for vagrancy."

"Maybe he knows someone there, or lives there himself."

"It doesn't matter," Billy said. "I'm not having him in my car. I saw him in the mirror. Forgive me, but he looks like the kind of person who would slit our throats to get the contents of the picnic basket."

"But he's from the Hundred and First," Harry said, realizing that, to others, and since it wasn't even his own division, this was hardly a powerful argument.

"I don't care if he's from the Million and Tenth. The war's over. He should get a job and wear shoes."

"The war isn't over yet," Harry said, "not for him. And it'll be a really long time, Billy, before it is. Eighteen months ago he was fighting in Germany. What does that say to you?"

"Not enough, Harry. I'm not going to risk my family by picking up a stranger on a dark road."

"But he isn't a stranger," Harry insisted. He knew this was weak, that anyone could be wearing a paratrooper's tunic.

"I'm sorry, Harry, to me he is." Billy accelerated, and soon they ran up the hill to Amagansett and left the area that was subject to inundations when hurricanes pushed the sea over the dunes and joined it with the Sound. There, a few miles back in the dark, James George Vanderlyn continued his unvaried pace.

Billy and Harry had never had words, with Harry always respectful not only of Billy himself but of his age and his position as Catherine's father, and with Billy trying hard to avoid the thoughtless and weakminded tyranny that so often seduces fathers-in-law. But rather than worry about alienating the Hales, Harry was concerned about the man walking along the lonely stretch of road between sea and sound. As the rain had strengthened, the wind had come up cold.

Although Catherine had been for a while fairly distant, she surprised him. Arriving at the pool house, where Harry had gone to allow Billy to cool off, she said, "Oh, he'll be all right. His point is well taken, but still, I think about that man out there. I wouldn't have last year, I just would have let it go."

"He's a brother in arms. We could at least have given him a ride into town, and a few dollars. Yes, there's a risk, but he's got no shoes. It could be me."

"Why don't you bring him here?" Catherine asked.

"Here?"

"Feed him, clothe him, give him shelter, a place to sleep, and some money, and then set him on his way."

"What if he kills us?"

"Hales don't like to be murdered in their sleep," she said matter-of-factly, "which is why Copeland will revert to his military self and stand watch all night if this guy seems even slightly dangerous. If not, locked doors will do."

"If your parents found out, they'd never speak to me again."

"Yes they would, because it's my idea. But they won't find out. He'll stay in the pool house, and you'll stay with me."

"I hate sneaking around."

She looked at him with not a little heat. "I kind of like it," she said, and thereafter nothing could have kept him from her room that night, where they would make love as if in a silent movie — except that there would be no piano.

"They'll hear the car," Harry told Catherine. "How am I supposed to retrieve him? We have an hour and a half until dinner. I can't walk to him and bring him back in that time. If dinner ends two and a half hours from now he'll be gone. He may be gone already, sheltering in the dunes."

"Come with me," she said. "I'll show you."

Moving like conspirators, they crossed the gardens quickly, unseen from the house, which glowed in the rain. The garage was dark and musty, but the cars, parked in a neat row like cows at milking gates, smelled of fresh wax and leather. Catherine held his hand and moved slowly, feeling her way to the back, where she pulled at a white porcelain knob on a paneled door. It was one of those doors that always sticks and that when it comes open vibrates like a reed. She threw a switch that lit a clear lightbulb. There before them, amidst mildewed badminton nets, surf-casting rods, and sports equipment of the twenties and before — varnished Indian clubs, rings, a mechanical horse — were three French bicycles.

"I'll bring him back."

Some rain was still driven on the wind, and it was cold and dark, but beneath the dripping trees of Further Lane Harry's spirits rose as he rode toward the Montauk Highway. Shepherding the second bike alongside, he held the yoke in his left hand. Sometimes the front wheels of the two bicycles left the parallel, but he brought them back and pushed on. The bicycles were solid and heavy, the kind that, in peacetime, postmen ride and that in war are used to carry packs and ammunition.

He glided down the big hill that descended east from Amagansett, the wind in his ears, the breakers barely audible to his right. He must not either miss his target or smack into him. Thinking of this man in the 101st jacket, with no shoes, he had a vision of himself in what had been the most vivid part of his life before Catherine. Perhaps he would have reason to fear a former soldier, were this man indeed that, but nevertheless Harry was a trooper of the 82nd on his way to aid one of the 101st. There was something very important about this, something he would neither deny nor forgo, not now, not yet, because it was written in him still that this was what one did even if it meant dying.

He sensed motion ahead, a slight turbulence in the black, which persisted and strengthened, the faint glimmer that a paratrooper had learned to extract from virtually nothing with the corner of his eye, the relaxation of focus and of expectation allowing whatever was there to make itself known more strongly than an image that preconception overlaid upon the field of view. Within a few seconds he had passed Vanderlyn.

They could barely see one another. Harry turned the bicycles around and came up alongside. He stopped, wheeled the free bicycle a few feet forward, and then looked at Vanderlyn with an expression unmistakable even in the dark.

Surprised, Vanderlyn surveyed the bicycle and asked, *"Pour moi?"* in a perfect accent.

*"Oui, pour vous,"* Harry answered, amazed that he was conversing in French on the Montauk Highway in the dark.

"*Merci bien,*" Vanderlyn said, mounting the bicycle. And then, with some amusement, "*Puis-je vous demander de m'aider? Pourriez-vous m'indiquer le chemin de Meudon?*"

"What?" Harry asked. "Are you French? What'd you do, swim the Atlantic?"

"No, but the last time someone handed me a bicycle, a French bicycle, no less, I said those exact words."

"The last time *I* was on a bicycle," Harry told him, "I was in Holland."

"It was a password," Vanderlyn said, "a pass-*phrase*. I knew he was all right when he said . . . what did he say? He said, '*Nathalie a vu écraser sa maison par une énorme roche.*' Yes."

"Nathalie saw her house destroyed by an enormous rock?"

"Didn't you have passwords?"

"Yes we did. Things like *Oil Can,* and *Betty Grable's Tits.*"

"Very elevated." They were pedaling now.

"I was the Eighty-second. I didn't think the Hundred and First was all that erudite."

"It wasn't. They dropped me out of their Dakotas but I was something else entirely, although I wore their uniform beneath my clothes."

"Oh," Harry said, "one of those."

Vanderlyn smiled. Harry still could not see his face clearly. "And you?"

"Pathfinder," Harry replied.

"What luck. Now, may I ask, where the hell did you come from with two bicycles?"

"We passed you in the car, almost hit you."

"That was you. And where are we going?"

"We're going," Harry informed him, "up the hill into Amagansett and then down Further Lane, to get you a pair of shoes."

After they replaced the bicycles, Harry led Vanderlyn through the back garden and over the tennis court to the pool house, so that even had Billy been looking out the window, and even had he been able to see in the dark, nothing would have seemed untoward.

Vanderlyn stood between the fire and the French doors, dripping slightly, his paratrooper jacket dark with rain, the pockets distinctively slanted, the belt hanging loosely, the eagle on the shoulder patch, laundered by hours in salt water and rain, glowing white. Although he was unshaven and disheveled, he seemed healthy and strong; and although he stood straight with a military bearing, he was relaxed.

An hour later, bathed and shaved, his clothes having dried by the fire and his hair neatly combed, he sat by the hearth completely at ease, the unease having been beaten out of him by the storm. The only discordance was that, his and Harry's shoe sizes not being the same, he was in his stocking feet. He looked like a general, but his jacket had neither insignia nor rank. Waiting for Harry, who had explained the situation and promised to bring him dinner, he studied the room and the beautifully lit house beyond the pool, and was aware that whoever had saved him had no idea that there were half a dozen houses in East Hampton and a dozen like them in Southampton where he might have gone to sit by the fire and recount his adventure to people he had known all his life. This was better. He was grateful that Harry hadn't known and still didn't know him, and entranced by the fact that Harry thought he was some sort of impoverished, French-speaking vagrant.

Harry came in, with Catherine following. They carried stacked-cylinder food containers of the type made for invalids (and which the Hales used for beach dinners), and silverware rolled in a pressed linen napkin. Vanderlyn stood for Catherine, who was preoccupied with closing the door with her left hand while she held a thick porcelain bowl in her right. Although he bowed slightly when she appeared, the conversation had already started and turned practical, and there were no introductions.

"Here," Harry said. "Corn-and-roasted-cod chowder, salad, bread. There's a bottle of beer in the kitchen." He went to get it as Catherine set an informal table.

"You really don't have to do this," Vanderlyn said to her. "I just need to get to the station."

"The last train's gone," Catherine stated. She looked up. "Do you have a ticket, or money?"

Remembering that his wallet had been in the lost rucksack, Vanderlyn turned red in what Catherine thought was a deeper form of shame. "Don't worry," she said. "We'll take care of that." And knowing about pride and honor, she would not slight his: "You can pay us back when you're able."

"Thank you," he said, his head slightly dipping with his heartbeat.

They set the dinner before him, and as he ate they made sure not to interrogate but to converse. When he offered, they offered, and soon this courtesy proved revealing, even if everything, on one side or another, and for differing reasons, was deliberately shielded.

"I lost my boat and all my money," he said, truthfully, but knowing that, coming as he had from the direction of the Montauk docks, what he said would be taken for what it was not.

"Your shoes, too?" Catherine asked.

"I'm lucky, Miss, not to be naked. And it wasn't a poker game, it was something a lot more serious and demanding than poker."

"Your family?"

"My wife and I live on the North Shore." Here he spoke with crooked ambiguity. "She helps to take care of a very big house, and in season I sometimes work in the garden — when I'm not out on my boat."

"Do they pay well?" Harry asked.

"Uhh!" Vanderlyn said. "The pay is nothing. I'm going to have to go into the city and really start to work. I prefer to be outdoors, you know, but I guess those days are over."

"Where'd you learn to speak French with virtually no accent?" Harry asked, wondering how a gardener-fisherman had become a French-speaking agent of the OSS.

"From my mother," Vanderlyn said, aware of the opening and delighted that with the simple truth he could continue his obfuscation. "She was French. She came over in the early eighties sometime. I was born in 'eighty-eight. When I was little, I spoke French first. I was over there in the First War, too." It was all true. Vanderlyn's unconcealable delight that he could use the truth to mask himself seemed to Catherine and Harry like a simple man's pride at having done things considered beyond his expected range.

"This is crazy," said Harry, "because my business is probably on its last legs. But I can give you a job if you want. It might not go for long, but it's there if you need it."

"What kind of business?" Vanderlyn asked.

"Leather goods. Briefcases, handbags, portfolios. We can use you."

"And why wouldn't it last long?"

For the next hour, with great relief and without mentioning a single name, Harry told him.

At the station in the morning as they waited for the early train to come charging over the flats from Montauk, the sky was clear and a cool breeze came all the way from the sea, waving grasses now dry and golden in the sun. Harry noticed that, as if Vanderlyn had done so many times before, he went to the spot on the platform where the club car would stop. "I'll get the ticket," Harry said, "be right back," and went to the ticket window.

The night before, as Vanderlyn lay in bed listening to the pounding of the surf, he had been filled with a kind of happiness that he had not experienced in a long while. The young couple had taken him for what he was, shorn of everything but his French. They had risked her parents' anger, gambled with their security, given of their time and now their money, expecting nothing in return. He saw in daylight when leaving the house that it was Billy Hale's. So she was Catherine, the daughter of Billy and Evelyn Hale, who was so strong in spirit and independent of view, while yet remaining lovely. But who was he? That is, Harry. His business was failing catastrophically, his life in danger. He would not, out of pride, take his future father-in-law's offer of help.

Vanderlyn, who had learned as a matter of survival to be uncannily observant, saw Harry by the ticket window, methodically placing bills in an envelope into which he had placed the ticket. From a distance, not many people would have been aware of this, but Vanderlyn had learned under the highest pressure to synthesize the most fleeting clues — flashes of light and color, the messages in someone's gait as far as a mile away, a concealed expression. In the pool house, as the night wore on and the sea surged, he had been filled with gratitude. Although he would not have been able to calculate or foresee it, what they had done had not saved him materially — that salvation was less than half an hour away in any number of places — but at his age it had given him new life. It was not something he had achieved, but something he had been granted. It was more than their simple and generous act, but he could not figure quite what.

Harry came back, walking anxiously because he could hear the train whistling through the crossings, although when the wind was right as it was that morning you could hear the locomotive's whistle blasts ten minutes before its blinding headlamp would come into view, daffodil yellow even in daylight. Harry put the envelope in his pocket because he didn't want Vanderlyn to see how thick it was until he was on the steps of the train.

"Write down your name, address, and telephone number so I can pay you back," Vanderlyn told Harry.

"You don't need to pay me back."

"But I will."

"Really, you don't."

The yellow light came riding in on decreasing exhalations of steam, far away, moving fast but slowing down. "Please," Vanderlyn asked. "I've got to return the boots" — a pair of Billy's rubber Wellingtons, expensive, British, and pre-war — "and what about the job?"

Harry quickly pulled out the envelope and a pen, and went over to use as a desk an ancient baggage trolley with steel wheels and a wood deck three feet off the ground. The smoothly rusted brown steel rim had grown hot in the sun, and the ink from his pen spread out beyond the lines, leaving archipelagoes of little dots.

"Copeland," Vanderlyn read. "Then it's Copeland Leather."

"Yes."

"We wouldn't want that to go out of business."

"You know it?"

"Sure. On the estate, they've got it all over the place."

"Who owns the estate?"

"You'll hear from me," Vanderlyn said loudly as the train pulled in and spread a cloud of water vapor over the platform, obscuring everyone's feet: all they needed were wings and harps. Vanderlyn had said *You'll hear from me* with almost a magisterial air, as if he were used to saying it. It wasn't the kind of phrase a destitute fisherman might employ.

Curious about this, puzzled really, Harry remembered that he had no name to go on. "What's your name?" he asked over the exhalations of steam and drippings of water that come from a halted steam locomotive.

For this, Vanderlyn seemed unprepared. At least before the age of seventy and after the age of four, one does not normally hesitate when supplying one's own name, but Vanderlyn let at least half a minute go by. He could not use any of the names he had stocked in his time in the OSS, so he cleared his throat to cover the delay. Harry couldn't fathom it, thinking that perhaps Vanderlyn was in fact a criminal. But then Vanderlyn said, "Baucus."

"Baucus?"

Vanderlyn nodded.

"Your last name."

"Yes."

"And your first?"

Vanderlyn looked up in the air, and, as if he had plucked a fruit, presented it, with strange satisfaction. "Phil," he said, as if he had just made it up, which he had. "Phil Baucus." He held out his hand, which Harry took.

"Phil Baucus," Harry repeated. "Somehow it seems familiar. I don't know why."

Vanderlyn gave him what he thought was a haughty look for an insolvent fisherman, but Harry remarked to himself that he himself was an insolvent manufacturer. "There are lots of us here. Goes all the way back," he said with a kind of twinkle, "to Queen Elizabeth's grant of cod-fishing patents to Humphrey Lemmon and Reginald Baucus. (My middle name is Lemmon.) Although they built only summer dwellings, my family was here before the *Mayflower* — it is said. Never mind."

"Okay. Phil, if you need a job...."

"I'm going to pay you back, you do know that?"

"I think you will, yes. I think I won't be able to stop you. Please don't rob a jewelry store."

Vanderlyn thought this was extremely funny. "I'll try not to," he said, "but if I do, it'll be Tiffany's." As he stepped up into the vestibule of the club car a corpulent man in horn-rims and a whipcord suit — it was after Labor Day, he was careless — the very model of an Ivy Leaguer gone richly to seed in a rain of alcohol and a hail of hors d'oeuvres — called out to Vanderlyn. "Jim!" he said. "Jim! What are you doing out here?"

"Fishing, as usual," Vanderlyn said.

The conductor helped the fat preppy up the steps, politely pushing on the small of his back when it would have been much more efficient to press against the big of his behind, and soon after that the train pulled out, conductors jumping on board as it moved, the best part of their job.

Harry stayed on the platform, looking down the track. Wives re-entered their wooden station wagons and headed back toward the ocean. The red lantern attached to the last car of the train, he knew, would still be glowing in the tunnels that led under the river to New York, and would burn in the dim light of Penn Station as the passengers disgorged into the beige rooms above, as busy and humming as a beehive, a world like no other, crossed by beams of dust-filled light.

# 31

## CROSSING THE RIVER

For Catherine, part of being rich was that she would get no sympathy from anyone but those closest to her. It is for some reason incomprehensible to many that owning a fair Persian carpet or a mahogany table is no compensation for the death of a child, a life without love, or a failure of ambition. Though money may make tragedy less likely, when mortality and matters of the heart come calling, they easily cut through the soft armor of wealth.

She was hurt and perplexed by the Boston critics' obvious enjoyment as they savaged her. Their mistaken notion that her father had bought her the part they took not only as license to destroy her, but also to overlook, merely for the pleasure of their cruelty, that which was right before their eyes. To sing arrestingly onstage requires courage, for the theater is a kind of killing ground, which is why she was impelled to protect George Yellin. One line of praise had been the only light to illuminate his last twenty years and would likely be the only light to illuminate the next. She had no intention of following suit.

She would either have to overcome what lay ahead, giving her performances despite the preordained reactions, and lasting through punishment for years, or abandon what she believed she had been born for. Despite much praise, she was hardly certain of her talents, and half the time she believed everything the newspapers had said. She wondered if ever she or her detractors would be distant or disinterested enough to feel either shame or pride, and which it would be and who would be right. But for the moment the temptation of the boards and the lights was such that she would not be kept away. The cast worked hard at revisions before the October opening, and every day she found new strength in her own voice, the music, and what she was still able to convey to an audience as the theater went dark. The energy of the craft itself and the work they put into it carried them through and promised to carry the audiences as well, but outside the theater itself, where the music stopped, it was not so.

One of Sidney's changes, all of which, given the success in Boston, were minor, was to have Catherine wear gloves during the first part of her second scene, a trick of timing to provide visual distraction as she removed them before going into her second song. "I'm not Gypsy Rose Lee," she told Sidney, and he replied convincingly that of course she wasn't, but that as she took off the gloves and bared only her hands and wrists it was not just for the pacing but also symbolic of her opening herself to the audience. "Think about it," he said. "It's modest, lovely, and it commands attention. In this scene the mood changes, and you've just been standing passively, as if you were a part of the audience. I want them to watch you and not vice versa, and so you have to move, and thus the gloves coming off, to catch their eye. The gloves should be gray so they won't shine in the spotlights like a traffic policeman's gloves."

"What kind?"

"Any kind. You know more about gloves than I do. We'll reimburse you, of course."

"That's all right." She could afford to buy a pair of gloves that she would keep anyway. In fact, she would neither ask the price nor ever see the bill, which would be sent down to Wall Street to a very efficient office that invisibly took care of such things.

Within an hour of Sidney's request she found herself staring into a display case of gloves, a quarter of which were gray. As she looked them over she heard her own clear but slightly misty voice echoing through the theater in a very sad song. She could hear it with the precision and power of real sound as if she were listening outside herself.

A light that had once been installed to make diamonds sparkle still shone strongly down upon the display case, making the kind of contrast she had always loved, and that in painting is called *tenebroso*.

It was the end of the day, and the salesgirl was anxious to leave. "Have you decided?" she asked, shattering Catherine's peace, which allowed the sound of an accelerating bus to replace that of the music.

"No," said Catherine, visibly upset. A disappointment in love, the salesgirl thought. "I don't know which one." She went from one to another, unable to decide. Then she looked up at the salesgirl. "I don't know what's good anymore." She shook slightly but uncontrollably as she asked, "Can you choose for me?"

"These," the salesgirl said decisively, pulling out the first pair of grays she touched.

"Fine," Catherine agreed. "I'll take them." It was most unlike her.

After she arranged payment and exited the store, she walked up Fifth Avenue, angry at the lights and the rush, and knowing full well that anger was fatal to song.

"Kill who?" Harry asked.

"Victor and Verderamé. They both begin with V." Coming from Catherine this was charming, because, never having killed anyone, she couldn't have been serious.

He knew that she had been behaving oddly. For two and a half hours on the drive from East Hampton—all the way in and relentlessly—she had engaged her father in a ferocious argument about patents and trademarks. No one knew what the hell she had been talking about, why she was so exercised, and how she had come to know so much about patent and trademark law, least of all Billy, who stuck to his guns but was left dazed and with a ringing in his ears. Harry, who knew a little bit about trademarks, and patents too, had tried to adjudicate, but she had turned to him as fast as a whiplash, commanding him to "Shut *up*."

He loved her in all her moods, not least when she was unreasonably passionate, so, as Ronkonkoma and Commack whizzed by, he had leaned back in his seat to listen to her furious disquisition. And now this. "You've killed people before. Don't get peanut-hearted about a jerk like Victor, or some gangster. Just shoot them."

"It was somewhat different, you see," he said, gently, because she was upset.

"Oh?" she said, as if he had said something implausible.

"It was a war."

"Well?"

"Why don't you kill them?" he asked her, regretting that he had.

"I don't know how, and I...."

"It's easy. They won't be in a tank or a pillbox. Just get a gun and shoot them. You've been to a butcher shop. That's what it looks like, only a lot bloodier."

"It does?"

"It's not a magic ray. The body gets torn apart. It's just a question of how much and where. We don't even know if Victor's responsible."

"You yourself said that was his chief weapon, and that it was to be ignored."

"But not as a sentence of death, Catherine."

"But what about Verderamé? You always say, in regard to what's happening to you, 'If you take my livelihood, you take my life.' 'The props that do support my house....'"

"*Merchant of Venice*," Harry said. "'You take my house when you do take the prop / That doth sustain my house. You take my life / When you do take the means whereby I live.'"

"That's what I mean."

"And what have I done about it?"

"Nothing. You've done nothing."

"And why?"

"I don't know. Because 'the quality of mercy is not strained'? Why? You tell me." She was twisting her pearls dangerously. He imagined them clattering onto the terrace floor and rolling out the drains to rain down on the garden below.

"Electric chair," he said, beginning the list. "Being caught by the mob. Not being caught by the mob and hiding for the rest of my life. Being caught by the police. Being in a cell with Louis Lepke. Not wanting to go back."

"To Sing Sing?"

"To the war," he said, now serious. "If there's no difference between the battlefield I left and here, what was the point of fighting? I'd love to snap my fingers and make Verderamé disappear. Snap twice and Victor goes too. But if everyone just killed whoever persecuted him, the world would be constantly at war."

"The world *is* constantly at war."

"Not on account of me."

"So, you'll surrender?"

"Not surrender."

"No, just lose, because he's willing to do what you're not. You're ethical, and he's not. So you'll disappear and he'll stay. He'll take from you, and you'll let him."

"Now the Hales are coming through," Harry said. "Somewhere not that far back there was a test like this, and some Hale — who knows who, maybe even Billy — was pure steel, and did God knows what, and won. It must be in the blood."

"Is that bad?"

"No. In fact, I love it."

"And I love you, Harry," Catherine said, "and if you want me, if you want to mix your blood with mine. . . ."

She didn't know where to go from here. A serious conversation that he had tried to lighten had become instantly grave. This was their past, the present, their future, and that of their children and their children's children. All he could do was comfort her. Once again he could see her heart moving against the mother-of-pearl iridescence of her silk blouse. For him there was nothing more powerful than the small touches of beauty a woman might not think about but that are regal, absolute, and appealing. And then, as if from nowhere, he said, "Catherine, one of the most beautiful things I've ever seen is when you lift your arms to tie back your hair."

"It is?"

"Yes. And the *most* beautiful thing I've ever seen is when a small patch of your blouse or your camisole — gray, pearl, and slightly blushing with red from your color beneath — will on occasion move with the beat of your heart. Do you understand that? Do you understand how unreasonably and completely I've fallen in love with you?"

She nodded.

"Now," he said, "listen. For a Jew, which is what you are as well, even if you're a Hale, even if you didn't know it, glory lies in something other than victory."

"Not in the Bible. I know the Bible," she said.

"Yes, in the Bible — unless you're moved by the slaying of Amalekites — and for thousands of years after the Bible."

"But look what happened to the Jews," she said, bearing down. "There's no glory in that. The murder of whole populations? Processing families as if in a slaughterhouse, the children butchered as casually as chickens? You think that's glorious? If that's glorious, it's time to end it. In big ways and in little ways. That is, it's time to make a stand."

"At risk...," he started to say.

But she interrupted him. "Yes, at risk. At risk of everything."

The blouse behind which her heart beat so truly had pearl buttons captured by loops. The top two were unbuttoned, the loops white and lavishly disengaged. The blood that had risen to her face had raised her color, and the heat of her convictions had raised her perfume. He slowly unbuttoned the rest, traveling downward, the progress of the loops falling away toward the side like a steady and sparkling fuse.

Vanderlyn called in early October. He asked Harry to meet him on the overlook at Weehawken. "Weehawken?" Harry had repeated. "Why Weehawken?"

"For one," Vanderlyn replied, "I like to hear it when people say *Why Weehawken?* It sounds like they're calling a pig. And then, there's the magnificent view of Manhattan."

"I know."

"I think you need it."

"Do I?"

"The trouble you're in requires it. You might want to see things as if from the outside, or looking back — as if you're gone, and danger isn't dangerous anymore."

"Do you want a job?" Harry asked. "This is a strange way to ask for a job. It's still open if you need it. Why don't you come here?"

"I have a job. I want you to cross the river."

So he did, and waited, because although Vanderlyn was late, it was a good place in which to pass the time. The benches were empty, the trees beginning to turn, leaves scattered in red and orange — some from early heat-kills and some from cold nights — like leaves pressed in a book. The overlook at Weehawken was one of those places from which everything can be seen in grand exposition and yet nothing that can be seen sees back, as if the vantage point were hidden or invisible, which it was not. Though in plain sight, it was positioned so that eyes were never drawn to it. Thus, to stand there was to look on as unseen as a narrator.

Harry was anxious about many things. He wondered why action was in real life so recalcitrant, when in films and books it always took place when it was fitting. Everything appeared to move but his plans and desires, and as if paralyzed he watched the seasons change and his lot stay the same or worsen. But on the overlook he forgot his anxiety as he watched the river, the ferries in constant motion, the busy commerce of barges by the hundreds lashed together in eights and tens, and oceangoing ships waiting shyly in the roads to be nuzzled by one of the eight hundred agile tugs that populated the harbor, tooting about like illustrations in a children's book the size of a city. As quick as water bugs or shuttlecocks, with each vessel leaving traces and trails of smoke carried on the winds and lofted to the clouds, all things waterborne crowded the bays and rivers.

The city was a perfect place in which to have fallen in love with Catherine. Not only was she, by speech shaped over two hundred years and by familiarity since early childhood, a part of it and as settled there as is the image of Liberty on the back of a coin, in Manhattan, with so little of nature and the little there was so expertly suppressed, the person one loved became the emblem of life. And now here was Manhattan under his eye, somehow innocent and unknowing. So much had happened there, so many interweavings, actions, and echoes, that it was easy for him to go back. All he had to do was to seek some high and lonely place from which to look across the water at the shoreline, the streets telescoping into infinity, foreshortened, compressed, and crowded with noiseless movement. It did not matter the weather or the hour, the frame and foil of towers and piers were armature enough and never fading. All he had to do was close his eyes and breathe deeply, and the past would glide forward like a warm breeze — plumes of smoke silvered in the sun, ferries sliding gracefully to land, their decks crowded with souls long gone but somehow still there as if nothing were lost or ever would be. It was loved too much to be lost, which is why it could rise long after, vivid, beautiful, and real, an emissary of eternal life. That was the challenge from which many turned away in fear, comforting one another in shared disbelief though many an agency made more than clear that the permanence of love could be etched even upon quicksilver.

It is remarkable what the eye can do, absent a telescope, by training and deduction alone. Concentration, practice, and thought can impart to anyone the power to see far into the distance. A flash of color, a speck, a contrast hardly visible, or a dream-like wavering can magnify a nearly invisible image and bring it up uncannily sharp. Halfway across the river from the Jersey side, the Weehawken Ferry, its stacks issuing floods of smoke and steam, was almost empty. Some cars and trucks, a bread van, and a slat-sided wagon drawn by two white horses had taken up the forward deck. Above, there were so few passengers that from the cliffs they might have been impossible to report. But Harry spotted one of them. The tall figure at the rail, staring west, was illuminated by the October sun as if he had been only a tiny brushstroke, a mere impression of what might have been a man, yet Harry recognized him. The movement of the ferry and the changing light made clear that he was wearing a suit. And not just a suit but — Harry could tell as if by magic at half a mile — a pinstriped suit. Although he couldn't see this across the wide stretch of spangling water, the suit fit well, loosely, lightly, and gracefully, and there was a handkerchief in the breast pocket.

The transformation of an indigent fisherman into a man whose excellent tailoring projected across most of the Hudson River suggested that something was going to happen. Coming onto the overlook, Vanderlyn had a magisterial air. "I don't think," Harry said when Vanderlyn arrived, "that Fred Astaire could dress better."

Vanderlyn waited for what he thought would be inevitable, and it was.

"You're a fisherman who lost his boat," Harry said, cuttingly.

"I do fish," Vanderlyn said.

"I haven't read about an America's Cup racer going down."

"Ah!" said Vanderlyn. "I would have been in quite a different mood had I lost that."

"Was it just an eighty-footer?"

"A Winabout."

"Do all you people have Winabouts?"

"I don't know what you mean exactly, but Winabouts are very popular now. It's a great little boat."

"You have the other one as well."

"I do, safe in harbor."

"And I don't know your real name, do I?"

"No, and you don't want to."

"Why is that?"

"I can help you, but I would prefer to do so from afar." Vanderlyn sat down on one of the benches facing out across the Hudson at 42nd Street, which was shrouded in smoke and mist.

"Why would you want to help me?"

"Why? Look out there." He lifted his right arm in a gesture to Manhattan that was part salute and part permission for it to carry on. As he surveyed what was before him, his eyes narrowed affectionately, leaping from spire to spire, focusing tightly on distant details. Something electric was flowing between the man and the city, something to which Harry himself was hardly a stranger. "You were born here, I take it?"

"In Weehawken?"

"No, not in Weehawken. Weehawken doesn't count. There."

"Yes."

"So was I," Vanderlyn said. "We'll probably die there, too. I hope so — I wouldn't want to die in New Jersey. No offense to New Jersey, but over there is our entrance and our exit. The portals of infinity spit us out there, and there they'll take us in. Meanwhile, what have we got? You know those Russian Easter eggs that you look into? I have a few, excessively bejeweled. When people come to dinner parties at our house, like an x-ray machine looking into their brains I can see who considers quietly pocketing one. When you look into these things — not the brains of my dinner guests but the interiors of my Fabergé eggs — you see something perfect, rich in color, mysteriously deep. As a child I wanted more than anything to be able actually to go inside them and enter another world.

"And there it is, self-contained, gold at sunset, red at dawn. And in between run all the blues, greens, and grays of every sea in every condition of light. An isle in the water, infinitely complex and forever giving, the hive of millions. Everything happens there, just and unjust, beautiful and hideous, joyful, painful, powerful — and it's all there for you threescore and ten if you can make it. Then it's gone.

"Thus, for me, the only thing that matters is the proper closing of the loops. Now, I realize that this is an idiosyncratic way of putting it, but...."

"I know what you mean," Harry said in clipped fashion, not curtly but so as not to disrupt the natural rhythm of Vanderlyn's explanation.

"Making sure," Vanderlyn continued, "that any one of the infinite number of stories into which you might stumble... ends properly."

"*Properly* meaning...?"

"Strongly. Justly. And perhaps tragically, but always beautifully," he said, gesturing again across the river. "That's what keeps the fires burning and the wheels spinning. That's what keeps what you see there alive, and what keeps it alive is what keeps us alive.

"You were plucked away by the war. When you came back, didn't all this strike you as a magnificent surplus, as if you had come back from the dead, and here was your second chance?"

"Yes."

"It's happened to me twice. Looking down upon all this from afar, privileged to enter the scene wherever I wish, I feel like a ghost. When I wake up, and when I step out onto the street, my interest is in the story, in closing the loop gracefully and beautifully. I have to do this. Otherwise, I can't live and I can't die. And you, Harry, if I may, are a very special case."

"Definitely," Harry said, mocking himself.

"You are," Vanderlyn insisted. "It's not that you helped *me*. I was half an hour from any comfort I might want. It's that you helped the person you thought I was. You and that lovely girl. You didn't know what you were doing. You had no idea that as you did one thing after another, putting yourself at risk, giving generously to someone you took as having nothing, you were building in me, with jolt after jolt, an irrevocable devotion. I knew then. I had no doubt or reservation. And then, unknowing of what I was feeling, when you told me what you yourself were facing you enlisted me to your cause — which seems to me like a loop that should be brought to a just and decisive close. A small story, but a big loop."

"I have no hope of ending it justly. It's impossible," Harry said, wanting to be realistic. "They have too much power. The strength it would take to fight them hasn't been given to the police, the government, or to the entire population."

"They own many of the police," Vanderlyn said, "and up the chain as well. I know that."

"No one has ever been able to take them on. The government has only symbolic victories against them. When they're forced from one area they just show up in another."

"All true."

"Then what can I do?"

"Tell me what has enabled you to last this long. You made no mention of it. Why haven't you closed down?"

"My father, mainly." Vanderlyn's expression encouraged Harry to explain. "He started the business from nothing. He taught himself to make fine things that people value. Some looked down on him because, what did he do, after all? He was a tradesman who made briefcases and belts. He didn't traffic in theory, he had no power, but he was faithful to what he did and he employed many fine people, organizing and then tending the structure that supported them. He was, as I heard my friends say in college, and I heard him say himself, 'just a businessman,' but he was my father, he was as good and as worthy as any man, and I loved him.

"It was all thrown in my lap when he died. I was going to be educated for the purpose, he thought, of surpassing him, but I was educated enough to understand that I have no need to surpass him and will be lucky to follow. He built this business with his whole life. Whatever it is, whatever its virtues, whatever its faults, as long as it continues he's still got some light left."

"How did he deal with these people?"

"I don't know, but I'm told he paid them. They said he begged like a dog."

"Did he?"

"I don't know, but if he did, I have reason to hold on until they kill me, and if he didn't, I have reason to hold on just as long, although that isn't what he would have wanted."

"But is it what he would have done?"

"It's exactly what he would have done, but it's impossible to close the story justly. Not in these conditions."

Vanderlyn put his fingertips together and rested his face upon almost prayerful hands so that the ring fingers lightly touched the tip of his nose. Brows knit, concentrating, slightly swaying back and forth, he would look up at the city — now, in the deeper color of the afternoon sun, burning with the commerce for which it was famous — just with his eyes, and then he would look down. He was not light in thought; he was in storm. Then he put his hands on the bench, straightened, and, lifting his head so that his eyes met Harry's, he said, "It can be done, but you can't go on without making a choice. You've either got to pull out and make a new start, which I would recommend...."

"I won't do that."

"Or you go all the way. That's dangerous, but if you neither surrender nor fight back they'll kill you, and I wouldn't want to see that."

"You would care?"

"I would, yes."

Sometimes in the war, by necessity or accident, a newly or inappropriately trained unit would be sent into battle. Everyone held his breath for these men, not only because of their dangerous inexperience but because they had not, like most soldiers, been properly acclimatized, as if to altitude, in stages. Procession through the army changed body and soul in gradual accretions and strippings away. Eventually battle and hardship were expected and normal, but to get there involved as many leaves and layers as have an artichoke or an onion: the draft notice, the bus ride, the haircut, the night marches, firing range, weight loss, hardening, sleep deprivation. And then the second stage: riding to the front, the sight of combat-weary soldiers moving in the opposite direction, the sound of artillery, the wounded, the dead, firing and being fired upon, losing friends, being hit, sleeping in the cold rain, dysentery, vomiting, bleeding, and perhaps dying. From the family dinner table to a shallow, unmarked grave in the mud, the procession moved tolerably in stages.

When Vanderlyn said "It can be done," it was for Harry the kind of shock a new recruit might feel when sent directly to the front. But that was where the conversation had led, and there they were. Harry posed the obvious question. "Who are you?"

"If we're going to do this, you shouldn't know."

"Why?"

"Deniability, compartmentalization. It's habit and the right procedure necessary for such an undertaking."

"What undertaking? What procedure?" Harry asked, thinking that this was too fast, too soon, and too indefinite.

Vanderlyn stated it simply. "Getting out from under the Mafia." He saw Harry's skepticism and that he might bolt, so he backed up a little. "All through the war," he said, "we ran operations that pitted a David against a Goliath. A few men would take on whole units of the Wehrmacht. I myself did that, in Germany before the Normandy landings.

"Like you, we had to parachute in, but we had no divisions following us. We had great difficulty passing as locals, we could never entirely trust our networks, none of our bases was ever really secure. You learn from that how to compensate. The compensations are not always what one might think, but they can be very effective.

"If you really want to do this, look at all the advantages you have. You'll have to avoid the law, but not attack it, and it will be delighted to look the other way. Your bases are safe at least until you open the fight. You're native born, and free to circulate. You can order food in a restaurant or walk down the street and you don't even have to think about it. You have many resources that we didn't have in the war, and your enemy has many weaknesses that you can exploit."

"That may be true, but I don't have license."

"Take license. They do."

"If I can't know exactly who you are," Harry said, "I'd like to know whom you're with."

"Fair enough. Let me put it this way. America really suffered in the war and a lot of people died because before the war our special services were undeveloped. It has been decided that we won't be caught short again, and that, therefore, people like me, who can't get this out of their system, can continue. What's under construction may go in a number of directions, depending upon the funding, the political reaction, and the international situation of the next few years. We're starting out now as we did: informal recruitment, relationships, improvisation. It worked well during the war, and we hope that whatever comes out of this is not too bureaucratic and stiff."

"You're recruiting me?"

"No."

"Then, what?"

"From what I know about you, you're ideal: a pathfinder with years of combat, the best education. Languages other than French?"

"A few."

"Good."

"I don't quite understand."

"And a businessman. It's what we were built on. I regret that you weren't in before, but I'm not recruiting you. This is personal. If in the future you want to come in, that's another thing. For now, for this, I told you why I'm here."

"And how can I trust you?"

"To trust is both to sense accurately and to risk, to neither of which, I believe, you are a stranger. Do you think I'm with *them?*"

It would have been absurd, and Harry said, "There isn't one among them who could pass for Fred Astaire, and there never will be. You don't do this full time, do you? What do you do?"

"Wall Street," Vanderlyn said, "just like the Hales."

"You knew."

"In the morning I saw the house. I was there once for a reception. I remember the daughter when she was about eight. She got to be really stunning, didn't she? She used to be a sweet little thing, with glasses, excited just to be passing out hors d'oeuvres. Every time someone took one, it was as if she had been given the Nobel Prize. Granted, the whole thing is a bit risky. But think about it. What needs to be done seems obvious. It'll have to be refined. I'll need more to go on, but I know the outline of these things generally and how they work. As for the methods and means, I'm hardly a genius, but I've been there before. I think it can be done, and I think you think it can. It would be interesting."

"Yes," Harry said, "it would be very interesting. You're talking about...."

"Assassination." Vanderlyn started to walk, and then turned. "They will never, ever, be expecting to receive what you are capable of visiting upon them. Like everyone else, they're creatures of habit. They have their systems and their rules. They know about crime, they don't know about war, and you do. It would be better to retreat and let them have their way. Don't you think? Just start a new life. But, if you need it, I'll help."

Vanderlyn turned placidly toward the city. Without looking back at Harry, he said, "You leave first. I'll take the next boat."

The play debuted in the midst of three days of Indian summer that threw open outdoor cafés and propelled not a few boys to jump from the rocks at Beekman Place into the early October waters of the East River. Audiences are cruel but understanding, as half the tension and excitement when the curtain rises comes from their imagination of themselves onstage doing the difficult and wonderful thing they know they cannot do. Looking upon the performers, they fear every potential slip, miscue, or mistake, so that when actors or actresses are lifted up and out of themselves, the audience, empathetic to the point of physical pain, rides with them on the same wings.

Because the theater filled with people who had arrived touched with sun and with neither the fur wraps nor greatcoats common to opening nights, the coat-check girls were despondent. Exhaust fans had run on full power since five o'clock to pull in the cooler evening air, and would be shut down only just before curtain time. It was hoped that a convection current would draw enough of a breeze through the lobby to cool the hot lights and exit through the roof vents, rising like a sea current into the pink sky of Times Square.

Catherine now had no choice but to sing for the sake of singing itself. She expected nothing or worse from the critics, and, no matter what Sidney said, to be booted from the production. This gave her songs a quality of defiance, emotion, and truth that paralyzed her listeners with admiration not for her but for the state she had attained. She carried them on a wave that made quite a few of them fall in love with her through the mystery of a voice that was evocative beyond reason. The way Catherine sang a single, simple word could summon memory, love, and the best graces of her listeners. Even the position of her body, the way she held her hands, the expression on her face (powdered and yet flushed), and the sparkle of her eyes were surpassed by the voice, most feminine, with which she conquered and commanded.

She dominated the first act. Had she been onstage more, she would have become a rising star of Broadway, pushing aside the doubts sown in the press. But her part did not afford her that, and she waited in her dressing room as the building vibrated with the cheers and applause that had begun to interrupt the action more and more as it built, and would have followed her songs and pressed her to an encore had her audience been as warm and relaxed as it could not have been at the beginning of the play.

Not wanting his exit to suggest disapproval to those sitting around him, Harry waited until the intermission to go to her. The lobby and sidewalk were packed with people eager to finish their drinks and go back in. The production was more than safe, as were Sidney and the investors. Harry circled into the alley and entered through the stage door. Left and right, stagehands, chorus girls, and people with clipboards were rushing in opposite directions like sailors summoned to general quarters.

Because the mirror was surrounded by eighteen clear bulbs that burned hot, a fan was turning in Catherine's dressing room. She had exchanged her costume for a silk robe. "Don't you have to wear that," he asked, referring to the wool suit of the girl from Red Lion, "for the curtain call?"

"Yes, but I must be an Eskimo. If I keep it on I'll be dripping with sweat." She took a drink from a glass filled with water and ice.

He told her that she had been without peer. He told her how much he loved her, how proud he was, and that, as she sang, he fell in love with her as if for the first time. Her answer was to look at him sadly, but lovingly, which was all he needed and every bit of the truth.

After intermission, the idea had been to shock the audience back into what Sidney called the *"Dramatische Weltanschauung,"* with a vigorous production number from the play within a play, in which the full chorus appeared in tap shoes and pounded the boards so rhythmically and hard that had a subway passed underneath, the blades of its fans and the brims of the last-of-the-season straw hats would have been bent down as if by ten-pound weights. The sounds of keening clarinets and hound-like trombones, and the very vibrations of the boards possessed the theater, moving Catherine's tumbler across the glass top of her dressing table as if on a Ouija board. "Those chorus girls," Harry said. "I wouldn't want to get in their way."

And then Catherine, hesitating just like her mother — she often had, even at twenty-three, the gravity and calm of long introspection — said, "They never tire. It's something in the flesh. Like Betty Boop, they were born bouncing. The other day I spoke to one who thinks that melancholy is a type of dog that loves fruit. Their energy comes from innocence. Oh," she said, holding up her right index finger and looking at the ceiling as a wave of laughter rolled through the walls, "they laughed for George. That's wonderful. It'll bring him back to life."

"And what about you? They applauded like a rainstorm."

"Like hail," she said. "And I'm not from Texas."

"Will that bring *you* back?"

"I have to be cautious," she answered. "I have to learn to do what I do and push through like an armored division. But I'm not like an armored division. I'm not armored, which is a problem, although if I were, that would be a problem, too."

"Play your part every day," Harry said, "until the end of the run. It'll give you strength beyond what you can imagine. That's how iron is tempered and hickory is cured. Nothing is born as strong as it can become." He took her into his arms and she stayed there comfortably until just before the curtain call, listening to the music from above, muffled and vague, the sounds of horns and traffic filtering in from the stage entrance, and the hard whirring of the fan like wind moving through sails.

Once again, Billy and Evelyn were astonished and proud. They believed that the quality of Catherine's singing, her magnificent presence, and her financial independence would allow her to outlast whatever difficulties Victor or anyone or anything else could throw her way. She was only a year out of school, and at the curtain call she had summoned that special burst of applause for which actors live. And this was not on a college campus or in Providence, it was Broadway.

Catherine, however, was not as sanguine. She understood what everyone told her, but she was the one who had to sing, and she had as well some of the impatience of youth. Even Billy had some of the impatience of youth. Perhaps because half his friends and associates were now dead, he was uncomfortable about wasting time.

Rather than await reviews as she had done in Boston, Catherine decided to follow the lead of nineteenth-century presidents on election nights and go home to bed. Billy proposed a stop at "21" to ease the transition, but she refused. In fact, she had little of the euphoric elevation that keeps the minds of actors spinning at high speed after their performances and long into nights often made quiet only by alcohol. Having decided that it might be years until she could collect the rewards of her labor, or perhaps never, she was all business. They went home, dropping Harry on Central Park West. By now Billy and Evelyn were used to seeing their daughter in his embrace, used to seeing them kiss. They knew by the quality of the touch that she had done right and was lucky, and at twelve-thirty, as the doorman at 333 Central Park West held the door open longer than he had thought he would have to, Catherine and Harry embraced in air that was now midnight blue.

The Hales drove off, and Harry rode up in the elevator, as always, almost stunned by Catherine's absence. It was unnatural not to be next to her, to be looking at her, to be kissing the side of her face. It was especially painful now because he knew that were he to decide upon what Vanderlyn had in mind, it would be dangerous for them both no matter how carefully he insulated her from what he would do, and that it promised long absences.

Before the Hales reached Sutton Place, Harry was able to fall asleep. Sleep was doubly magic. It would cut by half the time he would be away from her before they were to meet for lunch the next day, and as he slept he would dream of her. When you are in love, you dream about the person you love. After ten, twenty, thirty, or forty years, the dreams are so clear and real they shake you to the core. And if love be denied or suppressed, they are so vivid as to burn.

Early in the morning, as the sunlight invaded over the bridges from Long Island, though the cast was by now exhausted and asleep, Catherine was fresh and awake, up before anyone else, on the third and last day of the Indian summer. She dressed quickly and walked to the newsstand on 57th and First, and then hurried home with a stack of papers for which, impatient to wait for her change, she had paid too much: the *Times,* the *Trib,* the *Post,* the *Journal-American,* the *Daily News,* and one or two others that probably could not afford to send someone to write a review.

She opened them one by one on the massive kitchen island and read them at high speed. Then she read again, more carefully. When she finished, she stepped back and looked at the mass of papers spread out as if they were the white wings of dead swans or geese limp across the stone. All the reviews were good, some spectacular, but in not one line or phrase of any one of them was she mentioned: not her name, not her character, not the allegations that had failed to escape a single Boston paper.

She had been erased. It was worse than being attacked. It did not engage the emotions, but extinguished them. Silence was the cause of silence. She stood in the kitchen, staring at the newspapers as if, without shock or pain, her heart had simply stopped.

"It seems perfectly natural, doesn't it?" she asked. He was seated on her right, at a little square table covered with blindingly white cloth. His place had been set across from her, but he had moved closer, taking the heavy china and silver with him.

"What does?" They were many storeys up, as if flying, and the midday sun, now fairly low, was powerful enough to make things clear but not so powerful as to wash them out. The harbor was the color of the Mediterranean at Malta. Flimsy clouds of translucent mist sped above, at eye level, and beneath them. Sunlight glinted off glass and stone all the way to the Battery, and the wind was wonderfully cool.

"Being here, at lunch, all dressed up, looking as if we haven't a worry in the world. You'll go back to your business and tonight I'll perform in a theater on Broadway. It's New York. It's perfect to a T. Why do I feel this way?"

"Let's see," he said, which meant he would have to think about how most delicately to state the obvious. Meanwhile, it was not silent. A wash of sound came from the bar and joined indistinguishably the settling of crushed ice and the rhythmic brushing of a drum. There was a single red rose in the center of the table, the oil in its petals refracting a direct ray of sunlight into moving and uncountable flecks of gold, silver, red, and blue. Even without alcohol, it all seemed hypnotic. "Our food supply hasn't been interrupted." He said this in the tone of lists. "We have water. We're alive. None of us is wounded" — he wagged his finger — "physically. We're healthy. We're clean. We're free. And we're young."

"True. Why do I feel oppressed? I shouldn't," she said, lowering her voice modestly as the waiters set down before them a "bouquet" of shellfish, two glasses of the Hales' customary white Haut-Brion, and a basket of bread that had arrived from Paris that morning on a Pan Am Clipper.

"Because you've been told repeatedly and from many directions that you're no good. That would oppress even the Pope, and especially someone who has hardly ever been told anything like it. Have you?"

"Directly? I haven't. I mean, if you count Victor and the way he treated me, yes. But otherwise no, not really."

"That may explain part of it," he said. "In this regard there are two kinds of people. One extrapolates the unfortunate present far into the future, takes warning, and feels oppressed. The other fails to extrapolate, never knows what's coming, and stays happy until struck down. But if in extrapolating because you're in a difficult situation you dare not assume that you'll have some luck, because you're responsible by nature your projections become grimmer and grimmer. But, Catherine, you will have luck. There's no way to account for all the things that will happen and of which you have no inkling. Things will let up. Everything moves in a wave. Until the end, you never stay down and you never stay up. And at the very last, who knows? You might be launched like a rocket."

"I guess I believed, despite what I knew, that I was going to be the toast of Broadway, and then, look, I became the ghost of Broadway. It's because I'm so goddamned rich. I hate it. My father once said to me, 'At times in my life I've been so desperate that I behaved like a normal person, and I liked it, but then they threw me out. They always do.' Harry, does all the money get in the way?"

"Of us? Doesn't mean a thing, except that sometimes it's hard for me to keep up with you. Like this," he said, meaning where they were and how much it would cost. "But the starch and gleam of the tablecloth alone is worth it, not to mention my napkin. In June of 'forty-four I would have traded a month's salary for this napkin. The British, of course, have a different understanding of the word, and might find that quite funny."

"I'll take care of this," she assured him.

"No you won't."

"That's what I mean. The imbalance."

"There's one thing — I take it back — there's one thing that I do love about your being rich." She was pleasantly surprised by this. "You wear new clothes more than anyone I've ever known, including people in the garment business. I like the smell of new clothes. Whether its from mercerizing, or the scent of close-to-the-row cotton, or whatever makes silk new, I don't know. But, like bread baking or new paint, it has a lot of promise: starting fresh just by putting on a new shirt. When I was a child I loved when we were given our books on the first day of school. The smell of ink and paper still makes me feel that the world is open, that my mother and father are alive, that the summer heat has just broken and the suddenly clear September air is pouring gently through the windows."

"You can tell when I'm wearing something new?"

"Always."

"I can't say I'm not pleased. I just thought of coming here," she said, "because my mother would take me here for lunch when I was little. Once, there was a really strong wind, and a biplane struggling against it was perfectly motionless relative to the ground. It couldn't have been more than a hundred feet away. I could see the pilot's mustache. He finally gave up and fled, but after that I was always looking up on windy days, when sometimes you could hear a droning like that of an insect. On occasion when this happens, you see people unconsciously making swatting motions. But the war killed that. Now that the planes are more powerful, the city can't trap them. I wanted to come here because of what I remember. I didn't think of the expense. I'm sorry."

"No, it's worth it. Even the urinals. Instead of staring ahead at a dirty wall with phone numbers and bad sketches of body parts, you look through a little window at the clouds. Lindbergh didn't have as good a view, you know. He couldn't see out the front. So don't apologize, really."

Though she wanted to be, Catherine would never be released from the effect of her wealth. "In college, I had two roommates," she said, "Marisol—whom you've met—who's from Cuba and whose family is rich from sugar and tobacco; and Wendy, who's from Port Jervis. Have you ever been to Port Jervis? Forest as far as you can see. Her father is a *deer hunter*."

"Full time?" Harry asked. "It must be rough."

"I believe so. She's Marisol's size, so she used to borrow Marisol's dresses for dances and teas. She looked stunning. Everything was working out well. No problems. Once, before Christmas vacation, there was a tea with Princeton—very important for some girls. We went. Just before we left I saw that Wendy was putting perfume behind her ears and at the base of her neck—McCormick vanilla extract, straight from the bottle."

"She was a Christmas cookie?"

"She was one hell of a Christmas cookie. We were out the door before I could say anything, but I called my mother the next day and asked if she could order one of those big bottles of Guerlain. 'Like the one you brought to school?' my mother asked. 'How could you have used it up so fast? Did it break?' So I told her, and without hesitation she said, 'No. You and Marisol, you bring home your perfumes, and when you go back, you go back with a bottle of vanilla.'"

"She was right."

"She was so right," Catherine said. "When Wendy saw us putting on vanilla, she cried. The three of us embraced, and, I'll tell you, that little bottle of vanilla that I got at Gristedes was more precious than ten thousand flagons of Guerlain or Jean Patou. There's a bond now between the three girls, and it can never be broken."

"And?" he asked, pleased.

"I want to come to you rather than trying to meet in the middle. If you're poor, I'll be poor. If you're rich, I'll be rich. It doesn't matter."

"And what will be the destination of all the money that's aimed at you?"

"I don't know."

"I was going to tell you today," he said, "that I'm going to put to rest this problem of the business."

"Verderamé?"

"Verderamé."

"What are you going to do? I mean, how?"

"You shouldn't be involved."

She put down the teaspoon she had had in her hand, and at which she had been looking as they spoke, admiring the dull shine — it had been washed two thousand times — that emanated from its bowl, warm and slightly white. When she understood both the full import of what he had said, and that she could not press him to elaborate on it, she shuddered, and what seemed like an electrical jolt ran up and down her body. But she didn't try to dissuade him from what she was sure he had decided. She knew the risk, that she could lose him, and lose her life, but she didn't say no. By gesture, a tightly limited lifting and raising of her head, she assented. On the last day of the Indian summer, when the sky was a blue milder than Wedgwood and they were surrounded by dating couples and tourists who had come to dance, she felt what untold numbers of women had felt since the beginning of time. Her father had been safe at home, and the war had been abstract, but now that it was over it was as if she were in it, and it seemed almost to pierce her.

"You can't know anything about this," he continued, speaking in a restrained fashion that, even had a lip reader been observing him, would have given nothing away.

"You're not leaving me?" she asked.

When they linked hands under the table, she squeezed so hard that were she stronger she would have broken his. "Marry me," she said. She neither commanded nor begged, but simply stated it.

"Yes."

Had tears come, which they didn't, for she would not let them, she might not have been able to control them even with the blizzard-white napkin.

"We'll go north," she proposed, "to some place in the Berkshires or New Hampshire where they write the license by hand and record it in a ledger. No one will ever be able to find out until we want them to. Gangsters have no need for little towns with clapboard churches and mountain shadows that start in the middle of the afternoon. They'd stick out there like a moose at Toots Shor."

He liked that, about the moose.

"But the wedding," Harry said, talking beneath the noise of the restaurant. "I've been looking forward to the wedding. I thought that you would be so beautiful it would nearly kill me, that on that day I'd let a lot slip away and become someone new. I thought that even if there were a storm at sea it would be held at bay, that we could risk not having a tent."

"It'll be better than that," she said.

"When?"

"Now. Leave from here."

"Just like that?"

"Just like that."

"I don't have a ring," Harry told her. Of course he hadn't.

"We'll stop at Woolworth's, or use a blade of grass. It doesn't matter."

As they waited for the check, they looked out the tall windows at a sky crowded with moving clouds. One over Turtle Bay looked like England, Scotland, and Wales, and one to the east of the Empire State Building was a bit like Ireland. Though reversed in a mirror image, they were quite accurately drawn. The winds aloft were so unsettled and strong that the mountains of white were blown toward one another, the Irish Sea in cerulean blue lessening in width at a stately pace, and the broken fingers of Land's End moving toward a fictional spur south of Cork like two hands reaching out to touch, not to mention India and Pakistan ready in waiting where Novaya Zemlya was supposed to have been. Had it been a gray day it could not have been so arrestingly beautiful, as great things on a massive scale occurred modestly and silently above the city.

As they drove up to Egremont, Massachusetts, theirs was almost the only car on the Taconic. Not far north of Manhattan, on a rise just outside the Bronx, Harry looked in the rearview mirror and saw the towers of midtown veiled in a mist that crossed them like smoke. He pointed to the mirror, and Catherine rose slightly in the passenger seat and leaned toward the center to see. There in a rectangle of glass were her life to date and her life to come. There, hidden deep in the stone, were her parents, and the theater where at curtain time the next day she would on command rise above the profane. There was the war that her husband-to-be had chosen to fight. And there, perhaps, her children would be born and she would die. All in a smoky gray rectangle, sparkling at times, and jiggling with the rough surface of the road.

When people love one another, conversation is not a necessity but a pleasure, and when they reach, as at times they do, deep into the immeasurable part of what holds them together, everything can pass between them without a word. Even gestures become unnecessary. In a vast, continuous exchange, they need do nothing but glance at one another occasionally as if to remark on the miracle of so much transpiring so invisibly. That was how it was on the day they married. Each knew what the other was thinking. The car seemed to be in on it, too, as naturally as a dog. They never looked at a map, but somehow took the right exit off the Taconic, went up into the Berkshires, and found Egremont, although they weren't looking for it in particular.

They drove through the town in half a minute and stopped at a small cape covered in weathered brown shingles. Of crushed stone and wide enough for two cars, the driveway was empty. Only after Harry had sharply turned the wheel and the sound of tires on gravel rose from the skirts of the black Chevrolet did they see the sign that said *Town Clerk*. Harry turned off the motor and yanked the emergency brake. In childhood, the sound this made had always seemed to Catherine like that of a crocodile clearing its throat. They both looked up at the sky, and then, at the same time, opened their doors, knowing that they could leave the top down because it was not going to rain. And they knew — or perhaps they didn't but just counted on their luck, which was running more strongly than ever before — that the house would be open and the clerk would be in.

A tall New Englander in wire-rims, he seemed both intelligent and kind. "You made it just in time if you want the whole package," he said, not getting up from his desk. "You don't have it in your hand, so my guess is that you need a blood test." They did. "Across the street. The doctor's in. He can do it on the spot. Leave your driver's licenses here and I'll start on the copy of record. I can do the ceremony if you hurry up."

It was almost as if they were deaf-mutes. At the doctor's they had no need to say anything, having come into the office rolling up their sleeves, and they filled out their forms in silence. He told them it would take half an hour.

"You can do it that fast?" Harry asked. "Don't you have to culture...."

"I don't culture anything," the doctor said. "Just come back in a half hour."

They rolled their sleeves back down, giddily crossed the street, crunched over the gravel near their car, and, screen door slamming behind them, quickly filled out more forms before they went outside to wait on a bench in the sun. Shortly after that, the doctor appeared at his door, summoned them over to him, and asked them in. Standing in the waiting room, they received their certificates and paid for them. As they signed, by habit of observation the doctor took Harry's strong pulse by sight in his wrists, and Catherine's by the slight flutter of her lightly stretched blouse. Having many times before seen couples about to wed, he understood why they didn't speak.

Then across the street again, pulses rising higher, into the dark study where the clerk attended to his records. The forms were signed and dated, the seals affixed. "You want the ceremony," he did not quite ask. He could tell from her eyes misting up and his deep breathing that they did. They nodded, they paid. He moved them into a corner of the room where many lives had been joined, and asked if they were ready. Clearly they were. He knew that they would hear but not quite hear what he said. He knew that his words — old language, formal and legal — would move them more than any poetry.

"We are gathered here to unite" — he looked at the papers — "Catherine Thomas Hale and Harry Copeland in marriage, an institution founded in nature and ordained by the state. It is a solemn and binding contract uniting a man and a woman. It is a cause of joy and celebration. For on this occasion Harry and Catherine join one another and embark upon a new life, not as two individuals, but as one.

"Theirs is a union that is not to be entered into lightly, but, rather, discreetly and with due respect. For it is indeed the beginning of a new life. Do you, Harry, take Catherine to be your lawfully wedded wife, from this day forward, to have and to hold, for richer or for poorer, in sickness and in health, until death do you part?

"And do you, Catherine, take Harry to be your lawfully wedded husband, from this day forward, to have and to hold, for richer and for poorer, in sickness and in health, until death do you part?

"Do you both enter into this union and contract of marriage of your own free act and will, both fully knowing and accepting the responsibilities and obligations of marriage which will be imposed upon you by the laws of this Commonwealth of Massachusetts? If you do so agree, then both say 'I do.'"

As they said "I do," they shook with emotion.

"Will the groom place the ring on the bride's finger and pronounce these words: 'With this ring, I take you as my wife, and seal this bond and contract of marriage.'"

"We have no ring," Harry said, but Catherine lifted her hand and, taking it, he put on it an invisible ring that would outlast any ring of gold.

"Will the bride," the clerk said, "place the ring on the groom's finger and pronounce these words...."

Remembering that he hadn't repeated the oath, Harry said it at the same time she did, as she put the invisible ring on his finger. Her voice, of course, was very beautiful and distinctive, and, with his, normally deep but now even deeper, in the background, the sentence became a kind of music. She didn't sing it, but it had the beauty of song.

The clerk somehow understood that here was not only great love, but peril. This was an exceptional marriage, and he wished them well. Hesitating for a moment, and then breaking the silence, he said, "In accordance with the authority invested in me by the Commonwealth of Massachusetts, I now pronounce you husband and wife."

It was almost five o'clock. The ferries would soon be choking the harbor, and the winds tangling their smoke.

# 32

## THE HIGHLANDS

WARFARE ON THE MARGINS of Manhattan, troops marching in and out, battles fought in ancient Brooklyn, and sad news from many fronts over centuries, even if redeemed by victories in or on the main, confirmed that war was something from which, with nothing to lose, only the dead might be sure to profit. And this was especially clear in 1946, so soon after so many letters and telegrams announcing the deaths of fathers and sons had been received in so many dwellings that retained the memory as if they were alive, Childe Hassam's pointillist flags notwithstanding.

Almost every day had a touch of battle already. There was no need to fight Germans or Mongolians after having managed to conquer a taxi in the rain at five in the afternoon on a weekday, or facing down a six-foot-eight litigator expecting everyone on the sidewalk to jump out of his way. And that is not to mention surviving the terror of being transported to the wilds of the Bronx by a subway that the devil has made race through its customary stops. A day in the garment business or the commodity pits was equivalent to a day on Parris Island. Plains Indians and New Yorkers always survived best the rigors of war, the former as tough as snow-crusted buffalo, the latter as wily and indomitable as rats.

And then there was the opposite pull, the luxuries and distractions of Manhattan. Whether dazzling or soft, glittering or seductive, they were present at every turn. What man would want to go to war after watching for just ten minutes the passage of gloriously dressed women on a single block of East 57th Street; or wending his way through the

Met; or sitting in the white sound of one of the many fountains; or standing beneath the dark green leaves of a quiet Village street on a summer night when the rare but inevitable north wind descends like a fall of cold water through streetlight-washed emeralds?

All these things and a great deal more weighed against what Harry had to do, and yet, although the decision was his to make and his will to break, he knew he would do it. But to think it out, he would go to a more austere, more elemental place. An oratorio in stone, Manhattan was too possessive of too many things remembered and loved. For a while he had thought that he had come through, but when he dreamed now he was pulled back to when he was a soldier and peace was twenty minutes' sleep between artillery barrages.

From the highest points of Manhattan—the roofs or observation decks of the tallest buildings, next to the bells of Riverside Church, or at Coogan's Bluff—to the south was the sea, open and blue. To the east was Long Island, narrowing to a sandy spit of potato fields and summer mansions, and to the west, just New Jersey. But the north was different. There, distant mountains came into view. They began to rise at thirty miles and were fully risen at fifty, deserted highlands through which the Hudson wound, in winter often ice-choked and immobile, uplands so rough and wild that it seemed impossible for Manhattan to be so close. They might as well have been Labrador, though the fiery colors of October and the Hudson's royal blue took far longer than Labrador to change into the gray and white of winter.

The difference between children raised in these highlands and children raised in New York was so enormous as to be unspeakable. To feel as natural in a place like this as if he had been born there had taken Harry an entire world war. And this was where he would go, where battles had been fought and cannon fired, in the crags overlooking West Point, on the high rock ledges, in the bays of the Hudson, along the long ridges where the scent and sound of war had never faded and never would. Many of the children brought up there were born to be warriors, and would never be understood by those who were not. Both inexplicably and irresistibly, the spark was seated in the terrain.

# The Highlands    395

With a pack and in boots and a field jacket, Harry caught a nearly empty morning train that pulled out shortly after Grand Central had exhausted itself of half a million commuters who were by then taking off their coats and sitting down at their desks.

North of the village of Cold Spring, after a long climb to a granite ledge more than a thousand feet above the Hudson, he threw down the pack and allowed himself to take in a view to which all the way up he had forced himself not to turn. Pivoting south, he wondered how it was that such an open picture, which, like a painting on a scrim, he could only see and neither touch nor enter, could so easily strike down his doubts. And how the blue glare that burnished those surfaces of the river left unruffled by the winds could stop time. He had never known whether the few perfect moments in his life had occurred because the walls between past and present had fallen, or if those walls fall in deference to perfection. But he did know that perfection and the defeat of time ran together, and that they brought love, calm, and resolution as solid as the granite on which he now stood.

Southward, the last ranges of hills began to combine into disciplined ranks that eventually would become the tenement-like Palisades. One could tell that the ocean was somewhere near, even if it could not be seen. Ten miles or so to the south, the first ridges of the Appalachians leapt the Hudson. These ramparts, which can be seen from Manhattan on the other side, loomed large and high, their north cols and steeps in dark blue shadow, their lighted flanks slightly rust-colored in the midmorning air. Breaking through the mountain wall, the Hudson widened capaciously at West Point, then turned west and north into the narrow channel where the chain had blocked the ships of George III. The nearer the terrain, the more incendiary its colors. Trees flared in yellow. Marsh grasses and reeds swept back and forth like wheat in the wind. The sky was cloudless, the air bracing and cold even in the sun, and he was completely alone.

The outcrop where he halted was about six feet wide and twice as long, tapering to no width whatsoever at either end. Jutting from the south face of the mountain, it was well shielded from the north wind, though the winds at that height seemed to chase in a circle around the peaks. Toward one side of the ledge a crease in the rock made a shelter shaped like a lean-to or an attic without a knee wall, a right triangle about five feet at the base, five feet high at the peak, and almost seven feet along its hypotenuse.

After a few minutes of stillness in the open, Harry realized how cold it really was. He had been walking and climbing since Cold Spring station, and the exertion had made him sweat. Now, with a drop in temperature that was the advance guard of a change in the weather, with ascent to a thousand feet, and in a rising wind, the damp patch on his back where the pack had rested was achingly cold. The top of the water in one of his metal canteens had frozen, and to drink he had to shake it and break the thin plug of ice.

Because it would only get colder, he set about making preparations for his defense. He ate the small lunch he had brought. Eating makes heat, and to live outside one must stoke one's metabolism with frequent, carefully spaced meals. Then he set about gathering wood. To keep a fire burning for as long as he might stay there he would need as much dry wood as he could possibly collect in a high place of few trees, the gathering of which would occupy him until dark. To make his stockpile, he had to scurry up and down the ledges, find the wood, break it up, and then, on paths made more dangerous because he didn't use his hands, carry it without falling. Eventually he filled the cave with an eighth of a cord of grayed conifer limbs, splinters, and pine cones, enough for a small fire that could last for several days.

There was no water on the mountain, he had only two quarts, the air was dry, and he had been exerting himself for hours. He could always go down to a stream, but the idea was to hold out in one place and through physical deprivation cast himself back to the less tender state of mind necessary to serve his resolution. He thought he could last quite well, as he would be neither moving nor working, and he accepted the prospect of thirst.

As darkness fell, he made a fire beneath the canopy of rock, about two feet from the open. Like all evergreen fires but the wettest, it raged and crackled like gunshots and was as bright as Christmas on the ground floor of a department store. When the wind didn't invade it, the tiny cave was almost warm, though as yet there were no coals. Despite a dim, otherworldly red glow a thousand feet above Cold Spring, there would be no one sighting him in, no beads taken, no killing patrols dispatched or howitzers aimed. Not long before, he had mainly done without. That was when the night would become hallucinatory, when they lost their bearings as well as their fingers, when time had no memory, the heart beat too slowly to be safe, and flesh froze black.

Although he had come to cast himself back, he would never get all the way. He had survived the war, but he could not do such a thing twice. He was older, and had barely made it the first time. Having fought for years, he found the professional soldier hard to discern. What was it that made anyone want to fight again and again?

At about seven-thirty he bloused his cuffs into his socks, tightened and buttoned his jacket and collar, fed the fire until it was gold, and, saving one blanket and the sleeping bag for sleep, threw the other blanket over his shoulders. Comfortably sitting against the granite wall, feet tucked under him, he stared into the abyss. Because they were cut out by the ledge, he couldn't see the lights of the town below. In the far distance was a dim white haze, Manhattan's nightly shedding of the energy and emotion of several million lives. But though Manhattan and the boroughs were vast and spread across worlds of land and water, from a distance they were no more than the glimmer of a lost brooch catching a gleam of moonlight.

Even before Catherine. . . . Catherine—when she put down her purse on a bench the strap fell over the arm in two perfect, parallel sine waves, as if she were infused with so much beauty it had to find outlet even in her accidents. Even before Catherine, Catherine was there, somehow always present, as if watching invisibly, as if it had all been locked down, and the purpose of his life was to make his way to her through countries, over seas, in battles, and falling through the air.

Above, the sky was clear, the stars throbbed. But straight out there was no light, just a mass of black that the eye mischievously made gray and populated with chaotic figures arising ex nihilo, their voices incomprehensible as they ceaselessly tumbled. From this came something like sleep. Colors and faces appeared. And below the noise, in more than a dream, another time began to rise.

The Bay of Biscay, early in the evening, on a smooth, rolling sea: the bow of a destroyer was raised twenty feet in the air and lowered with each swell so cleanly that when it cut through the glassy waves it made neither foam nor whitecaps nor the slightest sound, as the sea was complicit in its quiet race north. Few things are as wonderful as a ship mated gracefully with the waves, and it was breathtaking to ride in the prow. Because the speed of the destroyer was the same as the speed of the wind from astern, the ship's noiseless strides were rhythmically accomplished in perfectly still air.

Harry and half a dozen pathfinders of the 82nd Airborne sat above the forecastle as the light dimmed and the sun turned a bank of clouds pink. They could feel the rumble of the engines. The narrow ship that was taking them to England was a spear in the sea more than ten times longer than it was wide. Always the vanguard, their detachment had been separated from the division and sent through the Strait of Gibraltar to make a left hook through the Atlantic.

They were going to England so as to go to France, which might be the last place for some or perhaps all of them. But the enterprise was so great, and they had been caught up in it for so long, that the intervals between battles now blended with the battles themselves as if there were no distinction. If they feared anything, it was that they would become wed to safety and forget that to carry themselves properly in combat so as to stay alive they had to forgo hope of living.

At sea this quality was not degraded. The warship cut through waters that held enemy submarines and were near an occupied coast from which attack aircraft routinely sallied. The sailors were tense, and when the paratroopers had done calisthenics on the afterdeck, their arms stacked, the gunners had remained at their guns, and lookouts had carefully scanned the sky.

Despite the English weather, and as bad as English cooking had been and had become, the spring would be mild and the food better than what he had carried with him in Sicily. There would be a long period of rest before the invasion, when he would be able to walk in London or in the countryside as if there were no war. He was going to England, and to get him there the sea was lifting and lowering him in air through which he was now well practiced in falling and floating.

# 33

## PATHFINDER

IN LONDON THE massive stone columns of the great financial houses still stood in the City, blackened by a hundred years of coal smoke, their ornamental bases now covered not with a dusting of snow but the dust of bomb craters and the ash of fires that consumed whole blocks. Each excavated crater or freely standing chimney, and every high wall bereft of supports, or formerly private room now open to the air, its wallpaper flapping, was yet another reinforcement of English resolve. Because of the way the bombs fell, striking at random and with devastating effect, and because everyone was always at risk, ready to be separated from a material state that could vanish instantaneously, London came alight not only with spark and fire but with holiness and life. Its muted colors, the famous whites and grays, the flashes of red and occasional blues, were now laden with longing and emotion as seldom before.

Harry Copeland, formerly of the 504th Regimental Combat Team, but now Captain, Special Advance Element, 2nd Battalion Pathfinder Team, 505th Parachute Infantry Regiment, 82nd Airborne Division, walked from one end of London to the other, with neither plan nor schedule except that in late evening he was expected at an address in South Kensington. Because he had last been at a dinner party in a different world and a long time before, and at such engagements had often been disruptive without intending to be, he was fairly apprehensive.

Though he had never stated it, he had felt from early childhood that life was magnificently intense, in splendor overwhelming, in sight demanding, and in time very short. And that therefore the only worthwhile thing other than a noble showing in the face of its dangers was the ravishing connection of one heart to another. This made him uninterested in the idea of people sitting at table, talking and posing. But occasionally he would attend dinner parties, because he recognized that not everyone in the world thought as he did, and he had always hoped that someday at a painful social event he would encounter a woman whose views were in this regard the same, and who, like him, was so naturally lonely that, for her as well, making small talk and holding cocktails was somewhat like being burned at the stake.

There was also the matter of army food. He hoped that though it was England of 1944, someone had been able to come up with something better, like a real egg. And there were other things, too, such as his desire simply to be in an elegant room in the company of women rather than in a tent with a kerosene lantern, a kerosene stove, and the murmurs of men playing cards. That is not to say that he was uncomfortable with privation or that he did not know that it had kept him alive and he owed it a lifelong debt of gratitude. Never would he assume, no matter what age he might be privileged to reach, that having once been thrown into war it could not happen again. And then, as time passed, he discovered more and more that the strength engendered by privation was not only a defense against death in battle, but that it had a purity and austerity that set existence ablaze.

He knew London well enough from before the war when he had come down from Oxford, *coming down* meaning not, as was commonly assumed, from north to south, but—Oxford being west of London—according to the flow of the Thames. Since his arrival in the city on his first leave, he had used a compass, which enabled him to avoid the illusory paths worn by others. You might walk west along a street or road that after gradually bending would point you north or east. Things often did not run as they promised, go where they announced, or stay constant as one believed. With a compass to correct his impressions, he formed an objective view of the lay of London, the beauty of which was not diminished. To get to his engagement, in proceeding from Marble Arch to the bridge over the Serpentine he crossed paths and walks and found his way directly. Going overland, finding and marking routes, staying true to what existed, and being wary of new features on the land were now part of his trade, and upon his trade his life and the lives of others would at times depend. In addition to formal exercises such as parachuting into Scotland or onto the sheep-dotted fields closer to his base, he practiced wherever he was.

But to attain Brompton Square he had to take the regimented streets, and his compass, folded with a click, was deep in his pocket when he arrived. As if he could neither remember what the world had been like before the war, nor envision what it would be like after, he found the color of the private house intimidating. Eighteenth-century stonework behind abbreviated gardens and an iron gate framed a red door amid windows glowing with the light of the rooms beyond them. As darkness fell, the blackout curtains were still open, and as he hesitated at the gate a woman went from window to window dutifully closing off the warmly lit tableaux.

He was received almost apologetically not by a servant but by the lady of the house, the wife of his former Oxford tutor. Almost white-haired, in a black velvet gown, she welcomed him and led him to what they called the salon, where upon his appearance conversation, though it continued, was muted as swiftly as if someone had thrown a switch. Heads turned tentatively to assess him. He assessed back, his initial nervousness giving way to confidence as he scouted the guests and marked them down.

There was his tutor, a heart-rending shock as Harry knew he would be, tall and stiff in a wheelchair, unable to speak, unable to lift his hand, which Harry took and squeezed. And when he did, Martin Cater's waxy fingers, the skin glossy and immobile, tried to squeeze back, but could not. An exploding shell somewhere on the desert coast of Libya had been the cause of that. A man who spoke so beautifully, knew so much, and formulated so well, could now only observe. His hair, white and wiry, had thinned to almost nothing, riding above the tightened skin of his scalp and a long scar that graphically signified his affliction. But he still hung on, all he knew was yet within him, and he was dressed magnificently, medals and all, in the uniform of his rank as colonel.

His was the place of honor, close to the fire, where conversations crossed. Opposite him was an academic colleague whom Harry had not met. Too old for this war, he probably had seen enough in the last, although one could not tell for sure. From him, inexplicably, Harry immediately received emanations of hostility, disapproval, and immutable arrogance. Harry thought, Either I'm in for it or he is.

Fortunately, to his right was an exquisite woman of Harry's age or perhaps a few years older, a New Zealander, a divorcée, a musicologist now working in a factory making field kitchens. She wore a silk dress somewhat darker than royal blue, and a glittering diamond necklace totally superfluous in drawing the eye to the majestically décolleté bosom over which it was draped. Sneaking a look, Harry knew that this was a woman of great and alluring density, not of volume but of solidity. Above all, her eyes and brows, almost Eurasian, were clean of line, high, sharp, and ethereal. And her smile, snow-capped, gave off more light than her diamonds.

And then two Americans, a journalist and his journalistic wife, both of whom had been living abroad since the early thirties and both of whom, of English descent, were by now almost British in speech, even if not for a purist. Among other things, they couldn't have cared less and they drank a lot. He was what by now he would have called a cheeky fellow, with a wonderful, mischievous, brave face, and she was almost as attractive as the New Zealand woman. She had a hypnotic, ancien régime birthmark to the left of her upper lip, so perfectly placed it looked artificial. Maybe it was. And she had thick, soft black hair and an expression that was simultaneously randy and sweet. Somehow it was appropriate that he was from Fort Worth and she was from Manchester, Vermont. Harry knew that in the battle sure to come with the choleric don, he would need allies, and though they were long-term expatriates and she had alluded to a sojourn in El Paso by saying, "It's da moon," they seemed spirited enough to stand their American ground.

Other than Martin Cater, Harry was the only one in uniform, and an American captain's uniform could not hold a candle to that of a British colonel. He was also the youngest, unattached, and socially inept. At least he knew he was socially inept, and, at first, tried to shut up.

He observed with mounting joy the contrasts with his life in camp and the field. Three women were in the room. No room could ever be alive without at least one, and here they were, with all the pleasurable tension they generate — like music, or the incline that assures the life of a stream. The New Zealand woman and the American were sufficient to produce waves throughout Harry's body that pulsed to his fingertips. So badly did he want to hold them that he wished there had been dancing, but it was enough just to be in their presence, to hear them speak, to watch them closely as each made her point. He studied the New Zealander's face, lips, her delicate hands, her devastating profile, the curve of her neck, the way her clothes draped. Inconspicuously and with hidden admiration and respect, he looked at one woman and then the other. They knew it, they always did, and it did for them at least as much as it did for him, which was the way it was supposed to be. Nothing would come of it but memory, neither action nor regret, and thus it could charge and be charged by civilization far more than just the enervated recollections, if at all, of a desperately fast, alcohol-fueled, lightning-quick fuck in a room above a pub, memories of which were brought back in the thick fog by a soldier returning at four in the morning, and who on other nights might wander off into the trees to no lesser avail.

This evening in Brompton Square the fire steadily flared, the lights were strong, the colors subtle and lovely as so often they are in England. A pair of Empire torchères stood upon the mantel flanking a Georgian clock that ticked like a bomb. The sole remaining seat was next to the New Zealand woman, who introduced herself as Claire.

"Claire what?"

"Jay."

"The sister of Claire Daloon," the don said, after which Claire gave him a look that could be likened only to a harpoon in full flight. She actually began to get up as if she were going to go over and smack him in the face.

As the don had missed the real pun — Claire Jay — Harry almost said, "Are you a woman of the cloth?" but wisely decided to refrain. Instead, he said, "What an excellent name, for its clarity, quickness, definition, color, flight, reflex, and beauty." (The don looked as if he had just inhaled a lemon.) "Are you related to John Jay?"

"Your revolutionary? Yes, I am, in fact, directly and not so distantly, as not that much time has passed."

When Harry had settled into the sofa alongside her, the cloth of his trousers crushed against the blue silk of her dress, and, although after that they did not touch, he kept on feeling the presence of her body next to his. Perhaps it was its heat, or his imagination as he leapt ahead and was overcome, or her pulse that, hardly perceptible over the gap of open air, reverberated through him. He turned red, and the redder he turned, the redder he turned. There was a natural limit, but by the time he had reached it he had stopped the conversation completely. As everyone looked on, Mrs. Cater inquired about his condition.

"Harris," she began, but he interrupted her.

"Please, Margaret, *Harry*."

"Sorry, Harry. Are you all right? Are you having an attack of some sort?"

"I'm not used to the warmth," he almost squeaked. "And the alcohol," he added, after looking around desperately and noting the drink in each person's hand.

"But you haven't had anything to drink."

"The suggestion is sometimes enough" — he took a deep breath, interrupting himself — "to...."

By this time, Claire knew that it was she, and, if truth be told, began to have a strong sexual feeling in regard to Harry, which was both persistent and magnified by his awkwardness and, perhaps, charm.

"Then let me get you something," Margaret said.

Harry, at this time extremely ignorant of alcohol, and whose last taste of it had been a thimbleful of grappa offered to him by a Sicilian peasant in the first flush of political rehabilitation, was now trapped. "Scotch," he said, "four up."

"What is that?" the Texan asked, "a quadruple shot?"

"That's right," said Harry, "in a glass."

"That's how we do it in England," the don said, "ever since Ethelred the Fat."

Margaret went to an array of light-spangled bottles, ice buckets, and glasses, where she took a cut-crystal tumbler, filled it to the brim, and gingerly sailed it across the room, with everyone following this as if she were building a house of cards.

So as not to spill it after being admonished by the don — "Don't spill it, it's Glenfiddich" — Harry drained half and, as his interior roasted in the tropics, thanked his hostess.

Now, as if drawn by an electromagnet a magnificent inch and a half closer, the brief rustling of her dress more powerful than the Scotch, Claire asked, "What part of the army are you in?"

The Texan answered, almost proudly, "Eighty-second Airborne. You can't do better."

"Oh," said Claire, "a para."

Harry, already more than relaxed, heard *parrot*. "What?" he asked.

"A para," she repeated, with time to calibrate her tone exactly, somewhat admiringly, slightly mockingly, certainly seductively, not completely clearly, and another half inch closer.

"Well," Harry replied, having heard *parrot* again, "if you say so." And then he turned to her, not leering, but very open and friendly, and said, "Polly want a cracker?"

She had no idea what he meant, but he had by this and his general maladroitness vaulted past all normal obstacles and come very close to the state — he himself had actually entered into it — where he and she could not look at one another without imagining the details of a very long kiss and what would follow. Every time they turned away from one another, they cooled, but when they turned back they heated up again. He had been in the room for only a few minutes. God, he thought, what's it going to be like in half an hour? To prepare, he drank from the crystal glass, soon asking for another.

"Why not just a double this time?" Margaret asked, understanding that he didn't know what he was doing.

"Please! Do you have any nuts or popcorn? I don't like popcorn, but I think it might act as a kind of batting."

The don, whose name Harry had heard and immediately forgotten (he struggled to remember it, and came up, inaccurately, with *Chester*), rolled his eyes.

"I'm afraid we don't," Margaret said. "Smoked salmon?"

Harry was dumbfounded. He hadn't seen a smoked salmon for years. "Lox!" he said, startling even himself.

"Lox?" Chester questioned, with a gimlet eye. "What kind of a term is that?"

"Yiddish," Harry replied, seizing a little knife and a cracker. "Also German, *lachs,* Scandinavian, *lax,* and Russian, *losos.* A venerable Indo-European root. Don't you know? You must be an economist." Chester was, in fact, an economist, who before the war had moved with Martin Cater from Oxford to the LSE. Paratroopers were not supposed to know about Indo-European roots, not American paratroopers anyway, but the evening had just begun and there would be plenty of time in which to turf him out no matter how many roots he might grab on to.

Harry turned respectfully to his tutor, also his friend. "Martin, I'm told you can't respond. How then am I to address you? You always found a way, and no matter how old I get — if I do — you'll always be ahead of me and everyone else, as you are now, even if they may fail to see it when it's right in front of them."

With perfect timing and consummate sensitivity, Margaret rose, took her place beside her husband, and put her hands upon his shoulders. "We like to think, Harry," she said, "that it's a question of timing. How often in his tutorials, in listening to, among others, me, would Martin respond with silence, the glint in his eyes, his expression, the silence itself guiding you along, bringing out the best in you as you yourself found it?

"Now, that silence is elongated," she said, pronouncing the *e* by elongating it, as *ee*, and putting the stress on the third syllable, as befitted her upbringing.

"And it ends where, in death?" Harry asked.

The shock of the chill that swept the room could have shattered glass, but Harry, who knew Martin, knew his courage, knew his detestation of nonsense, and also knew exactly what he was doing, saw a barely perceptible smile on the face of the paralyzed man. "Like hell it does," said Harry. "It must have been extremely frustrating for you, Martin, all this time." Moments passed, with Martin blinking as if in panic. No one knew what to say, and then Harry announced, deepening his jeopardy, "He says, 'Bloody hell!'"

Margaret leaned over her husband and saw his blinking, as if he had been pushed into some variant of a seizure, which is what she thought, as it had happened often. But it was not a seizure, hardly so, for as Harry had been electrified to discover almost immediately, it was Morse. Now Harry moved forward in his seat to the edge of the sofa, followed by Claire, who was still with him, and, slowly, as Martin blinked, spoke for him.

"'Harry,'" Martin said. Harry said it as he decoded it.

"Oh Christ," Margaret cried. "It's Morse code. We didn't know!"

"That's right," Harry said, "and you'll have to learn it starting tonight. He says

"'Those . . . blighters . . . don't know . . . Morse. Not . . . even . . . doctors. No . . . not afraid . . . of . . . death. Margaret . . . quick . . . learner . . . why . . . I . . . married. Hope . . . eyelids . . . hold . . . out. Harry . . . stay . . . safe . . . I will . . . just . . . listen. Come . . . back . . . for . . . slow . . . conversation. Tired. Don't . . . like . . . black . . . currant . . . jam.'"

Harry said, "Martin, when I came in you were blinking at me like a tart, and I remembered that once, in your office at Rhodes House, you told me that in the First War you were a signalman. Right before a drop, I talk to airplanes full of paratroopers by blinking lights at them. Think of how fast you can go when you and Margaret get abbreviations settled, when simple Y's or N's will convey a huge amount of information upon answering a series of questions." He lifted his glass. "Cheers, Martin. And you should know that if I have rendered anything to you, it is but a small part of what you have given to me."

This was all quite astounding, and as everyone was reflecting silently upon it, a woman in a white bonnet that looked almost like a nurse's cap but was shaped more like a mushroom, appeared and announced as stiffly as a six-year-old in a school play that the dinner would be served. The timing was perfect, and they rose, abandoning the fire, to file in procession to yet another room of quiet splendor as is often produced by limited resources and educated yet independent tastes.

Seated across from the exquisite Claire, Harry kept his gaze upon her immoderately, and she often returned it. He tried not to but could not help it, and nor could she, for neither of them could wait to exit, embrace, and kiss, right outside the door, in Brompton Square. But civilization, elongating anticipation and thus amplifying the connections between a man and a woman far beyond what barbarians, modern or ancient, can comprehend, forced them to. Immediately they joined the others in a collective gasp as the doors opened from the kitchen and a butler (a caterer, actually, no puns having been intended) brought out a platter of steaks as thick as Texas.

This was so unheard of in England at the time as to suggest illegal activity or perhaps treason. But from behind half a dozen burning candles Margaret was quick to disabuse them of false impressions. "Before you turn us in," she said, "because not even the king has such an allowance of beef, please take into account that these are whale steaks, what in Canada are called, I believe, *ookpik*. Choice *ookpik*, very chewy, very oily. You may be delighted. If not, you'll be reminded that we're still at war. We do have traditional potatoes, a semi-fake chocolate cake (no chocolate), and good wines from before the war. Why not?"

Harry looked at Margaret and thought that, should a woman grow old, she might still have her deepest charm. Should a woman grow old, she would still be a woman, the essence of being so being so inerasable as never to vanish. And if men were to understand this as they, too, grew old, the world would be a happier place. That charm was in Claire so strongly that it was wonderful just to be in the same room with her.

But the don had a bone to pick. He had been left on the sidelines because he had been demonstrably unintelligent enough not to know that with apparently spastic blinking his friend was pleading to be heeded and understood. He had been shown to be unobservant, and thus stupid — for a professional academician the most potent toxin of all. Slammed into his place as violently as a lorry spinning out after hitting a chuckhole, he rebounded in frontal attack.

"You know," he said, "Americans eat the real steaks they bring over. They have massive amounts of men and materiel. But they can't match our brilliance in fighting."

"You mean like Dunkirk?" Harry asked, "or Yorktown?"

"Nonetheless, man for man...."

"No no," Harry countered. "I'm from the Eighty-second Airborne, and you're treading on ground that will swallow you."

"And how is that?"

"That is," Harry said, "because the world has never seen — in initiative, imagination, courage, and steadfastness — anything like the American fighting man." He was still plundered by alcohol. "Not the Germans, the non-Germans, the semi-German Viennese, the British, the Scots, the Welsh, the Cornish, the Danish, or the Nepalese. You may in future" (here he resorted to British usage) "condemn us for it. You may continue to think that we are savage, disproportionate, and uncivilized. But we saved you the last time. And it is we, I guarantee you, who will liberate Paris and drive into Berlin. We don't like it. We don't like fighting and dying. But" (and here he held up his fairly intoxicated left hand) "when it comes time for that, we are *facile princeps*, and will always be. We were born for it. The terrain of the New World educated us in it. That in America every man is a king assures us of it." Here he made a kind of circular, magician's motion with his hand, or something that an eighteenth-century aristocrat might do with a handkerchief, and ended his peroration with yet another drink from the tumbler he had carried from the salon.

Backed into a corner, Chester, whose real name was Nigel something, could only repel. "Do you realize," he pronounced royally, "that I haven't understood a single word you've said?"

"Why? Because you're stupid?"

"Because your speech is hideous and unintelligible, not English."

"Oh," said Harry, having encountered this in his student days. "Not English. Not English. Let's explore this." He was angry, and used to fighting hard. What a dinner party it was, like eating whale hot dogs at a boxing match.

"My dialect versus yours. Were there a pure, uniform, consistent English in England, you might have a point. But there isn't, not even in London. Not even in Oxbridge. If you can understand someone from Southwark, much less Bristol, why not from New York or St. Louis? In India they speak as if they are floating on a cloud. In the Caribbean it's like singing. And by the way, you'd be better understood if, when you spoke, you removed the ball bearings from your cheeks."

Harry was an airborne trooper who truly expected that he would not live long. He didn't care about breaking up dinner parties, and all he wanted to do was to float to Claire.

"Tell me, then," Chester asked from a rather deep crevasse, "pimp of New-World-vulgar speech, what is *salpiglossis?*"

"What?" Harry asked, laughing. "Are you out of your mind? I may have had too much to drink. I'm sure I did. But you? Am I imagining you? You can't be real."

"I'm testing your command of English. What is *salpiglossis?*"

Harry had two options. He could laboriously demonstrate that his ignorance of the word *salpiglossis* had no significance, or he could pull a rabbit out of a hat. Though it would be nearly impossible, he prayed for a miracle, and God, apparently aware of the reading Harry had done on his cot at Camp Quorn, north of Leicester, in loneliness and cold, in the absence of women, in the scholarly devotion that for Jews is worship first class, sent him one. It came via the fire and the light, the magic of the evening, the vitality of London, the spirit of man and the beauty of woman, from the improbable, from love, from all he treasured, and from a required botany course that once had almost driven him crazy.

"*Salpiglossis,*" he said, with a long, dramatic pause, "as I recall from a difficult time, is a herbaceous, somewhat showy-flowered garden plant allied to the fucking petunia, its etymology deriving, I would guess, from the Greek *salpigx,* trumpet, and *glossa,* tongue, of course. Isn't it?"

"Unfortunately," Chester volunteered, "it is." And then, "And what am I to do now?"

"Eat your whale steak," Harry answered, "and I'll eat mine. We speak the same language, which makes us brothers. Imagine if we spoke German. We wouldn't know what the hell we were talking about. We'll drive on to Berlin and sort this out later."

Harry drained his glass and, lest he grow ill, refused wine. Embarrassed at having been the center of attention for too long, he glanced now and then at Claire, who, had there been another man closer to her age, by now would have begun to pay him attention for the purpose of influencing Harry, even were it the kind of influence that vanishes with evening and infatuation. She had turned to Chester, with whom she was engaged in conversation that on her part was for Harry's sake, the elevation of her voice reflecting this in reaching just the right level to find him across the table.

The excitements Harry had felt when first beholding her were quickly outdone merely by listening to what she said, for the things she said and how she said them were more attractive to him than anything he might see or touch, and vastly multiplied the powerful alchemy of her appearance and voice. Getting up between courses to go to Martin at the head of the table, with his napkin in hand trailing like a scroll held by a statesman in a monumental painting, he heard Chester say, "I have a general contempt for war," and Claire's reply: "What a coincidence! So do I! Let's send a telegram to Hitler and Mussolini. Maybe they do, too."

Harry found a side chair and positioned it next to Martin so they could converse, as far as possible, in relative privacy. From the corner of his eye he could see the fire in the salon and its reflection in a set of glass doors. This was a stand-in for all of London, which he imagined as if he could see it from the air, as if he could somehow take in all at once the careful labor and extraordinary judgment of centuries; the balance, restraint, and fairness of the English; their heartbreak and trials like a knife cutting at the city as it was turned on the lathe of time. The moonlit curve of the Thames, which could not be blacked out or erased, was a guide for the bombers that then with incendiary vengeance restored to London its darkened lights. In peril, every detail could sing, and did.

"Anything you want me to tell Margaret before she learns Morse, which, if she stays up all night, she'll know by tomorrow morning?"

Martin blinked out that he wanted lemon in his tea in the P.M.

"Milk at other times?"

"Y."

"I suppose it wouldn't be unusual," Harry said, "for me to present you with a monologue as I did in tutorial. But how will you bring me up sharp? How will you point me right and guide me along?"

"O-n y-o-u-r o-w-n."

"There are so many things I wanted to ask you, in that you've done this, been through it — twice now. Complicated questions that I didn't ask when I could have."

"Now you guide," he blinked. "I need to see this through."

"I see." It would be nearly impossible, like a son guiding his father, and not just in the ordinary things but in something far separated from Harry's youth, strength, and the frame of mind to which he had been brought by rigorous training and war itself. In a single moment, between courses, he would have to contradict his training, resist his predilections, open all the gates he had shut to survive, and put himself into the heart of the afflicted man. With the fire and its reflection vying with Claire on the periphery, he would have to backwater all the way up the Thames to a different time and a different self. But Martin was dying, as Harry would too, so Harry, who loved him, did his best.

How he knew where to go was a mystery, but it was given to him to know. "You once told me," he said, "that you believed the impressionists were the product of the Siege of Paris and the Commune. That the darkness and misery had bred an explosion of color, that the love of life cannot be suppressed."

Martin blinked a simple Y. He did remember. He had originated it.

"It didn't occur to me when you said that, but when I was in college I knew the most extraordinary person. At least, a person to whom the most extraordinary thing had happened. The tragedy of his wealthy family was that he was blind from birth or shortly thereafter: I don't know the circumstances.

"Though he lived in the dark, the decoration of his apartment had been accomplished as if in service to a client with the keenest appreciation of color and form. The blind can appreciate form, of course, but not by sight; and color, but only by heat. He had never seen proportions all together making a whole. He had never seen a face, or a color. He didn't know the beauty of one shade fading into another, or the attraction of changing light, like one of those precisely turned engines in Cavendish, its brass and mirrors casting rays according to the physicist's command.

"But"—Harry leaned forward—"one morning, as he was getting out of his bath, dizzy and disoriented with heat, he fell, hit his head, and immediately"—Harry violently snapped his fingers—"he could see. Strong light shone down from a lamp above. He had never seen light. The wall upon which his towel bar was mounted—these he knew by touch—was a deep green, and the towel bar itself a highly polished brass shining in the light. As he stood looking at this, having risen as if lifted, it was so beautiful to him, who had no conception of light, that he thought he had died, and that this—a towel bar on a bathroom wall—was heaven. He thought he was in the dwelling of God and the angels. Overwhelmed, he shook and he wept, partly from gratitude but in the main because the world, now written in full, was almost too wonderful to bear.

"There, in the light shining down from a bathroom ceiling, was the selfsame glory of the most massive suns. The man saw God in the towel bar in his bathroom. He was able to see and feel without the obstruction of training, conformity, necessity, or the ordered blindness of habit.

"I may never see you again. I may die before you. You may die before me. What can I say to a man of the widest range I've ever known, who is now made prisoner in his own body, except to keep in mind my once-blind friend, for neither of us has a fair or promising choice except to follow his lead and to see, I only hope, that concealed in the world we have is a world greater than we can imagine."

It was understood without announcement that Martin could not eat with the rest of them and had been fed before. Aside from blinking, with Harry his only interpreter, he could not participate. But this was not the first social affair after his paralysis. He wanted company and conversation, and had he the energy he might have told Harry that observing in silence was in some ways better than being on tap to be witty, or even just to speak. Being present without obligation was much like watching a movie, but with a realism unparalleled by anything in a theater — in full and perfect color, 195 degrees of view in three dimensions, stereoscopic vision, true sound, and the touch of air, aromas, perfumes. . . . By command of circumstance, Martin receded, almost contentedly.

"What do you do with your days?" Claire asked Harry, not quite out of the blue.

"Our camp is north of Leicester, at Quorn House," he said. "You may have heard of it. We have the great house but we live in rows of tents. Bouncing back and forth from one to the other makes us classless."

"It doesn't make you middle class?" the Texan asked.

"We don't do averages. It's feast or famine, like the classic problem of warming yourself by the fire. Unless you turn like a rotisserie, one side is too hot, the other too cold."

"So you pivot?" the Texan's wife asked.

"I spend as much time as I can in the house. Many of the boys feel uncomfortable there because they can't get used to the elegance.

They're always aware of it, as if they were in the lobby of the Roxy, staring in wonder at the high ceiling. But it's cold in the tents, and the smell of kerosene never leaves."

"But what do you *do*?" Claire asked.

"You really want to know?"

"It's why I asked."

"We rise in the dark and spend time cleaning our quarters, bathing, dressing. Then we eat breakfast. It's still dark when we start our run. My stick — that is, my detachment, the men with whom I will jump into France (I don't think that's a secret) — does twelve miles each morning." There was a slight gasp. "Not everyone does, but we do, in boots, with weapons, ammunition, helmet, and a light pack."

"Twelve miles?" Margaret asked.

"Every goddamned day. When we get back, we eat again. Then we go out on the field and do calisthenics and hand-to-hand fighting for an hour and a half. Every day."

"I hope you can take a nap," Margaret said, maternally, and, in Harry's view, insanely.

"No nap. We go to the firing range for a few hours. After that, maintaining equipment, map study, briefing. I study French and German every day, for less than half an hour but regularly. Then a shower, dinner, an hour's free time in which I usually read but most everyone else plays cards. It's like a casino."

"You don't play cards?" the Texan asked.

"I never learned how. The only game I like is chess. And then lights out. Sometimes we have a movie, sometimes there's no routine because we go on an exercise, or jump. Rarely do we get leave, but when we do I come to London. In camp the water's cold, the air's cold. After a while the cold, the mud, even jumping out of airplanes, become the default conditions of life."

"What weapon?" the Texan asked. Though old enough so that the draft passed way over him, he was an excellent shot.

"All weapons, including German, French, Russian, and Italian." Turning to his British hosts and Chester, he said, "We have bazookas, but sometimes the PIAT. The standard weapon is the M1, but I have a special situation with the M1 Carbine." Here it was as if he were describing a villa he had just bought in the south of France, and how he would refurbish it. He knew that this was in its way pathetic, but the hand he had been dealt was now so close to his heart he was ashamed of neither his enthusiasm nor his concentration.

"The M1 is long and heavy, almost ten pounds. With the stock folded, the carbine is half the length and less than two-thirds the weight, although I have a wood stock, because it gives the carbine a better balance. It's worth a little bit of extra weight and a fair amount of length. Because of its longer barrel and greater mass, the M1 is accurate out to a quarter of a mile. You need it for what the infantry does, so it's standard. The carbine normally is accurate to less than two-thirds that range, but in a pinch it does better. That's because the M1 has an eight-round clip and requires a pull of the trigger for each shot, but the carbine has a thirty-round magazine and can fire at seven hundred and fifty rounds per minute."

"What does that do?" the Texan's wife asked.

"It means that in two seconds you can put thirty bullets into a target, as opposed to two at most with the rifle. The thirty will spread to cover so much of the target box that you're likely to get a hit. That's why we have two designations, accuracy range and effective range. In practicing, you wouldn't waste ammunition that way, but you would if circumstances demanded it. Ammunition is heavy. You can't ever have enough of it, and you have to carry it. Just from the weight I save from carrying the carbine rather than the rifle, I can carry a hundred extra rounds. And loading the rounds into the magazine is easier than clipping them, and loading the magazine into the carbine is easier and faster than inserting the clip into the rifle. If the enemy is assaulting you and you have to reload once every thirty shots, you're a lot better off than reloading every eight. With all the other equipment we have to carry, the carbine's lesser weight saves us. It's superior by far."

"Except in accuracy," the Texan said. His small mustache accented his very blue, darty eyes. "I have a bias toward accuracy and against squirrels. Granted, squirrels don't shoot back, but I have to say that one accurate shot is worth its weight in — what's scarce these days?"

"Everything," said Claire.

Like a magician at the cusp of his trick, Harry was delighted with expectation. Lifting his head, he said, "That's where my special relation to the carbine comes in. Mine is as accurate as, or more so than, the M1."

"How did you manage that?" Chester asked. "Or is it a military secret?"

"Unfortunately it isn't a military secret, being of little value in that it can't be generally replicated. What we did was this: My detachment consists of seven men and is devoted to a special purpose. I went up the chain of command all the way to a lieutenant general and received permission for each of us to take two carbines to the range each time we went. We compared them for accuracy, and returned the lesser of the two. Every day thereafter, we would check out a fresh weapon, compare it to the one we had retained, and keep whichever was better. They vary, of course, according to the peculiarities of manufacture, quirks in metallurgy, how new was the blade of the machine tool that shaped them, the concentration of its operator . . . God only knows.

"By this method, after months of comparison and subjecting ourselves to double gun-cleaning and the armorers to an absolute hell of record-keeping, we nicked, as it were, those carbines in the top one or two percent of accuracy. But we didn't stop there. We applied the same process to the ammunition, which also varies by batch, putting aside the stable and accurate loads once we had discovered them.

"It comes down to this. My carbine, like those of my men, while shorter than an M1, lighter in weight, easier to load, and able to carry thirty rounds at a time and fire on full automatic, is, like the M1, accurate to about a quarter of a mile. And we are practiced to use it to the peak of its capacities. The squad has the firepower of a platoon. The individual has almost the firepower of a squad."

When Harry finished, no one said anything. It was as if he had committed some sort of faux pas, although he didn't know which one. And then he realized that they were not impressed. They neither admired what he had done nor shared in his enthusiasm. If not embarrassed, they were at least put off—and sad for him almost to the point of pity, because he had spoken too much and they had seen his exceptional intelligence made common by the needs of war. He didn't understand, and never understood, and had never been able to accustom himself to the society into which—as what he had called a Jew out of water—he had been only half, and even then merely provisionally, accepted once he had arrived at Harvard. He would never know the rules by nature or intuition, never know when force and brilliance are best reined in, or how to rein them in, never know what was right to say in dinner conversation in any setting but that of a boy and his father eating at a kitchen table on the eleventh floor next to an echoing alley off Central Park West, using just a few utensils so as not to make washing difficult, while, as he remembered it most, a cool spring wind whistled through the iron gates that closed off the back courtyards from the street. There he learned to speak freely, with consideration only of the substance of what he said, and not a thought about the intricacies of its reception.

So he ended, and perhaps added to whatever transgression he had committed, by saying, "I'm fond of my carbine, and have etched my name on the stock. I killed some Germans with one that was far less accurate, and now I may kill more, which may help to prevent little clouds of parachutes from blooming over the parks, gardens, and parade grounds of London, and keep the Germans swaying beneath them from landing on your roofs and crashing through your skylights."

After some time had passed in which silver upon china and the slight hiss of the candles were the only sounds, Harry, not solely out of politeness, asked Claire what she did with *her* days.

"I work in a factory."

"Making?"

"Field kitchens."

"Would you please make them so that the food tastes better?"

"'Fraid not."

"What part do you play?"

"Ophelia."

"Ophelia's the one," he asked, "who makes the fittings that drown the Spam in gravy?"

"No, she bolts on the clamps that hold the gas canisters and the lines that lead to the burners."

"All day long?"

"All day long, in Slough, and then she goes home to nothing."

"But she reads."

"Of course she does. She reads. She dreams of splendors. She remembers before the war and imagines after. And, someday, she'll get on a ship in winter and glide happily and sadly over two oceans, to summer and home."

"What if the war ends when it's summer in England?"

"You know what? Just the way you were sharp about your carbine, I've been sharp about that."

"About what?"

"About the schedule for when the war ends. I'll be dismissed from my factory, which will stop making field kitchens long before the fighting stops. They'll look at the battlefields and see that it's likely to come to a close within a certain length of time. And when the battles are still raging, the gates will shut, our war will be over, and I'll go home. If it's summer here, I'll wait until winter. If it's winter, I'll go, knowing that my job is done."

"You don't want to stay?" Margaret asked.

Claire shook her head back and forth, her eyes closed. She was lonely, too.

Two trains left for Leicester that night, one from Marylebone and one from St. Pancras. Harry was determined to make the first from Marylebone and keep the second in reserve. He simply could not be absent without leave, not only because of the penalties but because they had no idea where they might be moved before the invasion or when the camps would be sealed or struck. As an officer and a member of an advance element, he had to be available when it was expected of him — as it was also expected and required that he would without hesitation leave the warmth and color of London, and leave a woman alone in her bed when he should have been next to her, for a line of tents that he could hardly see in the cold fog.

He hoped at least that, availing herself of any one of the many trains that left Paddington and made a stop at Slough, Claire would walk with him through Hyde Park to the station, and he broached with his hosts the subject of leaving in time for this. But the Texan jumped in and promised a cab.

"There aren't any cabs," Harry said. "What if we can't find one?"

"We'll leave early enough."

So they stayed on, adjourning to the salon and talking about the war a lot, which Harry didn't like, because there was nothing he could do about it except what he was doing, and whatever that might be there would be no trace of it in history. They talked about British politics as well, which Harry found theoretically of interest but less so than the chance, now gone, of walking through the park with Claire.

Half an hour before her train from Paddington they rushed out as if from a sinking ship, politely but quickly, and with the women's heels clicking upon the pavement like castanets they double-timed to Exhibition Road, where there were no cars at all, much less taxis.

"What shall we do?" Claire asked.

"Walk toward the park." They were already doing that. "Maybe a taxi will come along. If not, we're headed in the right direction."

"No," the Texan said. "We should go down to Brompton Road. There'll be much more traffic there."

"We'll split up," Harry proposed. "You don't have to make a train. If you get a taxi, come along this way and pick us up. If we get one, we'll just go."

"Okay" was the reply, and the Americans turned on their heels and walked determinedly in the opposite direction. Everyone had been breathing hard and moving fast. Even so, Harry and Claire picked up the pace. "Can we make it?" she asked.

"If you can keep this up."

"I can."

"Then yes."

"Is there time," she asked as they sped forward on the deserted street, "or will there be time, for a kiss—or two?"

"I've been wanting to kiss you ever since I walked into that room."

"I know," she said.

In a single movement, he stopped suddenly and stepped in front of her so that she would run into him, and when she did they first clasped hands, and then their hands, like the receivers on rifles, slid up the other's forearms until each held the other by the elbows, which locked them tightly at the hips and enabled them to press their upper bodies together, and then he kissed her, lightly at first, like stroking, with rhythm in each touch, all in what seemed like seconds. He opened her coat, and then his, and found out how thin and conforming silk is, as if it were not there, but better because it is. He kissed her neck, and his hands found her back and then her breasts, which he bent to kiss. Harry and Claire, the war suspended by the only thing in the world that could suspend it, embraced in the dark, standing alone on Exhibition Road. A wind came through the trees, the kind of wind that comes only at night, and shook droplets of water rather gently from the leaves, in a shower that wet nothing. Because the street lamps were extinguished, the museums were closed, and the lights of London were blacked out, they could have been deep in the forest.

Both knew that he would soon go back into the war and had no say in when or if he could come down to London. Five years had been enough to instruct her in that uncertainty, and, for him, two with the shock of ten. When they had exchanged addresses on little pieces of paper in the hallway as everyone was donning coats and looking for umbrellas, the papers seemed more powerfully sad than paper was ever meant to be, and when thrust into their coat pockets the notes were like the lockets that hold remembrances of the dead. All they could do was kiss, and so they kissed, and the purest and kindest that was in them echoed from one to the other.

Until a horse-drawn cab came racing up the street, and as it stopped they did too, and got in, with the Texan and his wife pretending unsuccessfully not to have seen. "Paddington Station," the Texan said. "Can you gallop this horse?" The cab driver answered with a crack of his whip. Claire was all red and disheveled, but no one could see this in the dark, except everybody.

# 34

## GLORIOUS SUMMER

OTHER THAN IN replaying over and over the several minutes before the cab drew up on Exhibition Road, he never did get back to London or to Claire. Shortly after his return, leave was canceled, the camp was sealed in, and in May the division moved to the airfields from which it would rise sometime in June on its way to France. As they drove through the countryside to the departure point, Harry knew with each change of heading in which direction London lay, and as if the canvas cover of the truck were one of the many outdoor movie screens he had seen in desert camps and in Sicily, he envisioned upon it scenes of life as they played out oblivious of him: tugs puffing down the Thames; traffic crossing bridges; trucks rolling; horses trotting, clopping; women in scarves, wending their way to work; and Claire, who did not know that he was watching. In his imagination, as if in a film, she was in a great hall where here and there and never ceasing, showers of bluish-white sparks arose from welders' arcs and then died into cool smoke fleeing sadly on the air, and because of the way things were and had to be, her back was turned to him as he receded dimly on the road, goodbye, Claire.

The charm of northern European summers is that because they are so cool you do not need to yearn for fall. The summer light, the scents, and the sounds of warblers and owls at night and doves of any type in morning, and crows that caw for corn months before it ripens, come in England and in Normandy on currents of cold glassy air. Summer colors in high sun, vivid and clear, pierce the density of the atmosphere, which otherwise might be misty or vacuous, blurring sight and sound. The sun shone warmly upon rows of tents at the side of the airstrip, and refreshing air wound like a brook through their rolled-up sides. In the fields and woods, except when airplanes racing down the runway stunned them into silence, doves cooed with the precision of clocks.

At the beginning of June, when they were ready on the airfield, had packed and checked their equipment many times, and were as determined to live as they were at peace with dying, Harry and his men were visited by a colonel from the Combined Chiefs of Staff. The seven paratroopers were summoned to the officers' mess, where in a room with diaphanous curtains that rose and fell with the breeze they stood at attention and saluted the colonel, who was on the phone, and who, with the rocking of his left hand, had them stand at ease. Then, furthering his order, he pointed to the benches and chairs scattered against the walls.

"I have no idea, and they don't either," he said into the phone, "but it has to be done." The unintelligible response sounded like Louis Armstrong playing with the mute against the bell of his trumpet, and the impression given was that a creature like Rumpelstiltskin was on the other end of the line, a munchkin with three stars and a big office filled with maps, map cases, and telephones. "Two thousand here and another two thousand with the Hundred and First," the colonel said to the munchkin. "I'll let you know as soon as I can. Meanwhile, I'm talking to the blocking forces. Oh. Okay. Yes, sir." He hung up.

"Sorry about that," he said. "Good news and bad news for you, depending upon how you look at it, and depending on how it works out."

They were silent.

"We go on the fifth. You're first. You won't jump first, however. We're detaching you, and you're going farther south. Your plane has to swing way out into the ocean to get you where we want you and not conflict with the traffic, of which there will be so much that we fear that no matter what we do we're going to have collisions." The colonel stood and walked over to a map of northern France, which because it had neither indications of enemy dispositions nor invasion routes marked upon it could have been lifted from a high school French class. "Here," he said, pointing to a small town about twenty miles south of St. Lô, "rather alarmingly in the interior, is Tessy sur Vire, and somewhere around here is the Seventeenth SS Panzergrenadier Division. Very bad."

"Why, sir?" someone asked.

"Because they like to kill civilians—lock the doors of a church, set it on fire, machine-gun people who jump from the windows. When they take prisoners they have them dig long trenches and stand at the edge, so people can fall in conveniently a hundred at a time after they're shot.

"They've got a lot of Romanians with them. We've found that, for whatever reason, the Axis troops that fight alongside Germans are nastier than the Germans themselves. Either they want to prove something, they're more naturally barbaric, or they're homesick, but whatever they are, this is what they do and they'll give you no quarter.

"On the plus side, the Seventeenth SS is under-strength, like the Dutch a great many of them have no transport except bicycles, and they've been scrounging around for armor. They're a Panzer division, but they've got mostly French tanks and StuG IVs. You know what they are?"

"Yeah, we know what they are, sir," said a trooper who had destroyed one.

"Tell me, because I need to know if you're really aware of what you're facing."

"It's an assault gun," Harry said. "It's got a machine gun up top, but it's exposed, which means you can kill the gunner with a well placed shot, and the main thing is that the big gun doesn't swivel like a tank gun. That makes it a lot more approachable. Knock out a tread and the machine gunner, and you can kill it."

"Right," the colonel said. "But if they're concentrated and protected, their guns can do an immense amount of damage, and the Seventeenth has a bunch of them."

"Why the Seventeenth?" Harry asked. "They're pretty far away."

"There's nothing between them and the invasion area. We've got to concentrate on the center, but there's been a great deal of worry about the periphery. We can't spare much from the heart of the matter, but we're going to run a bunch of diversions. That's where you come in. Of course, they'll have had the hell bombed out of them, but, as you know, it's hard to bomb a dispersed armored force and it may not mean a thing.

"I had to present on the Seventeenth SS to the Combined Chiefs: Eisenhower, Tedder, and Bedell Smith. I did my homework. I knew about as much as it was possible to know about a newly formed — or re-formed — division.

"Because they've spent their lives in the military, the chiefs are very interested in detail. They can read it as well or better than any intelligence officer, which is what I'm supposed to be. Actually," he said wistfully, "in real life I was a chemist.

"The chiefs perked up about this division. There's not too much we can do — and you're part of it — because we're so stretched. As I was briefing them . . . I gotta tell you this. The divisional emblem of the Seventeenth is a clenched iron fist. That's because it's the Götz von Berlichingen Division, named after a German knight who had an iron hand after his real hand was cut off.

"The chiefs wanted to know more about this, and I told them what I knew, including that the division's motto is *Leck mich am Arsch,* which means 'Lick my ass.' How did that come about? they wanted to know. All I know is that it's short for something the knight is supposed to have said: *Er kann mich im Arsche lecken,* or, 'He can lick my ass.' *Arse,* actually.

"So Ike, without looking up from his papers, quietly says, 'At least they've got that right.' 'I beg your pardon?' asks Tedder, who, along with the other Englishmen — lots of staff — doesn't get the American meaning. Ike looks up over his reading glasses and says, 'You're goddamned right we're going to lick his ass, aren't we, Beetle?'

"At this, Bedell Smith says, 'All the way to Berlin, Ike.'

"And Ike says, 'And when we get to Berlin, we're going to lick Hitler's ass, and I'll be first in line.'

"It was as if someone had gone through the room and hit every Englishman a hard blow on the head with a blackjack. They looked like fish that are slapped against the deck. And then Admiral Sir Bertram Ramsay says, 'I take it, Ike, that we are not speaking literally.' Ike, who thinks Ramsay is referring to the individual combat implication about what Ike has said about Hitler, says, 'Maybe not, but if I had the chance, I'd take it, and I don't think I'd be disappointed at the outcome.'"

"That must have been some meeting," Harry said.

"It was," the colonel continued. "It was. And what it comes down to is that you are going to be facing the Seventeenth SS Panzergrenadier Division Götz von Berlichingen, 'Lick my ass.'"

"All seven of us?" asked Rice, a trooper from Ohio, a lawyer. "Is that fair to them?"

"We want to slow them down on their way north to meet us, and there's little we can do to accomplish that, given that the focus is on the beachhead. We're hoping to confuse and delay, sever communications, give the impression that we have an airborne force in their vicinity. At the very least, we make them unsure, cut the telephone lines, blow some bridges, and derail a few trains."

"Don't the Maquis and the OSS do that?" Harry asked.

"We've been unable to coordinate sufficiently with the Maquis. Stupid, I know. Coalition politics. Anyway, that's not the point. We want the Germans to see our airborne there, to report the uniform, to see the patch."

"If they can see the patch, sir," another pathfinder said, "shortly they'll be dead, or we will."

The colonel made no response, until finally he had to. "People will see, civilians. The Germans have binoculars. Maybe you'll release a prisoner or two, so they can report. And I'll tell you the truth and level with you. If you should get killed, you'll be of use even then."

"Please forgive us if we're not enthusiastic about that," Rice said.

"I would hope you're not."

"Sir," Harry put in, "they'll come after the seven of us with God knows what as soon as they get a fix, and that'll be that."

"No, they won't."

"Why?"

"This is not an infantry operation, it's a diversion and a feint. You'll be dropped five miles apart. Each of you will work independently. They'll be looking for a formation, but you'll be one apiece. After you strike, run. Go into a forest if you can find one. Hide under a log. The breaks between the fields are impenetrable thickets. Burrow in there and you'll be invisible for as long as you want."

"What's the good news, sir?" another trooper wanted to know.

"You don't have to take your Eurekas or anything like that. You don't have to pinpoint any particular spot. You don't have to hang around and get killed once you hit the ground. You can move. What you'll take in place of guidance and marking equipment will be extra ammunition, provisions, and explosives. If you get the opportunity, do something spectacular."

"Something spectacular."

"It's up to you. Although I spend most of my time in meetings and writing orders, I myself have always wanted to blow up an ammunition train, or at least a truck. You'll find something. We chose you because you can work alone and you like to work alone. That's unusual. And you're not the only ones."

"Who else?"

"Not for you to know."

"It's not like there's a whole regiment that's...."

"I can't say," the colonel said, cutting off the discussion. "Tomorrow you'll be briefed; you'll get maps and passwords. You can draw or exchange whatever weapons and equipment you want. When you've finished your assignments, or as you work them, make your ways north. Eventually, we'll meet you."

"Colonel," Harry said. "As pathfinders, we do work independently. Once our regiment is down, though, we form up together to fight. The seven of us are mutually supportive and we've been together since the beginning. We're very effective if we can work that way."

"Not this time, Captain. I wish you luck."

· · ·

Harry had anticipated the day when, as in North Africa, the division would assemble in its thousands, each man determined and trained, and with little talk line up to board planes waiting in the fading light. To soar over deserts and seas and then, the quality of landing undetermined, to fall, at first with great speed and then slowly and in silence into the flares of war — such things were without parallel in electrifying the senses.

One remembered everything in impressed detail: the smell of webbing and gun oil, the rattling of airframes, the burning line of orange as the sun set, and the sharp awakening, though not from sleep, when it was time to jump. Late in the evening of the fourth of June, Harry's stick boarded the first of the C-47s at the front of the queue, the propellers whirring and impatient to get the planes back to the night air over France, where in the attention paid to them by anti-aircraft guns they would almost come alive.

The seven paratroopers boarded quietly. Rice, the lawyer from Ohio, had a big face, a mustache, unbreakable strength, and an illuminating smile. Bayer, a who-knows-what from the Lower East Side, was six-four, fearless, and so quick of wit that tritely but truly he often had discovered a solution before anyone knew of a problem. Johnson, a stocky and sardonic English teacher who took all in stride, was totally reliable, and had read and seemingly committed to memory every book in Wisconsin. Hemphill, a Virginian who looked just like General Gavin and because of Gavin's unassuming dress and manner was often mistaken for him, had a certain sharpness and readiness of feature that said, accurately, that he was an uncanny shot. Reeves, a farmer from Colorado, was a big blond boy, forever good and forever young. And Sussingham, a steelworker from Gary, Indiana, was one of those people who seems to have taken on some of the attributes of his profession: he was unflappable, cool, terribly strong, and senselessly brave. They all were ever enduring and resourceful. Each one accepted his lot, not one assuming that he would come out alive.

The door of the plane was closed with a bang and sealed shut. All the delicate threads that tied them to home had now to be severed, as were their ties to the division and everything that had come before.

Alone in the dark, with only a dim red light showing the outline of the others, they had to say goodbye to all they had known.

With a thousand planes behind it, the C-47 faced an empty runway and the wind. It was an honor to be first. The engines were brought up and the plane began to roll. In France it was early summer, and if they were to die that day it would not have to be in the cold. Rising to full rpm, the propellers were deafening and reassuring. For anyone in the belly of the plane, the faster it went the better it was. Finally, hurtling forward was insufficient for it, and as it reached its full potential on the ground it lifted, dipping one wing and then another because it was not yet steady in the stream of air. Faster and faster it went, until it rose vigorously enough to press them down in their seats. They were the only ones it carried, and the lightness of the load had freed it for an unusually powerful rise.

As they came to the coast, the jumpmaster opened the door both to make sure that it hadn't jammed during takeoff and to let in some summer air. Harry leaned over and looked out. The open channels of a marsh gleamed in gold and red intarsia, and the sea beyond was a gem-like blue fading to black. As an A-20 returning from France passed below them, its huge engines easily pulling it home, the last rays of sun glinted off its upper surfaces but left the rest in shadow. Its twinned machine guns atop the center of the fuselage were relaxed to the left as the flight made it safely to base. What this plane had been doing in France Harry did not know, but it had been there, it had come back with the sunset, and in an instant it had passed. Then the jumpmaster shut the door upon the world below.

It was a long ride south-southwest until they dropped due west of the Channel Islands and made a ninety-degree turn east to enter France, so low above the breaking waves that German pickets watching by the sea would have been hit by the wash of the propellers. Then they rose in a steep climb, adjusting course toward the drop zones. Once over Coutances, they began to trace a gentle arc that would curve slightly north to St. Lô and end just beyond the river Vire. The distance was only about thirty miles.

They had hooked up as soon as they gained altitude. They knew what to do, although not how they would do it, and, paradoxically, they knew how to do what they had to do, but not exactly what it was. They would be forty miles south of the invasion beaches and perhaps weeks away from a linkup with their own forces, but they were free, and each man was now his own general.

Soon after the door was opened, the light flashed. First out was Rice, without a word, gone and on his own. Next, Bayer, with a joke that no one heard. Then Johnson, who calmly looked back as if for the last time and disappeared, his static line flapping against the plane. Harry, who would take the middle position, closest to the most direct route north, stepped to the door, outside of which was a black whirlwind. Ex nihilo, he thought, which comforted him. Even though he was heavily weighted with weapons and equipment, the rush of air made him feel light. The light flashed, the jumpmaster signaled, and Harry left not only the plane but, for a moment, everything he had been heretofore. He fell very fast, not just as one falls after stepping wrongly on the stairs, or off a roof, but hundreds of feet into an abyss. All was darkness, speed, and wind as he was washed clean, emptied out, and reset. Then his chute opened, unfurling slowly at first but finally holding him, swinging him to left and right — just as the plane's wings had rocked at takeoff before it found the fullness of the air — and opening into a cloud, a petticoat ballooning above him, visible in the dark as a faint, slightly bluish glow.

The plane gone, he drifted down in silence without sight of the ground. He released his leg bags. Now hanging below him, they made the descent more difficult as they became a pendulum to Harry, who was already a pendulum to the chute. At least the sudden absence of their pull would tell him when to brace. He hoped that upon landing he would clear walls, trees, and other obstacles, and break neither his legs nor his back.

The gentlest cross between a whistle and a hum, an insistent breeze through the silks made the familiar sound of tracking steadily to the ground. Alone in the sky, Harry surveyed the world as winds aloft moved the clouds across a lustrous moon that lit the landscape in silver. On the eastern horizon toward Paris, the sky was filled almost warmly with beckoning stars.

Then he sensed the ground quickly rising as the stars themselves appeared to shoot upward and the world below grow uneven. The tension of the leg-bag lines disappeared as the bags came to rest and tilted over. He braced, hit, relaxed, and rolled. He was in France. He had landed perilously close to a stone wall and tumbled over an exposed flat rock that he struck in such a way as to have pulled a muscle or tendon in his neck.

Fired by adrenaline, he raced through the things he had to do. With light wind and no need to control his chute, he readied the carbine to fire. Parachute lines trailing from him like a spider web, he stood, listened, and slowly turned. His eyes were used to the moonlit darkness, which seemed almost like daylight, and he saw nothing but the outline of trees, stone walls, and a small building in the next field. It was too late for frogs and crickets, and too early for engines, talk, footfalls, music, or the metallic sounds made by soldiers as they move — their equipment striking rocks and branches; rifles vaguely clinking; buckles and water bottles, willed to be quiet, rebelling. Not even any lowing or mooing. Nothing.

He took off his parachute harness and other attachments, gathered the cloth, unfolded his shovel, and began to dig, not daring to breathe hard, touching the tip of the spade to the earth each time before pushing it in, so as not to make the sharp sound of steel against stone. Every few shovelfuls, he would stop to listen. The soil was rich and not hard to pierce or lift. Seemingly without effort — though now he would not have felt strain had he been making a hole five times as deep — he finished after a few minutes, gathered the moon-white silk, and buried it, being careful to replace sod and turf so that at a glance it would seem undisturbed. Having buried the leg bags too, he distributed the contents into his pack and pouches and onto his straps and belts. His immediate undertaking was to find cover, the next to rid himself of excess weight. If possible, he would use the bazooka and its two rockets as soon as he could, which would subtract twenty-one pounds and, because the launcher was broken down into two sections, four awkward weights to carry. Once the rockets were fired he would be free to fight as he did best, light and from cover, with precise shots. But he would not, as the pilots said, drop his ordnance over water so as to get to this: putting the rockets on target would save lives.

By the radium hands and blazes on his watch face it was four in the morning. Somewhere west and south of St. Lô, he moved off toward the silhouette of the building beyond the stone wall he had missed on landing. It was not likely that there would be Germans anywhere about, or anyone at all, but soon the farmers would arise.

The building was an old, well kept, windowless barn with a double door. He waited, listening, and then went in. He might have used a flashlight, but he had chosen not to carry one, for without its weight and that of extra batteries he could carry almost fifty additional .30-caliber rounds. The carbine was the thing, the anchor of his world.

He took a stubby candle from his pocket, held it low to the ground, lit it, and, shielding it with his body, stepped inside, closing the door behind him. The only thing there was hay. He cleared a space on the floor, put the candle down, and as quickly as he could, because even the faintest flash of light might pass the cracks in the boards and give him away, took stock and rearranged. In his pack or strapped to it were rations for ten days, a ground sheet, a light woolen blanket the size of a throw, four hundred rounds of ammunition, a folding shovel, and two rockets that protruded on each side like horns. In his pouches and pockets were four thirty-round magazines, two grenades, two half-pound blocks of plastique, toilet articles, pressure bandages, candles, matches, sulfa powder, morphine, two signal flares, a mirror, a clicker, maps, and a monocular. On his belt were a canteen, a wire cutter, and a bayonet; hanging from him on their shoulder straps were the two parts of the bazooka. In his hands was the carbine, loaded with a magazine. And on his head was the helmet he detested for its horrible weight, heat, and the way it threw off every move and restricted both sight and sound, but was better than a bullet in the brain.

He could not know until morning even approximately where he was; he was not at all hungry or thirsty; he had landed safely and undetected; and although his heart had been pounding, it was now settled down. He blew out the candle, put it in his pocket, and backed into the hay, partly hidden from the door. Placing the pack and the bazooka to his right, he took out the blanket and threw it about his shoulders, loosened his collar, removed the helmet, and, the carbine in his hands, leaned back. All was quiet. His neck, he now realized, hurt rather badly. But that was nothing. He listened. Then he took the chance a lone soldier must always take, and slept.

Awakening a little after the light, he went to the walls of the barn and peered out the cracks on all four sides. He could see the spire of a church fairly close to the south. To east and west lay fields crisscrossed by stone walls, and to the north were palisades of evergreens. He had breakfast, brushed his teeth, took a drink of water, and buried the ration containers, all in about a minute. Then he shouldered his load and started toward the forest, where he intended to establish a base before determining his exact position and setting about his job.

As soon as he got close enough to the wall he had crossed the night before, he caught sight of a farmer using a long switch to drive cows down the hill. Harry started toward him and remained unobserved until he was about seventy-five feet away. The farmer started, drew in a breath, said something, and threw back his arms.

Here would come a test more frightening than engaging the enemy — speaking French correctly after many years in which it had been fallow. When he was much younger it had taken him weeks in Paris before he had felt vaguely comfortable, and here, despite the fact that he had studied, he was absolutely fresh and with other things on his mind.

"The Americans! You are American!" the farmer said, followed by four years of pent-up emotion expressed in a western French dialect and agricultural idiom that Harry would not have been able to translate even with a dictionary, and to which Harry answered only "Yes, yes," and, to his surprise, because it sounded like something straight from the music hall, "Here we are again."

"Thank God!" the farmer exclaimed, stepping back and again

holding out his arms. He had a mustache, a cap, and was old enough to be Harry's father. "Let me bring you some cheese! Some bread!" There he stopped, and looked about. "Where are the others?"

"Just me," said Harry, and then, seeing a look almost of terror on the man's face, adding, "in this sector. The others," he told him, "are in the north."

"How many?" The farmer was horrified at the prospect of invasion one soldier at a time.

"I don't know exactly," Harry said, carefully formulating his French and, he thought, doing rather well in regard to accent, "but a few hundred thousand in the first cut," he assured him, using the French idiom, "and, soon thereafter, two or three million."

"Two or three *million?*" the farmer asked, his eyes, above reddened cheeks, like moons seen from the soil of Mars.

"Yes," Harry answered proudly, "million."

Not knowing how to react to such greatness of scale, the farmer returned to what he knew. "Let me get you some bread, some cheese."

"I don't have time," said Harry. "I need information. I have questions."

"My house is right over there. It's safer. Sometimes the Germans pass by on their motorcycles, but they can't see the house from the road."

"What kind of cheese? I can't carry a soft cheese." Harry marveled at this turn. It was as if he were in a grocery store on Lexington Avenue.

"No, very hard, like Gruyère."

"Okay."

The farmer's wife was much less emotional, or at least she did not show it, channeling everything she might have felt into the intense provision of a breakfast that Harry ate, marking it down as lunch in advance. He spread his map on the table and then availed himself of intelligence to perfection, for the farmer had lived in this house all his life and knew everything about anything within three days' walk.

The night before, Harry had not imagined that he would be filling himself with an *omelette aux fines herbes*, bacon, bread, and butter. They pressed upon him two loaves and a kilo of cheese, which he stowed in his pack, the breads symmetrically next to the rockets, which they resembled. Then they got down to business.

Beautiful and detailed, the pre-war map was printed in red, yellow, blue, and green, and was unlike a military map except that now marked clearly, and as a result of reports from the resistance and the latest photo reconnaissance prior to June 4, were German echelons, their numbers, equipment, and the dates when last observed. War was overlaid upon peace in a rough and smudgy black. Like someone who knew he was a part of something great, even if only a small part, the farmer looked at the map as though looking into the face of Joan of Arc. This portrait of France now before him in the hands of a soldier who was about to fight for it, he found so exciting as to make him euphoric. He moved his index finger happily south and west of St. Lô, descending as if by magic to the exact spot where they were.

"Here," he said, "Soulles. We are between the village and the Bois de Soulles."

Harry saw that he could go east to lay an ambush on the main road to St. Lô, or north and west to where the railroad crossed a river, the Terrette, on a bridge that might still be intact. "Where are the Germans?" he asked. The farmer pointed to sections far south or on the coast. "When they come through here," Harry asked, "how do they travel?"

"Just a few, on motorcycles and sometimes in trucks. We're out of the way."

"I mean when they travel en masse, with tanks and big guns."

"Not on the road. The road is too narrow and it twists. They put the tanks and guns on flatcars."

Harry pointed to the intersection of the Terrette and the rail line to St. Lô. "Do you know this bridge?"

"I know it."

"Is it intact?"

"Yes."

"What's there?"

"Two anti-aircraft guns near the road, and some soldiers who guard either end of it."

"How many?"

"Three or four, maybe ten."

"What color are their uniforms?"

"Black."

"SS? Why would the SS be guarding a bridge?"

"I don't know. Maybe it's important to them."

"Do you remember what weapons they have? Do they have machine guns in emplacements? Is there a pillbox?"

"I don't know what weapons. When we drive we can't stop or stare for too long. There is no pillbox. You can get there without going on the roads if you go straight north through the *bois*. You'll reach a river. Follow that north, which will lead you to Quibou, only about two and a half kilometers. The road west of Quibou leads north about a kilometer to the railway, and the bridge is about a kilometer west of that. You would have to go on the roads a little. Isn't that dangerous?"

"Everything is dangerous."

"The Germans," the farmer said, as if this were a new idea, "must not be allowed to win."

"We think so, too," Harry said. He thought he should elaborate, despite his unpracticed French. "France will be liberated and Germany will be defeated all the way to Berlin. We've decided upon that. We've decided that it might be the last thing a lot of us do. I'm content with it. I have my task, my life is full." He stopped, and then said, "Against all reason, I'm happy." Changing the subject, he asked, "Have you ever seen the Germans in the *bois*?"

"Never. All they do is pass on the roads now and then, just a few, on their way to somewhere else and going very fast."

"Are there collaborators here?"

"Here? No. There isn't anyone to collaborate with."

"Resistance?"

"In St. Lô."

"I like the river," Harry told him, looking at the lovely blue line on the map. "I like the river very much."

"Why?"

"Dogs can't track you, and when you're forced into it, you come out clean."

With thinning patches of morning fog still gliding across the fields, Harry put pastures and walls behind him and disappeared among the tall pines of the Bois de Soulles, stopping every few minutes to look and listen. The preservation of forests in such ancient and intensively worked landscapes was no more explicable than the existence of villages untouched by war; or women so beautiful and radiant of the spirit that perfected imperfect form as to appear like angels floating above the things of the world; or soldiers who come through every kind of fire without being hit. He never prayed for such protection, thinking it would be to presume too much. But at times he felt it, an all-embracing beauty that knit everything together, and made sense even of death.

Deep in the forest, he went in directions opposite to those in which his senses guided him, rejecting the open and easy way in favor of the blocked and the difficult. Contradicting the contours of the land and ignoring the natural paths through it, he found himself in a hidden, cathedral-like clearing in which seven pines — he counted — rose straight and high into the blue, but were surrounded by a perimeter of dense brush woven with fallen boughs almost into breastworks. Because it was so much out of the way he doubted that anyone had been there in decades. Certainly all over the world were patches of ground, even in populous areas, where no one had ever or would ever set foot, and until he had arrived this could have been one of them. Unshouldering his load, he felt the illusion of rising. Then he sat down on a floor of dry pine needles and leaned against one of the trees, the carbine cradled in his lap.

The back of his jacket, pressed against the tree, was immediately spotted with heavy imprints of resin. He didn't mind. As dirt and dust adhered to it, it would soon turn from clear to black, but would not lose its scent until perhaps the end of the war, and it was a scent he loved. He tilted his head up and stared through the branches at the sky. The rich green and blue at this moment were all he wanted from the world, and the world provided.

That night he would leave his stores in the clearing, take weapons, explosives, and provisions for three days, and establish himself near the railroad bridge to wait for a train rushing the 17th SS toward St. Lô. He knew neither when nor if such a train would pass over the bridge, or if the terrain would afford him a position in which he could wait and from which he could shoot, fight, and safely withdraw. But having come this far with all going well, he was confident that he would find a target.

There was a pacing to things, not least in war, a rhythm of stops and starts as if preordained. He had followed this path in Sicily, and now he could almost hear the commands: go, stop, go fast, go slow. When they ran together, as often they did, they seemed to coalesce into music. His sense was that in following it he could stay alive and that in departing from it he might not.

By nightfall he was so well rested and alone that he wondered if he were still in the army and at war. Then he moved off to the north, carefully noting how to get back. Soon he found the river. Although in places there was a path, following it was difficult, but when he exited the forest he was able to move more rapidly through the fields. Coming to a road, he crossed in the open rather than mucking around in the river under the bridge. The countryside was so deserted that he might have sung at the top of his voice without an audience other than cows and sheep.

At around midnight, as the river arced gently northwest it brought him to the junction of two roads just south of Quibou. There he saw what he assumed were Germans, although because they were in a speeding truck he wasn't sure. The traffic was not even desultory. Five minutes after the truck came two bicycles. These, he was fairly sure, were civilians, for when they passed he had seen no gun barrels silhouetted against the sky.

This road was a lot busier than the first, so he had to weigh darting over it versus going into the water, which would be uncomfortable and possibly fatal, in that the bazooka's rockets were electrically fused and to wet their firing mechanisms might mean both failure and death. Nor did he want to immerse either his ammunition or his grenades. He waited for five or ten minutes, during which no one passed, and decided to chance going over the road. After crawling up the bank, he stared into the distance first one way and then another. The moon had yet to rise, and he lay there, listening.

Deciding on impulse to go, he bounded up and ran across the road as fast as he could. Only halfway, and unable to check his forward momentum, not least because of all the dead weight he carried, he saw what appeared to be a complication of the darkness. The instant before he collided with this apparition, it was lit in orange as a lighter was brought to a cigarette. Though unable to modify his trajectory, he registered, in shock, two helmetless German soldiers standing astride their bicycles, about to share a light. They had pistols but not rifles, and their heads were close to the flame as they focused upon lighting up.

They were less aware of Harry than he was of them, and, because of their proximity to the flame, blinded. Harry had no time even to think "Oh no," much less to say anything or alter his course. So, before he hit, he gave an extra push. Then he made contact, like a crashing locomotive.

He knocked the wind out of both of them and sent them flying at least five feet before they fell to the ground in a clatter of bicycles, one of which sounded its bell as it scraped along the pavement. They could not have had the faintest idea of what had hit them, and before they began to get up Harry was three hundred feet away, heart pounding, running under his combat load across a rocky field in the dark. The dumbfounded Germans didn't know from which direction it had come, much less where it went or what it was.

He might easily have turned and shot them. But it was too early for that. The invasion fleets were unloading. The airborne divisions were deep in their assaults. Let the two bicyclists have their peace for half a day more, and let them wonder what it was that came out of the dark and struck them like an enraged bull. They would be puzzled for the rest of their perhaps short lives, and, meanwhile, he was still on track to blow up their train.

It was necessary to approach the bridge slowly lest he stumble onto a guard or a patrol walking the railbed. To cover not much more than a kilometer took him almost two hours as he zigzagged, paused to listen, and made occasional swings north, away from the railway and the road that paralleled it. Although the shortest route between one thing and another is a straight line, between an attacker and his objective it is hardly ever the best. The virtue of meandering is that it lessens the chance that an enemy will observe you, and increases the chance that you will observe him. Harry broke his time and pace so as not to fall into a pattern, and he avoided places where, although not seeing it, he felt nonetheless the potential presence of the enemy. It was as if he had senses that he could neither explain nor name, but he trusted them to lead him. Well before dawn, he reached a spot that gave him a clear view of the railroad bridge. There were no lights, but moonlight now showed it, the road beyond, and a guardhouse at either end.

Just north of the river, the ground rose to the west. This would offer the best firing position and a means of escape if he could hide in the brush until a train approached from the west, fire the two rockets, follow with a fusillade from his carbine, light the long-fused plastique, run north along the river, and then recross it to the southeast to head back to the forest. Expecting the descent of paratroopers north and west of St. Lô, the Germans, were they able to pursue, would probably stay west of the river, as they knew that heavily laden airborne troops did not make a habit of swimming.

So Harry ran a half mile up the Terrette until he came to a rocky area that wouldn't show footprints on the bank, and there left everything but the bazooka, the two rockets, two blocks of plastique, his carbine, and four magazines of ammunition. He ferried over in four trips, and then went south toward the bridge. Though not exhausted, he was beginning to tire. As he was trying to settle on a location that would be the best compromise of cover and a good firing point, he felt the oncoming dawn. In summer, the temperature begins to change before the light. Currents of air move differently. Some animals alter the pitch of their cries, and some stop altogether. The sky is transformed in such a way that before one is able to discern the difference one is aware of it nonetheless. The coming of dawn, a knowledge that somewhere in the east the sun was hot and somewhere it was noon, that perhaps in India it was raining and people were already tired from their morning's work, gave him a sense of urgency. It was hard to find the right place, but he chose a clump of saplings not substantial enough to block the light, so that grass had grown high between them.

He could hide there, and the bar pattern of the saplings would break the sight of any movement he might make either by necessity or inadvertently. From afar and close on, trees and brush efficiently conceal something or someone one is not primed to see, as the eye registers the expected break in consistency and then moves on. Sentries are warned of this, but they forget.

Covering himself with grass, Harry then placed the assembled and loaded bazooka to his right. On either side, the plastique was long-fused for a minute and a half, the two fuses, meeting in front of him, twisted together so they could be lit simultaneously. The loaded carbine was on his left with two magazines next to it, the one remaining magazine in a left-hand pocket. Other pockets were unbuttoned, ready to receive the three other magazines when they were empty. As he waited for full light he made some decisions. The first was that for as long as he could hold out he would neither eat nor drink the little he had. Eating was not merely eating. Were he to lie hidden for hours or days, it was also entertainment and a reward. The second was that after his fusillade he would take the time to put the three empty magazines in his pockets and button them rather than trying to do this on the run. He was certain that he could make better time that way. The third was that, if he could, he would stand for a moment in the open, so the enemy could see his uniform. He hoped anyway that the abandoned bazooka and rations containers would give the Germans cause to believe that airborne troops were active in the sector.

The sun climbed, and when it was white above the trees it hit him blindingly, which meant that he had to stay still and, while thusly illuminated, could not use his monocular to examine the target. The minute flash of a watch crystal, wedding ring, glasses, or polished button or buckle had probably, in the twentieth century alone, led to the deaths of hundreds of thousands of young fathers, sons, husbands, and brothers.

It was almost as uncomfortable as a staring contest, and soon grew far worse. Harry had always enjoyed the occasional skillful use of foul language, which was like a hot pepper in a dish of rice. In the right circumstances and the right hands, it could be powerful and, at times, poetic. Often the use of other words instead would have been, in fact, obscene, but the thoughtless overuse of obscenities common in the army was annoying and painful because of its persistent insufficiency of expression. In his view, people whose every other word was *fuck* were like dogs that will eat themselves to death. As a consequence, he swore less in the army than he had at home, so as not to add to the ever-swelling symphony of curses. But now, blinded by the sun, beginning to sweat, unable to move a muscle lest something flash or someone see, and looking to perhaps another bout of this the next day, he said "Shit!" And he said it out loud, but so that even he could barely hear it.

For hours and hours he listened for a train to the west, knowing that its approach would sharpen everything. Were that explained simply by adrenaline, one might attribute to adrenaline the power of opening another dimension in life, in which the color of color, the sound of sound, and the depth of field were so intensified as to impart to time a limitless velocity while simultaneously rendering it completely still. For very long, he hardly moved at all, and dreamt of the moment when the sun would move high and southwest enough so that with the monocular he could take in the details of the target.

Without the monocular, he could see soldiers at their mundane tasks, milling on the west side of the bridge, sometimes walking over it to the east side. They seemed overfamiliar with their surroundings. This he could tell, for example, from their gait as they crossed the bridge. They took the ties, which have never on any continent been spaced to fit the stride of a human being, so smoothly as to suggest perfect adaptation. One soldier, filling a bucket at the end of a rope by tossing it into the river below, did it so skillfully Harry guessed that he might have been guarding this bridge since the summer of 1940. After so long a time in which nothing had happened, and as yet uninformed of the Allied tidal wave approaching, they were such an open and easy target that he could hardly believe it.

When the sun was nearly overhead, with the angle of incidence such that only pilots could be struck by the angle of reflection, Harry lifted himself on his elbows so that air could flow beneath him. It cooled him with evaporation—for his front, which had been pressed on the mat of grass, was soaking wet. He stretched carefully. He unbuckled his chin strap and lifted his helmet so that the air could cool his head. This small pleasure was here as satisfying as any of the major sensations constantly sought in civilian life. He thought that the feeling of his forehead cooling as the wet hair that had fallen from the rim of the helmet dried in the slight breeze would be better than a night with Cleopatra.

Through the monocular, he saw that the soldiers whom he was going to kill looked much like the soldiers he himself knew and commanded, and like himself. The heat and a rarity of officers had made them careless of their uniforms. They looked depressed and lonely, and had the air of those who cannot know what will be required of them next. New roses had begun to open on a bush lodged improbably at the juncture of the riverbank and the eastern abutment of the bridge. Though the guard force could not see them, Harry could. Close up and clear in the glass of the monocular, they waved in the air flowing beneath the bridge. He counted them: twenty, perfect for a florist. Late in the morning, smoke had begun to come from a pipe projecting from a small cookhouse. When the wind carried it to

Harry, he knew that they would have no meat for lunch. One of the soldiers was doing laundry. At each end of the bridge two helmeted men were on duty, with submachine guns slung from their shoulders. Not once did a sentry look toward Harry or upriver. They sometimes stared east or west along the track, but most of the time they looked down, they kicked gravel, they stopped to talk to one another or soldiers off duty. Probably at some fixed time there would be a patrol, but Harry saw that no path was worn anywhere near where he was: they would stick to the roads, the fastest and easiest way to cover ground in fulfilling their eventless obligations.

Lunch came and went, shifts changed, laughter rang out a few times, an argument, the sun cut a trail deep into afternoon, and still there was no train. The night before, Harry had judged that a long drink of water would see him through the next day, especially if he were motionless and in cover, but he had been so wrong that now he considered crawling down to the river to drink. He didn't, but he thought of water continuously, except when, because of the heat, he was only half conscious. Then, with extraordinary fidelity, dreams carried him elsewhere.

Another June, Cambridge, on the day of his graduation. His father was there, in an old-fashioned suit which that day was by no means the only one of its kind. In a portion of the Yard that now, after three hundred years, was pompously called the Tercentenary Theater, bow ties floated like butterflies, and morning wind made young leaves in the trees seem to applaud more vigorously than the self-conscious crowd. After the ceremony, of which Harry was almost completely oblivious, they sat for a while in the Yard as it emptied, and then his father gave him instructions that he did not hear, and left to catch a train back to New York. Harry was going to stay the two weeks until his lease expired, during which he would live quietly, pack up his things, and think of what he would do next. With his diploma in hand and his robe open to the breeze, he remained as the thunderous bustle came to an end and groups broke up and disappeared like ice melting in a stream, until he himself was the very last straggler. Except for a dog or two, usually a Labrador crossing the Yard as if on an official mission, everyone was gone. All afternoon the sun tracked across stone and brick, and only the birds were busy. In the near silence, Harry heard things slight and far away: the hum of traffic on Mass. Ave., the barely registered passage of an occasional breeze, air whistling past the wings of swooping birds — a delicate sound that stops at the instant the bird touches ground, and gives way to a throbbing vibration so minor it probably is that of the bird's beating heart. This long-ago summer was as prepossessing as storm. Nothing in his four years of study had prepared him for the stillness of the Yard when the business of the world had moved someplace else and only the shell of what once had been remained, echoing with an ocean sound, saturated with the beauties that present themselves only to solitude. He had remained there, hardly moving, his black robe pulling-in the sun, because of a presence that had filled the place and from which he could not tear himself away. At first he had thought about plans and problems, things to do and things undone, but in the end, after something had descended through the trees as invisibly as a current of cool air, after the birds had been pressed out of the branches by its passing and hopped about on the ground as if puzzled, he had no thought at all, just an awareness as taut as the string of the heaviest bow. That was when he finally understood, in language that could not be uttered, that those who are alone are never alone. And having been brought to this in such a way, with force both absolute and gentle, he was as confident of it as were the many physicists, in their laboratories nearby, of the elegant laws of nature they had so recently divined.

Listening for trains as if it were his profession, he found himself in a combat of endurance with the sun, until in late afternoon the shadows of the hill relieved him of this struggle so he could assume another. A train was in the west. It had chanced Allied strafing and was headed to St. Lô, its flatcars loaded with some of the tanks and assault guns of the 17th SS Panzergrenadier Division Götz von Berlichingen. Without knowing why, Harry stirred, having heard it before he knew he had heard it. And then he did hear it, and before he was sure of what it was, his heart began to pound anyway. As it got closer and louder, he could feel the rumble, and then he heard the sharp exhalations of steam from the pistons as, with their angry, stuttered rhythms, they seemed to curse the countryside.

He looked left, right, and behind. He checked his weapons. Though in the heat-filled hours he had mentally rehearsed many times what he was going to do, he began to tremble slightly with fear. It was the kind of fear, however, that never fails to be transformed into a heavy calm. And he understood that the next few minutes might be his last. At some point, uncontrolled by either will or the prospects of success, something apart from oneself takes over, working alongside and flooding the body with grace, or perhaps failing to do so entirely.

Fear turned to light and heat when Harry saw even puffs of steam scoring a cloud-white line against the sky above the sheds and hedges west of the bridge. Like the charge of a whole brigade, the oncoming train transformed everything into action. He sighted the carbine on one of the two sentries standing on the east side of the bridge. They had moved off the track and were looking into the headlight of the oncoming locomotive as it rounded a slight bend. Harry shot one, and then the other not a second later. Both crumpled forward onto the rails nearest them. The first remained motionless, and would be hit by the train; the other rolled back and fell into the river, where he would drown. By that time, Harry had shot the two on the west abutment, who, deafened by the train, had heard only muted reports or perhaps nothing at all. For the same reason, no one in the guardhouses rushed out.

As the first of tandem locomotives began to cross the bridge, Harry shouldered the bazooka, aimed at the boiler, and, following it in a smooth leftward traverse, pulled the trigger. Though he was close, he was still far enough away so that he had had to elevate for distance when he shot the sentries, but with a rocket no such reckoning was required: it was a point-blank weapon with no ballistic trajectory. It closed upon its unknowing target, passed through the bridge frame, and struck, its detonation followed by the great concussion of a pressurized boiler blowing with explosive assist.

Harry had already reloaded. Bringing up the bazooka, he watched what was left of the lead locomotive turn sideways and tip onto the track, squealing miserably as it ripped against the rails. The second then derailed and went into the river, taking with it three flatcars on which were two StuG IVs and a French tank that had been defaced with an iron cross. There was a terrible noise as the rest of the train derailed, tumbling its heavy vehicles upside down. Soldiers rushed forward, cocking their weapons, shouting, not knowing where to fire. Some looked up, thinking they had been attacked from the air.

Aiming at a boxcar leaning halfway over the water, Harry launched the second rocket. The soldiers running onto the bridge saw it coming and turned back, only to collide with newly dismounted guards from the rear of the train, but it was too late for all of them. The rocket went through the wood walls of the boxcar with a thump like that of an arrow in a straw target, and then it blew. Even Harry was thrown back. He had hit an ammunition carriage, which took down the bridge, all the buildings, and several flatcars behind it loaded with StuG IVs.

The explosion was so powerful that Harry was deafened and stunned. Nauseated and shaken, he picked up the carbine and waited for others to appear. None did. So he stood up. As his ears slowly cleared, he saw that what he had wrought was far beyond his expectations — although nothing more than what might have come from the single pass of a fighter plane. As he stared at the ruins he had made, some Germans who were doing the same walked into view as if from stage right. He saw them first, and could have dropped down, but he remembered what he was supposed to accomplish. He lifted the carbine and took aim, but waited until they would look in his direction. What seemed like a long time passed, but when they did, they saw him clearly enough in the instant before he started shooting to know that they were now fighting Americans. He hit at least two of them, and then both parties took cover and, to little avail, began firing. For Harry it was a question of emptying his magazines fast enough so they would think they faced at least a squad. He shot left and right, at the remains of the locomotive to make a series of pings from the east, at the one window left in a shack on the hillside, so as to smash it dramatically, and in a line across the entire front, as if the fire were coming from different angles. With half a magazine left, he stopped. His hands steady, he lit the twisted fuses. Then he put the two empty magazines in his right pocket, fired fifteen more rounds very quickly, reloaded with the full magazine, pocketed the empty third, buttoned the pockets, pushed himself backward down the slope, turned, and ran. In boots, steel helmet, and a heavy tunic, carrying a loaded carbine and three empty magazines, he ran faster than he had ever run in his life. The more speed he developed, the more he sought. Halfway to the bend where he would cross back, he heard the first explosion of plastique, but did not turn around. Then he heard another sound, another thump like an arrow, and he tumbled down and forward, having been pushed there by a bullet striking just above his left shoulder blade.

He gasped as he tumbled, still gripping the carbine with his right hand while the left seemed no longer to exist. When the second explosion came, he turned as best he could to fight, but saw no one. Surprised to see that the fields were empty, he resumed his flight, with pain at each step and blood running warmly down his front. Struggling for breath, he slowed to a walk, and while still walking removed a pressure bandage from a pocket, opened it, kept the wrapping balled up in his right hand for fear of leaving a trace, and, carbine slung against his back, applied the bandage as best he could. In a minute or two he reached the place where he had ferried the river, and threw himself violently into the water both from urgency and because he had lost his balance. He sank all the way and swallowed some of the muddy Terrette, but then began to swim with his right arm and kicks. He tried not to choke on the water that was choking him, to keep the carbine, to retain the bandage, to get to the other side. He thought that when he would reach the east bank his pursuers would take careful aim and he would die. But with no time to look back he fought through foam and bubbles, swallowing river water mixed with his own blood.

When he got to shore he pulled himself up on a flat rock and turned to see what was behind him. Nothing but the slight chime of the river. He half dragged himself, half scrambled on his knees to the thicket in which he had hidden the rest of his things, and there burrowed into the vegetation as deeply as he could. He tried to catch his breath. Using his good hand, he wrung out the bandage and began alternating applications to the entry and exit wounds.

Then, allowing the wound to bleed, he readied the carbine and peered through branches and young grass at the opposite bank. Six soldiers were coming up from the south, cautiously in fear of an ambush. They may have felt outnumbered. Though occasionally they would glance across the river, the ground there seemed empty, and they were focused north, where the invasion was in progress and where the train they had lucklessly been escorting had been rushing. Harry watched as they came level with him, and prepared to fight as best he could. But they moved on. Perhaps they didn't want to find him.

Before dark, he went east two hedgerows, south a field or two, and concealed himself in a thicket that long before had smothered a stone wall. Until it was pitch black, he stayed here and concentrated upon stopping the flow of blood, which he did after having torn the bandage in his teeth and applied half to the entrance and half to the exit wounds. At first the gauze was as soaked with blood as it had been in the river, but then the open air took away enough moisture from the surface to harden it, and the clotting worked its way down. He sat upright so as not to increase blood flow at his shoulder. Every minute that passed without bleeding was a victory. Rather than elation, what he experienced was both deeper and quieter.

It took most of the night to move six or seven kilometers. The roads were far more alive than they had been, with military convoys' red blackout lights strung like coals sometimes for half a mile. He neither saw nor heard any patrols, and what he feared most, tracking dogs, did not appear. Nor did their distant barks that, when heard by their quarry, would cause the unconscious and unavoidable production of a scent that for them made pursuit both easier and more exciting.

Though afraid to follow the river directly back to his hiding place in the Bois de Soulles, he was too weak not to. When he arrived, an hour before dawn, he threw down the pack and the carbine, sank to his knees, ate and drank methodically and for strength, wrapped the blanket around his upper body, lowered himself onto his right side, and slept. Were they to find him they would find him asleep, but sleep would be worth the trade. In the minute before he found his rest, the whole world spun before his eyes: trains moving, metal flying in slow motion, sounds deafening, men falling, water rising in white, saplings slapping him in the face, darkness, concussions, running, rocket trails, smoke.

Splayed out, hardly able to move, throbbing with pain and sweating with fever even in the morning, he awakened not with soldierly caution before dawn but carelessly late and facing a white-hot sun. It seemed strange not to be able to turn his head or rise, to be dizzy and weak and as vulnerable as a baby. As he lay there undiscovered, he was of a delirious two minds. One was almost pridefully appreciative of the hiding place that shielded him from the Wehrmacht and the SS. The other was aware of the soldiers missing in action as the armies passed on to further objectives. So many little clearings, tangles of brush, ditches, trenches, and canals were the quiet resting places of bodies that would never be buried, their graves as painfully open as the hearts of those who grieved until they would follow.

After half an hour of effort, he managed to roll fully onto his back. Some time later, breathing hard, he was able to turn his head and look at the exit wound. It was difficult to see exactly what was going on because blood, gauze, flesh, cloth, and dirt were combined in an unintelligible mass that was so hot he could feel it on the left side of his face. "God," he said to himself, dismayed that infection could gallop so fast.

He could neither move, nor defend himself, nor hope to be found. Were the Germans to find him, they would kill him. Were the farmer to find and shelter him, they would kill the farmer as well. There was little danger that anyone would happen upon him where he was, unless like the Germans they had dogs, and he wondered how long he could last, and, if he could last, how he would be able to make his way out. Very much unlike him, he thought he couldn't. Shock, exhaustion, and the pathogens liberally applied to his wound at the riverside as he crawled over open soil combined to make him less than optimistic. Because he had been deathly ill not a few times in childhood, he knew how sickness smoothes the way. It wasn't just a question of weakening the will, but of opening to the sick a vision of things they cannot see when life runs strongly — of rhythms, signs, signals, lights, and mercies that one can apprehend only as one falls.

Though it seemed to make no sense given what he knew of his injury, he was so intensely stricken that he would fall asleep and awaken without knowing how much time had passed, and then stay awake for how much time he could not tell. But somewhere in the in-and-out he reasoned with himself, inquiring if in fact he had another wound. To investigate, first he moved his legs, which seemed all right, and then he inspected his arms, which were all right, too. He unbuttoned his tunic and felt under his shirt. His chest was unbroken. These movements made him slightly more supple and freed him to prospect over a wider range. Doing so, he managed to get his right hand around his back, where he immediately felt a hole in the cloth. Following this with his finger, he discovered that it was only the preface to a small hole in his lower back that, though it seemed not to bleed, was still open. This, then, was why he was so sick. One bullet had passed through him, but another remained within.

Although he couldn't tell where it had lodged and what processes it had interrupted, he believed that it might kill him — which in those momentous years and that momentous week would have been no great distinction. It was so easy for the power of life simply to drain away. With the opening of an interior channel that must remain closed, or the closing of one that must remain open, strength once admirable and extraordinary would become weakness. And in a man, although his strength would never grow beyond a very small capacity — he would never lift a hill, run thirty miles in an hour, or swim the ocean — it was certain that one day his weakness would become infinite. All the soldiers Harry had seen stopped dead by a bullet or shell were instantly thrown back to the eternity whence they had come, and were just gone. This was the essential condition, the truth of the world, all life only a short liberty away from it.

As he couldn't move from where he was, couldn't treat himself, and couldn't know the full facts of his condition, and as night approached and he wanted rest, he did what he had hoped never to do. Not so much to alleviate the pain but rather to take himself away from the fight, he took out the box with the morphine, uncapped the syringe, and plunged it into his thigh as once he had been instructed. Even before it took effect, everything changed. He had willfully and at great risk removed himself from the battle. This was because he knew that were strength to flood back it would be only if every door were opened wide, every chance embraced, and his every trust made absolute. As the morphia began to stream through his system and carry him away, he looked at his hands, and when they seemed to become bodiless before the rest of him and to rise without weight, he knew he was almost gone.

Death leads either to the absence of light or to its omnipresence. One summer night in France, Harry Copeland lay in the brush, dying of a wound he could not see. For a few hours, the morphia had cleared away the frictions and regrets of existence, relaxing him to whatever might come, closing his accounts, dotting every *i*, crossing every *t*, winding every clock, locking every door, packing every case, and forgiving every sin. The only regret that stayed and that morphia could not erase was that he had yet to love or be loved as he had always hoped. All the majestical lights, airy and bright, the floating orbs, the effulgent stars, were lonely things and would not suffice. And here it was, deep in a luminous, moonlit forest, that he had wished for an angel, for as they lay dying all soldiers wherever they may be need an angel to carry them up.

# 35

## VIERVILLE

A MAJOR AND A lieutenant of the 82nd came to the field hospital in Vierville sometime in June. Like many paratroopers, they were strapping and tall. Their faces were as remarkably even and uneventful as those of bankers and brokers with houses in Scarsdale or on the North Shore. The major was in his late thirties, and smoked a pipe. The lieutenant was young, reserved, and from the South. Harry was too tired to try to guess the state, but nonetheless he could not help but think of Georgia, and left it at that.

Carrying chairs that, like overly cautious lion tamers, they held out before them with both hands, they walked down the center aisle between the invalids. Then they rooted the chairs next to Harry's cot and stepped close, speaking as if to a foreigner.

"Why are you talking to me that way?" he asked. "I'm an American. I understand English."

"Sorry," said the lieutenant. He handled apologies. "We just wanted to make sure you could hear."

"Why wouldn't I hear?"

"You're wounded."

"Not in the head."

"We've spoken," the major said, correctively but entirely without animus, "to a lot of men, many of whom were in terribly bad shape." He dipped his head forward, as if in a bow. "Can you answer a few questions?"

"Sure," Harry said, weakly. The energy that upon their arrival he thought was his had left him unexpectedly, which they could tell—

from his appearance, his breathing, and because now and then he closed his eyes as if he were asleep or wanting to be.

"You were in the church at Montmartin en Graignes?"

"I didn't know what it was called."

"During the massacre?"

"And before, and after."

"How did you get there? It wasn't your regiment."

"I know."

"Did you fight with them to hold the town?"

Harry shook his head to signify that he hadn't.

"You were wounded and already in the church? During the fight?"

"Brought there after the fight."

"From where?"

"The Bois de Soulles."

"Where is that?"

"South of St. Lô."

"How did you get *there?*"

"We were dropped to harass the Götz von Berlichingen."

"Who was dropped?" the major asked.

"My stick of pathfinders, detached from the Five Hundred and Fifth."

"So you were never with the Five Oh Seventh?"

"Not until the church. They were already there. The Germans put me with them."

"How did you get from St. Lô to Montmartin?"

"With the Germans who captured me. Look, why don't I just tell you what happened?"

"Please, go ahead."

"I can't speak too long: I'm tired."

"Whatever you can manage," the lieutenant told him.

Harry turned his head up, mainly for comfort, and saw the sun almost directly overhead through the weave of the olive-drab tent cloth. The oil that coated each thread acted as a refraction grid, plastering the patch of sun with millions of miniature spectra. He could see the sky between the threads in an uncountable number of little boxes faithfully holding the color blue. "I was dropped near Soulles. I made a refuge in the forest, went north to the railroad that leads to St. Lô, and blew up a train." He stopped to breathe for a while before resuming. "I blew up a whole train, and I killed a lot of them." He stopped again. "They looked like us. The ones who were left shot me."

"Then they captured you?"

"I ran north along the river — creek, really. I was going to cut back to throw them off. I did. But before I did, I was hit twice."

"You have three gunshot wounds," the major said, almost accusingly. In civilian life, he had been a prosecutor.

"I know I have three gunshot wounds, Major: I'm the one who has them. After the train, I was hit twice. I went back to the forest thinking I was hit only in the shoulder, but then discovered that I also.... Here." He motioned to the wound around his back. They nodded. "I was good for nothing. I couldn't even move. I thought I was going to die, and I would have. I lay there for I don't know how long. Used up all the morphine. I was out."

"Then what?"

"They found me."

"Who?"

"Seventeenth SS."

"How? You had lost them."

"Dogs."

"They took you to Montmartin? What for?"

"I don't know. I wasn't conscious all that much. I thought they were taking me to Germany."

"Did they interrogate you?"

"I think they tried. They brought a lot of officers to look at me. I remember a lot of black suits. Maybe it was a dream. I couldn't tell you if I were on a train or a truck or a donkey cart or what. For much of the time I thought I was dead."

"That they were going to kill you?"

"No, that I was dead. I was carried around all the time. It never stopped. I would wake up in the dark, in a strange place. I didn't know what was happening. Things wouldn't stick to my memory but just slide off. I thought I was a child again. I thought I was an old man. I thought I was in a cathedral. That I was flying. That my mother was there, taking care of me."

"There were nuns in the church. They were executed."

Harry took this in quietly. They could see that he was trying to remain composed, and they were not surprised, as they had discovered that wounded men are often very emotional. "They weren't your mother," the major said. "Your mother's okay."

"Yes, she is," Harry said. "She died a long time ago."

"I'm sorry, Captain. I wasn't thinking. Really, I'm sorry. Do you remember who shot you? I take it that this is how you got the third wound. Was it an officer?"

"Yes."

This animated them to the edge of their lion tamer's chairs. "Are you sure?"

"I'm sure. They went around shooting people. It was very quick. We tried to get up, but most couldn't. People fell over and were shot on the floor, sometimes as they were crawling. I was in the litter they brought me in on, and they hadn't taken off the straps."

"You hadn't been there long?"

"I don't know. The straps had been loosened, but not enough. I tried to get out, but couldn't. They moved down the row, shooting."

"What did you see, exactly?"

"I wasn't looking. I was using what I thought would be my last few seconds to prepare myself."

"How?" the major asked, though not as a part of his inquiry.

Harry remembered how, and always would. "To fill my heart with love," he said, "as if breathing in every moment of my life. That's what I tried to do. You know those wrappers that you can do a trick with by lighting them on a plate?"

They didn't have the slightest idea of what he was talking about.

"They come wrapped around an Italian cookie," he said, twirling his finger to help them along. "I can't think of the name, but if you fold them the right way they hold together after they burn. The ash that's left is so light it suddenly launches upward on the rising convection current that was made when it itself burned. The denser cold air that follows pushes them up, and they rise. I breathed in. I tried to take in all the love I had ever known, and then I felt that I was rising, really rising up. We've all been there, up there," he said, meaning airborne troops, although his questioners were not sure. "We know what it's like, but instead of descending, this time I was going up."

"But they shot you in the leg."

"In the leg." Harry looked over the sheets and toward his legs. "Did they miss?"

He moved his head from side to side.

"How do you know?"

"The pistol was pointed at my forehead. I thought that was it. I was sure. He shot me in the leg. I waited for the next shot to end the pain, but when it came it wasn't for me. He had moved on. Though it doesn't make sense, I was sorry that I was still there. Maybe it was because I was really ready to go, and it wasn't so bad. I wasn't afraid."

"They killed seventy of our men that way," the major told him.

"I didn't know how many," Harry said. "And I'll never . . . I'll never quite. . . . I mean, I'm still there, I always will be."

As field hospitals go, which isn't saying very much, the hospital at Vierville was excellent in many ways. By the time Harry got there it was far enough from the fighting that only occasionally and with a south wind did he hear the distant concussions of bombs and artillery. Small arms fire, as familiar to him as rain on the roof, was entirely absent. And yet, day and night, even though the port of Cherbourg was soon open, one could hear trucks and tanks on the road, streaming south from the artificial harbors at Utah Beach six miles to the north; and bombers, fighters, transport, and reconnaissance aircraft passing overhead at various altitudes, their sounds covering a range from angry and urgent to the intermittency of a fly in the winter sun. The twenty-four-hour flow into the battle was reassuring if only because the Germans had no such overbrimming supply and were literally stunned by its ceaseless swelling.

As soon as Harry was told where he was, and was well enough to keep it in mind, he was happy. The name alone, Vierville, had made him so, because of a Radcliffe girl, Alice Vierville. He couldn't remember how he had come to know her, but he had, enough so that they had stopped to talk on Mount Auburn Street sometime in late May of their senior year. It was burned into his memory. She was facing east; he, west. She was wearing a print sundress, and with her right hand in salute as she shielded her eyes from the light, her hair was so blond it shone almost violently. On his cot, grateful to be in Vierville, he remembered the deep crescents near the corners of her mouth when she smiled. And she had them, she really had them, and they were beautiful, as was she. Although beginning in freshman year he had wanted to, he had never approached her. Now he did, and her response was seductive, charming, and to tell him that she was about to be married. "Alice," he said, "why didn't you marry me?"

Her reply was kind, respectful, and perhaps wistful: "As I recall, Harry, you never asked." Then they parted, with Harry, at least, dreaming of the counterfactual and vibrating with regret. That was one reason he liked being in Vierville, a place from which the quintessentially American Alice Vierville had undoubtedly descended, though probably through many generations. And, that summer, Vierville was as sunny as she was.

The half-dozen tents that had seen so much triage, surgery, and dying were now filled with those who would be able to return to duty soon enough so that it made no sense to evacuate them to England. There were some who had just arrived and who slept most of the time, and some about to be sent back into battle. The latter were fully healthy and had organized physical training to get into shape. It was a wonderful place, and as no one was dying there, it was unusual.

And then there was the weather, which after the storms at the beginning of the month could not have been more splendid. And then the food. It wasn't army food, which was trundled past them by the ton in groaning, can-filled trucks on their way to the fighting. So as not to open a distraction on the route of supply, the army had contracted with the village. Four women with what was for them a nearly unthinkable budget cooked for the more than one hundred patients and staff. Just the bread, butter, and jam were almost beyond the imagination of the American soldier. The pâtés, cheeses, summer fruits and vegetables, meats, fish, and fowl were for many not only a relief from military cuisine but something they had never experienced and might never experience again.

It is most difficult to get something you want in an army rather than what the army dictates, but it can be done, and with patience and a trick that Harry figured out in his hospital bed, he did it. The trick is to be happy and optimistic. Unhappy soldiers who want or desperately need something are so numerous, and their petitions come in such a flood, that for bureaucrats to survive they must make them invisible, and they do. A joyful, confident soldier, one who is illogically cheerful, almost a lunatic, will stand out like a lighted sign. Clerks and even higher officers seem magically to seek the satisfaction of obliging him, and delight in sending him on his way as much as if they were freeing a bird by tossing it into the air. They see in him a possibility of which they might not have been aware but that they wish to nurture and support. They see him as an emissary from a place that holds the potential of their own happiness, which is how and why it works.

He needed to know about his pathfinder team — Rice, Bayer, Johnson, Hemphill, Reeves, and Sussingham. He wanted to hear their stories and tell them his own, but above all he wanted to know that they were alive and well. As an army in combat is a very hard thing from which to pry information, he would need help, so he went to the physician in command at Vierville.

"Sir," he began.

"*Doctor* sounds better to me," said the physician, a major who, like all practicing physicians in the army, was not quite in the army, if only because keeping people alive is different from killing them. And an army doctor was also supposed to be a kind of shelter from the army itself, as anyone, including illiterate privates, knew well.

"Doctor, sir."

"Just *Doctor*, please. Get out of the habit," said the doctor, who wore round wire glasses and had an unfolded surgical mask hanging over his chest, like a bib.

"Yes, sir, I wonder if you might be able to help me find out if the members of my unit are all right. I'm really happy about that."

"You're what?"

"I'm happy to imagine that they're all fine."

"Well that's good." The doctor looked down at his blood-spotted campaign desk and said to himself, under his breath, "Jesus Christ."

"I mean, I just want to know that they're okay. I'm sure they are, and that makes me happy."

"So why don't you just go with that?"

"I want official confirmation."

The doctor pursed his lips and looked down once more. "You and everyone else. Do you realize," he asked, "that almost without exception, everyone, of every rank, asks the same question? When they wake up, they ask where they are, how they got here, can we notify their families that they're all right, and where are their — I hate the word — *buddies*, if they're enlisted. Their *men* if they're officers."

"I don't like the word *buddies* either," Harry said. "It sounds like they're potatoes, but, whatever they are, I'd like to know that they're safe. Their names are Rice, Bayer, Johnson, Hemphill, Reeves, and Sussingham."

"I can't help," the doctor said, as, even so, he was counting on his fingers and then silently reciting the names he had just heard. The study of medicine had sharpened his memory. "Six, right?" he asked.

Harry didn't have to count on his fingers. "Six."

"They were here. Soon after you were admitted, I was in your tent when a truck pulled up and a bunch of rude, unmanageable pathfinders disrupted my ward. They were looking for you. They were a real pain in the ass, but fortunately they didn't stay long. And there were six. They took chairs without asking and arranged them at your bed, three on a side. It was like the bloody Last Supper. We don't keep records of visitors, of course. I don't know who they were, but given your probable social circle, will six pathfinders who had the unmistakable air of delinquents do it for you?"

"That's us. They were all alive," Harry said, not quite as a question.

"They were walking around. They weren't zombies."

"I wasn't asking, sir. I'm just . . . happy."

"Yes, be happy, and bless those of us who are alive, who are no different from those who are dead, except that we're not dead yet."

"In light of that," Harry asked, "when can I leave?"

"When you're fit."

"Who decides?"

"I do."

"The criteria?"

"Wounds healed, with no constrictions, no loss of normal movement, no infectious disease. Mental soundness; normal blood pressure, pulse, respiration, and muscle tone. The decision's mine. If you're going back into combat, ideally you should be as fit as when you went in. It takes a lot, but we'll send you back. That's what we do now. Those who are too eager slow what would otherwise be a natural recovery. Start gradually. Pace yourself. You'll get further, go faster, and join your unit more quickly if you don't push too hard."

Harry commenced his recovery by sitting in a canvas chair in the sun. In hours of silence his strength began to come back. He positioned himself at the edge of a field of hay that he watched thicken and grow until, as the wind swept through it, it undulated like the sea.

Ready for neither calisthenics nor marching, he started to take short walks that he lengthened by half a kilometer each day, until by the beginning of July, slowly becoming his old self, he reached the Channel, having passed through Ste. Marie du Mont many times and, with discipline, turned back. But finally he came to the edge of La Madeleine, right on the water, the horizon as open as that of a broad ocean. Throwing over his self-imposed limits, he didn't turn back but went straight for the beach. He ran to meet the waves, carbine bumping against his side, and when he bent down to touch their most advanced guard, upon which a necklace of foam was taking its very last ride before sinking into the sand, he felt strength welling up in him as before.

There can be in a soldier's heart many things that sometimes others fail to know, impressed there by sudden, irrational, clarifying fire, and that for the rest of his life will call forth loyalty and emotion that cannot be countermanded. In this place, memory knits together improbably a love of life and the acceptance of annihilation, and the great charge between the two will from time to time light the world in strange ways. When Harry stood, he looked over the beach to the northwest. There, beneath clouds scudding in strong wind the invasion fleet rode at anchor offshore, steady in the blue. Onshore, the detritus of the assault—barges, piers, bulldozed berms of sand and tangled wire, vehicles gutted and overturned—looked like the rough-hewn outskirts of New York. Storms had smashed the Mulberry Harbors and tossed ships and barges into islets of contorted steel. It looked as vacant and industrial as the piers of Weehawken or the Bayonne marsh across which were stretched the blackened girders of the Pulaski Skyway.

Ships were unloaded silently to feed the expansion of the armies as the front moved forward on the fuel of good lives fed to war as steadily as coal conveyed mechanically into the fire of a boiler. But here the sea was still cobalt and gray, the clouds as rough and full of life as in a painting by Boudin, the regimental pennants that flew from whiplike radio masts as colorful as the racing silks in a Manet. The movement of vehicles crossing the beach and dutifully accelerating to battle kept Harry transfixed. For all who, like him, were caught up beyond the power of will in such a wave, the likes of which had been repeated again and again over thousands of years, there was a compensatory light that at times allowed to even the simplest soldiers a penetrating and commemorative vision, which, were they to survive, would give them a quality unmatched in artists, philosophers, or clerics—a holiness now and then brought forth in sudden patches of memory that could ambush even old men with trembling and tears.

From the north over the Channel a flight of three Spitfires was coming in low and level. As they approached the beach they pulled up, showed their blue-and-white undersides, banked southeast, and in respect to what had happened below them not long before, dipped their wings in salute to the living and the dead. These planes and others like them were as deeply loved by infantrymen as if they were sword-bearing angels. It wasn't only that the infantry cheered them when they appeared above a battle, but that they loved them. Their startling presence and immense roar were salvation and vindication at once. That they moved so beautifully through the air, uniting power with grace, hardly slowed the racing hearts of those saved by them. Usually they came thundering from the back and were not seen until just before they went into action. They were watched closely and with great excitement as they fought with the grounded enemy, turning and diving like hawks, and as they did battle in the ether, flecks of light that could not be heard. Harry had watched the three planes for almost a minute as they skimmed like swallows over the sea, and, as they passed over the bluff, they flexed and turned in the sun.

He walked every day from Vierville to the sea and back, and the beach soon became familiar. The wind leveled the smoke of hundreds of ships and slapped taut their flags and ensigns from halyards and masts. Harry's round trip of twelve miles, sometimes leaving the road, had by the middle of July become a run that, if difficult and slow, and sometimes requiring a nap in the dunes, was a run nonetheless, made unavoidably unpleasant by the carbine (not the near-perfect one, which had been lost) bouncing against his back. Most mornings and late afternoons he would exercise with soldiers about to return to the front, and sometimes, overcome with fatigue that said he was not yet healed, he would go to his cot to sleep. Only when dinner was over, after a day in the sun or, sometimes, a swim in the Channel, the frigidity of which was both bracing and exhausting, did he seek his canvas chair at the edge of the now harvested hayfield to sit and read. On a little folding table that he had carried out, he would write letters and do paperwork by the flame of a candle after darkness fell. The fat homemade candle was set in a glass jar that protected it from the occasional breezes that had swayed the hay before it was cut. He discovered that not only could he work by the light of one wick, with no pantheon of mirrors, refracting crystals, or candelabra, but that this was comforting as well as sufficient. He would put the jar right on the page, and in its warm flickering light, center stage, surrounded by dancing shadow, his pen worked in a world of its own, sheltered and tranquil, yet active and free. And though the war, the past, and the future were stilled in the summer night, he knew it would not be long until he was carrying his carbine through the snow.

In Vierville he lived magnificently in the present, but the gorgeous summer embraced a continent in which every conviction and expectation were tested by emotions and tragedy that exceeded the human capacity to endure—children deprived of fathers and mothers, parents whose children perished before them in both senses of the word, whole families extinguished in an instant, on either side of the line, in suffering beyond imagination. Which was more true, that France, though ravishingly beautiful, was burning before his eyes, or that France, though burning before his eyes, was ravishingly beautiful?

On the eleventh of July, the entire 82nd Airborne departed for England via Utah Beach, leaving behind so many killed, wounded, and missing that it made the boats metaphysically light. Not officially recovered, Harry had obtained permission to remain at Vierville, and would not rejoin his unit until shortly before they were parachuted into Holland. There, though fully expecting to die, he would fight calmly and efficiently, for a great deal had been driven out of him and he was able to look upon things with a disturbingly neutral eye.

# 36

## SNOW

From the half-inundated, sometimes wooded country south of Nijmegen in Holland, where the 82nd landed and fought through insistently arising chaos and then into the winter Ardennes, Harry Copeland's stick of pathfinders was bounced from battalion to battalion and company to company supposedly according to need, but often it seemed according to someone somewhere rolling dice in a cup. Unattached to any unit on a permanent basis, they never knew where they would be going and with whom.

After the invasion, the immediate objective in the minds of the troops, if not the generals, was Paris. This imposed upon the constant improvisations of combat not only a direction and a plan but an artful theme with weather to match. Though hardly as glorious as France, cooler, and quite dark even in September, Holland still had the feel of summer's end. Like France, it was to be liberated; it had a definitive character that everyone knew, and a mild, waterlogged landscape.

After weeks of fighting there, the 82nd was withdrawn to Rheims for rest, but in December, in response to the German counterattack in the Bulge, they were trucked to Belgium to fight as never before. They struggled not only with the enemy but against cold, darkness, hunger, and filth: the countryside was so bleak that to be alive in it was torture. And the forward momentum they had enjoyed as liberators in the light of summer disappeared as they retrenched to hold the onslaught of German troops fighting for their country's survival.

The greater theme of the Allied armies was to reach and conquer Germany, and this they did in one broken step after another, in thousands of sharp engagements and occasional sprints forward where a line had collapsed or a town was left undefended. But the nature of the terrain, the fact that to the east the land did not end until the Pacific, and, most of all, the winter itself made this fight the closest thing to the infinite that the soldiers of both sides had ever known. A short time in the winter forests and fields, steadily watching men die after they had lived in cold and squalor, was enough to make anyone believe he had been and would remain there forever.

The closer the armies came to the German heartland, the more certain they were of victory, and the more slowly they moved. Their progress from Georgia, Louisiana, New Jersey, Massachusetts, across the Atlantic, across the western half of North Africa, in Sicily and through France, Holland, and Belgium; the passing of years; and the seas, deserts, forests, cities, plains, and not least the oceans of air through which they had fought were to what remained of Germany what the left nine-tenths of a book are to the remaining tenth on the right. They still could call upon the esprit de corps that in battle gave them powers they never thought they had, a determination unmatched by any they would ever feel again, a lightness of being that at times seemed to remove them from contact with the ground. They still could summon a willingness to leave everything behind, even life, in satisfaction of the imperative that takes hold of a mass of men in war. They had this despite their familiarity, in the lee of engagements, with the fields of the dead and the cries of the wounded.

The closer they came to war's end and the surer they were of victory, the more pointless both seemed. If by spring Berlin would fall and if in a year the armies dissolve, why die now? Worse than dying before one knew the outcome, was dying when one did. Not only did they pity the last man to be killed, but as each day passed they felt more and more like him.

They had practically nothing but snow — the feel of it, the silence it imposed with an almost beneath-the-threshold-of-sound hissing as it fell, the way it lit the darkness even as it smothered sight. Snow was God's scolding of the world for war. It suppressed and conquered legions and nations. It quieted continents, forced branches to bow in submission, and broke those that would not. It made a mockery of military power and pride in numbers, throwing into the world inexhaustibly its own soldiers, tiny crystals each with an inimitable identity, each fragile, temporary, frozen, resigned, but in such endless profusion that they could slaughter entire armies in absolute silence and bury them until spring. Snow muffled the sounds of soldiers who fought across it or waited in it; it sent them messages in its glistening whirlwinds; and like a wrestler who need not expend energy or breath, it effortlessly pinned them to earth.

Harry was saved by more things than he could count. On the battlefield, in the forests, fording streams, and crossing fields, the threads of chance were woven into a tapestry that could not have assembled itself. Nor, as whole armies of men were tossed and broken like puppets, could chance adequately account for the heart-piercing visions that came to those in great distress. Like souls departing bodies, meaning, explanation, and beauty rose and fused, and then, after fatigue and despair, could not be adequately recounted. Little things, however, seemingly inconsequential, stayed with them — and a soldier might wonder for the rest of his life how it was that they came to save him.

Preserved in Harry's memory was a flash of white, an object that flew in a weightless arc and landed softly in his arms. Then the choking exhaust of a truck moving off into the snow, and a cold wind herding the clouds in such a way that it opened lakes of blue in the sky, from which uncomfortably bright light rained down upon the motionless soldiers and briefly gilded them with warmth. The miracle of what flew into Harry's arms before the truck pulled away, and saved his life, is comprehensible only in light of the way they lived and died.

Bullets were important: soldiers carried, fired, dodged, feared, and relied upon them. Bullets, extricated from their casings so as to use the powder to make a fire in ice-saturated wood, are surprisingly light. They rest in the palm of the hand less obtrusively than coins, and when fingers close around them as they are about to be tossed into a pocket they seem as light as cork. Though they are mostly smaller than a lima bean, they do such grievous damage because their immense velocity imparts to them a power greater than that of a spear thousands of times their mass. Despite their speed, they are not, as commonly believed, invisible, and often can be seen, even if not clearly enough or in time to get out of the way, which leads to what is perhaps their most overlooked quality, which is that one becomes aware of them from the inside, not, as one might think, from without. They seem to emerge from the body — like an instantaneous sickness or eruption. The message of their arrival is unfairly sensed as a manifestation, blooming inexplicably from within, of one's self.

Because they often come unpredictably and as if from nowhere, every minute and every second is filled with their possibility, which makes life seem full if only because it can so quickly become empty. This in turn is more tiring than labor, and saps massive amounts of energy, which in unrelenting cold makes everything seem colder. Living outside in the winter without relief allows inurement to the cold of perhaps ten or twenty percent. Because the other eighty or ninety percent is unrelievable and therefore becomes cumulatively worse, the only way to deal with it is to suffer or outwit it.

To fight the enemy, the 82nd's paratroopers were armed with an array of light but deadly weapons. To fight the cold, they were less adequately equipped. Their wool uniforms, socks, gloves, and heavy overcoats were not warm enough and had to be supplemented, the best of all improvisations being a doubled wool blanket draped across the shoulders and held at the neck with a clasp or by hand. This kept more men alive than did the steel helmet, and worked well when standing, although in a seated position, or, worse, when lying down, it was far less effective.

The general-issue sleeping roll was too short, hardly waterproof, and filled with about half an inch of down, sufficient perhaps for a September night in a temperate climate, but certainly not for the winter of '44–'45. Despite blankets emplaced within and around the down, after half an hour of immobility the cold made sleep a torture.

Drinking hot water before sleep, when hot water was available, helped at first, but after a few hours it necessitated unwrapping, rising, stepping outside, and relieving oneself in cold that was close to zero. Any heat or imitation of heat that had slowly built up in the body would then vanish for the rest of the night. If, as often was the practice, three or four men slept jammed together, the one who had to get up would be cursed for shattering the equilibrium and letting in the cold air.

So close to the front, fires were often out of the question, as smoke by day and flame by night invited enemy rifle and artillery ranging. Sterno might covertly heat up a pot of something, but on such a small scale it hardly mattered, and within a hollowed-out earthen shelter half hewn from a bank of soil and covered with a snow-laden poncho or tarp, the fumes were stupefying. Still, anyone who could, did make a fire of some sort, kindling wet and frozen branches with liberal applications of gunpowder.

At four in the morning, if they were not pacing numbly on picket duty, even young men in perfect health would awaken with a feverish heart beating slowly, explosively, and booming in the chest as if calling for help. Their teeth chattering, their lips chapped and bloody, white or blue, they would look out at the darkness and imagine not only that they were about to die, but, despite the slow-motion thinking brought by frigid temperatures, that they saw, suspended in the air, things that were colorful and beckoning. In this unrelieved hell, Harry would see women dressed for a party on a bracing fall evening; the landscapes of the Hudson; animals cavorting above, like the constellations; flying fish rising on the spray of windy green seas; and his father, his mother, himself as a child; cityscapes; ferries; New York in summer, windows open, people speaking as if they did not know that they were suspended in the whitened air above a battlefield. Though they might have been classified as such, these were not hallucinations but, in a failing reality, memories and wishes risen in a new balance of power.

It might have been more tolerable had there been decent or hot food, but seldom was there either, for whatever came in a can was frozen or congealed. The bearded, blackened, rancid soldiers could not bathe, and their undergarments and socks became so filthy that many men were kept alive merely because they were determined not to be buried in them. Harry was too tired to resolve upon anything other than a simple—perhaps simple-minded—desire to come out of the war. This led to a focus on practicalities. He and his six men, fighting as a kind of flying squad, learned to construct in very little time a tolerable shelter partially dug into the earth and covered with ponchos, blankets, and tarpaulins. They survived in such things four or five at once, because at least two were on watch at any time. They learned how to sleep back-to-back, in a horrible clump, with whatever they had to cover themselves arrayed in feverish and inadequate tangles full of cold spots that grew colder as night progressed. When the watch changed and the heat seal was broken, the two men who came in, especially if they had been in the wind, would shiver for an hour before falling asleep.

Bayer, who was six foot four and 280 pounds, was the best heater. "I remember buying a bag of hot roasted chestnuts on Fifth Avenue in February," he said. "I walked from Fifty-ninth Street to Washington Square. The wind was blowing and the street was empty, but the chestnuts kept me warm all the way. I'm still warm. They were magic chestnuts." That he half believed himself was confirmed by a crazed look. "The war eats shit, and I shoulda dodged the draft," he would say, and then go out and fight like a seventh-generation West Pointer. He was such a big target, and yet he had moved through the war as if he were invisible or a sylph, fighting imperturbably, and fearlessly and smoothly working the bolt of his rifle as the enemy drew close.

Sussingham was the second-best heater. Just under six feet tall, he weighed 200 pounds but it was all muscle, so he burned a lot of fuel. This seemed to make sense for a steelworker who came from the hellish blast furnaces and mills of Gary, Indiana, where inside cavernous sheds filled with fleeing smoke winter was made summer as if by harnessed volcanoes. He was the best-humored person Harry had ever met, continually puzzled that other people were not as good as he was, although in his modesty he thought that he was no better than anyone else. He was as steady and dependable as one would expect of someone whose job it was to grapple molten slabs of metal gliding past at high speed.

Reeves, from Colorado, tall and lanky, was a terrible heater, and he had the temperament of a golden retriever. In the midst of war, after shooting people against whom he held no grudge as they cut through hell to shoot and kill him, he was still kind. He wanted to be a rodeo announcer after the war, and, as if people could not understand English, he would say, "Rodeo announcer, not radio announcer."

Rice, the lawyer from Ohio, was, like Harry, older and qualified to be an officer, but unlike Harry he had chosen to be an enlisted man. Like almost everyone from Ohio, he wanted to run for Congress, and thought that having been a common soldier would more honestly qualify him. "The mind of a general and the heart of an infantryman," he once had told Harry, "are what is required to make the decisions politicians make in regard to both war and peace." Clearly, he was getting ready to run, and not only was he right, Harry thought, but were he to survive he would go far if after the war courage and probity would still count.

Dan Hemphill, from the western mountains of Virginia, was not affable. Though courteous and efficient, he actually felt out of place fighting for the Union. Because his side had been defeated, he had to prove that he was a better soldier than anyone else, and time after time he did. "Go easy," Harry would tell him, and the look he got in return was one of amused contempt. It wasn't that Hemphill could not be trusted, but that he was distant, and remained so in spite of circumstances that alloyed all the others until they thought almost as one.

And then there was Johnson, studious and alone, an English teacher from Superior, Wisconsin. He didn't mind the cold, and was a good heater. He hated the war as much as anyone else, but his wife had died, and the war was his penance. He suffered it quietly, always soft-spoken, waiting for what he thought would inevitably be his death, to which he looked forward as rest and perhaps a reunion with the one he had loved the most.

Harry was Harry, and having crossed the Siegfried Line, with the rest of Germany to punch through—they never knew where they would meet up with the Russians—one of the many things that saved him started one night with a sound. He was on watch, it was 0330, and although with two blankets around his shoulders the rest of him was almost warm, he could no longer feel his feet. Falling snow presented him with the image of a dancer amid the snowflakes, appearing and disappearing in the dark spaces, moving when the wind bent the straight falling lines into curves and tangles. He tried to give her a face and a body, but he couldn't. Though she was inchoate and out of reach, she was as strongly felt as if she were there. Then he tensed his grip on the carbine and brought it level. All his senses came alive, charged by a faint but undeniable whimpering.

At first he thought it was a wounded soldier, or perhaps the imitation of a wounded soldier, made to lure him to his death. And if it were a child, lost in the middle of the night? In a war that left scores of millions dead, how many bombs, shells, and bursts of machine-gun fire had destroyed houses, killed parents, and left children to fend for themselves because their parents had hidden them in safe places? "Run and hide!" was a theme that predated history. But how long could a child continue to move and speak in ten degrees and wind that charged in from the distant Russian steppes?

As the moaning continued, it sounded hardly human. "*Kommen Sie hier,*" Harry urged, "*ich nicht schiessen.*" Whoever heard this understood it and drew closer. Harry had to keep the carbine trained on the sound and his finger on the trigger, but what if accidentally he shot a child? "*Kommen Sie.*"

He sensed movement directly ahead as a disturbance of the falling snow. It was low to the ground, crawling like an infant. But a very young child could not walk in a foot of snow. The first real sight of it was of snow being tossed forward of the movement of its legs. The whimpering had stopped. Then two eyes, briefly visible when the snow thinned and the wind paused, receded into the dark.

Harry took his flashlight from its pouch, held it away from him at arm's length should someone fire at it, and swept the area in front of him. A foot above the ground, electrically green eyes opened wide and were fixed in the beam. "Dog," Harry said, and it ran to him.

It was short-haired, lucky to be alive in the cold, a beagle, or, as it seemed to understand when Harry greeted it, a *kleiner Spürhund*, a "little detective hound," and like all beagles it was timid and yet devastatingly friendly. It wanted Harry to like it, but seemed to think itself unworthy. The combination of its modesty, trust, and apparent self-deprecation gave it a philosophical air, and its kindly look was commanded by its natural features into an expression of perpetual inquiry. By nature, it was immune to sin. Had it lived with Nazis, which it may have, it would not have known, on any level, what they were about, whereas a Doberman would know exactly. Because the little beagle was totally innocent, Harry had no choice but to take him in.

Soon they discovered that she was a she, and at Johnson's insistence they named her Debra. After she heard it twice, she responded to it. There was enough affection, and there were enough scraps — although at first she wisely refused to eat C-rations — to keep her going as long as she and they could stay alive. In that regard, she enjoyed better odds than they did. She was a smaller target and neither a valuable nor an active one, she was better camouflaged, she shied from weaponry, was terrified by artillery, and would dig herself into the snow or wiggle under a log at the first report of a rifle.

Used to fires, Debra would lie near them. Harry let her curl up next to his sleeping bag, threw a blanket over both the dog and himself, and for the first time since he had been sent into the winter was warm enough to sleep. She was almost better than a woodstove. He could relax, drift off, and not be awakened by fingers of freezing air or a world's worth of chill rising from the earth itself. In the daytime, others held her on their laps, but at night, because Harry had found her and she answered first to him, she was his hot water bottle.

She was so afraid of gunfire, and she could hear so well, that if a tank or an artillery piece were to report anywhere within a twenty-mile range she would tremble uncontrollably. There was hardly a minute during which a shell was not fired, a bomb not dropped, or a demolition charge not detonated within that radius. When the paratroopers could not hear a distant thud, she could, and no amount of petting could stop the trembling.

Harry thought that, stressed without letup, she would die. She seemed too innocent to die, but he could think of nothing that would help her except to stop the war or finish it more quickly. "It's a dog," said Bayer. "She's had a good life. If she dies, she dies — like us."

Reeves said, "In the mountains in summer, watching the flocks, we'll kill a sheep every four or five days. That's how we eat. That's just the way it is."

"What about earplugs?" asked Johnson, who was fond of disputations in which he represented both sides. "No, the low frequency goes right through her skull: earplugs wouldn't work."

"I don't know much about dogs," Sussingham told Harry. "I never had a dog."

"It's a pity," said Rice, "but maybe she can weather it. We're all under the same sort of strain, even if we're not dogs. Her trembling is equivalent to our worry."

"Swaddle her," said Hemphill, as if speaking to idiots.

"What?"

"Swaddle her. Wrap her up. That's what you do to a dog that's afraid of thunder, or maybe up there in Yankee-land you send it to a dog psychiatrist or get it addicted to dope."

"Yeah, that's what we do," Harry answered. "We get our dogs addicted to dope, then we take them to dog psychiatrists. How'dja know? And that was the cause of the Civil War. Lincoln wanted to addict the dogs of Alabama to dope. Aren't most wars caused by that?"

Hemphill snorted contemptuously.

"With what?" Harry asked about the swaddling.

"That's not my problem, Captain."

It was, however, a problem. In the foxholes and lean-tos they had no swaddling; every bit of cloth they had, had been sewn into a shape to clad or make a shelter for a body. As they moved slowly east, mainly on foot — fighting and resting in alternation — the dog, as if she did not want to go into Germany, became a mental case. One rifle report was enough to set her trembling for half the night. It seemed unfair to take her with them, but without them she would have frozen to death, starved, or been eaten. Winter came down so hard that they fought and moved in slow motion. To walk a hundred yards in thigh-deep snow dangerously sapped their strength. Many a soldier separated from his unit died of the cold, because no boy scouts or village search parties would be there for a private who, after his platoon had been outflanked, had been driven into the forest, where he then slowly turned blue, slept, and died.

Harry's stick was ordered to help hold a section of the front thirty miles east of the breached Siegfried Line. They reinforced a company that had dug in at the edge of a wood overlooking a broad prospect of open country dotted with villages and small stands of pine. Larger forces and armor would be on their way when they could disengage from what they were doing elsewhere, to push onto the peaceful-looking killing fields beyond the trees on the hill. Until those columns could be diverted, the task was to hold against counterattack. In the forest, Harry's men dug in on the south side of a snow-covered dirt road that led down across the fields and to the first village. Though they could see assembled German armor to the east, all they had to stop it were bazookas and PIATs. The ground was so hard frozen it could be excavated only near the roots of trees, where the loamy soil was relatively soft. So they dug in at the base of the pines flanking the road, and lived among the roots. Evergreen boughs burned well when thick fogs allowed the soldiers to make small fires that would go undetected. Nonetheless, the cold was doing them in, and it was dangerous to be among the trees, the branches of which could fuse enemy shells so they would blast down from above instead of partially slaking their force in the earth.

On the second day, a truck came up from the rear with ammunition for an anti-tank gun. "Where's the gun?" a master sergeant asked Harry after he rolled down the window, and then, when he saw Harry's insignia peeking out of the blanket Harry clasped at the base of his neck, "Sir."

"What gun?"

"G-Two says there's supposed to be a captured eighty-eight at the intersection of this road and the front line," the sergeant said over the rumble of the engine.

"How would they know?"

"Either 'cause someone told them, or from the air," the sergeant replied.

"That's the front line," Harry stated, pointing to where the field began a hundred feet from where they stood. "There's no gun here. We have an infantry company dug in north and south of the road. No armor, no gun."

The sergeant looked exhausted. "We'll just go back."

His driver told him that to turn around they had to shovel out a space. "Do it," he said, and then closed his eyes and sank back in his seat.

Harry walked to the rear of the truck. Two privates were shivering inside, sitting on crates of captured shell for the captured 88s. They also had quart containers of gun oil and carbon tetrachloride, ramrods, and dozens of rolls of new gun flannel. These were little bolts of cloth a foot high and as thick as a telephone pole. Every six inches or so, a blue line ran from edge to edge so the gunners would know where to cut the patches they slotted into the heads of their ramrods and ran through the barrels of the guns.

"Could you spare five or ten feet of one of those rolls?" Harry asked.

"Not without a trip to the stockade," said one of the privates, with blue eyes and a rosacean complexion waxen with cold.

Harry dipped into his coat pockets. "How 'bout for some cigarettes?" He often used his officer's ration of cigarettes as currency.

"How many?"

"What's your price?"

The rosacean private thought for a moment. "One cigarette per section."

"Per three," Harry said.

"Two."

"Okay."

"How many you want?"

"Twenty." That would be more than enough, he thought, to wrap around the dog. He began extricating half the cigarettes from a full pack as the private unrolled the flannel, counted the sections, and unsheathed a bayonet with which to cut it.

"Roll that up!" the sergeant commanded from where he had been watching in the snow.

Embarrassed, Harry put the cigarettes back into the pack. He hated the smell of tobacco on his fingers, but was able to make the replacement very quickly because of so much practice inserting cartridges into ammunition magazines. More than embarrassed, the private rolled up the flannel as if it were a window shade that goes berserk and rotates with a bang like that of a bomb going off.

"You," the sergeant said, addressing both privates, although only one was guilty, "get out of the truck and shovel. The driver shouldn't have to do it." They jumped out and dug with their hands. The sergeant stayed at the back, guarding the contents. Engaging Harry in forced conversation, he said *sir*, with obvious contempt, whenever he could: Harry, a captain, was just like any other scrounger. But Harry didn't care. The truck crew got back in, doors slammed, and the truck turned around. As it left, the back flap opened a wink and the rosacean private looked out to left and right as if the sergeant might be running alongside.

And then a whole roll of gun flannel came flying from the back like a depth charge catapulted off the fantail of a destroyer. Harry watched it find its arc. Many things now seemed to happen in slow motion, and this especially. The flannel was as white as the snow, *pace* the blue stripes, and when he caught it he said "Thank you," silently, and lifted his left hand to acknowledge the gift. The rosacean private seemed satisfied, and disappeared behind the flap as the truck itself disappeared in the snow.

When Harry wrapped the flannel around the dog's middle, then over the shoulders and around the neck and back crosswise under the belly, Debra, who had been frightened by a mortar barrage several miles to the north, suddenly stopped trembling. As if he had won the Nobel Prize, had a baby, or bet on a horse at four hundred to one, Harry went from position to position and handed out lengths of flannel. The troopers wrapped them around their heads like burnouses, deployed them more prosaically as scarfs, or pressed them into service as socks: they were tight in the boots, but clean, warm, and thick. "This is better," Bayer said, "than getting laid."

After everyone had taken what he needed, much was left. First Harry made a pair of ersatz socks for boots that, because they had stretched too much anyway, would not be tight even with the flannel. He wrapped a length around his head and neck, as the others had done, took off his coat, sweater, and shirts, and stood half naked in the snow, winding the flannel around his torso to serve as an undergarment. The risk to his core temperature was worthwhile, for when he put back his layers of clothing he felt clean and warm for the first time in weeks. This produced a pathetic euphoria.

He ate, drank a little hot water, brushed his teeth, and as it was quiet and he didn't have the watch until four the next morning, he retired, sitting the dog on a bed of pine needles next to his sleeping bag and pulling a blanket over them both. No longer trembling, the dog fell asleep immediately. True, the wind that blew across Harry's face was many degrees below freezing, but all else was covered and warm.

The cold air smelled especially good because there was no gunpowder in it. He could sleep until four A.M., and it was only six in the evening. After ten good hours, with no attack, no call to get up, no anxiety to wake him, he would be reborn. He slept, and dreamt not a dream but a precise recollection so vivid and exact that the illusion had no check, and was not only more desirable but somehow more real than sleeping in the snow on a front line pushed up to within easy range of German armor.

In the early twenties, after the Great War and its many casualties, the many more of the influenza epidemic, and the minor depression at the beginning of the decade, New York was as quiet and slow as an invalid who though he has crested his illness remains extraordinarily weak. Harry's formative years were spent in the dip before the bustle and prosperity that would signify the rest of the decade all the way to the Crash at its end. As a child, he roamed freely about the city. He swam in the rivers even though he was forbidden to do so; climbed girders and bridges even though forbidden to do so; hitched rides on the back bumpers of buses and trolleys even though forbidden to do so; and wandered through the many worlds that were New York's neighborhoods. This he was allowed. It was only one city, but no walker could see all of it even were he to walk forever, for it changed by the hour and no matter at what speed or with what duration one might try, it would never be compassed.

He liked to go to the Hudson River piers to look at the warships when they tied up — the gray four-stack destroyers from the World War and the gunboats remaining from the war with Spain, with their black cannon and white sides. This was in Hell's Kitchen, which was tame compared to what it had been in the nineteenth century, and now controlled by gangs of Irish children highly alert to invasion of any type, including that of a lone Jew from Central Park West. As urchinesque as Harry was, he was immediately recognizable as a Jew and a swell, and he paid for this in bruises and blood. Because his antagonists, like him, were not yet ten, he was neither killed nor maimed, although he could have been. The unusual twist was that he admired them. He believed, as did they, that because they were Irish and he was Jewish, they were clean and he was dirty. The fact that he was highly scrubbed and they were often filthy was irrelevant. They were taller and lighter-colored, and their English, even if they said *youse*, was authoritative. When he spoke to them, he filtered out any hint of Yiddish syntax or intonation that otherwise marked his dialect. In short, although he was never quite sure that he was an American, he was sure that they were — no matter how Irish they were, no matter when they had gotten off the boat (and some of them were still quite seasick). Not only did he want to be like them, he felt that somehow, fundamentally and indelibly, he really was like them. So he went there a lot, and was beaten up a lot.

"Why do you want to go to Hell's Kitchen so much?" his father asked, which, translated from the Yiddish idiom, was "Don't go to Hell's Kitchen."

"To see the ships."

"Go down to Chelsea."

"Chelsea's Irish too."

"It's less warlike."

"Still, Irish."

"Then go to Hudson Street."

"Too far away."

"So take the subway."

"It's too expensive."

"I'll give you the money. Why don't you go to . . . Little Italy? Do the Italians beat you up?"

"No."

"Why not?"

"They think I'm Italian."

"Really?"

"Yeah, I think so."

"They don't think you're Irish?"

"Why would they think I'm Irish?"

"I don't know. They beat you up so much you'd think it might rub off on you."

"I get along with them."

"You get along with them?" His father was astounded.

"In a way."

"Why not go to Yorkville?"

"I do go to Yorkville."

"Where the Germans beat you up?"

"No, they're too busy beating up the Negroes, who live on the edge of them."

"Do the Negroes beat you up in Harlem?"

"They always say they will, but they never do."

"Just don't go to Hell's Kitchen. Harry, they beat you up."

"No."

"Why?"

"Because it's America. I can go anywhere in America, I'm an American. Even Scarsdale."

"Okay, but you can also get beaten up."

"I can get strong, and learn to fight."

"Harry, Harry," his father said, looking at an eight-year-old with skinny limbs and muscles like shredded chicken. "Don't waste your time on that. You could be a neurologist."

"I don't want to be a neurologist."

"An internist."

"I don't want to be an internist."

"What do you want to be, Jack Johnson?"

Harry paid an Irish kid named Dennis O'Rourke ten cents a week to teach him how to fight. Dennis O'Rourke didn't know how to fight either, but for ten cents a week he gave it some thought, and between what he and Harry could think up together, learn from watching prizefights, and discover in practice, Harry did learn to hold his own, and could do so at times against three or four opponents at once, which, after the first time he did it, changed his life forever.

Then he began to exercise by running around Central Park on the bridle paths. Mocked and cursed by the aristocracy on their horses, he knew that his running six—and, later, twelve—miles was better than their riding the distance. When he was in high school he went over to Yorkville and learned to fence. He kept that up in college, where he also rowed and boxed. Although he was a welterweight, and then a middleweight, he trained with heavyweights. He was fast and powerful enough to do so, but as this was always to his disadvantage, the Harvard boxing coach once asked him why he kept it up. "In life," Harry had replied, "when you fight, you don't get to exclude the heavyweights."

After college, he stopped boxing. At the gyms where he might have continued, real prizefighters of much greater skill would have hurt him badly, and he knew it. But he did everything else that he had done, including rowing from the Columbia boathouse on the East River, which was unsatisfactory water. A college acquaintance whose full name was, truly, Allis Grosvenor Elliot Vliet Dukynk worked in an investment house that transferred him to London for two years. Harry had always dreamed of working in such a place, where the money was supposed to be, but being a humanities major he could neither be sure of nor imagine what kind of work they might actually require of him other than to wear the right kind of clothes. Because of the transfer, he was invited to use Allis's single shell at the Dukynk estate fronting an arm of the Croton Reservoir. Allis Grosvenor Elliot Vliet Dukynk was under the impression that if unexercised a wooden boat would fall apart, and was relieved that Harry undertook the task of rowing it once a week during the season. A car would be waiting for him at Harmon, the Dukynk servants would give him lunch after he rowed, and the car would take him back to the train. Being relatively asocial, Harry refused the lunch but accepted the rest. Allis had taken him upstate and showed him where the boat was hidden among a copse of pines near the water — which is what he dreamed of as he slept in the snow in Germany.

Every Wednesday, into November, weather permitting, he rowed on an empty lake with hundreds of miles of shoreline, tranquil bays, and extensions of water as smooth as glass. In August of '38, Harry was living at home and working in his father's loft without pay. He would take the New York Central up the Hudson to Harmon and be out on the lake by eleven. Fishermen were allowed in rowboats, which had to be licensed, but there were very few of them and so seldom did they go out other than on weekends that Harry had never seen one. The Croton Reservoir system, one of several that supplied water to New York City, was so huge, so surrounded by undeveloped buffers of forest land, and kept so empty of people that it seemed to be not forty miles from Times Square but somewhere in Canada or Maine. A few grandfathered estates came right down to the water, but even they had to comply with restrictions in view of protecting its purity. Allis's boat, because it was supposed to be a rowboat, had a serial number on its bows, and was thus perfectly legal. It glowed rose and yellow in the August sun and was almost as fragrant as the pines amid which it slept.

Harry woke it up by turning it over to prepare it for being hoisted onto his shoulders and carried down to the lake. In ninety degrees of windless sun there was no need for a shirt, and he had changed into a pair of khaki rowing shorts and hung his clothes on the stub of a pine branch. Through the trees was a prairie of blue water as still as a mirror. The heat had silvered its surface not with mist but with a diffusion of light. He carried down the boat and oars, then set it in the shallows and locked them into the oarlocks. Without a dock, entering the boat was not uncomplicated, but two strokes later he was in deep open water.

Felt through the oars, the smooth resistance as he moved across the lake was a beautiful thing not least because of its alliance with a steady cadence and the rise of the heart to meet it in propelling the boat at the speed of a man running. The oarsman was the motor, his steadiness and discipline of technique yielding a constant velocity. As the lake's hypnotic surface and rugged shoreline passed by, they made for thought and recollection as nature put anxiety and ambition on holiday and substituted in their place the genuine coin of the world.

Once, in the middle of October, when the sun was low, the open water, normally windblown, was flat except in his wake, which sparkled with a kind of light he had never before seen. Its flashes were triangular, their bases resting upon the surface. In a long line back, it seemed as if a group of sailboats were following his shell. But more remarkable still was that when a patch of water in the distance was disturbed by a gust of wind, the blinding triangular flashes, miniature sails bursting with fire, moved as if in an electric regatta. Turning, weaving, tacking, coming about, slowing, accelerating, rocking in the breeze and bouncing almost into the air, they possessed the speed and chaos of those swarms of white moths that sometimes hover over a field or take possession of a clearing. Each blinding flash was a perfect reiteration of the sun, each only instantaneous, its life too short to note much less to follow or record. Nonetheless, when and though it would disappear, it would appear again, or others like it would arise upon the same course resurrected, marvelously nimble and impossibly bright. Against a background of parti-colored foliage and a deep blue sky, this regatta of golden suns racing at high speed was so striking and hypnotic that Harry had almost rowed straight into the shore. Catching himself in time, he rested his oars and watched the hundred million flares, a world unto themselves and more joyful than swallows.

With every power within him, and against sadness he could not deny, he had hoped that these were souls, that they were free to come with the light, and that they could rise at will and hover in the air to overlook all that they had never left.

Now he would row eight miles, entering just before the midpoint an extraordinary extension of the reservoir, accessible only over a hundred yards of six-inch shallows pouring across a bed of small glistening stones. To row past this obstruction and against the current, he could not dip his oars as deeply as usual, and had to increase his stroke to the point where it looked panicky. Then he would glide off the bar and into a long, narrow lake rounded at its far end and encompassed by granite ledges and stands of pine. The trees were uniform, dense, and dark. All the land around the lake was owned by the City of New York. There was no access road to it; fishing boats could not get in over the bar; there were no predators, no people; and the water, issuing from deep springs, was purer and fresher than that of the pristine reservoir itself. This Eden was Harry's destination every time he rowed. At the end of the hidden lake, before he would start back, he would turn the boat and sit, listening to his heartbeat. In great heat, he would lift the water in the cup of his hand and drink, allowing it to cool him as it spilled through his fingers.

Now he raced toward the lake and its inlet, increasing speed as he closed, covered in sweat, burning up, and yet he was hardly exhausted, and each forward sweep invited the next as if with the easy assist of the wind. But the only wind in his final sprint to the bar was the ten-mile-per-hour breeze from the bow as a result of his forward momentum, which vanished as he glided over the shallows and was slowed by the exit current.

He always rowed slowly on the hidden lake as his reward for reaching it. Eyes stinging with salt, the heat from his body sometimes pulsing so that it felt hotter than sunlight, he turned in his seat to align the bow with the center of the lake's far end. His oars dropped protectively of his balance and rested on top of the water, but without turning back, he kept looking. Halfway up and in the middle was a commotion of white foam. At first he thought it was a drowning deer thrashing the surface with its antlers, but it was moving forward a great deal faster than a deer could swim. Low to the water, steady, at half the speed of a single shell going at a good clip, it was too small to be a rowboat and had no oars projecting from it. But it was moving and agitating like some sort of mechanism, impossible to identify. He decided to catch up, and began to row hard.

After a minute or two of speed, he turned again to look. Closer to it now, he could see that the object projected alternately from about a foot and a half to about three feet above the water. He still didn't know what it was or what it could be, and rowed furiously for a hundred strokes, counting them and afraid that he might overtake and collide with it. Having denied his curiosity during the hundred strokes, he turned again. Now he was close enough to see that it was a person, entirely unaware of him, kneeling on some sort of board and paddling violently. Fifty more strokes and he saw that it was a young woman. Twenty-five more and he glided past her. She was so surprised that she almost fell off her board, but then resumed, just as violently and as if to race him.

That, she could not do, and at the end of the lake he dropped his oars, came to a stop, and watched her approach. She straightened up and coasted over the last stretch, drifting to within ten feet of his boat. She was deeply tanned and completely wet, not with water alone but with her own glistening perspiration, breathing hard, visibly relieved to be able to straighten her back after however long she had bent forward to paddle. Never had he seen a woman with a body like hers, and musculature so well and beautifully defined, though not at all like a man's. He was immediately convinced that this was the way women were born to be, if only because the world offered resistance in all its aspects, and until the very end, opposition to resistance — life — creates strength. She was beautiful in many other ways as well, not least because of the heat that, though she was deeply tanned, made her almost scarlet.

"I've never seen anyone here before, anyone," she said, almost angrily.

"Nor have I," Harry responded.

She had said it to protect her dignity, because she was wearing only a robin's-egg-blue, satin brassiere and panties, and they were wet, tight, brief, and, though not entirely transparent, clinging. She did not hunch forward as she might have to minimize the glory of her splendid physique, but remained as straight-backed as her board. To stay balanced on it when its forward momentum had ceased, she had had to straddle it, and thus was he drawn to the two tendons that ran up each inner thigh, creating graceful, rounded channels that were perhaps the most inviting things he had ever seen (though he had seen others before in lesser examples).

Practically naked, in a lake of sapphire-blue, still water, in the high heat of Eden, they were aware of every detail of one another, with hardly anything hidden. Despite the magnificent way she held herself, he was drawn mainly to her face, now framed with partially wet chestnut-colored hair that shone in the overhead sun. She had the self-possession that came from intelligence, and he thought it had to be a great deal of intelligence, as it was a great deal of self-possession.

Still pulsing with heat, they stared at one another until he understood that she was daring him to pretend that he could not look at her forever, and that her near nakedness required of him some sort of polite speech. "Is this a sport I've never heard of," he asked, gesturing toward her board, and her, "or do I have heat stroke?"

She looked down and almost laughed, hiding it with a cough. "No," she said, "you don't have heat stroke. In my sophomore year we went to Hawaii for Christmas, and my father shipped this back. Hawaiians ride the waves on them." Her hair descended in long, accidental curls, and her eyes were blue. He could not stop himself from imagining her in a dress, décolleté, or a sundress and a straw hat. "Forgive me," he said, smiling, "but I'm dressing you with my eyes, and it's beautiful."

"That's a change, I'll admit. Do you also read from right to left?"

"Sometimes." She had no idea of what she had just elicited. "You go really fast on that thing. I think it's a lot more exercise than rowing."

"When I go to Hawaii again," she said, "I want to go out on the waves. They're so big they can kill you. To maneuver, you have to have speed, know how to turn the board, and place yourself on it. That I can do, and I've taken it to Southampton. Atlantic waves break rather than roll, but it's halfway there."

"Are you still in college?"

She nodded. "Are you?"

"I'm done. Where?"

"Smith."

"Senior?"

"In two weeks."

"And then what?"

"I'm engaged. I'm...."

Pushed below the waves, he managed to bob up. "Would that preclude having lunch in the city?"

"No."

"With me?"

"Yes."

"You would, or it would be precluded?"

"It would be precluded."

The sun was too hot, they were too close, and she was too magnificent for him to give up. "Might you be tempted out of preclusion?"

"Oh," she said, "I would certainly be tempted, pleasingly tempted, tempted so that I will think about it for a day or two, and perhaps even when I'm old, but I'll resist temptation, which is what you're supposed to do."

"Your character must be as strong as your body."

"Stronger."

"Can I know who you are, in case you get disengaged?"

"No" was the answer, given kindly.

"Fair enough."

The sudden infatuation and its definitive end was like being in a kind of car crash, and he didn't know what to say or how to break off and leave her. "Let's hope that neither of us," he finally said, "is arrested."

"Why would we be?"

"For swimming in the reservoir. You're soaking wet. The people of New York would be blessed to drink the water you were contained in, but the watershed police might not agree — especially if they're blind."

"Have you ever even seen them?" she asked. "Because I haven't, and we live here."

"I saw them once, when I was swimming after my row. I ducked underwater and stayed there longer than I thought I could. When I surfaced, their backs were turned. I went under again, and when I came up they were gone."

"Thanks for the warning," she said. He knew from the way she said it that it was time for him to row out, so he did. She turned her board around and faced him as he left, observing with sympathy that he could not completely conceal his yearning and loss as he forced himself to pull at the oars.

He reached the gravel bar and glided over it, accelerated by the water issuing from the smaller lake, and soon he was racing in the main stream.

Shaken awake by Johnson, who was drained of energy and so cold he could hardly stand, Harry was still on the lake. After emerging from his coverings, he tried to hold on to the dream as the heat and light began to fade. At first the cold air was refreshing, but as accounts began to square, he shivered. The dog didn't budge, so he let her lie. Many mornings and other awakenings had been worse. Now he was well enough and rested enough almost to enjoy the freezing mist. "You're relieved," he told Johnson, who rushed to get some sleep.

Alternately freezing or warmed by waves of heat that came from within, he thought of patches of the dream as he walked to his post at the edge of the woods. To the left and right, barely visible, were the sentries of other squads, who were looking out over the fields and straining to see or hear. At least a dozen squads were emplaced on a line perpendicular to the road, holding a space a hundred yards back from where the trees met the open prairie. Their fields of fire were focused on the road, in a pattern contrived to be a lens that would direct and concentrate the rays of heavy machine-gun fire, rockets, and mortars at an armored counterattack. Every one of these weapons could also slew along the edges of its emplacement to fight the battle the soldiers dreaded most — when German tanks, which could knock down many of the trees and maneuver around the rest, would run wild among them, individually hunting them in all directions, with neither a front nor a rear, as in the clash of medieval armies. In such a fight there was neither strategy nor tactics, and shelter and time disappeared in favor of terror. If only they had armor, they could fight on equal terms with the Tiger and Panther tanks. But that there was temporarily no armor was the reason they were there. Not a single soldier failed to harbor the image of a moving tank, cannon firing, turret swiveling and searching, its body pitching forward as the driver found men to crush in its treads.

Harry knew none of the men to his left and right, but the weight of their common circumstance defined them more than any of their previous distinctions. Only when settled at his post did he fully realize the extent of the artillery barrage all along the line, and the explosions of its shells far forward in the darkness. From miles away, the concussions both at the guns and where the shells burst vibrated pine needles, sometimes clearing them of snow. They shook the diaphragms of the soldiers to the point where it was actually easier to breathe. And they were felt on the skin through heavy clothing. The ground itself was lightly palsied.

But fog and snow were so thick that nothing could be seen. The barrage continued for an hour and a half after four, and then silence rolled up the line from south to north, making the night suddenly so still that the hissing of the snow sounded almost like a steam kettle. Like sentries everywhere, Harry fought to keep his eyes from closing; and, like sentries everywhere, he did not always succeed, and would wake with a start, having for an instant slept standing up. Then he would stomp his feet, take deep breaths, pace up and down, slap himself like a vaudevillian. He hardly felt it, because his cheeks and nose were stiff and numb. He would tap at his face out of curiosity to see which parts didn't register the announcement, and run his thumb and index finger down the length of his nose, fascinated because it seemed to belong to someone else. Sentries spend the night staring into nothing and shivering deep down. When dawn comes they know it whether in clear skies by the apparent dimming of the stars or, in clouds or mist, by a slight change to gray. Observed in this way, the dawn lasts much longer than its commonly recognized last hour.

When it was light enough to see the bark on the trees, the snow abated as abruptly as had the artillery. Now its hiss was gone, and the mist in front of the infantrymen staring into it was parted by the wind. You cannot see the wind or the air, and yet they're always there. Like God, air is invisible, and yet you feel its presence when you move through it or as it presses against you when it rises. The wind is a lesson always in play, and it revealed a low ceiling of white and soot-black clouds enameled with orange light that moved along their undersides as if a painter were stroking with an unseen brush. When the mist rolled east and the fields were cleared, the whole eastern sky flickered with orange. Half a dozen burning towns came into view at once. Spaced evenly on the whitened plain according to the dictates of medieval agriculture, they looked like campfires. Pillars of black smoke rose from yellow, flaming bases. The army would soon take these towns. Within or close to them, the Wehrmacht waited to defend or counterattack, their hopes shattered, their anger permanently annealed. When they would fight they would be as steadfast and tragic as the dead. Bullet for bullet, blow for blow, the Americans would meet and roll over them. The soldiers of neither side fought for what propaganda told them, or for principle, or for each other, as is commonly claimed. They fought because they had been set to it, and would hold fast to the impulse of which they were part, which had begun before the beginning of time.

Letting Sussingham sleep into his watch, Harry remained transfixed by the burning towns. Daylight revealed a nation of crows on the snow-covered plain. Thousands were in the sky or on the ground—flying in tightening circles, breaking off to glide down, running to take off, or walking like old people trying to dance. They fell from a white sky as if they had just been created, and their spirals echoed the columns of black smoke beyond them. In cold winters these crows flew west and southwest from Russia, above the armies or lighting among them, neutral and immune. This was the first Harry had seen of them during the war, although in the thirties he saw them in Vienna. There they lit to find warmth and peck in the snow on the banks of the unfrozen Danube after their start on the steppes and their flight over forgotten worlds in Bukovina and Bohemia and on the plains of Hungary.

What he saw ahead of him took Harry out of the orbit of France and to the edges of Eastern Europe. The Russian cold had sent the crows over the lands of bleak weather from which he himself had descended. He understood the language and somehow remembered the climate, the terrain, and how the rivers ran in full but beaten flood. If he closed his eyes, a hundred generations pulled him back as if the sojourn in America had been just a dream. Entranced by fatigue, he found himself in the Pale of Settlement. The powerlessness and peril of fighting through the winter onto the German plains brought him to the gatherings of his faceless ancestors, whose poverty, glory, and humanity were now entwined in fire and smoke swirling like the crows. Because he did not and could not ever know them, a condition to which the English euphemistically referred as the obscurity of one's origins, he envied for a moment the aristocratic families who had been able to keep records and paintings of preceding generations. But his envy vanished when he thought of how empty of emotion were records of achievement, how unexpressive the portraits — how, despite the brittle gloss that lined the walls of aristocratic houses, in citations of heroism, wealth, or lineage, so little of life was remembered or conveyed.

Instead, those from whom he had descended arose within him — forgotten men, women, and children too poor and oppressed for commemoration. The more exhausted, hopeless, and endangered he became, the more real they seemed, flashing with gold and red as if they were alive. They were so close and real he thought he might touch them. Whence they had come he could not know, but perhaps as he came closer and closer to death he was simply carried forward to them as they waited.

What he saw, imagined, and remembered was the convergence of immortal souls. These were more powerful than armies or empires and more radiant than sunlight. He could not see their faces, because they were swirling like dancers, having risen wildly from the darkness and been shot into the air in spark and flame. If he had been able to rise above the plain and join them, he would have. He stretched out his left hand as if to touch them, as if they would take it and bring him home.

In midmorning it began to snow enough to mute the glow of the fires and swallow up all the smoke. When Sussingham came up to Harry's position he saw that Harry was breathing sharp, infrequent breaths: the night exhaustion of a sentry in the cold, and hardly unusual. "It's your turn," Sussingham said.

"My turn to do what? It's your turn."

"Showers and hot food."

"That's funny."

"No, back a few miles they set up a kind of dog-face hotel with hot water. There's a truck taking one man from each squad every trip. You get an hour and a half before they bring you back."

"I'll go last," Harry said. He was the ranking officer.

"They want whoever was standing guard. That's the way it works. Go ahead. I'm next after you."

Not far from the line, COM Z, the supply and logistics command, had made a resort for soldiers on the front, planting a forest of large tents on a sloping field. Trucks were parked everywhere or going back and forth. Smoke poured from cook trailers as if they were racing locomotives. Harry could smell meat, gravy, and fried potatoes.

When he got off the truck, infantrymen in the line that had formed at the first station offered him a place in front because he was an officer, but he refused it. It was expected that they would offer, and it was hoped that he would decline. They appreciated this, and when officers were as filthy and ragged as they were, and despite their rank had not put themselves ahead, they would follow them wherever necessary. It was the way it was supposed to be.

In the first tent they recorded his name and gave him a towel, a small bar of soap, and a package with five pairs of socks and two sets of underwear. Before the cold had set in and the mud solidified, every soldier in the Seventh Army had been issued one pair of socks per day. No other army in the world had ever been so richly supplied. It was possible to follow the trail of battle by taking note of discarded socks. Some of the less intelligent men, trying to accumulate socks to sell after the war, had trench foot and bulging packs.

After receiving his linens, Harry passed into a gap between the first and second tents, where a furious snow squall made it almost impossible to see someone directly in front of him. Once inside the second tent, he stripped, gave up his old socks and underwear, and gathered his gunnery flannel, pants, shirt, sweater, tunic, and coat into a bundle. Naked for a short time, he went outside and saw many entrances to an immensely long tent. At one of these he was told by a soldier standing just inside, "Take number two, leave your stuff on this side, and close the curtain so water doesn't get on your clothing and your rifle. Get out your razor." Harry complied. "Not everyone brings one. When you pull the chain, the water'll run for eight minutes. After that it stops and you get out. Did you see the boilers?"

"No."

"They got big boilers and tank trucks on the other side. The water's real hot. Make sure you get the soap off pretty early, or you'll have to live with it."

Harry left his things on the duckboard outside the shower, pulled out his razor, put in his last blade, and entered. The walls were canvas and not particularly clean, and the floor was a freight pallet that was slippery with slime and moss. Though it was almost dark, he could see a gleam that marked the chrome shower head. Soap and razor in hand, he pulled the chain. A thick pressurized stream so hot it reddened his skin hit him with a shock. Sometimes even fancy hotels did not have enough hot water. Not here. For half a minute he just let the water play over him. Steam rose, and for the first time in weeks he was actually hot. He got to work frantically with the soap, lathering and cleaning as if he were something very rough and dirty, which he was.

Not devoting so much as a second to removing the soap, he let the water do it in the course of things as he ran the remnants of the bar over a week's worth of beard, until his face was covered by an inch of white mousse. Held under the stream of hot water, the new blade was supple and sharp, and by the time he was clean-shaven he had about four minutes left. He turned his face to the stream and slowly revolved so as to be covered everywhere. Never had water been so wonderful.

When it stopped, he dried himself, surrendered the thin towel to a bin, picked up his clothes and rifle, and staggered forward to the next station, a tent in which half a dozen lines of men were "puffed" with DDT. At the next station they dressed, combed their hair, and saw their new selves in clouded metal mirrors fastened to the canvas walls of the tent.

Fully dressed and armed once again, they went outside and waited in the snow before being seated in one of the huge mess tents. Everyone was so hot that no one wore a helmet or a balaclava, and while they were waiting their hair froze and snow dusted the tops of their heads. In the mess tent they picked up trays and went from server to server taking on food. At the end of this, Harry found himself sitting on a bench at a long table with a good space on either side of him. He had a knife, fork, spoon, paper napkin, and an aluminum tray upon which were a pound of pot roast, a pile of fried potatoes, corn, and a large piece of COM Z chocolate cake without icing. Hot tea with many sugars filled his canteen cup. The light that came through the high ceiling of the tent was silvered by the snow that had collected on the canvas, which in places sagged and dripped. From outside, the sound of gas burners penetrated what might have been a steady silence had it not been for the occasional huge thud of incoming German artillery. As the men ate, a hundred in Harry's tent alone, they hardly noticed the concussions. They were clean and warm, with clean linen, and they were eating real food. That was enough.

Though hardly a word was spoken, from somewhere behind Harry came the words, heard as if faintly echoed from the vaulted roof of a busy train station, "It's near Atlanta." And during the meal a name was called out—someone who had left his dog tags in the shower. It was almost like a monastery, until a captain walked in, banged an aluminum cup against a tent poll as if there had been noise to suppress, and went through a recitation he had made many times before and would make many times again.

"Listen up," he said. "General orders. I'm supposed to remind you of a few things, because we've been taking unnecessary casualties as people have gotten careless. Remember, European roads, especially in Germany, are intersected about every thousand meters by lanes at right angles. These are often swept by machine-gun fire. Don't walk down them. Cross fast. Got that? That's one.

"Two: How many of you are gonna die because you forgot how to attack a pillbox? Let me remind you. Don't do it unless you've got the right team. Wait for it. Put it together. Get it right. You need two BARS, a bazooka, a light machine gun, two to four riflemen, and two men with demolitions. That's a lot, but it works, and it'll get the job done and probably save your goddamned life. There's a method here. Follow it. Night approach. Dawn attack. Fire at the openings with everything you've got. Demolitions can then move to the rear. Blow the door. Toss in the grenades. Enfilade fire as the enemy exits if any are left. Okay? Don't forget.

"And three: Everybody keep this in mind. A vigorous attack pressed relentlessly and with surprise—don't slack—is the best chance you have of living through the war. It may not seem so even now after all you've done, but it is. If you plod toward the enemy he'll hold out five times as long and kill five times as many of us. If you run him down quick he can't and he won't. Officers, noncoms, squad leaders—everybody—keep these three things in mind. That's all."

At the very last station, Harry was given five chocolate bars and three packs of cigarettes. Just before he got on the truck he passed some sort of welfare officer, his insignia obscured by snow, who asked, "Do you need anything?"

Almost universally the reply was a stunned repetition of the question — "Do I need anything?" — followed by uncontrollable laughter that was a gift in itself, of relief. And on the truck back, for a short time, they were as happy as babies in their mothers' arms, because from start to finish, over a little more than an hour and a half, they were reacquainted with life, which gave them a reason to live.

The next day, after everyone had experienced three or four hours of happiness before things reverted to normal, a regimental combat team, one-third the fighting strength of a division, came down the road in several miles of trucks, armor, and infantry ready to press east. They were to pass through the several companies of infantry that had advanced to and held the wood, and who would follow them to their farthest salient, to hold once again as the main force recharged and waited for gasoline.

Everyone knew that soldiers rest and fight, then rest and fight, so the combat teams that were poised to thread through the lines onto the plain below thought no less of the soldiers who had been holding the position until their arrival. Some of the newcomers asked questions of Harry and the others, but most were quiet, depressed, sullen, or in dignified despair. As soon as they began to fight, their fear and melancholy would vanish, but now they stared at the pine boughs laden with snow, or rested their foreheads on their hands, and remembered things from childhood and things from not so long ago. Poets could not have been more contemplative, though some of the men drowned their fear in bravado and talked about what they would do to the Germans. Some would do what they said, if they could, if they found themselves in a house where they might kill the men and rape the women. They were very few, but they did exist, and they made the American lines less solid than they might have been, because their existence was a threat to body and soul.

The armor was in the lead, tanks ten feet apart stretching back on the road as far as one could see. The tankers spent the night as miserably as anyone else, because they could neither sleep in their tanks nor make decent fires. And because they were not as warmly dressed as soldiers who were outside for twenty-four hours a day in the cold and wind, they were like horses who find themselves in the field without blankets or their natural heavy coats.

Thousands of men were scattered unit by unit among the trees, waiting for first light. They were spared the stench of their own waste only because of the subfreezing temperatures and the winds that lifted warmth away from things so efficiently that a dead man or animal would hard freeze in less than an hour. Something hot to drink — from a thermos, a small concealed fire, or a can of Sterno's patient work beneath a cup — was as appreciated and desired as if Venus had presented herself in the nude. More so, because in the hours before the attack the great sexual charge that for an infantryman is either fully on or fully off, was fully off. They breathed carefully, and slept fitfully.

Just before dawn, officers moved among the masses of men and ordered them into roughly assembled formations. Having arisen from sleep into shattering cold, they tried to stop trembling, and when, disciplining their arms and shoulders, they forced them to be still, their teeth would chatter.

The tankers climbed into their tanks. At the signal of a dropped flag, they started their engines all at once. Not even the heavy snow would conceal the sound from the enemy dug in around the town, so, having alerted him, they rushed. But within seconds the huge rumble of scores of tank engines brought forth a barrage of heavy artillery that the Germans had been holding in reserve. 280-millimeter shells came in a shrieking arc over their heads and burst behind them. And then the explosions started walking back in a tightening pattern as if to spur the concentrated attackers out into the open. This may have been the plan, but the open, choked with delicately falling snow, was no longer a field of fire. Knowing that they could not be seen on these fields, because nature had covered them with a perfect smokescreen, the tank commanders were impatient to escape the walking barrage. A 280-millimeter shell could collapse a large house, shatter a concrete pillbox, or sink a ship. With a direct hit, it would obliterate a tank.

No longer needed in the line, which was about to be pushed forward radically, and desperate to leave the area of bombardment, the soldiers who had held the woods rushed to take their places on the tanks that were about to leave. No one was going to defy the incoming artillery. Leaving behind crucial items and smoldering fires, they ran to the tanks and climbed up on them.

From their lead position, Harry's stick climbed on the forward tank. This was not as foolish as it might have seemed. They knew from long experience that in open country tanks fan out and the one at the head of the line would take a position on the extreme left or right, away from the point of the spear.

As shells were bursting behind them they climbed onto the first tank and knocked at its turret with their rifle butts. But the tank wouldn't move until the officer standing in front of it dropped his flag to signal the attack, and he waited until everyone was on. Rice was on, Bayer was on, Johnson was on, Hemphill was on, Reeves was on, and Sussingham was on. But not Harry.

Harry, who was as athletic as any of the others, was unable to mount the tank because the gunnery flannel that he had wrapped around him made it impossible to vault onto the deck. He tried, but it was as if he were an old man with a bad back. As the column began to move, forcing aside the officer with the flag, Harry ran alongside and held out his hand. Bayer, whose weight was a steady anchor, went to the edge of the deck to help pull him up, but the tank made a slight turn and the track shot out toward Harry, forcing him to throw himself backward. Having lost his opportunity, he was left behind.

With hand signals, pointing to themselves and then the ground, they asked if they should jump off. Harry signaled back that they should stay on. Hemphill, who was holding Debra the beagle, asked by pantomime if he should toss her off. She was Harry's dog. Harry said yes, and she was pitched into the snow. She rolled, righted herself, and ran toward her master and benefactor as he whistled to her over the sound of the armor. Stumbling forward, his carbine banging against his back, Harry tried to keep up, but couldn't. Breathing hard and not thinking, he was driven on by the shells that, sighted-in during the retreat of the German artillery, had found their marks back along the road and blown whole truckloads of men into the air. The explosions were so massive that when they hit a vehicle they blew it a hundred feet or more off to the side. But when all they did was crater the road, they just as often flattened the small pines along it, allowing other vehicles to pass.

With the paratroopers riding atop it, the lead tank was about to move out of the trees when it stopped short. Harry kept running toward it. He saw its gun move and thought that perhaps it was going to fire an exploratory round dead ahead. The tank commander dropped into the turret. Harry slowed, as if to give himself time to understand what was happening.

During the night, shielded by the snow, the Germans — it must have taken fifty men — had pulled up an anti-tank gun by hand two hundred feet from the edge of the forest and set it down on the road just below a dip in the hill. The tank driver had seen it first, then the commander, then Harry, who shouted to his men to leap off. But as if in a dream the engines drowned out his voice.

The dog kept on running. Harry called to her. "Debra!" he shouted. "Debra! Come! Come!" It seemed insane to be calling so desperately, his heart breaking, in the almost blinding snow, after a dog named Debra, someplace in Germany, while looking into the barrel of a German 88. What happened, happened in a fraction of a second. But even as the light and flame burst from the dark spot that was the bore of the gun, and before he heard the sound, Harry felt sorrow, hopeless sorrow, and right before the shell hit, he exhaled as if he would never breathe again.

The first shot blew the turret off the tank and onto the north side of the road, where it lay like an overturned horseshoe crab, the cannon its tail. Harry watched his men launched twenty feet into the air and propelled backward, some over the tank that was second in line, landing on the road behind it, some onto the side of the road, beyond the turret. All in an instant, they were shot upward as if hit by a speeding truck. As they flew they tumbled, their limbs spread from their bodies. They knocked into each other, and they snapped like towels, with motion whipping through them from head to toe.

When the second tank saw the turret coming off the first, it hesitated and then started to back up. Paralyzed, Harry stood by its side, staring at those of his men splayed out unconscious in the snow behind it. Although it could not have been for more than half a second, it seemed forever before his nerves could communicate with his muscles. This half second would haunt him for the rest of his life. When finally he could move, he reached the backing tank, and, having unslung his carbine, beat the armor with the butt as he screamed for them to halt. Even as he was doing this, he knew that to the driver the sound would be only faint knocks, and that his voice could not be heard.

Anticipating the second shot, the commander had dropped down and closed the hatch. Nothing would stop the tank from its movement. Behind it, the motionless paratroopers lay, perhaps dead. Harry beat frantically with his carbine. His throat was raw with screaming. Then he dropped his weapon and ran toward the three men in the path of the backing tank. He had time to seize only the one nearest, whose helmet he grasped and pulled, dragging him out of the way. Though Harry didn't know until later, it was Johnson, and although Harry exerted himself to the point where he thought his heart would burst, the right tread of the tank rolled over Johnson's right leg from just below the knee down.

Harry was caught between freezing with horror at the sound of the treads crushing the two men he was unable to help, and the blood from Johnson's leg reddening the snow. The sound was the same as that of a pile of twigs and small branches when a man puts his weight on them to compress them into a cart or a wheelbarrow. Skulls, bones, and ligaments were cracking and snapping. Harry was shouting, not words but something from deep in his chest as, at the same time, he mechanically found a tourniquet in one of his pouches and tied off Johnson's leg. Then he started screaming for a corpsman, until a second shell hit and the crippled tank blew up.

The force of the explosion was like an incoming wave across a broad front. Harry thought he could see it, that it looked like the blurry, heated air above a highway in July or August. It propelled him back, parallel to the ground, sweeping over Johnson without effect. He was flying, and in the fractional moment before he blacked out, he felt and knew a thousand things. Among them, incorrectly, was that this was his death. Not only was it not terrifying or unpleasant, it was euphoric. It was the end of gravity and pressure and the triumph of light. As time began to stop, he sensed perfection. And although he saw no scenes of his life, and nothing was played for him like a newsreel, it was as if he could feel everything — not every emotion he had ever experienced, but only those that were deep and good — in a concentration so intense he would later recall it as resembling a slab of black stone. And as he flew without volition or control he felt as if the world were moving, not he. That he was the only thing that was still was a great comfort. And then, before he hit the ground, he found himself in a painless darkness that he did not even know was dark.

How much later he couldn't tell, but he awoke staring at a white sky from which snow was falling straight at him. Nor could he calculate how long he lay without feeling his body or being able to move. He wasn't sure at first that he was alive. Like something that wasn't a part of him, his right hand appeared before his face to clear away the snow that had accumulated on his eyelids. There wasn't much, not enough to completely obscure his vision. He felt his limbs and moved them. Then he rolled onto his side. He was looking back on the road, along which armor was traveling in a line, its engines deafening. Riding atop most of the tanks, as always, were infantry. He turned over to look in the other direction. The hulk of the first tank was burning gently. The second tank was gone. The armor had cut a detour around the scene, smashing down trees to do it. Now it moved fluidly in a crescent, and returned to the road, passing the upended German antitank gun, on the way east, from which the thuds of battle came rolling up the hill.

A corpsman who was bent over Johnson held a bottle of plasma high in his left hand. Harry rose to his knees. Unable to stand, he walked on all fours halfway, and then, somehow, rose and staggered. His carbine lay behind the corpsman, half visible in the snow. "Are these your men?" the corpsman asked.

"Get an ambulance," Harry said, as if he were on Central Park West.

"The road's not wide enough for traffic in the other direction," the corpsman replied. Harry knew this, but he had had to say what he said. "They're going to bring a field hospital and set up right down there," the corpsman told him, meaning just beyond the trees.

"When?"

"Should be very soon. We were behind the first five platoons. It should be now." He was working on Johnson, who had awakened. The corpsman was preparing morphine, and had laid out pressure bandages. As Harry moved toward the others, the corpsman said, "I can't help them. I checked."

Hemphill and Reeves were still on the road. Nothing was left of Reeves. Harry couldn't even look. Hemphill was not easy to see, either, but he was alive. Harry moved toward him. Rice, Bayer, and Sussingham were still where they had landed north of the road. Bayer was sitting up, staring into space. Rice and Sussingham looked as if they were sleeping.

When Harry got to Hemphill he saw that the tread had run over his middle, and that he looked like something in the cartoons they show before movies, which Harry would hate always. That Hemphill was alive did not seem possible, but he was. Everything was forgotten. All differences, sharpnesses, challenges, had dissolved. He looked at Harry as if Harry were his mother and he were a baby.

Seeing that he was shivering, Harry put his arms around his shoulders. "They're bringing up a field hospital to just beyond the trees. A whole field hospital."

Hemphill said "Oh," and looked toward the edge of the forest, where there was much more light. "Where's the dog?" he asked.

"I don't know," Harry said.

"The dog is gone," Hemphill whispered.

"Hemphill," Harry said, tightening his embrace, "I want you to do something for me. I want you to do something." Harry's wool uniform and the gunnery flannel underneath had begun to be soaked with Hemphill's blood, which was as warm as bath water. "Just one thing."

"Any fuckin' thing, Captain, any fuckin' thing."

"Live."

Smiling, Hemphill expelled a weak breath as if to laugh. "Captain, that I can't do." And he didn't.

Untouched himself, soaked with blood, holding a body that was still warm, Harry turned his face upward, as if inquiring, and the only answer he received was the snow falling evenly and impassively, its pace unvaried, spilling from endless reservoirs above.

# 37

## CATHERINE

Just after dawn, surprising gusts of wind moved the falling snow off the perpendicular as the cloud layer broke to show light blue. Harry was still lost in memory and nothing was left of the fire, but time was recalibrating with the steady clearing of the sky. The Hudson was azure, its flanking auburn, rust, and yellow hills now covered in a quickly disappearing blanket of snow. Like the sound of an alarm clock that seems unnecessarily hysterical to someone who is already awake, a train from Beacon clattered down the tracks and tooted its whistle as it approached Cold Spring. In the fall of 1946, the war had been won, and the great landscape he saw before him—including West Point, clinging to the hillsides on the opposite bank of the Hudson—was at peace. But shortly after the train passed, the faint notes of reveille drifting across the water suggested that although war might sleep, it would never fail to wake.

By the time Harry reached the station at Cold Spring the morning trains had gone. Pacing on the platform, he waited for at least an hour until a desultory local arrived, and on it he slept to recover his strength, until the train rushed into the Park Avenue tunnel very near the place where as a boy he had swung from the girders of the El. And with a whoosh that rattled a hundred windows, shades, floor plates, and doors, this put a temporary end to crossword puzzles and news stories about the rebirth of Europe.

In Grand Central, he looked up at the representation of heaven and was moved by the unboundedness written into it by art. Perhaps those who made it had known, like Michelangelo, that when someone looks up and stretches into immobility as his eyes focus and lock, he is taken further than he might go on the level, cut-off paths of the world. Add to that the flashing of the constellations, the oceanic green of the vault, and the white noise roiling above the sea floor of travertine, and never was a station more like a cathedral.

Harry crossed the concourse and dodged through the crowded arcades to the counter in the Oyster Bar. Although no one could know it, he was a soldier in a dream. Still not quite sure what was real, he was determined to enjoy it even so. All around him the advertising men, accountants, and lawyers were the infantry and sailors of just a short time before, but now in tweed jackets, pinstriped suits, and hats. They had returned, and were grateful. Theirs was the energy of those who had survived and were at the beginning of new lives. Every reader of English at Harvard College was required to know the Bible, as Harry did, in English more than in Hebrew, which he always thought a failing. The sight of legions of soldiers now in suits brought back Deuteronomy 24 from the King James: *When a man hath taken a new wife, he shall not go out to war ... but he shall be free at home one year.* It had a very sad ring to it, because years end.

And now, for the sake of the ones who hadn't come home, Harry lived the dream they had dreamed — of ordinary things, of pedestrian routine, of the small and quiet actions that to the less experienced might seem worthless or oppressive, but that were secretly laden with the beauty that graced the quiet lives that those who had not returned could not live. Here were the dead in the hearts of the living, to whom the living spoke without speaking, saying: Here is a bustling restaurant and its whited sound; here are the lights of the theater; the halls of the Metropolitan; the afternoon sun deepening the fall colors of the park; the wind rising on the avenues, blowing dust in your eye; and here is a woman, her touch warm, her breathing deep and delicate, her skin fragrant, her patience loving.

They carried the dead as lightly as if they were the newly born infants in their arms, the children to whom they would gladly show the wonders of the world. They might stop in an alley at a stage door, so that the fallen of the Pointe du Hoc could listen to the sound of a chorus line, the music rising from the orchestra pit like smoke in the trees, or stare transfixed at a brass banister under strong incandescent light, praying, literally praying, that the gleam of its refraction would skip to another realm to shine in eyes that could no longer see.

As Harry ate, he remembered the invisible others: Hemphill, nasty and unapproachable, had at the last elicited from Harry a deep love. Harry would never forget Reeves, who would forever be a boy, and Townsend Coombs, gravityless in his last and infinite moment, fixed in the night above the sea near Sicily, never to disappear. The living as well drew upon his loyalty, and would always have a place in his heart and trust: Bayer, who spoke of the necessity of compromise and imperfection, even corruption, yet ducked and weaved to make whatever he did as pure and ideal as it could be; Rice, who should have been a general, patiently taking orders from young lieutenants; Sussingham, irrepressible, never at a loss for a joke even as in the collapsing world he held the ground that ten men could not; Johnson, both brilliant and kind as rarely one sees.

And he saw the living and the dead in the men working fast behind the bar, who were like the best troops in an army. Fully equal, absorbed, and taken up by their tasks, they had surrendered to the objective and transcended themselves. As they polished cups, served soup, poured bottles of beer, wiped counters, carried lobster on a plate, and opened clams and oysters at high speed, a dozen men in starched white — black, white, Irish, Italian, Chinese — worked furiously, interweaving without collision, calling out, checking off, making change, greeting, bantering, and moving through the rush like a platoon holding off a counterattack or a deck crew launching carrier planes. United by the deeper rhythms of their work, their reward was a steadying happiness.

Harry was both fully there and elsewhere. He blessed the food and ate for those who could not eat: oyster pan roast, as he remembered it, almost scaldingly hot; broiled lobster eaten slowly and carefully, as there was never enough; a tall glass of beer with foam that lasted; a salad; French fries; and then chocolate mousse and tea. Then through the great hall of Grand Central and its twinkling lights; onto the street at midday; out to a city perpetually strutting and never asleep; to the streetcars and bells, and the buses running along the avenues like unhappy buffalo inexplicably tamed to their routes; to weak, white, nearly winter sunshine that could almost be blown aside by the wind, straining to penetrate the blue-tinted diesel exhaust of paradoxically hoarse trucks and strike the glass sparkles in the sidewalks, where it would echo until exterminated by the shadow of a passing cloud; to the rare silences that would implode amidst the commotion, and lay down stillness like a pool of water in fractured ice; to the deft traffic on the rivers at evening, tugs, barges, cruisers, and launches, their moving lights a diamond necklace for Manhattan; and to Catherine, his wife.

Except for two matinees each week, Catherine's was evening work. On rare occasions, Harry met her and they walked home (his apartment had become theirs) in the dense late night air of fall, which was somehow cold without being cold, never having been in winter. As opposed to thinner summer breezes, it flowed around them almost like water and gave the impression of having color — perhaps gunmetal blue or dark gray. Mostly she would arrive home by taxi at around eleven, far earlier than others in the cast, because she did her curtain calls in the coat she wore in the first scene, with her street clothes underneath and her stage makeup already removed. Perhaps because of this, at curtain calls she looked wan, almost as if she had been reprimanded. And she was out of the theater like a shot, beating to the street and the taxis ahead of even the standees. Sometimes she didn't bother to stay for the curtain call.

These were the best times for her, late at night when she was full of energy and disappointment, and there was Harry, who adored her. For a long time before they slept they would touch, stroke, kiss, with things said, cries cried, requests made and answered, shame courted and shared, eyes open and staring at climax. There was nothing they kept from one another, nothing they did not know, and it seemed as if there would be no end to it, as if they were always just at the beginning. Deeply in love, they were easily lost in the sea of the other's body.

In the light of day, however, though he could not match expenditures with revenues, Harry tried to save Copeland Leather, and although Catherine volunteered to help, and sometimes worked in the loft alongside Harry or wherever she was needed, she had to save her strength for the evening performances. You would not find her at Sardi's or cocktail receptions. She did not receive the kind of invitations received by others in the cast — even George Yellin — to read to sick children (in front of the press), to speak to ladies' groups and at schools, to sell things on the radio and pose for stilted magazine portraits: "Here is Miss Cucuando, the leading lady of the new Broadway hit *Brazil!,* tending to her tomato garden in New Rochelle with her husband Xavier and their dog Vicky" — in six pounds of makeup (Miss Cucuando, not the dog), lit by half a dozen klieg lights powered by a generator truck in the driveway, with safety pins out of camera view tightening her bodice until she could hardly breathe, and after four and a half hours of art direction and trying to get the dog to smile. Such things did not come Catherine's way, although at one time, when she thought they would, she was sure she would turn them down. Now, after too much silence, she was not so sure.

In the light of day — and for the five non-matinee days a week she was free into the evening — she could be found where perhaps no ingénue of the musical theater had ever set foot, in the reading rooms of libraries, where the world could open quietly to infinity and she could visit and consult remnant souls in traces of themselves and their efforts on shelves deep in the stacks, in obscure places past which the stack workers flew on their roller skates, unconscious of them, popping bubble gum, thinking of money, dinner, and sex. Here were books that had not been opened in a hundred years and yet had not died and would not die even if no one would ever open them again. How such life is impressed forever upon time Catherine did not know, but she felt strongly that nothing was ever lost, that the world was so full of faint echoes that the air was almost solid.

She served her sentence of anonymity anonymously. Who would

ever know the people moored to the green glow of the lamps in row after row upon the long tables of the main reading room of the New York Public Library? The famous, for the most part, had never seen the place, at least those who were famous by face. Mainly scholars filled the chairs, and if scholars are assertive it is only with other scholars, for when they come up against the rougher sort, especially in New York, they shatter, cower, or melt. While she was teaching herself to deal with her wounds, Catherine was delighted to be in such timid company.

She would order from the stacks something she picked at random from the card catalog, and then make of it what she would. She might spend an afternoon reading a book in French about Marcus Aurelius, dictionary by her side, immersed in the language, satisfied, delighted, and speaking to herself by the end of the day in the Parisian dialect she had learned as a child. A description of the Hudson Valley, 1824. A technical manual for making steel. An essay upon the English Revolution. She followed her nose. October fled by. Sometimes, she would close the book, or not, direct her gaze at the far spaces of the reading room, where no one ever looked — red dragons could have been battling in the dark as long as they did so in silence — and think about her situation.

She had been done an injustice by the press, or so it seemed to her, although she could not be sure, and she believed at times that her singing and stage presence were simply not worthwhile. Nor could she be sure of or separate the involvement of Victor Marrow. Perhaps he had been the instigator, or perhaps not. It was possible that every critic failed to notice her, failed even to dislike her, or thought she was not quite untalented enough to attack. The way the tendrils of all such possibilities intertwined left her with no means to judge either herself or others. Deprived of bearings, she suffered a kind of motion sickness, a continual nausea the effect of which was rapid corrosion.

She fought this as best she could. Except for George Yellin, the other cast members now took obvious if unstated delight in her fall — which had cleared the way for them — and expressed the kind of sympathy they might have for a great racehorse that had broken its leg. They said their piece with as much politeness as they could, and then, only as quickly as did not appear ruthless, turned away and instantly forgot. George himself, who was in the last effulgence of his life, could not endanger his good fortune by allowing his sympathy to cast him too far back toward what he had just escaped. Sidney no longer thought she was as desirable, and now that she was not an asset, seemed not so sure of his high opinion of her singing. Everything changed in the great currents of fashion, and Sidney had to put on plays to suit the public taste. He had investors to please and actors to sustain, not to mention himself. Like a statesman or a general, he had learned to move forward unaffected by the people who were left behind.

At first she was puzzled as to how one might fight complete disregard. But when she thought on it, she came up with a strategy. She understood that no matter what audiences might feel directly, they could be made to ignore their own convictions. Such was the social power and that of the press. She had seen it time and again. So she could not rely upon the natural reaction she had elicited at the beginning of the run. As attention gravitated to the new stars, she noticed that this reaction changed. Within weeks, the ovations for her went from the wind-driven downpour of large hail upon a metal roof, to the obligatory drizzle reserved for those whose appearance is an opportunity to rest the hands between more emphatic bursts of applause. It is not just that actors who live with the polite drizzle eventually die inside, but that their performances then conform to what is expected.

Determined to avoid this, her method of resistance was to recognize that she could not for long overcome the currents of fashion — not one young woman, not alone — and that no matter what she did, she had only a limited time. Given that, she need not conserve her energy as any wounded animal or person might, and she could be reckless with emotion, technique, and conviction, for her own pleasure if nothing else. Though she might be forced to retire, when in the field she would move with all her strength.

She could not rely upon opinion at all, even that of those whom she loved and who loved her. Of course Harry and her parents would tell her that she was wonderful, as Evelyn put it time and time again, but if she could no longer trust her own view, how could she trust theirs? She was out on a ledge. She would take her cues only from the music. All she could have, and ever have, was this, and if it took her up, and lifted her as she sang, that would have to be enough. Suffering throughout the day and after her performances, she held through with determination so that when the orchestra was struck her singing would be cut loose from the things of the world, and the song itself, fragile and evanescent, could spar with the background of silence.

She opened the book in front of her. It had just been delivered from the stacks: *A Survey of Flowers and Floral Ornamentation in European Painting, with Identification According to Biological Principles.* You could not major in music at Bryn Mawr without taking required courses in art and aesthetics. Because she had often sat in libraries with this kind of book, which had elicited intricate observations and comparisons, she looked at it unintimidated.

The page to which she had turned was in the section on lilies and irises. They were depicted in French and Italian paintings, in patterns on cloth of blue and gold, literal, abstract, or emblematic. Immediately she saw that the hierarchy of virtue in flowers was the opposite of what human intervention might create. The fleur-de-lis of Louis XIV was as dead as a horseshoe nail no matter how many courtiers subjugated themselves to it. As an emblem, it was lifeless. In a Botticelli or a Monet (although Monet was left out of this survey) flowers were beautiful, of a much higher rank than those that served as stilted emblems. Of a higher rank still, though hardly recognized and celebrated, were those in someone's garden. She imagined a woman tending them on a summer's day, lifting them in the sun, arrested by their color and scent. But of the highest rank were those that were never celebrated or seen, blooming by themselves in a corner of woods or at the edge of a field, never to be beheld. Distinction had no more effect on their essence or their glory than love or remembrance have upon the resurrection of the dead. In the few hours when flowers catch the sun, she realized, all are equal, then all are done. And in the reading room crowded with anonymous scholars amid long rows of sea-green lamps and in a dull murmur like that of the ocean in a shell, no one looked up but Catherine, whose face was upturned, as always when seeking courage and faith.

On the night when snow fell in the Hudson Highlands for the first time that October, it had brushed lightly over Manhattan on its way. Fluttering like a veil, it descended in confused spirals that trembled on winds channeled by the high towers, the upper floors of which were drowned in cloud. As Catherine walked to the theater, snowflakes sparkled on her coat. At the lamp over the stage door they plunged into its light before the storm moved north and left the city pleasantly breathless with its first intimation of winter.

As Harry had once gone into battle, so Catherine had entered the theater. Upon her demotion, the confidence of many generations of Hales had vanished, and she was put to the test anew with each performance. It was not nothing to sing into darkness, blinded by light, with just a glimpse of the hundreds of judges trying to relax in stiff formal clothes. And although she was strong and courageous, blessed with the vitality of youth, quick of wit, seductively hot of temper, and could fight with great spirit in everything from sharp debate to the waves of the Atlantic, she was in essence tender, and all the fight that was in her was there to protect her faith in the gentle and the good.

When, trying to control the nervous trembling that these days would escape from her hands were they extended too long, she had put away her coat, changed her clothes, applied stage makeup, and donned the gloves she wore at her entrance, she had some minutes before she went on. Although she was given warnings—a rap on her door, and the calling out of time left—she told time by the orchestra swelling in its overture.

A few minutes before her cue, she locked the door, sank to her knees, put her hands together palm to palm and fingertip to fingertip, closed her eyes, and did not quite pray. This was what for thousands of years warriors had done before going into battle. Her lips moved, but she spoke no words and asked for nothing. Given her posture and expression, she might have been in armor or mail, and a sword might have been stuck in the ground before her, her forehead lightly touching it. She was no different from Harry when, before the jump, hands in the same position, head bent or upraised, he leaned into his reserve chute as the plane rose and fell on the wind and he, too, not quite prayed, asking for nothing. From Catherine and from Harry came absolute surrender, and to Catherine and Harry came the deepest strength. The current was strong and magnetic, the exchange electric and warm as everything came alight from what the blind of spirit took for darkness. Catherine felt her heart swell with strength and love, and then she rose and unlocked the door.

She hurried through the corridors and to the edge of the stage, and from the shadows she watched the lights come up as if in an explosion. She could never see much beyond them, for her song was sung in the brightness of day, when every effect was intended to carry the city into the theater. As soon as the lights went on the orchestra burst into action. Someone pounded on piano keys like the police hammering down a door, and then came the strings, bells, horns, whistles, flutes, brass, and drums. By this time she was already front and center. And because she never tired of the greatness of the city that her task was to convey, she never had to pretend to astonishment. It was always real. She had it in memory, from childhood on, in a hundred thousand scenes.

She took the crucial breath that the audience had to hear. The music rose in a minor key, and when the melody took over and began its riverine flow, this was where she was put to the test every night. For it was not enough for her voice to be beautiful, as it was; to be powerful; and to be pure. She had to embrace the song until it almost broke her heart, to devote herself solely to what was true, and to ignore the judgment of the world in favor of the judgment of heaven.

Their apartment overlooked the park through a bank of three double windows, each with a window seat. The Sunday after Harry returned from up the Hudson he and Catherine sat across from one another in the southernmost alcove. She looked out at the park, over the reservoir, and toward midtown, its towers dark at dusk with not a soul working in them, not even the cleaning ladies, who that night could sleep in Harlem. Harry's view was to the northeast, where the lights of the Triboro Bridge, having just come on, had begun to sparkle with a slight blue-green tint. The pueblos of Fifth Avenue, which in noonday sun were as pale as the White Cliffs of Dover, had turned butter-colored and then deep red with the very last of the sun. This light broke the buildings into color planes of scarlet and black as darkness climbed them from the ground up. In the silent afternoon of late October the light would briefly glow like a coal and then go quickly. Strings of street lamps now decorated the park asymmetrically because someone, somewhere, had thrown a switch, and clouds, the last pale things, floated regally over Queens.

She didn't want to break the silence, but she had a question. "Harry," she asked, "what's a nudnik?"

"How can you have lived in New York all your life and not know what a nudnik is?"

"I don't know what it is."

After a long silence, Harry said, "Why do you ask?"

"I went into a candy store on Columbus Avenue to make a phone call. While I was in the booth, fishing out change from my purse, a man came in with his son. The boy, who was about eight or nine, burst into the store, screaming 'I want a monkey! I want a monkey!'

"Naturally, I noticed. I couldn't help it. What he meant was one of those little plastic monkeys that slides up and down a red stick. If you put the monkey at the top, it takes a minute to jerk all the way down."

"Yes. George the Sixth gives those out at state dinners in Buckingham Palace."

"They're very clever, actually. The father took one down, bought a cigar and a paper, and was about to pay when the kid showed up from the back of the store with another monkey on a red stick. 'I have one,' the father says. 'Put it back.' Then the kid says, 'I need two.' 'Two?' the father asks. 'Why?' 'A spare.' 'A spare? Why would you need a spare monkey?' 'In case one breaks.' 'No, put it back.' 'No, I'll take two.' 'Uh-uh, put it back.' 'No, I need two.' 'Put *it back!*' 'I want it! I want it!'

"Then the father looked at him more than sternly, and said, 'Cyril! Don't be a nudnik!' What's a nudnik?"

"Cyril is a nudnik."

"I know. I mean, I understand the context and I have a general idea, but I can't fix it precisely. The West Side is new to me. Don't forget, I grew up in the East."

"A nudnik," Harry said, as if lecturing the assembled French Academy, "is a person — male, usually below middle age — who is simultaneously annoying, demanding, irritating, preposterous, cloying, deeply limited, insistent, energetic, needy, innocent, crafty, amusing, clueless, destructive, distractive, disconnected, monomaniacal, totally without self-awareness, off-putting, magnetic, haunting, whiny, horrible, exasperating, and, most of the time, Jewish. That's the short definition."

"It's Yiddish?"

"It could only be."

"Can you point one out?"

"Look out the window."

"I never heard of such a thing."

"Really? Well, guess what. Cyril has a brother. The brother's name is Irwin. He's going to grow up to be a pharmacist and a mass murderer. He's four years old but he looks like a miniature Harpo Marx, with curly blond hair and a crazed expression. On the scale of nudnikism, Cyril is a three. Irwin is a ten. When Irwin enters a room, he knows instinctively a thousand ways to make everyone insane in less than half an hour, and when he contemplates this he's filled with joy, like the Pope or the Dalai Lama."

"But Harry, how do you know?"

"It's in the blood."

Then Harry sniffed the air, raising his head progressively higher as one does when trying to catch a scent. "What is that?" he asked. Never having had much opportunity to cook, Catherine was daring to roast a chicken. She was quite unconcerned, because she was relaxed about household matters generally left to servants, and because for a while it had smelled good in the kitchen. But she had misread a digit in the cookbook, and the chicken, left in the oven for more than six hours, was getting fairly dry.

That day they had walked from the highest point of the city, in Kingsbridge, down to the Battery and then back up to 93rd Street, stopping in Chelsea for the most imprecisely named beverage in the world, the egg cream, which had neither egg nor cream, and at Fulton Street for clam broth and a salad. They were now so hungry that they had lost their hunger to a state of mild intoxication that made it all the easier simply to stare at one another as if in a trance. Just one look, just a touch, was like a strong surge of narcotic. On the rare occasions when instead of walking they took a subway, a bus, or a taxi, they would automatically and simultaneously reach out and take one another's hand, which would make them feel levitated.

"Tomorrow," said Harry, "I'm going to meet someone at the Niagara, the fisherman we almost ran over."

"Did you ever find out his real name?"

"If I find out too much about him, he won't help me."

"Help you do what?"

"The Niagara's on Wall Street," he said, not answering the question.

"I know. I've been there. Have you?"

"No."

"Oh, well, you'll see. In the center is a huge waterfall twenty feet high and fifty feet long. It's almost impossible to converse if you sit near it, and there's so much noise and activity you can't hear anyone else's conversation or keep track of who's there. They do business deals there so they can speak privately and still be in a restaurant. Help you do what?"

"We'll talk under the noise. It works, I'm told. That's probably why he chose it."

Catherine stood up next to the window seat, put a thumb and a forefinger next to one of the windowpanes, then turned, took a step toward the middle of the living room, and pivoted back toward Harry. "You really are going to kill Verderamé." She didn't have the gallant though half-serious air she had had when, at times, she had petulantly argued for it. Now it was real. "That's it?"

"It is."

"Then I've got to be involved."

"No, you've got to be uninvolved."

"That's not true. I've got to share the risk."

"I'm expendable," he said. "You're not. What would be the point if something happened to you? You're the future. It's my job to protect you."

"And what about me protecting you?"

"To put it as simply as I can, if I die, you can have and raise our child."

"But I'm not pregnant."

"Not even after what we did last night?"

"Well, maybe."

"But if *you* die, Catherine, everything stops dead."

"You could marry someone else."

"I don't want to marry someone else."

"Look," she said, "this man has no idea you're going after him, not in a million years. Otherwise, you couldn't even begin: you'd already be dead."

"That's right."

"So, in the initial stages, when he doesn't suspect...."

"He can never suspect."

"Let me be more precise, then: when it would not be possible for him to suspect."

"Okay."

"Then I can help. Afterward, I'll go live with my parents until it's safe. You can decide when I leave and when I come back, but you must let me help. You're not the only one with dictates. If I don't share in the risk I become nothing, just as you would. We're going to die anyway. If you hold as tightly to life as you propose, you'll smother it. For richer or for poorer, as one. We took an oath. The man is a killer. He's killed our own and he almost killed you. The law is paralyzed. He threatens our future. Look, I'm like you."

"How do you mean?"

"I wasn't born to run."

With this they stepped onto a higher and more dangerous plane, but she was right. He asked what she might do.

"You've made a plan, or you will have made a plan. You're not going to just charge in with guns blazing, are you?"

"A surgery, Catherine, would not be better organized."

"You'll need surveillance."

"Yes."

"And who would have done it? You? One person? Don't you think that might be noticed?"

"Not if it's done very carefully, over time."

"Patterns change with time. You can't age surveillance, I would imagine."

"Granted," Harry allowed, "and that with you it would halve the chances of discovery."

"No, reduce them by much more than that. I'm a woman. I'm an actress. I can speak in dialects and accents and I have closets full of clothes. I know costumes and makeup. I can be many different people. Someone like Verderamé looks at women only for sex. . . ."

"How do you know?"

"I'll bet. For him, a *dame* is not someone he has to worry about."

"But we don't need that kind of thing. It's more straightforward."

"But what if you do? Do you know where he lives?"

"Not yet."

"Do you know where he takes a walk?"

"I doubt he does."

"Do you know his routes when he travels?"

"Not at this point."

"Well, then, it's pretty clear," she said with irresistible authority, sounding so much like a Hale, "that I'm in." And she was.

# 38

## COUNSEL AND ARMS

NEW YORKERS OFTEN FORGET, and some may not know, that theirs is a state of truly vast forests, spectacular rivers, fjords, and lakes, long pastoral valleys, and a huge, vertiginous fall of water that through a single spigot drains an area the size of Western Europe. And sometimes they remember, which is why Harry was able to wait for Vanderlyn in front of the Niagara, where hundreds of people were eating or serving lunch, and the noise befitted the name. Intermittently but unceasingly the front doors flapped like elephant ears as people entered and exited. From the hard-working, blue-jacketed Wall Street runners in white bucks half constructed of cardboard, to the top, pompous, stately, plump investment bankers in Florentine leather shoes, people came for the broiled fish, the mulligan stews, raw shellfish of fifty types and twice as many cocktails and beers, including beer from Mongolia, Anatolia, and the interior of Nigeria. The floor was made of little white tiles, the same mosaic found in millions of New York bathrooms, but here they were covered in sawdust that twice a day busboys swept up and dumped into the harbor. According to tradition, one threw one's oyster and clam shells aside. This started in the eighteenth century, no one had ever thought to stop it, and now, close to midcentury and after two hundred years, the discarded shells still hit the floor like bullet casings.

As Harry waited, he looked through a window into the restaurant. The thin mistresses of fat men; the fat mistresses of thin men; secretaries in mouton; waitresses with strong, straight backs, because they carried heavy trays; and other women, business women, wives, college girls who had drifted downtown, God knows who from God knows where, were inside, working the fields of force that directed the actions of men, who could, without seeing, feel the presence of a woman walking by or sitting near them, and who adjusted their glances, positions, and thoughts accordingly, their breathing involuntarily, and their behavior summarily. The presence of a woman was such that if she walked into a restaurant and sat down at a table, the vital signs of every man who could see her would change in proportion to the inverse square of the distance between them, and some might even die. This was the subtext not only of restaurants but of the world, a metaphysics that would forever overlay everything.

Harry scanned the room. Each of the five or six hundred people within seemed intent and absorbed, on fire with ambition, dreams, memories, resentments, and thought on many levels: how much horseradish to add to the cocktail sauce or which oyster to eat first; would there be time after lunch to go to the bank; how to pay for college; why the head of the foreign currency trading desk had cast aspersions; what movie to see on Saturday; was Dewey going to run in '48; ah, the girl in high school, with the spectacular red hair; how could God have allowed children to have been blown to bits in the war; *Rhapsody in Blue* echoing without cease in memory; let a shoeshine seat be open at the stand in the Schlumberger Building after six (if you could say it); who was right, Hamilton or Jefferson; I wish my father were alive, sitting next to me now; do birds have nightmares; two days ago, above Central Park, a skywriter wrote "I love you, Jill"; how much will it cost to rent a summer house for a week on Lake Winnipesaukee; how the hell can a grasshopper jump so far; he (not a grasshopper) makes more money than I do, or anyone else in the department; Cleopatra's Barge; here comes the check; if nothing is the absence of something, then nothing is something; I wonder if I will die in a hospital, and will it be on a beautiful day in September; what the hell, exactly, is a prairie dog, is it a dog, how could it be — and so on, all proceeding at a fantastic rate, interweaving as much as the sound of voices, cutlery, crockery, and china, rising to hang in silence like the smoke of a waterfall, leaving only a frozen picture of five or six hundred people eating lunch or bustling about, their hands busy in reaching, their eyes reflecting, their souls invisibly weeping.

Then Vanderlyn touched him on the right shoulder. Not tapped, which would have been too low for Vanderlyn. "Hello," said Harry, taken by surprise. (How did Vanderlyn get right next to him without his knowledge?) "I don't want to go in there."

"Why?"

"I don't know."

"Where do you want to go?"

"I don't know that either."

"Come with me, then," Vanderlyn said, moving in the direction of the Battery, "and we'll figure it out."

They went right to the rail, where the wind was up just enough to ruffle the water into leonine whitecaps that would rise and then sink with a hiss into the rocking of the waves. October light made the harbor glow and shine in blue so intense that looking at it hurt. Ferries, barges, and tugs glided by, and a gray warship headed toward the Narrows as an ice-white Caribbean freighter backed into a slip at the Brooklyn piers. Every now and then a ship's whistle more powerful than a thousand tubas thundered across the gaps and echoed, if you listened closely, off the walls of St. George.

"I'm hungry," Vanderlyn said. "Where would you like to eat?"

"In the private dining room," said Harry, "after we walk into the bank with your name on it and you're greeted by smiling women and deferential men."

"Why do you assume," Vanderlyn asked, "that I have a private dining room?"

"Because your suit costs as much as a car."

"That's it?"

"You want more? You know the Hales; you work on Wall Street; your schedule is up to you; from the way you speak you must have gone to Yale; you were, or are, in the OSS; you have a manicure and a Patek Philippe; you're about to embark on some sort of dollar-a-year-type government service; you've risen above caring about money;

you're about sixty; and despite the fact that it was the Winabout that sank in the storm that day, you still have the yacht."

Vanderlyn smiled.

"In a package like that is an excellent chance of a private dining room, not far from here, which is where I want to go. What we've been talking about is dangerous and illegal, and if you're going to know all the details of what I might do, I want to know at least who you are."

"Tell me why," Vanderlyn commanded in a neutral tone, saying it quickly.

"How do I know, for example, that you're not the FBI, and this is not entrapment?"

"What for?"

"I don't know."

"You do know," Vanderlyn said, "that they have to have law degrees."

"The FBI? So?"

"So here's some etiquette from Emily Post. Never inquire of an FBI agent if he passed the bar: you'll make an enemy for life. If I had been a lawyer, I would have passed the bar, Harry, I wouldn't have had to join the FBI. The FBI is trying to shut us down even before we're established, because they don't want us to intrude upon what they think is their territory, and so what if they know less about operations abroad than they do about shitting in a milk bottle."

This was all news to Harry, who had drawn Vanderlyn out far more than he had expected.

"They've been looking into anyone involved, trying to blackmail us into abandoning it. They're on me, they're on everyone in it. That's one reason for a buffer between us. Given what you may do, you don't want them to be thinking about you in any way, not that they would give a fig—except that they might try to force me to stand down by threatening to put you away. Needless to say, that wouldn't work. We can take some casualties, including me, including you, because what we're trying to do is very important."

"But they must already have some things they can use," Harry speculated, "unless you and everyone around you are absolutely pristine."

Vanderlyn was amused. "Of course we're not," he said, sweeping his hand toward what lay in back of him. "Wall Street, Harry. Its mother's milk is corruption. We shepherd and maneuver capital, and the country couldn't exist without us, but why are our rewards so exceptional, except that because we turn the valves we drink from the tap when we want? It doesn't require a Pascal or an Einstein. Government employees — generals, cabinet secretaries — who have more skill than we do, and more responsibility, make a hundredth, a thousandth, of what we make. And capital, in the free-market countries, is almost a public trust, so dependent are they upon it. We don't even pretend it's ours. It just passes through us as we siphon and divert. It belongs to other people, but, you know, you'd hardly know it as we sit at their table and sup. Diamond miners don't get to fill their pockets with diamonds, Harry, but we do."

"How do you propose to continue whatever it is you're setting up," Harry asked, "if they can blackmail you?"

"Blackmail them back."

"The FBI?"

"The FBI. They're not the only ones who can find things out. We had people in the Chancellery in Berlin. Why wouldn't we be able to penetrate an agency of our own government?"

"Because they don't speak German."

"They might as well, because they hardly speak English. Believe me, it wasn't too challenging, but it was unpleasant."

"The bureaucracy will merely sacrifice a clerk. I was in the army. I know."

"Not if the person responsible is the person at the very top," Vanderlyn said with unconcealed delight.

"J. Edgar Hoover?"

"We've got that crumb completely covered. Believe me."

Shaking his head in both disbelief and disengagement, which Vanderlyn found annoying, Harry said, "He would claim that whoever actually did whatever was done was a rogue employee and probably a low one, too. As I said, a clerk."

"Unless he did it himself."

"With his own hand? J. Edgar Hoover?"

For some reason, Vanderlyn thought this was very funny.

"What did he do?"

"You don't want to know, and you can't know. At least until we get established, knowing it and keeping it contained is our shield. Probably no one will ever know, but had he not slipped up we couldn't have begun. They're still waiting for an opening, just in case, but I can't think of anything that could happen that would get them out of check — and, oh, we've got them in check, even if Hoover dies. But if we go to my office — I don't have a private dining room, I like to get out — they'll get your picture and they'll want to know who you are. That's no way to begin."

"They're not watching us now?"

"It's easy to lose them. They're idiots, after all. But they've got my firm covered. They've got someone inside my private office to whom we feed false information. She's lovely, so it's easy to be dazzled, which covers all the signs that we're playing her like a lute."

"Who's 'we'?"

"Would you like me to give you a personnel roster? Remember, gentlemen don't read other gentlemen's mail, which, of course, is what we will overturn."

"I want to know at least who *you* are."

"And if I don't tell you? How would you proceed without me?"

"Somehow. Or not."

"Must I?" He had already come around.

"Yes."

When Vanderlyn thought, he looked like someone playing chess . . . well. He said, "You know I want to take you in anyway, afterward. I have deniability, I trust you, and I want to help you." He put both hands on the rail, and looking not at Harry but out at the harbor, spoke as if addressing the distant gulls following a Staten Island ferry,

"Why not, then? James George Vanderlyn, with a *y* before the terminal *n*. You have to say that, or people spell it any which way."

They started walking. As they rounded the bend of lower Manhattan and the East River bridges came into view they were both struck by the color of the light in the north wind, which was enough to wake the dead.

"Take this," Vanderlyn said, handing Harry a thin leather wallet.

When Harry opened it he was speechless. On one fold was a gold shield, the badge of a New York City police detective, on the other, police department identification with Harry's photograph over a different name. "What is this?" he asked.

"If you can't figure out what it is, you'd better give it back."

"What am I supposed to do with it?"

"I'm serious," Vanderlyn insisted nervously. "You tell me."

"To get out of tight spots," Harry reasoned, "smooth things over if necessary."

"That's right. It works wonders. Not only can you cross the street during parades and park anywhere you want—don't—but let's say you're loading a truck and you excite the suspicions of a passing patrol car. Again, don't let it happen. But if it did. . . ."

"What if they called it in? They'd know at any precinct who their detectives are, and that this one doesn't exist."

Vanderlyn shook his head. "Look," he said, "we're not amateurs. This is real. It's a prerogative of the mayor. It's legitimate except that you have a false identity. Should anyone ask, you'll be okayed at police headquarters. You can carry a firearm. You can go into a police station and get their assistance. You can, if you want, stop traffic on the Brooklyn Bridge," under which they were walking at that moment, "and you can speed and get out of a ticket."

"Ah," Harry said, entranced.

"But don't. It's only to give you a way to cover a mistake. Everyone makes mistakes."

"My driver's license is in my real name."

"Driver's license, passport, birth certificate, Colt—all coming," Vanderlyn said. "Sorry about the delay."

"Jesus."

"James, his brother."

"You have a brother named Jesus?"

"It's his middle name," said Vanderlyn. "My parents may have had a bit too much to drink when they named us. The baby arrives, you break out a good Lafite. I'm James George, he's James Jesus. We're twins. They started out calling us both James, but that didn't work, so they called him Jesus. It became much more of a problem for him than it did for me, as you might imagine. People tend to think he's from Mexico. It's always been his cross to bear, so to speak. I was the lucky one."

In struggling to keep pace with Vanderlyn, Harry was almost breathless. "Two questions," he said. "First, I find it somewhat difficult to keep up with you, and I run six miles around the park every day, often twelve. How is that?"

"I run ten, invariably. Even in blizzards. You have to."

"You have to?" Harry was astounded. "All right, you have to. Second, how did you get this picture?"

"Look at it."

"From the army," Harry said. The uniform was retouched into a suit.

"No one can tell the difference with certainty. Anyway, no one would try."

"What you do is like magic."

"To do what we have to do, it has to be that way, which is what makes it so attractive now and what made it attractive during the war. For example, we didn't know that the Czechs would beat us to it, but to prepare for assassinating Heydrich we found someone with a photographic memory—he was in the film business, a Columbia graduate. He looked a lot like you. We trained him at the Field estate and at Camp X in Canada. He spoke German because his first language was Yiddish, so we parachuted him into Germany so close to the target that after they caught him they kept him in the building where

Heydrich worked. For several months they interrogated him. That is, they tortured him. We had made him a major. Wanting to know why an American major in full uniform was nonchalantly walking down the street in the heart of the Reich, they were too curious to kill him.

"He committed to his photographic memory every document, every schedule posted on every bulletin board, every shift change, to the minute, every coming and going of cars and trucks, every rank and every insignia of everyone he saw, names, plans of wherever he was taken. He counted paces when he was marched blindfolded through halls, and knew when he passed doorways, because the echo of his footsteps changed. He speed-read (is that a word?) all the documents on all the desks that he faced during questioning. They were, to him, upside down. Didn't matter. Then he escaped, floating on the rivers of Germany down to the sea. He was a great swimmer, and the currents did most of the work, but it took two weeks and when he finished he thought like a fish. In Hamburg he climbed onto a neutral ship, and as it passed through the Channel he dived in and swam to England. Three hours after they arrested him on the beach he was in my office. It took him a week to disgorge everything, which he did as if he were reading it.

"We put him up at the Connaught. We said, 'Order anything you want from room service. Go out and buy a suit. We'll get you a Swiss bank account.' We all had them, after all. And when he was finished with the debriefing we asked, 'What do you want to do now? Would you like to go home? You've earned it. Just tell us.' He looked at me and said, 'If we're going to kill Heydrich, you might need me.'

"That's magic, Harry, and I never want to leave it."

"But there's no war."

"There will be. Or perhaps we can prevent it. What we could have done to Heydrich, we might be able to do to another Hitler before he's unleashed."

"And the unintended consequences?"

"How many millions have to die, Harry, before we stop worrying about unintended consequences?"

"What if all nations decided to kill off what in their eyes was mortally dangerous leadership? It would be a Hobbesian world."

"The world just lost fifty million dead. Is that Hobbesian enough? Politeness can be a form of collaboration, or suicide. Besides, our focus is primarily intelligence. You have to play it by ear. As you know, as you must know, having fought your way through Sicily, France, Holland, and Germany, your responsibility is not to be morally pristine but to preserve the maximum number of innocent lives. How many men have you killed?"

"Too many."

"Yes, and probably most of them were as innocent as you," Vanderlyn said, "or more so. You know that. And yet you had to kill them, and you did, because all in all, in the gross and scope of it, scores of millions are alive now who would not have been, or who would have been enslaved, had Germany not been defeated—children by the millions, Harry. They are the reason you killed men. Now you are forever morally impure, but, Harry, if only by the weight of the flesh and blood in the balance, you're purer than those who refused."

"What if your judgment of these things is wrong? What if mine, in the case of Verderamé, is wrong?"

"That's a chance you take as a consequence of your imperfection."

"Doubt and sadness for the rest of your life," Harry reported. "And it never leaves you."

"Doubt and sadness for the rest of your life, so that others may live. I thought we were already beyond that."

"We are," Harry said.

"Good, then tell me what you need."

"I won't know until I've done a lot of preparation."

"When you're ready, call my office. You know my name now. Say that you need specifications for framing a painting I left with you. They'll ask for your number. Tell them I know it. They wonder about calls like that, and the occasional rough-looking character who shows up, but that's okay: the curiosity of a certain kind of employee is mysteriously limited. If they have the kind of curiosity they need, they either rise to the top or they're fired. It's a defining difference, curiosity. I've never known a stupid person who was curious, or a curious person who was stupid."

Vanderlyn shook Harry's hand and then veered left toward the Municipal Building. Harry headed into Chinatown. He was addled all the way to Washington Square.

"What's all this?" Harry asked Cornell, referring to a pile of cardboard boxes that almost blocked the entry to the office.

"Returns."

"Returns? We don't sell on a returnable basis. Why did you accept them?"

"They're damaged. Workmanship." Cornell picked up a leather portfolio and turned it over so Harry could see a deep scratch that ran across it. Then a briefcase, with loose and broken waxed threads projecting from a seam.

"We've never sent out anything like that," Harry said angrily.

"Of course not." He gave Harry the briefcase and a little loupe. "You can see where a stitch puller went into the hole. It cut a slit at the edge."

"Then we should refuse all these."

"I did at first, but a dozen stores came in, just yesterday. A customer wants to buy something, takes it to the counter, and discovers the damage. The store apologizes and asks him to grab another one. He does, and it's damaged, too. So the store inspects, and sees that most of our products are that way."

"Then it's a matter of security."

"They don't think so. I tried to refuse. They said if we do they won't reorder. If we take it back, they will. What this means is that however long we have to work to replace the damaged inventory—and who knows when this will stop—we'll be working, paying salaries, paying suppliers, but giving away what we produce. I have a horror of working for nothing, Harry. I don't want to be pulled back into that nightmare. My father, my father's father, and his father all had the same dread all their lives. It never goes away, and it makes me very angry that anyone, *anyone*, would presume to own my time and my labor, and, therefore, me."

"I don't understand," Harry said. "They beat us and they kill us, and then they pull threads and scratch the leather? Since when do you escalate down?"

"However they work, with what we're paying them it'll mean the end for us. I guess this is just to speed things up."

"And if we don't pay them?"

"They'll kill us. You know that."

"I mean if we didn't have to pay them."

"If we didn't *have* to pay them, the weights and chains would be removed. It wouldn't be easy, but we could get back. We'd survive. Orders are down so much I was about to reduce our hours again, but if we're going to replace this stuff, we're going to have to work."

"Can we restitch?"

"Only by hand. The needle holes are already in the leather. A machine would make another set."

"What about the scratches?"

"Every one I've seen goes too deep to buff out."

"So what do we do?"

"We job-lot it for five cents on the dollar."

"So people will be walking around carrying Copeland Leather with the stitches coming out."

"We're still alive," said Cornell. "With starvation wages, all the money you have, the practically non-existent sales revenue, no extortion increases, and an easing off on the sabotage, maybe we've got a year. Then we'd have to shut down. In conditions like that, Harry, a year goes by both very fast and very slow."

"I understand, but we've got a year, and then one way or another we're done. Look at it that way. In a year, no matter what, it'll be over."

This did not cheer Cornell, who said, "I forgot to tell you. Catherine's father was here. Billy Hale. The man can dress, but I felt comfortable with him."

"What was he doing here?"

"Looking for you."

"That's strange. He does have a telephone. Was Catherine with him?"

"Just him. I showed him around. He was interested in everything we do."

Harry met Catherine in front of her parents' house. As they approached one another from opposite ends of the street it was as if they grew lighter. In Catherine's eyes and her smile was Harry's memory of her voice, which came from deeper within than there was a within. Although she was unaware of it, the breeze lifted the collar of her coat up from the shoulder and suspended it in the air. A thousand lights of buildings and bridges came on as night fell, a halo that could not do her justice as she rushed toward him, in the wind, on an October evening, with the whole world glittering behind her.

As it often was in the autumn, the house was heated by three or four fires and the light of many lamps. Had the central heating been on, it would have been like an oven, but now the temperature was just right, and as they threw orange and gold rays across slate or marble hearths, the fires made a pleasing noise like that of streams. Billy greeted Catherine, as he always did, as if the last time he had seen her he might never have seen her again. Evelyn was more hopeful that neither she nor her husband were likely soon to drop dead, perhaps because unlike Billy's friends most of hers tended not to keel over at their desks.

They sat down in the dining room, a fire burning nicely. The first course was soup. "What the hell is this?" Billy asked.

"*Yosenabé*," Evelyn reported.

"Yosen what?"

"*Yosenabé*. It's Japanese."

"Why suddenly are we having Japanese soup?"

"I read about it." It was a clear soup with shrimp, scallops, clams, and seaweed.

"In what, a war-crimes tribunal?"

"They killed us, Billy, and we killed them," Evelyn said.

"They started it."

"I know, but it's over."

"Not for everyone. I'm sorry, Evelyn, but it reminds me too much of the Taylors, the Drews, the Vanderlyns, the Davises...."

"Which Vanderlyns?" Harry interrupted.

"James."

"James George?"

"That's right."

"Why does it remind you?" Harry asked.

"They all lost boys in the Pacific."

"The Vanderlyns, too?"

"Their son died on Guadalcanal. He was a marine."

"How old was he?"

"I don't know, maybe twenty-four or twenty-five. Not long out of Harvard, but he must have gotten there after you left. That was a big thing, at the time. His father went to Yale. Stupid stuff, but not really serious. He was proud of him but he would joke about being betrayed. He used to say that his son had converted. Why do you ask?"

"The name is familiar," Harry said.

"Of course it is. They're a bigger firm than we are. Deadly enemies of the Marrows, like almost everyone else. In the early days, Willie Marrow screwed Vanderlyn out of more deals than you can count. He had — what do you call it, a mole, a plant? — in Vanderlyn's office. This was before the Crash. We were about your age and, excuse me, we didn't know a goddamned thing, but we thought we did. Vanderlyn's uncle ran the firm, but Vanderlyn was the hot one. He would set up a deal, working eighteen-hour days, doing all the research himself, and then Willie would come in at a couple of thousand dollars under. And Willie was smart enough sometimes to come in over. Vanderlyn found out because he followed the mole uptown to Grand Central — *rat* would be more precise — where the rat, mole, whatever he was, went into a telephone booth and Vanderlyn took the next one, pressing his ear up against the wall and listening as his trusted aide fed everything to Willie Marrow. Even though Willie Marrow has mellowed, God has made the very report of it a tongue twister to let you know that you still must be careful of him. Vanderlyn then began to feed Willie some very wrong information that caused Willie to lose a great deal of money. Then he dispatched the rat to someplace in Southeast Asia, to wait for six months for information about a deal that never existed. While the rat was there, Vanderlyn sent him a cable that said, 'Go to Tibet immediately, using your own funds,' and then shut him out of his firm and his mind forever. Vanderlyn is not the kind of man that I would ever, ever, want to be my enemy. While his son was in the Pacific, he himself was in Europe. He doesn't have much to do with anybody anymore, at least socially. It was his only son, their only child. You don't get over that." Billy shot a glance at Catherine.

Harry was more or less unable to speak. Catherine kicked him under the table, and then changed the subject. She had invited herself and Harry to dinner for a particular reason, and she wanted to glide up to it gently. So she talked about the now steady performances, and how she was learning to do her job without thought of recognition, merely to face the audience and do her best. This made her parents feel not only proud but right about having prepared their own moment.

Whereas Catherine had drunk her soup using the right hand to grasp the spoon (with her left hand hidden beneath the table), during the main course her left hand was busy with the fork, holding it while she cut, handing it off to the right hand, and taking it back. A simple ring Harry had bought at Tiffany's took the firelight, and she knew that her mother would notice the dull gold sheen. And when her mother did, it was no small thing.

"Catherine," she asked, her voice grave, "do you have something to tell us?"

Billy, who didn't notice things like rings or shoes, had no idea what was coming—an announcement for which, by feminine observation, Evelyn was now fully prepared.

"Yes, we do," Catherine said, carefully choosing her words.

Billy obliviously speared potatoes.

"What, dear?" her mother asked, in a tone that would not have been different had a tidal wave twenty storeys tall been racing up the East River.

"Well, we got married."

Billy had just put a slightly too big potato in his mouth. It shot out like an artillery shell. Before it landed—somewhere—he lunged forward as if he were choking, which he wasn't, and knocked over his water glass. "What did you say?"

"We got married."

"Who?"

"Who do you think?"

Billy stared at the puddle of water on the table and tapped it rapidly with his right index finger. His hand looked like a woodpecker. "When?"

She told him.

"One would have thought that you might—might—have invited your parents," Evelyn said.

"I'm sorry," Catherine told them. "It had to be quick, and secret."

They readied for what was next, but were relieved when she said, "I'm not pregnant. And at the right time we can have a ceremony and reception in East Hampton, an orchestra, announcements, all those things. We'd like to do that, but it could never be better than what it was. We had no choice." She told them why, leaving out what Harry and she were going to do. Billy and Evelyn knew of course that Harry had run afoul of the mob, and understood the reason for dissociating their daughter from Harry publicly. Although they could not help but be shocked, they were grateful that it had been done. It was sensible. It was what they would have recommended. And it led right into what Billy had prepared for them.

"I can't eat," Evelyn said. "Can you eat?" she asked Harry and Catherine, who could. "Billy, can you eat?"

"No."

"We'll go into the living room," Evelyn told her daughter and, now, son-in-law, "and when you're finished, come in. With my encouragement, your father has something to tell you."

They left, Evelyn moving with the dignity of a fully rigged clipper, Billy walking unselfconsciously and erratically, like either a schoolboy fascinated by cracks in the sidewalk, or a goose. Harry and Catherine ate quickly. "That wasn't so bad," Harry said. "What do you think they want to talk to us about?"

"My guess," Catherine told him, "is that they want to get us out of New York, set us up in Paris or somewhere with something that would be lucrative and dignified if we had accomplished it ourselves, but lucrative, demeaning, and destabilizing otherwise."

"You know I can't do that."

"You know I can't either."

"Okay," said Billy. "Okay. So. Congratulations. Would you like dessert?" He lifted his eyebrows.

"We had dessert, Daddy," Catherine said. She took a seat by the fire and crossed her legs. Harry sat down next to Evelyn, catercorner from Catherine so he could look at her. She was wearing a suit of beige satin, stockings with a whitish tinge, and pearls. When he was kissing her he hadn't noticed in detail how she was dressed, but only the sweetness of her kiss. Her power and sophistication were increasing, and he guessed that by the time she was thirty they would be formidable. What made this even more magnificent was that as she was beginning to know it, she was discovering how to deploy it. Sitting by the fire, perfumed, her legs crossed and ensilked, her jewelry occasionally clinking softly as she moved, her hair glinting and elastic, she was impossible to resist.

Very beautiful women — whether mainly from the physical attributes that can radiate even over a distance, or from some combination of body and spirit in proportions decided not quite here on earth — sometimes soften their overwhelming presences by adopting imperfections: a slight stammer, a dipping of the head, a deferential lowering of the gaze, like someone who is very tall accommodating someone who is short by bending forward to greet him. Not Catherine. Her full effect, amplified by her lack of ameliorative gestures, was almost cruel, the very silence and stillness of their absence allowing the shock of her beauty to penetrate like infrared. To say that her lack of mannerisms was artificial would be to state a contradiction. It was just that she was too interested in the truth of things to waste time stammering even slightly with her soul. She was, to those who appreciated it, painfully beautiful, and that was that. There was no cure for it.

"I haven't," said Billy, so late in delivery that no one knew what he was talking about.

"You haven't what?" Evelyn asked him.

"Had dessert." Then he forgot dessert and navigated ahead, after a fashion. "You've heard of the Gordiani? Or maybe it was Gordioni?" he asked, standing up and walking close to the fire. "The consul and his son in Roman North Africa who were pressed into rebellion against the emperor Maximin? Maximin was literally and figuratively a barbarian. He was an Ostrogoth, or something like that—I hate Ostrogoths—a giant whom the troops called Hercules. He started out not as a soldier but as a servant and camp follower. There was a wrestling match...."

"Billy?" Evelyn said. He turned to her. "Get to the point."

"All right. I will. You're married now?" he asked Catherine. She nodded. He turned to Harry. "Legally?" Harry nodded. "Then it makes even more sense."

"What makes sense?" Catherine inquired.

"Today I went to Harry's workshop . . . factory. I thought you'd be there. I thought we could all go out to lunch, Evelyn joining us, where I would have proposed what follows. You weren't, so the colored fellow showed me around. It's impressive, what you do there, but you're in trouble. A man has died. You've been beaten almost to death, and you're continually threatened. That's no way to live, and obviously you're in danger. Catherine is your wife. Therefore she's in danger. She's my daughter."

Now he spoke very deliberately. "I understand that you're young, that you're brave, and that you want to see this through on your own. No one knows better than I the price of the deus ex machina: I was literally born in one. For people like me, who are responsible to family and fortune, it's the greatest threat. That is, living as if in a glass case. I envy you, Harry, for having been the right age for the war, for having risked everything, for having been broken and for having come back.

I was never broken, and I think that means I've never really known myself.

"But you've been there, you've proved yourself, and your strength isn't in question. Let's say by way of illustration that you're the Olympic gold medalist in the marathon. Whoever he is, I assure you that he sometimes takes the train or rides in a car, and over distances less than twenty-six miles. Why risk your life, and that of every man and woman in that workshop, fighting a force from which the police and government will not and cannot protect you?"

"I can't just fold," Harry said. "Your decision was made in responsibility to your family and its fortune. I have a family, too, and its fortune, not in money, has a call on me. A part of life that fortifies you against death, and transcends it, is keeping promises."

"To the dead?" Billy asked, although he knew the answer.

"Especially."

"But you didn't promise this to your father."

"Yes I did. When I was born, my soul took shape in the promises I would keep. They were there by the score, waiting for me, and this was one of them. Catherine will be safe. That's another. I'll keep her safe, and if it gets really bad she'll come home to you. I can't just surrender the business, if that's what you mean."

"I don't."

Catherine shifted in her chair. Even her elegance shifted, as if it were a body in itself. Like most adult children, she oscillated between underestimating and overestimating her parents, which made her vulnerable to puzzlement and surprise.

"What I mean to do is to buy the business from you, take it off your hands, and end the problem there."

"What would you do with it?" Harry asked, as if no one could do anything with it. No one could.

"Dissolve it and write it off as a loss. It would cost very little if that's what we did." He saw that Harry was not excited by the prospect. "Because it's possible to offset profits from another area. You'd get a good price, I'd give a very generous severance to the employees, sell the inventory, machines, and the loft, and abandon the trademark to the public domain. Your adversaries would be left with nothing, and you and your workers would be whole."

"And what would I do?"

"Whatever you want. Start fresh. Isn't this what your father would have wanted?"

"Is it what your father would have wanted for Hale and Company?"

Billy was an honest man and probably would have been so even had he not been able to afford to be, so he said, "No."

"What would you do?"

Billy thought, and surrendered. "I'd fight."

"That's what I'm going to do, Billy. Catherine will be safe."

Now Catherine stood. Perhaps for the first time, her parents saw not the child whose image and memory they would always love, preserve, and carry with them to the end, but a woman who, just like them, was moving in the shadow of mortality. She hardly needed to say what she said, for they had read it in her stance and in the straightness and strength of her body as she rose, in the way she held herself, in her expression, and in her eyes. And before she said it, they had accepted it.

"I don't need to be protected," she told them. "I'm not immortal. Just like you, I won't last forever, and anyone who won't last forever has to live courageously and well, or she's left with, and leaves behind, nothing. If defiance gives you life," she said, turning to Harry, "it gives me life, too. What do you think I do when, every night, I face an audience primed to disapprove of me? What do you think I do when I persist through what I'm told is failure? And why do you think I chose Harry? I didn't choose him for certainty or protection, but for his courage." Addressing her parents, she said, "I'm just like him, and I'm just like you. You should know this, starting tonight."

Evelyn rose, and then Harry, the only one left seated, stood as well. It was a kind of standing ovation from love and respect. Her parents did not have to go to Catherine, for their embrace magically crossed the air. A tug sped down the East River, its lights shining through the dark. They were apprehensive, but never had the Hales stood prouder, except perhaps long before, when they had gone out to chase whales, or cross the sea, or rebel against the mother country. It was dark outside, but an edge of blue remained above the horizon, and the fire came alive as if someone had thrown open a window and the wind had rushed through the room.

Only a short time before, when Catherine had lived in a dorm with a curfew, little allowance had been made for either her natural powers or her durability. All the while that she was contending with Victor, her parents had assumed that she was as protected as when she was a young child, though she had understood by then more of the world, its sadness, and its risks, than they knew. Even then she had fallen deeply in love with an image that, though it might be lost, she could not dismiss, not even, she thought, for Harry. It had never left her. She would never let it leave her. For in it she had been given the gift, early on, of knowing who she was.

Now she tried, tentatively, to stretch her mandate. As she and Harry walked up Fifth Avenue before cutting across the park, she said, "I can handle a gun, you know. I've been out on the heath with a shotgun."

"What heath?"

"The dunes at Hither Hills."

"You shot birds?"

"Well, no, I wouldn't do that, but I was excellent at clay pigeons, which is why I was asked to go along. I'm a very good shot, and I'm not afraid of the noise or the recoil."

"Why are you telling me this?"

"I want to share equally with you."

"There's a lot that you can do. Then you go to ground."

"But why?"

"Because when it happens, unless you have experience, you tend to go into a daze." She seemed skeptical, as he knew she would. "You know what a shotgun sounds like, even a four-ten? Very loud, right?"

"Yes."

"Most people don't know. They think it's like the pop they hear in the movies. It isn't. It rattles you. It's a little like being hit. Ever shot a deer rifle?" She hadn't. "Much more dramatic. It makes a twelve-gauge shotgun seem minor. In a sharp action you've got hundreds of these concussions all at once, over and over, for minutes or hours. It's possible to have ten, twenty, forty reports simultaneously. If you add artillery, rocket, and tank fires, the sound of the tank engines, aircraft, bombs, and the detonation of mines, it's. . . . I think what it does is overload your voluntary capacities and throw as much as can be thrown into the involuntary nervous system. You hardly know what's happening. Time, slow or fast, disappears. It's like moving through a dream. But if you don't function physically and you don't make the right judgments, you can't come out of it except by accident."

"Have you ever heard all that at once?"

"Almost all of it."

"But don't they just kill each other with a little gun, drop it, and walk away?"

"Gangsters, maybe, but I don't know how to do that, and neither do you. We don't have access. I'm not an assassin. I can't do what they do, but I can do what I can do. When I attack him, his lieutenants will be with him. They'll be armed, some probably with Thompsons, and it will have to be planned and executed as a military action and nothing less.

"He travels with an entourage of bodyguards. Like others of his type, he doesn't trust anyone too intelligent or too ambitious, and surrounds himself with goons because the goons' limited abilities constrict their imaginations and make their intentions transparent. If they get ambitious he knows immediately and quashes them. The operations aren't as efficient as they could be, which is one reason that, to make up for the inefficiency, they're often so ruthless and extreme.

"Verderamé has five or six men who are always with him, some right on him, some where you can't see them—pickets. I counted them before they beat me. I counted them at his place. They're stupid and dangerous and they all have to go."

"Can you take on seven people, alone?" Catherine asked. She saw it now in a different light.

"I wouldn't even consider that."

"Who's going to help you?"

"I don't know yet. There are a lot of things that have to fall into place. The first is to find out where he lives. You can't just look it up. It's not necessarily in Manhattan, or the city at all. We have to find out directly, which is where you can help. And because everything has to be done with extreme caution, it might take a long time."

"How long?"

"Months."

She was astounded. "Months? To find out where someone lives?"

"So that he doesn't know or suspect. And during that time other things have to be prepared as well."

"How do you know he's not in the telephone book?"

"I looked."

"What about the city directory?"

"I looked there, too. There was no listing under 'gangsters.' We have to follow him one turn at a time, sometimes with days between observations. People like him use their rearview mirrors a lot. We can't fall into a pattern. We let him show a pattern, and then we read it. The first thing is to find out where he goes when he leaves his place. That's going to be difficult now because it's getting cold—fewer people on the street and no reason to sit outside. If we knew exactly when he leaves, and it probably varies, we could just be walking by. But we don't know, so we have to figure something out."

When they got to the door of the apartment they heard the telephone ringing. Harry rushed to put his key in the lock, missed the first time, then got it, and Catherine ran in to pick up the phone. It was her father, who wanted to speak to Harry, who took the call while Catherine moved from lamp to lamp in the living room until their light glowed out upon the necklaces of streetlights draped across the park.

"I forgot to add, Harry, and I don't know why—well, I do know why: it was Catherine's declaration that threw me off—that I know you're not interested in finance, and I can't blame you. I wasn't either. I am now, but it's only because once I had made the decision to enter the firm I was broken to it like a horse. You're old enough and you know other ways, which is just the point. We're a financial house, the war's over, Europe will get back on its feet, and most of the world will be open to American trade and investment. It's really going to take off. Nobody except missionaries knows anything, really, about the rest of the world.

"Every major firm will need as much foreign intelligence as it can get. Lots of it will be contracted out, but who'll mind the contractors and weigh what they say? There'll have to be in-house departments to supervise, check, and interpret what's received, and to make their own independent or blended assessments. The position, or positions, will be very important. With a couple of thousand brokers, mistakes tend to balance out and the risk is divided and fragmented. But if a company decided to build a steel mill in, let's say, Greece, everything would ride on the assessment not only of the country but of the region, and the great powers and their motives and likely actions. Build a steel mill in Greece, and you'd better goddamned well know the domestic situation, the military balance with Turkey, the naval developments in the Mediterranean, and Soviet, British, and American capabilities, potential, and policy."

"I think I know what you're driving at, Billy."

"I'm sure you do. We need such a department, and at the moment neither we nor anyone else has one to speak of. You have academic training, foreign languages, and during the war you were at the tip of the spear. There's a place for you. You can start the department, run it, hire the people you need. You wouldn't have to worry about working for me, for two reasons. First, I'm not going to last forever. I might retire, I most certainly will die. Second, by necessity you would have to have complete independence or your advice would be worthless. And third (although I didn't say three reasons), if your advice did prove to be worthless you'd be out of that job. So it isn't nepotism: you'd have to perform, and it's a demanding task.

"I'd make sure that you'd have your own untouchable budget, total insulation, total protection, and that you'd be judged only by the accuracy of your estimates. You could go get a Ph.D. if that would help. Good strategy comes from knowledge and genius, not from punching a time clock, and the higher the level of thought the more necessary is relaxation. That's why I fish and play golf. At least it's a good excuse.

"When Catherine owns the firm, you will, too, and then your descendants. Not only do you have an interest and a stake, but a job, if you want it."

Harry thought for a moment. "Thank you, Billy, but I want to keep my business alive, and because my father is dead, my obligation to him is never-ending. I am grateful, very much so."

"We'll hold the position for you as long as we can manage. Think about it. Don't feel rushed. Do what you have to do." The last was difficult for Billy to say.

It was a day of clear October sunshine. All the way from 93rd Street to Little Italy they said almost nothing, but each step they took brought them closer to one another. Though it was against Harry's every impulse for Catherine to assume the risk, once she had insisted and he had relented, sharing even the lesser part of the danger intensified his love and respect for her, which then shone back. One loves one's comrades-in-arms in a deep and everlasting way, but when one's comrade-in-arms is also the woman one loves, there is no limit.

On Prince Street they walked past Verderamé's and Harry identified it under his breath. At the corner, they turned right and Catherine broke off to go back uptown. Harry circled and ended up at a shoe repair shop almost directly across the street from the private club where he had met the man he was going to kill. All the way from 93rd Street, the sole of Harry's right shoe had been flopping, because before leaving he had cut the outer edge toward the front. It was four o'clock when he walked in. The cobbler was dark and heavy, his eyebrows joined together in matrimony. "Can you fix this?" Harry asked after removing his shoe.

"Do you want to resole both?"

"How much?" All the while, Harry was watching the door across the street.

The cobbler turned in the tight space in which he worked, and held up a pair of soles bound together with twine. "High quality, three dollars for the job."

"Okay." Harry took three dollars from his wallet while the cobbler wrote out a ticket.

"When would you like to pick them up?"

Harry stared at the cobbler, who looked Harry over, leaned across the counter to see more clearly, and realized that Harry was carrying only a newspaper. "Can't you do them today?" Harry asked.

"Ooh, wha?" the cobbler said. "I close in an hour. Here." He tried to hand back the shoes, but Harry wouldn't take them.

"Can you loan me a pair?"

"I'm not an ice-skating rink."

"You see," said Harry, as if he hadn't thought it out, "I've got to go to a dinner, and I can't go looking like a bum."

"Then you'd better not go."

"Thanks. It's for a job. I won't get the job if I don't go."

"Go home and get another pair of shoes," the cobbler said. "I'm not your mother." Harry just looked at him. "You don't have another pair of shoes? Buy one." Harry remained immobile. "You can't afford to?"

"I have five dollars, that's it. I'll give you that if you do it right now."

"I'll do it for three," the cobbler said, "because the glue won't dry."

"Do the best you can. If I get the job, it'll be well worth it. Take the five dollars. I insist."

As the cobbler got to work, Harry sat on the shoeshine stand and opened up the newspaper, over which he stared at Verderamé's door, although now and then he did glance at the brassiere ads and movie announcements. He was afraid to start reading, lest he miss what he was there for. An upcoming movie, *Dear Ruth*, with William Holden and Joan Caulfield, was announced in a full-page ad as if it were the second coming of Christ. The names *William* and *Joan* sat above their last names in tiny letters, but the last names were in enormous block type, Holden's first, so that when Harry glanced at the page — all he could afford was a glance — it looked like the movie starred someone named Holden Caulfield, writ large. He wondered if anyone had that name and would be shocked to see it. It seemed genuine, the name of someone Billy and Evelyn might know. Then he turned the page and forgot about it.

At Copeland Leather, machinery had to be clear of oil. Oil from a spurt or a leak, from touching a surface, or from a hand that had touched an oil-covered part could stain even highly waxed leather, leaving a kind of birthmark or dark cloud. Birthmarks on people had to stay, and were often the stimulus of character or the sign of beauty, but they were unacceptable on wallets and briefcases, which, so adorned, would not sell except to eccentrics. When leather was cut, the surface was pale and absorbent, and even a little stain had to be avoided before waxing or dying, for when it was covered it would only darken. Nor was the thread, imbued with paraffin, entirely immune. Thus Copeland Leather was rich in rags — delivered and taken away by a rag trader — with which every machine and every surface near every machine were wiped down assiduously until, for example, the heavy sewing machines shone silver wherever they were constructed of chrome or stainless steel, and were a flawless, grime-free, deep black wherever they were painted, although the polishing and cleaning had removed the brand names leafed in gold across their metal flanks and backs. The habit spread to other areas. Copeland Leather was the cleanest manufacture Harry had ever seen. People visiting the loft might think of the Columbian Exposition and its shiny engines, the Royal Navy, or the gleaming palaces of the rich, where a finger run across the most obscure molding would collect no dust.

The cobbler's shop was the opposite. Shoe polish, oil, wax, machine grit, and dust from leather, rubber, and steel nails covered everything in black or brown, with the steel sparkles from the nails everywhere like mica in rock. Where there was light, the silvery parts of the machines flashed through the oil on their surfaces, sometimes radiating a refraction broken up into more millions of tiny lenses than there were windows in Manhattan.

When the cobbler finished, he said, "The glue's not dry. It should dry for a day but I'm usually closed by now. They have new glues, but leather is porous...." At this moment, the door across the street swung open and, though it was still too warm for overcoats, men in hats and overcoats spilled out as if in a fire drill. The first two went left and right, scanned the street, and stayed in position while Verderamé, preceded and followed by guards, came down the few steps and turned right on the sidewalk. Then they all briskly walked away.

Coughing violently, Harry excused himself, jumped from the shoeshine stand, and stepped outside in his socks. Still making the motions of coughing so the cobbler could see them through his window, but with no sound, Harry watched as the overcoats sailed up the street and went right. This was all he needed to know that day. The picture would be built painstakingly piece by piece. But a few minutes later he was pleased when, as he was looking to see if another perch was available for looking up the street where they had turned, two cars appeared. One was a polished black Cadillac, and the other a humpbacked Nash. The bodyguards were recognizable in the front seats of both cars, as was Verderamé himself in the back seat of the Cadillac, where he was reading a newspaper. They went down Prince Street all the way to MacDougal, where they doglegged out of sight.

Catherine, who had never had her hair done, had it done the next day at the junction of Sixth Avenue and Prince, where she sat under the dryer and pretended to read *Town and Country* while she watched traffic out the window. There was nothing to report, and she went back the next day to have her hair cut. "How much would you like me to take off?" she was asked.

"About an eighth of an inch. Subtle differences can really change a look."

"They can," the hairdresser said.

"But to really change a look, you have to be bold."

"Absolutely!"

"Don't you think the new styles this year herald a wonderful change?" Catherine asked.

"Yes. After all those years of war — drab, drab, drab — they certainly do, but it's almost too late. Anyway, it's about time."

"I favor the classic, unchanging look," Catherine stated. "Do you?"

"Of course I do. It's classic, it's timeless, it's chic, it's elegant. Give me that any day rather than all that ridiculous experimentation."

"Oh damn," Catherine said. "They went by and my hair's wet." They had turned up Sixth Avenue.

"Who went by?" the hairdresser asked.

Catherine's eyes darted. She had given too much away. "The Pygmies."

"The Pygmies?"

"Yes."

"What Pygmies?"

"Pygmies from the Congo. Or someplace. They're chasing me."

"Oh," the hairdresser said.

Catherine rose from her chair, her hair still dripping, and rushed out the door.

"You've already paid!" the hairdresser shouted out after her. "Come back anytime you'd like! I'll cut it!" And then, "She took the smock. Bitch!"

Not quite as raggedly over the following weeks, they reconstructed Verderamé's route. They didn't want to use automobiles until they had to, and after long waits, patronizing businesses using various pretexts, and chilling exposure to the elements, they were able to trace Verderamé's way home, up Sixth Avenue, west across 14th Street, onto the West Side Highway, over the Henry Hudson Parkway through Riverdale and on to the Saw Mill River. It was in December when they finally got to use a car, but only Catherine, who waited by a public phone in Riverdale. When it rang, it was Harry, who was in a telephone booth on Riverside Drive and 145th, where he had seen the two cars pass. He had timed how long it would take to get to where Catherine was waiting, and when she should turn north onto the highway, driving slowly until she saw Verderamé in her rearview mirror. This she did and then picked up speed so as to keep them behind her all the way until they would turn off. They would never think that a car in front of them was following them. Even after dark, Catherine was able to keep track of them because they drove closely together and the Cadillac had widely spaced, powerful headlamps. Every mile was a step closer to the goal, and she went steadily north, past Hawthorne Circle, onto Route 9A, across the Croton River, and toward Peekskill, holding her breath at every juncture. Verderamé's cars moved at a steady rate until they turned off at Croton.

Catherine was ecstatic. When she got back to New York, with great excitement she told Harry that she had made them, without their knowledge, for almost fifty miles. After a week had passed—among other things, Catherine had her performance schedule—she parked pointing north on the street in Croton where Verderamé had turned off and continued in that direction. There she waited until he passed her, and then followed. As he turned onto a small, rural road, she continued straight. They waited ten days. By this time it was the end of January, and in late afternoon it was, if not light, lighter.

Harry used his false identity to rent a pickup truck. He drove up the road into which Verderamé had disappeared, and at the first junction parked and began to cut fallen wood. He was dressed like a farmer, in a watch cap that made it difficult even for Catherine to recognize him. Cutting half a truckload of wood, he worked until dusk, hoping, because a farmer would not be cutting wood in the dark, that Verderamé would come by before then. But not a single car passed, and he had to leave. Because he hadn't been seen by anyone, he was able to return the next day in the same guise, his truck bed empty after he had surprised the Hales with a gift of unseasoned wood to keep in the garden shed for the next season's fires.

The next day, just before dark, the two cars passed. Harry hardly looked up. The ground was littered with wood chips, and he was working hard. Verderamé turned left and west, toward the Hudson. When Harry had almost filled the truck, he drove in that direction. After a little way, he passed a wall on the right side of the road. A short apron led to a double gate of solid wood or steel, and beyond this, sited above the river, was an enormous house, the upper storeys of which were visible over the wall. Fittingly, it looked like a prison. Floodlights illuminated the open space between the battlements and the house. A man stood in front of the gate, and Harry saw in the mirror that he stopped his pacing, looked after the truck, and then started again. It had taken three months, but now they knew Verderamé's tight schedule and where he lived, and he didn't know they did.

The next stage of the preliminaries was far less time-consuming, although for its second part they were obliged to wait until March. On a glass-shattering cold day at the the beginning of February, Harry went down to Prince Street, walked casually past the social club, turned right at the corner, and went north until he came to the empty lot where the Cadillac and Nash were parked. Despite having only four spaces, two of which were unused, the lot was attended even so. At night, Verderamé's cars slept in his Croton compound, and during the day they were carefully watched.

The attendant was a miserable yet arrogant wretch of a youth with a repulsive jejune mustache of the type that Catherine called "jump-the-gun facial hair." He sat in a little wooden hut that he shared dangerously with a charcoal brazier. The only thing that kept him alive was that several windowpanes were missing. Still, he was groggy.

"Do you have any spaces available for daytime parking?" Harry asked, sounding to himself like a phrase from a Berlitz language manual.

After a delay appropriate to a crucial move in the world chess championship, the answer was "No."

"When do you think one might be available?"

"It's a private lot."

Talking to the kid was like talking to cheese. "Who owns it?"

"None of your business."

"Just curious. They got a Cadillac, huh."

"Yeah, they got a Cadillac."

"I always wanted one," Harry said, moving toward it.

The attendant ran out the door and around his hut. Harry was already at the car. "Hey! What are you doing? Get outta here!" the attendant said.

"What a car." Harry knocked on the driver's window. "It's really solid."

"Yeah, it's solid. Now get outta here before I call somebody and you regret it."

"Just admiring the car." Harry kicked the tires. "Can I sit in it?"

"No, you can't sit in it."

"I'll give you a quarter if you let me take a nap in it."

"Are you crazy? Just get going. One . . . two. . . ."

"Okay, okay." Harry began to leave. "A week ago I saw a Rolls-Royce on Park Avenue. Park and Sixty-eighth. That makes this look like nothing."

"Terrific," said the kid, who, as Harry departed, went back into his hut to sacrifice more brain cells to carbon monoxide. He wouldn't tell anyone about this, because the car was safe, Harry seemed to him to be a harmless jerk, and he himself was an idiot, although he was the last one to know, and what had happened, just like everything else, sailed through his mind like a dime dropping through a subway grate. But now Harry knew that the windows of the car were bulletproof, its solid tires were able to run flat, and, likely, the body was armored: it sat very low and both he and Catherine had noticed how ponderously it turned.

On the third of March, when the snow had melted and the ground was dry, Harry took an express train to Harmon and then a local to Oscawana, a mile or so north of Verderamé's compound in the woods overlooking the Hudson. With the ground such that he would leave neither tracks in the snow nor footprints in the mud, Harry set out to make a map. By the time he found himself looking up at the house, which was walled even on the western side, high over the river, it was dark.

He sketched every angle and dimension, scaling the cliff, measuring with a metal tape the height of the wall, and crossing the road into the thickets of pine beyond. There, using a red-lensed penlight, he completed his maps while he waited for the two cars to pull in. Although less than fifty feet from the gate, he was completely relaxed as he watched. The leaves of the gate swung open and two men from inside appeared as the Cadillac and Nash rolled through. They then looked down the road, backed in, closed up, and threw a heavy bolt, securing the closure. While this was happening, a man appeared waist-high above the wall, a long gun or Thompson cradled in his arms. The parapet on which he paced appeared to go all the way around.

Lights went on in the house one by one. Harry watched for another half hour or so and then began to walk to Harmon, noting that the pines grew thickly on one side of the road. Until he was near the station, he went into the woods whenever a car passed, which, while people were returning home in the evening, was often. Because the headlights gave him much advanced notice, no one saw him. On the train back to Grand Central, he kept his notebook closed but he recapped. There would be at least seven guards. The wall was twelve feet high. Verderamé was punctual, as they had observed during their slow-motion tracking of his route. And in line with his precise style of dress and rigidity of bearing, he was a man dependent upon routine, perhaps as a refuge from a business in which the only routine was collections and everything else was dangerously and continually improvised. Whatever the reason, he checked his watch often and was hesitant to disobey it. Harry prayed that no children lived behind the wall.

The easiest place in the world for shaking off a tail is in the subway in midafternoon, when whole cars or entire trains can be empty. Vanderlyn shuttled from train to train and line to line as skillfully as an eleven-year-old boy who has committed the system map to memory, and when he found himself in a nearly empty train hurtling toward the Bronx with a deafening and continuous rattle — tourists whose mistakes kidnap them this way often descend into panic, terror, and regret (and sometimes they never return) — he was sure that he was in the clear. It seemed to him that the wicker seats, the open windows, and the overhead fans, their blades of varnished wood, were sad things that, like so much else, were soon to disappear. Then he was alone in the station, in the shocking silence after the train had rumbled north and disappeared. Water dripping onto the blackened track bed thundered in his ears as the cool, moist air of early April fell from the grate on the street above. Incandescent lights gave off a pale, ashen glare onto white tiles as if in an icebox. Nothing is quite as brassy and cold as a New York subway station dazzlingly lit for the benefit of no one. At 96th and the park, Vanderlyn emerged from this into a world of the lightest green. In the rain the new leaves held as much water as they could and then bent to let go. Taxis drove by, full because of the rain, their windshield wipers making a sound that can put small children to sleep better than a cradle endlessly rocking. Water quieted and soothed the world, relieving it of ambition if only in promising its dissolution.

It was Harry's idea to invite Vanderlyn for lunch. Harry wanted to speak with him openly and at length, and in the dining room where he and Catherine had never before entertained a guest, he did, over consommé, smoked trout, and French bread, as rain cascaded down the dining room's one window.

"Billy Hale," Harry said, "my father-in-law, brought you up out of the blue when he was talking about people who had lost a son. I'm sorry."

For a moment, Vanderlyn's eyes seemed unable to focus on anything except the tablecloth, which was as empty as a snowfield. "Then it wasn't out of the blue, and, yes," he said, "I did."

"I need to know more about you," Harry told him, "because I'm about to gamble my whole life on an enterprise from which you are inseparable."

"But gambling," Vanderlyn replied, "is in its essence acting despite a lack of information — when you don't know, and yet you move — or you don't move."

"There are degrees."

"There are. What would you like to know?"

"Anything at random."

"Not a bad technique, and not new, either. All right. I'm teaching myself Russian."

"How's it going?"

"Very difficult for an old man, but I just finished a Chekhov story. I'll never be able to work in Russia. It might as well be Chinese."

Vanderlyn also read every day in French, and in regard to a language he had known since childhood, was distressed by his weakness of memory. "I have to look up words I don't know, and when I encounter them again, they've left me."

"That doesn't matter," Harry assured him.

"You're very kind."

"No, not at all. Think of it. Throughout your life you've read thousands of books, newspapers, journals, monographs, letters, documents, magazines — millions of pages, scores of millions of sentences, hundreds of millions of phrases, and perhaps a billion words. Of this, what do you remember? How much can you quote? Most likely not a thousandth of a percent, perhaps much less, which, of course, is why it's written down.

"And yet your reading, your education, what you have seen and learned, have shaped you. Although the exact form falls away almost immediately, the essence remains. In what you read, the difference between the great and the pedestrian is something very subtle that rides above the static form. The clarifying spirit can't be memorized, and the essence is in what's elusive, which is why those who can't grasp it other than willfully tend to deny it, because they can't see it."

"Go on."

"To know what you have read isn't necessarily to understand or to benefit from it immediately, as its central qualities exist above its mere form. If you and a cow listen to Mozart, you both know exactly the same sounds, the same notes, but you and presumably not the cow would hear a lot else, beyond the sounds, meaning, and meter. You would hear something the cow would not, and that the cow, if he could, would strenuously deny — I imagine."

"*He?*" Vanderlyn inquired.

"I like to refer to a cow as a he. Cows don't seem to me like shes."

"That's — almost — sane," Vanderlyn stated.

"What I'd like to know," Harry asked, "is who you are other than someone who spends his time on languages, sailing, and parachuting into France."

"I haven't parachuted into France for a while, and apart from work, I don't do much at all. I take very little pleasure in things. Either it's a sickness or part of growing old. With a few exceptions who are incomprehensible to me, and whom I envy, I find that happy older people are happy because they're idiots. Frankly, I'd rather be dead than go to a sing-along with Mrs. Buford at the piano and a dozen geriatrics who can neither remember lyrics nor clap in time. Have you ever noticed that the vigorous young talk to old people as if they were dogs?"

"No."

"You will."

"But you're not old."

"I'm forever old. My son, before he died, had begun to pull away from us, as I suppose he should have, and as I suppose is natural. Our job with him was done, my friends were dying, my wife and I sensing more and more the envoys of mortality that begin to visit you at a certain point whether you want them to or not. By nature's command and to protect his heart, my son had to put distance between himself and me. But, unlike Charlie, who had a full life to look forward to, it left my wife and me in a very lonely place.

"During the war, I convoyed over to Liverpool. I didn't have to — I had been taking a flying boat — but I felt that I should. We were hit at night in the North Atlantic. It was in the summer, but it was still miserably cold. Nineteen ships went down. Everything was in chaos. We tied the lifeboats from my ship together, but as the weather worsened we had to cast off the lines. We tried to stay in sight of each other's lights, but it rained, we soon lost sight of anything, and in the morning, when the sky cleared, we saw that we were alone in the middle of an empty sea.

"That's what happens when your children leave, but it's bearable, because you know they'll continue. When you know they won't, you know as well that you'll be on the sea forever, and that for you the sea has had no purpose. My son was estranged from me when he died, and I was waiting for him to come back.

"So now I work. I don't really care about it, but, just like you, people depend upon me — not only the living but the dead, to whom I owe a certain conduct and constancy. It's odd how people struggle for position and spend a whole life building a résumé that no one will read. A résumé follows you into the grave, a piece of paper that jerks like a moth. We get them at my company from seekers of employment. I never look at them. I find them offensive. If I can talk to someone for an hour, and watch his face, his hands, his eyes, I don't care what he's accomplished or what schools he's attended. Every second, you start over, and I want people who, second by second, can hew to the good and break the mold. That's what I see or don't see in their presence."

"And you?"

"I have no future. What I want to do, second by second, is that which is worthy in itself, that which I would do even if no one in the world were living, that which I would do at the cost of my life, in return for nothing, with great difficulty, and against terrible odds."

"Which is like war."

"Whatever it is, Harry, there's always plenty of it without my having to make it. As long as blood never cools, I'll have a place. I was in both world wars. It's time for me to retire, but there would be no point, so I'll step into the breach and perhaps spare someone else from having to do so. You're welcome to come along if you feel the need. Or you can run. Nothing wrong with running. Most people do. Perfectly honorable if that's what you decide, especially if you never want to kill again. You'd be entirely right."

Harry walked to the window. Water went on streaming down the panes. "Sometimes," he said, "my wife, who is twenty-four, and still like a young girl in many respects, has more sense and courage than almost anyone I've ever known. In very difficult conditions, she keeps at what she does steadily and without complaint. There's something in her that's admirable and instructive, inbred from so far back that it's breathtaking. As for me, this terrible thing is hanging over us, someone has been killed, the dead have been dishonored, and I'm going to clear the air."

# 39

## OFFICE IN MADISON SQUARE

SOMETIME AT THE END of April, when the whine of distant lawn mowers had returned to the parks, Harry had a two o'clock appointment with Bayer at his office in Madison Square. With everything garlanded in light green, it was neither too hot nor too cold, and now and then the wind billowed gently, carrying the scent of new grass. All morning, Harry and Catherine had left the windows open and lain together, sheets peeled back and trailing on the floor like a wedding gown. Their nightclothes discarded, her satin and lace splayed on the bed, time vanished until they heard the one o'clock bells from a church on Columbus Avenue.

After bathing and dressing at high speed, Harry passed the doorman, jumped the wall, and ran across the park until he disappeared into the haze of taxi horns and jackhammers that rolled out of the East Side like a fog bank. If he didn't have to wait long at 96th Street for an express, he might make it. He didn't want to be late for Bayer, whom he respected immensely, and arriving at even 2:01 would not be right. Long before any noise, the light of an express appeared far up the tunnel, jerking slowly and silently from side to side, yellowish white with traces of electrical red. Then came the cool air and the sound, pushed forward by the first car as if by a ramrod. Harry would be able to make 14th Street and then walk the nine blocks north to Madison Square, but with only minutes to spare.

Carrying Harry and remnants of winter air, the number 4 train squealed into the 14th Street station of the Lexington IRT like a screaming harpy, made a dead stop, gave up, and opened its doors.

Harry exited into the harsh light between the rows of steel columns at the edge of the tracks and a food stand tucked against a wall of white tile. As layers of air fell from the gardens of Union Square through many open grids, people ran to throw themselves into the downtown express and then sat breathing heavily as the doors stayed open and the train, humming tensely, did not move. All that time to spare was both embarrassing and like money in the bank.

With the rumble of idling electric motors in the background and the scent of their metal-infused oil issuing from under the train, Harry stared at a machine in which a dozen hot dogs were trapped on stainless steel rollers and spinning like torpedoes. "What is that?" he asked a squat, sweating man with a mustache and distressed eyes.

"What is what?"

"That machine."

"It for hot dogs."

"If it cooks them," Harry said, "aren't they terribly overcooked? And if it's just holding them at a warm temperature, isn't that dangerous after a while?"

"No one is ever been sick."

"How would you know? They take them, and then they get on a train to Brooklyn."

"Not just Brooklyn. And if they sick, they come back, and no one come back."

"You don't come back if you're dead."

"Mister . . . what you want? You want hot dog?"

"Are you kidding?" said Harry.

"Orange drink?"

"If it had anything in it related to an orange, which it doesn't."

"You crazy. You don't want nothing."

"Yes I do."

"What you want?"

"I want you to change the name of this place to Angel of Death Hot Dog Stand."

"Where you live, Los Angeles?"

"No."

"Yes. Everybody Los Angeles. Always talk. Tell you who they are. Lazy!"

"I beg your pardon?"

"Go back to there!" The proprietor moved to the western extremity of his empire, near the cheaty, pointy-bottomed cups and the giant, dangling pretzels coated with salt crystals as big as snails, and would not look at Harry. Harry took the stairs and found himself once again in the sweet air of April, when all is in balance and the world, like something tossed into the air and hesitating at the top of its arc, is momentarily ardent, motionless, and perfect.

With every step he took toward Madison Square he grew less and less certain not only of the chances of recruiting Bayer or anyone else to his plan but of the plan itself. "My enemy is not the law," he found himself saying under his breath as he walked—talking to himself was not a good sign—"but the enemy of the law, against which the law is too weak to defend itself. If the law is complicit in crime, is it the law? If, when not complicit, it not only fails to protect but proscribes self-protection, then it is not law but fraud. Anarchy arises not from those who defend themselves by natural right, but from officials who fail in their calling, look the other way, succumb to threats and blackmail, or who are themselves criminal. If without defending me the law says I can't defend myself, it is no longer the law, and I have to defy it."

As rationalization usually follows rather than precedes motivation, it was not likely that Bayer would be convinced by such abstractions. Harry faulted himself for seeking to lead his friends back into danger after they had come through so much of it, and by the time he got off the elevator on the ninth floor of a building on the south side of the square he was almost despondent enough not to knock on the door, except that through a frosted-glass panel upon which only a number had been painted he saw movement—of the friend to whom he had many times entrusted his life. This made him so happy he almost forgot what he had come for.

"Ha!" Bayer exclaimed when he saw Harry. North light flooded in through large windows overlooking the square, making Bayer, who was enormous, look like a crowned figure in a Flemish painting. "Have you had lunch?"

Harry said yes, though he hadn't.

"How about a Scotch?"

"No. Don't need it."

"An orange drink?"

It could only have been a coincidence, Harry told himself.

"Straight peanuts, then," Bayer said, going to a desk drawer from which he pulled out a small burlap sack of roasted peanuts. "How about these?" In one motion he moved a gray wastepaper can from beneath his desk to the space in front of them, and as if they were doing piecework they began to shell the peanuts and toss the husks, missing only rarely. Feeling a sense of joy merely in sitting with Bayer, whom he had seen blown into the air by a German cannon, but who now was alive, he felt that they were two schoolboys. All rationales fled from him.

"What are you doing now? Are you married?" Bayer asked.

"I am."

"So quick. I'll bet she's beautiful."

"She is. Not everyone thinks so, but for me every imperfection is like a sharp cut driving her in deeper — every time I think of her, and I think of her all the time. I think I'm crazy."

"I wish I could be crazy like that."

"I could marry her ten thousand times. She's twenty-four years old. She has the charm of a girl and the wisdom of a woman. I've never seen such grace or beauty." An awkward silence followed, during which Harry was embarrassed for having gone on about Catherine as if Bayer didn't exist. "And you?" he said, now almost fearfully.

"Ah well," Bayer answered, throwing a whole, unshelled peanut into the wastepaper can so that it sounded like a distant shot. "Marriages are made in heaven, but not mine. She left me."

"I'm sorry," Harry said.

"Yeah. It's nothing new, either, although I found out about it only after I got back. In 'forty-four — can you imagine that? I could have died and I wouldn't have known, which is maybe why she didn't tell me — she took up with some Jewish fucker and they moved out to the Island."

"*You're* Jewish," Harry said.

"Yeah, but my name isn't *Jewish Bayer.* His is *Jewish Lucky.*"

"That's his real name?"

"It's at least his nickname."

"Probably just a nickname, wouldn't you think?"

"That's what it is in the telephone book."

"You're kidding."

"Check if you want. They have a kid. I know it's Jewish Lucky's kid, but somehow I think of it as my own. Even if it doesn't know it, I'm a ghost in its life. It's either a boy or a girl."

"Right," Harry said.

"It'll probably grow up to be the president of the United States, and I'll be ninety years old, living in a cold-water flat on Avenue D. On the day they light the White House Christmas tree, if that's what they do, I'll eat dinner alone at Horn and Hardart. On the way home I'll slip on the ice and lie in the street for two hours before I die. My last words will be spoken to a Bowery bum who's too drunk to understand them, and the president, who would have been my kid, will be waltzing in the White House, eating rondalays of beef. Why are you laughing?"

"Because you've got it all planned out," Harry said.

"From the time we jumped into Normandy.... God, had I known, I almost certainly would have been killed. All that time, all the blood, and the snow: you can't describe it — and I loved her, I yearned for her. Thinking about her saved me."

"I'm sure that's why she didn't tell you."

"You think she was that decent? I'll tell ya, when I got home . . . there was a stranger living in the apartment where we used to live. He had forwarded my mail to her for a year and a half. She was gone. He told me that she was with this guy Jewish Lucky, and he was sorry to break it to me. He gave me her number. I called. She said it would be best for us not to see each other. 'Ever?' I asked. She said, 'Ever.' 'What if I run into you on the street, like at the Macy's parade or something?'

'You go to that? What, are you ten years old?' 'I mean in front of Macy's, or *in* Macy's.' 'Then you do, that's all, but it's over.' I said okay, and she said goodbye as if I was talking to some sort of clerk in an office. She was very curt. She cut me off. Just after the line clicked, I told her I loved her."

"You'll find someone," Harry said.

"Yeah, eventually."

"You will. I saw my wife for the first time on the Staten Island Ferry, and I fell in love with her instantly. She was far away, her back turned, and though I could hardly see her it was as if I had known her all my life. Then she disappeared, and I lost her. But on the way back from St. George later in the day we were on the same boat. At first I lost her again, but then she came right to me, and she was standing — I don't know — a foot away. What caused her to do that I can't tell, and neither can she, but the instant I saw her face-to-face I knew I loved her, that I wanted to spend the rest of my life with her, and that if that meant the rest of my life would last only ten seconds, so be it."

"For me," Bayer said, "that may take awhile."

"Have you heard from the others?"

"Just their addresses. Rice moved out west. He got a law job in California someplace. Has to do with farming or ranching or something. Everyone else went home, and the dead ones are in heaven, even Hemphill."

"What are you doing now, for a living?" Harry asked. There was no way to tell from the office: two visitors' chairs, filing cabinets, telephone, typewriter, shelves lined with folders, a cabinet with office supplies, but no pictures, diplomas, or any other direct evidence of what Bayer did. And the door had just a number, as Harry had noted.

"I'm not proud of what I do."

"I thought you were a draftsman. I don't see the table. I always wanted one as a desk. It seems to me a more comfortable desk than the blocky things most people have to lean over."

"You can have mine if you want. I still have it. I'm a draftsman by trade. In high school I was really good. It caught me at the right time, and I loved the little wooden box I had, with German drafting tools set into the recesses. Other kids had cheap ones, but my father gave me these from when he was in school: Solingen, expensive and indestructible. I felt I had to live up to them, so I did. I worked four times as much as anybody else and they misinterpreted that as natural talent. My own school sent me to technical school during the year and over the summer, actually paid for it. I got an associate degree in technical drawing before I got my high school diploma.

"Before the war I worked at Otis Elevator in Yonkers and then at Bulova out in Queens."

"That's right," Harry said, remembering.

"Not fun to get there, but I did well. Then I came back from overseas. To make all the tanks, ships, and planes, they trained so many draftsmen you can't count 'em anymore. Now that production has ceased, there's such an oversupply that if you do find work you earn less than you would breaking pavement.

"After a while I got a job with an architectural firm. I can draw anything to specifications, and it didn't take long to learn how to do building plans, but the architects weren't happy with me."

"Why not?"

"They were making astoundingly ugly buildings, and I told them so."

"The diplomat."

"Really, they pollute the world. I mean, how much does it cost to have a peaked roof, for Chrissakes? This whole country is messed up with flat roofs. We have a beautiful landscape, you know? What if New England towns with village greens had flat roofs? It's gonna happen."

"How long did you last there?"

"I'm still there."

"What, they put you in a quarantine office?" Harry asked, looking around the small room.

"And they fired me, too, but I got a big raise, a really big raise."

"*Comment?*" Harry asked in French. It was an expression that his men used frequently and with a great deal of amused irony when they were in France.

"They said, 'You can't work here anymore, but you can be our expediter.'"

"What's an expediter? I mean, what do you expedite?"

"That's what I myself said. What's an expediter? I didn't know what it was, much less that they had one, or that it would be me."

"What is it?"

"Let's say," Bayer told him, tossing a peanut shell, "that you and your wife buy a co-op in . . . you tell me."

"Brooklyn Heights," Harry said instantly. "They've got peaked roofs, no aluminum trim, and tree-shaded streets."

"In a brownstone?"

"The whole building," Harry told him, "if things go right. If we have a baby. Our apartment's too small, and it was mine. We want to go to a place that's ours."

"Okay, a brownstone. That's not a co-op, but so what. The problem is that it's divided up into four apartments, with four kitchens, four cruddy bathrooms. You're going to have to redo the whole thing."

"Maybe."

"You definitely will. So you go to an architect. The architect tells you that you need a certificate of occupancy, a set of plans (or otherwise he has to send people to make them, which is expensive), and a building permit. You say, 'Can you get them for me?' And he says, 'Sure, it will cost such and such,' a small amount — fees. He doesn't do anything for two weeks, because to know what's going to happen he doesn't have to, and yet he knows that you're going to have to be made anxious in order to do what he has in store for you. Life is a series of traps, and unless you've already been in one, it's hard to see it coming even if it's right there."

"What do I have to do?"

"Your wife is pregnant, your lease may be expiring, you're already paying taxes on the building you bought, you need the proceeds from selling your apartment if you own it, or you're paying rent if you don't. You want to stop paying interest on the bridge loan. You want to get on with your life. Everyone knows this.

"And what the architect tells you is that he went down to the building department — he didn't; he didn't have to — and they can't find the certificate of occupancy or the plans. They 'lost' them. Do you have a C of O? No. Does the previous owner? You call the previous owner. He says he'll look. You bother him for a week. He doesn't. You call the architect. By this time you're ripe for the picking. 'What can I do?' you ask. The architect says he'll try again.

"Another two weeks go by. You feel what it's like to be in prison. He calls. He went down to the building department, and they suggested that you get an expediter. And you say. . . ." Bayer held out his left hand, inviting Harry to say . . .

"'What's an expediter?'"

"Ah, but you know now, right?"

"I think so."

"You go to the expediter the architect recommends — me, if it's my firm or one of several others I work for — and you present your problem. He says, 'I'll go down to the building department and see what I can do.' He doesn't. He doesn't have to. In a week he calls you. Good news. The building department will allow him to search the records. They themselves can't do it expeditiously because they have a shortage of funds and personnel (most of whom spend their afternoons at the track or in a steam bath). 'How long will it take?' you ask. 'It varies,' I say, knowing that it doesn't, that it's complete bullshit. 'Sometimes you can find what you're looking for in twenty minutes, and sometimes, if the papers have been misfiled, it can take a year. That can cost up to twenty thousand dollars.'

"I listen to your inward collapse. Despair. But then I lift you out. I tell you that because of the variability, one can pay a fixed fee. It may be more than you might have to pay, but it's guaranteed to save you from catastrophe. It's the same principle as insurance.

"And then, then the sad part. You leap at the chance to pay me two thousand dollars and rush down here with it in your pocket. I see hope and relief in your face as you hand me the check that could help pay for your child's college, medical bills if someone in your family gets sick, food on the table. But you give it over gratefully, because now your life can move forward.

"I let some days pass. I amble on down to the building department, and in a back room I give a guy fourteen hundred dollars, cash. Then I go to the counter, and they give me the stuff you need, which they always had and which they can find in three seconds, because other than steal that's the only thing they do.

"Then I go to the architects, and in another back room I give a guy three hundred dollars, cash, and I keep the rest for myself. No one ever complains that the building department asked for a bribe, because it never did. The expediters — of whom there are quite a few — will always say that they were paid for looking for documents, and that they did look for documents. We keep fake time sheets. The client is as happy as the crooks who take his money. When you deliver the necessary materials, he's virtually glowing.

"I'm a thief. I steal from good, innocent people, from young couples who need the money and have no idea what's happening to them, from old people with canes, from anyone."

"Why don't you go to the mayor?" Harry asked, "or the mayor's office?"

Bayer looked at him with amusement. "The mayor?"

"Yes."

"You think the mayor doesn't know?"

"Really?"

"Really. And the police commissioner. And the heads of the departments. They know, they know. It all runs on graft. The government that's supposed to serve and protect steals and lies. I'm going to get out as soon as I can, but of course that won't stop it. It'll continue, and long after we're dead it'll be the same. If I refused, it wouldn't make any difference. The process begins and ends at the counter, when the city employees tell you that they've lost your records, and everyone above them knows exactly what's going on, and so you pay. And you know who owns the whole scheme, who provides the protection, makes the payoffs to the higher-ups, launders the money, invented the process, and gets a very big piece? The Mafia. It's part of the city government. While we were fighting a war, it was here, digging in deeper.

"Where's the law? I hate people who steal. I hate myself. If I could,

Captain, I would take my carbine and kill those guys, just as sure as I would kill an armed man breaking into my house to rob me."

"They are armed," Harry said.

Bayer continued Harry's sentence. "Like an army, with all the powers of government. But killing someone like that wouldn't make any difference, and besides, they haven't killed anyone."

"What if it would?" Harry asked. "What if they had?"

"*Comment?*" Bayer asked.

"Listen," Harry said. "Let me tell you what I've been doing."

## 40

## THE TRAIN FROM MILWAUKEE

WHEN JOHNSON LEFT the Apostle Islands, a curtain of snow had descended upon the lake, obscuring alternating bands of white ice and blue open water that disappeared northward toward Canada. Like almost all things in the Apostles, it was cold, sharp, and well defined. No gray, each crystalline flake falling with a hiss on pine needles that did not bow to the winds of winter. The Apostles were the standard to which Johnson returned. He referred to them, the sentinels of Lake Superior, when he faltered, and the memory of them gave him strength.

After the war, he had returned to teach English — a language they did not yet speak or understand in its subtleties — to young people whose chief regret was that they had missed what he had been condemned to suffer through. Apart from teaching them that sometimes you can end a sentence with a preposition, he taught them that one way to be grateful for being alive was to say it, hear it, and sing it in the song of their language. His work did not produce bales of cotton or stacks of lumber, it filled hearts, opened long views, and allowed the sons and daughters of miners and mill workers to rise in air so metaphysical it might lead them ready and armed to meet the ghosts of sorrow and death.

To get from Bayfield to Milwaukee was not the easiest thing in the world, but, after that, riding the train from Milwaukee to Chicago was what some commuters did every day. Harry had proposed that he and Johnson meet in Chicago, which was fair in that Harry would come nine hundred miles and Johnson less than half that, although Harry would ride the sleek Twentieth Century Limited, and Johnson would have to board a Greyhound at Bayfield and will himself into the kind of Buddhist trance necessary to ride without distress on a bus.

That Harry had prepared a meeting at Johnson's convenience meant that he wanted something. That it was in Chicago meant that he could have done without what he wanted, for otherwise he would have contrived to get himself to Bayfield, or at least to Superior. It was intriguing especially because Harry had said his father-in-law had a suite at the Drake, where he and Johnson could stay and eat on the company dime. The Drake meant big money. At the very least, it would be luxurious, unlike most reunions, which took place in cheap beer joints or restaurants by the waterside where gulls stole French fries from paper containers that sat on picnic tables like German industrial towns waiting to be carpet-bombed.

This was something else. At Milwaukee the steam locomotive, unsuspecting that in time it would be replaced by a boxy, foul, predictable diesel, was bristling with stilled arms, pistons, rods, and pipes, a black triceratops that could push its way past every Wisconsin cow insolent enough to block the tracks and impede the path to Chicago.

The rhythm of such an engine, heard in every city and town and across open fields, invited Johnson to think high. It was April of 1947, and the tall buildings of Chicago were lit with innumerable lights above the darkening blue of the lake. For Johnson the sounds of the steam locomotive opened past and future. They were assurance, encouragement, a message of faith. This was America's time. Its engines exhaled and pushed forward, never missing a beat.

He descended at Union Station and walked toward the northern end of Michigan Avenue, thinking about the red shingles he was going to put on the roof of his house in the Apostles. They were guaranteed, it was said, to last and not to crack in the frost, and they were the color of the tiles he had seen in Sicily.

Every day, the great and famous train backed into its berth in Grand Central and waited to be filled with New Yorkers who would throw themselves at Chicago as if on a mission to conquer its superior *lebensraum*. Then it raced north, dusting past commuter trains all the way up the Hudson. Approached from the rear as it sat ready on the track, it was fluted and modern, the wasp-like rounding of its last car squared off in a cream-colored, lighted sign that read *20th Century Limited*.

Countless passengers had seen this upon striking out for the Second City. For New Yorkers it is always painful to leave New York, no matter how much they dream of escaping, because when they turn their backs on it they feel as if they are going to prison rather than leaving it. Racing along the Hudson at what seemed like spectacular speed, Harry closed his eyes. There was Catherine, caught in the net of streets. The registers and years of the city would shift and turn, and its shafts would spin, while he was not there. Flying away from her, he saw her in a silence that rose as an inaudible fume.

The ice on Lake Erie that had accumulated in slowly melting thirty-foot moraines resulted in a chain of red lights that halted the Twentieth Century and forced it to stay stock still, breathing like a charger, dripping as if hot from its run, and vibrating with the strain of stopping somewhere west of Cleveland, which meant that Johnson would arrive at the Drake before Harry. It didn't matter. One thing Johnson had learned in recent years was to give someone time to show up alive. Whereas in Bayfield the richest colors were the greens, whites, and blues of the islands and the lake, here they were overwhelming and intense reds, browns, and gold, with a touch of royal. Neither snow nor ice covered Lake Michigan, only dusk made duskier for Johnson by the yellow glow of little lamps spread across the tables at the Drake. The silverware glistened with a muted shine almost like nickel. The war was over, he had lived, and here he was, waiting, with a bandage on his nose, now fairly well soaked in blood.

"How did you get that?" Harry asked as he guided his suitcase in the air and around the table, having come straight in because he was late. "I want to put this down where the waiter won't trip over it." They didn't need to shake hands. A hundred years might elapse and they could still speak to one another as if they were walking down a snowy road in France, numb from cold and exhaustion.

Before Johnson could answer, Harry had another question. "Why didn't you order something?"

"The prices."

"The company'll pay for it."

"Are you sure?" Johnson asked.

He had not fathomed what was involved. Harry said, "They keep the suite year-round and no one was scheduled for it. It's got two bedrooms, on a high floor. I've been told you can't hear anything but the wind, and you see the lights blanketing the North Shore."

"What about the food?" Johnson asked. "If no one were here, they wouldn't be paying for that."

"They said the budget is set in such a way that they assume someone will be here on an expense account eighty percent of the time. An ordinary mortal can't quite understand this — I never will — but Billy Hale said to me, If you were in an office and you took a drink from the water cooler, would you worry about what it costs?"

"What kind of water cooler?" Johnson asked. It was a very odd question. "You mean, one that has those conical cups you can't put down unless you're Houdini? That's about a hundredth of a cent's worth, if that, if it's delivered. If it comes from a pipe, it's a millionth."

Surprised to hear that Johnson was also irritated by the Houdini cups, Harry continued on in the line of conversation. "That's what I said to him, more or less. And he said that, proportionately, given the resources of the firm, if we ate like hogs and stuck to Russian caviar, it would be no more than taking a drink from the water cooler."

"I can't grasp that," Johnson said, "but I'll have a Champagne cocktail. I've never had one. I don't even know what it is. But it sounds good."

"I'll bet Catherine knows," Harry said.

"Who's Catherine?"

"My wife." Harry's anaesthetized look told Johnson exactly how far gone he was.

"I can tell," Johnson said, "that though she may be an heiress, it's not for the money."

"No," Harry said, still intoxicated with thinking of her, "it's not for the money."

The waiter came to them, gliding over the thick carpet as gracefully as a manta ray. Everyone's face was slightly red-orange in the light of the table lamp, its shade chosen to show to perfection a woman in makeup. But without makeup, anyone in this light looked like a pumpkin. They ordered four Champagne cocktails. "Are you expecting other diners?" the waiter asked. He was a horsey-looking Slav with huge mother-of-pearl cufflinks as round as the moon.

"We aren't," said Harry. "We just like to have our reserves in place."

The waiter returned with the four drinks and put them down so daintily as to indicate resentment, then disappeared into near darkness lit only by a painting light over a canvas of either starving racehorses or really fat greyhounds. Although they didn't know what a Champagne cocktail was, it was lemon juice, sugar, bitters, and Champagne in a glass so cold it was frosted. "It didn't make Milwaukee famous," Johnson said, "but I like it. It's festive."

"Yeah," said Harry. "It's festive. You know, you're still bleeding."

The gauze taped to the ridge of Johnson's nose was getting heavier and redder. "Oh, that," he said.

"What happened?"

"Nothing. Well, almost nothing. I got to the hotel and I was looking up at it and not at my feet. I don't walk around looking at my feet. At the entrance there's a lectern which is the doorman's post."

"I noticed. The doorman is seven feet tall and dressed like Frederick the Great."

"Did you notice that there was a tent-like structure where people waiting for taxis can get out of the wind and rain?"

"No."

"Neither did I. That's because the canvas part is gone. The frame, however," Johnson said, finishing the first cocktail and searching for the second (there would be a third), "remains. Including the brass bars at the bottom. Excuse me, the *fucking* brass bars at the bottom, about four inches above the ground."

"Ah," said Harry, who was taking yet another chance on what he was drinking, "it's coming into focus."

"I fell flat on my face, not holding my arms out, because I was reflexively reaching down to free my feet. All right, so I smashed up. It happens. What really bothers me is the doorman."

"The doorman."

"First, he laughed. Then he sneered at me, lifting his upper lip like a garage door and moving his head from side to side. And then he turned away. If a dog got hurt it would excite more sympathy than that."

"Did you complain?"

Johnson had a determined look. "I have better plans. The way I'm dressed, the way I look, he didn't think I was a guest. People who stay here don't carry U.S. Army packs." Near Harry's Copeland Leather suitcase was an olive-drab knapsack.

"But then he saw you go in."

"I went around the other side. He doesn't know I'm staying here, which is good. And he won't, because I'll never go out the front door."

"Why?"

"Because, on the day we leave, and I'm flexible about that, it's the weekend...."

"That's why it's so empty in here," Harry commented. "It's for businessmen, not for taking a date or your wife."

"And maybe," Johnson said, "that's why the waiter was a bit put out to bring Champagne cocktails. I would say it's a woman's drink."

"Do you think we shouldn't be drinking it?"

"What the hell. The day we leave, you're going to take my pack and wait for me in a taxi on Michigan Avenue. The lectern that that son of a bitch stands at is quite complex. It's got a lamp, some sort of log or ledger, guidebooks, umbrellas, a pitcher of water, glasses, flashlights, probably the lunch of the son of a bitch, and a telephone."

"What are you going to do?"

"I weigh a hundred and ninety pounds. When the tank tread ran over my leg, the plate settled on an unevenness of ground, and didn't crush it as it might have. I'm okay now: I don't even limp. I coach the track team, so I run with them a lot. I still can move fast. So what's fourteen miles an hour times two hundred pounds — include clothing and shoes — in foot-pounds?"

"Two thousand eight hundred."

"Like a car. He won't know what hit him. The lectern will shatter. Its contents will explode in all directions. He'll be knocked five or ten feet, and his hat will fly twenty feet. He won't be hurt much unless he tries to get in a punch, but he'll wonder for the rest of his life what it was that came flying down the sidewalk like a bat.

"And that's me."

"I'm in the taxi?"

"You're in the taxi. I get in, we drive five or ten blocks. I take my knapsack and get out, you go another few blocks. We mix with the crowds. To the Union Station . . . just like Lenin. Then home."

"Unlike Lenin," Harry said, "I'm going to Indiana to see Sussingham. And I can tell him that you haven't changed."

"Should I have? My values are timeless, but my morals are flexible where required."

"Revenge?"

"Symmetry. The universe not only consists of it, it demands it."

"I'll tell you what, Johnson. Let's have a great dinner, charge it to Hale and Company, and go up to the suite, pull two chairs to the window, prop up our feet, and have a long talk."

"About what?"

"Symmetry."

When they opened the windows, the sound of traffic on Lake Shore Drive, occasionally muted by gusts of wind shot from the looming darkness above the lake, gave body to the arc of red and white lights moving in two streams far below them. A white voile curtain swept back and forth with the spring breeze, and they were able to sense the humidity of the air coming from over the water, because the left sides of their faces were slightly drier than the right.

"Even with a view like that," Johnson said, "I mark it for ranges." He meant for rifle, BAR, machine gun, mortar, tank, 88, and howitzer. "Do you still do that?"

"No, but sometimes I'm afraid to go to sleep, because I think civilian life is a dream and if I let go I'll wake up in a freezing hole in Germany. What haunts me is the men who never came back, and the ones now hidden away in hospitals, without a jaw, or half a face, no legs, bodies scarred with burns; the ones who'll go back to their towns or neighborhoods and the people there will freeze when they see them. The luck we had, that saw us through . . . ," Harry said.

"But you're not scared of anything anymore, right?"

"Nothing physical, not yet. My father-in-law—who just paid for our dinner—is almost sixty. He says, when you're young—and from his perspective that would mean us—take the risks you're going to take in your life, because risk hates the old. Make your dangerous moves when you still have the ability and time to recover. Which is why I asked you here."

"I figured something. The Drake. . . ."

"To ask a favor. More than a favor."

Johnson turned from the high view to Harry. "Whatever you want, I can tell you in advance, I'll do it. You know that. As long as I don't have to kill someone or rob a bank."

Harry was absolutely still. Then he looked down.

"Uh-oh," Johnson said, leaning toward the windowsill, like a judge about to get up from a massive leather chair in his club. "Which is it?"

"A bank would be no problem."

"It's a person?"

"More than one."

"How many?"

"Maybe half a dozen."

"Half a dozen? The war's over, Harry," Johnson said.

"Not for some people."

"It is for me."

"That's fine. It's okay. I would never expect this of anyone. Don't worry."

"I didn't say no. What is it?"

"In essence, it's this: If you have a fire in your house, you call the fire department and they come as fast as they can. If someone is robbing a bank, the police and the FBI come as fast as they can. There could be a gun battle. They could kill the robbers, and die themselves. But for organized crime it's different. If you're being shaken down, and they beat you, set your place on fire, kill you if you resist . . . if they steal from a whole city, intimidate a whole nation really, run prostitution and burglary rings, murder for hire, pay off police and judges, kidnap children for ransom . . . for these things, if you go to the police, not only will they not do anything, someone among them will report you if you persist, and you'll be killed."

"This is happening to you? You're really going to do this?"

"I'm being driven out of business. They killed one of my workers. They beat me to within inches of my life. They rule the city and they enjoy it. You can see it on their faces. They walk around like kings."

"What about the FBI?"

"That's what I wanted to say. If there's a fire in your house, you call the fire department and they come to put it out. If the Mafia is shaking you down and murdering your people, you go to the FBI and they say that they're working on it. What does that mean? It means two things. First, they may have a task force or two, let's say in Newark. Maybe in ten years they'll arrest some guys in Newark and it'll be all over the front pages. It's as if you report that your house is burning down and the fire department says, We're working on putting out a fire. Well, it's in Phoenix, not that they can tell you that, or any details, so you don't know if in ten years they'll put out a fire in Phoenix or not. It's left to your imagination. And the other thing is that when you go to them they ask if you're willing to testify. What that means is that you're going to die, because they can neither protect you nor keep a secret. You're dead when you open your mouth. They know that no one testifies. They ask it to get rid of you and to make you feel responsible for their failures. Because, you see, they know who's committing these crimes, how, where, and when. They could get the evidence themselves with surveillance, wiretaps, and presence at the scene. And they do, every now and then symbolically, with their well publicized task forces. To put it simply, they have a modus vivendi, and for some of them there's even what we would call a 'relationship.' You don't know who knows whom or what will be reported to whom."

"Who else?" Johnson asked.

"Thus far I've spoken only to Bayer. Sussingham tomorrow. Then Rice."

"What did Bayer say?"

"He'll do it."

"What exactly is *it?*"

"A road ambush in a fairly remote area, with a wide river across which to escape in the dark. Any reaction from the law or the mob will be channeled north and south, which is how the roads run. No one will cross the river to look, as the nearest bridges are forty and twenty miles away."

"The Mafia knows how to protect itself, Harry, doesn't it? This kind of thing is their business."

"Not like it's ours. We're not going to do it their way. We don't know how to do that. We'll do it our way. We'll have heavy weapons — bazooka, light machine gun, explosives. They have, at most, a few Thompsons. Before the war, who would have known how to do something like this? Now it's like brushing your teeth."

"It would be the softest target we ever had, but where would you get the weapons?"

"From the government."

"The government? I don't understand. They won't do it, but it's okay if we do? What is it, a do-it-yourself thing where they lend us the tools?"

"I can't explain. I hardly know myself, but it's true. We don't go without them, and it's not the FBI."

"Then what is it?"

"Some sort of offshoot of the OSS, but I really don't know. It's forming now."

"This is not going to be a regular thing, is it?"

"One shot."

"A year from now, maybe six months," Johnson said, "and I don't think I would have done it. Now it seems kind of natural. I need to know the details, but it feels more like reality than what I've been living of late. It would have to be my last shot, though. I mean, it's crazy, but I'll do it."

"Why don't you sleep on it?"

"I don't have to. Many times, my life was in your hands, yours in mine. It's a habit that's hard to break. You knew that."

"I did, and I don't feel good about it."

"You don't have to feel good about it. That's the point."

"I'm sorry you had to come all the way down here," Harry said. "I couldn't tell you on the telephone."

"Hey," said Johnson. "I love Chicago. I gotta get outa Bayfield now and then. And think of what I'm going to do to that doorman."

"No," Harry said. "Fire discipline."

Johnson thought for a minute. "No, Harry. If I'm going to help you possibly kill half a dozen mob soldiers, you're going to help me tackle an officious doorman."

"You're right, you're absolutely right," Harry told him. "I'm sorry. But I want to be able to see it. The taxi should be where I can witness the impact."

"Yeah, I'd like that."

"I forgot to ask you," Harry said. "Did you remarry? Because I'm not going to risk breaking up any families — other than my own."

"No."

"Do you have someone?"

"I tried to have a girlfriend but I couldn't give her enough. It was as if I had reins and someone was pulling on them. It wasn't fair to her or to anybody. She got married and moved to Menomonie. It's better for her. She weighed about ninety-five pounds. She was very pretty. Petite. I'm all right. I won't ever love anyone but Ann."

# 41

## RED STEEL

THOUGH THE ATMOSPHERE was choked with soot and sulfur, and everything was black but for an underbelly of orange billowing from fires in the mills along the lake, the town was alive with spring. The air that trapped the smoke was also saturated with a clean mist that was winning a battle with the blast furnaces. Like a wrestler, it pushed down its antagonists, and nature prevailed. The reason that on a spring night in 1947 life was lit up in Gary, Indiana, and the streets were as active as Times Square, was that even at midnight they were making steel.

After taking the steps of a brick boarding house, Harry knocked on the first apartment door. A giant melon of a man in an undershirt appeared, and, without speaking, lifted his eyebrows. Inside the apartment, a mother and daughter were sitting together at the dining room table, working on something. The girl, whose face was from a Botticelli, was nonetheless tough and raw, with pulled-back hair and skin blotched with acne, all of which somehow made her more alluring than someone softer. Harry had to speak or the door would shut in his face.

"I'm sorry to disturb you," he began.

"No, not disturb," said the man, who hadn't been in the country long, or had lived only among his own.

"I'm looking for Sussingham. Sussingham."

"Not here."

"He doesn't live here?"

"On shift. Work now."

"When does he get off? Finish."

"Morning." The man pointed toward the U.S. Steel works, miles away but so huge that they seemed like a cliff face of hell. "You can go. Tell them at gate. They send man with you sometime. Sometime no."

As the door shut, the girl smiled. Harry guessed that she worked very hard in a factory or a bakery, someplace where there was heat and sweat, where things were made in great numbers in production lines or on conveyors that set the pace for the makers, challenging them to keep up or die. On the surface she was tough and coarse, and yet she had, as much as anyone he had ever seen, the kind of beauty that can come through fire day by day. As he walked toward the mills that stood beneath ropes of dirty smoke twisting in agony as they rose, he couldn't stop thinking of her.

After he talked his way in, they put him in a place where, although Sussingham didn't know it, he could watch him work. It was as if Sussingham were still at war. The noise of the steel furnace was like the roar of tank engines or bombers. Sirens, claxons, and engines, and the wind blowing through as if the enormous shed were a mountain range, made a counterpoint that stood up the senses.

Harry could not suppress his awe when a bucket as big as a building glided through the darkness, tipped, and spilled out a waterfall of molten steel redder than lava. In the confusion that followed — rollers rolling, traveling cranes passing above, little locomotives dashing about, huge electric motors spinning to move the machines that cradled and formed the steel — glowing rectangles began to course like ice floes in a river, dangerous things that had just been born. Sussingham stood on one side of the river of rollers and, like a logger, guided the nearly molten slabs with a long steel pole hooked at its far end. Though everything about them was deadly, they went helplessly to their execution in immense machines that cut and compressed them.

Currents of heat lifted in serpentines and seared the air. Smoke rocked back and forth fifty feet above the rollers before it was carried upward through giant fans in a long row at the peak of the roof. The men on the floor moved like soldiers, and Harry ached to join them not because he was oblivious of the danger but rather because his life had taught him to run to it.

In making steel, as their strength flowed out, it also flowed in. It happens to soldiers, girls who work in bakeries, and sailors on an undulating sea, and it was happening to Sussingham in the mill. He had not resigned from battle and probably never would. Someone there has to be who carries on for those who are forever silent. That was Sussingham, of all of them the one who was still at war and unaware, the one who would not let go.

In the morning, spring sunshine gave its silvery-white veneer to towers and sheds hundreds of feet high and thousands of feet long. The fires of the night before were washed out by the light, which now illuminated the structural complexity of what in darkness had seemed to be solid cliffs. Beams, trusses, cables, and buttresses cloaked the soot-blackened buildings and shone delicately against the blue lake. The donkey engines and their tooting were hardly something from hell, and Harry noticed that there was plenty of green, even if not a single tree, as nature marched grasslands right up to the concrete aprons of the mills, and that the roads crossed the surrounding fields as if on a prairie that had never felt a footstep. Gulls soared over the stacks and spinning ventilators, lifted by masses of bracing air that had traveled half the world before shooting unobstructed down the length of Lake Michigan. Colliding with Chicago, a rude shock, they then arched over and punched through it on their way to becoming motionless and water-laden in New Orleans.

"I'm stuck," said Sussingham, entirely unbidden.

"You're not stuck, you're exhausted," Harry told him.

"Not yet. On this shift I usually can't fall asleep until ten or eleven in the morning. It throws you off."

"Why do you do it?"

"Work rules. I have no seniority, and the money's good. Demand for steel isn't consistent, but we'll be making it forever. It's secure, and I feel trapped."

"Then why don't you" — here Harry stopped and made a freeing, tossing-something-away gesture — "free yourself?"

"What am I going to do? In the war I knew what to do. Get to Berlin, move forward, dislodge the enemy, kill him if necessary. As difficult as it was, it was clear. After all that" — he meant North Africa, Italy, France, and Germany — "it got in my blood. Nothing less will make me feel alive."

"So re-enlist."

"Making steel is more exciting than the peacetime army. So is watching concrete dry. I think about the last four years all the time. I can't see settling down, which is funny, because when I was in, all I wanted was for the war to end so I could go home."

"What about becoming a cop or something?"

"Cops don't invade Normandy and smash through the *Westwall*. They don't jump out of airplanes into enemy armored divisions. They rattle doorknobs of dry-goods stores at night and yell at kids for opening fire hydrants or smoking corn-silk cigarettes."

"Become a pilot in Alaska."

"That might be something."

"What you're talking about is like swimming in a cold river," Harry went on. "When you swim through cold, active water, you're on fire with life. Every one of your senses is elevated, you feel things you don't otherwise feel, the world is fresh and promising. But when you get out and get warm, your heart stops beating so fast, your breathing slows, your muscles relax. That's normal. You object?"

"No."

"And are you sure that it's not just that you haven't come down from work? My wife's an actress, and when she comes home from the theater she finds it impossible to sleep. She gets a little crazy, thinking of all kinds of things to do and places to go. She wanted to go riding at two o'clock in the morning, not in the park, which would have been one thing, but through lower Manhattan, which was dead still. There's something very attractive about thundering on a horse down the middle of Fifth Avenue at three A.M."

"You did that?"

"We did. We also rode across the Brooklyn Bridge, on the boards, raced through Brooklyn Heights, and crossed back. At dawn we ended up at Ratner's."

"What's Ratner's?"

"It's a dairy restaurant on the Lower East Side, famous for its early breakfast, onion rolls, and sour cream, none of which I like, but you can appreciate them for being the best of what they are. My wife . . . well, women of a certain temperament and class sometimes do things like this."

"Galloping horses around New York in the middle of the night? Whose horses?"

"Hers. And, given what she can do, they might have been zebras. When we got to the restaurant, she goes up to an astounded cop who doesn't know what to say because the horses are so beautiful and the woman is breathtaking, and you know what that does to you. And she says, 'I'll give you ten dollars if you hold these horses while we're in Ratner's.' And he says, 'Ma'am, I can't do that. It's illegal.'"

"Not in Chicago," Sussingham said.

"Not in New York either, really. And she says, looking at him straight, with her paralytic beauty, and not missing a beat, 'Apiece.'"

"Did he take it?"

"Of course he did. I don't live that way. Neither, most of the time, does she, but on occasion what she can do slips right past what she should do. It makes me love her even more, as if for the first time. All over again, you get a shot of whatever the hell it is — happiness, elation. What about the daughter of your landlord?"

Sussingham stopped, looked at Harry, and started walking again. "You noticed." They were on a long stretch of dry macadam whitened by sand from the Indiana dunes. Someday it would crumble, but now it shone in the sun. "He's not my landlord. I know who you're talking about, though: first apartment on the right. She works in a factory that makes window glass. Her face is always red from the furnaces, like mine, but her skin is more sensitive, so she broke out. She's young.

Doesn't speak English very well, but her accent is beautiful. She's a Slovak. When she sees me she gets as red as a tomato."

"You could teach her English."

"I could," said Sussingham. "I could teach her a lot more than that, and I think she'd be a willing student. I think that in a short while she'd be teaching me, that's what I think."

"I'm serious," Harry said.

"So am I. That's a girl that loves. You can tell from the blush. Bad people don't blush. When a woman does, you know she's pure inside, she has a conscience, and she can love."

"I saw the same thing in that girl's smile and in her eyes," Harry said. "I may be crazy, but when I saw her in the apartment, I thought you should marry her."

"If I can get past her father. Then I'll learn to fly, and we'll move to Alaska."

"I apologize," Harry told him, thinking he had overstepped.

"No. Really. I mean, what the hell, I'm up for anything. You got me at just the right moment. If you asked me, I'd jump off the edge of the earth, if it had one."

"Didn't we just do that?"

"Yeah," said Sussingham. "We did."

# 42

## A PASSION OF KINDNESS

ALMOST A YEAR of steadfast work had given to Catherine's voice and her stage presence a depth exceeding even that which came naturally. But as rumors could not be withdrawn and reviews were set and printed, she had to prove herself performance by performance. There was no coasting, the way some actors did, allowing reputation to outshine defects. As much as this took from her, it gave more, for as her voice filled the theater she herself was filled, from what source she did not know, but it had never failed. When the song flowed through her in notes of incandescent beauty she experienced the physical sensation of riding a stream. And although grateful for the applause, she never could understand why she was applauded. Sometimes, to the storm of sound when it was directed toward her, she would silently mouth the words "It's not me, it's not me," and although they couldn't hear her, the onlookers saw in her expression a modesty that could not be feigned, and then they would make the theater sound like a box holding a hurricane. She discounted the praise, because that was the way she was, it would not carry beyond the moment, and it was anything but the general impression of the world. At each performance she made the same extraordinary transit, and by August, with a full heart and the gravitas and power of a woman much more than her age, she was ready for a vacation.

Having already been to East Hampton a few times that summer, she went with Harry to California to recruit Rice. Recruiting Rice would be either successful or unsuccessful in only a day or two, or perhaps just half an hour, and then they would have the rest of the time together.

Harry had never been to California. She would show it to him, having been there as a girl at an ideal age and in an ideal season, discovering a Garden of Eden in Pasadena, where from her parents' capacious suite she could see the great expanse of a green valley splashed with the reds and saffrons of hibiscus and date palms and backed by a steep mountain range laden with shining snow. The light alone was a barrier to the sorrows of the Old World.

In sun unfiltered and uninterrupted by cloud, they stood on the bone-white tarmac at Idlewild in a breeze coming off the sea. Harry was in a blazer. Catherine was gorgeous and overdressed. To left and right were two identical planes of polished aluminum buffed by sand and hail into a semi-golden sheen that embraced the fuselages and rested lightly upon the wings. The landing gear was so leggy it elevated the planes high off the ground, and their streamlining was such that both aircraft seemed like starved swans. Harry noted that the engines were oversized and the aerodynamics better suited to a fighter than a transport.

The people boarding the aircraft to the left were headed to Cuba, and some already had straw hats. Those on the right were flying to San Francisco. Stewardesses in navy blue, their hair up under jaunty caps with white piping, guided the passengers on the steps and into the planes. As ocean wind swept through the reeds at the edge of the field, Catherine asked Harry if he missed his parachute and rifle, and he said no, though it would forever be unnatural to board a plane without both. Blinded by the dazzling airliners even though both Catherine and Harry were in sunglasses, their hair lifting in the wind, they filed slowly toward the stairs and then up them. Briefly turning at the cabin door, they saw over Brooklyn and the marshes the great towers of Manhattan as waves of morning light broke against their iridescent stone and glass.

. . .

During the war, because it was for many couples the last place they would know together before the men went to fight in the Pacific, the Mark Hopkins had, and would keep for years thereafter, a special significance that made it more than just a high tower on a steep hill. In the somewhat indelicate idiom of the bellboys, there was a whole lot of fucking going on, nineteen storeys of it, day in and day out, as if the hotel were a station on a conveyor belt that led to the troopships and fighting vessels parading from the bay into the banks of North Pacific fog, and then into a world of azure seas, and green hills riddled with Japanese machine-gun emplacements. The bellboys, being boys, misunderstood, for the tower they served was like a cathedral, and its sacrament, which they called fucking, was the deepest and at times the last expression of love between a man who might not come back and a woman charged with the especially difficult task of waiting for him.

How many times had her whitened body, resting upon turned-back sheets a thousand feet above the ethereal blue of the bay, been offered to husband or lover perhaps to leave behind the last of his life in her charge? Where ordinarily desk clerks would enforce the code of marriage, here, during the war, they did not, lest they deprive a man of his continuation or a woman of her love. And these nineteen storeys were indeed more church-like than the cathedral up the street, magnificent as it was. Here they parted, and here they conjoined, in an altar of the Pacific war, leaving without a living father many a child who did not know his elegant and vertiginous origins.

And here Harry and Catherine made love as if he, too, were departing for the Pacific. It was not simply having sex in a hotel, and they understood this. The way they held tight as if in a struggle, the way they looked into one another's eyes, and the sadness they felt were almost as if they were spending their last hours together. And yet, as had others, lying together exhausted and totally united they felt that a knot had been tied forever and that everything that had unraveled had been knit back up.

As it got dark, Catherine led Harry upstairs to dinner. They watched the lights coming up and the bay darkening to indigo, and looked calmly over the world with no fear of leaving it, having, although they did not know it, fulfilled the task for which they had been born.

It took an hour to go from San Francisco — where the ocean was a frigid blue and the light was cool — to the Sacramento Valley, where, to the left and right of kiln-fired yellow prairie, dry mountains stood in long golden lines. The wind was hot, and carried the smoke of burnt fields and the scent of things growing. If the coast belonged to the Pacific Northwest, the valley clung stubbornly to Mexico — in its shimmering dryness, the supremacy of the sun, and its emptiness of nearly everything but agriculture, light, color, and heat.

Although finding their bearings in the great north-south valley was not complicated, the roads were poorly marked, and in a rented convertible as big as a boat, the top down, they found themselves raising dust on dirt tracks that ran between fields stretching endlessly in every direction. To be lost in such intense sun-beaten color was a pleasure, and if they took an extra day to get up to Redding it hardly mattered, for they had no precise appointment. Still, after an hour or two of elated cruising with their radio supplying Mexican music that could not have been better suited to the terrain, they saw an ancient truck parked in a field ahead, where a man was stacking long irrigation pipes.

"Let's ask," Catherine said. Harry reluctantly threw the wheel over to the left as the car followed into a fallow field and crossed it like a tank. As they approached, the man loading pipe stopped and stood straight. A bracero the color of tanned leather, he had a broad mustache and kind yet cautious eyes. When the car came up even with the truck, Harry took it out of gear and, while still seated, greeted him with a little bow. "Can you tell me where the road is that will take us to the road to Redding?" Harry asked.

For a second the bracero stared at him, then widened his eyes and spread his hands casually and asymmetrically to the sky, to say that he didn't speak English. That was all right, because Catherine spoke Spanish of a sort. Pulling herself out of her seat, she turned and knelt, so that now she looked over Harry's head. The chrome fitting she grasped to hold herself steady was pleasantly hot. "Where is the road to Redding?" she asked in Spanish that, though it may not have been correct, carried the inimitable loveliness of her voice.

"Oh, the road to Redding," the bracero said. And then, in the hot wind, he began a five-minute dissertation. Each time he mentioned a junction where they had to make a turn, Catherine counted on her fingers. At the end, she had gone through both hands and started over again, logging fourteen turns. "There are fourteen turns," she said in Spanish. "It's impossible."

"I know," the man said.

"Are the crossroads marked?"

He thought this was funny.

"How do you get out of here?"

"Me, I don't," he said. "I live here." He smiled at their predicament. "It's pretty."

"Yes, it is," Catherine told him. She looked west toward the line of mountains and shaded her eyes with her left hand, her right resting on the top of the seat back.

"Ask him if there's a town near here where we can stay," Harry said.

She did, and, still kneeling, reported back. "He says about ten miles that way — her right arm swung like a compass needle, clearing the top of the windshield — there's a town with a hotel and a restaurant. He says that everybody goes there because they can get vanilla ice cream in a big glass of root beer. How does that sound?"

"It sounds like a root-beer float."

"I can see that," Catherine added.

They thanked him and drove off toward the root-beer float, Catherine still kneeling on the seat, facing backward and waving like a little girl.

They didn't need to know the name of the town, and didn't ask. And because everyone there knew it, it wasn't written anywhere. "It's like New York," Harry said to Catherine as he watched her in the shower in the best room — it was clean — in the hotel.

"It is?"

"Because in New York there aren't signs everywhere that say 'New York.' I've seen a sign at the northern extremity of the Bronx that says 'City Limits,' but it doesn't say which city. My guess is that it's there to keep out the savages of Yonkers."

"Are you staring at me?" Catherine asked as shampoo foam ran down her body in streams of hot water.

"I am."

"Do you enjoy it?"

"Do I enjoy it? Oh!"

"Even after all this time?"

"I could watch you for a thousand years, naked or clothed. Each is better than the other."

"I have to confess," she said, "that I enjoy it when you do . . . tremendously."

Two hours later, having used up a great deal of hot water, they were sitting in a booth in the only restaurant in town, not surprisingly the Café Mexicana, where because it was so near closing time they had only one option: steak Mexicana, salad Mexicana, tortillas, beer, and root-beer floats. Their steaks were actually fajitas hot in temperature and otherwise. The salad, with hot sauce and chili, was such as they had never had, and they got the hang of buttered tortillas after the proprietor explained how to handle them.

"I've been to Mexican restaurants in New York," Catherine said, "but they're so fancy that everything was unrecognizable. This, however. . . . If you brought it to the East it would really take off."

"After French rules for a while," Harry offered. "All the soldiers coming back from France. It happened in the twenties as well."

"Why didn't it last?"

"The Depression."

"You know," Catherine said, "I like this restaurant better than any I've ever been to in New York. In New York, you go into a restaurant and everyone looks at you. Not here."

"That's because there's no one here but us," Harry informed her. "And look over there."

She turned to see. The proprietors were staring at her as if hypnotized. "They want to go home, that's all. But in New York, it's like entering a contest. The other diners stare at you."

"They stare at *you*."

"Not just me. Everyone's measure is taken. Even the waiters are engaged in a great, never-ending Olympics of station. I think that's because, although they lose all the time, they can win if they spot a phony, of which there are many." She looked around. "But not here." She glanced again at the very dignified middle-aged man and his wife, both of whom seemed happy, but eager to close up. "*They're* not in combat with us."

"I may be out of my mind," Harry said, "but I've been thinking about maybe living here. Pulling the plug in New York and coming here. I can't run away, or can I? I could live with dishonor, guilt. I could stand knowing that I'd run away and let evil run its course. All I need is you."

As Catherine put down her fork, it clanged on the plate. "I've been thinking that, too," she said.

"Catherine, I had a vision while we were driving. We lived in a white cottage on the slope of the mountains, overlooking a sea of golden fields. I don't know whether they were ours or not; it doesn't matter. It was quiet, private, sunny. It was as if there were no people in the world, or it was not even in the world. You were in the garden, planting flowers. You wore a white blouse that was open quite far down, and you were a sort of light olive and tan color but with so much red underlying it and showing through because of the heat, though now and then there was a cool breeze. Sometimes you wiped the sweat from your brow with your forearm and you blinked. And there was a rhythm to your work. Your hands shaped the loam in a floating kind of way, quickly, sometimes thrusting down into the dark earth but then gently healing the wound, as if your hands themselves knew exactly what to do to cultivate and plant."

"We can do that," she said, "if we want."

"No. It's just a dream. It wouldn't work."

Catherine was young enough to say, "Why not?"

• • •

## A Passion of Kindness  593

They stayed in the town, but because their rest had refreshed them they got in the car and drove as if they hadn't driven all day. They might have driven all night, had they not suspected that at four in the morning their clarity and energy might desert them. So rather than pushing north they followed long, straight farm roads into the darkened valley, navigating by the stars, with no place in particular to go. They had done this before, coming in from East Hampton.

In the midst of the many paths that lay across the land and beneath the gliding stars was one that branched off in a curve. For a time it followed a huge irrigation channel. The water rushing headlong in the dark was so loud they could hear it over their engine. Then the road abruptly changed direction and climbed a projection in the valley floor, as out of place as a volcano and a hundred or more feet high, at the summit of which the road came to an end with hardly any room to turn around. They stopped here, facing south, stunned by the pellucid night.

Lined with blue at its western edge, the sky was heavy with stars that, sparkling gently, showed a barely perceptible hint of yellow. An uninterrupted horizon was visible in the direction they were facing, they were high up, and many stars seemed to be below them, others straight on. More like gentle lamps than stars, their blinking was not cold and quick like the disinterested stars of winter, but slow and seductive, as if they were speaking in a code that all mankind understood, even if it did not know that such a language existed, much less that it was following its benevolent commands. And along with the stars came the inexplicable illusion that the warm wind was visible in a procession across the valley floor. While Harry and Catherine were suspended among these stars, for three hundred and sixty degrees the world was as calm as if it had never known anything but peace and perfection.

"I didn't know the world could be like this," Catherine said. "I've never seen the sky in such a passion of kindness."

The next day, the sun was dependably hot, the air reliably clear. Just as after two days at sea, out of sight of land, you become a sailor as the boat moves ahead, rising and falling on the waves, as they sped north they were separated from almost everything they had left behind. In the valley it was as hot as molten silver, dust devils arose and played in the fields, and the golden summits of the mountains were lost in glare.

"We'll make Redding by evening if we don't get sidetracked," Harry said. Catherine was content just to be driving through the summer air. After a silence of ten minutes or so, Harry said, "I've been thinking about your father and your mother."

"You have?"

"I have. You're their only daughter, their only child, and they've entrusted you to yourself and to me. I was my parents' only child as well. Everyone in my family is dead except my aunt by marriage, who's older and not a blood relation. I never knew our relatives in Europe, and they're all almost undoubtedly gone—if not murdered, then broken and scattered only God knows where.

"The two of us are kind of a slender reed. If the car blows a tire and flips, two families come to a sudden end. I've never quite understood how brave and disciplined your parents are and mine were. I've never quite felt the way they must feel when they look after us as we go out into the world. Maybe I should drive more slowly."

Catherine said, "No. You're not driving too fast. Just drive well. There's no guarantee, no safety. That's what—between us and them, and between us—clarifies love. That's what the songs that they pay me to sing are about, and I want nothing but that. Of course, I've already got it."

As she put her hand out into the wind, her arm was lifted by an insistent and invisible force. By rolling her hand slightly left, it was forced down until she rolled it back to the right and it was lifted as smoothly as a sea bird. The afternoon passed in confident silence, and then Redding appeared in the foothills. The plain of the valley had subtly vanished, and although here just as dry, it was rolling. They had no idea how they were going to find Rice, but the town was not that big.

By the time they checked into a hotel, settled, showered, and dressed, it was almost dark. They stepped out on the sidewalk unsure whether they were going to find someplace to eat or look for Rice. There weren't many streets and they didn't know where to go, but when they heard the sound of distant music coming over the air they walked in its direction, and as they crested the top of a hill what appeared to them a quarter of a mile in the distance was a lighted dance floor, about fifty feet square, beneath strings of colored lights.

Musicians were arrayed on steps at the platform's north end. The music was strong, and on the boards were scores of dancing couples moving gracefully beneath Japanese lanterns waving in the wind. As they do at such times, children chased around the perimeter. Adults who were not dancing were engaged in conversation at the edges. Sometimes the wind took the music, but then brought it back with a slight slur. The mountain wall in the distance was black at the base and purple at the top beneath a rim of vanishing royal blue.

As they approached, now in the spell of the music, Harry said, "I see him."

"How can you tell at such a remove?" Catherine asked. "You can't see anyone's face."

"I can tell by the way he moves. I've never seen him dance, but I've seen him walk a hundred miles. He doesn't know we're coming. Let's go up there. We'll dance, and see how long it takes for him to recognize us."

Partly because of their clothing, which hadn't been bought at the two or three stores that supplied the town, they stood out as they danced. Some men wore their war uniforms, some were almost formally dressed, some danced with their hats on, others not. The women's attire was more varied, although none of it matched the elegance of Catherine's simple white dress, with pearl buttons in a line down the front, a sheath cut that her figure could bear easily, and the partially built-up shoulders of the period, which if not done well looked stiff and off-putting but if skillfully done gave the impression of an upper body as wide and noble as that of a goddess. Harry had no hat, much less a cowboy hat, and was one of the few men without a string tie. Though obviously they were strangers, they were cordially welcomed.

He wanted to avoid Rice for as long as possible so that Rice would see them in the corner of his eye and become accustomed to them, and the surprise would be that they had been there all along. Catherine didn't know this was what Harry was trying to do, but was happy just to dance beneath the strings of colored lights, the brighter stars, and the Milky Way, which despite the lights was visible in the desert-clear sky.

As they danced they saw one another's faces, constant, steady, and close, as the background passed by in a blur. Pulling apart and coming together; held gently; hands clasped and positioned almost aloft and leading through the air; with no need to speak and yet every word that was spoken elevated and made lovely. Nothing was quite so promising, beautiful, and exciting as dancing with Catherine in the mild air and open sky of California just after the war, when the valley was forgotten and at peace. They would think of other things, and then they would come back to where they were. The pleasure of re-entering was more exquisite than the pleasure of the dance itself, and, like the caesura in Catherine's song, it was the silence that perfected the sound.

The lights made Catherine think back to a time before the Crash, when none of her father's friends whose ruin she had seen and grown up with had yet to be destroyed, when the bank had yet to face its own difficulties, and when she was only four or five years old and her house was her world. In the library, facing the East River, was a cherrywood table upon which were two sterling trays. On one was a crystal ice bucket and crystal tumblers. On the other were eight or nine bottles of liquor: a frosted-glass bottle of vodka, a green gin bottle with a red sealing wax medallion, a brown bottle of sherry with a reproduction of El Greco's *View of Toledo* on the label, and bottles of Scotch, some with colorful caps in red and gold, others with more prosaic tops to fit their printed labels in black and white. Between the trays on the polished and glowing wood was a Wedgwood vase — in muted blue and white — in which on most days was a splay of red roses. The rest of the room matched this with the elegance of its rugs, furniture, and paintings, and views of the garden and river through French doors.

In those times, when her father was much younger and things were flush, without anyone's knowledge Catherine would go to the library after breakfast, because there at all times of the year, although at different hours and from different angles, the sun climbing across the eastern sky would illuminate the concentrated colors in such a way that the child greeted them every morning she could, as if they were not mere effects of the spectrum but a living being, or a message of some sort, both of which spoke to her fluently, although she could not have translated.

The rich early morning light struck the roses and was refracted in a billion tiny gleams. The silver followed suit with the same microscopic glinting. And the reds, greens, and browns of wood, glass, and wax took fire, deepened, and glowed in caramel, emerald, and scarlet. In the very early morning when the sun was trapped by the stubby buildings across the river in Long Island City, it sent out weak rays to scout the gaps between the tenements, and these rays would leap the river and hit the bottles, their dim light making the room glow in preternatural brown, bringing up the colors so gently that they showed even finer than the blazes of color that would follow. Catherine watched this closely and was open to it as only a child can be. It wasn't that it was speaking to her in particular, but that it was speaking of things that, though supposedly far beyond her understanding, she comprehended nonetheless. Some children have friends, and some who have no friends have imaginary friends. Catherine had neither. She had the light.

Once, her father, passing by, saw his daughter motionless as if hypnotized by the liquor and crystal. "What are you staring at, Catherine?" he asked after a few minutes. She motioned at the blaze of color. "I hope you don't plan to drink it," he said. She wrinkled her nose. "That's a 'no,' right?" She found this amusing, because she had smelled the stuff in the bottles and found it truly horrible. Somewhat reassured, Billy left for work in a city delirious with prosperity. Completely unknowing of the difference between riches and poverty, Catherine remained in the library, patiently observing.

Decades later, she was dancing beneath strings of lights that hung in the air like planets. She was embracing and embraced by her husband. She was loving and content, and yet aware that with the movement of time everything was slowly overturning. On how many platforms in mountain ranges overlooking summer plains or the sea in crescent bays or coasts from Maine to Catalina had heaven come down to bless a couple gliding across the floor beneath a string of colored lights? "Am I chasing you? Do I have you?" he asked as they moved together.

"You're chasing me," she answered, "and you have me."

Rice was older than Harry, a lawyer, a superb soldier, but because he preferred not to be an officer, Harry had outranked him. His parents had died when he was young. His first wife had died, childless, in the thirties. Of all of Harry's pathfinders, Rice knew the most and said the least. He was always good-humored, often taking the lead to spare others danger, and his life before the war had led him to believe that he was not going to come home. Shocked and surprised that he did, he left behind everything he knew except his profession, which he carried out to California when he settled in the great country north of the Sacramento Valley.

He was dancing with a woman almost as tall as he was, and he stood at six-three. Her bearing and dress suggested that she had been born on a ranch, and that she might have been the daughter of the man who owned a great deal of the valley, and the granddaughter of the man who founded the town, and she was, in fact, all of these things. Slightly wavy blond hair fell to her shoulders. Her eyes were blue, and, like Catherine's, her face was enchanting for its beauty and character. Merely from occasional glances, Harry and Catherine were impressed by and attracted to this couple that they carefully avoided. Many of the other dancers, though they may have enjoyed what they were doing, were burdened with an ineluctable stiffness that was less physical than emotional, and some with obviously long histories danced not only as if they hardly knew one another but as if they did not want to. In such circumstances, an alert divorce lawyer could make a fortune.

After an hour that went quickly, Harry said, "Let's intercept."

"You're not a fighter plane, Harry," Catherine scolded, but she agreed.

They moved toward Rice, staying close for a few seconds rather than allowing the distance that etiquette demanded, and then, still undiscovered, bumped him. He turned with an irritated look, but immediately recognized Harry. "Who's *that?*" he said, referring to Catherine, recognizing the force of her beauty.

"My wife, Catherine," Harry answered. "Who's *that?*" he went on, returning the compliment.

Almost speechless, Rice said, "*My* wife, *Catherine.*"

The four of them had stopped in the middle of the floor, and everyone had to find ways around them.

Because the moon had risen just before they left, they could see their way in the dark. Ordinarily, in that they weren't yet acquainted and were walking two by two, conversation would have been strained as everyone tried not to miss anything and to project so that all could hear. But the two Catherines, immediately comfortable with one another, silently came to the conclusion that they did not have to say anything until they reached home. Because they didn't have to alter pace or posture to hear, they made good time through the few streets and a little way into the hills, to a large stone house that Rice explained had belonged to Catherine's grandparents and was built of granite quarried in the Sierra Nevada. This broke open a line of conversation that was continued in the kitchen, where Catherine Rice, without tension or missing a word, began to prepare a light dinner.

Her parents still lived on their ranch. "Which is where?" Harry asked.

"Almost everything you see," Rice said. "They were farsighted enough to buy land surrounding the town on all sides. Whichever way the town expands, as it will, the land will provide for their descendants."

Soon after she had started her preparations, Catherine Rice excused herself, saying, "Hulda just beckoned to me." As soon as her name was mentioned, Hulda disappeared. "She's shy," Catherine Rice said. "I think the baby's up. I'll go see."

"Ten months," Rice said.

In a few moments, Catherine Rice reappeared with the infant in her arms. He turned his head to his father, and then, upon seeing Harry and Catherine, buried his face against his mother's right shoulder. With a little patting and a few kisses, he was reassured, and studied the new people. Harry looked at Catherine to see if this would be the next step, and to say that he wanted to take it. He expected perhaps a nod or a smile in return, but received far more when he saw that her eyes were brimming with tears that she would not let fall.

Catherine Rice moved forward decisively and placed the child in Catherine Copeland's arms. No one saw, but a tear dropped on the baby's gown. Catherine took in a breath through her nose, laughed a little, and smiled. As she began to talk to the baby, the baby took to her. "What's his name?" she asked.

"Gordon," Catherine Rice answered. "After Jim's father. Kind of a strange name for a baby, don't you think? Sometimes when I talk to him and call him by his name it's as if I'm talking to a lawyer."

"He's half lawyer," Rice said, "and half nurse." He gestured to his wife.

"I was a nurse," Catherine Rice said, "during the war."

"And Catherine," Rice said to Catherine Copeland, "you're so young... I hesitate to ask."

"I'm a stage actress," Catherine replied rather painfully, remembering every bad review and every review that should have been better, and every review that might have been written and was not.

Rice could see her shame, and didn't know what to say, but Harry immediately filled in. "She has a good part, a strong part, in which she sings beautifully. The play's been running for almost a year, with no end in sight."

"Where?" said Rice, hoping that it would not be someplace like Trenton but assuming that it would. "I don't even know where you live."

"It's a Broadway play," Harry told him. "We live in New York."

Relieved, Rice said, admiringly, "That's really something." The conversation continued, until Catherine Rice served the dinner, and, conquering her shyness, at the sound of plates being set upon a marble table in the center of the kitchen Hulda appeared and took Gordon, now fast asleep, from Catherine Copeland's arms. It was hard for Catherine to let go.

"This was a baking surface," Rice said. "You spread flour on it and it's possible to roll dough without it sticking. They did a lot of baking then. We still do, if not as much, and we eat most of our meals right at this table. I put that light in." He pointed to a translucent cone of green glass, lined with nacreous white, from which came the light of a shielded bulb. It hung over the table and lit the marble without glare.

Catherine Rice served a dinner that although it was centered around slices of the steak ubiquitous in the ranchlands, was otherwise Southeast Asian, with dipping sauces, rice, and some things that neither Harry nor Catherine could identify. The hostess explained. "I was in the South Pacific," she said. "Most of the time we set up in villages at some remove from the battles, where we had the local foods as well as our own." This was familiar to Harry. "When we had them, theirs were fresher, and we learned not only how to cook the way they did, but how to treat what we were issued as they would. So what you have here is a mixture."

"Not Chinese," Rice added, "although people think it is."

"How long were you there?" Catherine asked.

"Late 'forty-two through May of 'forty-five, the whole time: it was too far away to come home. We started in Australia and went almost to Japan, and never knew whether we had a lot of rest punctuated by war or a lot of war punctuated by rest. I was quite young when I went in, and not young at all when I got out." She said this with an air of deep, earned authority, and ruefully. As if to set a seal on this, as Catherine Copeland moved her hands her woven bracelet with the jeweled signets clinked and reflected the light that Rice had hung above the table.

The war had not really touched Catherine. She had been young and safely far from combat. Hardly unaware of the loss, she had not, however, been damaged by it, and here she was the only one of the four who had not been on a front. "What kind of work did you do?" she asked the other Catherine, hoping that the answer would be that it had been something auxiliary and removed from the fighting, not too much unlike what Bryn Mawr girls did when they rolled bandages.

"Recovery," Catherine Rice answered. "After surgery, they were sent to us. Although there had to be triage, we were generous with surgery even for those for whom surgery was just a gesture. Because there were supply ships right offshore and we were never far from the coast, we could afford to be less frugal than the field hospitals in Europe, and for the most part we were. When the surgeons tried to save those who could not be saved, we had to struggle to keep them alive, though we knew they were not going to live.

"The surgeries were often very fast, and then it was up to us — doctors of course, but mainly the nurses — to see them through. And so many of them didn't come through. This lasted, periodically, for more than three years. There was so much death the hospitals were churches. I feel very bad because I can hardly remember their faces, and there were thousands, and each one. . . ." Here she stopped, overcome, but she recovered.

"Each one . . . was a soul. Each one had been a child. Each one was loved. Perhaps coarsely, perhaps not well, but loved. And they died out there, without their mothers, their fathers, their wives and children. Not a single one wanted to go. Everything was regret, I saw so much regret. If only they had been near their families: they missed them so much. Especially for those who died on the battlefield, something was opened that can never be closed.

"Every time a soldier died, we were taken, for a moment that seemed never to end, on the very same wave. In Australia, before it all started, I used to swim in the surf. Sometimes it was so powerful, the waves so fierce, that you couldn't move your arms or legs to try to guide yourself. That's what it was like at each death. Defeat. You cry, you hang your head, your heart breaks, you see what we are, and it shows you that the only thing we have, though we may imagine otherwise, is love."

Though stunned and moved, Catherine, the daughter of many generations of brave men and women, maintained her composure, as did Catherine Rice. "Did they fall in love with you?" Catherine asked. "You're a beautiful woman."

"They were going to die. They were apart from their families. And I was the woman who was there. Because of childbearing, a woman is more than half of life. Their strongest impulse was not to survive, but to love, so that even as they died they might live. They would come to us by scores and hundreds, and when they became conscious and in not too terrible pain, they would fall in love so strongly and purely, each and every one of them. And then they just vanish. They're gone. They don't appear again, or write letters from beyond. Silence. And then forgetting."

"Perhaps I shouldn't ask this," Catherine said. "Forgive me. But did you fall in love with them?"

"I did," Catherine Rice said weakly, and bowed her head.

"You helped them," Catherine asserted. "You did help them."

"Yes, I did." She lifted her eyes to the others. "On Guadalcanal the Pacific is turquoise and blue, and the tents of the field hospitals were dark green, with red the only occasional contrasting color. It was way too heavy, a lousy way to die. There was a boy, a marine, and he was just about to go. I could see that he was oppressed by the heaviness of the canvas, and the red was no good — the red crosses that were on a lot of things. So I said, Would you like to see the Pacific, the blue? And he moved his head to say yes.

"I rolled up the sides of the tent and turned his bed around. You could see the sea straight out, empty except for warships riding at anchor, which looked very small. Beyond the surf, heat waves welded the sea to the sky in a kind of border. He stared at it. It was where he was going, and he felt no fear, as if he had said to himself, That's where I'm going, it's beautiful there, and there's nothing to be afraid of. It was so much better than some shitty olive-drab canvas that in the shadows inside is so green it's almost black. I opened the flaps and turned the beds whenever I could. We all did. The blue comforted them. They went with less suffering, less fear, when the sea took them. That's what I did. That's all I did."

Catherine then embraced Catherine Rice, resting her left elbow on the smooth white marble, as Catherine Rice did the same with her right. "Now I have a baby," said Catherine Rice, "a husband and a baby." She took a sharp, involuntary breath in.

Harry had already had a bond with Rice that could never be broken, but now they were all united in a way that time and distance could not defeat. After a long evening easily talking about everything, Rice insisted upon driving them back to their hotel, until they stepped out of the house, and the moon was so huge and close, the air so perfect, that he said driving them would be a sin. After they parted, Catherine and Harry walked down the road toward the lights of the town.

"We could move here," Catherine said. "They're wonderful people. They would be our friends. We'd have them; we could buy a ranch; San Francisco isn't that far: for pearls, books, and ocean liners to Japan. After a war you have the right to start fresh. You can leave everything behind and make a new life." She paused. "You didn't ask Rice, did you?"

The two men had been alone for a while, looking over maps of the valley that Rice was someday to own with his wife.

"No. Married, with a newborn?"

"*We're* married."

"Catherine, the time for something like this comes, and this is mine."

"It was yours during the war," Catherine argued, thinking about the baby she had cradled. Now she could almost feel his weight, and the sad lightening of her arms when she had given him up.

"I know."

He stopped and pulled her close. They always came together easily. With building affection he felt her hair and breathed the sweet air that rose from her body. "Look at that," he said, meaning the town resting on the silvery ridge, its strings of lights still glowing.

The wind was soft, and they were happy and unafraid. Then the strings of colored lights over the dance floor were switched off. The moonlight brightened, the town receded, and in the quiet on the silvered black road, Catherine said, "Just like the theater, except that in the theater there was never so much art."

# 43

## THE LETTER

JOHNSON WAS THE first to arrive, on Tuesday, the twenty-first of October. Compared to Wisconsin, New York was like Miami, and when he stepped off the Twentieth Century Limited at Grand Central he had to remove his coat because the air on the platform was so humid and hot. By the time he got to the cavernous great hall, he was sweating as he hadn't since summer. Crossing the marble floor at speeds so high it seemed as if they were being chased were the first New Yorkers he had seen in their native habitat. They put their feet down like campers stamping out a fire, launched themselves forward like divers off low boards, and seemed not to see anything, by reason of having seen it before. It was as if they possessed such a dense registry of memories that they could fly through reality on instruments, thinking their thoughts, solving their puzzles, and doing their sums while seeking Lexington Avenue on autopilot.

He stood in the middle of the floor, slightly east of the information booth, astounded by a room so big it had its own constellations. The sky is not green. How did they know that virtually no one would say, "Why is the sky green? Because it isn't." He could hardly believe the speed at which everything moved. The lines at the ticket windows advanced and spit out ticket holders the way Coca-Cola plants put the caps on bottles. The stairs from Vanderbilt Avenue were like a waterfall down which people cascaded long before rush hour. In Chicago's Union Station, the biggest he had previously seen, early afternoon was a mausoleum. But in Grand Central it was as if someone had set off a thousand rockets and they were bouncing crazily against the walls.

As he had on the train to track things of interest as they flew past, he fastened now on a woman who was almost leaping over the people ahead of her on the stairs. He stuck with her so tightly that the rest of everything became a blur. You could not say she was pretty, but she had a strong face, with a thrust-out nose that matched her thrust-out breasts, except that her nose was not restrained by a brassiere and the top of a dress striped like a candy cane in white and off-white. A belt around her waist was as thick as a cummerbund and at the back it was a bow. Her hair was chestnut, swept from her face, shoulder length. She wore wire glasses, her heels clicked on the travertine like a machine-gun belt ejecting links, and her crazed forward motion, like someone running after an escaped rabbit, was stabilized royally by a disc-like, aerodynamic, white hat three times the size of a pie plate.

She seemed to be coming right for him, as if she knew him, as if she loved him, as if she were about to attack him. Because he knew her in part already, having concentrated upon her, he thought that maybe she did know him, and that she would suddenly stop and say, "Where were you?" or "I love you" or "What's playing at the Roxy, and if we don't get there in time for the afternoon show we'll miss Velez and Yolanda, the world's most exquisite dancers." Or perhaps she would say, "This is my time, and I'm bearing down hard upon it, which is why I walk so fast and why you should, too. Come out with me, walk down the avenues, look across the river at the steam clouds rising for a mile and looming like mountains. Take off my hat, stare at me, touch me, kiss me."

But she said nothing. She didn't even see him, or if she did she gave no sign, and she blew past, a foot away—her guidons of striped taffeta flapping—like the mail train in Wisconsin. Said train does not stop, but pushes on to Chicago, dropping off and picking up with its deadly hook the wasp-waisted sacks of mail with letters that could come from Mozambique, its stamps green, coffee-colored, and red, the tropics made miniature to tempt the souls of snow-covered stamp collectors. She was gone in a puff, but when she was gone it was indeed as if she had kissed him. And that, he discovered, was New York.

. . .

Already changed and left standing like a rube, he then humiliated himself by asking where his hotel was. It might have been less humiliating had he not asked at the information booth, which sat in the center of the marble sea, encased in brass, beneath a giant turnip that thought it was a clock. At the information booth, questions were suffered indignantly. "Excuse me," he said, his first mistake. "Can you tell me how to get to the Waldorf-Astoria?" What he should have said was, "Ha-doo'wai geh tu d'Wawldawf?" Because he didn't say it that way, the man in charge of the western front thought that he was being mocked, despite the fact that Johnson was carrying a suitcase. Sometimes college boys, and Johnson looked young for his age, went to elaborate lengths to torment the prisoners of the information booth, asking, for example, "How many balls are there in New York?"

"Track seventeen, leaving two-oh-seven."

"The Waldorf-Astoria Hotel?"

"Step aside, there are real people out there."

"I'm real," Johnson said.

"In your dreams, big ass."

Dumbfounded, Johnson eventually asked a policeman, who was, if abrupt, not impolite. Then he emerged somehow onto Park Avenue — another name for the rocket-launching rails to Westchester and beyond, ornamented on either side by people who rode horses and tried to send their sons to Princeton. The policeman said the hotel would be on the right, five blocks north, look for the flags. Johnson did, and it was. Another deal like the Drake: all paid for; peacocks, jewels, and gold; a piano being played elegantly in the bar; an elevator that popped his ears; a room that looked out upon the smoothest, most relaxed view he had ever seen, a city stretching languidly to infinity, dotted with parks, lakes, and trees that even at the end of their autumnal haze were explosively yellow and rusty scarlet (who was playing the piano at the bar).

Apparently the maid had left the radio on. Johnson walked into his room at exactly three-thirty and regretfully parted with fifty cents for the bellboy. As he stood mesmerized by the roiling city made lovely by distance and altitude, he heard, "Welcome to *What's on Your Mind?*,

WQXR's forum, with Iphigene Bettman. Today's guests, Dr. Mary Fisher Langmuir, Mark McCloskey (headmaster of the Scarborough School), Ethel Alpenfels, and Benjamin Fine, will discuss 'Are we creating a nation of adolescents?'"

After what he had been through in the war, and looking upon this airy view of a great city, Johnson found this amusing, but he did not rule out the effect for the future and listened dutifully until four, not so much as taking off his jacket, because the riveting north light and the very scale of things held him in place.

Sussingham had been to New York three or four times as a child, bundled up like baggage as things passed by, his head bent in looking at a comic book or a game. Now he came as an adult. On the twenty-second of October, after a detour in Pennsylvania to see an uncle, he got off a commuter train on the Jersey side and took a ferry across the Hudson. It was almost as warm as summer, as if New York were in another world.

The ferry nosed out of its berth and made an arc slightly upriver before turning straight for the Manhattan shore. Sussingham stood at the bow, clasping the shaving-mirror gate, his lungs filled with the balmy air over the water and his eyes knocked back by the spectacle of the city rising before him like a steel mill shrouded in smoke and steam, backlit in white and gold by the morning sun. Its towers stretched in a line as far as he could see upriver to the north and to the edge of the harbor to the south. The palette of blacks and grays was irrationally varied. Some of the buildings were dark and inexplicably in shadow while others behind them were light gray in the mist, and still others behind these black and dark again. Sunlight and shadow in almost infinite alternation made for a depth never-ending, from which things were produced as if by the fires of the earth to issue forth from stacks and chimneys and pipes, while kicking off from the docks were ferries, ships, and barges rushing to open water.

Harry had paid in cash both for Sussingham's stay at the Astor and Johnson's at the Waldorf. He left envelopes for them with money, tickets to shows and movies, and no instructions, as the understanding was that they would simply be visitors to New York, soldiers who had once promised themselves Broadway and now had come to grant their own wish. "Enjoy yourself," he had said, "and when it's time for us to meet, we will." This seemed unnecessarily mysterious, but it was a result of Vanderlyn's experience in occupied France and in Germany itself during the war, not just a habit but rather a method of operation that had been proved under the greatest stress. Harry would not contact them or bring in Bayer until Saturday, the twenty-fifth. So they had a few days in which to wander around, doing anything they wanted except leaving their names promiscuously or attracting the attention of the law.

"You mean," Johnson had asked, back in the Drake, "we can't jaywalk?"

Harry had looked at him blankly.

"Cross the street against the light?"

"That's not *illegal*," Harry said.

"It's not illegal in New York?" Johnson asked.

"I wouldn't think so. At least, I've never heard of it."

With money in their pockets, orders to relax, and the freedom to cross against the light, they hit the streets like Baptist sailors on liberty. They both knew Chicago fairly well, especially Sussingham, who although he was from Indiana went into the city at least once every few months. Both had thought Chicago the epitome of cities, but after an hour in New York they abandoned that belief, for Chicago can have all the tall buildings it wants and as many millions as it can hold: it's still a suburb. If you take a cord of wood and lay it out evenly over half an acre of field, you have, in a pretty good stand-in for Chicago, something that will neither kindle nor light. Take the same cord of wood, stack it high into a structure with broad and intricate channels for the air to race through, and you have, in an approximation of New York, something that will easily take fire, burn, flame, whistle, roar, and wake up the world.

Each had in mind things to do and sights to see. Being from somewhere else, they actually thought they could check them off one after another. These were men who were capable of marching a hundred miles in the snow and then attacking an entrenched enemy. They found, however, that when they stepped out of their hotels they were introduced to new forms of being. Every foot of travel offered resistance to the senses, an overload upon eyes, ears, and everything else. The crush of things, the speed, the way all the billion moving parts wove like fighter planes in a dogfight and yet went right to the places where they belonged, all without direction or, seemingly, broader intent, was exhausting to behold.

Johnson decided to walk the length of Fifth Avenue, only to discover that he was soon plotting a route back to his hotel the way a swimmer in a rip tide focuses on the beach. A quick study, he learned from department store windows, and from ducking into Lord & Taylor in hope of respite that he did not find, that most of the women he passed that morning in the office districts were wearing what was called a "ballerina suit." These came in two basic varieties. Although both comprised close-fitting, short jackets and full-swinging, gracefully swirling skirts, the notched-collar suit (he was overwhelmed by such detail) was rib-hugging and handsomely tailored in fine wool gabardine with notched revers and a high-waisted skirt. The round-collar suit, on the other hand, was a cutaway with a sculpted, tiny-waisted jacket accented by shiny crown buttons. Its high-waisted skirt was notched, all in worsted crêpe. He had no idea what the hell was going on, but it looked good.

He studied the suits on mannequins as he took shelter from the chaos of the street, trying to understand the meaning of the minor variations. There seemed to be a subtle class difference, or perhaps an age difference, between the two, with the older, richer, more sexually devastating women in the notched-collar suits, and the younger, more demure, recently-in-from-Smith-or-Mount-Holyoke secretaries in publishing or import/export, in the round-collar. The notched-collar went for $55.00, and the round for $49.95, which didn't speak volumes.

Back on the street, real women in the sunshine pushed against the light and wind, their hair lifted by gentle masses of air touring languidly south of the park. How these women did this he did not know, but as they sped forward like corvettes or PT boats they often appeared to have closed eyes. Was it possible that they could see without seeing, or navigate like bats, or were guided by some unseen hand? Of course, most of the time — given the great numbers of people on the street; the rounded, dashing taxis; the green-and-white double-decker buses moving slowly like loaves of bread on wheels; the trucks and carts and racks of clothes pushed by teenage boys who had just missed the war; the signs, obstructions, opening doors, flashing lights, elevators rising from basements right up through the sidewalk; and accountants walking blindly in a fog of figures — most of the time, the women on the street kept their eyes open. But when for the brief moments they trusted in the harmony of things to guide them, and turned their faces to the sun, resigning their vision to something higher, they were then achingly, movingly, almost unbearably beautiful.

On West 57th Street, having sailed up Sixth Avenue against a Victoria Falls of office workers pouring into midtown, Sussingham ran aground temporarily in front of Fraser, Morris — purveyors. He held his position on the sidewalk, staring in wonder at a placard in the window. According to Fraser, Morris, two and a half years after V-E Day each limey in England was limited by law to one egg a week, if he could get it. This was incomprehensible to a near-Chicagoan in whose proximity agricultural commodities ran like rivers in flood. But the New World was ready once again to supply the Old, by hook or by crook, as the restrictions did not apply to direct imports. For its part, Fraser, Morris, which claimed already to have dispatched four million food parcels, was willing and wanting, for only $14.95, to send six dozen freshly laid eggs by air express to Great Britain. They would arrive two days from the laying, and the Englishman who received them would be up 7,200 percent on his egg ration.

Shellacked by all this, Sussingham thought of the many egg flights, the English iceboxes full of eggs, the egg recipes, egg parties, and egg thefts. He turned to a passerby, a man who looked like Melvyn Douglas, and said, "Boy oh boy, they could take a bath in eggs." The man was unaware of the sign and thought Sussingham was just a New Yorker of a certain type that could never be eradicated.

Like Johnson and like Harry, when Sussingham made eye contact with a woman, even if she were a photograph on a billboard, something happened — to him, and to her, although not if she were just a photograph — which is why at lunch he found himself in his hotel room, exhausted, looking at a three-pound box of Loft's chocolates, because the salesgirl was an Irish beauty from Queens who spoke to him without words about what she wanted of love, and he spoke back. If he had been in New York for other, less dangerous reasons, perhaps instead of buying three pounds of chocolates for 79¢ a pound he would have married her. But he didn't, and had he wanted to find her he would have to exert himself at some future date. Among other things, he thought that she was in the only Loft's chocolate shop in New York and that all he had to do was look it up in the telephone book. He didn't remember where it was, but in only the half hour it took him to carry what he had bought safely back to his room, he knew when he passed his fourteenth Loft's shop that his luck had deserted him.

And then he suffered through a quiet struggle in regard to Miss Rheingold and the Trommer's White Label beer girl. They looked like sisters. They were everywhere, on giant billboards and posters, in magazines, newspapers, and cardboard cutouts in restaurants. Chicago had plenty of advertising, but not as much as New York, where word was more important than deed. Sussingham felt obliged to choose between Miss Rheingold 1947 and the Trommer's White Label girl — bypassing Ruppert entirely, because Sussingham didn't like the name *Ruppert*. It was hardly a serious matter, but somehow he could not dismiss it as easily as he could the exhortations to "Smoke Camels" (perhaps as opposed to hams) and to eat Planters peanuts because "a bag a day" would give him "more pep." Miss Rheingold was holding a rifle and a target with eleven shots through the bull's-eye. He counted, and wondered at what range she had shot, or if she had shot at all. She seemed sporting and Irish, and her name was Michaele Fallon: maybe she was half Italian. The Trommer girl, on the other hand, had spectacular teeth and so open a smile that in the end she won, and when each day that Sussingham had both lunch and dinner at the White Turkey on East 49th Street or the one at Madison and 37th, or the one in University Place, he always had a Trommer's White Label. Being a regular gave him a certain sense of stability that New York otherwise was quick to take away.

As Bayer labored sadly and with growing anger, "finding" supposedly lost plans at the building department, Johnson and Sussingham went separately to the Statue of Liberty, the Empire State Building, and Rockefeller Center. Johnson went to the New York Public Library and there, happily melancholy amid the glowing green shades and a consistent unintelligible murmur that sounded like a stream in a cavern, he read. Although neither of them knew, he and Catherine were at times in the same room, bathed in the same light. Sussingham, on the other hand, went to see the elephants in the zoo.

But for both of them all these things, delightful or exhausting, wondrous or taxing, were moved aside like mental scenery pushed by imaginary stagehands when they thought of why they had come to New York. Away from home and the ordinary, they had their doubts. Would they go through with it, should they, and was it right in itself and for them? Opposed to their hesitation was their habit, formed in years of war, of operating together ruthlessly and violently to accomplish with discipline an objective about which they had never, not for one second, felt the slightest passion, but only a grim determination to do what had to be done. The more time passed in loneliness, the more they were thrown back into what they had been in the war. It rose from within and took its place without shame. And as they hardened back into place, they, like everyone in Manhattan, eventually got down to business.

Thin, white-haired, rugged, his gaze piercing, Cornell was calmly fighting to the end. Though now convinced that they were going under, he kept at it without flinching, his initial anxiety having fled before the winds of certainty. He knew from a long life of privations and indignities that what mattered was not winning but how one holds to one's part. In that, he was a cousin to Catherine, who had come to it by a different route, and a father to Harry, who, not as far along as Cornell or even young Catherine, was on his way and would soon be there.

As Copeland Leather was stripped of assets and options and driven toward bankruptcy and dissolution, Harry had become more active in its management even if for naught. Early one morning, as Johnson and Sussingham slept in their hotels, Harry sat with Cornell in the office. A third of the employees had had to quit because they could not get by on the forty percent pay cut everyone was obliged to take. Harry and Cornell had long since put their own funds into the company. No bank, upon looking at the balance sheet, would lend them money. Nor should any bank have done so, because among other things any banker with experience could tell instantly that they were being bled dry by protection payments. Accountants and loan officers knew how to spot this under "miscellaneous expenses," "cash payments," and, most often, especially if large sums were involved, "fees and services."

"The buyers are in town," Cornell announced without energy. "Are you ready for our three appointments today?" They had customarily received a dozen a day when buyers flocked to New York. "That guy Swanson from Hudson's in Detroit. . . ."

"Never buys anything," Harry said. "According to my father."

"Sometimes he buys a little. Miss Mahoney from Lansburgh's in Washington. She's good for fifty or a hundred bags, as is Miss Levy from Hecht's in Baltimore. It's as if they're in competition."

"They are, because the people who live in between the two cities have the choice of either," Harry said, as if he knew what he was talking about.

"Who? Dairy farmers?" Cornell asked.

"Other people live there: bureaucrats, politicians, spice magnates."

Cornell, who was born in Washington, said, "Harry, the suburbs are tight. Washington in some senses is as far from Baltimore as it is from Boston."

Corrected, Harry jumped to Boston. "What about Filene's?"

"Haven't heard a peep. And we missed the boat this fall with the box bag."

"It's insane," Harry said. "They're too small, they don't carry well next to the body, and what woman wants to open a trunk-like lid to get at her stuff?"

"I know, Harry, but they're the fashion. Altman's is selling one for thirty-five-forty, including the twenty percent federal tax."

"How do they do that?"

"European labor costs and the dollar, that's how. De Pinna has a cigarette case for twelve-seventy-five. We'd have to sell it to them for four dollars. That's our cost, depending; and we never had much volume and we have less now, so if we squeezed out twenty-five cents of profit from each sale we'd have maybe twenty-five dollars a week to show for it, at the cost of shifting production from more expensive items."

Harry said, "There's a Chekhov story, 'The Fat One and the Thin One.' The thin one made cigarette cases. He did well with them, but in the end — unlike the cigarettes in his cases — he was crushed." Harry looked down as they both listened to the deep whistle of an ocean liner that had backed out of its berth in the North River and was signaling that it was headed out to sea.

"Let's keep going, Cornell," Harry said, "'til it's running on fumes, and then when the fumes are gone we won't tell it, and maybe it'll run without fumes."

"Do you know how to do that, Harry?" Cornell asked, because he knew, and he had seen it many times. He had seen men go down, some bravely, some not.

"Yeah, I do," Harry said. "To the last."

At the end of October the weather had been May-like, with some readings in the seventies, but the audience at the chamber music concert in the Great Hall of the Metropolitan Museum was dressed as if for winter and the racks in the coat room threatened to snap with the weight of cashmere and mink. For the most part, the listeners were old, their circulation was poor, and they had lived long enough to have been caught by sudden temperature drops that in the mountains of New Hampshire, on the plains of Nebraska, or in the ice-boating bays of the Hudson had almost carried them away when they were small children. The young, too, of whom there were not just a few, were more heavily dressed than the air outside required. They did this out of pure conformity, as people do.

Harry wore a blazer and a bow tie, which was inappropriately informal, but he had his reasons. Some of the older people looked on disapprovingly. He was not a college student, and this was not a picnic. What was he trying to prove, or was he just careless, or a boor? "Sit between Catherine and me," Evelyn said to him as they stood in an alcove near the coat room. "We'll protect you. Do you like this kind of music, or for you is it like sawing wood?" (She had invited Harry and Catherine mainly as an excuse to see them.)

Before answering, Harry opened the program. "To tell you the truth," he said, "I don't really care for anything in the program except the first movement of the Brahms Quartet Number One, which I really love. The rest is like grasshoppers complaining at the Department of Motor Vehicles."

Billy thought so, too. "It's the hors d'oeuvres," he said. "I myself came for the shrimp." A very dry-looking old woman with the face of a starving coyote gave Billy a look that was supposed to make him wither, but which made him laugh. "Let's get to it," he said so that she could hear. "In tiny voices, the shrimp are begging to be eaten."

Billy and Evelyn went in, leaving Harry and Catherine in the echoing alcove. He looked at her, and she looked back. He loved her so much, so hard, always more, always driven deeper. "Are you okay with how things are now, Catherine?"

She was surprised. "Yes, why shouldn't I be?"

"You were shocked when you found out that all your life you hadn't known who you were, and now all this."

"I got over it, and it's not true. I knew who I was. I always did. If you know what you love, you know who you are. Harry, I know what I love." She smiled, as if she knew, and didn't know, what was going to happen. One way or another, it would somehow be the same.

And then they went in, together.

Luckily for Harry, they played his favorite movement right off, and luckily for him Catherine was by his side. Despite the room's high ceiling, it was hot. He leaned slightly toward her, so that as she leaned toward him they touched, ever so gently, and each put an arm around the other, at the waist. It was like a kiss. Catherine's suit, of light, soft wool, smelled of her perfume. Sitting so closely together, yet modestly, they felt their pulses. When, as a student long before the war, Harry had listened to the *allegro non troppo* again and again, he had dreamed and desired that someday there might be a woman like Catherine, who loved him, with whom he might listen just as they were now, not wanting anything else in the world. And, for a moment, there was.

Running down the front steps of the museum to catch a bus that would then swing to the right across the park, he felt his heart break as if with grief. But when he leapt into the open vestibule as the bus began to move, action made him feel somewhat better. As he settled into his seat, the heat rising from him carried with it not just the remnants of Catherine's perfume but its scent after her body had changed it and made it better. He breathed its last for as long as he could.

Having crossed the park, transfer in hand, he went south toward midtown, eventually losing patience with the speed of traffic and alighting to walk the last few blocks to Madison Square Garden, there to see the fight that would bring together not only Gitano Morales and Marcus Joseph, welterweights, but the greater portion of his pathfinders now living, synchronized to arrive from various parts of the city and converge upon four seats close enough to take in the whole spectacle and far away enough to do so without craning one's neck or catching droplets of sweat as the boxers' heads were whiplashed by punches. Harry had written on each ticket, "Be sure to attend."

The fight crowd poured in tensely: a few women, but mostly men. It was not like going to a movie. Adrenaline rose long before one got to the arena, because this was not just something to see but rather a form of simulation and training. Every blow was followed for its technique as every man transported himself into the ring, senses alive, to give and to receive it. The connoisseurs of boxing could talk of its art all they wanted to; it was primarily a ritual of transport and preparation in which the ordinary man who did not have to fight reclaimed within him the man who did.

In the midst of a navy, black, and gray river of gabardine and wool, upon the tide of which rode an undulating flotsam of hats, stood a girl of about twenty, perhaps a student at Barnard or Vassar. She could not have been more than five feet tall and a hundred pounds, and would appear and disappear in the stream of coats, bobbing, absolutely blond, her hair tied back. She had even and unblemished features, and luminous blue eyes magnified in the crystals of gold wire-rims. She was handing out broadsheets in protest of boxing.

Most people ignored her. Some took her sheets without knowing what they were. Some read them as they walked, crumpled them, and threw them to the ground. Harry took one and stood between her and the relentlessly moving stream of men as if to shelter her. He read carefully, looking down at her a few times as he did. She was much like a somewhat younger Catherine, and for the first time in his life in regard to a young woman who was not a child, he felt what it would be like to have a daughter.

"This is beautifully written," he said. "Did you write it?"

She nodded.

"Really wonderful."

"And in substance?" she challenged, bravely.

"Not a single point with which I can disagree."

She smiled. It was her first success of the evening. "Then will you go in?"

"Yes."

"Why?"

Harry didn't answer immediately, but thought for a while. "Because two propositions can be true at once," he said. "Because the world is imperfect. Because we are imperfect. Because sometimes we're called upon to do terrible things. And because we define ourselves in dying, which is," he indicated by motioning with his head toward the arena, "what this is. Give us at least that."

"I don't understand."

"You don't have to. You're beautiful and you have courage. You're already there."

"Am I not right?" she asked as he started toward the interior of the arena.

"Of course you're right," he answered.

In the pulse of the arena before the lights went down, Harry, Bayer, Johnson, and Sussingham sat together as if inside a transport plane before a jump. Tensing before the fight like everyone else, they said nothing. The house grew dark. Kliegs suspended over the ring came on in blinding shots straight from above like beams of light in a Bible story. The ring announcer, in shirt and tie, climbed through the ropes as a microphone was lowered to him. He had a good sense of drama, and after he gripped the microphone he hesitated before he spoke. Other than a hum like that of distant traffic, nothing could be heard but the attempted silence of thousands waiting to listen to what he was going to say. They already knew it, but there was pleasure in hearing it even were it to be heard a thousand times.

As first Morales and then Joseph entered the arena they were accorded the respect that is accorded to those who put themselves on the line, whether they be boxers, soldiers falling through the air into battle, or Barnard girls, in wire-rims, standing alone upon principle. After the fighters came from their corners and were announced, the crowds cocked like a crossbow. Then the fighters went back, and were impossibly overwhelmed with advice from little bald trainers. They bit into their mouth guards, had perhaps a last jolt of fear, and before they knew it the bell rang for the first round. After that was no more fear but only automatic action. The gods of war abbreviate time, put a mist before the eyes, and, if you are lucky, you last until the mist dissipates and the world clears. Time is slowed to allow the blocking and delivery of blows precisely as intended. Spectators, too, can rise into this gift of grace and fly with the fighter along the rails of victory, or fall with him in defeat.

When it ended after seven rounds, everyone had sore muscles from following each punch and dodge. Pity and joy for loser and winner were balanced with exhaustion as people filed out, mentally or actually counting the money that they had just lost or won, or trying to remember the particulars of the expertise they had just witnessed in case they would be called upon to do the same, without realizing that what the fighters knew and put into play was not visible even to those in the front row. What made them professionals was something that came in two parts. The first was born with them and could not and did not need to be learned; and the second could be learned only after years of labor and suffering, all of which allowed them to see as if through a clarifying lens the microscopic differences in action and deployment that pass right by those who have not done the work and those who look like fools when they imitate those who have.

As the arena emptied but the lights blazed on, the four former pathfinders sat together quietly. "Are you still in?" Harry asked.

They answered with barely perceptible changes of expression. Barely perceptible but, nonetheless, like the ignition of lightning and the roll of thunder. He told them to make their ways, individually, to an address in Newark, and he knew that he could count on them to arrive exactly on time.

Bayer and Johnson found themselves coincidentally on the same train to Newark the next day, as did Harry and Sussingham on another train, having crossed over on the same ferry. They had no need to avoid speaking, and when they walked from their stops to a warehouse in a semi-abandoned industrial area they did so with the relaxed but burdened air of people going to work. As Bayer and Johnson walked down Johnson Avenue, to Bayer, who hadn't made a comment but had looked at Johnson in a certain way, Johnson said, "No more than aspirin is named after you."

"I didn't say anything," Bayer protested.

"I read your mind."

With a longer distance to cover, Sussingham and Harry spoke mainly about the Slovak girl who worked in the glass factory, Sussingham doing most of the talking, all the way to the gate of the warehouse, which was opened for them by a security guard in a peaked cap after they told him they were there to "unload Norwegian sardines." Bayer and Johnson were waiting amid civilian trucks and a few surplus jeeps parked in a huge fenced yard. In the center was a brick building with rows of arched doors on each of its five floors, but no windows. Not a single one of the wooden doors was open. A canal had once run right by the building, and these doors had facilitated the loading and unloading of barges. But that was in the nineteenth century, and the canal had been filled in. Black iron fire escapes clung like ivy to the brickwork at the corners, and cast-iron rosettes ran in rows across the façade, signaling where, inside, beams were attached to the wall.

As in a speakeasy, Harry pulled a bell cord. A little port opened in the entryway. The man who let them in said, "Everything's on the second floor except the truck, which is the one on the lot as you came in."

"I saw it," Harry said. "The bales aren't stacked all the way through, are they?"

"There's a space in the center, with supports and ventilation. To get to it, you remove two rows of four bales apiece in the middle of the back. The tailgate swings clear, and the bales that are to be moved around are triply strung so they don't fall apart."

"Who thought of that?" Harry asked.

"Who do you think?" was the answer, meaning Vanderlyn. "He left lunch, too, figuring you might stay awhile."

As they walked up a wide staircase built of heavy beams and planks, Bayer asked, "What is this place?"

Before Harry could answer, they reached the second floor. Half of it was partitioned off, but what remained was vast and dark except where it was lit by huge turn-of-the-century bulbs as big as champion squashes, with giant filaments, the size of buggy springs, glowing in solar yellow. The floor was a mosaic of end-grain, hard-cured oak dented with the use of a hundred years. It was warm inside because the brick had been soaking up the sunlight of the unusually intense Indian summer. Arrayed upon tables gathered together beneath one of the great gourd-like lights were carbines, magazines of ammunition, a light machine gun and box of belted cartridges, a bazooka with three rockets, a plinth made of five bricks of plastic explosive, fuses, a collapsible stretcher, a rubber assault boat with four paddles, four hand grenades, four individual medical kits, rations for light duty, and, on a different table, a lunch catered by Sardi's, although it was doubtful that any Sardi's employee came anywhere near the warehouse to lay it down.

The weaponry was as familiar to the four of them as a toothbrush or a pen. On one level it made them feel comfortable, but on another it did just the opposite. "You can't buy bazookas and machine guns in a store," Sussingham stated. "What is this place, and who supplied it?"

"I don't know exactly," Harry told them. "His name is Vanderlyn, someone I picked up on the road during a storm. His boat had sunk. He looked like a derelict, but he was wearing an airborne tunic. Because of that I couldn't leave him out there, so even though my father-in-law — who wasn't my father-in-law at the time — wouldn't stop the car, I went back and got him. He's quite a big deal, although I didn't know it then."

"Why would he do this?" Bayer asked, because in New York everything was either bought or sold.

"He's returning the favor, I guess, and it's a good thing to do. So far this year Verderamé has been connected to half a dozen murders, including that of a man who worked for me. The way it's been is that we play by the rules, he doesn't, he gets away with it, he becomes our master, and it goes on forever.

"In the war, the OSS made its own rules, and killed the wolves to protect the sheep. It gets touchy here, where we have law . . . and it's dangerous, of course. But the way he put it to me was quite simple. He said, 'Do we have law? Because if we do, I'll go home and knit tea cozies. If we do not, in fact, have law, and just the unfulfilled hope of it, then how can what we do threaten something that doesn't exist except partially or as an always unrealized hope?'"

"That's simple?" Sussingham asked.

"For him."

"Everything has a price," Bayer added. "What do they want from us?"

"He wants nothing," Harry said, "not from me, anyway. But you're right. I don't know who they are, but when they get started—and they're starting something big—don't be surprised if you get an offer of employment. I already did, and turned it down."

"They went ahead anyway?" Sussingham asked.

"Decent of them," Johnson said. "Do they know who we are? They know you, but do they know us?"

"*I* didn't tell them," Harry said, "but who knows?"

"They know," Bayer announced. He had veered toward the lunch, and stood two feet away from the table, pointing at it. The others walked over. Near a kettle above a can of Sterno were a chafing dish, similarly warmed, and trays of sandwiches, hors d'oeuvres, and cookies. On four china plates cutlery was rolled in cloth napkins, and on each plate was a folded card with a single letter written on it: C, J, S, and B, for Copeland, Johnson, Sussingham, and Bayer. "They didn't have to do that," Bayer continued, "but they did. I suppose there could be a hundred reasons for it, but we'll never figure it out."

"I would think," said Harry, "knowing him, that it was for fun. Where's the blackboard? There was supposed to be a blackboard."

"There," Sussingham said. The blackboard stood apart from everything else and was hard to see in the shadows of the powerful lights. He and Bayer approached on either side, lifted it, and silently led it closer. They tilted it forward slightly, but not so much that an eraser and chalk would roll off its curled ledge. As it flew at them, they pulled up their chairs and Harry seized a piece of chalk.

"If anyone wants to go home, don't worry about it and don't hesitate. That you've come is way above the call: there is no call," Harry said, and fell silent. After a few moments, with no response, he went on.

"Okay. Thank you. We've done this before, both together and separately. We trained for it, we exercised, but when we actually did it we sometimes threw it together in seconds, and never once as I recall had we the benefits we have now. What I proposed is illegal, but, in light of the target, law enforcement won't hold us to account. I've always assumed, and now people I trust have affirmed, that other than showing up at the scene, making a conjecture or two, writing a report, and looking good in the press, the police don't actually investigate attacks on criminals, which would be for them sort of like bailing out a sinking boat by putting the water back in. As they see it, their job is mainly to clarify and limit the interest of the public, which fades after a day. Who ever got indignant when a gangster was killed? If anything, people are quietly delighted. We might offend some who live strictly by principle were it known that the gangster wasn't killed by other gangsters but by regular citizens. In other words, if the wolves kill the wolves, that's no problem, but if the sheep kill the wolves, then you have holy hell. Vigilantism is dangerous, of course, but that's not what this is. We're not a parallel system of justice. We're confined to one case, my own, responding to a mortal attack and the threat of others—just as I would were someone smashing down the doors of my house. The danger is imminent, although its timing is deliberately unpredictable. The threat is constant. Protection on the part of the state is nil. This is self-defense.

"I harp on this because it's against our instincts and upbringing to do what we're going to do. Certainly against mine, but my instincts and upbringing never took account of being the target of a killer who enjoys the favor of authority."

"We're okay," Sussingham said.

"Good," said Harry. "When we ambushed a German convoy, the people we killed were likely more innocent than our targets now. And half the force on the battlefield was determined to prevent it and to take revenge. Now, within a ten-mile radius of where we're going to strike there may be a dozen cops with pistols and a shotgun or two, whereas then we had to look out for far more interested, motivated, and skilled Wehrmacht divisions, or even corps, and their tanks, artillery, heavy machine guns, grenades, and occasional air support. And we're not going to come in contact with the police. We'll be finished and away long before they know what happened. We're on the same side: we can't harm them. You never know which cops are on the take, but most aren't, so rather than fight I'll surrender to them if it's necessary, but it won't be."

"No one has done this kind of attack, with these weapons, in civilian life," Bayer said.

"It'll be an item of tremendous interest for a few days. And here's where we may provide a public service. When the other crime families hear of this, to protect themselves they'll seek out similar weapons." Harry swept his hand over the heavily laden tables. "Evidently, there's a parallel arm somewhere ready to supply them. The dealers are federal agents, and when the buyers are arrested the charges will weigh heavily against them because of their prior records."

"Are we acting for the government, or not?" Bayer asked. "Because if we are, why don't they do it themselves? Okay, they can't, but they're part of it anyway, right?"

"It knows," Harry answered, "or a part of it knows, but it will never acknowledge. As to what exactly it is, apparently even it doesn't know yet. It's brand new."

"But with a lot of resources," Johnson said.

"That's how we won the war."

"With blood, too."

"I know," Harry said. Then he moved it forward. "It's a road ambush. The target is named Verderamé, a gangster, as you know. He's a creature of habit. The only variation we've observed in his timing is due to traffic. We have about a ninety-minute window in the worst case, so we don't have to wait there all day, and that reduces the chances of discovery. We'll advance, arrive, execute, and retreat in darkness. The area is heavily wooded. One side looks out over the Hudson, which at that point is just under two miles wide, a lake-like stretch called Haverstraw Bay. Only one road leads to the house. These days they return home from the south. There's a lot of mud on the north side, and I think they don't want to dirty the cars.

"We'll blow a tree ahead so it blocks the road, drop one behind before they can back up, put a rocket into each vehicle, rake them with rifle fire. The machine gun will be placed so that anyone running from the house to help won't know what hit them. Let me stress. These are murderers. There could be a dozen or more in the cars and inside the compound. They've got a lot of pistols, shotguns, probably some

Thompsons. Most of them will go down in the first seconds. If any remain to put up a fight, they won't even see us. We'll shift positions right after opening fire, so they can shoot at the spaces where our muzzle flashes were. They won't panic, but they don't know how to fight as a unit and they've never been confronted by this kind of force. It should be over in a couple of minutes. The cars can't run off the road: it's too steep and treed. If there are women and/or children in the cars — I've never seen it — no one fires a shot, and we go home."

"Positions?"

"Facing west, I'll take center, Bayer on the far left to cover the rear-blocking, Sussingham near left. Johnson, with the machine gun, off to the far right to cover the gate and the walls of the house. Let me draw a schematic."

Harry went to the blackboard and mapped out the site, taking pains to draw well. As he worked, Sussingham asked why they would bother to fell trees across the road and rocket the cars. Wouldn't automatic fire from three or four points be sufficient? "The tires will run flat, like agricultural tires," Harry answered. "And the glass is bulletproof, so that means that the car is probably armored. It's very heavy and rounds corners like a boat — wanting, unlike Verderamé, to go straight."

"How'd you find this out?"

"I inspected the car in the parking lot near where Verderamé holds court."

"No one was watching it?"

"A kid was. I pretended I was excited to see a Cadillac. I had to do it after I watched it drive, because either they were transporting pig iron or the thing was armored."

When his diagram was completed, Harry continued his presentation. They would get there in the hay truck, two in front and two secreted with the weapons and the boat in the back. "The boat, do we really have to go across the river?" Bayer asked. They had all been wondering.

"After the attack we have to avoid police dispatched to the scene and to block the roads; possible reinforcements called in by someone in the house; and witnesses who might see us and the truck. We have to get back here and then disappear. We can't just disperse, because there are very few trains at night going south. They sleep at the Harmon yards, ready to carry commuters to the city in the morning. This is by far the best way. All it is, is crossing a river, which we've done before."

"We crossed, we never went back."

"I know, but it's the best option, we have only so much time, and that's the way it is."

"What if we're stopped in the truck," Johnson asked, "by a traffic cop?"

"I have a forged license," Harry answered. "I'll be driving. If I can't drive, someone else will use it. Read it before we jump off."

"We won't have identification?"

"You're farm hands. You won't be expected to."

"Draft cards."

"The war's over. No cop is going to ask you for your draft card or your orders. The roads are deserted on the east side of the Hudson. From a spot on the river between High Tor and Haverstraw, we'll paddle over in the dark. To the right of the target about a quarter of a mile there's a railway signal light that's always on. That's our reference point. It'll take less than an hour to cross. We leave the boat, climb the bank — no one will be there at night — and when we're done, paddle back, drop the weapons in the deepest channel of the river, where they'll be scattered by the current and the tide, cut open the boat and sink it, and drive south with a truckload of hay and nothing else."

"What if there *is* someone on the bank?" Bayer asked.

"Then we turn around. We don't kill innocent people."

"But he will have seen us."

"It's all right. We won't have done anything. We'll say we're duck hunters."

"Some ducks," Bayer said, looking at the weapons. "And if it's a goon?"

"If we can't kill him quietly before he fires a shot or sounds an alarm, we'll retreat."

"Who's gonna kill him quietly?" Johnson asked.

"I'll have to" was Harry's reply. "But I'm sure there won't be anyone. I've been there."

"And the people in the cars, exactly?" Sussingham wanted to know.

"His soldiers. They're the ones who shoot people in the head, beat them to death, stab them in the temple with ice picks, kidnap children for ransom, and dismember bodies. That is, when they're not burning down houses or raping young girls."

"How do you know this?" Sussingham pressed.

"He reads the papers," Bayer told him, "and he lives in New York. Their protection is supposed to go all the way up to O'Dwyer. Who knows?" To Sussingham's puzzled look, Bayer responded, "The mayor."

"He'll be quite surprised," Harry added, "if it's true. But everyone will think it's a gang war in which one side escalated."

Using the diagram, they went over the plan second by second, which was not so difficult, as the action was supposed to run for no more than a few minutes. Each man knew his part, his place, and the part and place of the others. They weren't nervous about forgetting the details, for not only were they practiced but they knew they could improvise as they had many times before. This led to a question, over lunch, that had to come up. Johnson was the one who raised it.

"Casualties," he said.

"I would hope we can do this safely," Harry answered. "We'll have surprise, superior armament, cover, darkness, and whereas we're practiced in assault they have no experience in defense. But if there are casualties, we have medical kits, we evacuate the wounded, bring him, or them, here, where they will be treated by a surgeon who will be waiting."

"And killed?" Johnson asked.

"We'll bring him out. I have cards for you to complete: next of kin, where you want to be buried, that kind of thing."

"I want to be buried in Arlington," Bayer said. "Do they take Jews?"

"Of course they do," Sussingham said, "but not you. You're too big."

"And your wills," Harry said. "Informally. Nothing will see a judge."

"I don't need a will," Sussingham declared. "I don't have anything to leave or anyone to leave it to."

"You're insured," Harry told him. "We all are."

"They thought of everything," Bayer said. "How much?"

"Thirty thousand."

"For all of us together?"

"Apiece."

They were astounded. "That's three big houses, Harry," Bayer said.

"Six in Wisconsin," Johnson added.

"I told you, I don't have anyone to leave it to," Sussingham insisted.

"What about the pretty girl in the apartment on the first floor? She's apparently all you think about."

"Yeah, I'll leave it to her. That would make me feel. . . . It would almost be like kissing her, which I always wanted to do."

"Then kiss her," Harry said.

"I'd leave it to my sister," Johnson announced.

They looked at Harry. "My wife, Catherine. She doesn't need it, but as you said, it would be like kissing her. She'd be moved, I know. It would be as if, for a second, I was there."

Then they all looked at Bayer. "No one," he said. "Absolutely, no one."

They met twice more in Newark, going over the details again and again; stripping and cleaning their weapons so that they would feel wed to them once more; and getting back to what they had been. In the eyes of a soldier whose life may end at any time, the things that weigh upon him heavily are vivid in proportion. If much is lost, much is gained.

They were going to go on Thursday, the thirtieth of October, arriving in Newark at two and driving north an hour later, but it didn't work, because there was a fire in the Hudson Tubes and they couldn't get across on time. When Johnson and Bayer got to the station it was closed off and smoke was issuing from the doors. This was just as well, as heavy rain might have thrown them off schedule anyway. High tides and street flooding paralyzed traffic, shut down air operations at La Guardia, and made Friday uncertain in terms of both what they could do and the effect upon Verderamé's usual punctuality. Also, Friday had been ruled out in general not only because they wanted a business day for the day following their strike, but because it was more likely that on Friday Verderamé might stay in town for dinner or go to a show. And had they set out that Friday they would have been frustrated yet again. The Tubes were flooded at times and the ferries backed up, their crossings made difficult by high winds, and boats that had broken from their moorings and were running unmanned on unusually powerful currents.

They decided to go on the first good day of the first week in November. Everyone except Harry went back to his routine. Sussingham went to a lot of movies and ate repeatedly at the White Turkey, alternating from one to the other out of embarrassment that despite the thousands of restaurants in New York, all he wanted to eat was turkey. Johnson settled into the library and ate mostly at the automat. Bayer went back to work on Thursday, again on Friday, and, receiving various clients, noted that their umbrellas held so much water that as the owners sat talking to him the umbrellas would drip for half an hour, that water ran off people's hair onto their shoulders as if it were raining indoors, and that his windows streamed perpetually as sideways rain was swept against the glass. Everything was gray and wet, and when darkness came it was worse.

Harry and Catherine had agreed that she would stay with her parents and not return home until it was over. He told her, and it was true, that if she were with him beforehand he might not be able to come out safely. He had to leave behind her world and everything feminine. To do what he had to do, he could not think at all of things that were tender or of what he loved. He had seen too many men disengage from the rhythm of war and then die for their want of ferocity and fighting grace. Though the best of them fought to return to love, to return to it they had to put it out of their minds.

The delay was not propitious. It is true that had Catherine been with him he would have been thrown off, but in her absence he could not help but think of her, and the more he thought of her, the more he missed her. As he read, he saw her on the page, more beautiful than anything that was ever written. And when he slept, he dreamt of her.

At the beginning of the week, when the weather was still a problem, he was sitting in the living room at dusk. Lights across the park came on a score at a time until thousands lit the stone cliffs of Fifth Avenue. They twinkled gently, as they were for the most part just table lamps, shaded in silk, glowing in warm apartments. A burst of sun beneath the clouds momentarily washed the off-white façades with an orange-tinged red the color of molten steel. Behind this, the sky was blued as purple and black as a gun, and the trees in the park, leafless and thin, were for a moment like flames the color of white gold.

Although he had always been unwilling — so as not to tempt fate — to have his picture taken or write a farewell before going into battle, he decided to write to Catherine. He had in mind a short note, like that which would have announced that he was going out to buy groceries and would be back at such and such a time. But though it would be short, he thought to leave something rather than nothing. He wanted it to be almost breezy, certainly informal, and not too serious. He wouldn't be away for long, and would see her on the Esplanade at eleven o'clock on the day after the action. That was set in stone. He didn't want her in the apartment. It wasn't safe. They would meet in the park and then see how things played out, what the papers said, how it felt. He would be seeing her soon enough, so just a paragraph or two, if only because writing it would be as if she were there.

He searched the house for the right paper upon which to write. Though it might be casual, it couldn't be like a telephone message or a grocery list. On the other hand, stationery was too somber and out of the question. At first he searched mentally, thinking about what could be where, and then he got up and started opening drawers. Since Catherine had moved in, these held many surprises. She carried things from home or from elsewhere, and, being neither as neat nor as organized as he, simply threw them into anything that might hold them. In one of the compartments of a breakfront she had installed in the hall, Harry found a half-depleted pad of musical notation paper. Six by eight and stiff enough to fold into a card that would stand on the marble-topped table in the entryway, it was printed with staffs only on one side, and he would write on the other. Whether it was from the music department at Bryn Mawr, a long-ago voice teacher, or the theater, didn't matter: it was a small part of the many things that had made Catherine's song.

He sat down to write, intending not to touch upon anything too grave, and aware that were things to turn out well, he and Catherine would return to the apartment together and there would be no need for a note — a note that, despite Harry's wishes, and though by necessity it was short, became a letter.

He folded it in two and stood it up on the oval marble top of the table that had been near the front door since Harry was a child. She couldn't miss it, especially because she had left a bracelet there, abandoning it on the way out perhaps because she discovered that it was not right for her outfit. Or perhaps because the clasp had broken. It lay as she had left it, open and empty, the fragile safety chain of almost gossamer gold links lying bereft on the cold marble, not quite glowing in the light that came from over the rooftops and across the deeply shadowed courtyards.

# 44

## IN THE ARCADE

PHILOSOPHERS, MATHEMATICIANS, and logicians would not have given it a thought. But dyslexics, those with right-left confusion, women whose sense of direction was not quite equal to that of a carrier pigeon, and men who could not fathom the idea of a Möbius belt were stopped for at least a moment by the fact that 28 West 44th Street was also 25 West 43rd Street. How could this be? The post office had long before reconciled itself to the paradox. People who wanted to put on the dog could write: "Please send to me at my offices either at 28 West 44th St., or at 25 West 43rd St., and my staff will see that I get it, even if I'm in Paris." And visitors who walked through the arcade, entering at one address and leaving by another while in only one building, sometimes found it pleasing.

This was the arcade in which Eugenia Eba worked beneath the symbol that apart from memory was all she had left of her husband, a gold star to which she would be faithful—which would inspire within her a feeling of holiness as if he were in her embrace—for the rest of her life. Reweaving was an art that soon would be lost, but all day long it is what she did, working amid travertine walls beneath a vaulted ceiling and separated by her little window from a constellation of highly polished fittings that gave off a golden glow. She had always loved how, hour after hour, the brass arrow of the elevator indicator moved like a weathervane in the wind.

She worked in a silence made soft by many sounds mixing in tranquility—footsteps and heel clicks on the marble floors; sewing machines whirring intermittently like orgasmic crickets; and lost voices rising invisibly to the ceiling. Murmurs, cries, or singing, their meaning was unintelligible but their import was felt as little explosions upon the heart.

When finally the beginning of November had hesitantly returned to fall, bands of rain remained nonetheless to sweep over Manhattan in alternation with sun and blue sky. As Eugenia Eba finished mending a particular English wool jacket she had fixed many times before, the streets were wet and dark or just as often sparkling with sunshine. Business was slow thanks to ready-to-wear, so she was grateful for the work, strange as it was, and it was not hers to question why the tear in the sleeve kept on tearing. The second time the garment was handed over to her, she recognized her own work, and offered to restore it for no charge. "I wouldn't hear of it," the owner had said commandingly. "It's my fault. A hinge on the tiller of my boat keeps on catching there. I can't change that. It's a fast boat that wins races. You can throw over the tiller in such a way that it turns on a dime, coming about with the stern elevated rather than depressed. No. I wouldn't hear of it. If you don't mind fixing this, I'll just bring it in when it tears."

Knowing that the tear was made with a thread hook and not by a sailboat hinge, she acquiesced anyway. At first she thought he was interested in her. He was, but it was not the kind of interest that often stopped men at her window, as, young and old, they pretended fascination with reweaving but could not take their eyes off her, her hair shining in the light. He was wealthy and of an age when he might have been seeking a mistress, but the way he spoke to her, and his expression when he did, said that this was not the case.

It was at least the tenth time he had brought the jacket in, always cut in the same place. She knew no more about him now than the first time she had seen him, and he no more about her, as he was not eager to make conversation, and of all the things of the world, conversation was one of the foremost that Eugenia Eba did without. She was grateful and at the same time somewhat resentful, for over almost a year the work she did for him served to keep her accounts in the black month after month, even if not by much.

In January she never pointed out that he almost surely could not have been sailing, or, in July and August, when the sun came close to boiling the waters of the Sound, that he was unlikely to have been sailing in a wool jacket. It was understood that such things would pass without comment. For him, whatever he was doing was not a duty. Nor was it pleasure or displeasure, but only somehow written in. Time after time he would bring her the jacket he cut and she would gently reweave it. Perhaps he took pity on her. Perhaps he had lost a son and seen her star, or had been commanded in a way he did not know, or was simply generous, as some people are. Perhaps, after the war, he was a bit crazy, and thought that an exquisite woman sitting alone in a little shop was reweaving and repairing with gifted persistence not just the torn jackets, pants with cigarette burns, and coats with fraying edges upon which she worked every day, but the whole wounded and suffering world.

Harry stared out his windows high over Central Park and watched as bands of rain clouds would raid the city and then run from blue sky. The elements had begun to fuse. Sussingham and Johnson would leave their hotels, Bayer would flip the sign on his door early that afternoon and his clients would have to come back another time. Vanderlyn's people were waiting in Newark, and the surgeon knew to arrive later. Verderamé was holding court amid walls of gray and green, sure of his role and the justice of what he did. He was what he was, he thought, because the world was unfair to him, and the license he had granted to himself because of this injustice was an endless source of enjoyment as he revenged his slights and struck at everything before it could strike him. Though the wheels on his Cadillac were still, they would roll at dusk. Everything was poised for what would happen, even if not everyone knew it was coming and no one knew exactly how it would occur.

Catherine told herself more than once that Harry had fought through the war with the 82nd Airborne, that he and the others were naturals to begin with and had learned all the lessons they might need as they had pushed the Germans into the heart of Germany, that they were used to hard combat and knew what to do, which would not daunt them.

Still, sometimes she trembled. But she would go onstage that evening and give the best performance of her career. The applause would rival the recent downpours, but she would not hear it. She would disdain and leave it behind as she was carried away by her song. All she could think of was the Esplanade, where everything would come clear.

Harry made his way toward the ferry, leaving earlier than planned, hoping to walk off all that was unsettling him. He had never been in a city just before going into a fight. It had always been on some quiet airfield when he could listen to the cicadas in the desert, or on an English weald after a long truck ride. These surroundings, lacking in complexity or action, had allowed him to catch the pacing of war and unite with it, to alloy with the battle and cast away the hope of life, as a trick to preserve it.

Now and then the remnant bands of rain, which could last for a minute or half an hour, would pound down furiously before running north to die in the highlands of New England. Not long after he left the park, Harry was caught outside a piano store on 57th Street, where he found himself standing with half a dozen people in the vestibule while a young girl inside tried out a piano. As her parents watched, she played sections of Beethoven sonatas and concerti, and fragments of Mozart, all joined together by her own superb cadenzas. She didn't know that she had an audience, that it had been raining, that it had stopped, that they had left, or that Harry had stayed to listen when he might have gone on. The last thing she played, before she put down the cover in a way that said that this was the piano she had chosen, was the second movement of the *Pathétique*.

When Harry pushed out from the vestibule onto a wet sidewalk reflecting dashes of blue, he had begun to get a little of what he had always sought before he went into battle — a sense that time does not exist, that he himself was of no account, that all things were connected and orchestrated far beyond human will, and that the world was saturated with beauty no matter what the loss. This he began to receive from the music, and then from the motion of the streets and what seemed like the purposeful racing of the clouds.

After he went ten or twelve blocks down Fifth Avenue to 46th

Street it began to pour. He thought he might outlast it, but was forced by wind and water to seek shelter west on 44th. He thoughtlessly imagined that he might duck into the Harvard Club. On occasion, he could fake it, walking in with an expression of aristocracy, pleasure, and irritation all compressed into one odd look. Still, the porter sometimes checked, asking, "Are you a member, sir?" in tones that could touchlessly dissect a frog. The one time Harry had been intercepted he had had no need for counterfeit nonchalance. He was there, legitimately, to meet Howard Mumford Jones, with whom he had formed a connection after the eminent professor had asked Harry, who one fall had been the only student in his course he had not recognized, what he thought of literature in service to politics and ideals. In the thirties it was assumed that literature would be. Harry replied, improvising and out of conviction, "My view is that literature should move beyond opinion, where music already is, and old age, if we're lucky, may lead." That was the beginning of their acquaintance. After Harry returned to New York, they sometimes met for a drink at the Harvard Club.

One entered via a brilliance of architecture—first through a reception hall that was elegant but hardly overwhelming. Then, as if to dash expectations, the ceiling was lower toward the interior and darkness made the senses adjust to a lesser scale. But the third chamber opened up breathtakingly, three storeys high, vast and wide, richly appointed in crimson, dark wood, and gold, its heroic paintings staring down through silence so capacious it absorbed sound like a pillow slammed upon a mosquito. It would have been the perfect place, tranquilly by the several fires, in which to wait out an angry bout of gray rain, but during the Depression Harry could not afford to join. He was of course unavailable during the war, and when he returned he had put off joining until, once more, he could not afford to do so. Also, other than waiting out a storm, he didn't know—being impatient of luxury and a stranger to normal sociality—exactly what he would do there.

But now when he had to get out of the rain he found himself in the arcade, the normal logic of which would have been for him to have walked through to 43rd Street, past Eugenia Eba in the reweaving shop. Most of the time, she was looking down into a magnifying glass, as big as a dinner plate and as clear as ether, suspended above her work while strong light illumined the strands of wool she wove and twisted together.

He would never love anyone the way he loved Catherine, but he loved Eugenia Eba all the same, even if only from a distance. Though still beautiful, she was no longer a girl with peerless charm, but no matter how old she might be, she retained for him all the magic she once had had. Were it an illusion, it was yet a finer, more solid truth. If when she is aged you cannot see in the eyes of a woman the youth she was at eighteen, then it is not she that is old but you that are blind.

Harry began to move through the narrow arcade, slowly progressing toward her shop. With each step the cares of the world drained from him, and he grew more and more content. It was not the false and misleading equanimity of success, but that which comes of failure and truth — after darkness and restriction would come a feeling of holiness, an ocean of clarity. He came to the little window, through which he saw in cameo the ideal of loveliness from his youth, now seemingly immortal. Protected from all comers by her golden star, her face lit by light more benevolent than on any nearby stage — and there were many — she was patiently weaving, and although he could not explain it, Harry thought that she would do this contentedly and forever.

He forced himself to move until he stood at the 43rd Street door. The rain had begun to subside. In only moments he would again be on the street and in the invisible clouds of air that often linger after a downpour. In harmony arising from dissonance came the hum of the arcade, like the propeller noise of an airplane stationary on a runway, ready to release its brakes and rush forward. Like sheaves of wheat in the sun, a thousand shafts tied together as one, the revolving blades of propellers were invisible except as a gleaming disc. This insistent, lapping frequency and pitch, which announces that one is to be borne away on high, was the sound he heard in the golden arcade.

• • •

As intermittent squalls crosshatched dark lines upon waters normally speckled with whitecaps, Vanderlyn was out of commission in his office, keeping track of the ferries as they trudged through curtains of rain. Unable to work, he would rest his elbow on the desk and hold his chin in his hand, and then drop his hand, nervously knocking his thumb against the wood, like someone who has come to a conclusion. At times his heart fluttered as if his blood had mixed with air.

He pressed the first lever on his intercom. "What time is my appointment with the lawyers?"—meaning Sutherland, Dwight, his personal attorneys.

"You don't have one" came the answer.

"Oh, I thought I did. Please get them on the phone."

A minute later Vanderlyn's secretary told him that they were on the line.

"When can you see me?" Vanderlyn asked Sutherland, who had once been a terrified little boy in the next cubicle on their first day at Groton—terrified, Vanderlyn would later say to him at innumerable family gatherings, because his extrasensory perception had informed him that in the future he would have to settle for Princeton.

Sutherland knew from Vanderlyn's tone that he wanted it to be soon. "When would you like?"

"Today."

"I'm free now. I usually make it a practice to eat lunch. Where are you?"

"At the office."

"If you shoot yourself out of a cannon you can get here in a minute. Shall I open the window?"

"Come on, Squeaky." (People of their station called one another such names despite their fear that immigrants of very tough fiber might hear, and make a mockery of their class.)

"Whenever you can get here. It's not so busy today."

"I can't wait."

"I'm sure you can't."

. . .

When the rain stopped, Harry looked at the clock in a store window across the street and, knowing that he was early, left without urgency. He walked slowly east and south toward Kips Bay on quiet blocks of brownstones immune to the frenzy of midtown.

The rain, however, had one more shot, and took it as Harry crossed Park Avenue somewhere in the Thirties, suddenly driving down like chorus lines of jackhammers. Not wanting to be soaked or chilled, he ran for the first wide portal he saw, a neoclassical monument on a small scale a third of a block toward Lexington. He hadn't had time to see what it was, but once inside he realized it was a hotel, one of many in the area, of medium price, mainly for businessmen, and largely unknown. It was usually safe to assume that such places were deficient in elegance, not a single one having a great name.

But New York is a city of open secrets, and this hotel, the name of which Harry had no need to find out and would never know, was luxurious in an uncanny way. The entrance was so dark that it was almost as if he had either stepped into a cave or was in a quick eclipse. The darkness was relieved every minute or so by flashes of lightning as a thunderstorm crossed Manhattan. The lightning would burst, fixing a still image then falsified by subsequent movements in the dark.

There was no front desk. No doormen or bellboys. To the right was a bar at which a few people sat absorbed in conversation. To the left was a sunken seating area at one end of which was an extraordinary fire. Two rows of gas flames each a foot or more high ran for ten feet within a fireplace of black slate. The gas pressure that shot the flames a foot into the air, sixty in each row, also made them dance wildly. Their heat was warm but not excessively dry, and the dancing light, the only illumination in a large room, changed everything as it shifted second by second.

Harry walked down two steps and sat in a leather chair close and at eye level to the flames. It would be a good place to get dry as the last of the storm departed. He had time. A waitress appeared on the steps. She held a tray under her arm, and looked more like a schoolgirl than a waitress. "What would you like?" she asked.

Harry had the trapped-animal feeling of someone who, to stay in place, must spend money on something he doesn't want. What she was asking for was a kind of rent, but for the tenants to save face she would bring them something on a tray. It was early for anyone to drink, especially Harry, but he had to pay the rent.

"What kind of Scotch do you have?" he asked.

She named half a dozen. He thought to hell with his inability to drink, chose one, and asked for a glass of water to go with it. This he had observed at the Connaught, among people who appeared to know what they were doing. Back quickly, she set down the Scotch and a glass of water on a low table at Harry's knees, took payment, and left after flashing a pumpkin smile. That so small a woman had so wide and shocking a grin was mysterious and disconcerting. Harry drank a little Scotch, and then a little water. He waited for a few minutes and then repeated the process. Given the amounts in the glasses, he thought he would take about twenty minutes to finish before he left to catch the Weehawken Ferry, which was the right interval in terms of getting dry, especially because of the fire. He closed his eyes and slipped into the kind of sleep that commuters sleep between stations, a slumber that despite its great heaviness does not compromise keeping to schedule. The roar of the fire divided time into precise increments of which he was somehow aware.

As if on cue, he opened his eyes, and the light refreshed his wits. Across from him in a chair that was the twin of his own was a man staring at the flames, his body turned three-quarters to the fire. His face was long, strong, and gaunt. Even in a garden restaurant in May at Cap d'Antibes he would have looked like a man who had spent the previous six months fighting across the desert or the steppes, or so it seemed to Harry, who thought as well that he might be a Hungarian or a Turk. His face, though European, was also incalculably Asian. It told of untraceable places lost in time, of taut, weatherbeaten Mongols, Sarmatians, Kazakhs, and Finns.

He was dressed in a tweed jacket and taupe slacks. His hair was thinning and pomaded, his teeth very large, white, and straight, his gums receding with age. Looking at his hands, Harry could see from their size and the structure of the tendons that his grip was powerful. He was in some senses frightening, and yet Harry felt warmly toward him. Although he was wearing round, horn-rimmed glasses, the passport of the Ivy League, they were reddish orange. Harry had never seen such frames.

Easily legible in his expression was the faraway look of the refugee, of whom tens of thousands had begun to pour into New York. Though Harry had seen much and suffered some, he had escaped the tragedy that so many had borne and were yet bearing. It was not just the age of the man but what he had endured that drew Harry magnetically and made him deferential. He stared as if waiting for an answer to a question that had not been asked.

The older man saw from the corner of his eye that he was being watched. He turned to Harry as if to say, What do you want? And, without words, the way Harry looked at him told him, so he answered the question that had not been posed. He shrugged. He motioned toward the flames, his left hand flipping at the air in almost the same movement as a hand scattering crumbs for the pigeons. "My whole family," he said. "How could they have this here?"

"Have what?" Harry asked.

The Turk looked his way to verify that Harry truly didn't know, to check Harry's spirit, to see if he were worthy of telling. "This," he said, with a motion to indicate the fire. "It is the apparatus, unmodified, of a crematorium."

"It is?" Harry asked.

"It is."

"Are you sure?"

"I am sure."

"How can they have such a thing in a hotel bar?" Harry asked.

"That, of course, was my question."

"Perhaps they don't know."

"Perhaps they don't," the Turk said. "I came in to escape the rain, and when I saw it...."

"Why have you stayed?" Harry asked. "The rain?"

"The rain is really nothing."

"Then why?"

"I see my child," he said, "my wife, my parents, in the flames. I can't leave them. Of course, they aren't there, but that's the point: in holiness, they are. Oxidation," he said professionally. "In the grave, slow. Here, rapid. In the grave aided by foragers minute and otherwise. Here, aided by, or, rather, I should say, it is pulled along as if by the hand, by the oxidation of methane. It's all the same. The difference is velocity."

"You're a chemist?"

"At one time," the Turk said, "I was a physicist."

"Where?"

"Budapest." He said it in Magyar: *Buda-pesht.*

"I thought you were Hungarian. I didn't guess that you're a physicist."

"*Was.* Physicists have a penchant for philosophy in the abstract, which is a sin. If I were to return to physics, I'd be tempted by that sin. It's the sin that gave rise to the war that took everything. I'm no longer interested in the truth of nature, or any other such cold thing. We're too delicate for that. It won't do us any good." Here, he stopped.

Harry tried to come to his rescue. "What does one do then," he asked, "when one ceases to be a physicist?"

"Work in a restaurant," the Turk said, almost cheerfully. "Not far from here. It's kosher. I know how to do that. I was not religious, but my wife made me observe those things, although we made many exceptions that we were not supposed to have made."

"Like what?" Harry asked, wanting to distract him further, although it could not have been a distraction to have asked him about his previous life.

"In Italy and Dalmatia, eating shellfish. And now I work in a restaurant. For me it seems strange to be among Jews who are alive. It's as if they're ghosts."

"*You* are alive."

"Not really, and not for long, which is as it should be."

"You're a waiter?"

"I wash the dishes. Because I lived in England when I was a child my English is, well, you can see. They wanted me to wait. It would be more money and a lot more pleasant."

"But you have to do penance."

"I have to do penance. And I have to die. But tell me why I have yet to die."

"You keep them alive as long as you live. You're a vessel that must not sink, or they sink with you. And you stay washing dishes because...."

"Because it is holy," the Turk said, finishing Harry's sentence for him. Harry had no need to prod, for the Turk wanted to explain, and did so, not like the professor he once had been, but with conviction and emotion that the world had burned into him. "Souls," he said, "like rays of light, exist in perfect, parallel equality, always. But when for infinitely short a time they pass through the rough and delaying mechanism of life, they separate and disentangle, encountering different obstacles, traveling at different rates, like light refracted by the friction of things in its path. Emerging on the other side, they run together once more, in perfection.

"For the short and difficult span when confounded by matter and time they are made unequal, they try to bind together as they always were and eventually will be. The impulse to do so is called love. The extent to which they succeed is called justice. And the energy lost in the effort is called sacrifice. On the infinite scale of things, this life is to a spark what a spark is to all the time man can imagine, but still, like a sudden rapids or a bend in the river, it is that to which the eye of God may be drawn from time to time out of interest in happenstance." His expression hardened, and then softened a little. "But so what," he said, rising. Pointing to the fire, he added, "That's where I want to go, and I will, and there I'll find peace — but not yet."

In making his way through the tangle of tables and chairs, he touched Harry on the arm. "I didn't mean to burden you. At my age, I have no fire, and can only reflect. I'm sorry to talk so much about myself, except that, and here you have my apologies, I was, of course, talking about more than just myself."

"I know," Harry told him, and they parted.

Here by the fire, half in darkness, the light still dancing, Harry understood that those left behind — the failures and the deformed, the suffering and the dead — are not just equal in soul, but that they are we and we are they. Struggle as we may for distinction, soon enough we fail, and, without exception, follow.

Vanderlyn took the East Side IRT to Grand Central, where he stood in the reduced traffic on the main floor as it ebbed between rush hours. He had calculated that he would have no time for a restaurant, so he bought a pretzel and a celery tonic, remarking to himself that he paid the same price for these as he had in the twenties, and that by this measure the Depression was over. He was most likely the richest man in New York who ate a pretzel lunch while sitting on the Vanderbilt steps.

Grand Central had been the scene of one of his greatest triumphs. At the beginning of the war he had been sent to Camp X in Canada to be trained by the British special services. The final exercise required him to make his way back to New York, saddled with what most people might have considered the disadvantage of having been parachuted — blindfolded — into the wilderness of Ontario, shoeless, bootless, with only reichsmarks in his pocket. A warrant had been issued to the RCMP, and — in perhaps the most challenging part — he was dressed in the uniform of an SS major. Less than two weeks later, attired in a Savile Row suit, shaved, bathed, silk tie, pocket square, and shined shoes, he arrived in Grand Central. Before reporting in, he stopped for oysters. This as much as anything else had caught the attention of Colonel Donovan, who was also Vanderlyn's lawyer, and Vanderlyn was almost instantly packed off to London, with the order simply to do everything he could to win the war. He thought then that he would never return home. Instead, the one who never returned was his son and only child. At that point, Vanderlyn despaired. Psychiatrists were becoming the vogue, and he was urged to consult them for his own good. "I'd be happy to," he had said, "if they can bring back the dead."

Sutherland, Dwight, so white-shoe that its partners could walk in the snow and not leave tracks, was on three rosewood-paneled floors of 30 Rockefeller Plaza, so high that it had an internal, windowless conference room for the use of clients who feared heights. The city spread out on all the firm's comfortable sides, glinting magnificently in silver and gray. Clouds rushed in on Atlantic air, light ricocheted in blinding incandescence from streets and avenues that shone like burning filaments, and all was quiet except for the muted whistling of the wind.

Vanderlyn never had to wait long in the waiting room and Sutherland always came out to greet him. They had no need of saying anything, as they had been acquainted since their chief excitement was catching tadpoles. Sutherland's huge office was beautifully and sparsely furnished, and from his windows, even while sitting in a visitor's chair, it was possible to see the Ramapos to the west, a lightship anchored off Sandy Hook directly south, and the disappearing plains of Long Island to the east. Aircraft rose from Idlewild as delicately as house flies in a squall, flashing like mica as they banked to set their course.

"We're going to have to bill you, you know," Sutherland said. "I don't like to do that. Actually, I do, but you could have just come to my house and it wouldn't have cost a cent."

Vanderlyn literally waved away the cost. "I want to change my will."

"That's relatively easy assuming that you don't want to alter the nature of the trusts or do anything for which we would have to petition the court. I assume you're not cutting out Elyssa. I won't do that."

"Elyssa is my wife and your sister. What do *you* think?"

"It would be a tragedy all around."

"It's a change for after her death."

"What happened? Did the chairman of an institution you're going to endow tell you to fuck off?"

Vanderlyn said, "I wish they had the courage, but they're too good at sucking up. Maybe sometimes they go out on the beach and try to scream the truth into the wind, but I'll bet they can't."

"Too many wealthy dames at the beach. Depending on which beach. I'm not going to tell you," Sutherland said, "as I've told you all our lives, not to be impulsive. We're too old for that now, and you are impulsive. As long as Elyssa is protected, it doesn't matter to me if you leave your money to the circus. Is it the circus?"

Vanderlyn shook his head dismissively.

"I do remind you, however, that soon after we met you told me that. . . ."

Vanderlyn knew exactly what Sutherland was about to say.

"You would cut off your right arm. . . ."

"Left. I was hedging, even then."

"For five chocolate bars and twenty minutes alone with a naked girl."

"I would have. I think I might now."

"All you had to do was wait. That's my point."

"I'm too old to wait." Vanderlyn pointed to the Rolodex on the credenza behind Sutherland's desk. "When did you get that?" he asked.

"I don't know, a long time ago."

"Look at it."

"Look at it?"

"Yes."

Sutherland looked at it. It was, as he well knew, heavy with hundreds of cards.

"What percentage of the people on that are dead?"

Thinking for a moment, Sutherland made a calculation that he did not accomplish with numbers. "Half. Maybe more. When they die, I can't take them off the wheel. It would be horrible just to toss them in the wastebasket."

"I'm much better at making decisions now than I was when we were nine, and I've decided."

"All right." Sutherland took out a legal pad and picked up a pen. "Shoot." He was much like Vanderlyn — fit, self-contained, modest, thoughtful, all of which could be read in his bearing and in his face.

"I don't want to leave what I have to institutions, Gibb. I know it would help charity and art, and a lot of people one way or another, but I do that from income anyway, and so can my heirs. All things — everything material — are useless unless they're fed into the fire of the living. My son is gone, and he won't be honored by having his name on a building. That's not my idea of how it should be."

Sutherland listened attentively, having not yet made a note.

"I've discovered of late . . . this morning . . . that perhaps the greatest pleasure and relief in life, and I know this may sound strange, is to trust your heirs, and the heirs of your heirs, in a future you cannot and will not know.

"When Charlie was a kid, we. . . ." Vanderlyn stumbled, but, with resolution, went on. "We fought a lot. I thought that sometime in his twenties it would be over, as it was with my father and me, but he never got there. Even so, even at the worst of it, I saw in him a man as steady and as good as any I've ever seen. You trust in that. You cast your bread upon the waters, and in so doing, in expressing confidence in those who follow, you give them the greatest gift, and the gift you get in return is even greater."

Sutherland agreed, but he still hadn't made a note.

"So the institutions will have to wait. I read biographies now, Gibb. In a life, or a portion of a life illuminated, there's a fullness and a balance that no theory or abstraction can match. Why do people waste so much time on abstraction? The life that is given to us, that we play out, is something that you cannot any more grasp with systems and ideas than you can tame an elephant with a tweezers."

"What about powerful ideas, Jim? The atomic bomb, gravity, the Magna Carta, and all that?"

"Stabbing the universe with a needle."

"And a life? What's bigger about a life?"

"All the great forces working in miniature, perfectly. That's where to look. That's why I want everything to go to living flesh and blood. Specifically, to someone who I know is courageous, honorable, faithful, charitable, and has no expectation of me in this regard. To someone who reached out to help me when to him and everyone else in the world I was the least among us."

"In the war?"

"After the war."

"Is he married?"

"Yes."

"Children?"

"I'm pretty sure not."

"Do you want his future children to inherit, *per stirpes,* or some other arrangement?"

"Yes, his children. I'm not doing this halfway."

"The cousins will fight it."

"He's semi-criminal, and his son is worse. Make it shell-proof."

"That I can do." Sutherland tossed the pad onto his desk, having written nothing on it. "If it's all for after Elyssa is deceased, the terms of the trusts are the same, and there's no messing with the inventory, the only things we have to do really are some typing and signing. I won't have to blow off U.S. Steel this afternoon, though God knows they deserve it. They're real pricks, you know. Come back before the close of business and we'll have everything ready, just like a dry cleaner's." He thought this was amusing, and he picked up the pad and opened his pen yet again. "Give me the name, accurately spelled, and an address."

"I don't remember his address, but I can find out. I'll do that."

"Then come back at" — Sutherland lifted his wrist to look at his watch — "five." He positioned the pen. "What's the name? And what's that?"

Beneath Vanderlyn's arm was the roll of canvas that he had carried all the way from Wall Street, hardly giving it a thought. "It's a garment bag," he said. "I'm going to pick up a jacket that's being mended."

"Don't you send someone?"

"No, it's something I attend to myself." He turned and began to leave.

"Jim? The name?"

When Vanderlyn replied, naming his heir, it was a little like getting his son back, and he stopped his turn, because he did not want even his friend of such long duration to see how this affected him. Sutherland's pen moved smoothly over the legal pad, in the quiet of his office except for the wind hissing past the windows as it moved across the world in great currents as clear and cold as ether.

# 45

## CATHERINE RISING

BEFORE HARRY SAW Eugenia Eba in the arcade, and Vanderlyn recast his will, and four pathfinders converged on the warehouse in Newark, Catherine awoke in her childhood room. The East River was shrouded in gray, and pigeons cooed on the terrace. She felt thrown back in time as surely as if someone had lifted a tone arm in the midst of a song and set it upon the smooth and soundless rim of the record. Though she had great affection for times past, to relive them would be the saddest thing, if only because she would know exactly the way they would end.

But soon, in an almost painfully hot shower, with the water singing through the taps, she returned to practical matters. The night before, after an unusually strong performance at the beginning of the week, she had faltered, and was unsure that she could get back. Everything in this regard had always come naturally, with labor merely to confirm it. Whence it arose she did not know, and now as things that had always seemed effortless collided in chaos she had no access to their origins for repair. It had happened in the theater not twelve hours before.

First, she had hurriedly put on her costume in such a way that it ripped and had to be patched together with safety pins and tape. Whatever had distracted her grew in strength until it seized her entirely. In the dressing room, after her dress had been jury-rigged, she knocked over a bottle of rubbing alcohol, which cracked the glass top of her makeup table. The corridors refused to impart the customary momentum that enabled her to burst out onto the stage as if she really had come from the interior of a railroad station into the light and cacophony of New York. Instead of traveling them like someone riding down a flume, she was hypnotized and held back by the friction of what she saw—a folded fire hose in a glass box, electrical switches, a bucket of sand for cigarettes, a statement from the New York State Department of Labor.

In the opening, which she had never done other than masterfully, she proved slow and uninterested, as if she were not her character but only someone playing it. Unable to convince herself of where she was supposed to be, her singing was uninspired. The other actors knew, the chorus knew, the musicians and of course the audience knew. They almost stopped breathing. George, who was like a horse that has been broken and gratefully draws the plough, watched from the wings in pained distress. How could Catherine fall? How could she fail?

After her last song, she left the theater, so upset that she neglected to take off her costume or remove her makeup. She explained to the puzzled guard at the stage door that she would have the dress fixed the next day, since she would have to be in it anyway while it was pinned. He didn't know what she was talking about, but he agreed that it was a sensible idea. The taxi that picked her up had the midperformance luxury of gliding across town on empty streets before intermission, when the crowds drinking gin and tonics or chilled orange juice would spill from sidewalks lit by a hundred thousand bulbs onto streets as black as ebony. She wept in the cab. Because she was in a ripped dress and heavy makeup, the taxi driver was reluctant to offer comfort, seeing that what ailed her was too complex to fathom on a crosstown ride.

In the morning, simultaneously as weak and as strong as someone emerging from an illness, she left the house, carrying the dress in paper wrapping, and an umbrella for the intermittent squalls. One of her mother's dressmakers, on First Avenue, was pressed into emergency service. The woman was an expert, and for her it was nothing. After pinning it, she told Catherine it would take no more than an hour. Catherine waited, trying to read a magazine, staring out at traffic as if her heart were broken, occasionally checking her watch. She would drop the repaired costume at the theater, have lunch, go to a doctor's appointment, return home to rest, and then go back to the theater again, where, while Harry did something that not long before she would not have dreamed of, she would sing to redeem herself.

Catherine had never arrived so early except during the period when they were rehearsing and the theater was rented to them on the condition that each day they vacate promptly in favor of the real play. She remembered how deferential she and the rest of the cast had been when encountering anyone associated with the ongoing production, even though it was a play about physics. Their deference was that of the aspiring to the successful, the untried to the tested, the amateur to the professional, the young to the old, and even the short to the tall, the poor to the rich, sometimes the rich to the poor, and just about everyone to a cop.

Now she discovered that there was another aspiring production making use of the theater during the day, which Sidney had not bothered to mention. As she passed its hopeful cast, they slightly lowered their eyes. They admired and envied her. And, yet, when she came to her dressing room, closed the door, and felt the thunder of the chorus line pounding the floor with their taps, and the brass piercing the darkness like a golden ray, she envied them, for as they were rising all the life in rising was theirs. For them, nothing was certain, and she, who had a role, had by definition begun to fade. As she unwrapped her dress and placed it on its hanger, the music from above saturating through the boards, she took an irrevocable step in growing up, recognizing and embracing the duty to step aside for those who follow, as others had stepped aside for her.

She looked at the little watch that no one but a hawk could see well, and suspected that the hands were somewhere close to noon. Then she clicked shut her door and was halfway down the corridor on her way to lunch when suddenly she stopped. She didn't know why, but she stood in place, tapping her right foot to the music raining down from above. She hadn't forgotten her umbrella, which she held in both hands. She had intended to leave the dress behind: it wasn't that. Then she realized. On the makeup table, on the newly cracked glass, was something that had briefly caught her eye for being out of place. Whatever it was it couldn't have been important, and anyway she would see it when she returned in the evening.

She started forward, but then stopped and turned around. "Don't stoop when you turn," she heard from long ago. A choreographer had said, "Just because you're dancing doesn't mean you have to make yourself small. Dance tall." When she switched on the light in the dressing room she saw a Western Union telegram wedged into the crack of the glass. In show business, they called it a cable, and in no business was it ever ignored, if only because it was the messenger of death, birth, windfalls, and disappointments.

Without closing the door behind her she walked to the makeup table, grabbed the telegram, threw down her purse and umbrella, and opened the envelope as if she were starving and it was the wrapper of a Swiss chocolate bar. She had heard from her father and mother that morning: it was not likely about them. It could not have been from or about Harry. Whatever might happen, Harry would not announce it in a telegram. And the war was over.

On the white tape glued to yellow paper were her stage name— Catherine Sedley—and her address at the theater. The message was short: WOULD LIKE TO SEE YOU AT YOUR CONVENIENCE STOP PLEASE CALL PL 9 2472 STOP MIKE BECK. She stared at the message written on what looked like the name tapes on her tennis whites at camp. The Beck Organization—which at any one time had half a dozen shows on Broadway—was four blocks away, and they had sent a telegram. Her father had told her of how, once, when he was having lunch with a producer (who, like all producers, wanted to borrow money), the producer had called for a telephone and dictated a cable to be sent to a colleague whom he could clearly see at another table across the room. Ten minutes later, a Western Union messenger had appeared, handed the cable to a waiter, and the waiter had brought it to a bald man with a pipe—as opposed to thirty or forty bald men with cigars. Opening it immediately and reading it gravely, the bald man with a pipe had called for a telephone. Ten minutes after that, Billy's lunch companion ripped open a yellow envelope and threw the cable down in front of him. When Billy picked it up, he read: NONE OF YOUR F-----G BUSINESS STOP MEL. So it was in show business.

She put the telegram in her pocket and left for lunch. Only when she was on the sidewalk did she remember to call the Beck Organization. Once again, they asked to see her, and would not say why. "I can come late this afternoon," she said, adding unnecessarily, "I have a doctor's appointment."

The secretary left the line and returned a minute later. "Mr. Beck will be delighted to see you then. What time?"

"Four?"

"We look forward to it."

Other productions had tried to raid everyone in the cast except Catherine. She often thought that this would be her last part, and was reconciled to it. But many different parts on the lower rungs were hard to fill well, so perhaps her time had come. She worried that her father had pulled strings to get Mike Beck himself to call her. Every father wants the best for his daughter, but it was not likely to work out that way if now he had done what before he had only been accused of doing.

Already at noon, Times Square, which made night day and day night, was beginning its tawdry and energetic celebrations. Catherine had always wondered who it was who went to nightclubs in the daytime. Whoever they were, there were enough of them to keep clubs and bars full at all hours. From a dozen establishments came the sounds of saxophones, drums, and dancing. Boys who should have been in school and were too young to go inside stood in small groups at the doorways of such places, straining for a glimpse of strippers, frightened that someone they knew might see them. To camouflage themselves should their headmasters or priests pass by, they pretended to be tying their shoes, or reading—by happenstance, just beyond the entrance of the club featuring Miss Gloria Seins and Her Nude Mesopotamian Snake Dance—the *Christian Science Monitor*.

Spilling out onto the street, music inundated the barkers, bouncers, and truants. The doors to these places were like valves that sprayed out rays of light and flashes of sequins, and the colors within — purple, mauve, metallic silver and gold, lipstick red, ultraviolet, black velvet — were largely unnatural and unfailingly exciting.

Catherine hesitated at one of the doorways. The barker/bouncer was dumbfounded. As she was neither a potential victim, customer, cop, nor kid, he had no tools in his kit with which to deal with her. Her tailoring, bearing, and self-possession were entirely out of place in his world. Inside, an orchestra played as if it were Saturday night. Except for the bartender and a skinny sailor trying to keep up with the other dancers, everyone in the place, and the man at the door, was colored. Heretofore, they would have been confined to Harlem, but the war had brought them downtown. Women with immensely long legs were dancing to the blasts of trumpets, drums, and saxes. They wore flower-petal-like dresses, upside-down yellow roses that, like skaters' costumes, stopped at the top of the thigh.

Thousands of sequins were dashed in the strong lights that shone upon the dancers and musicians. A mirrored ball revolved like a water wheel pushed by light. This was a portal to the south, which suddenly, in New York, had pushed up like a daffodil. It seemed that they were celebrating something that, though yet to come, would come unstoppably; something that, in truth, was already halfway there. In her childhood Catherine had been in the presence of many people who had in their own childhood been slaves. The climb out was slow, but it was steady.

"This is new," she said to the doorkeeper, who had begun to get nervous.

Relieved that she had spoken, but still puzzled, he said, "Yes, Miss, this *is* new."

She leaned slightly toward him and asked, "Do you have to be Irish to go in?"

He thought this was rather funny, and as she left he smiled at her and gave a thumbs-up. The women were still dancing, no more tired than locomotives running across the flatlands early in the evening, lights shining onto the straight track ahead.

Having added the appointment at the Beck Organization, about which she tried not to think, Catherine had to manage her time very closely. She had half an hour for lunch before arriving at the doctor's office on Park in the low Seventies. After her annual checkup, he had called her back, which she hadn't mentioned to Harry or her parents, being too young to think that anything might be seriously wrong. She thought less about this, in fact, than what kind of part might be offered to her—if indeed it were—by Mike Beck, and less even than about where she might eat. She decided on a Schrafft's that she knew was on Madison somewhere in the high Fifties: she would find it.

The food would be light, the service fast, and no one would recognize her. It was not that she was ashamed of herself, but that she knew that many servile people of the upper class, with whom she was loosely acquainted, and who took their direction faithfully from newspapers whose truth and wisdom they did not doubt or ever question, might believe that she should be ashamed of herself. It happened often enough and she hated the way they enjoyed it. They would be at various restaurants and clubs that were definitely not Schrafft's, so she went in and sat safely at the counter.

The trick of the place was that it was almost luxurious and neither expensive nor pretentious. Perhaps it was the name, which always made her think of the sound water makes as it flows through a weir. Perhaps it was the lighting, or the way they somehow muted sounds, unlike in most restaurants, where sound was sharp and aggressive. Here it was a cross between a low murmur and the sibilance of wind and water, with sometimes the sparkling clink of silverware or glass. The food was quite acceptable, no more, no less, and always the same. She did not have to look at the menu, for she always had a BLT and a chocolate milkshake, which, this time, came at her before she finished ordering it. She asked the waitress how this could have happened.

The waitress pulled out her pad, studied it, and seized one end of Catherine's oval platter. Catherine grabbed the other end with her left hand, and half the sandwich in her right. "What are you doing?" she protested. She was tired of people taking, assuming, and attacking, just tired of it, and she wasn't going to let it happen anymore.

"It's someone else's. I gave it to you by mistake."

"What are you going to do, take it back?" Catherine asked.

"It's not yours."

Catherine took a large bite out of the sandwich and said, "Now it is."

The waitress went for the milkshake, into which, after letting go of the plate post-conquest, Catherine stuck her left index finger. The waitress took it anyway. "They won't know," she said.

"I'll tell them," Catherine told her.

"You wouldn't."

"I will, and your manager, too."

"Fuck you," the waitress said quietly, and slammed down the milkshake so that a bit of it flew out of the glass.

"Dream about your tip," Catherine commanded.

"People don't tip at the counter."

"*I* do."

"I wouldn't ever come back here if I was you," the waitress said.

Catherine was preternaturally collected. "Because I don't like eating food that has been touched by a monkey, I'll wait until you're dead."

"Fuck you."

"You said that."

The waitress went to the other side of the horseshoe-shaped counter and traded places with another waitress, who upon taking her station asked Catherine, "Is everything all right?"

"Everything's fine," Catherine said.

By this time, two women had sat down on either side of Catherine and were having a conversation behind her back, which for her was a very strange feeling. She asked the one on her left if she would like to exchange seats (the stools had backs). "Oh no, deah. We can stretch awah back muscles. It's bettah than going to a chiropractah."

"Okay," Catherine said.

As she ate her sandwich and drank her milkshake she could not avoid hearing their conversation.

"She takes twice as lawng to type the wholesale invoices as Oiy do, and she gets a raise!"

"She's new."

"So whoiy should she get a raise?"

"Becawse, she's new. It was too low to begin with. Then it'll stay, like ahwas. I know it'll stay fa-evah."

"That my poynt, Dawris. That's what Oiy'm saying. Nothing evah happens. It used to be that it did, in the olden days, but not now."

"But the waugh. Theah was a waugh!" She looked at her friend in astonishment.

"Dawris, let me clue you in. The waugh's ovah. Like Oiy told ya, nothing evah happens."

Catherine finished her milkshake, and like all courageous people, made a huge noise with the straw as she pulled in the very last of it.

She hated doctors' offices, for what they looked like, how they smelled, how they sounded, and Park Avenue had as many as there were berries on a holly. In suites of rooms where once families had lived, now the floors were covered with coarse gray carpeting or black linoleum, the moldings laced with the thin lines of indelible soot that embed themselves forever in New York paint even after it has dried. And when the heat was on, doctors' offices were terribly dry. No one took showers there, washed dishes, or boiled water for spaghetti, so the air was never moistened except by the escape of alcohol from sterilization trays.

Where once there had been libraries, newspapers, drawers full of fliers and letters, now there were overthumbed copies of *National Geographic, Life, Time, Look,* the *Saturday Evening Post, and Gynecological Abstracts*. In what had been bedrooms, studies, and dining rooms, lovemaking, sleep, study, and family dinners were banished in favor of unpleasant and painful examinations for which one had to pay. The rooms held Prussian-looking white cabinets with glass fronts through which one could see kidney-shaped vessels of white enamel or stainless steel, in which rested sharp and unbending instruments — scalpels, probes, calipers, and spreaders. The furniture was born on the banks of the river Styx, with stirrups, and with rolls of white kraft that, for reasons of sanitation, extended over it like Brobdingnagian toilet paper. And on the walls were very bad oils or watercolors, which sometimes could not compete aesthetically with the pink and yellow renderings of viscera staring out from just above a drug company calendar.

Why did she have to come back? She had been through the indignity of putting her feet in the stirrups and wanted to be done with it for at least another year, when she would read about the Ubangis yet again in *National Geographic*. She already knew that despite the soothing light and bubbles in the water, the fish tank was bereft of fish. "The doctor will see you now...."

The appointment had been quick and her parents' house was close enough that she went there to rest before going to see Mike Beck. No one was home, not even the servants, who had their day off. No longer shocked, with neither a welling up of tears nor fairly heavy breathing, she climbed the stairs to her room, closed the door behind her, and sat where she had sat as a child and a girl, though at the beginning the furniture and other things had been different. She remembered her crib in the nursery before she moved upstairs. She remembered using her weight to rattle the sides by holding the rail with both hands and pulling and pushing, pulling and pushing. She remembered the toys, the dolls, the pictures of penguins, and then horses. The things of childhood were all gone except for a few books she could not part with, and one doll, whom she loved.

At some point the furniture and paintings, too, would go and the room would be empty, awaiting someone else. Although Billy swam in high surf, could walk for twenty miles, and was as strong as a man half his age, he often didn't remember things that had happened only a short time before, and Catherine sometimes found him, in the middle of the afternoon, sleeping upright in a chair, a book or newspaper splayed on the floor where it had been dropped. His laugh had changed. It was an old man's laugh now, awkward, almost insincere, as if he were trying to pretend that he could still laugh. At least half his friends and contemporaries were dead, and in East Hampton on the most glorious days, when Catherine and Harry never stopped moving in the waves or on the sand, he now sat quietly and looked out to sea as if a fleet were passing in review, even if nothing was there but a fine blue emptiness and a beckoning horizon.

Evelyn had no problems with memory, and her friends were mostly alive and would live forever, as dowagers tend to do. But she grew increasingly delicate. Handsome, commanding, and still beautiful, she seemed at times as fragile as a chrysalis. She now walked in smaller steps, and instead of rushing down the stairs, like Catherine incapable of losing her balance, she held the banister every time and moved deliberately. And although she kept up to some degree with fashion as the garnishing ornament of her timeless dress, it was more and more the fashion of the previous decades, as with every advancing year she earned the privilege of paying no attention to the present.

Catherine now felt this in herself. That is, being content as the world passed by, without the urge to join in. The house was empty when she left, and it would eventually pass to others as generations stood and fell. Until this very day she had not known how wonderful, steady, and implacable the rhythm of this was, how comforting, how it made sense of everything, and how it quieted one's fears.

Though she knew her appointment was with Mike Beck himself, she was somewhat taken aback to be ushered into his office. She was used to the eminent and the powerful at her parents' dinner table, yet she was still nervous, for whatever was intended and however it had come about, here she would be judged solely on her own merits.

Everyone knew that Mike Beck was blind, but it was strange to see a man with hardly any hair, dark glasses, and a cane, his head cocked as if he were staring at the joint between the ceiling and the wall. It had something to do with hearing, or another sense not known. "Come in," he said. "You know, I'm blind, so don't hesitate to speak. I can't see your reactions but I can hear them, and I'm neither deaf nor a foreigner, so you don't have to shout or carefully enunciate."

"People often do," his secretary, a man, told Catherine.

"And you are?" Mike Beck asked. "I can't see you."

"Catherine." That she said only her first name was lovely. If she hadn't had him already, she had him right there. He smiled when he heard the quality of her voice.

"Shall we call you Miss Sedley or Miss Hale?"

"My stage name is Sedley, my maiden name is Hale, and my married name is Copeland," she said. "Frankly, I don't know who the hell I am. Just call me Catherine."

"And on the billing? You're not a porpoise or circus bear."

"Am I hired?"

"Not yet. But if you are . . . ?"

She thought, and, under her breath, tried out her names. "Catherine Sedley, Catherine Thomas Hale, Catherine Copeland." She decided. "I like Catherine Copeland, and I think people would remember it."

"It's a beautiful name," Beck said. "They're all beautiful names."

"Is there a part available?" Catherine asked.

"There is a part," Beck told her, "in a new musical." When he named the composer and the lyricist their magic enveloped the room. They had never failed. Even their least was better than others' best, although the critics compared them only to themselves, which was fair but misleading. "We hope it will be the kind of show that can run for ten years, clean up on the road, and then go into revival and high school productions forever. What you're in now is terrific, but not like this. The theater will be twice as big—we own it, and we've booked it—and the ticket prices much higher. If we hit, it'll sell a million phonograph records and there'll be a movie. Of course, it could close on the first night. It's that danger that makes this business what it is. You have the part if you want it."

"Without audition?"

"We've heard you sing."

"You have?"

"Of course. We go to all the plays. Among other things, it's deductible. Why pay for an empty audition hall when you can audition people in full costume and makeup, with an orchestra, lights, sets, and a packed theater?"

"I have the part?" she asked, somewhat amazed, unconcerned about money, because she had never been concerned about money.

"We very much want you to take it. Who's your agent? We couldn't find out."

"I don't have an agent."

"You should get one, *after* you appear for us."

"I can't accept," she said. "There's something I have to tell you. It's very private. I haven't even had a chance to tell my husband, because I won't see him until tomorrow."

"What?" Beck asked. "You don't have to tell me."

"I'm pregnant." She was quite rattled. Too many things were coming at once. "I never thought of a Jewish name," she said, to no one in particular, as if she were talking to the air. And then, apologetically to Mike Beck, "My husband is Jewish." She dipped her head and brought it up again, as if breaking the surface. "I'm Jewish, too," she said as if she had just found out. She looked amazed.

"Since when is Catherine Thomas Hale Jewish?" Beck asked.

"Since I was born, but I didn't know."

"You didn't know?"

"I didn't."

"Well, you got me," said Mike Beck. "Name the baby anything you want. My name used to be Meyer Beckerman, and now I'm Mike Beck. I could have been George Washington if the judge had been a little more flexible."

"I can't take the part," Catherine explained, "unless it's a sort of constantly changing part in which the character gets pregnant and then has her baby and then isn't pregnant anymore. That's probably not what it is, is it, and I doubt that you can write it in."

"It's really not a problem."

She found that hard to believe.

"It isn't. I'll tell you why. We have a spectacular cast. It could be a runaway. But they're all such big stars that they're committed, just as you are."

"I have no contract," she interrupted.

"They do. The earliest we can begin rehearsals is at the end of next year, when, unless you're an elephant, your baby will already be crawling. And as far as being with a new baby, Wednesdays and Saturdays would be difficult but every other day of the week you can be with him all day long until eight."

"I see."

"I'm sorry," Beck said. "Would you like something to drink? Tea? Coffee?"

"No, thank you. I don't have to try out?"

"I've heard you sing." He shook his head, smiling. "You don't have to try out. We don't manufacture drugs or bomb sights. It's all in the heart, and we know what we have to know in about two seconds."

"So it's a singing part? I have a song?"

"Miss Hale," Mike Beck said. "Mrs. Copeland. Miss Sedley, whoever you are or want to be, I've been told that you are very beautiful, that although you don't have the wide planes of face that make stars of some, men find it difficult to take their eyes off you. That's good."

"If you believe it," she said. He couldn't see that she blushed.

"I believe it. I have it on good authority." Now his secretary blushed, but Catherine wasn't looking at him. "I do. But here I must confess that I myself went to hear you sing—seven times. The first time, I didn't know who you were or anything about your part. Then I heard you, and I returned again, and again."

"But the reviews...."

"Victor Marrow screwed you."

"I know," Catherine said. The double meaning echoed within her. And then she realized, and she said, "How do *you* know?"

"You may not know in full detail," the secretary said, adding to her amazement.

"You do?" she asked.

"Yes, we do," Mike Beck said.

"How is that?" It hardly seemed possible.

"Since it concerns you, I'll tell you. But since it concerns us, I have to ask you not to mention it to anyone — anyone — until it all comes out, as it will."

Mentally excepting Harry from the prohibition, Catherine shifted in her chair, leaned forward a little, and smiled in a way that said, "I'm fascinated. What could this be? But I'm slightly wary." This expression was conveyed in her eyes. Harry loved it so much that he would think of it when he was riding in the subway or sitting at his desk, and in recalling it he would feel much the same as when, wounded, he felt the first strong shot of morphine. "Tell me," she said, only because Mike Beck could not see what Harry so loved. But the same quality was in her voice, and this he perceived exactly.

Mike Beck said, "Start with a professor at Wharton. He's a Saltonstall. You know the Saltonstalls?"

"Some of them," she replied.

"I don't mean personally. You know them personally?"

"A few."

"Do you know *him*?"

"A professor at Wharton? No."

"Anyway, a New York paper, which I know you know, as do we all, hired this guy to write a major piece to explain the Bretton Woods agreements to the general public. During the war, no one was interested. But now that whatever they decided there is beginning to shape the economies of the world, people are, but no one can understand it, and no one ever will, really."

"Except economists," Catherine interrupted.

"No. Economists are paid to pretend they understand such things so that people will think the world isn't riding a wild horse, when in fact it is. And, okay, maybe a few actually do understand it, but I don't."

"I was joking, Mr. Beck. I grew up with economists."

"Oh. Anyway, this guy was supposed to be one of the ones who really did understand. He wrote his article and sent it in. They could make neither hide nor hair of it, so they brought him up here and put him in a hotel, with instructions to rewrite it so it would be clearer.

"He struggled to do so all night, walked into their offices in the morning, and gave them a revised piece, words counted to the exact length. 'What the hell is this?' says the editor. 'Did you write this with a quill?' The guy had eighteenth-century handwriting. 'You gotta type it,' the editor tells him.

"He's a Saltonstall, he doesn't type, but he's got honor, so he assents without protest, swallowing the indignity. What do they do? They take him to the Week in Review section, which works on a different schedule because it comes out on Sunday, and on the day he was there it was completely deserted. They set him up with a typewriter, at which he pecks away. But he gets tired after a few hours and falls asleep in his chair. No lights. Dusk. He's resting against a glass partition, like a passenger on a train.

"He awakens to a telephone conversation taking place on the other side of the partition, and although he can hear only one party, what's going on is quite obvious even to an economics professor. The guy on the other side, who thinks the whole place is empty, is whispering nonetheless, low. But it goes right through the wall. The desk lamp on the other side is burning, and the Wharton professor sees the silhouette moving in the wavy glass.

"It's the theater critic, taking instructions. Protesting that he can't do exactly what they tell him, but agreeing to come close, and asking for more money. There are organizations that are our competitors. On the other end of the line was one of them.

"The next day, literally, the professor reads this guy's review of our just-opened show and recognizes the phrases he heard the evening before. We were panned. It cost us hundreds of thousands of dollars, and for the playwright and actors it was heartbreak and misery. He understood this, so he came to us."

Catherine was speechless at the unbidden workings of justice.

"We knew this guy had been biased against us: Malan — oops, I shouldn't have said it."

It was as if lightning had struck Catherine. His was the most influential review of her show, in which all had been praised but her.

"Keep it under your hat. It'll come out.

"We didn't know what to do," he continued. "It was the professor's word against Malan's, and although in Boston Malan wouldn't have stood a chance, this is New York, where most of the eight million people would think a Saltonstall is a place where you keep a horse, or some sort of machine used in the manufacture of pretzels. We really didn't know how to approach this.

"My wife solved the problem. She said, It's simple, bring in Malan's wife. We did. It turns out she's what we call, forgive me, a society dame."

"I know," said Catherine. "That's what I'm supposed to be when I grow up."

"I guess so, but it's up to you."

"It is. And I see that woman sometimes at the Colony Club. I mean, I pass her. I've never met her. My mother probably has."

"It turns out that her family thinks of Malan the way you might think of a particle of food that gets stuck between your teeth. He was taking money because he wanted to impress them. Of course, he couldn't do that, no matter what. They think show business is for the Irish and Jews, who, they think, are lower than apes. She doesn't think that, but they do. He's Irish for Chrissake, Catholic. He's drinking as well. Their marriage is almost finished, but she loves him, so when we told her she said, really and truly, 'You wait here, and I'll be back in ten minutes.' She meant business, this dame. As she saw it, she was saving the honor of her family, her children, her name, herself.

"Carmichael . . . ," Mike Beck went on.

"I'm Carmichael," the secretary said, giving a little bow to Catherine, at whom he had been trying not to stare.

". . . was perspicacious enough to get our lawyers here, because he guessed what was coming. The paper's around the corner, but she had to fish him out from Sardi's, where he had evidently had double his normal overage of alcohol. That was lucky for us. He was teary and afraid, and by the time he was ready to give the full account, we had lawyers, a stenographer, and witnesses in the conference room.

"He kept saying, 'It's like an execution! My career! My career!' And every time he would say that, his wife would say, 'Shut up, Irish shitbird! This is America and this is New York. Nothing can ruin a career, because no one cares about anything that anyone else does, and no one remembers anything, and no one has standards anymore.' And he would say, 'But Nancy . . . ,' and she would say, 'You just tell the truth, you stupid bastard, and the truth will set you free — or I will.'

"It was dramatic. He's Catholic, so he confessed like a pro. Trained to do it. The drinking, the womanizing, everything. Including that he took five hundred dollars from Victor Marrow after Victor Marrow tried and failed to persuade his editor to get him to pan *you*. In fact, he wanted a thousand to pan you — a man of principles — but Victor settled for five hundred if he would just leave you out.

"When Victor and he met for payment, overlooking the ice-skating rink at Rockefeller Center, Victor told him that he liked the idea of just ignoring you, and had adapted it for the other critics and editors, though Malan was the first one he went to. Neat, huh? And we've got it all down. With witnesses. Notarized."

"But it's his word against Victor's," Catherine said.

"Nope. Like the royalty he is, Victor doesn't carry cash." Catherine smiled. She knew this, and foresaw what was coming. "He wrote Malan a check. He actually noted on it what it was for, which numbs me, I'll tell you. Malan, being a drunk, neglected to cash it. We've got the check. What a scandal," Mike Beck said, leaning back in his chair. "We're going to make it the publicity narrative of the opening. It will set the newspapers back on their ass. The only way you can push those behemoths, to the extent you can, is not to sue them but to embarrass them. It will shame Victor Marrow and damage Willie Marrow's company and standing with the press. And it will redeem you, Miss, because you deserve it, and it's the kind of story the public loves. They'll come to hear you because you've been wronged, and then, when they do hear you, they'll keep coming for the rest of your life."

"So I do have a song," she said.

Mike Beck and his secretary, Carmichael, were moved by the modesty of her expectations. As gently as if he were telling her that someone she thought had died was in fact alive in the next room, Mike Beck said, "Miss Hale, Mrs. Copeland, I've never heard a better singer, and indeed you have a song. You have more than one song. Catherine, I apologize. I haven't been clear. I'm offering you the lead."

Shaken, she could hardly believe she had heard correctly. "How could that be? You said there were big stars."

"Yes," he said. "The royalty of Broadway." He named them. "Big egos. Big salaries. They'll draw everyone in during the advance ticket sales, and the critics will come to see them, although they'll wonder why you have top billing. Then, after the opening, they'll know.

"We're not going to pay you what we're going to have to pay you next time. We've got one free ride. Then you'll break us."

"I don't care about money."

"I know. And I know another thing. I've been listening to singers since — if you can believe it — the eighteen seventies. I was a kid, but my mother was a costumer, and by the time I was ten I was an old hand in the theater. I've heard Caruso, Nellie Melba, Jenny Lind. Very few people alive today have heard Jenny Lind. Now, don't let this go to your head. I don't think anyone will ever equal her — except maybe you. You don't have her range, you never will, but your voice is as beautiful. It isn't mature yet, but when that happens I think you'll probably leave the musical theater and go to opera.

"It's not just that you don't have to do any acting, because nobody believes the acting in opera anyway, but that as powerful as a musical can be, there's something much higher, almost ravishing, about the great operas. In my case I went blind before I could really see it, but in general you learn it when your heart is broken. You should stay in the theater, Catherine, as long as you can. It's your youth. Only later, as you grow older in the world, will you see light in darkness, and that's the most beautiful thing, the saddest thing."

It was as if her future had been laid out for her by an oracle, and it seemed so real that her heart began to pound.

He brought her back. "But don't think about that now. You've got a lot of work to do."

"The composer? And the lyricist?" she asked. "Don't they have to approve?"

"They approve. They've heard you. I brought them with me several times."

"They were in the audience? If I had known...."

"Don't be ridiculous. Here's a trick I learned when I was younger than you and I could see. From the beginning, from the first dress rehearsal, even before, as soon as you're blinded by the light and the theater goes black" — he tapped the bridge of his glasses — "convince yourself early on that in the audience are the Pope, the president, the king of England, William Shakespeare, Helen Hayes, Enrico Caruso, Archimedes, Abraham Lincoln, and, not least, your parents. If you get used to this before opening night you'll never have stage fright, and when the curtain goes up you'll rush out there eager to begin, because all those guys and Helen Hayes and your mother will be like old friends, and you'll want to sing for them as you've done for months."

"Oh," she said. It was a rather long *oh*.

"You have the part if you want it. The lead."

Trying not to cry, she was barely succeeding. With a voice that despite all its training she could not keep from trembling, she said, "That's because nothing ever happens."

"Is that a yes?" Mike Beck asked.

She closed her eyes and nodded her assent. The secretary said, "It's a yes, Mr. Beck." It was a yes, but she was frightened, frightened for herself, frightened for Harry, for what he was doing, and for leaving him behind.

In the hours between the interview with Mike Beck and dressing for the curtain, Catherine wandered, overwhelmed and astonished. It was as if now she had assumed the part she sang almost every night. Everything was in flux and at risk. A new life was within her, and if all went well would carry on for her and for Harry long past the end of their lives in a future she would not know. The constriction of her early twenties was about to end. She had been born to wealth and success, then had been forced to earn it, and it seemed that she had, although she was wise enough to know that struggle never ends but always comes in new forms.

She was frightened but euphoric. The natural course and alternation of things meant that a heart lifted to the empyrean was then cast down. It never failed. And yet the liveliness she felt because of her success and the promise of a child deepened her emotions and sensations into art. She saw things, and she longed for them—shadows in gray, people who will never return, days of sun and clouds that vanish like smoke....

As Harry had wandered only hours before, so did she, taking in faces and forms, not that she was a stranger to this, to seeing in the city a portrait arising with great energy as if random, but then becoming with momentary shock and telltale beauty a poignant composition that fled upon the winds. She could freeze these images and hold them forever, even as they vanished. Although she could never quite understand them, she knew that they all pointed to one thing and had come of one origin, and that should she never give up trying to penetrate their meaning, should she never relinquish them from memory, should she hold them in her heart until she died, perhaps then she could relate one to another and hear with piercing clarity the song they were singing in silence.

She wandered, overwhelmed by images—by thousands of faces, each telling of deep or despairing lives; by clouds garlanding the great buildings; by the engines of the city's commerce; the wind lifting briefly the hem of a woman's cream-colored coat as she glided south at the edge of Madison Square; the sun in blinding flashes upon a hundred thousand windows; bridges sailing high above blue waters and whitecaps; pigeons rising in almost exact synchrony from sidewalks darkened by rain, banking in a mathematically perfect curve, wings still, their perfection the gift of the omnipresent and invisible air.

With the gravity and concentration of a bullfighter adorning himself, Catherine dressed and applied her stage makeup, the lights of her mirror fusing in peripheral vision into a ring of suns. North on the

Hudson, four men guided their boat unseen across the broad reach of Haverstraw Bay. No other boats were anywhere near on a November evening, and the only lights those of Haverstraw, High Tor, and the muted glow of towns on the east bank. As trees swayed in the wind and the rubber boat bobbed in small swells, street lamps and the lighted windows of individual houses appeared to blink. But it was mainly dark, for what moon there was, was largely hidden by cloud. The November waters, their boat, their weapons, as in the war, were black.

Neither at the warehouse in Newark, nor in the truck on the way up, nor when they had armed themselves and inflated the boat, had they been pulled back to the France of 1944 and 1945. But with their paddles dipping in unison, sometimes flashing when the moon appeared, and as they fought the wind and moved slowly and smoothly across, they became once again the proxies of history: silent, awed, working entrained with death. They felt again the tragic satisfaction of soldiers separated from time as everything fled before the concentration of battle. Something beyond and apart from the noise and the pain was always there, comforting and strong, the river upon which, if they did not survive, they would be borne away. Perhaps it is God's merciful gift to soldiers that they can look upon themselves as if from the future or afar, that even the most terrible sounds are silenced, and time slows so as to lift them gently from the things of the world. The wind across the black water was cold, and with each stroke they knew whatever it is that is the opposite of fear.

By the time Catherine heard the rap on her dressing room door she had been pulled deeply into the magic of the theater. Here, just as powerful as the real scenes on the street, was the touch and elusive afterimage that brought and held audiences and always would. In the wave-like progressions of the songs and the glare of the lights was something that, though never directly apprehended, was sought by every soul. And like so many other things, the theater was an attempt to come near it.

Tonight, Catherine was stronger and more radiant than she had ever been. It was as if she were actually in the scene and could not tell the difference between what was real and what was not, her life and her part having fused until she was in two worlds at once. As she stood in the wings she had steadiness and strength she could not account for. She couldn't wait to go on, for she was certain that this performance would flow through her as if she did not exist and as if she offered no impediment to perfection.

Right on cue, she stepped onto the stage, the girl from Red Lion or wherever it was, and the lights found her. The color rose within her, and was stronger. Perhaps the way she stood, her energy rising, made the audience aware, even before her famous drawing in of breaths, that they were present at a remarkable moment.

The music began, the pounding of the kettledrums, the bells, all the things that brought the chaos of the city into the shining set, and she took in her breaths, and began to sing. What a song it was. Everything was in the balance, nothing settled, all uncertain, which lifted her as never before. The sound was so strong it filled the theater like a wind that fells the trees, and yet it was so pure that it was perfectly tender. When a gull flies across the waves, sparingly moving its wings, taking energy from the crests to stay close and just above them, this was how Catherine sang.

All was at risk, all the time, and ever would be. Therein lay the greatness of her singing, eternally clarified by the oppression of mortality and the rebellion of love. It was almost as if she were singing to the rhythm of the paddles, and the paddles were dipping in time to her song. As brave as her husband, she sang into the darkness beyond blinding light, and time stood still. Evenly and steadily, with strength newborn within her, she carried the audience, through sunlight and shadow, effortlessly upon her song.

# 46

## THE HORSE AND HIS RIDER
## HE HATH THROWN INTO THE SEA

THE HUDSON IS an estuary. Ocean tides surge in and out, making its waters variously brackish and fresh depending upon the time of day, the distance from the sea, and the strength of the sweet streams that tumble into it. The life of the river always changes. Sometimes beaches, sandbars, and shallows appear, placed by new eddies and currents. Coves can fill with silt and cattails, and then empty of them so that deep water returns once again. White sandspits stretching into Croton Bay come and go over decades, so that the river of childhood and youth vanishes with one's maturity and old age, and children can hardly believe old men who point to open water and say, There, when I was a boy, was a peninsula of white sand so fine that high winds lifted it and blew it into the waves, which eventually took it all.

Isolated from the influences of the Croton River, from which it is protected by Teller's Point, Haverstraw Bay is relatively stable, its eastern shore rocky and high compared to the western shore after the heights that run from the Palisades to High Tor flatten before rising into the Highlands.

Verderamé's house stood like a battlement on a rock overlooking the water. The gravel-and-shell beach where the rubber boat made landfall was no more than three or four feet wide at high tide. Any footprint made upon it would not need the waves to wash it away, as by its nature gravel, though impressed, refuses to record. The wind was high and noisy, so even had the boat slammed into shore no sound would have carried above. It was impossible from beneath the cliff to see the house, or from the house to see what was below. Nor was it likely that in a cold wind on a November night anyone would have been stationed at the base of the cliff, and no one was.

Probably no one had ever stood watch there or been tasked to look down from above. Still, they brought the boat up so smoothly and slowly that the gravel made no sound. They breathed quietly; communicated with hand signals; scanned right, left, and upward; and stepped as lightly as burglars in a house with dogs. Sussingham took the painter and tied it on to a gnarled pine projecting from a fold in the rock. They stood for a minute or two, staring up and to the sides, carbines cradled in their hands. Then they slung their weapons, adjusting them to keep them from moving as they climbed, so as to prevent them from banging noisily against the rock or causing a loss of balance. They waited some more, banking into their accounts as it were the water and ground across which they had already moved without incident. By training and experience, they did everything patiently and in small, highly controlled steps, and rather than simply rushing ahead, they would listen and then move.

When they felt that in staying still they had sunk into the quiet and dark of night almost enough to become a part of it, they began to climb. Johnson was burdened the most, with the light machine gun, and he stopped to rest frequently. The cliff was not terribly steep, and it offered wide, open seams, broad ledges, and solidly rooted trees to grasp. One could go up it or down rather easily. The challenge was to move so slowly and deliberately that not one rifle butt or barrel would clatter on the rock. If they had sung at the top of their voices it was unlikely that anyone in the compound would have heard, or, if they had, would not have assumed that the noise came from a car passing innocently on the road. It hardly mattered, though, for the standards of assault were such for Harry and the others that to hear their own footsteps or breathing would have been a breach.

It took them nearly half an hour to climb the cliff, so slowly on the way up that, in anticipation of the rapid withdrawal, they were able to memorize every hand- and foothold. At the top they saw the lights of the compound a few hundred feet left and north. Here they did not hesitate, if only because at the edge of the cliff their silhouettes were visible against the background of the river, which was imperceptibly lighter due to its collection of moonlight and the faint glow of New York reflected from the clouds. Off to the north, in a gap between land and cloud that looked as if it had been cut into place with a razor and straightedge, stars shone through the Catskills' colder air.

They crawled twenty or thirty feet from the cliff's edge to the road, and hid themselves beneath laurel and rhododendron so that if a car had suddenly approached, its headlights slewing at every turn, they would not have been seen. But no cars came, and they were lined up from north to south as they would be for the assault: Johnson, Harry, Sussingham, Bayer. Although they had discussed precisely what they were going to do, and gone over it many times, they never doubted that the plan would be forced to circumstance, and when they moved according to the design they also improvised, so that if their expectations were confounded there would be neither shock nor interruption. Their ability to do this was the dissociated sum of their experience together and individually all across wartime Europe.

Harry turned to Johnson and made, had any sound escaped his lips, what would have been a clucking noise. No one could have guessed the meaning of this shorthand unless he had served with these pathfinders. Harry had told Johnson he had to be "the chicken." Johnson was then the first to cross the road. He hesitated on the other side, standing straight, listening carefully, then dashed perhaps a hundred and fifty feet north toward the house, made a sharp right, and disappeared into the woods. Bayer, the southernmost, his head raised like a hound's, then crossed directly and was soon invisible in the woods. Then Harry and Sussingham, twenty feet apart, went at the same time, Harry at a slightly northerly angle and Sussingham at a slightly southerly, and in this way when they reached the other side they were twice as far from one another as at the start.

While Harry and Sussingham found firing positions with as much cover as possible and open ways to north and south so that after their initial bursts they could move quickly to escape the return fire directed at their muzzle flashes, Johnson and Bayer moved slowly about, looking for tall pines close enough to the road to fall across it.

This took quite a while, and more time yet was required to strap the charges onto the trees so that they would keel over in the right direction. Branches at various levels would have to be in the clear if they were not to catch on other limbs or trees and redirect the course of descent. Then the detonation wires had to be strung down and up to Harry. It was okay to run them along the road: no one in a moving car, at night, would see thin black wires, and if by chance they were discovered it would be too late to do anything about it.

After half an hour, they were set. Farthest to the north and just beyond the gate of the compound, Johnson was positioned with the light machine gun he had hauled up the cliff. They assumed that the guards inside would rush out and toward the trapped cars. Johnson would not let them get far. Next down the road to the south was Harry, in front of whom were the two detonators. To his left was Sussingham, his carbine resting against a rock, and the bazooka, rocket loaded, ready to be lifted to his shoulder. In the southernmost position, Bayer was ready to move across the road and shoot anyone trying to escape on the lee side of the assault.

To make sure that they would not kill innocent people, after the trees were felled Harry would first identify the cars, and then move closer to determine whether Verderamé was inside. To be absolutely sure and not mistake for their target two other automobiles of similar make that might nonetheless be driving on a deserted road in front of Verderamé's compound and at his habitual hour of return, Harry was to move close enough to identify exactly. Were it not Verderamé, as unlikely as that might be, they would take everything with them, retreat, and leave behind the mystery of two trees felled one after another with burns at their bases, which to someone who didn't know explosives might seem to be the work of lightning.

By now they were allies of the dark, completely absorbed in their task, far removed from hesitation about what they were going to do. The evergreens, wind, and cold brought them almost all the way back to what they once had been, and they waited, not quite relaxed, listening to the sounds of branches swaying and creaking. Though they would have to remain motionless in the cold for perhaps an hour or two, not long before, they had passed a bitter winter in snow-covered forests and on whitened plains across which crows and ravens that had fled the cold of Russia had been scattered like pepper.

Their discipline was such that after an hour in which they neither moved nor spoke they themselves hardly knew the others were there. Waiting motionlessly in ambush, they found their bodies sinking into the terrain as smoothly as silt that calmly settles after flowing into a lake. Their sight and hearing were intensified, and unlike in the first moments of getting into position, they knew from which angles they were completely invisible, or only partly so, and could achieve total concealment by minor adjustments of posture, shifting an inch or two in one direction or another, or flattening themselves to the ground. As they had come to the ready, they had felt that they were making waves and ripples, but after an hour the lake of their surroundings was unruffled. By 9:30, they were confident that they were as well seated as the rocks and trees.

Forty miles to the south, in the most incandescent part of Manhattan, Catherine had stayed in her dressing room rather than go home. It would help to pass the time, and she wanted to take the curtain call. After her song the audience had stood in ovation, their applause increasing several times to a peak that reminded her not of hail but of a squall beating down upon water enough to turn it black. Like rain pummeling the sea, the ovation had continued, sometimes strengthening in unison for many heartbeats, and she accepted it calmly, having risen to another level, never to fall back. The regard that had been denied was now hers, earned many times over. The equation was in balance, and, like the weather that had rolled in from the west, the sky was clear. She had arrived.

At a little after 9:30, a man appeared, half visible over the wall of the compound. He was thick and stocky, but because one could not tell where the rampart was it was impossible to judge his height. He might have been five feet tall, or six foot ten. He lit a cigarette and was thenceforth a tiny red disc in the darkness, no brighter than the lights across the bay, which were blinking through the remnants of wind-driven clouds. Harry could see, interrupted through the foliage, the diamonds blazing across the water, and they brought him back to when he and Catherine had climbed the dune and seen distant lights gently pulsing in the summer wind.

But the tiny red spot above the rampart kept him in the present, because it meant the guards were expecting the return of Verderamé at any moment. Though the lights across the bay seemed to plead another case, there was no going back. They were slightly blue in cast, and they were beckoning, but up the road the red spot glowed in challenge and held its ground.

At 9:43 — Harry checked the luminous dial of the watch he had strapped to his wrist for the first time since the war — a car suddenly appeared from the north. Had Verderamé varied his route to approach that way even if it meant going through the mud, dirtying the cars, passing the gate, and backing in? The car moved beyond the compound and continued slowly down the road. They noticed that beneath the red dot the image changed. A long gun had been unslung and was now held just beneath the glowing cigarette. As the car moved on, the gun moved back to its resting position.

The relief didn't last, because the car stopped on the road, opposite Bayer, who although he was well concealed could not help but suspect that he had been seen. After a long moment, it moved slowly to the right onto a patch of ground that served as an overlook. The view of the bay was open here. Harry hoped that the occupants would take it in and go, but the engine was killed, followed by the lights. Ringing silence ensued, and then the sound of the wind could be heard once more. The hoarse ratcheting of an emergency brake announced that someone was going to stay awhile. Nothing could be allowed to happen as long as whoever it was remained. As if counting the seconds, Harry tensely anticipated the restarting of the engine. He told himself to have patience. Then the car jerked. They had moved to the back seat. Not too many minutes later, the windows began to steam up.

He tried to think of how to move them out of there. Anyone who crossed the road would be visible to the guard on the rampart. The only thing he could come up with was to throw a rock at the car to scare it away. People having sex on a deserted road had to feel rather vulnerable and might run like hell as one pebble, then another, and then another, hit metal. On the other hand, they might be so engrossed in what they were doing that they wouldn't take anything in. It was a tossup, but irrelevant, as Bayer was not thinking along the same lines, and he was the only one within range. Harry decided to move opposite the car and do it himself, but before he started out he saw the red dot vanish, so he held. At that moment, Sussingham appeared, having moved up to Harry instead of down to Bayer. "What are we going to do?" he whispered.

"Go back quietly," Harry told him. "If in a few minutes nothing changes, go down to Bayer and throw a few small rocks at the car. See if you can scare them into leaving."

"There aren't any rocks," Sussingham whispered, "just pine needles."

"Then throw a cartridge. They're all wiped clean."

Sussingham went back, his footsteps on the pine needles inaudible. Then the gate opened. Two men came out, only shadows but one identifiable by his bulk and the red dot of the cigarette. He walked forward, looking to left and right, the long gun (as he got closer, Harry saw that it was a shotgun) held in the ready position as he moved down the road. He walked right past Johnson though he clearly was wary of an ambush from the woods. He passed Harry, who had him continuously in the sights of the carbine, and he passed Sussingham, who sat quietly and did not move, knowing that Harry would be covering. When he neared the car, which was rocking with coitus, he moved the shotgun to his shoulder, depressed his stance a little, and looked in the right rear window.

Even Johnson, the farthest away, rapidly switching his gaze from the gate to the car to keep track of both, saw that the guard next to the car had relaxed his posture. The red light flew through the dark toward the center of the road, sparked orange as it landed, and lay there, glowing. The muzzle of the shotgun was rapped so hard against the window it might have broken the glass, but didn't.

"Get the fuck outta here!" everyone heard.

The car stopped rocking for an instant, and then dipped forward violently as, undoubtedly, the driver threw himself into the front seat. The engine turned over, the lights went on, and the car was thrown roughly into reverse. It lurched backward and stalled. The sound of the emergency brake being released, like a falling piece of metal, was followed by another sharp, single rap on the glass. From inside came the scream of a nude woman a foot and a half away from a huge, angry man with a shotgun. The engine turned over again, the car backed onto the road, ground its gears, and roared south, its tires having missed the still-burning cigarette. The guard slung his weapon and started to walk back to the compound.

It was perfect, Harry thought. Driving at speed down the road, naked, the two people in the car—he assumed there were two—would be forever impressed by what had happened. They would know the approximate time. They would, perhaps, come forward with a sanitized story (they had stopped momentarily to look at the view) and report that in the woods they had run into a bull of a man with a heavy New York accent, a threatening manner, and a shotgun. His cigarette would be found in the road, his footprints by its side in the mud, through which the four men now waiting in ambush had been careful not to walk.

The gate opened and closed. A minute later, breathing hard, the big man was again on the rampart. He didn't give himself a chance at the wonderfully fresh air the wind would have blown into his lungs, but lit another cigarette, and as things settled down the red spot appeared once again.

At about eleven, early for Broadway but late for Croton, and as Catherine took her curtain call to deafening applause, the Cadillac and its escort came up the hill from the south. It shifted into third while rounding the bend from east to north, and then, on the straightaway, lights blazing, moved into fourth.

Earlier that evening there had been a problem with Catherine's stage exit: the audience would not let her go. Amidst their applause they shouted for an encore and reasonably expected that she would oblige. But Sidney's rule about encores was that they were to be husbanded for the curtain call rather than that they interrupt the action. This was to apply throughout, but especially at the beginning, when, as Sidney put it, the audience was still "learning the idiom of the next few hours." Before the Boston tryouts, he had said, "I don't direct like everyone else. They've got to get used to my language, and then, when they do, they come along."

Honoring this, Catherine had refused the encores. She could have left the theater early, but outside its confines that night she had nothing, so she decided to take the curtain call, which meant that she would have to sing at least twice. Although it would keep everyone late, she wanted to sing — as if to keep Harry safe, as if to lift him and her parents aloft, to keep them afloat, to lock them into the buoyancy of a world that could raise the living above the passage of time if only in the brief moments when music holds the heart. This was why she had chosen the theater, a status far below that which she could have claimed without effort. But from the very beginning, early in childhood, Catherine had known exactly what she was about.

There was a problem with the detonators in that they were the kind used by the OSS, which was not at all surprising given from whom they had been obtained. The standard detonator generated its current as a long shaft was pushed down to spin gears that turned a magneto. But detonators like this were too cumbersome to be carried easily and surreptitiously. The ones that Vanderlyn had known were much smaller, with heavy clock springs wound with a key. That key was then moved to the trigger, another hole in the apparatus, in which the detent, which held back the triggering mechanism, was recessed. After winding, the key was moved and set for release. To prevent accidents, the detent was grooved according to the key. Setting the key properly took a second or two and required a steady hand.

Harry had wound both detonators and set a key in the one that would fell the tree north in front of the cars. Somewhere along the way, perhaps in the river or on the cliff, one of the keys had been lost, which meant that in the dark, amid the daze of explosions and gunfire, the remaining key had to be withdrawn from the north detonator, moved to the south detonator, made to find the hole, set properly, and turned to fell the second tree, which would then complete the boxing-in of both vehicles. This was the first instance of fact diverging from the plan, although they all knew that, as always, there would be others.

Now, amid the spotlights' mitered rays, Catherine sang again. The genius of the play had been that when she entered the scene, with the honking of horns and knocking of cowbells to express the bustle of the city, and the audience expecting something as light and frothy as the musings of a kewpie doll set to music, she launched instead into the breaths of astonishment infilling her lungs with air as if she were a newborn child, and then into a pure and heart-rending song such that, as Sidney knew, everyone was so deeply moved that they were not merely surprised but disturbed. For they had been taught that opera was European — and this was an aria, an American aria, inimitably beautiful in its own way, and by the time Catherine finished they knew what it was, and she had them completely, especially now, when she put everything she had into the song. At the curtain call they made her sing it three times. Though the cast was not happy at first, they forgot their unhappiness and their envy and they, too, came along. And although Catherine could not know it, her song was the accompaniment to the battle from beginning to end. But in a way she did know, and in a way Harry could hear it, in memory and at the present as the two combined, as in great and stressful moments they often do.

The Cadillac and the chase car approached. In the dim light the Cadillac's whitewalls were visible as they rolled like earthbound moons, and the hubcaps, polished that day by a boy in Little Italy, glinted with suppressed light. As the Cadillac passed him, Harry said to himself, "Here we go," and started it all with a clockwise one-quarter turn of his right wrist. He heard the detent snap up and the magneto whir violently. Before the whir ceased the charge was detonated and it lit up the scene like a star shell.

Sussingham lifted the bazooka to his shoulder, waiting for Harry's order to fire. Johnson embraced the light machine gun, ready to pivot as needed. And Bayer aimed his carbine at the rear car. The tree fell like a man dying, slowly at first but then with hopeless surrender. It settled like a cross between a railroad gate and a discarded Christmas tree.

The Cadillac jammed on its brakes. Reacting more slowly, the chase car hit it from the rear and, as if to make up for its lack of alertness, put itself into reverse with a major grinding of gears and roared backward. Harry had lifted the key from the north detonator and was trying to get it into the hole of the south detonator, but in the dark this was not easy. He still hadn't done it when the chase car sped past him in reverse, veering wildly as the driver overcompensated in one direction and then another.

Harry found the hole and plunged the key into it. He found the right position. Then he made the quarter turn to unlock the detent, and another explosion lit up the night. As the tree fell — a dignified fir that, because it was bigger, went down even more slowly than the first — the chase car sped up as if to beat it, and didn't. It was not, however, as blocked as the Cadillac. The tree fell across it. Gunning the engine, the driver tried to escape the net of fragrant branches, but all he could do was spin his tires and make ruts in the road.

For a moment there was silence, and then pistol shots and bursts from two Thompsons erupted from the chase car, unaimed, it seemed, sweeping the woods at random, so that limbs and twigs fell, severed or hanging. Seconds later, gunfire from the ramparts swept the woods. They had no other option and plenty of ammunition. The Cadillac remained motionless, doors closed.

Bayer could see the car amid the evergreen boughs. He fired his carbine, to what effect he was not sure, but when they saw his muzzle flashes they shot at them through the back window, to no avail, as he had already moved to the other side of the road and, seeking adequate cover, was getting ready to enfilade them. Sussingham held, waiting for the order, and Johnson was quiet, holding for what he was sure would be the opening of the gates and the charge of reinforcements.

Before checking the Cadillac to make sure that Verderamé was in it and neither women nor children were with him, Harry took careful aim at the figures on the rampart.

The one who still held a cigarette in his mouth as he pumped a shotgun would be the first. Harry adjusted for the distance and the rise, calculated to hit not quite a foot below the red dot, and fired. The bulky shape tumbled backward from the rampart and disappeared, the red dot with it. Just after that, the others vanished. Johnson expected that within moments they would charge out the gate, with no idea that after a few seconds' run a mounted machine gun would be trained on them.

Harry bolted toward the Cadillac, his carbine pointed at it in case they opened a window to fire at him. Unlike the chase car's, the windows were bulletproof and would have to be cranked down before a shot went out. When the firing from the rampart had ceased, the living occupants of the chase car were aiming to the rear where Bayer had been, and the Cadillac remained inert. Harry stepped into the clear, except that he doubled over in pain and almost went down, as if he had run straight into a sharp branch.

Recovering, he went right up to the Cadillac, carbine at the ready. He peered in through the thick glass. There, illuminated by the muzzle flashes that came from a Thompson in the chase car and Bayer's carbine that in a moment or two would silence it, was Verderamé, pistol in hand, sitting in the back seat, waiting. In the front were two guards, their pistols out as well. It was as if they had been frozen in molten glass. None of their weapons could fire, contained as they were by the bulletproof glass.

Now the gates were thrown open and eight men armed with Thompsons, rifles, and shotguns ran out, some firing as they moved, most waiting to find a target. No one saw through the branches of the first felled tree clearly enough to see Harry, locked in place, staring into Verderamé's car. Before they ever would, Johnson — the English teacher who had spent four years as a paratrooper and pathfinder, and had another self with which he could not reconcile and would not abandon — opened fire at six hundred rounds per minute, easily and justly cutting down these cruel men who for so long had been so confident in their numbers, armament, and ruthlessness. They were used to beating people, tossing Molotov cocktails through store windows, shooting bound captives, and raping helpless women. They didn't really know how to fight, never having come up against anyone but those who were weaker than they were. Their power and their terror, when resisted with determination, evaporated. They were cowards, murderers, and easy to kill.

Bayer silenced the last resistance in the chase car. Johnson had already dismantled the machine gun and was moving toward the center. It was suddenly quiet. Clutching the part of his abdomen that he thought the sharp end of a limb had penetrated, Harry peered into the Cadillac in a way that frightened Verderamé beyond measure. It seemed to those inside to make no sense that Harry pressed against the glass of the rear right-side window and raised his head almost to the roof of the car. They had no idea what he was doing, but he was checking to see that Verderamé had no passengers — a child who had been at a friend's house, a servant coming back after a day off, Verderamé's wife. If this were so, the woman or child would be on the floor, half hidden, and he wanted to make sure that no one was there. It was hard to see inside, and several pistols were aimed at him. But he knew that, if fired, the bullets would ricochet and probably kill them all. This made them helpless and it terrified them, as did Harry, because they didn't understand what he was doing as he looked in, and they never would.

Satisfied that only three men were inside, Harry gave Verderamé one last look, and fell back. Verderamé knew he was going to die, and, to his credit, he smiled.

As Harry retreated he called out to Sussingham, who had been waiting in a standing position to get a shot above the brush. "Clear," Harry shouted. "Fire."

Sussingham pulled the trigger and the rocket blazed from the tube. It went easily through the armored door and exploded in the interior, blowing the sides and roof off the Cadillac in a flash of orange, and killing everyone within.

From the first tree felled, to the rocketing of Verderamé's car, less than four minutes had passed, although to Harry and the others they were indistinguishable from either four hours or four seconds.

They had known from the beginning that the local police, state police, and FBI would quickly determine what weapons they had used. From bullet fragments or whole bullets lodged in people, cars, soil, and trees, they would know their calibers and the types of guns that had fired them. Two hours of collection and a day of putting the pieces together would identify the rocket that had killed Verderamé. And at first glance, from the lines of bullet holes stitched across the targets, it would be possible to see the signatures of the carbines and the machine gun.

Nor did they suffer the illusion that, having to flee immediately, in the dark, they would be able to collect shell casings, some of which would have been ejected out to ten feet or more, at all angles, landing in pine needles, rolling under fallen branches, or sinking in mud. Each cartridge had been wiped clean. Although the four pathfinders had crawled across soft ground when they could, as a diversionary measure they had worn new dress shoes in a larger size than what fit them, and which they would discard in the river; and they had been fairly heavily weighted down, making footprints attributable to heavier people. Each man had a checklist of things to take with him upon leaving. The weapons themselves and detonators, wire, surplus ammunition, and anything that might cast suspicion on them if their truck were stopped on the way back to Newark would be dropped in the ship channel of the Hudson. There, a scouring current would eventually sweep everything south into the many miles of the Tappan Zee, fingerprintless and, according to Vanderlyn, untraceable.

The cigarette that had been thrown onto the road by the stocky guard manning the rampart was a perfect dead end. Adding to this, Harry would drop a sandwich wrapper from a delicatessen in Bensonhurst known to be frequented by Verderamé's rivals of both low and high status. One wrapper. That was all. Several hundred shell casings.

The traces of new weaponry. Footprints here and there, of very large men who wore fancy shoes in the woods. The tire tracks, a gift of coincidence, of a car that had come from the north, stopped at the overlook, backed onto the road, and gone south at high speed. And then, of course, the wreckage of Verderamé's cars, and the bodies, every single one of them a known gangster, every single one armed. Who would think of an English teacher from Wisconsin, a steelworker from Indiana, an expediter in Union Square, and a former student of the humanities married to an heiress?

Often in France, Holland, and Germany — not in Sicily, where the country was more open, and not when the forests were simplified by a cover of snow — Harry had had to move very fast through branches and brush, or throw himself down without thought of where he would land. Descending by parachute into a forest could be fatal if a broken branch acted as a spear or the edge of a sword, and as they sliced through the trees paratroopers held themselves in odd-looking ways to protect their arteries. In the speed and desperation of battle, sharp cuts and penetrations often went unnoticed for a long time. More than once, Harry had removed his shirt or pants and been surprised by a mass of dried blood that had sealed shut a wound he did not know he had.

His first thought was that the terrible pain in his abdomen was the result of a freakishly sharp, strong, and long broken branch that as he had run toward the road had penetrated as deep into his body as an arrow. He felt for its shaft in case it had broken off in him. Even when he felt no shaft he wanted to think it wasn't a bullet wound. In France, he had been unaware of the wound in his back because his senses had been monopolized by the wound to his shoulder. Here, there was only one area of distress, but it had to have been caused by just a branch. The shots flying from the chase car had been directed toward Bayer far to the left. With some things of a mortal nature, what one knows and what one wants can exist with equal strength at the same time. Harry knew he was shot, but he also knew it was a cut from a broken branch. It wasn't a matter of one prevailing over the other in his mind;

both were and would be true until in the passage of time fact would assert itself as eventually it always does.

With the checklist on the ground and a penlight in his right hand, he held his left hand over the wound. Detonators. Bayer and Johnson were walking-in the wires. Carbine. Five magazines of ammunition. Penlight. List. Wrapper. Etc. Everything was in order, and he needed two hands to get things into the rucksack for carrying them out. But when he moved his left hand he felt a sharp, almost electrical lash circling his waist. It was bad enough that he cried out. Then he shone the light on his hand and saw that it was red, covered in new blood. The wound, when illuminated, was a round hole. "Oh, Christ," he said, sitting down to wait for the others. It wasn't a long wait, but during it he noticed that his right arm had gone almost completely numb. He could move it, and grasp with his hand, but he couldn't feel it anymore, and, despite the numbness, both hands felt cold.

"Are you all right?" he asked Bayer. "Are you all right? I need a pressure bandage."

"We're all okay," Johnson told him. Johnson was the medic. They were in the boat, halfway across Haverstraw Bay. "We stopped the bleeding. Can you feel your legs?"

"No." Harry wondered how he had forgotten packing up, descending the cliff, rowing halfway across the river. He was very cold, and there was a wind. Water splashed over the sides of the rubber boat, from the paddles and the waves, and being wet made him even colder. He felt that he had a fever, but just in his head. And he had no blanket. Oh, how he wished for a blanket.

"Look back there," Johnson said.

On the east bank, high on the bluff, was a chain of lights atop police cars and ambulances. Little white flashes like stillborn lightning, or perhaps fireflies, pulsated on the ground. These were flashbulbs going off as photographers did their work. "We're almost across," Johnson told him. "I have to paddle now," and he went back to paddling.

Harry was in and out. He woke to feel the boat swept quickly as they reached the middle of the shipping channel. Then the boat lightened as armaments, shoes, and rucksacks were tossed into the current. By now the line of lights, even though it had grown longer, had been made by distance to look shorter and more intense. And although Harry, whose head rested on the air-filled gunwale, did not see, and the others, paddling furiously in a race for his life, could not have noticed, for a short moment the tops of Manhattan towers, shining with encrusted lights, were visible over the lower ground west of the Palisades. Foreshortened, they sparked and shone like a crown of fire, and then went dark.

They had driven as fast as they could, with Harry and Johnson in the compartment amidst the hay bales. Johnson had useless tourniquets, pressure bandages, and a suturing kit. The external bleeding had stopped, and his forceps were far too shallow to retrieve the bullet, if indeed it could have been found, so he used morphine liberally and with sadness.

During the several hours in the truck, after he had been carried into the warehouse, and waiting for the surgeon, who had stepped out to get something to eat in an all-night diner near the railyards, Harry could hardly say a thing, but he was eloquent and longing within.

Readily and quick, a hundred thoughts, the kinds of things that fill the lives of philosophers, came to him as if from a gun set on rapid fire. As he lay dying, he realized too late that although he might never know the purpose of things he did not have to know if only he could somehow draw as if from life and out of love the city, his times, and Catherine — all destined to vanish into silence. How he regretted that he had not devoted himself to portraying them, and, because he loved them so much, to make an echo, fix them in the light, halt them for a moment in their rush to God knows where.

Sussingham and the surgeon ran across the railyards near the warehouse, jumping rusted tracks covered with weeds and trash. The surgeon was apologetic. And as they were running, beyond their hearing, and before they arrived, Harry was saying, "Catherine, Catherine," and trying to bring her to him in his senses rather than to think useless thoughts, for what good were they when life was so short and time so limited? If you are dying, what good is thought or speculation compared to love? Love simple and unadorned, that forgives and embraces all regrets and imperfections of judgment, and holds you in its arms as you fall away.

# 47

## IN THE ARMS OF AN ANGEL

CATHERINE AWAKENED, AFRAID to look at the time. After so much rain, warmth, and unsettled weather, the city had finally surrendered to fall. The air was clear, and the weakening sun, bright nonetheless, intensified all colors, especially blues. The winds that barreled down Kips Bay, colliding with Corlears Hook and the shoulder of Brooklyn massed awkwardly against the East River, pushed barges and tugs gliding on the current out toward the open sea. Everything glittered or was lost in deep shadow, and things were moving on.

She had slept in a slightly worn satin-and-lace camisole, and when she sat up the straps descending from her shoulders stretched taut and her hair fell about her neck more fetchingly than if it had been carefully arranged. She could not wait to arrive at the Esplanade at eleven, and yet she also wanted time to stop so that she could look forward to it always and never have to be disappointed. But unlike clocks that tell just time, the clock of the city is unimaginably complex, its gears set at all angles, with so many millions of them running off and intersecting and curving back 'round again in a mechanism that transcends all mechanisms. And although now and then the clock stops and time stands still, these are the rarest of moments, and time always begins again, and pulls you out of bed.

Seeking refuge in the shower, she turned her face to the strong stream and the bright light and held in a position that she knew was prayer, that every Renaissance painter knew was prayer, and that the body, tensed with looking up to receive, knew was prayer. There she stood, naked, gorgeous, and straight, the water cascading over her until she was rose-colored, but, eventually, the capacity of the hot-water boilers notwithstanding, she had to wind down the nickel taps and choke the stream that had seemed to hold her safe as long as she was in it.

Wrapped in a towel, she opened her bathroom door and watched the steam rush out, as white and visible as alpine cloud, to disappear into the colder air of the room as if it had never existed. Steadily and slowly, she accomplished the ritual of dressing. Each movement had been taught to her by her mother, and she honored every one of them. She chose the elegant clothes she had worn at the parley by the fireplace, when Harry hadn't been able to take his eyes off her — pearl and gray, tight against her body, overwhelming. Yet again, as in the theater, she dressed as ceremonially as a bullfighter, as if what she put on would protect and sanctify her. She had no idea how or why this was so, but the notion was impossible to dismiss. She applied her makeup. She was a grown woman now, an actress who knew how to make up far better than even the women at the continents of counters — veritable Ross Ice Shelves — on the first floors of department stores. She knew exactly, as a stage actress, how to accommodate light strong enough to wash out everything but white, or the dimming of the light almost to darkness. The world was generally more moderate than the stage, but although she was made up more than usual it matched the elegance of her clothing, her mien, and the resplendent sun that day. It had always been her mother's expert ornamentation, and now it was hers.

The servants were gone, her father had left for somewhere in Asia, her mother for San Francisco, where she would wait for him. Catherine was so alone in the house that she was reluctant to go downstairs: not out of fear but because no one would be there. As a child who spent most of the time by herself, she understood that coming into an empty room was to experience the distant traces of infinite sadness.

Perfectly attired and turned out, moving with the grace and power of the natural-born royalty she was, she walked down the staircase that went by the many windows looking out on the street. The Hales had taken some of the windows from houses they had owned for generations, carefully restoring them, and these filtered every day's new light through old experienced glass neither so disciplined nor so clear, like modern glass, as to be nothing. Light passing through them was changed, light reflecting from them reinterpreted. When she passed one of these windows, from which house in the past she did not know, her rapidly moving reflection was like the fluttering of birds that had suddenly taken flight. She saw not the picture of a young woman in her prime descending a staircase, but of white doves rising as quickly as the puff of a flashbulb and then vanishing in favor of the motionless façades across Sutton Place.

In the entrance hall, she looked at the tall-case clock, not because she could not have avoided it but because she had decided not to avoid it: 10:23. Breakfast was out of the question, even had she had time.

The strength of the sun seemed such that after walking a little she would not need a coat. She took one last look at the empty house, opened the door, and went out to the stoop. There she hesitated, her hand still on the pull. Eddies of air entered the house. She closed the door and listened to the brass click as the bolt sprang shut. Walking down the few steps, she left her childhood behind. Now she was on the windy street.

This wind combed through the blocks of Manhattan, sometimes gusting cold, sometimes dying down as if to let the sun warm the sidewalks and trees as in spring. Catherine knew that, even in the shade and the wind, as the day progressed she would be glad not to have worn a coat. For the wind would subside, and in walking everything would come right.

Just after leaving the house, she went west through streets that seemed by law to be open only to maids and to old ladies in mink. The maids walked half as fast as they might have had they been happy, and seemed never to look up, to the side, or far down the street. They were shopping for foods of which they would eat the leftovers, and flowers that would not show up in their minute quarters until they had wilted. And, as Catherine knew, because she had once been a little girl who had eaten with them and listened to their stories and complaints, they bore the burden, entirely within themselves, of reconciling a true affection for the employers whom they knew so well and who treated them, almost, like family, and the natural desire to steal their jewels and slit their throats, or at least to walk out, slam the door, and run to children and families just as precious, just as holy, just as deserving, with whom they could not be, for the sake of others whom they were serving.

The old ladies in mink were equally to be pitied as they walked slowly and looked down to guide their timid steps. Bent with age, they could not fight the cold with bodies that could no longer grow hot. Catherine felt the strength of her own body, its extraordinary balance, the straight shot from the top of her head down to the sidewalk, every muscle, tendon, and joint in perfect order, yearning for strain and challenge and overflowing with energy. Her breathing was slow and deep, her stride long, vision sharp, voice strong.

She might grow old, but, like her mother, she would swim, she would strain, she would walk great distances, lift things that were heavy, and dig in the garden. Even were she to die early because of the physical discipline to which she had been bred, she would never abandon it. Struggle was necessary to self-possession. Even from a wheelchair it was possible to struggle against the natural forces that eventually always win. "Spit in their eye," Evelyn had said, cheerfully but with the tranquil acceptance of her own fate. "Defiance, Catherine, is a gift of God, who is superior to nature. When nature comes to get you, honor God by treating it, as He would, with neither fear nor respect."

Once, when Catherine was eight or nine, they had gone to a Long Island beach club as the guests of friends of her parents, people whom she had never met. They were very famous and owned a movie studio, and had arrived in a chauffeured limousine with their daughter, who was a few years older than Catherine and who ignored her and spent the hours of the visit with a gymnastics coach who looked at Catherine, sized her up, and then turned away as if she didn't exist. Catherine went swimming, played in the sand, and was left lonely enough to go sit with the adults. She remembered nothing of the conversation except one thing that would stay with her for the rest of her life. Speaking to his friend, or, perhaps better, acquaintance, her father got up from a cushioned wicker chair, went over to her mother sitting opposite, and said, "Look." He traced the gracefully curved line between the top of Evelyn's neck and her shoulder. "I believe this is called the trapezius muscle," he said. "In some people, it hardly exists. In Evelyn, who swims, it's so beautiful. Isn't it, Catherine?"

At that moment, the daughter of the other family was exercising on a motionless trapeze. Billy had been aware of how Catherine had been treated, and now he was defending her. He was telling her that she would be like her mother, that in time she would grow into a splendor that would far overshadow what she felt now of powerlessness, awkwardness, loneliness. This she remembered as she walked through the quiet, tree-lined streets of the Upper East Side, because Billy, after delicately and provocatively holding up Evelyn's strength and beauty as a challenge, had kept his eye on Catherine, never looking away, speaking to her rather than the somewhat stunned couple he was addressing: lovely in remembrance, perfect in execution. She had received a lifetime of confidence almost as if by magic.

It was different for Harry. Although he did his best to ignore the many ways in which he was broken and weakened, he had lost his mother early, he had lost his father and not been there to bury him, he had been forced away from his studies enough times to make it for good, into a business that he was not born for, and a war that no one had been born for. She could only imagine what he had seen and done, and she knew that he had carried into it not only the strength of a man but the delicacy of a child. Where she herself had observations, visions, and ambition, he had unanswered questions and sorrows. That he forged ahead as he did, and had in the face of death all around him come out with his ability to love unbroken, was perhaps why she loved him so much.

She knew that all the busyness of the world, its infinite mechanical actions in city, in surf, in molecules rising in light, in machines and speech and clouds of sparkling dust, and trains and sounds and crowds and blades of grass that dance in the sun, all pass into silence, leaving only the soul, which cannot be proved and cannot be seen. And she knew that the brightness of day and the passions that flare within it are just a flash of light to fix the soul into an afterimage that will last forever.

This she had known, without knowing that she had known it, since infancy. It was what she was supposed to see in the play when she emerged from the station, the source of her breath and her astonishment. And it was what she was driving toward — walking in such a way that it turned men's eyes to her magisterial beauty so that some of them would never, for the rest of their lives, forget the sight of her as she made her way to the Esplanade.

Crossing Lexington Avenue, she had seen arrayed in front of one of the little green huts that served as newsstands a fan of papers, each and every one announcing what she knew Harry had done the night before. She could hardly bring herself to look, but could not help but read the huge headlines in the tabloids. "Gang War," was what they thought. There was a photograph, on one front page, that she had seen from the corner of her eye. Though she had quickly averted her gaze, what she saw was horrible enough to make fear rise from the places where she had forced it to wait, and now Catherine's gait was not quite steady, and she felt, though her body had warmed, the sun had strengthened, and the wind had lessened, a coldness rising within her from just above her waist all the way through to her shoulders and back.

Surely she would not now be brought down by the most unlikely chance. It was the kind of thing that could happen, but, to her, never had. It wouldn't. He would be there, as promised, and the fear and despair that almost brought her to a halt, that made her want the ground, and to lie down scandalously on the sidewalk somewhere in the Sixties between Park and Madison (it had probably never been done), would serve only to bless the joy of the moment with contrast and relief. Had anything happened, they would have contacted her by now — if it had been in the plan, if they had known how, if the timing had been right. Perhaps the phone was ringing at that very moment in the empty house.

She resolved to banish such thoughts and move forward. The Esplanade was not far, either in time or distance. The Esplanade, between the castle and the town, once a battleground, now a place of ease, was where war and peace conjoined, each colliding with the other and sinking back, like two waves, into still water that vibrates with the power of both. This was the Esplanade, where everything came together, and the story came to its close.

In the midst of her fear and uncertainty, she thought of how close she was to Harry in feeling and in thought, and that this would never depart. They both had had a vision of the ferries on a summer's day, the women in white, the men in boaters, hats everywhere like moths in a meadow. And together they had once seen a woman in Grand Central as they walked through the south waiting room, a deeply troubled, elegant woman, with a sadness they could not name, trapped in a beam of light, her chin resting on her hand, her eyes fixed upon a horizon far beyond the walls. Perhaps from some wound or incident of childhood, or by inheritance or accident or ineffable command, both Harry and Catherine had a deep and abiding love for all those who have been and vanished, who were left behind, expectant and surprised, trapped in time that will not die and is lost to a blind world yet as full as our own because it is our own, or soon will be.

Within sight of the park, on a street of many mansions of the type that were being felled by the wrecker's ball to make way for more efficient high-rises, Catherine passed the small garden, soon to be buried beneath layers of steel and brick, of a house that seemed almost uninhabited, so resigned and faithful was it to the beauties and emotions of an age that had passed.

She stopped so suddenly, it was as if she had walked into a street lamp. In the garden, illuminated by morning sun that reached back into a deeply shadowed place, was a bronze relief, almost life size, a memorial of the First World War. A soldier, his life gone, his rifle and bayonet cast aside, lay motionless in the arms of an angel. Winged and strong, she looked upward, undisturbed, about to rise. For soldiers need angels to comfort and carry them up, and if they are lucky, the angels will be sent to them early, so that in one form or another they will know them for all the days of their lives.

This could only have been a cry and a prayer occasioned by the death of a young man who as a boy had played in that garden beneath the watchful and loving eyes of his mother and father. It was the truth of the world, that all the world's busyness could not subsume, that all the world's illusions and beliefs could not override or dim. Catherine could hardly breathe. For a moment, she managed only the short gasps that come to small children after they have cried, a breathlessness that though it should have a name, does not.

She crossed Fifth Avenue and went through one of the entrances into the park. The stone wall was black with the soot of a century, for some of the smoke of a hundred million fires, risen to be carried away with the wind, had curled long enough near the ground — perhaps on a winter's night many years before Catherine was born — to leave a part of itself before it disappeared. From the playing fields near the Sheep Meadow, to which private schools marched their elementary and middle school students, children's voices rode on the wind, sharp, distant, and gentle. Once, Catherine had been marched there as well. Soon, on the Esplanade, she would tell her husband that she was carrying their child.

From its south end, the expanse of the Esplanade is both majestic and comforting. The trees in their raggedness and imperfect perfection are far more beautiful than the precise columns of a temple. They lean over the center, the branches on high reaching one for the other and sometimes succeeding, like clasped hands soon to be pulled apart. Their leaves were down, golden and red, playing in the whirlwinds that had dried them, and though the long walk was empty, the time was not yet eleven.

As she waited, it was as if her life were draining away. Why was no one on the Esplanade but she? Why were no latecomers on their way to midtown to work, no cops walking toward the precinct in the park, no nannies wheeling babies, and no Harry? Still, it was only a quarter after eleven.

She stiffened with courage. He had been late before. And when he came, she knew, he would not quite understand why she would cry. He would be philosophical, and she would forgive him. He would come up with something like what he had once said to her, out of the blue, in front of a restaurant—"There's so much I look back upon with affection, but when I was there, I couldn't quite grasp it. I didn't love enough"—and she would guide him to look ahead, happily. What would they do now? How would they live through midcentury and beyond?

"You'll see what comes," she would say, generations of confidence and calm reaching out to heal a man wounded by war, elevating him, as if in the embrace of an angel, to float and glide slightly above the Esplanade, when walking was somehow a thing of the past, and to love him, and carry him up.

She thought of the relief, set into the garden wall, a soldier in the arms of an angel. "You'll do what you've always done," she would say. "We'll do it together."

In a generation or two, we vanish without a trace, and if against all odds we manage to engrave a line in the stone, to impress upon history an act or deed, we become it and nothing more, and so depart according to the original premise. This is why Catherine's singing was so brave, and why Harry loved her for it so much. Day after day she went onstage and played her part, devoting herself to a song that disappeared even as she sang it, like the wake of a ship, a brilliant stroke that shines and sings and gently falls back into the quiet of the sea.

She knew he was gone, but he was there as well, as if he were with her, for everything within her called him forth, and for a precious minute or two that the practical might call hallucination and the faithful might call love, she pulled him back from the blind world and he appeared.

Neither spoke even the other's name. Alone on the Esplanade, when they met they linked hands, turned, and began to walk north, whence he had come. It was a dream they had had since they were children, dreamt in loneliness and in war, in their best times and in their worst, when with others and when not, while flying through the air beneath the pillars of the El, or falling into the Battle of France, while riding in her parents' car, powerless except to dream, or when onstage singing into the darkness. It was what gave him hope and courage and made her song searing to an honest heart, and now that they had it they would need nothing more.

Although she had not known it was Harry she had seen swinging beneath the El, she had fallen in love with him then. For most of her life she had been waiting even when she had not known that she was waiting. And now she knew, she remembered, and when she realized that, then as now, she loved him most when he was flying away from her, she shuddered, and in astonishment and grief she took in the short, involuntary breaths that she took onstage.

Had the story come full circle in the way that stories end, they would have walked quietly, Catherine and Harry, into the rest of their life, knowing that in the end the whole world is nothing more than what you remember and what you love, things fleeting and indefensible, light and beautiful, that were not supposed to last, echoing forever — golden leaves swept across the Esplanade, wind-polished bridges standing in the winter sun, the sound of Catherine's song.

# EPILOGUE

Sometime before Thanksgiving, Catherine returned to the apartment. In the weeks that had passed, the heat had gone on and despite newly cold nights the air inside, freshened because the window had been left open, was as warm as if no one had left.

The doorman, who didn't know that Harry was dead, smiled at Catherine, who smiled back and tried not to cry. With exemplary control, she rode up in the elevator, but could not help feeling as she ascended that when she opened the door Harry would be there. Although she knew it could not be so, she believed it because she so wished it, and as she turned her key in the lock, she felt hope, excitement, expectation, and love.

It was a lovely thing, the turning of a key, the brass tumblers as they snapped to attention, the sound of someone coming home. When she opened the door, the silence and desertion hit her hard, and her grief rose all over again. But then she heard the shade-pull tapping against the window frame. Lifting her head sharply and looking toward it, she said "Oh no!" and ran to the living room, expecting a miracle, believing the impossible. And there in the living room, when she saw the pull and the cord swaying in the wind, she cried until she could cry no more.

When she was done, she walked back to the hall, where she stood, almost insensibly, until she became aware of the bracelet. She instinctively clasped it to her wrist, as if to ratify her love for Harry forever, and then she saw the note, on musical notation paper from her first year in college.

Before she opened it, she touched and held it as if it were part of him. Before she opened it, she knew she would keep and read it until someday it was yellowed and brittle, and that she would keep faith to it until the end. Before she opened it, she knew it would be full of heartbreaking instruction. And then, because she knew that this would be the last, and that whatever was left of him was about to depart, she slowly unfolded it, and with all her courage, she read.

In it, Harry told her that, because she was so young, she had to marry, and that he wanted her above all to live to the full. He told her that for her the world would start again, imperfectly, but that it would start nonetheless. This he knew. He told her how much he had loved her, more than anything in life, and that even were he to die, and except that he wanted more time with her, she had been enough, she had been much more than enough, and he would die well.

He left no message for his son — who would hunger for such a message all his life, for it was not just Catherine who had been left — because he did not know he would have a child. And at the end, after bidding her once again to marry, he wrote: "I thought I had come through the war, but apparently have not. If that's so, and I'm one of the later casualties — the hospitals are full of them, and in other ways the war will continue, in silence, far longer than anyone may now imagine — you must not fall with me. Catherine, I beg of you not to withhold the smallest part of your love from your husband and your children. I know you will think of me now and then, but with time I will leave your memory except in symbols and traces. Let them be enough for you. Let me pass into the things we love: the motions of the city; its whitening sunrises; the ferries that glide across the harbor, trailing smoke; the avenues where once we walked toward an open horizon, holding one another comfortably pressed together at the hip; the bridges diamond-lit and distant; and all the millions, who should never be forgotten, and never go unloved."

And this she did, she married again, and fulfilled his wish, but when she thought of him it was not just as he had asked. For although she could not see a ferry lonely in the distance moving smoothly and silently toward the Narrows, or a snowfall that muted the streets, or any other such beautiful thing without thinking of him, she thought of him most of all as she had seen him first, swinging beneath the El, rising and falling, rising and falling, rising and falling through another time permanently set within her heart.